Janny Wurts

STORMED FORTRESS

The Wars of Light and Shadow

VOLUME 8

FIFTH BOOK OF
THE ALLIANCE OF LIGHT

HARPER
Voyager

HarperCollins*Publishers*
77–85 Fulham Palace Road,
Hammersmith, London W6 8JB

www.voyager-books.com

Published by Harper*Voyager*
An imprint of HarperCollins*Publishers* 2007
1

A catalogue record for this book
is available from the British Library

ISBN-13: 978-0-00-721780-9

Set in Palatino by Palimpsest Book Production Limited,
Grangemouth, Stirlingshire

Printed and bound in Great Britain by
Clays Ltd, St Ives plc

*For three, whose enduring commitment
to the literature of the fantastic
has enriched so many.*
Betty Ballantine
Ellen Datlow
Terri Windling

Acknowledgements

The culminating volume of the Alliance of Light could not have been accomplished without the grace of many helping hands, extra sets of eyes, and no end of cheerful encouragement. My heartfelt thanks to the following people who have been unflagging in their assistance:

Jeff Watson
Andrew Ginever
Lynda-Marie Hauptman, Betsy Hosler, Jana Paniccia,
Gale Skipworth, Karen Shull and Mark Timmony

Jonathan Matson

Jane Johnson, Sarah Hodgson, Harry Man,
Dominic Forbes and the Voyager crew
Bob and Sara Schwager

and not least,
My husband, Don Maitz, who never blinked when the wife was dreaming 'off planet' and talking to herself in Paravian.

Contents

Fifth Book

Maps viii
Story Time-line 1

    I. Binding Ties 9
   II. Recoil 43
  III. Obligations 75
  IV. Feint and Assault 111
   V. Blood Debt 145
  VI. Counterstrokes 179
 VII. Siege 211
VIII. First Turning 245
  IX. Schism 283
   X. Hammer and Anvil 317
  XI. Second Turning 353
 XII. Third Turning 387
XIII. Stormed Fortress 425
XIV. Sortie 463
 XV. Athir 503
XVI. Scarpdale 535

Glossary 575

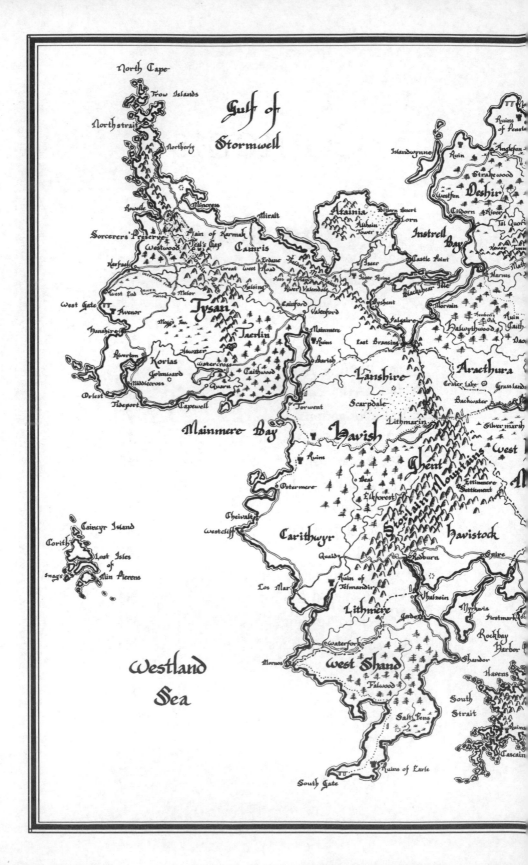

Athera
Continent of Paravia

Age of the Mistwraithe

N

Cildein
Ocean

Los Lier

South Sea

Fallowmere
North Ward — Grimwood
East Ward
Plain of Araithe
Valhaym River
Jorn Mountains
Eltarra
Perlorn
Valey Gap
Werpoint
Crescent Isle
Minderl Bay
Ithilt
Rathain
Earl Rocks
Ramon
Camris
Ivory River
Skyshiel Mountains
Eastwall
Highscarp
Minderl Ruin
Minderl Strait
Saint's Point
East Gate
Athir Ruins
Narms Barrens
Shelsend
Caolot
Bay of Eltair
Vaststrait
Northstor
Tharidon
Whitehold
Farsee
Eastair
Shipsport
Varens
Firans
Perdith
Atwood
East Halla
Firans Ruins
Anllain
Midhalla
Tiriac Mountains
Mirthlvain Swamp
Alestron
Kalesh
Adruin
Orvandir
Methisle
Methlas Lake
Ganish
Durn
Ishlir
Six Towers
Thirdmark
Kenton
Forthmark
Shand
Atchaz
Alland
Selkwood
Eltaire Tolzen
Skimlade Tip
Merior
Sickle Bay
Shaddorn
Southshire
Mountains
Janish
Desert of Sanpashir
Sahlit
Ruins
Sanshevas

○	Town	⚬	Grimward
ⱬ	Ancient Ruin		
✿	Unvanquished Town		
⬛	Worldsend Gate		
⌘	Paravian Marker		
‐·‐·‐	Kingdom Boundary		
∿	River		
🌲	Forest	▨	Preserve
⸜	Marsh		
⸗	Waste or Desert		
⌇	Roads		
⛰	Mountains		

0   10   25   50   100

© 1994 Janny Wurts

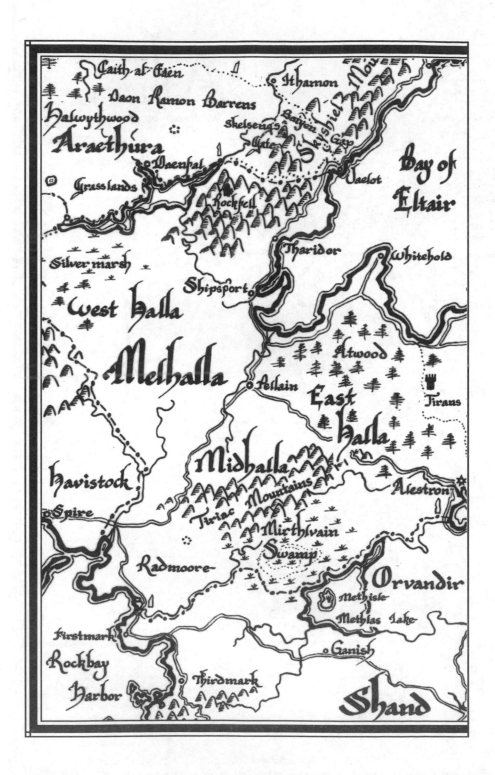

Story Time-line
What Has Gone Before

Third Age Year

5637—The half-brothers Arithon s'Ffalenn, Master of Shadow, and Lysaer s'Ilessid, gifted with Light, exiled through West Gate, are met as they arrive on Athera by the Fellowship Sorcerer Asandir and Dakar, the Mad Prophet, whose West Gate Prophecy forecast the defeat of the Mistwraith, Desh-thiere, and return of the sunlight that had been lost to Athera for five hundred years.

Arithon meets his beloved, Elaira, who is under a life vow of service to the celibate order of the enchantresses of the Koriathain.

5638—The Mistwraith is contained at Ithamon by Lysaer and Arithon and driven into captivity through their combined powers of Light and Shadow.

The Fellowship Sorcerers' effort to crown Arithon as High King, and re-instate Rathain's monarchy fails when the Mistwraith places the half-brothers under its curse: they will be enemies, bent upon each other's destruction until one or the other lies dead.

War follows. Lysaer, whose cardinal virtue is the s'Ilessid gift of justice, leads a war host ten thousand strong from Etarra against Arithon, who is backed by the clansmen in Strakewood Forest. Lysaer and Etarra lose eight thousand men, and the clans suffer the Massacre at Tal Quorin, when Etarran head-hunters destroy their women and children to draw the fighting men into the open. To spare his allies, Arithon is forced to use his mage talent to kill. And in the aftermath of this massive insult to his royal gift of compassion, he loses access to all facets of his trained mastery. Survivors of the debacle made possible

1

by his sacrifice include fourteen young boys, named as Companions, and Earl Jieret, twelve years of age, who becomes Arithon's 'shadow behind the throne' – or *caithdein*.

Lysaer returns to Etarra to begin the alliance of town forces against Arithon and court his beloved, Talith.

Arithon apprentices himself to the Masterbard, Halliron, and takes on the disguised persona of Medlir to deny his half-brother, and the directive of the curse, a fixed target.

5643—The Fellowship Sorcerers reinstate crown rule in Havish, under High King Eldir. In redress for irresponsible conduct, Dakar the Mad Prophet is assigned to Arithon's protection.

5644—Dakar tries to escape his charge and links up with Halliron and 'Medlir' on the eastshore, whereupon his scapegrace behaviour with town authorities in Jaelot leads to Halliron's death and Arithon's breaking his disguise, then achieving the title of Masterbard of Athera.

Arithon relocates down the eastshore en route to the southcoast, with Dakar's escapades earning him the enmity of the powerful clan family of Duke Bransian s'Brydion of Alestron.

Elaira receives her longevity from the Koriani Order for the purpose of keeping track of Arithon, since the sisterhood considers him a danger.

Lysaer solidifies his alliance of town interests, rebuilds the ruined citadel at Avenor, marries Talith, and begins his manoeuvres to claim ancestral title to rulership of Tysan.

Against the climate of building war, Arithon founds a shipyard in the fishing village of Merior, where he constructs blue-water sailing vessels with intent to escape to sea. He meets and befriends two fatherless twin children, Fiark and Feylind. He encounters Elaira, under orders from her Prime to involve herself in Arithon's affairs. Their affection deepens when a joint attempt to heal an injured fisherman creates an empathic link between them.

5645—Lysaer leads a war host to Rathain, with intent to sail south and crush Arithon in the fishing village of Merior. But Arithon hears, and uses wiles and Shadow to trigger the Mistwraith's curse beforetime. Inflamed to insane rage, Lysaer burns the fleet he intended to transport his war host, leaving his campaign stranded and delaying his assault through the winter.

Arithon's escape plan suffers a set-back when a rancorous, displaced field-captain from Alestron burns his shipyard at Merior, with only one vessel left fit to be salvaged.

5646—On the run as war builds, Arithon takes refuge in the strategically difficult terrain in Vastmark. Faced by a war host and impossible odds, he takes Lysaer's wife Talith as a captive to stall the onset of open war.

5647—Talith is ransomed by Lysaer, under auspice of the Fellowship Sorcerers and High King Eldir. Although she is safely returned, the experience leaves an irreparable rift in her marriage.

Lysaer masses his war host, thirty-five thousand strong, and marches on Arithon's smaller force in Vastmark. Arithon resorts to desperate measures to turn them, including the Massacre at the Havens, in which five hundred of Lysaer's men are killed outright. The tactic fails, and is followed by the main engagement at Dier Kenton Vale, in which twenty thousand Alliance troops die in one day in a shale slide.

The campaign collapses at the onset of winter, with Duke Bransian s'Brydion of Alestron changing sides and forging a covert alliance with Arithon.

Faced with a ruinous defeat, Lysaer decides to create a faith-based following and cast Arithon as evil incarnate.

Arithon escapes to sea to search for the lost Paravian races, who, as Ath's gift to redeem the world, offer hope he might break the Mistwraith's curse. Feylind sails as his navigator, and Fiark is apprenticed with a merchant-factor in the town of Innish.

The Prime Matriarch of the Koriani Order casts an augury showing that Arithon will cause her downfall. Since she is aging and has only one flawed candidate in line for her succession, and her death will cause an irreparable loss of the sisterhood's knowledge, she becomes Arithon's inveterate enemy.

Still in love with Arithon, Elaira saves the life of an infant during childbirth in the grass-lands of Araethura. Named Fionn Areth, he owes her a life debt, and a prophecy entangles him with Arithon's fate.

Back at Avenor to rebuild his following, Lysaer sets the clanborn who refuse to join his alliance to eradicate the Master of Shadow under a decree of slavery. His estrangement with Talith leads to her incarceration.

5648–9—For endorsing slave labour, Lysaer is cast out of the Fellowship's compact, which allows Mankind the right to inhabit Athera.

5649—The Prime Matriarch of the Koriathain confronts the Fellowship Sorcerers to lift restrictions imposed on her sisterhood and the use of their grand focus in their Great Waystone. The petition meets with refusal, sealing her determination to take Arithon captive and use him as leverage to force the Sorcerers to accede to her order's demands.

5652—Arithon fails in his search for the Paravians. He returns to the continent and discovers Lysaer is enslaving the clanborn. This leads him to infiltrate Lysaer's shipyard at Riverton, to steal vessels and assist the clansmen in their effort to escape the persecution of Lysaer's Alliance by fleeing to sanctuary in Havish.

5652–3—The Prime Matriarch of the Koriathain sets a trap to take Arithon by suborning his covert colleagues at the Riverton shipworks, only to have her grand plan undone by ambitious meddling on the part of her sole candidate for succession, Lirenda. The trap springs, but Arithon escapes into a grimward, chased by a company of men allied with Lysaer, under the captaincy of Sulfin Evend.

5653—Lysaer's wife Talith is murdered by a conspiracy in his own council, with her death made to appear as a suicide. Sulfin Evend survives the grimward and is appointed to the rank of Alliance Commander at Arms.

The Koriathain fail to forge an alliance with Lysaer against Arithon, and in disgrace for her meddling, Lirenda decides to claim the life debt owed by Fionn Areth to Elaira. The child is shapechanged to mature as Arithon's double, to be used as bait in a second, more elaborate trap to achieve his capture.

5654—Of their own accord, the s'Brydion duke's brothers decide to avenge the mishap at Riverton, against Arithon's better judgement. When an argument with Parrien leads to injury, Arithon is awarded the service of two trusted s'Brydion retainers, Vhandon and Talvish.

5654—Lysaer marries Lady Ellaine as a political expedient. On the day of the wedding, the s'Brydion vengeance plan destroys Lysaer's fleet and his shipyard at Riverton. Sulfin Evend's uncle, Raiett Raven, joins Alliance service as Lysaer's advisor and is eventually appointed as High Chancellor of Etarra.

5655—Lysaer and Ellaine's child, Prince Kevor, is born.

5667—Ellaine learns that her predecessor, Princess Talith, died as a victim of murder, arranged by Lysaer's council at Avenor.

5669—The Koriani plot to trap Arithon using Fionn Areth sends the boy into the town of Jaelot, where he is taken and condemned, mistaken for the Master of Shadow. Arithon is drawn ashore to prevent the death of an innocent accused in his stead. On winter solstice day, Fionn Areth is snatched from the scaffold. The Koriani conspiracy fails, with Lirenda disgraced and Elaira exonerated.

Now desperate and dying, with no available successor, the Prime Matriarch seizes her moment and distracts the Fellowship Sorcerers by inciting a sweeping upset of the energetic balance of the world. Although she fails to take Arithon captive, she successfully resolves her predicament by taking over a younger candidate, Selidie, in possession. As 'Selidie' assumes the mantle of Prime power, the Sorcerers' hands are tied. The upset has left the Mistwraith itself on the verge of escaping from containment, and other, equally dangerous predators left by the absent Paravian races pose further perils.

As the terrifying portents unleashed by Morriel's meddling cause sweeping panic, young Prince Kevor settles the riot that erupts in Lysaer's absence at Avenor. The brilliant statesmanship earns the young prince the love of the populace and the undying enmity of Lysaer's High Priest, Cerebeld.

5670—Fionn Areth's idealistic belief that Arithon is a criminal spoils the free escape from Jaelot. Alone, under pursuit by Alliance troops and Koriathain, Arithon is set to flight over the mountains and into Daon Ramon Barrens.

Young Prince Kevor is entrapped by the machinations of High Priest Cerebeld, and although he survives to become an adept of Ath's Brotherhood, his presumed death sends his mother Ellaine into flight to escape Lysaer's corrupt council at Avenor.

While Dakar and Fionn Areth are diverted to Rockfell Peak to assist the short-handed Fellowship Sorcerers' recontainment of the Mistwraith, the clans of Rathain, under Jieret, are left to face the combined Alliance war host, under command of Lysaer and Sulfin Evend. With their help, Arithon escapes the troop cordon that has closed to take him, but at cost of seven Companions' lives and Jieret's execution by Lysaer.

To evade capture, Arithon is driven into the dread maze under Kewar cavern, built by the Sorcerer Davien the Betrayer, whose hand originally caused the uprising that unseated the high kings and heated the conflict between town and clanborn. Arithon survives the arduous challenge of the maze, achieves mastery over the Mistwraith's curse, and recovers his mage talent. He takes sanctuary there, under guest welcome of Davien.

Defeated, since none dare follow Arithon's passage through the maze, Lysaer and the disheartened remains of his troop depart for Avenor.

After the successful reconfiguration of the wards containing the Mistwraith, Dakar and Fionn Areth are foiled in their plan to rendezvous with Feylind's ship, *Evenstar*, when the Koriathain attack them in a wayside tavern. To rejoin Arithon's retainers, Vhandon and Talvish, who await them at Duke Bransian's citadel at Alestron, they must continue their journey afoot. When they reach the fortress, a prank of Dakar's runs Fionn Areth afoul of their s'Brydion hosts, resulting in the grass-lander's imprisonment in the duke's dungeon.

5670—Across the continent, the defeated remains of the Alliance war host are en route to Avenor, when Lord Commander Sulfin Evend discovers that Lysaer is trapped under the influence of the Grey Kralovir necromancers, through dark blood rites initiated by the priest scryer used to locate the enemy. To salvage his liege from evil practice, he solicits the learned help of the wise woman Enithen Tuer. She informs him that he is directly related to the s'Gannley lineage, in outbred descent, and, in return for knowledge and a knife with the arcane properties needed to free Lysaer from enslavement, insists that Sulfin Evend swear a *caithdein's* oath to the land. Sulfin Evend is forced to compromise his honour by accepting, since he knows no other way to save Lysaer from Kralovir influence, or defend against the cult influence that also has suborned the high council at Avenor.

Arithon, still in recovery in Kewar with Davien, learns that he has awakened the ancient rogue talent for prophetic far-sight, latent in his mother's lineage.

Meantime, the stress introduced to the earth's lane tides by the Koriani bid to upset the Fellowship Sorcerers resulted in aberrant weather and crop failures in the western kingdoms. Threat of famine sends Feylind's brig, *Evenstar*, to Havish, bearing relief supplies. There, to avoid open war, King Eldir asks her to transport Lysaer's runaway wife, Princess Ellaine, eastward to sanctuary with the s'Brydion. The duke dispatches her to a safer refuge with the master spellbinder, Verrain, at Methisle, who in turn, remands her case to the Fellowship Sorcerers, who arrange for a permanent residence with Ath's

Brotherhood, at Spire. There, she is met by her lost son Kevor, now become an adept. This information, returned to Avenor by spies, gives Lysaer's cursed nature the opening to move for war against Alestron, on grounds of treason. He bides his time to launch the campaign, preferring to determine the truth in the charges himself.

At Alestron, Feylind boards Dakar and Fionn Areth upon *Evenstar*'s departure, only to have her brig targeted by Koriathain, who send a plague of fiends to sink the ship and force Arithon to leave his refuge at Kewar to defend his friends. Arithon defeats the assault by tapping the powers of the Paravian sword, Alithiel, and in the process, learns that his shadows have the power to suppress and even manipulate the fiends to do his bidding. He then turns the tables, with Selidie Prime left with the Great Waystone polluted by an *iyat*, as his machination turns her own spell in reverse.

5671—During their winter return, Lysaer and Sulfin Evend successfully curb the Kralovir cult's incursion at Avenor. The council hall is left a total ruin in the aftermath. While both men know an enclave still infiltrates the Alliance in Etarra, the active influence of Desh-thiere's curse makes Lysaer too murderously unreasonable for Sulfin Evend to act on the danger.

Meantime, the Alliance and Lysaer's religion have won enough towns to their cause to threaten the clan enclaves that protect the free wilds across the continent. Throughout the spring and summer, Arithon uses every talented skill he possesses, including *iyats*, to engineer embarrassing incidents and humorous attacks on the Light's followers, knowing the ridicule will eventually draw Lysaer into the south. His tight and intricate plan aims to pin Lysaer down there, then stop the spread of the false faith, end the persecution, and bring a lasting peace between town and clan to protect the free wilds that the Paravian presence requires for survival. But he fails to win the powerful and cantankerous s'Brydion duke into support. This forces Arithon to sever his relationship with Alestron and refuse them his backing, since his rogue talent forecasts the involvement of Desh-thiere's curse, and the near certainty of their utter defeat. He will not countenance being a party to war, and the brutal sack of Alestron that will likely follow should the Alliance come to attack.

On the heels of such set-back, the Fellowship Sorcerers lay a summons on Arithon to help them curb the Kralovir necromancers. The cult's invasive foothold in Lysaer's following at Etarra now poses a consummate danger, with Lysaer on the move with determined intent to muster the eastshore to arms to destroy Alestron. The hope of peace Arithon has worked to achieve is brought to a premature end and leaves his clan allies in deeper jeopardy than ever before, as he must abandon his efforts and travel at speed to Etarra.

His journey takes him by way of Halwythwood, where his effort to console young Jeynsa s'Valerient for her father's loss also misfires. Further, his one opportunity to consummate his undying love for Elaira is forced to an unrequited end by the dreadful discovery that the Prime Matriarch has laid a spell seal on his beloved, with intent to engineer the birth of their talented child for the co-opted use of the order.

Left emotionally raw, aware that Lysaer is building another armed campaign to ruin every trust built among his vulnerable clan allies, Arithon must move on to Etarra where, at risk of his life and sanity, he uses innovative tactics and successfully annihilates every standing member of the Kralovir cult. In the aftermath, the Sorcerer Davien rescues him and transfers him to the focus circle at Sanpashir to recuperate.

Now, with the peace plan ruined, and the demise of the Kralovir taking out several of the Light's highly placed officials, including Etarra's High Chancellor, fear has galvanized town interests against the Master of Shadow. The curse of Desh-thiere is wakened, driving Lysaer and the Alliance of Light to target the s'Brydion as Arithon's collaborator. War is building to raze the citadel at Alestron, with a troop muster sweeping the entire eastshore of the continent and Sulfin Evend recruiting on the southcoast. The season is summer, and the year, Third Age 5671.

Alestron the Bull whipped Adruin at darts.
Kalesh slipped behind with a knife in the dark.
Atwood's secure,
but East Halla's at war,
and the widows are ever in mourning.
– From an eastshore water-front lay, Third Age

I. Binding Ties

O n the night that the portents had named to the elders, stars blazed in white splendour over the obsidian sands of Sanpashir. Their icy light flooded the vista in mercury, knifed with black shade where the ruin cast shadow over a landscape of crumpled dunes. As the signs had bespoken, when the hour foretold by the seers became manifest, the laid pattern of the Paravian stone circle did not arouse to harness the raw powers of the elements. Lane forces did not waken. The indigo coils of starred light did not bloom, as they would for the workings of Sorcerers.

Where nothing had been but barren stone and the trackless waste of bare sand, the figure of the man just arrived seemed to shimmer, then settle into firm form. Naked, he sprawled as though asleep at the grand junction of the ancient focus.

His appearance summoned the tribesfolk who lurked, alert and waiting amid the cragged ruin. They sang. Soft chanting that whispered under the starlight: of a hope renewed, promised to them for millennia. They moved out of cover, silently approached. Their seamed hands were gentle as they gathered him up and wrapped his chilled frame in rough blankets. His skin was not marked, except by old scars. Yet the rifts that he bore in the weave of his aura ran deeper than flesh, bone, and blood.

'*Keir've arish,*' the oldest cautioned in dialect. 'Take him most softly.' She pressed forward, brushed back the man's tangled, black hair, and touched a crabbed finger to still the lips that quivered as though to cry out from a nightmare memory of an unbearable agony. 'The shock to his life-force has been deep and harsh. He must not arouse through our handling.'

Such damage demanded their vigilant care. Many hands lent assistance. Attentive to need, swift and silent, the desert-folk lifted his form, without jostling.

Respectful, they bore him on, past the looming, brick walls of the ruin. Through the cracked, weathered arches that marked the east gate, they turned their steps towards the dawn and made their way into the desert.

The path they walked held no sign-post. Shifting, dark sands erased all past traces of the ancestor's steadfast footprints. Here, guidance lay in the notes of the stars, heard by the ears of their wisest old man. Staff in hand, with slow steps, he led the company bearing the litter.

Yet before they reached the rock outcrops and the spring that promised them shelter and ease, the crone in their midst raised her palm and charged the procession to stop. 'I will require eight dartmen to serve. For there is another. Before night is done, a traveller will set foot on our shores from the decks of a ship bearing in from the west.' To the chosen handful of warriors, she pointed the way, and declared, 'I name him as our guest. Fetch him back.'

The waves crashing onto the black shingle at Sanpashir's cliff head had a muttering voice all their own. From the decks of the Sunwheel Alliance's flag-ship, under the ghostly flutter of the gold-blazoned banners, Sulfin Evend watched the white spume jet up and subside, bright and brief as the sparkle of diamond. Sable waters reflected the brilliance of stars, small light to his dark apprehension. This brooding shore-line of rock was a desolate destination. Only adamant use of his superior rank had brought the state galley to anchor. This territory was proscribed, demarked as free wilds, and no town-born man's place to trespass. Even the lord who held the command of the Alliance of Light's amassed war host should shun the prospect of landing.

Sulfin Evend took no comfort from the disciplined industry of the deck-crew, launching off the small tender at his insistence. His charge to leave the safe decks of the galley and pursue the unknown course of a promise was unlikely to settle his wracked peace of mind. He could scarcely stem the dread course of the future. Yet the hand-wringing nerves of his subordinate troop captain failed to unseat his resolve.

'Why should you do this?' Gold braid and Sunwheel surcoat reduced to pin-prick glints under starlight, the kindly man tried one last time to dissuade his conflicted Lord Commander. 'The desert tribes are not lenient with strangers. They poison the barbed points on their weapons.'

Sulfin Evend breathed in the sea air, freighted with blown salt and the rock-scented dew swept off the crags of the headland. 'Because the cause that we serve is grievously flawed. I cannot engage Lysaer's orders to recruit, or bear the Alliance standard to assault the s'Brydion citadel. Not before doing all in my power to secure a defensive talisman against the wanton destruction posed by Desh-thiere's curse.'

'Such strength and courage may not save your skin,' the galley's master broke in from the side-lines. Experience backed up his claim, that no task in this wasteland should ever be tried, even for dire necessity.

'What is my life, if not the desire to stand true at the side of a friend who's endangered?' Sulfin Evend shrugged under the weight of a mail shirt that offered haphazard protection from darts. 'Best I die here than fight at Alestron, leading a force of deluded fanatics blinded by Light, with no heart.' Beyond any words, the thought never spoken: the memory of Lysaer's private anguish, turned into a pillow to silence an onslaught of weeping fit to tear spirit from flesh. The stamp of the Mistwraith's design on such greatness was a sorrow not to be borne.

The davits squealed, and the tender struck the face of the sea with a splash that slapped wavelets against the state galley. Its crew of four oarsmen scrambled down the side battens. The coxswain assumed his post in the bow and pronounced the craft ready to board.

Since danger was unlikely to change the granite set to the Lord Commander's intent, the galley's master stepped back, his face creased with concern under the glow of the deck-lamp. 'Fare safely, then, and may the Light's blessing guard you until your return.'

Sulfin Evend snapped off a nod, then strode to embrace the poised jaws of his fate.

Settled in the boat, he claimed a seat in the stern, where his anxious, hatchet-nosed equerry awaited, clutching his hobnailed boots. 'I've brought your cloak,' the servant added with diffidence. 'The night wind has a bite.'

The Light's Lord Commander clapped the man's shoulder as thanks, while the reluctant rowers threaded their looms into the rowlocks, and slashed into black water with the launching stroke. The prow of the boat knifed into the darkness, towards the restless thread of cream surf and the stark shore of Sanpashir.

A landing through snags of rock and tumbling breakers taxed the seamanship of the men, accustomed to harbour-side docks, and the light chop behind sheltered jetties. When the craft reached the strand, the keel jarred against the obsidian sands, tossed like a chip in a mill-race. Sulfin Evend leaped the thwart, boots clutched to his chest, his cloak left behind in the white-knuckled grasp of the servant. Soaked to the waist, and buffeted by cold combers necklaced with foam, he helped steady the boat, shouting against the thundering waves that he would require no escort.

Since the craft would upset if the men stalled for argument, the coxswain shrilled orders for the oarsmen to change seat and reverse stroke back to the flagship.

Sulfin Evend strode free of the clawing surf. Barefoot and chilled, stumbling in the ebb currents, he stepped onto the wet sand under the vertical crags of the cliff head. Here, the clammy sea-breeze smelled of flint. The forbidding summit reared above, punch-cut against pre-dawn stars. Except for the wind and the tide, nothing spoke. The night of the dark moon cloaked the rock-face in secretive shadow. All civilized movement seemed far removed from this vista of primal wildness.

Or so Sulfin Evend was wont to presume, until he arrived at the weathered rock above the shingle. He had little chance to stamp on his dry boots. A male warrior issued a challenge out of the night. His speech was in dialect, most likely a fierce demand that the stranger stand forth and declare himself.

Sulfin Evend lost the last hope he had to soften his moment of reckoning. Answer, and he would be tagged by his town-bred, Hanshire accent. Stand silent, or try to run, and his infringing presence must provoke a lethal reaction. Never mentioning the fact that his Alliance rank as Lysaer's first commander, and his birth as the son of a mayor, marked him out as an enemy.

'I come on a mission of peace,' he announced, and gave nothing else but his name.

No sound attended the flurry of movement arisen out of the shadows. Eight men stepped forth, clad in loose, desert robes, with blow-tubes and darts at the ready. Sulfin Evend's blood ran chill at the sight. No routine patrol, this many warriors suggested the uncanny thought that his arrival *had been expected*.

The man at the fore changed tongue and addressed him again, clipped as sparks hammered off hot steel. 'Whom do you serve with your heart? Whose loyalty binds your body? Whose cause rules your mind?'

Sulfin Evend clamped his jaw. A year ago, he could have given the query an honourable, direct answer. Then, his oath to Avenor and Lysaer had not yet been flawed by the shoals of moral conflict. His hesitation drew the eyes of the dartmen, measuring him with cruel calculation.

Courage could not stem the blank well of his terror. Yet he answered with truth. 'Heart, body, and mind, I'm blood-bound to the land though the ache of that weighs like a shackle.'

The leading desertman arched his brows in surprise. 'What would you give for release, then?'

'No coin is left,' Sulfin Evend replied. 'None that won't cost me my life, or far worse, the ruin of a friend who's endangered.'

Again, the ring of robed dartmen advanced, the one at the forefront closest of all. The dusky features under his hood held a scouring intensity that might read a man's very thoughts through his skin. 'Sacrifice brings you to Sanpashir's free wilds?'

The sorrow welled up, then, too fierce to deny. Sulfin Evend shook his head. 'No. Concerning a pledge to a Fellowship Sorcerer, I have come to your tribe to consult.'

If that startling statement was greeted by murmurs, the lead dartman's gesture restored his warriors to formal silence. 'Your friend,' he said carefully. 'He needs no defence. Not if he still lives, and so has the power of choice.'

Sulfin Evend disclosed the unsavoury fact. 'He is cursed. A vile binding that clouds his sight and warps his nature until he cannot know how much his will has been compromised. I have given my pledge to stand guard for him, and for that claimed burden, I place my appeal.'

The lead dartman bowed his mantled head. 'By your will, then, disarm. All your weapons. You will also strip off every item you own that is not woven or braided from sun-ripened fibre.'

At Sulfin Evend's stiff resistance, the lead dartman smiled, a flash of white teeth in the gloom. 'This is our way, town-bred! You are advised. One chance is given to respect our customs and stand on the truth that has brought you. Do you merit?'

Sulfin Evend shot back his most cynical smile. 'Surrender, or else I'll be taken?'

The lead dartman bridled. 'Did you think the least step of your path is not known? Our eldest has Seen you! Your trespasser's foot on our shores bears a portent, locked tight in the wheels of destiny. You will come, town-bred man. Though how you embrace the fate that awaits you as yet remains to be written.'

Sulfin Evend caught back his self-deprecative laughter. Had he wished to turn back, the moment was forfeit, gone with his past consent to a Sorcerer's knife cut. He had no option but to lift off his helm, doff his belt and surcoat, shed his coat of mail, then peel off his laced leather gambeson. Stripped to his linen shirt and soaked breeches, and still braving the cruel rocks, barefoot, he unhooked the thong that secured the wrapped bundle that hung at his neck. The sheathed knife inside should not be left with the other steel weapons abandoned to rust on the beachhead.

He extended the wrapped dagger. 'This blade is flint, and not fashioned for killing. The deer-hide still shrouds it, as it was entrusted to me by the woman who made me its bearer.'

The lead dartman stepped forward, a wraith in jet robes. Backed by his tense dartmen, he lifted lean hands. His clasp, light and warm, briefly caged the slim bundle, overtop of the townsman's cold fingers.

'*Feiyd eth sa!*' he snapped to his dartmen, in dialect. The inflection sounded amazed. Then he tipped his head, perhaps with respect. 'I will take charge of this knife, town-bred man. It will be unveiled, and its purpose made known to you if you come to win the petition you've asked for.'

Upon his signal, the robed dartmen closed in. They offered no word, no grace of assurance. Sulfin Evend found his hands strapped at the wrists. A blindfold obscured his vision. Then an impatient prod urged his stumbling, first step into an unknown future.

The same stars that wheeled above Sanpashir's headland bathed wan light over the vista of waste, due east of the Paravian circle. The ruin's gapped wall, with its forlorn tracery of carved arches, was not visible from the barren vale where the desert tribe's elder signalled her people to pause. The litter-borne man was let down on black earth, his blanket-swathed frame aligned to the north.

'Softly, now. His deep shock will release, soon.' The wise crone who spoke as the voice of the tribe settled herself on the ground at the crown of the unconscious one's head.

Stillness reigned then, while the night sky revolved around the pole star that glimmered at its fixed axis. The dark moon passed nadir, reversed its fierce grip, and gave way at last to the hush that preceded the dawn. At that hour, the life tide that swept through land and air breathed through all things on Athera. First herald of the paean that came with the sunrise, its current was acknowledged by the circle of male elders, also seated in cross-legged stillness.

To their listening presence, the subtle quickening recharged the nerves like a sweet flare of lightning. The wounded survivor tucked in the blankets would not be overlooked by that benison. In thanksgiving for all things that lived, the ancient woman raised her voice and sang welcome, eyes trained upon the man at her knees as though his limp flesh held the flame of a lamp indescribably precious . . .

Arithon Teir's'Ffalenn recovered the full range of his senses one disparate strand at a time. The alkaline tang of dry mineral came first: the unmistakable, signature scent of the wind hissing over the bleak sands of Sanpashir. With sound came the lilt of an old woman's voice, crooning over his head. His limbs were kept warm by a rough, goat-hair blanket that bristled his sensitized skin. That discomfort lost meaning, undone by the joy that moved through the song. Though the crone's aged tone held a rasping quaver, her wise intent showered his mage-sense in glittering waves of sweet harmony.

Terror lurked outside, a drowning, black fear held at bay by the singer's lines of protection: the agonized memory, *not formless*! of bone knives and unnatural, dark seals wrought to seed dire torment and ensnare the spirit at the threshold of death.

Arithon loosed a shuddering sigh and wept through a flood of relief: first for the clean air that entered his lungs, then for the gift of mage-guided company.

He responded in thanks with his eyes shut. 'Mother Dark's blessing. Increase to the tribes, for your kindness.'

The grandame's evocative melody ceased. Not her warding, which shimmered still, an ephemeral embrace wrought from moving light that laced her guest's form in sealed quiet.

'What can a destitute *teidwar* return?' said Arithon Teir's'Ffalenn, quite undone by the piercing tenderness of her insight. The word he had chosen was in deep desert dialect, meaning *'outland, strange person, who fares through another's place, kinless.'*

Clothing rustled, to movement. His benefactress laid her tender hand on the blanket. Even that brief instant of pressure over his heart caused a flinch.

Her murmur held sympathy. 'There, do you see? The scar remains, yet. Though your body has knitted, and the ritual cuts are closed over, the etheric mark you still bear is not healed. Lie calm. Here is safety. Nor are you *teidwar*. Spirit who serves the true light, and this land, *D'aedenthic* himself has delivered you.'

'Fire Hands?' whispered Arithon in puzzled translation. The desert-folks' habit of speech often wound through convoluted, layered meanings. Since given names rarely were spoken aloud, he guessed with a wry twist of irony, 'Kewar's Sorcerer. You know him? Then I must apologize. Given the choice, I would not have burdened your people with my infirmity.'

The crone clicked her teeth. 'We asked. Yes, harken! You are here because your distress is our provenance.'

That direct claim shot Arithon's eyes open. As refined vision darkened to sensory sight, he stared upward: into crinkled, brown features, framed in wind-tangled snags of white hair. The woman sat against the wide, lucent sky, tinted aqua by on-coming daybreak. Her fringed head-dress was patterned with the beautiful yarns the tribes spun from silk and dyed goat hair. The gaudy colours seemed fit to stun his uncertain grasp on recovery.

'Your problem, old one?' He searched her burled face. Respectful, as Masterbard, he chose to use her cultural phrasing for absolute clarity. 'I don't see how our lines cross. Therefore, I don't understand.'

She cackled, amused. Seamed fingers brushed his cheek like a child's, while her patience chided his insolence. 'Lines! They are ancient. Older than Biedar have lived on Athera. Mother Dark has shown us your name for that long. The winds speak your voice, at each birthing.'

'I don't see how our lines cross,' Prince Arithon restated, the edge to his tone all but warning.

'Torbrand's get! Truly.' Black eyes glinted. The elder settled back on her heels. Ever restless, the breeze whirled stray sand on the blanket through the moment she peered at him, slantwise. 'You wish to leave, naked?'

Outplayed, not yet irritated, Arithon sighed. 'Fire Hands was remiss not to leave me a cloak.'

'He knew you that well,' the old woman agreed. Her dry grasp shifted, cupped over the frown that troubled his brow. Since he was tired, he chose to allow her: the touch brought him sleep that carried him, dreamless, into the gold of new morning.

Since the desert tribes travelled by night in deep summer, he was not aware of the strong, younger hands that tucked him in a litter and bore him into a cairn of stacked rocks. He slept the day through. When sundown came, the aged crone rubbed his wrists and his feet with sweet oil, and set a fresh warding to ensure that he did not awaken. Her nod roused the camp. The young men who stood guard shouldered the litter again, then resumed their careful trek eastward under the slender sickle of the waxing moon.

Arithon rested. The trackless, black wastes erased the night's journey from memory, while the wheeling stars passed overhead without record. The soft lilt of voices, and the bright *ching*! of the goat-bells glanced off his unhearing ears.

No nightmare struck until the dark just past midnight, when the spirit tide ebbed, and frayed boundaries were most wont to weaken. The horror that stalked was not real, *not present*; but the dream-state both altered and rippled the veil, blurring the line between time's world of substance, and the vistas beyond, that lapped at the unfettered mind.

Hammer to anvil, the emotional impact shuddered through breathing flesh. Arithon thrashed. The insufferable feeling lived with him, still: a remembered horror that *had occurred*, as his being was drawn by arcane constraint, then forced into shackling bondage. The experience of being disbarred from death shocked a howl that began in his viscera and opened his throat in raw agony.

A callused palm muffled his outcry. Other hands, agile and youthfully strong, caught his battering wrists and his ankles. While spoken words that meant nothing tried and failed to bring surcease to his torment, he struck out with deranged ferocity.

'Nay so!' rapped a voice of incisive command. The restraint – *not bloodied rope ties, or wax seals* – fell away.

Abruptly freed, Arithon curled on his side. A knot laced into himself, trapped in misery, he trembled, until a tentative, kindly touch laid a strung lyranthe against his clenched fingers.

His shuddering breath took in the familiar: a fragrance of citrus-waxed wood and old varnish. The clean scent of the resin used to stiffen the instrument's tuning pegs raised the forgotten echo of joy. Closed fists unbent. Tortured, Arithon reached out and stroked the cool, silken finish of shell inlay and gemstones. These had voice in the darkness. A beauty that whispered through mage-sense, imprinted by generations of masterbards, each devoted, unswerving, to harmony. Most recent of these, Halliron sen Alduin, still seemed to be chiding him with the wise vehemence given to elderly men before dying: *'If a masterbard's music can one day spare your life, or that of your loyal defenders, you will use it . . .'*

Successor now bearing his mentor's title, Arithon fought the surge of his nightmares to listen. His outer ear heard the brushed voice of the wind, drawn across ten courses of silver-wound wire, with the bass drone strings, thrumming beneath. No matter how emotionally raw, his sensitized talent could not refuse their sweet resonance.

Arithon gasped a ripped word of gratitude. Reunited with the heirloom lyranthe last played at Sanpashir to raise the lane flux in transfer two years ago, he shoved erect and acknowledged the desert tribes' generous stewardship. Then he gathered the instrument into his arms. His trembling clasp traced over the fretboard. Desperation guided his tuning. When the first chord rang out in corrected pitch, he immersed his torn faculties into the weaving of music.

His measures plunged into the well of blind fear. Sliding falls carried him deeper. He wrought his brutal despair into melody, carving out the courage and calm to plumb the most ravaging depths. In harmony, he sought to shatter the terror and break the cycle of endless reliving.

He would heal by such art, though recovery took days. The Biedar crone allowed him that space. Her dartmen pitched camp and kept watch at her bidding, until the afflicted had played his horrific dreams to a state of prostrate exhaustion.

Then their journey resumed, with Arithon litter-borne. Once they reached the haven of Sanpashir's deep caverns, they slipped into the womb of the earth. In the split cavern they called by the Name of the air, they granted their guest a tight, warded circle of privacy.

There, his days passed in silence. By night, his cascading spill of struck notes drilled through rock and wind and raised tears in the far-sighted eyes of their gifted.

That incongruous, sheet-silver curtain of sound was the first thing to greet the outland intruder brought in tribal custody from the sea-side. Herded in before dawn a moon's quarter hence, this one the Biedar still held under blindfold. Town-born, he had come uninvited, bearing forged arms to the headland. Because his outspoken protests were ignorant, his escort maintained their precautions. Besides the rag, this trespasser's wrists were lashed behind his stiff back.

Since sunrise eased the dread pull of rank dreams, the new arrival need not bear the heart's cry of the other guest's lyranthe for long.

While the final, struck notes spun dying echoes through the maze of Sanpashir's caverns, Sulfin Evend was pressed, stumbling, down a steep incline of stone. The deft hands of four dartmen guided him through the narrows that guarded a cul-de-sac. There, the tied cloth was pulled from his eyes. A silent young woman swathed in veils cut the rope from his wrists. She replaced the rough bonds with soft rag, more graciously knotted in front of his waist. A damp cloth was offered to cleanse his dust-caked face. Then dried meat, sour cheese, and an unleavened biscuit were set into his anxious grasp. For the first time since setting foot on the shore-line, Sulfin Evend was permitted to eat and drink on his own.

His escort of silent, robed dartmen remained. They tracked his least move with inimical, dark eyes and answered none of his questions.

Then, as now, they refused to soften despite his peaceful entreaty. An impatient man, Sulfin Evend leashed rage. He had little choice. A dead seeress's loan of their elder's flint knife had been the *sole* grace that once defended his sworn liege's life. Since the talisman had delivered the spirit, intact, from the hideous rites of Grey Kralovir's necromancers, the Lord Commander of the Alliance's war host stifled his rampant frustration. He was not such a fool, to transgress arcane bargains. Neither could he evade the harsh charge of his oath to a Fellowship Sorcerer.

His overtaxed nerves would have to be nursed, one hard-set breath at a time. Sulfin Evend ate the simple fare without savour. Wary of the poison that tipped desert darts, he would endure till these uncivilized people chose to grant his appeal.

The haunting strain of the lyranthe remained silenced when at length his warders allowed him to sleep. Yet somehow the searing measures lived on, unleashing a torrent of unquiet dreams. Sulfin Evend catnapped upon the damp stone, while the taciturn dartmen kept watch from the dark, their vigilance stubborn as bed-rock.

Later, an older man came with a torch. Words were exchanged in thick dialect. Then the elder departed. The robed dartmen allowed Sulfin Evend a brief walk outside to stretch his legs and relieve himself. Under daylight, he snatched the opening to ask once again if he might be given a fair hearing. As usual, no one deigned to reply. The desert-folk hustled him out of the glaring white sun. Dazzled and stumbling, he was prodded back into the gloom of the rock cave. While he was still blinking and cursing stubbed toes, they rebound his wrists with their twisted rag ropes. Then he was ushered back underground, but not to the same cave of imprisonment.

This pass, he was led through a narrower cleft, worn smooth by the footsteps of centuries. The close wall on both sides had been carved. Sulfin Evend need not be a scholar to recognize the interlaced coils of Mother Dark's mystic serpents. Heart pounding, unprepared, he realized his hour for audience had arrived. The reddish gleam of a lit cavern loomed at the far end of the corridor.

'There, you will go,' the lead dartman instructed, and although no other order was given, the escort of warriors melted behind. The outland stranger was left the choice to proceed of his own free will.

Sulfin Evend steadied his harrowed nerves. Past turning back, he advanced to confront a power of mystery that had stood in the breach to curb an entrenched binding of necromancy. Such strength, perhaps, fit to rival the arcane reach of a Fellowship Sorcerer, whom none but a fool approached lightly.

Across that carved threshold, rinsed in carnelian glare, a crone sat beyond the embers of a neat fire. She was shrouded. Black silk veils melted at one with the shadow thrown off by the coals. Her motionless presence might have been overlooked had the intricate whorls of embroidery that patterned her hems not chiselled her form in the darkness. The rock floor underneath her tucked knees had been channelled with similar patterns. Their looping spirals confounded the eye, while the gravid air wove an uncanny dance with a fragrant blanket of herb smoke.

Afraid for no reason, Sulfin Evend stopped cold. Instinct insisted that he should take flight without any care for the consequence. Before he risked death as a dartman's pinned target, his trailing escort grabbed hold. They shoved his reluctant, awkward step forward, then pressed him face-down on the earth.

'She is eldest!' snapped one in the stilted accent imposed by his wilderness dialect. 'Here, she rules. All others brought inside of our circle must show their seemly respect.'

The townsman submitted until they let him up, though the sensitivity brought by his errant clan lineage prickled his nape with unpleasant warning. An odd charge of awareness seemed to attend the ancient woman's rapt stillness. Almost, the cave's stone seemed to whisper and speak, while the flickering fire hissed in the cold air like the breath of a thousand vipers.

Sulfin Evend crouched on his heels. A brave man in battle, he could not stop shivering. The crone never moved. She looked unassuming in her rags and raw silk. Yet her wisdom spoke volumes through silence. Worse than Enithen Tuer's, her eerie knowing unsettled his calm as she uncovered her wizened face. No matter how seasoned, the grown man wrestled dread, while her black, shining eyes stared him through.

The well-rehearsed greeting Sulfin Evend intended stuck on his paralyzed tongue.

The crone motioned him closer.

The skilled dartmen behind disallowed his insane urge to try protest. Sulfin Evend edged towards the fire and sat. Hands tied, he could not refuse the goat-horn flask the barbaric matriarch uncorked and pressed to his lips. He managed the trial, though the swallow he took seized his breath like a fist in the guts. The bitter taste of strange herbs made his eyes water, while the bite of alcohol kindled a bonfire inside, wringing his body to sweat and rushed pulse.

The old one nodded, apparently appeased by his effort to honour her customs. She opened without need to ask for his name, or inquire what purpose had brought him. 'Your kinsman who lay under threat of the shadow that consumes the spirit is dead.'

'Raiett?' gasped Sulfin Evend. 'Lysaer's appointed Lord Governor of Etarra? He can't be!' The shock left him stunned, that the crone's uncanny faculties might read even the branching ties of his blood-line. 'I wished to petition your people for knowledge! Beg a stay of protection, that my uncle might be permitted the chance of salvation.'

'Done!' said the old woman. 'The cult you knew as Grey Kralovir has been sundered. Already, the one you name Raven has passed from this world, cut free from the ties of black craftmarks. Your need was released on the hour his remains were consumed, cleansed of all taint by white mage-fire.'

She moved. Paper dry as the scald of sun on baked rock, her crabbed finger tapped his moist forehead. 'You need not plead for our help, town-born man! Nor do you owe any debt to Biedar. Not for your kinsman, departed.'

Rattled by the uncivilized drink, or perhaps by the jab of her censure, Sulfin Evend wrestled the scatter of his wheeling, irrational thoughts. For in fact, the dire peril to his uncle had been the lesser of two threats that brought him. 'I bore a flint knife, made by your ancestry, that your warriors reclaimed at the time I made landfall.'

Unblinking, the crone nodded. 'The knife you brought back here has always carried but one written Name on its destiny.'

Sulfin Evend gathered his courage. 'Then I ask leave to plead for your favour.'

The old woman strummed a hand through her necklet of bone, jangling its strings of carved fetishes. If not encouragement, the gesture suggested he had her due leave to explain himself.

'I once gave my word to a Fellowship Sorcerer to return the knife's legacy to your keeping. This, I have done. The boon I would ask of your grace is to loan me the talisman for additional protection. I make the appeal on behalf of my liege. Lysaer s'Ilessid lies entrapped under a vile curse by the Mistwraith. Could you grant a stay to defend him when the madness saps his right mind? As the prince's sworn man, pledged to safeguard his virtue, I speak the truth. The Alliance behind him is built on false cause. I petition your people for assistance. Don't leave me stripped of all recourse as my liege loses ground to the blood-lust imposed by Desh-thiere.'

The crone laced her seamed fingers. 'Your obligation not being ours, you shall meet the one whose true gift has arranged for your uncle's deliverance.'

Sulfin Evend bristled. 'Did you hear nothing? Lysaer's misguided policy seeks to cleanse every trace of initiate knowledge from the five kingdoms. Backed by the fanatical, armed might of the towns, this self-righteous crusade may yet come to threaten the ancient roots of your heritage.'

'Refuse?' snapped the crone, not one whit inclined to reverse her lofty dismissal. 'A fool's errand, truly! Do you realize whose Name you spurn to know? His hand is the same, that will wield our ancestor's knife! Through him, the Kralovir's vile works have just been undone for all time. Ahead, *if his strength stays the course of his fate*, he bears the very flame of your hope.'

Frowning, his throat left seared raw from her wretched decoction, Sulfin Evend forced the stark inquiry. 'You claim that this man has brought Lysaer's salvation?'

'Past, and perhaps for the future.' The crone bent her head, deferent. 'Alone on Athera, he is the key to secure your liege's deliverance from jeopardy!'

Sulfin Evend lost his breath. Rocked dizzy, he ventured, 'Whose Name, then, Lady?' Sweating beneath her discerning, hard stare, he barely sustained without cringing. 'Do you speak of a Fellowship Sorcerer?' No other power abroad, that he knew, could have routed the works of the Kralovir.

The crone hissed in the negative. 'Mother Dark's chosen is not of the Starborn.' Both wrists chinked with bracelets, twisted of blown glass and copper, as she spread her red-dyed palms in a gesture that acknowledged the forces that lived and moved through the world, unseen. 'Know him, and the boon that you ask of Biedar is well answered. For there will come the dark hour. His life thread crosses the palm of your hand. The choice is yours, *seithur*, whether or not to stay blinded.'

Head spinning from the heat of the fire and the searing influence of the strange herbs, Sulfin Evend grappled to make sense of the crone's oblique phrases. She insisted the threat at Etarra was cleared. If so, the dread taint of necromancy had been expunged from the core of Lysaer's Alliance *already*. Sulfin Evend cradled his head in roped hands. Prompted by gratitude, he yielded to the tribal elder's request to confront her prodigal champion.

What would her folk show him, after all, but another primitive shaman, steeped within the queer, uncouth mystery of her nomadic tradition?

Blindfolded once again by the dartmen, Sulfin Evend found himself ushered away from the crone's revered presence. His steps were not steady. Either the pungent drink or the smoke from the coals had befuddled his natural senses. Drawing deep gulps of clean air in the passage, he let his escort draw him farther into the caves that riddled the deeps of Sanpashir. They guided him downwards. The way turned in switchbacks upon a steep slope, sometimes carved with the semblance of steps. Generations of inhabitance had smoothed the limestone into worn hollows. The dank tang of mineral mingled with smells of rancid fat and cold soot. Sulfin Evend was held back while someone lit a torch. Footfalls echoed around him as he was prodded leftwards, into a passage. The air changed, the last of the desert's dry heat smothered out by the bone chill of underground bed-rock and damp. He heard the trickle of fresh water, and waded through cold, shallow pools. The cavern whispered with the splashed plink of springs, no help to salvage his bearings.

The dark and the blindfold unstrung his mazed faculties. Now, each stumbling step and the close taint of smoke wrung him to visceral nausea. He lost count of the turnings and thresholds he crossed before the path wended upwards. He panted, distressed, though the sharp ascent seemed not to trouble the desertmen. He tasted the scorched flint of dry, outdoor air. The grave chill of the deeps gave way to close warmth, threaded through by the fragrance of embers reduced from a birch fire.

There, Sulfin Evend was steered to a halt.

The warrior beside him gave warning. 'Take care, town-born man. Do not stray too near. The one you approach is a sensitive, and for this, we ask your respect. A warding circle laid down by our elders keeps guard for his fragile peace.'

The blind was removed. Though no one came forward to untie his wrists, the armed escort stepped back and stood down. Their cloaked forms melted into the shadow behind, leaving Sulfin Evend alone to regain his strayed bearings.

He stood at the verge of a narrow rock-chamber. A raw crack in the ceiling let in the fresh air. The errant, hot breeze from outside winnowed smoke from a clay pot packed with coals, several yards from his planted feet. That carmine glow, and the pallid scatter of ambient light glanced lines of reflection off a lyranthe's silver-wound strings.

The instrument leaned against the far wall, its lacquered wood inset with a shimmer of jewels. Sulfin Evend shivered. The instrument owned a spare symmetry fit to pierce a man to the heart. Such beauty bespoke nothing less than the grace of Paravian craftsmanship.

Startled to find an heirloom beyond price in this unlikely, rough setting, Sulfin Evend peered into the gloom. There, he picked out a supine form, sprawled on a woven blanket.

The stranger the elder dispatched him to meet was no swarthy offshoot of tribal heritage. This man was pale-skinned. His arched feet were bare. Healed abrasions gleamed white on his ankles. The rest of his frame was obscured by the loose, silk garb of the desert. He did not seem either unsettled or dangerous. Asleep, his slight stature and angular face appeared refined, even strikingly vulnerable.

The contrary fact that he looked unimposing jarred every natural instinct.

First the glossy black hair, then the savage old scar, half-twisted the length of his right forearm, cued the uncanny awareness. Sulfin Evend realized he beheld none else but the Master of Shadow: for three decades, the author of unconscionable massacres and the sorcerer whose conniving wiles had once lured an elite band of Hanshire light horse to a nightmarish ruin inside a grimward.

Reason fled. Tied wrists notwithstanding, Sulfin Evend surged forward. His graphic memories of lost comrades, undone one by one, and consigned to hideous slaughter, lit his primal urge to retaliate.

Fierce hands jerked him backwards. Jabbed at the knees, knocked down by brute force, Sulfin Evend was cuffed and pinned flat by the hands of his wrathful escort. The tribesfolk were not a forgiving race. They gagged his mouth, trussed his legs, and rendered him helpless before they abandoned him to his fate. Their matriarch's decree left him sprawled at the feet of his liege's most merciless enemy: the same wanton criminal he had striven to destroy on Lysaer's failed campaign in Daon Ramon.

The last warrior to leave shed his dusty robe and tossed it over the prostrate outlander. 'To spare the sight of the one you offend, since our revered eldest has charged us to keep you here!'

Encounter

Hard-breathing and furious, Sulfin Evend could not thrash off the light cloth draped across him. Its clinging folds masked his prone body and face. Each breath, he inhaled the barbaric musk left ingrained by its owner. The mélange of strange herbs, ginger spice, and old wood smoke added a vicious kick to his vertigo. He found no recovery. The chill stone where he lay seemed alive with queer flashes of light, while his ears became overwhelmed by the force of plain silence.

His effort to curse entangled a tongue that rejected the habit of speech. Such uncanny malaise had to mean the old woman's welcoming drink had contained a narcotic infusion. Sulfin Evend regretted his manners, too late. He panted, pressed prostrate by his gravid flesh, while the bounds of his mind came undone, then up-ended, and dissolved his perception into spinning confusion.

He reeled, unmoored, beyond count of time. The earth did not measure by minutes. Magnified senses marked each indrawn breath, then entwined them with those of another man, sleeping. Identity blurred. The Light's Lord Commander lost track of himself. When his enemy shuddered, gripped by black nightmares, Sulfin Evend felt his own heart constrict. Shared dread rode him, roughshod. He quaked with terror. Tormented shadows that he could not see gibbered and wailed, hounding him into a darkness more vast than the deep. No fight availed him. He could not break free. His raced pulse drummed to his shredding fear, while his staked spirit languished, shackled between his locked limbs.

Far worse than helpless: Sulfin Evend felt as though drawn on unseen wires out of his hapless flesh.

The throes of rank horror *would not release*. Without training to harness the

23

gifts of his outbred clan blood-line, Sulfin Evend lacked the self-command to awaken. Suffering entrapped him in vivid distress. Every nerve he possessed felt redrawn in flame, until he lost his grip, crushed to madness. Shattered past recourse, he floundered, unstrung, when a lyranthe note speared through the dark.

Its ringing, sweet pitch snapped out of nowhere and sliced the unravelling thread of stark terror.

Another note followed, then another, cascading into a seamless run of ineffable, scalding purity. The graceful progression burgeoned into a chord that engaged formless dread, and *from nothing*, raised a bulwark of shimmering harmony.

Suspension ensued, upheld by a steadfast commitment that denied the chokehold of despair. Hope danced, forged into melody that rejected insidious dissolution. Where abased torment reigned, beauty unfurled the adamant fire of will.

Lifted free, Sulfin Evend wept without sound, while the cry of the other man's heart refigured itself in the soaring majesty of music. Fingers wrought light out of silver-wound strings and invoked exaltation through Ath's gift of unvanquished freedom.

Peace returned. What darkness remained had been cleansed of all stain, reduced to mere shade cast by moonbeams. The master musician laid down his last line. Exquisite, his closing chord faded. The quietude, after, still gleamed with raised power, even when he damped off his strings.

Left with a fragile, cathartic scar to offset an experience of lacerating separation, Sulfin Evend heard the sigh of stirred air as the superb instrument was set aside. A whisper of fabric described movement. Senses torn raw caught the near-soundless step that approached. Through drug haze and dull sickness, the shock of encounter carried an unbearable clarity: the looming fierce presence of the sorcerer took pause, brought short by belated discovery. An explorative touch traced the mantle that masked Sulfin Evend's prostrate shoulder.

'Dharkaron Avenge!' swore the Spinner of Darkness, sharpened to startled annoyance. 'A bound prisoner? What uncivil trick left you here?'

The robe draped over Sulfin Evend's gagged form was grasped, then snapped away.

Since nightfall left the cave dark as pitch, the initiate mind would use mage-sense: the Master of Shadow surveyed what lay at his feet. Wide open still, sensitized by his music, he exclaimed in shocked anguish, 'Ath's mercy forgive! *You're the same one who maimed Jieret!*'

Talented Sight and narcotic trance brought the past to collide with the present: still snagged into unwitting rapport, Sulfin Evend was hurled back into grisly recall, as a red-haired victim's hot blood splashed from the vengeful cut of his dagger.

He curled on his side, retching, while his enemy recoiled above him.

Barraged, caught stripped of defences as well, Arithon sucked a fast breath. He owned the strength of training to wrestle his unleashed emotion, but not the gush of a far-sighted talent, run irretrievably wild: *for he was not yet healed*. The traumatic assault on him by dark necromancy still faulted his natural barriers. The breach entangled his crown gift of empathy with flaring aggression and rage.

No less volatile, *and* just as viciously mirrored: he matched an antagonist also unstrung by deranging hallucination.

Equanimity shattered, Arithon gasped, staggered by the blazing ferocity that reached for instinctive revenge. Brute discipline triumphed. *He did not strike to kill*. The curbed stress discharged into his auric field and released as a burst of gold light.

But the stripping exposure laid his face bare to the force of his unassuaged grief.

Then darkness resettled. Sulfin Evend braced for a knife in the ribs, or a fist, as such a fury of towering, unexpressed pain triggered reflexive violence.

No mangling blow fell. The stilled, charcoal air gave nothing back. Not a sound, or a breeze, or a footstep. Unable to fight, unable to speak, unable to vent through his helplessness, Sulfin Evend shut his eyes. Strapped hand and foot, teeth clamped against nausea, he feared to breathe lest the tension should break him in pieces.

The touch, lightly trembling, grasped his shoulder again, to a ragged line spoken in Paravian. Met by a flinch, the Teir's'Ffalenn cursed. Then he said, still distressed, 'Relax. I wasn't expecting the Alliance Commander at Arms as my afternoon's idle company.' A deeply drawn breath, and his composure steadied. 'Despite what you've heard about my reputation, I'm truly not planning to murder you.'

But of course, Sulfin Evend held no grounds for trust. A confirmed enemy must understand that. Trussed as he was, he could do little but heave and try not to choke on the gag left by the barbaric dartmen.

There came, moments later, the soft hiss of flame: Arithon had rekindled the coal-pot. 'Drugged *and* held speechless? No wonder you fear. The flash-back similarity to your mishandling of Earl Jieret must sweat you with dreadful anxiety.' To the whisper of silk, he came close. His agile fingers loosened the knot and unwound the uncouth strip of rag.

Despite nausea, Sulfin Evend twisted his head and glared up at his looming nemesis. 'I don't fear death. You won't hear me beg.'

Slight of bone, neat of movement, the Master of Shadow tossed the fouled cloth aside in distaste. Unfazed, he moved on, then released the rope that restrained the Lord Commander's numbed ankles. 'Shall we drop the predictable, boring exchange? The pain my *caithdein* suffered is past. The same for your uncle, dead at my hand. He might have been saved had he not been so quick to dismiss the goodwill of an adversary.'

As his wrists were freed also, Sulfin Evend discovered he needed an enemy's help to sit up. Stiff from confinement, embarrassed by shame that thwarted all rational courtesy, he rubbed his gouged skin to restore circulation.

Scrambled wits forestalled even tact. He could not contain reckless bitterness. 'Where was goodwill, when Lysaer s'Ilessid was tricked into burning his own troops in Daon Ramon?'

The mistake was immediate: mention of *that name* with hostile intent could not do other than trigger the curse of Desh-thiere.

Arithon froze. Eyes darkened, he transformed on a breath to a mindless predator coiled to spring. Too late for even foolhardy regret, Sulfin Evend stared at death, poised to rend him apart without conscience.

There, the savage moment suspended. The inflicted pattern that sparked deranged madness hammered into an initiate sorcerer's singular will. The Master of Shadow shuddered. Griped as though body and spirit knew agony, he twisted and rammed his outflung hands against the jagged stonewall. Braced there, hard-breathing, he turned into himself with a focus no less ferociously frightening. His form appeared fleetingly wrapped in white starlight; or perhaps the unearthly effect was another offshoot of drug-birthed imagination.

Watching, transfixed, Sulfin Evend felt his hazed senses flung wide. Gooseflesh raked over him. As though he heard strains of intangible music, or pursued the cry of a thought hurled beyond reach of the mind, he gasped to a burst of wild ecstasy.

Ephemeral, sourceless, the emotion fled.

Arithon's tension snapped all at once. He sustained a series of disciplined breaths. Then he blotted his face on his sleeve, shoved erect, and crossed to the far side of the fire-pot. There, he sat down with his quivering fingers laced on his drawn-up knees. As though no break had happened; no razor-edged conflict had danced at the abyss to drive him to geas-bent violence, he resumed the brutal interrogation.

'Should I answer, for Daon Ramon?' His cool regard assessed his adversary, alert, but without sign of rancour. 'If you want to pick fights upon treacherous ground, I'll walk away. The bully can't punch with no victim to hand. For the dead on both sides, I have no stomach for mud-slinging, self-righteous argument.'

'I have earned my demand,' Sulfin Evend declared, shaken. 'The curse-driven killer did not arrange the acts of piracy that happened at Riverton. Nor its cold-blooded aftermath. Of forty good men, I alone survived your run through the Korias grimward.'

'The fox called to blame for the huntsman's demise?' Arithon laughed. 'That is a bit specious, since after all, the whim of the Biedar arranged this encounter.' Aware Sulfin Evend's suspicious regard sought to measure him for concealed weapons, he stood up, then hooked off his sash. His loose robe fell open. The unclothed flesh beneath served his bitter assurance that he was unarmed. 'My half-brother hates me because Desh-thiere wants us dead. Tell me, or better, examine yourself: what reason do you have to follow him?'

'Should I answer?' Sulfin Evend shot back.

Not large, though endowed with a neat, feline grace, the creature that four kingdoms raised arms to destroy resettled himself, stripped of humour. The thin glaze of flame-light played over his ironic gaze as he added, 'No just cause exists. No rhetoric can brighten the geas the Mistwraith has dealt, and no redeeming virtue at all can excuse the debacle between us. If this was a lie, you would be cut dead. Not invited to juggle a trying conversation.'

Such stabbing satire strangled reserve.

Sulfin Evend rested his forehead on his marked wrists, while his naked unease battled reason. When he found his voice, he dared a cautious truce. 'I have seen enough to allow you that truth. My best efforts have failed. I could not make Avenor's crown regent hear sense or abandon pursuit of his blood feud.'

Green eyes resurveyed him, sharply awake. 'Ath's sweet grace! You have tried?' Through a moment of desperate, excoriating pain, the Teir's'Ffalenn dropped his glance to his unrelaxed hands. 'You could gain a knife through the heart, for that risk. We are cursed, and not trustworthy, though we are both served with the gift of such adamant loyalty.'

'I swore oath to the land,' Sulfin Evend admitted, too mazed for the sense to withhold the confidence.

'*Caithdein*, to my *half-brother*?' Now, Rathain's prince stared, shocked. 'And the Fellowship backed this? You split your loyalty with the Sorcerers at Althain Tower?'

Sulfin Evend folded his abraded wrists in his lap, too flat tired for subterfuge. 'No way else could I spare the guiding light of the Alliance from falling to usage by necromancy.'

'Brave man! Since you have accomplished your victory, you also must know that the aftermath dooms you to failure.' Neither man courted pretence. The Alliance's troops were already marching. Towns in all three of the eastshore kingdoms now girded for war to take down this calm, dark-haired criminal. Given a stubborn lack of response, the Master of Shadow laid open his heart and bored in. 'An end like Jieret's could become your lot. You might die on the sword of a vengeance-bent clansman, or worse: Desh-thiere's geas can't honour your principles.'

'So Asandir warned.' A coal popped in the fire-pot, flurrying sparks that blinked into darkness. Sulfin Evend said carefully, 'My lord's fits of madness notwithstanding, I find that I still have to try.'

'Who else has the fibre to shoulder the load? I salute you, and grieve,' stated Arithon Teir's'Ffalenn. 'Before s'Ilessid, you could break my spirit.' He tightened his sash, perhaps reamed by a chill, though the desert air wafted in through the cleft carried the baked warmth of summer. Then he said, 'I am glad that you're with him. His ruler's vision has become so dreadfully lost. Lacking the disciplined guidance of training, my half-brother has little chance to resist. Past question, such caring as yours could offer the stance for salvation. As Earl Jieret's did, thrice over, for me, not least on the field at Daon Ramon.'

Sulfin Evend winced, wounded afresh by the genuine absence of anger. Drug-heightened perception made him see too far. Now, the yoke of old enmity haunted, that had led him to cut a courageous man's tongue; made him part and party to grotesque hatred, waged upon twisted political viciousness and geas-bent misunderstanding.

Nor could this unwanted, intimate encounter do aught to ease his raw conscience. 'How can you sit there and not break my neck?'

The creature that Lysaer named Spinner of Darkness did not take offence at the outburst. 'Within Kewar,' he said gently, 'I accepted the gift offered up by a centaur guardian.'

Sulfin Evend hauled in a shuddering breath. Fists jammed to shut lips, he stamped down the sudden upsurge of past vision: of a presence and majesty beyond the bounds of his mortal mind to encompass. He had witnessed such wonder: been overawed and crushed to his knees. Every day since, he survived by the sword, and the force of his abject denial.

This moment, as well, he could not match the grace of an enemy's sorrowful understanding. The drug's effect heightened their entwined emotions. Set under such stress, Sulfin Evend could not bear the tearing weight of remorse. Not without smashing the foundation that saw him oathsworn to command the Light's armies.

'Death can't restore what's already been lost,' the Master of Shadow declared. 'Does vengeance or blame ease the sorrow of heart-ache? We all make mistakes. Life can't be lived without harm to others. Worst of all, I have seen Jieret's path was self-chosen. That sting was the hardest trial to bear. We can't buy self-forgiveness. Can't pay for redress through our sorry penchant for guilt-fed lament and self-punishment. I would have you set free,' said Arithon Teir's'Ffalenn, 'since the man you support with such steadfast care is none else but birth kin, and my brother.'

The tears welled too fast, for that tender release. Sulfin Evend masked his wet face, while the soft voice resumed, and pierced his remorse with compassion. 'Some gifts of friendship cannot be earned. They exist, beyond price, and we cannot hope to match up to them.'

Never so clearly exposed to the debt he might leave to his liege, as survivor, the Alliance Lord Commander crumpled and wept. *Did this adversary not know?* Sulfin Evend lost the frank speech to inform that he held the sealed order to raise all of the southcoast to arms, a duty now made insupportable by the perverse strait of his quarry's free-will absolution.

The initiate master whose work had undone the Kralovir's deadly incursion, in cold fact, was no prejudiced town's mortal enemy. A bard of such gifted stature would have loved peace, before the pointless strife of Desh-thiere's cursed war had upset his natural destiny.

'What brought you here?' Sulfin Evend snatched dignity, and blotted damp cheeks. 'Why do the nomad tribes hold you in reverence?'

That woke wry humour, mixed with vexed irritation. 'Though frost should freeze water, I can't warn them off.' Arithon tucked lean fingers under his sleeves, discomfited and defensive. 'Their seers claim a prophecy. There, our interests collide, since I won't endorse the bizarre obligation.'

Grey eyes matched green, across open flame, while the well of earth's silence extended. No man to retreat, Sulfin Evend chose challenge. 'They say your fate's written into the flint knife I returned, that Enithen Tuer loaned on my behalf to spare my liege from the Kralovir's depredation.'

'Did they so?' stated Arithon s'Ffalenn with soft venom. 'Perhaps you don't want to hear this. But the knowledge that founded all three cults of necromancy originated with the Biedar.'

'Three cults!' Sulfin Evend still refused to back down. 'With the Kralovir gone, that leaves two more. Carry on.'

'I see why you were set in charge of the troops,' Rathain's prince said in nettled rejoinder. Nonetheless, he had the fibre not to recoil. 'The seals that stay death were once part of a sacred rite, used to commune with the ancestry. The Biedar don't write. Their tradition is inherited. They waken their talent through a trial of privation that opens initiate memory. Long before mankind settled Athera, Koriathain used arcane channels and disclosed the content. They catalogued everything. By rights, they claimed, since the dedicate purpose laid out by their founders held a mission of preserving all records of human achievement. The library they guarded was not discriminate, nor was it kept with integrity. Somebody tinkered, mixed forms, and experimented. Dark sources were tapped without wisdom. Sigils with binding aspects were forged. Worse forms evolved later, recombined with blood ceremony, which warped offshoot was leaked from the order. As I understand, the breach happened before today's stringent oath, which shackles each sister to unswerving loyalty. I have observed the knot tied by their Matriarch, first hand. It is utterly unforgiving.'

Arithon lapsed into silence. Whatever the bent of his personal thought now, Sulfin Evend was loath to disrupt him. Where Lysaer was wont to mask pain behind the trappings of royal deportment, the dark half-brother retreated, inscrutable. One recalled that this creature had endured Davien's maze at Kewar. He had walked out sane. Mage-taught, and fathomless as a pool of black water, his stillness had walls.

Shortly, Arithon came back to himself. 'Biedar would not be encamped on this world, but to see a responsibility to fulfilment. They are bound, so they say, to recoup the mistake that brought their sacred legacy into ill usage.' A rustle of silk, as he shifted the unsettling topic towards closure. 'Beyond that point, for my own peace of mind, I informed them I'd no longer listen.'

Sulfin Evend digested this statement, well warned. 'The elder said the Kralovir cult had been cleansed. If so, then the danger posed through the Alliance of Light is now culled. I doubt that my liege would repeat his error, or dare give consent to another pandering ally's dark ritual.'

'Lysaer will remember the knowledge exists.' Arithon exhorted his half-brother's officer with caustic honesty. 'Never blind yourself to complacence: Desh-thiere's curse will not rest. One day, if we cannot find means to prevail, your liege could be driven to use it. *Or I could.* The pitfalls if I should become cornered might seed a future that dire.'

'What can I do, except slow down the muster?' Sulfin Evend responded at tortured length. 'Though how that could matter, Ath knows, at this pass.'

The devastation left after the Kralovir's demise had already branded its relentless legacy: the governor's command struck dead to a man in the scouring cleanse at Etarra would now set all of the north into flame. Sulfin Evend balked at treason. No matter the cost, he would not reveal Lysaer's picked target as the citadel at Alestron, since the s'Brydion duke's family were exposed as spies, bound to suffer the brunt of the wrathful consequence. 'If I resign,' he said straitly, 'or if I obstruct Lysaer's thrust by an outright refusal to engage you, my liege will be left without any bulwark between Desh-thiere's geas and insanity.'

'You will not face me,' Rathain's prince cracked back. Nor were Lysaer's martial intentions a well-kept secret, before such piercing attentiveness. 'Attack the s'Brydion, and nothing you try can draw me out to participate. No alliance exists. I have severed all ties.'

Outfaced by every unimagined complexity, Sulfin Evend gaped, shocked. 'You? Turn your back and disown your most steadfast supporter? Forgive me, but I can't believe it!'

Shoved to his feet in sharp rage, Arithon lost his carefully held equanimity. 'After Vastmark? Tal Quorin? The dead of Daon Ramon? For what *reason* should I endorse another campaign that cannot but end in red slaughter? By Ath, you're a fool! No less than Duke Bransian, who would not hear my warning to stand down. Yes, I walked away! The man's damnable pride in his ancestral seat will bring ruin on all of his innocent holding!' Flame winnowed, as Arithon paced through the cauterized pain of past anguish. '*Nothing* I know could force me to this! No concept of honour will be made the cause to destroy another clan enclave of women and children.'

Again came that sheet-gold flare through the aura. No matter how brief, the fleeting light showed that Arithon was in fact chafed to exhaustion. His bearing and features were haggard. The nerves that tried his leashed talent suggested the hurt his adamant stance must have cost him. Silenced by pity, Sulfin Evend sat, torn, entrapped by his role as Alliance advocate.

'How can you sustain this?' he managed at last, when Arithon's caged movement threatened to scorch the eddyless air with each passage.

'I have seen,' said the Master of Shadow, worn by the cut of his forebears' wakened far-sight. 'To the last slaughtered babe, and the tears in the eyes of the women who will be forced on the hour the siege breaks, as spoils.' He stopped there. Black hair sifted over lean knuckles as he buried his face in his hands. As though applied pressure could anneal his agony, he recontained his emotion. When next he looked up, Sulfin Evend beheld all the terrible depths that victorious passage through Kewar had cost him.

'I will not live their death,' said Arithon Teir's'Ffalenn. 'Not ever by my willing consent, nor as the Mistwraith's curse-blinded accomplice.'

'If you stand out this war, the citadel must still go down in defeat,' Sulfin Evend felt obliged to point out.

'I have seen,' repeated the Master of Shadow. 'Let the town fall as a monument to stupidity, and not for self-righteous sentiment. Depend on my absence. I will weather the conflict inside the free wilds and assist the escape of survivors.'

Aware the discussion was finished, Sulfin Evend unbent his sore knees and rose also. Weaponless, empty-handed, he had no solace to offer the initiate master who had saved all of Etarra from an insidious corruption. A man of the sword possessed no statesman's gift, only the steel to admit his threadbare regret. 'I would give anything except the life of my liege, that we had never been adversaries.'

Arithon returned a grave smile, then offered the wrist clasp exchanged between clanborn. 'Guard my brother,' he said. 'If we meet at blade's edge, I would have you know: you fight as my nightmare, but never my enemy. This much I promise. Though you should pass the Wheel in pursuit of your duty, my blade will not be the weapon to reap Daelion's justice.'

Footsteps approached through the underground corridor. With uncanny timing, the dartmen returned to resume the lapsed charge of their vigilance.

'The Biedar revere courtesy,' Rathain's crown prince assured as he released his fingers in parting. 'Give them patience and calm, they must treat with you fairly, since their code demands no act of redress unless they are shown provocation. Rest well. You are safe. Eat whatever they bring you. When the seer's herb that opened your senses wears off, the tribesfolk will guide you back to your people unharmed.'

Sulfin Evend stepped back, erect but still sickened with vertigo. 'You've had meetings like this one before,' he accused.

Arithon's grin widened with piquant delight. 'Ath, no! If I had to guess, the old grandame here connives hand in glove with the Warden of Althain. Do you gamble?'

'Not with arcane powers, or seeresses given to drink,' Lysaer's first commander shot back. 'They both want you alive, depend on that much.' Startled by movement, closed in from behind, he stiffened as the dartmen grasped his upper arms.

31

'We must use the blindfold once more,' they informed, their quiet insistence as near as their kind would come to an open apology.

Against his grain, Sulfin Evend submitted. He did not resist as they led him away. If masked sight spared him from the sting of regret, the knotted rag did nothing at all to impair his sensitized hearing. Behind, in the cavern, the s'Ffalenn bastard who was not his foe engaged his own style of courage. The lyranthe spoke out of the echoing dark. Notes sparkled, and lingered, lilting an exquisite air, plangent with a beauty to transcend all hopeless sorrow.

Too late, the prisoner recalled the debt still left unacknowledged. Sulfin Evend had neglected to voice decent thanks for his kinsman's deliverance from necromancy. Now he hoped the lapsed opportunity would stay lost for all time. Strapped by his oaths, burdened by Lysaer's charge to engage the siege that must raze Alestron's proud citadel to rubble, the Alliance commander prayed the course of his fate would be kind. Let the Biedar matriarch's prophetic warning prove to be empty. In life, he wished he might never cross paths with the Spinner of Darkness again.

Late Summer 5671

Chase

Eight days' rugged travel were required to cross the free wilds, after the belated discovery that took the Halwythwood camp by grim storm: young Jeynsa s'Valerient had not ventured north, after all. Her feckless pursuit of her crown prince had never planned for an apology. Instead, folly sent her due south, with but one of her elders the wiser. She sought a ruler's counsel in Atwood, where, as she had confided to Eriegal, she meant to press a scathing inquiry into the moral probity of her sovereign.

Uninvested *caithdein* to Arithon of Rathain, and still enraged over the death of her father as sacrifice to salvage the royal blood-line, the girl was not faulted for her misplaced flight. Seventeen years of age, and outspoken, the daughter shared the impetuous dedication of her late sire.

'No bad thing, that the minx has the spit to stand up to his Grace's insufferable temperament,' her brother, Earl Barach, had declared, astonished to fierce admiration at the time. No coward, his sister, to seize her shirked post with such brazen daring. The result would peel skin if she tried formal stature to cross-examine her prince. 'The escapade should expose her, red-faced, for a rash idealist run riot.'

Except for the fatally explosive risk: that the Light's active muster now converged for war in East Halla.

Sidir had lost his tolerance. 'I'll haul her back, trussed and gagged in a game sack!' Become the firm arm that supported the bereft mother, the tall, grave Companion had gathered his weapons forthwith. 'Fiends plague that girl for her idiot timing!'

Jeynsa's volatile grief, heated by young-blood ignorance, outstripped the concept of dangerous. Etarra was unhinged by the cleanse of a death cult.

Every sword-bearing Sunwheel fanatic frothed to burn suspect talent for liaison with Shadow. No kinsman stepped forward to argue the need, that the Teiren's'Valerient must be fetched back by the scruff of the hair she had cropped in defiance of custom.

Sidir was not sanguine with the perils he faced. Now arrived at the verge of wide-open country, he knew that he shouldered an effort predestined to fail. The girl was a fit tigress, and she had an eighteen-day start on him. Worse, his hopeless journey was not made alone: the Koriani enchantress whose fate was entangled with Arithon's packed her satchel in stride alongside.

'You will need arcane help,' Elaira insisted, against the innate distrust her kind aroused from the clans. 'Or else waste the time you don't have to go wrong, chasing hunches down a cold trail.'

Since no forest-bred talent could challenge her power, Sidir took charge. He would take her from Halwythwood, if only to keep her order's suspect machinations under his direct sight.

Their hot-foot chase after Jeynsa had brought them to the fork in the River Arwent five nights past the dark of the moon. Now that the safe forest coverts must be left behind, the enchantress prevailed against the Companion's rife urgency: she would take pause and use her arcane knowledge to measure the outlying territory.

'You should heed my counsel,' Sidir resisted, his impatient grip on his sword reflecting his disapproval.

'We're not at odds,' Elaira reminded, loath to rattle the thorns under-lying their mismatched alliance. Steamed by worry herself, she crouched with the wood at her back and pressed her spread palms to the earth. 'I won't risk letting our crown prince know why Jeynsa's bolted hell-bent into trouble.'

The liegeman viewed her stifled need as transparent: to reach for heart's ease through subtle awareness and link with her distant beloved. The concern was not groundless: her longing desire yearned towards the south. The same, searing stars that Arithon experienced at Sanpashir glimmered here, but not softened by late-summer heat haze. The torpid air would not wear the scent of high grass, or the song of the nightjar that stitched lonely notes through the shrilling of nocturnal insects. Elaira kept her firm hold on restraint. She limited her trace to the deep strata of bed-rock, listening for the delicate, shimmering current that carried the local lane flux.

Looming above her, Rathain's grim Companion unleashed his overtried nerves. 'This is no secure place to dally for scrying. We should cross the north ford and push into the Barrens by daybreak to avoid the risk of a sighting by trackers.'

The enchantress persisted despite sound advice, stubborn beyond her slight build. She did not look the part of the initiate Koriathain. Clad in cross-laced leathers, her braided bronze hair tied with deer-hide, she could have passed for a forest-bred scout, searching for game sign; except her response second-guessed a man's mind, before he set words to his thinking.

'I won't need a fire,' Elaira demurred. 'This near the fourth lane, just a rock-pool at the verge, where shoaling rocks don't riffle the current.'

Which choice seemed the worse, to a forest clansman whose instincts were pressured. In this border-line country, where the Arwent's deep channel could float an east-bound, keeled barge, more trespassing merchants each year dared to route their perishable freight through the lake-side town of Daenfal. Free wilds or not, no clansman crossed them without an armed company at his back. Never mind that traders caught flouting crown charter must be waylaid, or that the fools born outside of blood heritage did not perceive how their venal invasion disrupted Athera's grand mysteries. The compact that served the aware heart of the land could not tolerate any compromise that degraded the harmonic flow of the fourth lane.

All the worse, that Jeynsa had tried this passage alone, when impending war drove invasive town interests to ever-more-vicious reprisal. Sidir shifted his sweating grip on his blade, not liking the fact his back was exposed as quarry for league-hunting bowmen.

Scalded at last by his smoking unease, Elaira broke off and stood. 'Sidir, believe me, your fuming is groundless. The flux lines are pulsing in natural harmony. If any townsmen are hanging about, they will be peacefully dead!' Against his stiff quiet, she finished off, clipped, 'Anyone living who isn't mage-shielded would stamp an emotional signature.'

Sidir raised a dark eyebrow, the silvered hair at his temples distinct even under faint starlight. 'I should rely on your vision?'

Elaira sighed. 'My dear man, are we dancing in blindfolds through hoops? I've stood tours of lane watch for my *meddling* order since I was a starving waif culled from an alley. Seen mirrored in earthforce, your distrust of my character may as well be a deafening shout.'

Not caught aback, Sidir chose his words to avoid a pitched fight. 'I don't like the fact I can't fathom your motives.' Grey eyes that discerned with birth talent for truth never flinched from unkind reservations. 'If you're wanting that pool, I'd as soon have this done with.'

Nonetheless, his guidance was considerate as he threaded the rough course through the overgrowth to the river-bank. Southside of Halwythwood, where Daon Ramon Barrens crumpled against the plateau of Araethura, the buttressed seam opened into a gorge. Beneath, the boisterous sluice of the Arwent thundered over its bed of split boulders. Poured ink since the set of the waxing moon, the misted air smelled of wet mineral. Game trails left by otters skeined through the scrub, raked to a leaning tangle of thatch by the floods at spring thaw.

Summer's drought tamed the rampaging spate. Scoured stone scalloped the water's edge, lapped by the cold depths where the trout swam.

'Here.' Elaira caught Sidir's wrist before the tall clansman withdrew. 'Stay as you wish. I won't have secrets that fan the least doubt that I'd use my powers to betray you.'

'To seek Feithan's daughter, perhaps not,' Sidir challenged. 'But a man who serves Rathain's crown has to wonder. Whose hidden cause *are* you backing?'

'The civilized mask was already stripped, that night in the glen by the Willowbrook,' Elaira snapped, a touch acid. Day upon day of exhaustive, harsh company chafed the barbs lying under the skin. 'From chastened, need I grovel to beg a reprieve from the on-going punishment? I have no desire to harm your clan interests! My order's knowledge will not be engaged, even for straightforward scrying.'

Sidir watched her elfin features turn haunted as she strained to recoup equilibrium. Not callous, at heart, he stripped away pretence. 'Dare I suggest your concern for Jeynsa might further your sisterhood's plot to trap Arithon Teir's'Ffalenn?'

'You helped tear him from me,' she shot back, uncowed. 'What could have changed?' Her tight smile followed, both poisoned and wry. 'My oathsworn obedience is not all-encompassing. Life has another facet called choice. You'll see that girl safe because you cherish Feithan. Is my care as an honest woman no less? Or must one bad thread condemn the whole cloth? Which one of us isn't embroiled in mankind's stewpot of intrigue? *I've* been magnanimous,' Elaira said, stung. 'For the bitch in blind heat, my balked need's in plain sight. It's your mulish candidate for Rathain's *caithdein* whose spiteful agenda might fray Arithon's personal integrity.'

Sidir fielded her accusation, flat calm. 'The crown liege whose shoulder I guarded at Vastmark would never abandon his oath of protection, sworn before death to her father.'

'He wouldn't,' the mettlesome enchantress agreed. 'That's the reason our hopeless mission can't fail and why you might want to muzzle your next slashing leap for the jugular.'

Epiphany struck with splintering force. 'Your orders from Prime Selidie have not been revoked!' While the sheeting curtains of spray smoked between them, the Companion most renowned for his tact found himself lashed to rare venom. 'Should you not stay the course and refashion the snare so narrowly thwarted in Halwythwood?'

Which dart pierced too deeply: Elaira's caught breath tore a pause.

Nor would Sidir relent, though she struck him. Not with the last prince of Rathain's crown lineage become the marked target for Koriani malice. 'Tell me you don't endanger all I hold dear!'

'I can't.' The enchantress bent her head, hands pressed to her face. Whether she masked agony for the unconsummated love that Sidir had invoked charter law and the help of a Fellowship Sorcerer to thwart, steel honesty would not prevaricate. *Elaira had never pretended her passion was not the prime bait in her sisterhood's bid to seize Arithon.*

Although genteel instinct yearned for reprieve, if only to soften discomfort, Sidir held firm. He carried the charge of an aggrieved mother's trust, as well as a kingdom laid open through the perils stalking its crown prince.

'I'm duty-bound to keep contact with Arithon's interests,' Elaira ventured at last. She rejected bitterness, despite the straits that seized her affection as the killing piece on the political game-board. 'My Prime's command leaves me no other path. But, pleas to Ath, I will seek my beloved after I'm certain you've secured that young girl from harm's way. She's your task, after that. Rope her wildcat fury to heel, then use every persuasion to make sure she wields her feal office from the safety of Halwythwood!'

Such blistering courage deserved better grace. 'I don't like the need,' Sidir allowed. 'But I can't drop my role as the diligent sentry.'

'Don't neglect the cold fact you're my enemy?' This time, Elaira's sarcasm bit. 'Then stay at my back. Keep your guard with drawn steel for as long as you think I lack basic human integrity.'

'Your heart's intent was never distrusted,' Sidir corrected with stickling firmness. 'The truth grants no quarter.' Oathsworn over crystal, the enchantress could not enforce any claim to free will.

'Let me enlarge on your view-point,' she said. 'If not me, you would have another Koriathain appointed to your prince's fate. She would be a huntress, ruled by vicious hate. This was the choice I was given, at Highscarp. When the Prime's bidding was laid before me, I claimed the burden upon the belief that the precepts of love would not hasten defeat, but instead seek a way to find triumph.'

'A queen of the realm would be as courageous.' Sidir swept her a bow, moved despite himself. 'Consider my sword at your back as a friend. Let my stroke fall as Dharkaron's own Spear and be welcomed, if ever your Prime tries to twist your resolve and enact my liege's destruction.'

The tears rose too suddenly. Throughout the brutal rip tide of release, Sidir did not try the demeaning palliative of soothing her anguish. Wise man, he knew which wracking griefs could be tempered and which must abide, unconsoled.

Nothing was left, except to move on. Elaira turned from the Companion's staunch calm. Too desolate to indulge her deep sorrows, she knelt on the jumbled rock by the river-course, then rallied her adamant discipline.

Water with fast-flowing current was never easy to tap in rapport. Most impressionable of the four elements, in liquid state tumbling with gravity, its bonding properties unravelled as bursts of electromagnetics. Such whirlpool turbulence rejected all pattern. Yet that same effervescence, harnessed with skill, might key a scrying that could not be traced. Elaira's affinity was an inborn gift. She let her active awareness dissolve into the flow of the Arwent.

An ephemeral thrill raced over her skin, leaving her momentarily deafened and blinded. Then her dissociate senses cleared: she became the black pool, scribed with whirling eddies, and the exuberant splash, necklaced with foam under starlight. She was the rampaging gush through the gorge, then the broad, placid sheet of Daenfal Lake, wind-ruffled and hemmed with plumed reed-beds. The expansion rushed through her, tingling her nerves, as near shore to far, she traced the meandering loops of the outflow, winding away towards the sea.

Elaira declared her bounds of intent before her reach encompassed the bay, and dispersed in the salt deeps of the ocean. Poised, she *became* the essence of water, inside a radius of one hundred leagues.

And water, an impressionably volatile medium, reflected the flows of the lanes, receptive as an echo to the harmonics struck off by human emotion. Awake to such whispers, Elaira could plumb the dreams of sleepers in Daenfal. She sensed the lampsmen and sentries on watch at the walls, and the individual moods of the goatherds encamped in Araethura. The scout patrols and the clan hunters of Halwythwood also were made known to her. Each living presence moved as liquid light, stamped into the streamlets and marshes, with exchanged conversation a subliminal resonance, laced through the underground springs.

At the cusp where earthly form bordered the mysteries, the innate cry of her hampered spirit burned for sweet return to the linked empathy only Arithon could partner. Elaira checked that yearning flame short. Since his late mission to curb the deadly cult at Etarra, she had promised him solitude for safety's sake. Though a Sorcerer wearing the form of an eagle had brought word of his triumphant survival, his silence since suggested he was still in healing recovery. Ache though she might to touch his close presence, news of Jeynsa's escapade would stress him. Elaira would not shake his peace, or breach polite ethic and invade the privacy of strangers. She quested, instead, for the signature presence of Jeynsa s'Valerient. The Fellowship's marked choice for a *caithdein's* inheritance, the girl's imprint should stand out like a brand.

Yet no match arose to receive the sought pattern divined through the element. The essence of Water spoke across time. Had Jeynsa died, her passage would have left ranging echoes of the event. *Unless she was warded.* That thought raised ugly questions.

What covert motive would drive a candidate whose duty spoke for the law as a crown prince's conscience?

Uneasy, Elaira refined her approach, sweeping for the resonant wake left by the girl's spent emotions.

Those residual traces emerged, one vivid imprint embedded in Daenfal Lake, stamped just after midnight at the recent dark moon. Jeynsa's terrified scream had distressed a young waterman and the steersman of the boat that had ferried her south towards Silvermarsh. The nightmare raised by the girl's Sighted talent now bled through: *a vision of the realm's crown prince, strapped to a stone slab, his bleeding form ringed by tormented ghosts. The bound shades were young girls, wracked women, and boys, entrapped by the practice of necromancy . . .*

Elaira smothered her visceral outcry. Cut free of gestalt awareness, revolted to nausea, she crouched on her knees and used merciless discipline to smother her stark bolt of fear. *This event was the past!* Arithon had confided his plan to bait the Kralovir to their downfall; yet his spoken word could *never* prepare for the impact of the horrors just witnessed. Elaira steadied her rattled nerves. Choked back springing tears for the glimpse of a suffering that defied endurance. Beyond sparing Sidir from a hideous explanation, her fierce reaction risked drawing Arithon himself into sympathetic rapport. Such carelessness could disclose Jeynsa's ill-starred defection and, worse, inflame the fresh scar the traumatic ordeal must have set on his spirit.

The humid night wrapped the enchantress like a blanket. Plumed spray off the thrashing falls braced her skin. Life's concert of crickets still pealed from the grasses, small balms to lean on until calm returned and overwrought pulse slowed and settled. Elaira steeled herself to proceed. No way else could she hope to trace past the warding that cloaked Jeynsa's movement from scryers. Determined, the enchantress plunged back into immersion, aligning her search south and east.

She sounded the bogs and the turbid reed-beds that fringed the lake-shore, into Silvermarsh, and there, detected a dark thread of silence that stitched a straight course through the landscape. *A talisman would soak up the natural flow of electromagnetics.* Jeynsa's trail led into Melhalla, where she did not move alone. Elaira's tuned senses detected a glimmering fan of pack-focused intent closing in on the girl from behind. The pattern fitted a tracker's array, running dogs for the head-hunters' league.

Elaira wrenched out of trance, shoved erect much too fast. Her staggered step encountered Sidir, his alert courtesy charged to alarm by the sight of her stricken face.

'What's wrong?' Just as fast, his bracing grasp steadied her. 'Has Jieret's daughter been killed?'

'No.' The enchantress shivered. 'Not yet. She's endangered.' Displaced senses still reeling, Elaira unburdened. 'Jeynsa's already crossed Daenfal Lake. She's set on the run through the game trails of Silvermarsh, pressed by a bountymen's ambush.'

'Fatemaster's mercy!' Sidir pealed in anguish. His grey eyes held the urgency seen once before, that unthinkable night when he had forced the breach of his crown prince's intimate privacy. 'How can I tell her mother we've failed? Dharkaron avert the cold hand of necessity! That girl's got a lead of sixty-five leagues, too far to hope we can help her.'

'Not if we chase her,' Elaira agreed. 'She's ahead of her enemies. She may outwit them. If not, the trackers will haze her into West Halla.'

'Straight into the swords of the Alliance's muster, by now choking the trade-routes through Pellain!'

As Sidir loosed his grasp, lashed frantic, Elaira captured his sleeve. 'Wait. There's more.'

Restrained at the edge of explosive impatience, the Companion still listened.

'Jeynsa's bearing a talisman,' said Elaira, aggrieved.

His sharp wit took stock. 'Then why didn't Eriegal decide to tell us, since he saw her off back in Halwythwood?'

Elaira met that probing dissection with silence, reluctant to suggest a conspiracy. Since the man at her side would shatter himself in a doomed attempt to best fate, she strove to avert suicidal disaster.

'I know you're loath to rely on my trust. But, Sidir, if you ask, I can hasten our journey. Snag a ride on the deck of a trespassing barge, and my resource can buy a swift passage. From Daenfal, we could fare southward by river.'

'You could disguise my origins?' The clansman's bleak glance mapped that prospect, displeased. 'Perish the thought! Far more than my life will reside in your hands.'

'I know.' Elaira withstood the balked heat of his rage. 'Dharkaron's revenge strike me dead if I'm false, since I don't see a more hopeful recourse.'

'On your head, then,' snapped Sidir, his staunch courage proof of his iron-heart character.

No use, to pretend that his stakes were not desperate. For every step taken to speed their pace to Melhalla, the Light's call to war would raise obstacles. The inns and the roads would be seething with troops. Each officer bearing a stamped requisition would be clamouring for transport, alongside contingents of Sunwheel priests, with the eyes of their zealot examiners. Should her power of arcane concealment fall short, or should her Prime Matriarch's fickle interests command Sidir's betrayal, he would be condemned. Clansmen caught inside town precincts were granted no trial. She asked Rathain's most loyal liegeman to run the risk of a death that began with public dismemberment.

Three Riders

A fast galley from Jaelot docks at Varens, with the Light's avatar rushed ahead down the trade town to Tirans bearing the shocking news: that the Spinner of Darkness has dared to strike at Etarra's high council by sorcery, and that the s'Brydion duke at Alestron has betrayed the Alliance in liaison with Shadow; therefore, the citadel and its corrupt defenders must be destroyed for rightful cause and by force of arms . . .

Galled from exhaustive days in the saddle, the Mad Prophet spurs through the town gates of Darkling amid the Skyshiel pass, only to find the spectacular demise of the Light's cult-tainted priest has ignited the troop muster ahead of him, with no horse, no cart, and no transport available to hasten his urgency to reach the Eltair Coast . . .

Beset while reforging Scarpdale's torn grimward, Asandir kneels beside his dying stallion, torn for his dread choice: to consign the burden of his unfinished mission back into Sethvir's taxed hands, and not leave the beloved horse's left shade to be subsumed by ravaging chaos; in mourning, he voices the Name for Isfarenn, binding the freed spirit under secure ward for return to Athera's continuum . . .

II. Recoil

On the day that event struck the anvil of fate, the ambassadorial courier from Varens rode into the trade town of Tirans. He came in the company of four mounted men and passed under the northern gate of the teeming, walled rise that guarded the industrious hub of East Halla's peninsula. Amid summer haze, the carnelian brick watchtowers arose, sturdy and square, gold-rimmed against an egg-shell sky. Beneath, the dust stirred up by labouring caravans spread a choking, alkali cloud.

The lumbering farm wagons emptied since dawn crowded past eight-in-hand ox teams, hauling inbound drays from the coast. Wedged in the crush, the sweating courier glanced sidelong at the rider clad in sweat rag and hat and anonymous leathers beside him. 'You were mad to come here without a state retinue.'

The shaded face turned. Fair-skinned, handsome features wore the same grime that coated all summer travellers. A haggard expression bespoke the rigors of three harried days in the saddle. Yet the glint in those wide-opened eyes stayed as steel, struck off azure ice. 'So we'll see.'

Turned forward again, Lysaer s'Ilessid never acknowledged the anxious men-at-arms paired at his back. His magisterial manner also refused to draw rein for the tender young talent who straggled behind: today's royal page was the gawky get of a Korias crofter. He still showed his plough-boy's fist on the reins, more at ease with a scythe than a weapon. If the Light's Lord Commander might have bade to correct the appalling lapse in formal panoply, Sulfin Evend was at large to muster the southcoast. His absence left the daunted dismay of his overruled, second-string officers.

The Blessed Prince remained unfazed. He surveyed the jostling backs of the draught teams, then the craft quarter shop-fronts with their gaudy signs. Adroit, he avoided the flower seller's child, darting to hawk posies to the silk-clad matrons in their parked carriages. Tirans' three-storied mansions framed the scene with established elegance, from door-sills agleam with new paint, to the carvings on marble cornices. A balladeer's notes braved the hubbub. The civilized populace adorned their dwellings with statuary, while the potted ivy and gardenia trailing from the upper galleries trumpeted nonchalant affluence.

Against the courier's outspoken concern, Lysaer observed, 'After all, we're not visiting a den of barbarians.'

His informants' reports had not been remiss: unlike the seaports, this town's ruling council had yet to embrace the cause of Avenor's Alliance. If the merchants and well-set craftsmen were aligned with the leanings of trade, Tirans supported no head-hunters' league. Her standing garrison did not chafe to impinge on the designate bounds of the free wilds. The canny mayor reigned without jostling to upset traditional diplomacy. Here, at the core of East Halla's prosperity, a frail-but-established truce had held sway since the downfall of Melhalla's crown. Charter law still kept tenuous influence.

Atwood's clans were too powerfully placed, allied as they were in tight interest with the warmongering s'Brydion dukes. Which stew of old order and defiant town enterprise primed the stage for an uncivil welcome.

The men-at-arms and the page trailed Lysaer's horse with closed mouths and inflexible orders. The Light's avatar had declared war against Shadow. Independent or not, Tirans' citizens soon would be commanded to muster. No town-born adult might resist that decision, not if he expected to thrive.

Therefore, the five riders on their lathered mounts breasted the moil at the main cross-road. They parted ways with the laden carts serving the craft quarter market, joining the smart, lighter vehicles and lackeys bound on genteel business uptown. As the press slackened, the Varens courier slapped the dust from his blazoned jacket. He assayed a sly glance. The expression under Lysaer's felt hat appeared reasonable enough to try a last appeal. 'The mayor's played fire with politics for more years than I've been alive. Blessed Light, Lord, you cannot expect your grand cause to be served by a routine man bearing dispatches!'

'I expect you to deliver my sealed writ, nothing more.' Lysaer tipped a nod to acknowledge his two armsmen, then gave an encouraging smile to ease the fresh nerves of his page-boy. 'That inn, the Flocked Starling, should do very well. My company stops there for a bath and a meal, followed up by a change of clothing.'

While the Varens man gaped like a trout, the Light's foolishly sparse retinue reined over to the curb and dismounted. The page took smooth charge of his master's hot horse. Foamed bits and grimed reins brought no disdainful comment, raised as he was at the ploughshare. His birth-born talent was as matter-of-fact. 'I sense nothing amiss, here,' he said after a moment. 'No untoward workings or sorceries.'

Lysaer clapped the boy's shoulder. 'Well done. Carry on.'

The yokel ducked, hiding his blush. He had never known privilege, unlike the silent, paired veterans behind, who once had served as honour guard for Avenor's lost prince. Now, Ranne and Fennick's taciturn competence headed the avatar's personal train. Their appointment had been Sulfin Evend's replacement, after the late, vile strike by cult sorcery destroyed his three elite captains.

Hawk-nosed Ranne never showed second thoughts. His whistle rousted the Flocked Starling's grooms, while his more personable, ruddy companion unbuckled their scant baggage and stayed to attend the unsaddling.

'Don't want your stashed coin rifled out of your gear?' Ranne needled his comrade-in-arms.

'Sweet life, I don't!' Fennick's quick glance appraised the poleaxed rider from Varens, caught still astride in the bustling street. 'Don't rush the occasion to sour my fun, or are you too gutless to try a hen's wager?'

Ranne tipped back his helm, while the master self-named as the Light's Blessed Prince continued discussion with the stalled courier. Then he shrugged and declared the importunate odds: 'That we're going to have Tirans declared for the Light before the hour of sundown?'

'Midnight,' corrected Lysaer, who had overheard through the clatter of hooves as the brow-beaten rider spurred off on his errand. 'We'll have Tirans after sundown, because her stiff-necked Lord Mayor has too much experience to bow to my overture.'

Which feint of sly statecraft left the Varens courier shamed scarlet under the lion's share of embarrassment. Alone on the carpet before the high council-men ensconced on the governor's dais, he was left standing in his dusty clothes, redolent of horse and greased leather. He did not have an ambassador's grace to disarm the pitched tension before him. The attendant High Magistrate looked furious in his lace. Worse, the suffused ire on the Lord Mayor's face suggested the Light's dispatch sparked a diplomatic explosion.

Packed in volatile ranks on the floor, and parboiled by sun through the windows, the guild ministers steamed in their lappet hats. Their whispered distress stretched the pause, dropped since the moment the finicky secretary had knifed through the Sunwheel seal.

'What appeal is presented?' a guild spokesman ventured across the stuffy atmosphere. 'How daring a claim does this royal presume to impose on our free city of Tirans?'

For answer, the Lord Mayor raised acid-sharp eyes, and instead accosted the courier. 'You know what this says?' Rings sparked to the pitiless snap of a finger against the unreeled parchment.

The tired rider sweated, trapped by the authority lidded under the vaulted ceiling. 'I'm a Varens man, your Worthiness. Routine messenger, only. Not my place to know, far less to opinionate on what's written and sent by my betters.' Which statement admitted no more than the service badge sewn on his jacket.

But the vulture wearing the seneschal's robe lashed back in jaundiced suspicion. 'You could be the Light's dedicate, come under plain clothes.'

'No.' The questioned man shifted, to the chink of rowelled spurs. 'I'm a hired rider, paid by the route. The scrolls in my dispatch pouch bide under seal. The state contents are never my business.'

Nor had the wax been breached beforetime, a fact witnessed by everyone present. First to crack, the town's acrimonious advisor slapped off his velvet hat.

'We're wasting our strategy grilling the messenger! What does the Exalted Prince have the gall to demand?'

The Lord Mayor's cheek twitched. 'That by sundown today, we are to be flying the Sunwheel banner from the most prominent pole on our watchtower.'

'Ultimatum?' The Minister of the Treasury bristled. 'Sheer arrogance!'

'A plea of insanity, more apt to spark war than move us to grant an alliance.' The advisor sniffed. 'Beneath our grace to respond, I suggest.'

'Ignore this? Are you mad?' The dimpled treasurer stabbed out a finger. 'This showman has tied the port towns in silk wraps! They embrace errant creed for a menial bargain that secures their defence against piracy!'

'Then let's hear the last line of that writ!' The armed veteran wearing the garrison's blazon banged the table with his unsheathed dagger. 'We hoist the Light's flag, or else what is threatened?'

'Or nothing,' responded the Lord Mayor, fixed by icy thought in his upright chair. His frown stayed perplexed. 'No ultimatum has been presented. We have no other statement. Just the one sentence, which also poses us an impertinent impasse.' The pause lagged again, while his fish-eyed glare raked over his disgruntled council-men. 'The rank challenge lies here: the questionable banner we've been asked to raise has, thanklessly, not been provided.'

The miserable courier cleared his dry throat. 'Your pardon, Lordships. And no fault, by Varens. But on my ride in, I was also charged to leave a wrapped bundle, addressed to the day's standing gate captain.' Set at risk by the more volatile jab, that the Light's avatar was in fact present in Tirans, unannounced with a retinue of three, the rider settled for malice. 'I don't broach state seals. But a hare-brained fool knows that packet held cloth, set under the Sunwheel blazon.'

'Black Sithaer, the rogue nerve!' pealed the gaunt justiciar.

If the garrison captain stayed his ill temper, the less-disciplined officials heaved to their feet. Amid declaiming shouts, and the chorused hysteria of trade ministers crying for reason, the fire of singed nerves prevailed.

'I will not give way!' The Lord Mayor pounced on the presumptuous parchment and ripped it to fluttering shreds. 'I grant this upstart nothing! Never, for anyone, will we discard our town's pride and independence!'

'Then stall diplomatically!' A fat bursar swiped through the small blizzard, ranting, 'Do less, and we're likely to cut ourselves off! Don't forget that the ports supporting the Alliance could freeze our trade by embargo.'

The arms captain howled. 'You would choose out of fear, for the sop of security bought by the gold in your ledgers?'

As the upset devolved to a fist-shaking knot, the dispatch rider ducked in retreat and quietly let himself out. To his novice's eye, the brash avatar had brought the Light's cause no genial accord: just a single, shrewd line that had driven a wedge through Tirans' steadfast high council.

Word leaked on the tongues of the lackeys and guards. Their talk took wing, that an officious dispatch issued by the Light's muster had demanded outrageous terms and been spurned by the council of Tirans. By then, Lysaer's sly order had Ranne installed in the Flocked Starling's packed tap-room. The beer jack in the man-at-arms' capable hand was scarcely tasted, although he had been at his ease at the trestle for some time. Since the inn yard's grooms had gossiped about his arrival, and marked his acquaintance with the Varens courier, natural curiosity moved the florid bar-keeper to approach his available silence.

'Yon message, just dispatched to our mayor,' he inquired. 'Did you know aught of the contents?'

Ranne dangled the question just long enough for the hush to acquire an edge. Brawny craftsmen and smiths stilled at the bar, and a sweating glazier elbowed two journeyman coopers aside, the better to hear the reply.

'I witnessed the secretary who set the Sunwheel seal,' Ranne admitted with loaded care. 'Hard not to know what the document said. The scribe had penned only one line.'

Jeers, speculation, then ribald encouragement, as hecklers begged Ranne to continue. The wise bar-keeper said nothing. Arms folded over his apron, he waited. Few drinkers, shown such undivided attention, could bear to hold out for long.

Ranne sipped his beer. With his dark hair sleeked back from a bath, his fresh cool was a provocation. Challenged, the inn's patrons dug into their pockets. Lysaer's armsman accepted their impromptu kitty, if only to dare Fennick to cram more loose silver into his overstuffed saddle-cloth. 'Just one demand,' Ranne relented, while the near trestles quieted, and a maid's laughter drifted, cut free of droned conversation.

'Is it true the Light's avatar wants a recruiter's rights to flesh out his latest campaign?' a bearded teamster called from the side-lines.

Half-smiling, amused, burly Ranne shook his head. 'Nothing like. The scroll contained the genteel suggestion that the Light's banner, now left with your gate watch, should be raised to fly above Tirans' town standard by sundown.

Damned odd request, I felt at the time. No thought over beer's made much sense of it.'

Now, having roused the crowd's blank astonishment, Ranne raised his jack in salute. He forestalled the rising clamour of questions by gulping the contents, then wiped his moustache, tossed a coin to pay up, and arose with a shrug of apology. 'Time to go. There's the master's demand for my service.'

And on cue, Fennick's straw head appeared at the railing that fronted the stair from the upper-floor chambers. The reluctant crowd parted, while across the inn's tap-room, voices exploded in speculation.

Arrived in alert form at the top landing, Ranne cast a glance towards his stalwart companion.

'White diamond,' snapped Fennick, in cryptic summary of Lysaer's current mood. 'He's blithe as an oyster chock-full of new pearls. No one can wring a frown out of him.'

'Not good then,' Ranne murmured. The pair were anything but Lysaer's confidants; just two trustworthy fighters Sulfin Evend had ordered to guard in the uneasy breach. 'Minding the young heir was the happier charge.' For no mind kept pace with the forsaken father; not since Avenor's young prince had decamped to join Ath's adepts. Granted reprieve from a state execution for their lapsed vigilance on that score, the salvaged men-at-arms had been re-assigned by their Lord Commander's adamant word. Only a few in the regent's honour guard shared the damaging secret, that their master was warped by the on-going influence of Desh-thiere's curse. They numbered a steadfast handful of officers, and two fighting men snatched from death by a felon's pardon, who formed the frail shield to stem Lysaer's unnatural fits of insanity. *If any man could.*

'We're not here to shape policy,' Fennick reminded.

In fact, Sulfin Evend's instructions remanded them to the role of observers who would, at need, draw their steel to defend the divine regent's back. Not that any commonplace hazard should have power to threaten the life of the man hailed as avatar.

'Dead is dead,' murmured Ranne, despite his elite skill not liking the prospect of risking a murderous mob.

Fair-skinned and freckled, Fennick's round face was not smiling as he tapped the shut door to the Divine Prince's quarters.

The knock brought the diffident page, who admitted the senior men-at-arms. Inside, late-day sun slanted through the unlatched casements and brightened the inn's threadbare carpet. Lysaer sat at ease, eating bread and stewed chicken. His masking sweat-band and hat were discarded. Golden hair still tarnished with damp from his bath fringed the snowy collar of a fresh shirt. Overtop, he now wore the gilt fire of an emblazoned Sunwheel doublet. The sight arrested vision: even without the Alliance insignia, his presence shouted with the magisterial force of birth-born royalty.

The paired retainers stalled upon entry, challenged by gemstone-blue eyes.

'You question the wisdom of state dress, but no retinue?' Lysaer stated with sanguine charm. His magnanimous gesture offered two chairs, followed up by his striking smile. 'Sit. Eat your fill, share some excellent wine. Since I've paid for the privilege of privacy, we aren't going to need your bristling vigilance until the hour of sundown.'

While the watchtower with the controversial flag spire lengthened its shadow across the slate roof-tops of Tirans, far to the west, the downs of Atainia hung layered in cloud like a vein of blue jasper. There, the warded stone of Althain Tower cut a stark silhouette, with only one casement illuminated. Candles pooled light where Sethvir languished in his debilitating fight to check the corrosive charge that leaked from destabilized grimwards. His compromised straits had turned for the worse without warning: Asandir's exemplary hold on the Scarpdale vortex had faltered. No means existed to assess the set-back. The Fellowship's field Sorcerer might be hurt, even dying, beyond reach of immediate help.

Althain's Warden endured that concern in fraught silence. From two minor vortices with minimal damage, once again, he had no viable choice but to shoulder the crushing burden of three. The increase already took its sapping toll: his aura displayed the febrile blaze of a spark reduced by a gale-wind. Sethvir maintained his obstinate grip on little more than dedicate will.

'We are not victims,' he reminded, the statement fierce at odds with the suffering etched into the face propped up by heaped pillows.

The draught he addressed took pause by the window, mingling chill with the breeze. 'Say that to Ciladis, wherever he's gone!' Kharadmon snapped, frustrated.

Hands stilled on the coverlet, Althain's Warden sighed. 'Would you be so angry if you thought him lost beyond all recovery?'

'Rage before grief,' the discorporate shade temporized.

Yet his colleague's point set a virulent sting. The posited chance could not be dismissed, that Ciladis might have abandoned their Fellowship's interests: the wounding left by the Paravians' withdrawal could well have broken a spirit beloved for his matchless tenderness.

Kharadmon added, 'Asandir would be first to remind that the gentlest nature is never least powerful.' Then, in ripped sorrow, 'though I'd rather hang trust in the mouth of a fool than wait for the gleam on a pearl to stave off our defeat!'

'No doubt to the pearl's everlasting relief,' Sethvir said, made tart by near-desperate duplicity. He scarcely dared breathe. If his irritable colleague should guess that fresh trouble now embroiled their interests in Scarpdale, the bitter predicament could not be salvaged: even a Fellowship shade could not survive the chaotic flux of an unshielded grimward.

'Surely you haven't come here to rant,' Althain's Warden pressed with weary delicacy.

'No.' Kharadmon had none of Luhaine's stuffy knack for diffusing rough news with a lecture. 'Raiett Raven's effects at Etarra have been searched, down to the last jewelled cloak-pin.' This testy spirit always delivered his impacts headlong. 'My best effort failed. The dragon-skull wards copped from Hanshire's state treasury are still at large in the world. My scour of the empty cult lairs at Etarra found no sign of the coffer that guarded them.'

'The Kralovir never acquired the talismans,' Sethvir agreed, unsurprised. 'If the grey necromancers had ever laid hands on that asset, presumably they would have put it to use?'

Kharadmon's savage eddy set the candle-flames fluttering. '*Davien*? Are you daring to suggest the Betrayer's involved? Did he flit in and make off with the contraband before Luhaine and I reached Etarra?'

Sethvir's wide-lashed eyes stayed a vacant, pale turquoise. 'For all your distrust, Davien's never been secretive. He may not pause for leave, but the thrust of his works has always been in the open.'

'My question's not answered!' Kharadmon cracked. 'If not one of us, then who else is left?'

'Not who, but where,' Sethvir defined, too aware of the stick that prospect kicked into the wasp's nest. 'I think we want Luhaine's persistence, if our search must be widened to include Avenor.'

'Lysaer's private treasury!' Kharadmon's vexed presence recoiled. The vault in question lay beneath the caved ruin of Avenor's state hall. The keys never left the false regent's sole possession, even after Lysaer's explosion of light had blasted the keep's lower dungeon to rubble.

'Where else?' Sethvir said in dismal conclusion. Flame or magma could never destroy the skulls of Athera's great drakes. But the strapped wood and silk that wrapped the arcane instruments under a passive protection would have been torched. Fire also would damage the skulls' jewelled settings, in which case the ghost remnant of four foetal hatchlings might be cut loose in a state of unrest.

'I have not sensed them stirring!' Sethvir added, fast. 'Let Luhaine confirm this before you rant! There's every chance we might not face the disaster of seeing the birth of a new grimward.'

'We need Asandir's hands freed!' Kharadmon skirted the bedside, riffling the blankets. 'I don't trust the Betrayer. Not his wild-card, cavalier handling, nor the means by which he has made himself corporate!'

'Davien hasn't troubled to offer himself, yet,' Sethvir reminded with level simplicity. Eyes like mirrored cloud, he fanned old dissent to further his bald-faced dissembling. Behind conversation, the strain bled him, relentless. While the room seemed to reel with unnatural shadows, Kharadmon rounded, suspicious.

'Ath above, what's gone wrong? What else are you hiding? What crock of ill news? Is your prodding meant to divert me?'

Sethvir snatched command of the blistering pause. 'It's the fool with the torch who picks fights with the wind.' His dead-pan expression might have been chipped from chert. 'I don't have the strength to chase every black vision. The true voice of hope never fades, though without Ciladis, one tends to forget.'

'We're drowning in chaos, while you shoulder a load any three of us would beg to delegate!' Frost on hot iron, Kharadmon added, 'I would take your place.' With no such grace possible, and no opening to challenge the Warden's prostrate regard, he circled again. 'What's left, but Lysaer?'

Sethvir pounced. 'That busy brash rogue is forcing his claim on new Tirans. A sly plan, in full swing.' The Sorcerer stirred a tremulous hand, inviting the timely diversion. 'You're certain you wish to bear witness?'

'Sight before ignorance,' Kharadmon groused.

Eyes shut, his face touched by ineffable sorrow, Althain's Warden engaged an active link through his earth-sense and traced a circle onto the coverlet. Inside, demarked by his measured intent, a sequence of images unveiled the thrust of the self-styled avatar's strategy . . .

As dusk falls in the trade town of Tirans, a lamplighter strikes a spark to a wick that ignites. But the flame fails to steady. An unnatural darkness swallows the flare, to a gasp of bewildered confusion. . . . while, down the street, the sconce by a tavern doorway goes out, its brilliance stolen away. . . . the fires in the bake-shop, and the spit in an inn's kitchen, and the candle on the desk of a scribe do the same. . . . across town, as night falls, every burning light fails amid gathering gloom. Havoc ensues. People rush outside, crying. Terror drives them to huddle in knots, while atop the gate watchtower, the flood of purloined fire coalesces into a raging beacon that illumines the flagstaff still flying the mayor's device.

No other light breaks summer's night but stars. Wild rumours fly house to house. News of a Sunwheel banner in the hands of the gate watch drives the seethe of a gathering crowd. The mob storms the door to the garrison keep. Deafened by the shouts, under assault by desperate citizens wielding craft-shop tools and pried-up cobbles, the acting captain cannot make himself heard. Two men-at-arms fall to a stoning. The town mayor and council find themselves helpless as well, unable to quell pandemonium.

Torn by riot, driven by panic, Tirans' populace batters the grilled door of the gate tower, howling for divine Light in relief . . .

'I see where this is leading,' Kharadmon broke in, while the disturbing flow of scried images on the blanket faded into release.

'The watch captain will raise the Sunwheel banner,' Sethvir murmured with sorrow. 'The same instant, Lysaer will step forth, clad in white pearls and state panoply. He will seize command through raw fear of the dark. We've already seen the voice of the mayor drowned by the uprising clamour. His council can't lead, though they'll try to hold out. The probabilities converge. By dawn, Tirans will be as softened clay in the trumped-up avatar's hands.'

'Like sheep, we'll have veterans and recruits alike flocking under the Alliance banner.' Kharadmon reversed course. The tight wind of his passage scattered the white hair spread over the Warden's pillow. 'What's to be done?'

'Visit Alestron,' Sethvir said, pale as bone. 'Pray the s'Brydion duke will hear the voice of old law and take warning.'

'Why in Sithaer do I wish that Luhaine were here?' Now poised to depart by the cracked open casement, Kharadmon snarled of his longtime adversary, 'He's the one better suited as a harbinger of doom.'

Sethvir widened his eyes. 'You'd rather dig for the lost hatchling skulls beneath the charred vaults, at Avenor?'

For answer, a white rose spiralled out of the air and dropped on the bed-clothes. 'I'll bear-bait the wolves,' Kharadmon responded, 'before I sift through the trash buried under that abhorrent site.'

The next instant, he was gone, leaving Althain's protections still as a premature tomb. Left in vigilant solitude, savaged by dread, Sethvir savoured the rose, while outside, the daylight bled out of the sky, and stained the layered cloud-banks blood crimson.

Bransian s'Brydion always knew by the wintry nip of the draught when a discorporate Sorcerer breathed down his neck. Burnished with sweat in his rolled-up sleeves, he hunched his obstinate shoulders. 'Take your blustering elsewhere! I don't want advice.'

Frost became tempest that raised a blue rime over his gorget and chain-mail.

The duke swore, stripped the armour, and planted his feet. Choleric as a bear in the faded surcoat his wife had thrice tried to retire, he cupped massive hands to his bearded mouth and bellowed downhill to the crew at the trebuchet. 'Another wedge! Crank up the elevation! Then reload and release her again!'

Sunburned industry swarmed on the field below. Bare-chested men laboured, shouting. Ropes creaked and timbers counterweighted with a stone basket groaned and moved. By arduous effort, the massive throwing arm was levered erect, then cocked back.

'Fire, you slugs!' Duke Bransian howled. 'No pissing off, and no slacking for beer bets! Who stalls to break wind will be grubbing with shovels to clear the latrines with the recruits!'

On the field marshal's signal, the huge engine let fly. With a vast whoosh of air and a pendulous arc, the trebuchet lofted its missile. The launched boulder tumbled, reached height, then plunged, whistling earthward like vengeance unleashed. Outside the lower citadel walls, the ponderous thud of its impact smashed a log target into flying slivers. The crew cheered amid the trembling noon air.

'That should hammer the teeth out of yon swaggering pretender's front ranks,' pronounced Bransian with fierce satisfaction. For the benefit of the sorcerous eddy that now iced the sweat at his collar, he added, 'That's precisely how I shall serve the land, this time. No matter what errand Sethvir's flipped a shade to dispatch! I won't play the toady with mincing ambassadors or hang out my flag for diplomacy!'

Silence. Even the tough, summer grass had stopped rustling.

Bransian glared mulishly forward, pulse soaring. 'Is it Luhaine, again? If so, speak up quick! We're busy as coupling may-flies, which means I can't dawdle for carping yap from a gas-bag.'

'Luhaine should hear you,' Kharadmon snapped with relish, 'the more since he treasures his grudges like fossils.'

Bransian stiffened. Red-faced, he folded his arms. 'If you've come here to plead against an armed fight, a straight pin in the arse would be kinder.'

'You may not have a living arse to offend,' Kharadmon pointed out. 'Lysaer's taken Tirans. Varens, Farsee, Northstor, and Easttair have all received Sunwheel sealed orders to march. Need I repeat that their harbours are already swarming? Perdith will join them, with Kalesh and Adruin primed to fuel that bonfire by week's end. You will see your gates stormed. The Light's minions will blockade your harbour within weeks, if you care to credit my warning. Carping yap!' the Sorcerer cracked with offence. 'Should I waste my time here, or try the reasonable course and visit your lady?'

'Liesse?' Bransian's lip curled. He kicked his dropped gorget, then spun towards the cold dust-devil that marked Kharadmon's seething presence. 'My wife's will backs mine. No women will leave. If they went, they would strip the steadfast heart out of the citadel.'

'Send Sevrand, then,' the Sorcerer persisted. 'At least leave your heir to the refuge of Atwood, if only to safeguard your lineage.'

'No get of mine would embrace such dishonour!' Bransian's glare showed blazing contempt. 'Shame on your words, Sorcerer! Such as Sevrand's become, he would run himself through, first. No cousin of mine forsakes his courage, or fails to stand in defence of his heritage.'

'So would the compact that binds charter law fail,' Kharadmon stated, ruthless. 'If each man sheds his blood for his personal turf above the weal of this land, we are lost. Prince Arithon was right to disown you.'

Since drawn steel could not silence an insolent shade, Bransian hit back with complacency. 'Alestron has always endured, undefeated.' He squared challenging shoulders, large fists hooked on his sword-belt. 'Or is the power of Lysaer's false godhead much worse than the fire of Athera's great dragons?'

'Apparently you are hell-bound to find out,' Kharadmon said, frustrated beyond storm or heat. 'If I thought earnest prayer could soften your pride, I would beg every power alive that innocents who rely on these walls do not pay the harsh price of your folly.'

'Over the wrack of my dead enemies, they won't,' Duke Bransian insisted.

But the Fellowship shade had already left, without the flourish of a rejoinder.

In his absence, the sunlight beat down like hot brass. The revetted walls danced through shimmering haze, while the glass fragments set into the mortar glared white. Yet even noon's wilting humidity could not blunt s'Brydion temper. The duke stalked ahead and snatched up his tossed mail. Straightened up with the links wadded in his bare hands, he harangued his available men. 'Damn your shirking hides! Who asked you loungers to park on your rumps? Hop to! There's a war bearing down on this stronghold! Load up the next round of stone-shot!'

While Alestron's titled lord drilled his field-troops, his brother Mearn was not gambling. Found in the smoking, red heat of the forge, the youngest of the duke's siblings was whetting one of his stiletto daggers. The whine of steel on the grindstone lagged only an instant as Kharadmon's chill presence sliced in, flaring the smith's coals bright ruby.

Mearn straightened, astute enough to shout through the clangour of hammers and dismiss the journeymen armourers. The knife in his fist remained poised in fierce irony as the grumbling men filed out. Too soon, he was facing an empty doorway across the brimstone hiss of the coals.

'You've knocked heads with Bransian, now it's my turn,' he supposed without formal greeting. Youngest by ten years, he avoided his sibling's mistake of presuming his visitor was Luhaine. Mearn mopped his wet blade on the leather apron tied over a dandy's trim doublet. Unhurried, he inspected his work, then stamped a dissatisfied foot onto the grindstone's treadle.

Were Kharadmon still embodied, his smile would have befitted a hunting tiger. 'I could edge that blade for you, without need to sweat.'

Mearn raised refined eyebrows. Thin as a whip, and crafty since birth, he shrugged with exquisite disinterest. 'For what price, pray tell?'

Kharadmon also liked spare debates. 'The safekeeping of your pregnant wife in the *caithdein*'s lodge tent in Atwood.'

'You foresee our defeat?' Not waiting for answer, Mearn grinned. 'Bransian will be smoking with temper, for that. Nor, I imagine, did you waste the breeze chasing down brothers Keldmar and Parrien.'

Kharadmon's snort flared the coals in the pit. 'That pair? Thick as they are, like two stones in a sack? Though in naked truth, any word from a rock is dulcet and politely reasonable.'

'You couldn't expect courtesy,' Mearn agreed without heat. 'My brothers see nothing more in a rock beyond dinging the heads of our enemies.' His quicksilver grin showed sharp teeth. 'When Bransian wants us complacent in council, he tells our women to ply us with drink. Personally, I'd stuff the lot with red meat. Drowsy and parked like swilled hogs in their seats, they're less apt to start hammering fights.'

'Our Fellowship should stoop to such tactics, you think?' Kharadmon pressed with snide irony.

Mearn deigned not to comment. As the wheel lagged, he resurveyed his blade. Since the finish seemed pleasing, he tucked the glittering weapon back into the wrist sheath beneath his lace cuff. 'You realize,' he said, thoughtful, 'I would set my manhood at risk if I dared to speak for my wife? That's if she deigned to address me at all. Since Arithon's rebuff, she's been thick with Dame Dawr. I will tell you this: if she wanted to birth our first child in Atwood, she would have gone there directly.'

Kharadmon's sigh riffled dust from the shelves, all but worked bare of the ingots the forges were smelting for weaponry.

'You're perfectly free to try swaying Anzia,' Mearn invited. 'You've no skin to blister. Nor ears to be thrashed till they ring like whacked chimes. The wife swears,' he admitted. 'I'm amazed the grandame's endured for this long without tossing her out on her petticoats.'

Kharadmon did not laugh. 'If the grandame's hand selected your match, she'll have balanced your badgering wits.'

'She did, the sly bitch.' Mearn shrugged. 'Gave me a woman intelligent enough to split hairs with a glower. At least on those days when she's not ripping mad. Then it's cut to the tenderest parts straightaway. She'd snip a man's bollocks with pincers.' Fishing his next dagger out of his boot, he gave the wheel's pedal a vengeful kick. As the stone whirred, the knife was applied with neat fingers. 'Our child's near term. If I want another, or hope for a kindly welcome in bed, I know when to keep my douce distance.'

'But unlike your brothers, you've never liked hunting,' Kharadmon admonished with piercing persistence.

'No.' Mearn stopped his sharpening, brown eyes intense. 'But try telling that to the rest of my family. As you've said, dumb rocks clapped in a sack have more sense. Nobody weans a s'Brydion from war. Long before Dawr, the cock's hens were hand-picked for hatching their get for the battle-field.'

'Not for this accursed fight!' Kharadmon said. This time sorrow scalded. 'You were never the fool, Mearn! You snarl in the pit for no cause but display. This stand in defiance is going to sow all manner of wrong-headed principles.'

'I know.' Mearn's admission came without pride. 'Prince Arithon spoke with a prophet's conviction. I never was deaf to wisdom. Yet these are my brothers. I would run this dagger through my own heart before I desert my blood-kin.'

'And Fianzia?' Kharadmon ventured at last, the lady's full name spoken with tenderness. 'You'd risk her to the rampage of Lysaer's crazed following?'

Mearn's level stare never faltered. 'She carries our child. Whatever she thinks now, that babe *is* our life, made in wedded union between us. Be sure I will sacrifice all that I have to ensure she survives to give birth.'

No more could be given; nothing more said. Kharadmon would have bowed, had he still possessed flesh. No such parting salute was left to a shade. Just regretful silence, followed by a retreat to visit the comfortless news on Dame Dawr.

Three days later, still held in close seclusion within the rock caves of Sanpashir, Arithon Teir's'Ffalenn paused where he knelt. He remained oblivious to Lysaer's bold claim at Tirans; was yet unaware of Jeynsa s'Valerient's resolve to question his royal character. The hands that secured the hide covering over his heirloom lyranthe poised with the laces half-tightened when the soft, barefoot step he expected intruded upon his kept solitude.

He finished the last knot. Turned his raised head, aware who approached well before the arrival emerged from the underground corridor. He arose with respect. Flawless in courtesy, he offered a seat on the folded blanket that had lately served as his bed. No fool, he did not make the outsider's mistake and try to lend an elder assistance.

The aged matriarch of the Biedar therefore took her imperious time to make herself comfortable. She circled the rock-chamber. Her fathomless interest peered into the dim corners; stared everywhere else but at the royal guest standing at her attendance.

Arithon waited. He might have been stone, so deep was his courteous stillness. The overhead crack that admitted the day's failing light dropped a shaft of hazed gold through the gloom. The mote shifted slowly from citrine to rose, then faded into still twilight.

The crone settled at last. A young woman arrived with a fire-pot, then a man bearing strips of raw meat on peeled sticks.

Arithon stayed on his feet, while the revered one roasted her meal. She watched him with bright, bead-black eyes, and as thoroughly chewed each steaming bite.

'You would not have answered my summons,' she revealed at length, though not before the evening wind moaned its chill serenade through the gap.

Arithon suppressed his most combative smile. Empty hands remained clasped at his waist. 'You would not take my gift for your tribe's hospitality. Therefore, we both suffer hardship.'

The grandame's cackling laughter bounced off the rough walls, waking a thrum of muffled resonance from his wrapped instrument. 'One might knap a flint knife with your tongue. Dare you leave? I have not released you with the tribe's blessing.'

The threatened curve turned Arithon's lips. 'And do you bless prisoners who should be set free?' Regarding her, serious, he added, 'The one who came armed was dispatched to his ship with no such presumptuous ceremony.' He considered with care, then selected the term that meant 'unwitting, ignorant stripling.' 'Do you halter the *m'a'hia* who comes to you naked?'

'You are not healed!' the grandame said, angered. 'A warrior not in fit state does not travel.'

Arithon resisted the need to lash back. 'Yet I bear no arms.'

Bone trinkets and fetishes clinked: one deft, ancient hand clapped the clay lid on the fire-pot, and night swallowed the blood glare of the coals. '*M'a'hi*! Grown but foolish! You should. Men are burning the standing crops in the fields. This I have seen, in East Halla.'

Cold despite his borrowed silk clothing, Arithon shivered. 'But I am not bound for East Halla. My path leads to Atwood, by way of Alland, and my sword was left, safe, back in Halwythwood.' Other messages lay rolled in the wood cylinder, bundled beside his lyranthe. The scroll-case bore letters for Fiark, at Innish, releasing the trade factor and other sworn allies from lists of detailed obligations. 'Old mother, your care is a dangerous gift should it cost me the lives of my friends.'

The crone arose at his chiding plea. Glass and copper chimed gently as she raised her creased hands and cradled his face with a feather touch. In darkness cut by the pearl gleam of the starlight let in through the overhead crack, she stared into Arithon's eyes. Her intensity raised the hair at his nape as she said, 'Mother Dark's mystery walks in your tracks, while we are the wind, chasing after the wisdom to read them. You will cross through the far side, and visit death twice again. When we meet, I will be with the ancestry.'

Cloth rustled within the deeps of the cavern. Already, a robed band of dartmen assembled to serve as his tireless escort. Arithon reached up and gently unclasped the aged woman's confining embrace. 'I do not leave your people, unblessed, after all?' he challenged with tender humour.

'You bless our tribe, not the other way round,' the ancient woman corrected. Then she stepped back and released him, though clear mage-sight would show him the tears cascading down her weathered cheeks.

Late Summer 5671

Foray

A man's heart could grow sick, watching the smoke-plume spread on the wind across the scorched fields of East Halla. Yet a veteran captain of Talvish's stature knew better than to criticize Duke Bransian's pre-emptive strike. Never mind the fact, that the order to raze the earth's bounty was an ugly defiance of charter law.

Sited beyond the bounds of the free wilds, Alestron would not incur direct censure by any Fellowship Sorcerer. Melhalla's *caithdein* held the steward's right to cry debt in the name of crown justice. Her concern for clan survival in Atwood came first. This razing of crops could scarcely incite the town garrisons to invade her domain any faster.

Already, the Light's call to arms swept the peninsula with a brush-fire's kindling speed. Galleys raced Lysaer's summons the length of the eastshore, while word winged its way inland to Shand by pigeon and post, through Six Towers, Ganish, and Atchaz. The onset of winter would bring no relief: fresh troops from the south would bolster the ranks as rough weather thrashed the northern harbours. Faced by an assault of unprecedented scope, the brothers s'Brydion ripped off the muzzle of peace and torched their last hope of diplomacy.

Today's standing grain would never supply the war host inbound to besiege them.

Retainers since birth, Vhandon and Talvish had fought such brutal campaigns under Alestron's banner before: the same reiver's tactics would be launched at Kalesh or Adruin, or both towns at once, when hostilities caused by a bottle-necked shore-line progressed from hurled threats to bloodshed. Alestron's harbour mouth was flanked by armed adversaries. No s'Brydion duke could ever afford to negotiate peace with complacency. When enemy galleys cut off the narrows, Bransian's field-captains deployed their light horse like hawks and burned out the hayricks and crops. Ships' crews could not hold a determined blockade without provender to sustain them.

Yet where Talvish once wielded the torch under orders, now his scouring silence reflected a new-found frustration. He and Vhandon had been stretched for too long to keep pace with Prince Arithon's astute innovation. They had experienced the cross-currents of Alliance politics at first hand. This time, a pitched stand against Lysaer's hot cause would not wane with the advent of snowfall.

Both men remained too determined for despondency, when Vhandon strode from the outer-gate ward-room at dusk, armed and dressed out in a new surcoat bearing Alestron's bull blazon. His shout sent the officer's equerry running to fetch him a saddled mount.

Talvish looked on with half-lidded, green eyes, fast to notice the crested officer's badge stitched to the senior campaigner's left shoulder. He said nothing. Just collected his stakes from the barracks dice game and crossed the vacant parade ground. He nipped through to the stables in time to measure his companion's squared jaw, then the rock set to stout shoulders. Without reference to the late meeting gone bad, he said only, 'You've chosen to stay the brute course.'

Vhandon shrugged. 'Old habits die hard.' He had served as Bransian's field-captain for twenty years, before debt of honour had seen him transferred into Arithon's service.

Yet Talvish saw past the stark front of the stoic. His quiet held drilling intensity.

'The duke asked!' Vhandon stated, his raw burst all but drowned by the racket of armourers' hammers. 'Should I have refused?'

'Not my call to make, friend.' Talvish side-stepped the lamp-man just arrived to snuff the wick by the entry. Before the flame died, he measured the grief masked behind the rapacious decision. 'I know there's been word from a Fellowship Sorcerer. What went down when the grey cult fell at Etarra? If Arithon had perished on the dark moon, you'd be off to get drunk. Not leaving the keep with a captaincy.'

Vhandon unburdened. 'The duke's raised his stakes. Called us to lay waste to more crop-land. Southward to Six Towers. Westward as well, clear over to Pellain.'

Talvish sucked a sharp breath. 'Better say what ill news has blown in from the north. Was it Luhaine? Seems he always bears the rough tidings.'

The equerry dashed up with Vhandon's fresh horse. The reinstated veteran accepted the reins, checked the girth, then ran down his stirrups. 'Kharadmon delivered the worst to Dame Dawr, since the s'Brydion men weren't minded to listen. The gist?' He shrugged, helpless. 'You have no idea.'

'With Prince Arithon involved? Say again!' Talvish collared the servant, sent him back for a second mount. 'Shall I guess? There's not a Kralovir cultist left standing, but half the north's mayors pissed their sheets out of shock. Dead bodies consumed by white mage-fire aren't subtle. When Rathain's town-born are done being scared, they'll draw steel for revenge. Cheek by jowl with everyone else in East Halla, they'll be ramming our gate, mad as hornets.'

Vhandon laughed, bitter. 'Fate wept! Did you eavesdrop?'

Yet Talvish could not be hazed off. The shrill clang of steel and coal fumes from the forges did not cause his closest friend's headache, tonight.

'Aye, you're right,' Vhandon cracked at due length. 'The grey cult's destroyed. But Arithon's tactic unleashed Desh-thiere's curse. We're not going to face necromancy, but elemental light. The Fellowship's sent warning that Lysaer's come undone, verging on geas-bent madness. He's swayed Tirans from fixed independence, *that fast.*'

The worst followed, quickly: that Kharadmon had pressed on to awaken the matrix of the old centaur markers and seal the free wilds of Atwood. Some forest clan families could withdraw to the Tiriacs. The rest would shelter at the ruin of ancient Tirans, where Traithe stood in residence to advise Melhalla's *caithdein.*

'The duke refused sanctuary,' Vhandon summed up. 'Nor would the wives relocate their families, or send out the young heirs to protect the core strength of the blood-line.'

'The siege would be lost on morale, if they tried,' Talvish allowed, brushed by dread. Nor could Bransian change his chosen course, now. Lysaer's muster had progressed too far.

The seasoned campaigner, looking ahead, must take icy stock of the walls and the gates, the trebuchets, and the causeway and winches. Against force of arms, the citadel was secure, if not very near to impregnable. But faced by the mage-gifted mastery of light, wielded by a curse-driven fanatic, no mortal might answer except for the one the fearful named Spinner of Darkness.

'I am not made as his Grace of Rathain, to forsake my loyalties over a principle.' Vhandon jammed his foot into the stirrup, laid raw. 'This is my country, and my parents' and grandparents' before them. If Alestron goes down, where else would I go? I can't stand to watch from the side-lines. Our day for defeat is not written, besides.' Astride, he deliberately gathered his reins. 'The Mathiell Gate's stonework was laid to stop drake fire. Before we're starved out, the moment may come when a cool voice for reason might spare a disaster.'

Talvish raised his eyebrows. 'Keep on wasting your breath to explain. I was hanging around to hear orders.'

Vhandon stopped in midtirade. 'You want to serve with me?'

The blond swordsman grinned. 'Damned well not under anyone else! Tell that laggard to hurry along with my horse. Then we'll argue in earnest, or maybe toss straws.'

'Over which of us trims that jackanapes goatherd into something resembling a soldier?' Vhandon shook his head, as close as he came to flummoxed exasperation over the temperamental young grass-lander left in their charge. The Araethurian had won their affection, a frank complication since a bad turn by Koriathain had shapechanged him into Arithon's double.

'Daelion's bollocks!' the elder campaigner ran on. 'Keep Fionn Areth here, and Mearn or Sevrand will crash heads to unwind his insolent tripes. That's if Parrien can't ram a pike through him, first. We daren't turn the yapping fool loose with that face! Not with the country-side swarming with spies and encampments of Sunwheel skirmishers.'

'Well, we could,' Talvish argued. He accepted the mare trotted out by the groom and vaulted astride. 'Though you're right. With nobody watching, the yokel might march off to Kalesh. Find himself slaughtered as Shadow's own self, as he hops into line to enlist.'

The next morning's dawn, Talvish took charge of the sweep down the trade-road to Pellain. Under his handling were eighty crack horsemen with standing orders to raze the fields through the back country. When the reiving was done, they were to fall back to the Tiriac foothills, in position to send warning should the town salve its wounds by trying an east-bound invasion. Since Fionn Areth was too much underfoot, and offensive with inflamed opinions, Vhandon attached the young man to the foray with hopes he might learn through no-nonsense experience.

The tight-knit troop of veterans rode out. All speed and grim purpose, they skirted the southern fringes of Atwood, doused by the squalls that raked off the Tiriacs. Scorching heat did not faze them, or fireless nights. They slept on rough ground and ate hard-tack and cheese, and met a greenhorn's complaints with clipped laughter. Fionn Areth's brash ideals and drawled, grass-lands vowels were made the butt of crude jokes.

Jaw set, the young man shouldered detail with the shovel, night after blistering night. His riding improved, and his sword-play became less classically neat and more dangerous. While his face tanned in squint lines, the hazy horizon revealed only flocking blackbirds and galloping post-couriers. The empty road was the precursor to war. The caravans spurned the land route through East Halla, the merchants staying well clear to avoid the outbreak of hostilities.

Talvish bolstered his scouts. Into the rolling hills south of Pellain, his picked company took to the brush. Half mounted, half on foot, they fanned out, all business as they slipped like grey wolves past the verges of Atwood. Kharadmon's warning forbade them to enter the forest. The old centaur markers were realigned for protection, and to broach their tuned ward without Fellowship leave might well cost a strayed man his life.

'Damned well makes things dicey,' the watch scouts complained. 'Flush an enemy, we could easily become cut off, or get ourselves hazed against the defences and shot down like cornered rabbits.'

Yet day followed day, with no movement sighted. Each evening, Fionn Areth dug the latrines, cursing his blisters in the ripe dialect once used to malign stubborn goats.

'You haven't figured, boy?' cracked the scarred veteran wringing his shirt by the river. 'A soldier's life is all grinding routine. Who sold you the rosy notion of honour, trumped up in bright flags and glory? We're here to burn barley. Tossing a torch takes a damned sight less practice than trenching hard ground with a spade.'

'Don't listen,' admonished the rear-guard lieutenant sent to string up the evening picket line. 'Keep your sword sharp, and both eyes open. Pellain's patrols won't be sleeping. We're six times outnumbered, and if we're attacked, a slacker's mistake'll drop you stone-dead in a second.'

Yet the sultry night passed without disturbance. Men tossed and turned to the shrilling of insects and the cries of rodents razed down by an owl.

Pre-dawn, under a dank scud of fog, the advance line spied a head-hunters' party on foot with three couples of dogs. The man with the report came in breathless, his professional summary bleak. 'Onto somebody's trail, tracking south-east from Silvermarsh. That points to a clan runner with news, moving hell-bent to reach Atwood.'

A ghost presence in his dull brigandine and blacked helm, Talvish weighed the development. 'That's a damned problem.' The Sorcerer's sealed warding might not let a messenger through; this, alongside the confounding snag, that the bounty hunt posed a hindrance to his skulking task force. 'Listen up, men! I want ten, armed for skirmish. By daylight, we'll have that league squad cut down. No noise, without fuss! Sink their dead in the river. Can't have a batch of circling vultures to warn off the couriers from Spire.'

Those chosen strung bows and slipped off to snipe headsmen. The unsavoury chore of weighting the corpses would be handled without complaint. They were too small a company, camped amid open land, far too deep into unfriendly territory.

Talvish moved next for chance-met opportunity. 'I'll have a cordon. We'll net the live quarry as well.' He would hear what grave need sent a fugitive clansman at risk near the towns of West Halla. 'I'd know what's afoot at first hand, and not wait on the pickings of rumour.'

The company's reserves assembled at speed, with Fionn Areth on fire to go with them. Three weeks tasked with menial chores had pitched his quick temper to snapping. 'Leave me in charge of the horses again, I'll go out of my skull slapping flies.'

Talvish scarcely paused. 'You want the assignment? Then streak your face, bantling.' The suspect, cat gleam to his glance should have roused second thoughts, under daylight.

In darkness, the veterans smiled, unfooled: the testy Araethurian was going to be dealt an arduous lesson in patience. Bagging forest-bred talent amid covert thickets called for hours of motionless vigil. The insect bites, nettle rash, and tedium could drive even a seasoned man fidgeting crazy.

Even so, Talvish was not complacent. Entrusting a greenhorn with critical action, he finished his raking review. 'Keep your wits, goatherd. Stay self-reliant. Don't think for one second you'd be here bearing arms if Vhan hadn't left his word with the duke to vouchsafe your weathercock character.'

'I won't fall short,' Fionn Areth insisted, absorbed with the fit of his baldric.

'Fall to napping, more likely,' Talvish tossed back.

The effect was predictable: Fionn Areth huffed in retort, 'A month's beer to my promise I'll stoop to fleece goats, first!'

Talvish clapped the young man's rigid shoulder. 'Should I pity the goats? It's not my place, but I have to presume that a sword makes a hack job of shearing.'

The duke's captain strode on his self-assured way, aware his brisk handling had whetted the edge he required of hot-blooded new recruits. If league trackers had flushed a clan runner crossing Melhalla on desperate business, the creature would sense Alestron's fixed line. The mistake must not happen, that forestborn instinct should snatch the least chance to slip through. 'Bring this scout in safely! Such news as he carries might become critical to holding Alestron's defence.'

Sunrise over East Halla dispersed the ripped tatters of mist. The rolling land emerged, its crabbed briar and crowned oak as a layered etching stamped on dull foil. Heat followed. The late-summer sun beat relentlessly through, bleaching the hazy sky powder blue and silting the parched vales in shadow. Jeynsa s'Valerient stirred as the first breeze riffled the leaves of the oak where she hid. She ached. Her tucked posture amid the crooked boughs had stiffened the muscles stressed hard by the zeal of league trackers. Her moment to catnap had lasted all night, a fool's lapse and a perilous set-back.

Thirsty, still tired, in need of the meal she dared not pause to forage, she took wary stock. In hindsight, she should never have shortened her route by choosing the east way past Backwater. Either the boatman she paid for her crossing had talked, or a child sent out to pick brambles had seen her; or else an inquisitive crofter's dog had dug up the warm ash of her campsite. Whatever the cause, the league pressed the chase. Her capture by townsmen would see Eriegal branded by Feithan's undying, cold fury. Sidir, as well, would decry the bold course that had led her into Melhalla. Her predicament should have borne deadly stakes, except that her mother and Halwythwood's council had been duped by Rathain's corrupt crown prince. His vile practice left Jeynsa no choice but to win through regardless of danger. In a country-side busy with pennoned outriders, armed skirmish parties, and couriers mustering troops, she had been chased, every step, since leaving the sinkpools of Silvermarsh. Though she was well trained to elude close pursuit, seventy-five leagues across open terrain had sapped her youthful resilience.

Now beaten lean, with the refuge of Atwood a day's run past the Pellain road, Jeynsa confronted the desperate fact she had lost her cover. The mist had burned off. Worse, a snapped twig from below revealed someone's unwelcome company.

Jeynsa silently unslung her bow. Prepared for a bountyman, she swiped back her hacked hair and peered downwards.

Another stick cracked. A snagged briar rustled. A slinking form wearing town cloth paused in step, while gingerly fingers unhooked the thorny grip of the underbrush. Her stalker was armed, and masked with streaked walnut, though clearly he was not woodwise. He never inspected the boughs overhead. The bumbler parked himself under her tree, oblivious as a straw target.

Jeynsa chose not to shoot him. Aside from the fact she had killed only deer, a dead body would attract scavengers and flag the dog-pack. This man was no scalper. Her indistinct view through the foliage unveiled a jerkin sewn with a troop badge. Which device did not matter. The town-born rooster would have armed companions. She dared not risk a redoubled pursuit, dizzy with hunger and wracked by exhaustion.

Past help, her niche in the oak was a trap till the fool on the ground chose to move.

Jeynsa curbed her impatience. He *would* fall asleep. Flushed by the scald of the sun on her back, she must bank on the rankling certainty. Amid sultry air, fecund with summer greenery, a man by himself on a boring patrol would nod in the shade and succumb.

But an hour passed; two. The young man remained standing. Back braced to the oak, he raked his dark hair from his streaming forehead. Jeynsa chewed her lip. Inwardly swearing, she wrestled her need to climb down, find a bush, and relieve herself. The man-at-arms, whoever he was, had not picked his vantage at random. She had detected the rest of his company staked across the next vale. Their placement deepened her growing anxiety, that their cast net had marked her as prey.

Noon came and went. Burgeoning cumulus fluffed into columns, then flattened to towering anvilheads. Unlike a town-born anyplace else, this soldier maintained his vigilance. He wasted more time than her straits could afford. Jeynsa smothered her insults maligning his ancestry. She had to move, or her bladder would burst. The squall line that darkened the sky would deliver its cloud-burst too late to shield her.

Helpless, she languished, draped on her branch, while the torpid air pressed down like a lid. Her nemesis continued to sweat and slap flies. He did not sit, did not sleep, failed to shirk his post despite itching discomfort. Ready to kill out of broiling frustration, Jeynsa endured. Before her survival, the warning she carried must reach the clans in Melhalla. *Her crown prince was involved with dark sorcery.* Sighted vision had unveiled his vile rites at Etarra. Against the grim charge of collusion with necromancy, Jeynsa required a witnessed accusation, then the formal backing of a Fellowship Sorcerer.

She suffered her impasse, until the young man below her tipped back his head.

Jeynsa went cold. Past question, beneath the smeared dye, the sharp cast of those features was royal. *As if thought had conjured him, she confronted the very same prince that her duty must challenge for criminal conduct.*

'You!' she exclaimed, furious. 'What conniving dishonesty brings you here!' She discarded her bow, shoved out of her eyrie and pounced.

The man she accosted startled and yelled. He snatched for the sword in his scabbard.

Jeynsa bore in, caught his wrist, then grappled as Sidir had taught her. A wrestler's move a clan child would know hooked his ankle and tripped him. Thrashed into the brush, her bared knife at his throat, he slammed at bay against the tree trunk.

'Dharkaron avenge!' she railed through her teeth. 'You won't escape justice. I've seen your foul works. As I live, I won't rest till I see you deposed for those sacrificed girls in that crypt!'

'I'm not who you think!' gasped the dishevelled victim. When the jab of her steel said she was not convinced, he ran on in a twanging Araethurian accent. 'Cutting my throat won't resolve a thing. The murdering bastard you want will be laughing, since I'm not the Prince of Rathain!'

'Liar!' Jeynsa snarled a vicious phrase in Paravian.

'And may I couple goats on your grandparents' grave,' Fionn Areth retorted. 'Whoever they are. If you had any.'

'*Say again*?' Jeynsa snapped. 'You laid out their burned bones in Strakewood. Built their stone grave cairn yourself!'

'I did no such thing,' her prisoner insisted. 'Though thinking I did will end my complaint and send you past Fate's Wheel straight after me.'

'Ath above!' Jeynsa swore. 'I should fall for a shameless mouthful of mimicry? Do you think I'm flat witless?'

'Aye, so,' said her captive, agreeably limp. 'Probably worse, since armed men on both sides of this thicket have you sighted under drawn bows.' As she stared at him, vexed, he risked bleeding and qualified. 'We're sent to pluck one of your woods-grubbing countrymen out of the teeth of a dog-pack.'

Set aback, moved to check the device on his jerkin, Jeynsa shoved upright and crouched. 'You're Alestron's sworn man?' She blinked, overset. 'Daelion forfend! The made double?' Shaken, incredulous, she pulled her bared steel. 'Then you're the poor wretch that almost got roasted for my liege's misdeeds in Jaelot!'

'His other associates are equally rude,' Fionn Areth declared as he brushed himself off.

Jeynsa watched him rake the caught leaves from his hair and dig a trapped beetle from under his collar. The face underneath the brown dye was alike as a rendered masterpiece. Yet as he stood up, his movement lacked the Teir's'Ffalenn's hair-trigger grace. These green eyes were not deep. Only prosaic as he sized up her cropped hair and torn leathers, then her gaunt state of privation.

'You'd better sit down,' he determined at last. 'At least sheathe the knife. You look faint enough to fall over.'

'Not just!' Jeynsa huffed. 'Warn your bowmen away. All night in a tree, I've got needs that won't wait.' Pink with embarrassment, she unclipped her quiver and flung it beside her dropped bow. 'If you see any hounds, shoot them down. They're league trackers. Stand guard for our lives, that's the least you can do, since I've lost my lead to the slipshod fact that you failed to look up, or declare yourself.'

Dagger poised, she shoved off with indecorous haste and burrowed into the privacy of the brambles.

She managed to give them her lineage and name before she collapsed at the feet of the acting sergeant. His cursory check encountered no injury, beyond a few festering thorns. 'Nothing that rest and good food won't put right.' He settled Jeynsa's limp wrist and regarded his men, gathered under the tree where Fionn Areth had flushed her. 'Do I have volunteers? Good. You'll need thick skins. I don't fancy she'll stay unconscious for long. Bound to fight like a cat once she notices she's being carried.'

Fionn Areth surveyed the unkempt girl they disarmed, then slung over the shoulder of the first burly man who stepped forward. Her filthy, cropped hair, tattered soles, and starved face seemed too young for the courage that would dare a black sorcerer's morals at knife point. '*The* Teiren s'Valerient? That sniping chit is *caithdein* to Arithon, and steward for the realm of Rathain?'

'In these hills? That name becomes an endangerment. I'd say she's all that she claims to be. If not, the problem's not ours. It's our duke she'll have to answer to.'

'Melhalla's *caithdein*,' Jeynsa interposed. Slung upside down, she should have had no standing left, and nothing resembling dignity. Yet her sharp demand was delivered forthwith. 'I ask for safe escort to Atwood.'

'Not possible.' The sergeant glanced at the darkening sky, as an icy gust tossed the oak leaves. The summer squall line threatened to break and douse them in a white torrent. 'Move out!' he barked. 'Keep ahead of that storm. This is no sort of place to leave footprints.' Fresh mud would hold an impression for days; Pellain's constable would not need a tracker.

To Jeynsa's protest, the officer repeated the news that dispatched their troop through the country-side. 'You can't go to Atwood. Access is closed. Kharadmon's resetting the Paravian markers to guard. We've been forewarned that our lives could be forfeit if we try to enter the free wilds without a Sorcerer's escort.'

At the end of her strength, the Teiren s'Valerient allowed them to bear her without further argument. The field company would see her through to Alestron. Denied other choice, her sensitive news must be brought to the ear of Duke Bransian s'Brydion.

Prophet

The last time Dakar crossed the high mountain pass through the Skyshiels, he had been piss drunk in his self-absorbed effort to thwart a Fellowship directive to stand guard for Arithon s'Ffalenn. This time detained by a renegade Sorcerer's meddling, he rode himself ragged to rejoin the same prince's service. Wayside inns where he had once dragged his feet now chafed him with obstructive delays. The after-shock of the cleanse that had expunged the grey cult's grip at Etarra made fit post-horses in scant supply. A fat man plagued with inept balance astride could not hope to outpace the state couriers bearing bad news. Nor could he bribe the deep treasuries of guildsmen, or overrule the sealed writs of Alliance requisition, unleashed by the imminent war.

The upset seeded at the moon's nadir had sparked Darkling's whirlwind muster as well. Clear down to Highscarp, the road had been choked with ox-drawn supply trains and foot-troops. Fast transport by galley across Eltair Bay became priced to extortion by the same demand. Jammed inns and a crucial shortage of provender made Dakar's need for haste a trial of sapping frustration. Even fishermen's luggers had been pressed in service to move men and arms to East Halla. The Mad Prophet fumed, coughing dust on the by-ways through the hamlets, cadging rides in lumbering farm drays. Forced to stage his way by the south route to Jaelot, his scapegrace past left him haunted by irony at every bend in the road: hung-over after a staggering binge, he once had endured the same, winding drive in the bed of a masterbard's pony-cart.

Such memories wore daggers. *This* smoky tap-room, and *that* gabled inn recalled the arduous care with which Halliron sen Alduin had shaped the talent of his successor. Twenty-seven years might have passed in a season: each painful detail remained vivid. The ghost echoes of the old bard's remonstrance, then

Arithon's diligent hours of practise notes lurked in the flickering shadows of the ingle-nooks, or else wafted down the backstair of some wayside tavern's tawdry lodgings.

Often, the spellbinder flushed with fresh shame, as informed hindsight brought wounding discovery: the guise of Medlir from those bygone days had masked s'Ffalenn features, and nothing else.

The laughing wit, and the quizzical patience shown to Dakar's complaints and slack living had never been feigned. The gently barbed tolerance granted to rage and eruptions of poisonous rancour had been Arithon's true nature, released to a care-free existence.

Now, the same tap-rooms were crammed with armed men, loud with their boastful intent to tear down the turncoat clan duke who had spied for the Spinner of Darkness. As the town garrisons marched to assault the s'Brydion, other factions that thrived upon strife positioned themselves to grasp profit. The boys in the smithies stoked the forge-fires, while farmers and merchants clustered in knots, concerned for their loved ones and livelihoods.

Dakar heard the bent of such rumours, and ached. Today's trouble came too late for regret. His vindictive lapse years ago now enacted its tragic conclusion: Halliron had died, and Desh-thiere's curse gave scared men a name for their doubts and a cause to vent feuding hatreds. Maturity did not excuse the mistake. The drunken buffoon who had run from himself now faced his irresponsible legacy. The uncaring act, however small, had unleashed a round of savage consequence.

'Dogs die!' cracked a bearded troop captain. The sweaty crowd packed into the tap-room raised cheers. Here, Alestron's clan families posed no more than an abstract target.

The swaggering noise wrecked Dakar's appetite. If wisdom had sprung from mismanaged experience, the deep scar remained. Some events that shifted the course of a lifetime might never be mended. One forgave the weakness of *why* one fell short. Yet the light of remorse scarcely eased burning shame.

The events that sent Arithon Teir's'Ffalenn into Kewar could not be reversed, or rescinded.

Dakar left a coin for his unfinished meal. Though blistered until thought of the saddle held torture, he stepped out and bullied the head hostler until he obtained a fast horse. The gelding had the white, rolling eye of a rogue. Dakar mounted anyway. Striving to honour today's steadfast friendship, he gathered the reins and spurred southward. He could not mend the past. But the possibility drove him half-mad, that he might fail to reach Prince Arithon's side for the hour that guided the future.

Concern only grew as day brightened. The spellbinder choked on stirred dust from the recruits, press-ganged to fill Jaelot's troop rolls. He sensed the raw fears of the young dragged from home, and the grim apprehensions of veteran officers whose comrades had died under Shadow and sorcery in Daon

Ramon. Another dew-soaked night in the open gave him no respite in rest. Here, where the range of the Skyshiels hemmed Eltair's coast, the quartz veins that laced the mountains amplified the stream of the lane flux. Cold sober, wrung sleepless by his sensitized talent, Dakar tracked the volatile elements, awakened and called to stand sentinel: he felt the Fellowship working to close Atwood. No prior demand in Athera's Third Age had ever enacted such dire expediency.

The spellbinder stole his next post-horse and galloped. Aching, bone deep, he could not outrun the tuned chord of the centaur markers, or escape cringing from the ubiquitous clangour of hammers forging steel for bloody destruction. The eastshore's industry girded for siege, while the cream of its men loaded stockpiled supplies, and burdened galleys embarked from every available harbour.

The charged atmosphere heightened Dakar's talent for prescience. Threatened, while waking, with chaotic, seer's dreams, he dared not linger in public. Private rooms were commandeered by troop officers, with the tap-rooms, haylofts, and craft sheds jammed full, rented to billet fresh conscripts. The rainy night he bribed a bed in a garret, he aroused in tears, his head spinning. Stung yet by the reek of phantom smoke, he regarded the rafters above, overlaid by the image of burning fields as far west as the Pellain trade-road.

Shivering at the window, while the gibbous moon swam through the tissue of errant vision, the Mad Prophet recalled the familiar blond head he had Sighted among the duke's reivers: Talvish now wore Alestron's bull blazon. In his company rode Fionn Areth, and worse, *the Teiren s'Valerient, Jeynsa.*

'Ath wept, this can't happen!' Dakar whispered, sick. He groped into yesterday's discarded clothes, barged into the stable, and extorted the grooms. Then he risked his neck in the mud and the dark, pressing his commandeered mount off the road, deep into the Tiriac foothills.

When the post-horse exhausted its wind, he reined up in a hidden copse. Sunrise and seclusion would give him the chance to scry through the lane tide.

A seer's trance demanded inflexible calm, if his unruly talent could be self-directed. Dakar selected a flat rock and settled. Wrapped in the resinous fragrance of pine, he wrestled his nagging anxiety. Basic discipline failed. Entangled in fear, he felt crushed by uncertainty. The pre-dawn gloom hung chill as the grave. Too often, the etched silence of spontaneous prescience ruffled his disrupted consciousness.

Dakar resisted that drowning current. His heart raced, and his shallow breaths whistled. Thin air and altitude had never agreed with him. He had no sorcerer's cast-iron nerve, to face death and heart-break, unflinching.

Yet on this hour, dread outfaced the most shrinking cowardice. He held fast. And the quiet sank deeper, first losing its shrill, surface ripple of worry. Next the undertow drag of his doubt smoothed away. Detached, Dakar waited. When the shuddering tingle spurred through his flesh, quickened by the rising lane tide, he slid into the flow and framed his willed intent.

Sighted vision responded. He saw *into* now, untainted by *maybe*, and the forest surrounding his physical senses dropped out of awareness . . .

. . . he was a breathless messenger, debarking from a fast galley at Varens and bearing the urgent tidings of deaths inflicted by Shadow at the Alliance stronghold of Etarra . . . and he was the choleric Mayor of Jaelot, exhorting his captains to redeem the defeat that disgraced the lost company slaughtered in winter upon Daon Ramon Barrens . . . and he was the weeping wife of Pellain's magistrate, decrying the wanton destruction of livestock, and the ash of the summer harvest . . . and he was a pall of etheric mist, raised by a Sorcerer's summons to bind the free wilds of Atwood into protection . . . and he was the goatherd, Fionn Areth, arguing with the Teiren's'Valerient over the ethics of the Fellowship of Seven . . .

That thread, Dakar snagged. Aligned with the charged flux, he let the bright burn of emotion flow through him . . . *as though he shared the ache of a harried night's ride, keeping pace with Talvish's veterans, he observed the gauntlet Fionn Areth hurled down over a breakfast of hard-tack with young Jeynsa . . .*

'I don't see!' snapped the goatherd, his yokel's drawl stubborn. 'Why should the Sorcerers defend hill-sides and trees but not set the same stringent wards to safeguard the clan lives at risk in Alestron?'

'The Fellowship can't.' Jeynsa's frown was her father's, stuck like nails through old oak. 'The duke's domain is not the high seat of Melhalla's crown capital. His citadel isn't sited inside the free wilds. You don't know the old law?' She swiped back her cropped hair, looking sorrowfully drawn as she stabbed home her point, out of patience. 'Such towns where men dwell are set outside of the Sorcerers' marked jurisdiction.'

Shown the grass-lander's blank incomprehension, she rolled her eyes and rapped out a clipped lesson. 'Fellowship power does not rule mankind. Free will is an inalienable right under the Major Balance. Yet this world of Athera was not given as ours. The Sorcerers stand surety for our human conduct. They will not intervene, unless the greater weal of the compact that serves Paravian survival becomes threatened. Before the uprising, charter law and royal justice kept the balance. Town coexistence was supported by those born and tested to bear the burdens evolved through old lineage. The High King acted as intermediary. With Melhalla left crownless, no force can gainsay. Since Bransian rejected his *caithdein*'s appeal to abandon the citadel and claim clan right to sanctuary in the forest, no recourse remains unless he breaks his titled covenant.'

'She means,' broke in Talvish, arrived to roust laggards, 'that Alestron has chosen to stand or fall alone on the strength of its merits.'

The Araethurian took brazen issue regardless, never able to withhold an obstreperous opinion. 'Then why has your prince forsaken his allies?' Outraged, he challenged the fixed resignation that stared him down on two fronts. 'Why, when his Grace's elemental Shadow might spare thousands of lives and save hapless families from certain destruction?'

Jeynsa bristled to frame her reply . . .

Contact snapped. Dakar lost the unreeling thread of true vision as the lane's crest subsided with daybreak. Tumbling unsupported amid the flux, he stretched to recapture the dialogue still exchanged in the Tiriac foothills. The ephemeral moment slipped beyond reach. Desperation, concern, and his forced need *to know* unravelled his grip. Set boundaries tore, fast followed by the chaotic surge that kindled his unbridled prescience . . . *and vision spiralled him forward in time, to an afternoon meeting two fateful days hence. Late sun would be streaming in blades through the arrow slits in the keep where Duke Bransian conducted closed councils . . .*

A blank interval later, the Mad Prophet aroused to a deafening chorus of bird-song. Daybreak had fled. The new morning was grey. His overhead view through the pines showed a lowering sky that threatened cold rain. Dakar sat up, befuddled. The storm's rising gusts harried his clothes and buffeted his spinning senses. He rested his aching head in his hands. His breaths came too fast. The galloping pound of his heart pained his chest, and sweat trickled under his collar. He scrubbed a stray beetle out of his beard; brushed scattered leaves from his shirt front.

Through disorientation, he groped to recall why he perched on a rock in the woods.

'Fiends plague,' he grumbled. The horse he had ridden had broken its bridle and wandered away while he maundered. Its thrashing excursion had carried it down-slope, where it browsed, munching leaves.

Dakar started to curse, then coughed, ripped double by nausea. The sickness recalled his troubled night; then the shattering of his tranced vision of Jeynsa, leading into an uncontrolled fit of prescience. After-shock always destroyed his digestion. Dakar gouged at his temples. *What had he foreseen?* He retained no memory, not the least clue. His chill lashed up goose bumps. Such bouts of amnesia foreran events of dire consequence. *When the auguries escaped him, they always came true.*

Black dread harrowed him to his feet. A clutched pine branch saved his wracked balance.

Cruel fragment, what knowledge he had bought no comfort: Jeynsa s'Valerient should be *nowhere* near the hostilities in East Halla. The short-handed Fellowship could not intervene. Since the risk of informing the Teir's'Ffalenn was tantamount to insanity, the Mad Prophet rallied his wits. He clawed his snapped reins from the tree trunk, determined. He had no choice now but to waylay a fishing boat, brave a rough crossing, then plead for a stay to send Jeynsa home through the auspices of Melhalla's *caithdein*.

Dakar clenched his jaw. Stumbling with sickness, he set after his horse. At least his wild talent had claimed him where no eavesdroppers could hear him raving. Yet though he believed that the rogue prophecy had been lost, on two deadly counts, he proved wrong.

Observations

Far south, in the Koriani enclave at Forthmark, the seeress attending the lane watch at dawn importunes the sisterhouse peeress: *'I ask leave to present a fresh record in crystal directly to Selidie Prime. We have captured the imprint of a true prophecy, made by the spellbinder, Dakar. He fumbled his boundaries in his distress, and the flux running through the quartz vein in the Skyshiels disclosed our view of the event . . .'*

In a seamless, domed chamber of rock, Davien the Betrayer regards a black pool welling up from a virgin spring; the water sheets over a carved ring of ciphers, raising rainbow mist, through which a drop falls, unveiling the prophesied scene to unfold two days hence in Duke Bransian's citadel . . .

Raced south by galley from Highscarp, the first-hand account of the sorcerous strike at Etarra reaches the port town of Varens; and mounted state couriers depart at speed: one to Lysaer s'Ilessid, commanding from Tirans, while two other riders pound on through the night to Perdith, bearing sealed orders for dispatch by sea to raise Kalesh and Adruin to arms . . .

III. Obligations

rime Selidie granted the unscheduled audience to review the captured lane imprint just picked up from the Fellowship Spellbinder. More, she called in her seniormost staff: opportunity walked in Dakar's slipshod vigilance, given his tight association with the crown prince targeted as her sisterhood's quarry.

'We have gleaned forewarning of a momentous event that will shift the course of the Alliance campaign at Alestron,' the duty watch seeress pronounced. If her ambitious claim at first raised disbelief, the purloined content of Dakar's late vision unfolded with clear vindication as she unveiled her imprinted quartz. There, etched in light through a west-facing arrow-slit, the scene foretold to occur would take place inside *what should have been* a warded keep within Alestron's citadel . . .

There, the duke glowered across an oak table left grooved by the ropes that strapped spies for interrogation. Prophetic sight showed the scarred boards spread across with a chart, salt-stained from last use on a galley. The corners were weighted with Parrien's whetstone, a tankard with dents left by Sevrand, and two impaled stilettos, pinched from Mearn. The youngest brother s'Brydion never relinquished such prizes, except under bitter duress. Mearn presently stood, decked out as the dandy, a negligent shoulder braced to the stonewall. His claret doublet agleam with seed pearls, he held the drawn blade from his shirtsleeve in hand, paring his nails like a dilettante.

That warning, no one who knew him misjudged: Mearn's affections infallibly masked the murderous bent of his rages.

The duke's wife, Liesse, was advised to tread softly. Her mere female presence an invasion of male authority, she had positioned her raw-boned frame in between her quarrelsome spouse and his snake-tempered younger brother.

'You want the truth?' Mearn contended. 'We're pickled.'

Bransian sweated in mail shirt and helm. Brows knitted, he leaned upon planted fists, spitting nails over the tactical map, which already reflected the blood-letting frenzy touched off by the grey cult's demise at Etarra. The inked shore-line of the East Halla peninsula lay inundated by the enemy. Black blocks representing the massed Alliance force threw long shadows across the wood plugs used as counters to mark the defenders: two veteran strike companies in the field under Vhandon, and the garrison troops entrenched by Keldmar's directive to safeguard Alestron's unharvested crops. Longer shadows striped the Cildein's scrolled waves, cast by the carved hulls representing Parrien's fleet of armed galleys. While they matched the sea-going might of Kalesh and Adruin, their numbers were too sparse to counter the warships inbound from Durn and Ishlir.

The advent of autumn could only bring worse. Elssine and Telzen downcoast flew the Sunwheel. Their standing companies would flood in, hard followed by spearmen and horse from Shaddorn. Then that menace soon to be augmented by Sulfin Evend's massed muster, sweeping the towns on the south-coast under the false avatar's banner.

Tottering piles of blocks sketched the outcome: the duke's men would be hard-pressed to hold their field entrenchments long enough to secure the harvest.

While Liesse laced tight fingers, too canny to comment, Mearn flipped a nail paring out of the arrow-loop, and glared, slit-eyed, at his brother. 'Stewed,' he insisted, 'and for stiff-necked pride. On the hour you jettisoned Arithon's goodwill, we might have attempted to reason with him.'

'*Reason*? With a bastard stripling whelped on foreign ground, witch-bred in descent from no less than Dari s'Ahelas?' The duke bristled, his wiry beard shot with grey, except for the side singed to frizz during yesterday's testing of fire shot. 'Fiends plague! You forget. Parrien fought the wretch to a bleeding standstill, and *still* had to break his damned leg.' Bransian swiped at the offensive document that had launched his tactical argument: a ribboned edict, dispatched from Tirans, and stamped with the Sunwheel. The flourished signature was no delegate secretary's, but Lysaer s'Ilessid's own hand.

The parchment fluttered towards the stone floor, its language demanding Alestron's surrender, upon charges of s'Brydion conspiracy in concert with powers of Darkness. The elaborate seal cracked off as it struck, crushed to powder by Bransian's boot-heel.

His baleful glance accosted his duchess, composed in her rose linen and shimmering cincture of pearls. Her hopeful expression pushed him to snipe first. 'Don't bother advising a plea for apology! We don't know where among Dharkaron's damned the Master of Shadow might be!'

'His Grace doesn't shift his fixed principles, anyway,' Mearn reminded. 'Thinks all his strategies through in advance. Like a plague-bearing weasel bashing a hornets' nest, you don't tend to notice his damages while you're bent double, nursing the stings. I should know. I spent enough time as his captive at Vastmark to learn how he works from his captains.'

Liesse awarded such carping short shrift. 'You could be wrong, this time. When Arithon delivered his ultimatum, he had no idea he would become summoned to rout a cult cabal out of Etarra. Given he has set that spark on dry tinder, don't you think civil words might make him reconsider?'

'Send my wits ahead of my carcass to Sithaer!' Bransian swore, while Mearn straightened.

'Besides the bald fact we've no clue where to look?' The duke's younger brother sheathed his vicious, small knife. 'As soon try conversing with Daelion himself, to wheedle your way past due reckoning. His Grace would rightfully tell us straight out to suck eggs in our well-soiled nest.'

Dame Dawr's cross-grained assessment agreed, that s'Brydion had spurned their last chance. Liesse pressed a taut hand to her lips. Regrets salvaged nothing. If the duke had abandoned the citadel as Arithon had asked, today's mustering cry to retaliate would have left Lysaer's cursed rage no fixed target. Now, the bone-crushing silence extended. The black blocks and red counters opposed on the map lent vicious hindsight to the Prince of Rathain's urgent argument.

'Dharkaron's immortal bollocks,' cracked Bransian, pinned under the pleading calm of his wife. 'I'm no weathercock ditherer, to spin about at each puff from the arse of town-bred politicians! No, don't start again!' He had made his grim point: the Fellowship's come-lately offer of sanctuary would have laid Alestron's civilian population open to attack on forced march to old Tirans, if not see another third slowly starved from inadequate stores through the winter. Aware of the tears Liesse held in check by the mulish set to her chin, Bransian hammered a fist, sending counters and tin ink-wells flying. 'We fight, and survive without grubbing for a miserable existence in the free wilds! You'll not see me kiss this false avatar's boots. Nor should I recant and risk getting burned for the skins of a handful of faint-hearted relatives!'

'I'm loath to bring comfort with difficult facts,' a cooler voice interjected. 'But the roads at this point are no longer an option, either for children or caval-cades.'

While Liesse startled, and Mearn grinned like a fox, more words spiralled up from the stairwell outside. 'Don't forget that Lysaer once burned his own troops in a curse-driven fit in Daon Ramon. Such madness as that can't be trusted by anyone.' Paused, breathless, at the last landing, the inbound newcomer added, 'Recant or not, none of ours would gain quarter. The damned fanatics can't rest till this citadel has been sacked, with every clan blood-line eradicated.'

Footsteps presently crested the stair-head, and Talvish strode in, road-dusty and redolent of hot horseflesh, cinders, and goose grease. 'You're one counter short,' he admonished the duke. 'We've more smoke-hazed enemies scuttling our way from Pellain.'

'Show me!' snapped Bransian, an arm clamped to secure his mail shirt as he bent and pawed under his chair for his scattered markers.

The lean swordsman advanced to the table. He snapped a courtesy nod to the duchess, then scrounged two spare broadheads from his gear and used them to replace Mearn's knives as corner pins holding the map. 'More than enemy troops happened by the west road,' he provoked, quick enough to avoid the duke's youngest brother's rabid snatch to recoup his weaponry.

Mearn's face lit. 'Trouble you can't trust with Vhandon's division?'

Talvish tipped his fair head towards the door, where other footsteps and more conversation flurried echoes up from below. 'Judge for yourself.'

At least one of the voices was recognized. Duke Bransian shoved back upright, distempered, and snatched the pinched hairs of his beard from the links as his chainmail resettled. 'If Arithon's dimwit double tried running away, I'm astonished that you didn't help him.'

Talvish stood dead-pan, with Mearn at his side perked to a weasel's fixed interest. As the duke dumped the counters and began to restate the array of the Alliance deployment, Liesse unwound her laced fingers, and said, 'That's a maid's voice, with Fionn. Whose daughter?'

'Earl Jieret's and Feithan's,' Talvish murmured, then shook his head, crushing out revived hope that the Teiren s'Valerient might bear an official reconciliation from the Prince of Rathain. 'Jeynsa was bound for East Halla, unaware that the borders were closed into Atwood.'

Then trouble itself strode through the door, the girl's rangy form clad in holed boots and forest leathers that broadcast her need for a bath. Too thin, she moved with instinctive grace, the ruthlessly cropped hair fronding her face as rich brown as her scattered freckles. Eyes the sparkling, pale brilliance of aventurine dismissed every person who was not the duke. To Bransian, bow and bone-handled knives rattling, she bent her proud head and offered the crossed wrists at her breast by which clanborn acknowledged titled rank.

'Jeynsa, Teiren's'Valerient, Lord,' she opened with point-blank formality.

While Mearn watched, avid, and Talvish stayed neutral, Liesse tucked her impulse to frown behind the bland stare she used on suspicious ambassadors.

Bransian slapped down a block for the vengeance-bent company riding the Pellain road, then flicked the red plug for Vhandon's reserves to harry their bristling advance. His inimical stare raked the tall girl, without deigning acknowledgement of Fionn Areth's come-lately arrival, behind her. 'You look like a stick dragged in by a dog, and for what? By Dharkaron's Spear, you have some strong nerve! What kind of fool would dare soil my presence, whose ungrateful liege washed his finicky hands of our years of *unbroken* service and loyalty!' While Jeynsa faltered, outfaced, Bransian surged forward in anger. 'Where is his Grace, anyway?' accosted the duke. 'I have some choice words to blister his ears concerning the enemies his doings have pitched like hazed rams against our defences.'

Liesse spoke, fast, her warning meant to deflect the girl's brazen approach. 'Child, be at peace. My husband has already heard that Prince Arithon was dispatched by the Fellowship to destroy a cabal of necromancy. Bluster though he will, Bransian knows a Sorcerer's summons could not be refused.'

Jeynsa flushed, shamed for no obvious reason. 'So Talvish told me,' she admitted. Threatened by Bransian's livid affront, almost anyone would have cowered. This sprig squared her shoulders with mulish bravado. 'I have seen your walls, your gates, and your fortress, and heard the ground-swell of complaint in your streets,' she addressed the duke. 'I make no excuse for my liege's defection from sharing Alestron's defence.' Jeynsa lifted her chin. Gaunt from the trail, irresolute in herself, the core of her stayed determined. 'As Rathain's chosen steward, I say his Grace was wrong to hand you his callous desertion.'

'Toss us a tit-bit we don't already know,' Mearn snapped, disgusted. 'Can you tell us where your skulking prince went when he left his charged task at Etarra?'

Jeynsa tossed her head, no. Grubby hands to scraped leathers, she looked as she was: a half-starved child called onto the carpet by strangers for a thought-less escapade. Except the steel in her glanced as the weapon's trued edge, whetted and deadly past compromise. 'I don't care where his Grace has hidden himself. Your cause was ill served. I won't sanction his choice, which leaves innocent families at risk before Lysaer's raised armies.'

Bransian's iron gaze narrowed. '*Caithdein* of Rathain, are you officially here to depose a Fellowship-sanctioned crown prince?'

'No. Better yet.' Jeynsa brushed off Liesse's startled alarm and knelt with bent head to the duke. 'Alestron, for need, has only to ask. By your leave, *I can bring him.*'

'What foolery is this?' exclaimed Talvish, astonished.

Mearn gave the girl his most fixated stare. 'Do say how you plan to bid that wild spirit! Even the Fellowship can't rein Arithon in. Or I daresay events would have taken a different, *safe* route through his recent affray at Etarra.'

Bransian's roar overruled his wife's chiding. 'Say *again*, you insolent chit!' His ice-grey eyes raked with dismissive contempt. 'Shadow behind Rathain's throne, you may be, girl, but no possible loop-hole in charter law appoints you the right to command your crown prince's presence. No sovereign charge can force his defence inside the realm of Melhalla!'

Flushed purple, now dangerous, the duke advanced, while Liesse's protesting grasp locked his wrist, and Talvish tensed, a hand closed on his sword for a suicidal prevention.

Yet the girl spoke first.

'No sovereign charge,' Jeynsa agreed, uncowed before brittle tension. 'I hold the sworn bond of Rathain's prince. Last month, in Halwythwood, he sealed a mage's blood pledge that binds him to my protection.' Insolent, aware she stopped everyone's breath, Jeynsa hooked the nearest empty chair. She sat down, not caring that Liesse trembled, or that Mearn's whiplash loquacity was finally shocked still. Behind her stiff back, even Talvish's aghast face had drained white.

Jeynsa shrugged, while the duke's menace loomed over her. 'I need do nothing at all but stay here. His Grace will hear word. When the siege closes, his sworn debt will come due. Prince Arithon must come for me if I'm endangered.'

The point was inarguable: a mage-trained master constrained by life-oath would have no other choice.

Liesse found her voice. 'My lord, you won't! We can't stoop to extortion, far less on a sanctioned crown heir!'

'That's risky business!' cracked Mearn. 'We'd call down the wrath of a Fellowship Sorcerer for sure!'

Jeynsa's eyes stayed upturned on the duke. 'There will be no opening,' she insisted, too crisp. 'Sethvir is gravely ill. Paravia is not endangered. The prime tenet of the Major Balance itself will allow for no grace of appeal.'

Mearn's fast wit flanked her. 'Alestron's governed by town charter, that's true enough.'

Outside the free wilds, unless the compact was threatened, the Fellowship would not effect a direct intervention. By written code, no Sorcerer dictated the fates of a people inside of established town boundaries. Excited, Bransian snatched a chair, spun it backwards, and straddled the seat. An unholy glee transformed his distress as he grappled the wicked obstruction. 'You were chosen as heir. Jeynsa s'Valerient, are you here to tell us you never stood for your investiture as Rathain's *caithdein*?'

The girl raised her chin. 'My sire's murder gave reason enough to stand back. For Arithon's sake, my father died under torture.' Trembling at the edge of exhausted hysteria, she added, 'Should you cavil at honour? Clan tradition would mediate the loss to my family. Would you not say the prince owes a life debt?'

'Dharkaron's Black Chariot and Spear!' Mearn swore.

'That's scarcely fair play,' Liesse interjected. 'If a just call for a clan injury exists, your lady mother should be the one to sue for redress!'

'It's survival!' Duke Bransian contradicted. 'And a compensation that's due to us, after Mearn's faithful years of spying on s'Ilessid policy.' Arisen again, he gestured to a dissonant clash of steel weaponry. 'Let's not omit our provision for supply and shelter. Or our staged withdrawal, that reversed Arithon's straits back in Vastmark.'

While Fionn Areth watched, wide-eyed, and Talvish clamped teeth to keep his own counsel, Liesse blotted damp palms. 'Such questionable policy will go hard with Dame Dawr. Ath wept, who will dare broach this news to her?'

The duke's beard split into a sharkish smile. 'What possible point could the old besom raise?'

A nitpicking magistrate must back the sweet gist: no investiture meant that a steward's oath did not *yet* tie Jeynsa's feal service in direct line to the Fellowship's compact. Therefore, her case devolved to royal justice, through the dictates of charter law.

'A damnable irony,' Mearn crowed, despite himself moved to triumphant amazement.

'Victory!' roared Bransian, rubbing his hands. 'By Sithaer's black pit, our weaselly masterbard's leashed. Legally snagged by his short hairs, in truth, and may Daelion Fatemaster spit on the hindmost! We will win the day, and see Lysaer's cause forced to a cringing standstill.'

The scried image that unreeled in the quartz sphere flicked out, leaving a breathless stillness. Afternoon at the Forthmark hospice, the southern heat was oppressive, closed behind the domed chamber's leaded windows. Rippled patterns cast by the lozenge glass washed across the clandestine gathering. The four robed enchantresses might have been trapped in amber, for their stunned lack of movement and noise.

The order's wizened senior healer laced her narrow fingers at length. 'You named this an augury?'

Few others might question the Koriani Prime, just twenty years of natural age, and scarcely seasoned since her accession. The young woman stared back in her formal state dress, a willowy coquette who seemed displaced in her high seat of office. Yet a steely authority wrapped her slim form. Flame from the bronze brazier at her feet spat glints through her traditional tiara of amethyst and diamond.

'Our preparations for compassionate relief are in force,' the sisterhouse peeress prompted gently. That on-going activity jammed the courtyard outside, with snappish drivers handling the mule-teams cut through by the voices of boy wards packing the wagons with supplies. For days, the sisters in grey robes of charitable service had assembled chests of crystals, philtres, and remedies, set coughing under the sulphurous smoke, as the first-rank initiates wrought the copper talismans to repulse *iyats* and settle the unquiet dead, soon to be sundered by violence.

'Why rush our departure,' the peeress ran on, 'or squander more of our resource over clan politics? The siege is inevitable. This forecast could extend the damage, but may not come to pass as we've seen it.'

'This pact with Duke Bransian is fated to happen,' Prime Selidie contradicted. Fair as frost on ripe wheat, she tipped an imperative nod to the seeress, who dutifully veiled the blanked quartz sphere that fire-scarred hands were too crippled to tend. 'Past question, Jeynsa's revenge will prevail. The duke is desperate. The dowager duchess may cringe over principle. But preservation of the s'Brydion lineage must force her support in the end. We're forewarned and poised to act on this opening.'

The Teir's'Ffalenn would stand in defence against Lysaer, and the curse of the Mistwraith would unleash a debacle.

'Prescience is not proof,' the old healer insisted. 'You would move our order to prying acts for a feckless spellbinder's maundering?'

'This time, we have a true prophecy.' The matriarch's smile was peaches and cream. 'Dakar awakened from his errant trance, and could not remember his vision.'

There, even Forthmark's sceptical seniors lost their last footing for argument. The spellbinder's gift was a wild talent. The intuitive leaps that outpaced his consciousness always held dazzling accuracy. Even the Fellowship Sorcerers had never fathomed the reason. Despite years of scrutiny at Althain Tower, Dakar's precocious Sight remained one of the world's greater mysteries, the source he tapped far beyond the veil, past the limit of cognizant reckoning.

'Jeynsa's extortion will leave us free rein.' Prime Selidie savoured the moment, the ruined, claw fingers masked under silk a gall she would never forgive. At long last she was granted the wedge to sunder clan hierarchy and thwart the Fellowship's compact. 'Make my palanquin ready. I intend to lead the order's relief for the war in East Halla myself.'

Forthmark's peeress gasped, swept to epiphany as the telling facts behind Selidie's eagerness finally slid into place. 'S'Brydion never sundered the terms of the charter!'

'I should live for the day!' Selidie loosed a satisfied laugh. 'This time, my sisters, the Fellowship Sorcerers have fully and finally tied their own hands.'

Asandir's lawful sanction had affirmed Rathain's prince. The royal oath of succession, and the formal, initiate ceremony at Etarra had sealed the authority of crown rule. Arithon Teir's'Ffalenn, *and no one else*, possessed the right to prosecute Jeynsa's betrayal.

Soon after Jeynsa s'Valerient made her fateful pact with Alestron, the Master of Shadow left the black dunes of Sanpashir behind. He journeyed alone, his mood knife-edged from the delicate persuasion needed to detach his escort of tribal dartmen. Fourteen days on foot through inhospitable terrain had done little to restore his hale strength. Still thin, worn yet in spirit, he bought their protective release by accepting a quiver of darts and a blow-tube. The knife at his belt was for hunting, not ambush. For cover, he preferred to weave shadow.

Few ventured the brush to the east of the waste. Where tribal tradition bordered upon the proscribed territory kept under clan vigilance, the road-bound silk caravans went heavily armed. Town dispatches were carried by pigeon.

Arithon crossed into those wilds, unseen. The dusky weave of his borrowed robe melted into the scrub. He carried his lyranthe slung from a strap and paced his progress with patience. At twilight, he buried the tribe's gifted weapons, and more carefully disposed of the poison phial, transmuting the toxin through magecraft. Then he crouched in a thorn brake, seized his moment, and slipped unnoticed across the baked ruts of the trade-road that carved inland towards the walled settlement at Atchaz.

By nightfall, the evergreen fringes of Selkwood closed over him. The milder breeze lost its flint, reclothed in the pungency of pine resin. Arithon lit no torch. Light-footed by nature, he moved without sound over the dense mat of needles. Such care bought no safety. The most furtive intrusion would draw the rapacious notice of Alland's patrolling clan scouts.

Since Arithon was tired, and efficiency mattered, he leaned on a tree by a game trail and settled to wait.

He was seen by starlight in under an hour, then challenged at weapon's point by three strapping men and a woman bristling with knives. To judge by the game bag bulging with pigeons, the party was inbound from a raid to intercept Alliance dispatches.

Arithon showed empty hands and gave them his name.

The armed scouts stood down. Unlike his previous visits to Shand, his slight stature received their combative respect.

'Not Kyrialt,' they admitted, when he asked whose gossip had made free with his reputation. 'It's the vixen wife with the runaway tongue. If you're wanting to flay her for that, we'll take wagers.'

Arithon laughed. 'With odds on the woman, dare I suggest?'

A flash of teeth in the surrounding dark, as the rambunctious speaker grinned back. 'What, trust a redhead for mild behaviour?'

The ringleader bearing the day's feathered trophies added his rueful shrug. 'The she-fox has scarcely been married two months. No sign yet, the husband can handle her.'

Night-singing crickets filled the slight pause. Still being measured, and fighting the stress of foot travel that spent his reserves, the Master of Shadow forestalled further by-play. 'I bring urgent news for your High Earl. A guide to his lodging at speed would be welcomed.'

He was not to be humoured. Too many pairs of sharp eyes assessed him. A soft swish of leather bespoke a hand signal exchanged out of sight. Then the ranking scout said, 'The outpost is four days' brisk journey from here. We will rest in the open and send on a runner. Can I hazard a guess that you're famished?'

Lent such grace, Rathain's prince gave his grateful assent. He managed the league's hike they could not spare, for safety, to a ravine deep enough to risk fire. While the scouts shed their gear, Arithon sat. He fell asleep, tucked up in the folds of his tribal robe, before the coals roasted the day's by-catch of messenger birds.

Much later, he wakened. The rocky surrounds, curtained over with ivy, glinted dull orange by flame-light. His escort of four now had additional company. A milling commotion of horses mingled with the muted talk of the arrivals. They already knew they were hosting a prince: from the awkward instant he opened his eyes, they were on him like hawks, falling over themselves to share their savoury stew and hard biscuit.

'Luhaine advised us you might not be hale,' somebody mentioned, then hastened, 'We have been told, your Grace. The cost of your victory came hard, at Etarra.'

Arithon recoiled from hands that would help him erect. Swore under his breath and tossed off the blanket a presumptuous nurse-maid left tucked around his thin shoulders. Embarrassed by the attention fixed on him, to see how he meant to respond, he bent his head and accepted the hot food with a nod, since his voice was not going to be trustworthy. Bad enough, that the lady who offered the bowl could not miss the humiliation. His fingers were chilled to the bone, and not steady, despite the sultry air of high summer.

He managed to spoon down the broth without shaking. The meat was fresh venison, not tough shreds of pigeon, which bespoke a skilled hunter's foraging. Only a churl would not finish the meal. When the bowl was scraped clean, the raw streak of dawn glimmered through the trees above the ravine. Eager hands had his lyranthe strapped to a saddle ring. Another scout steadied the horse. Someone else, deferent, hovered nearby should the prince need assistance to mount.

Arithon stood. He shook out his robe, swung astride without help, took the reins with a nod to the handler. He delivered his thanks with a masterbard's tongue. Then he salvaged his chafed dignity by clapping his heels to the gelding and setting a brutal pace.

The forest clans that served Alland's free wilds were practised at seamless efficiency. They kept swift horses, sited throughout the forest for riding fast relays. Noon saw them remounted for the third time, while zealous youngsters stripped the gear from their spent string, now blowing and streaming white lather.

Each rider was handed a pouch of jerked meat and dried fruit. They ate astride and shared a flask of Sanshevas rum, driving on at speed through the sun-slashed pines, with the chatter of sparrows stilled in the midday heat. At the fourth change of horses, Arithon lost his balance on dismount. Only the fist in his mare's steaming mane kept him on his unsteady feet.

'Your Grace,' a deferent voice ventured, behind. Someone else's hand gripped his robe and braced his awkward weight upright.

'Do you make the same allowance for toddlers?' Arithon gasped through clenched teeth.

The scout laughed. 'Would you rather sit down arse first in fresh horse-piss? I thought not,' he added, as the prince's knees gave.

Past rejoinder, the Teir's'Ffalenn slid into strong arms, dropped as though felled by a potion.

They installed him under the shade of a tent and eased fevered flesh with a compress. An elder whose lineage was practised with herbals was summoned away from the watch-post. She arrived with her remedies, measured his pulse, and, with talented hands, scanned his aura. His collapse was declared the effect of exhaustion, foolishly pushed past the edge. 'Whoever attended this man in Sanpashir ought to have chained him in bed.'

'Tried, no doubt,' said the captain of horse, his head poked in through the tent-flap. 'Simpler to rein in Dharkaron's Black Chariot. If we paused for rest, that devilsome royal threw away sense and outstripped us.'

The kind, white-haired woman jerked shut the strings on her satchel. 'Next time, use a net. Bring him down. Such strain as he's seen lays him open to risk. Keep on, we'll be treating an illness.'

'I do know my limits,' the victim protested, flat prostrate. Eyes shut, he remained wrung ghastly white. 'We have come halfway. Your scout raiders won't sleep. Or aren't they bearing a hot packet of tidings purloined from an Atchaz guild's dispatches? Among the batch news, your mettlesome High Earl will hear of my presence by sundown. Expect his quick response. Our history's too rife with contention.'

The healer snorted and made her way out, while the scout at the entry said nothing. His suggestive pause stretched, the hushed calm before thunder-storm.

Then the invalid raised his black eyebrows. 'You're deaf to the gossip? His lordship's irked with my matrilineal heritage. I dislike the concept of dynastic reign. But the bone in the craw gets picked all the same. My hackles rise with *caithdeinen* who try to impose their crown sovereignty over my choices.'

Through springing sweat, Arithon's lips flexed. *Almost*, that smile of combative malice matched the warning the scout had been primed to expect.

'For my part,' finished the Prince of Rathain, 'I'll need the recovery to master your High Earl's fractious audience by morning.'

'Maybe Lord Erlien will eat you alive?' The watch scout eased back the tent-flap, and chuckled. 'Ath above, let's see who stirs the pot first. I think we should bet. Odds on, you offer more sport than the vice of the town-born, who bait a chained bear with riled dogs in a pit.'

In fact, Arithon was on his feet sooner, arisen in the late afternoon with none of his keepers the wiser. His time in the desert had left him unkempt. Unnerved as he was by the fuss of the scouts, he enforced his preference as initiate master. A moment's working masked him well enough to leave the stifling tent and slip through the wood to a stream-bank. There, he indulged in the solitary ease beyond his reach in the waste of Sanpashir.

The Prince of Rathain slipped off his soiled robe, washed his clothes, and himself, in a trout pool. The languid sun striped his damp skin as he basked.

Firm earth and clean daylight cleared his rifted aura, and burned away the residual imprint of terror. Since wet cloth eased the heat, he donned his sopped robe, then settled beneath an ancient willow, whose thick, gnarled roots laced the river-side. Immersed in healing peace, he let the slow swirl of the current and the breeze through leafed fronds work their effortless tonic upon him.

Whether Arithon intended to fall back to sleep, the lesser warding to hide his presence had not been fashioned to last. Since his secluded hollow was sheltered from the campsite, he did not hear the stir as more horses arrived, hard-ridden as the relay mounts now loosed to graze in concealment. His being stayed wrapped in the calm of the willow; lulled by the eddy of free-flowing water. Vulnerable, he lay oblivious when the woman rounded the tree bole and happened upon him.

Her inquisitive step paused. Sultry eyes widened, surveying her find. 'Fatemaster's blessed weaving of chance!'

Poised as a vixen, she parted the greenery and dared a stalker's step closer.

To her delight, and his provocation, those exquisite, fine limbs and musician's fingers remained sprawled on the moss in abandon. Arithon's repose stayed unbroken, though she did the unthinkable: invaded his haven and stood over him. The casual drape of the damp, tribal robe hid nothing from her avid stare. Not the bronzed skin of desert exposure, or the welted scars he always kept hidden by natural reticence. His seal-black hair had dried, ungroomed. Tangled strands nested his unshaven cheek, softening his angular profile.

'Where is your vaunted dignity, prince?' Her vibrant smile exposed even teeth. Bold as a weasel, she flicked back fiery hair, crouched at his side, and dared to extend a pared nail to trace the old burn, seared down his right forearm from elbow to wrist by the strike of his half-brother's light-bolt.

Her touch never closed. Aroused and aware, no more dulled by exhaustion, Arithon Teir's'Ffalenn opened his eyes. 'Glendien, for shame! The same tricks, again?' With malicious speed, he recoiled, caught the robe closed before she could snatch, then folded his knees and sat up.

She had tiger's eyes, hot for teasing mischief, or else the taste of fresh blood.

Telling which could be murderously difficult. Arithon stifled his first impulse to wound. No grace for surprise, or the awkward timing: he would be a match for her challenge; or not. If their last, memorable encounter had left him the advantage, too apparently his wit still intrigued enough to provoke her.

'Should a wedding have tamed me?' Glendien licked her teeth, her linen blouse halfway unlaced in the heat, and the sweet skin beneath lightly freckled. 'This round, I'm not the one compromised.'

'You say.' Arithon smiled. With enviable quickness, he surged to his feet and offered an open, clean hand. 'Where do I look for your husband?'

'Kyrialt?' She accepted his grasp. 'Too bad he's not here to divert you.' Latched hold, she dealt Arithon's knuckles a lingering kiss. Her busy mouth burned, while her loosened hair slithered over his wrist like spilled lava.

'My dear!' chided the Prince of Rathain, his trapped hand unresponsive to her steamy attention. 'Is there no charity in Alland, that such beauty as yours should go hungry?'

'Invalid! You've been laid so low?' Her throaty laugh mocked as he tugged her erect. 'Or is the excuse to gloss over the claim there's no pith to Rathain's royal lineage? You're still bloodlessly cold as iced fish-bait.'

'To a fish, that's a banquet. You have a rank tongue. Here's your husband to lick the sauce off you.' And again, his evasion came fast enough. Her lightning pounce missed the robe that protected his modesty.

All insolence, he presented his back just in time to greet the mate who raced to catch up with her.

Glendien's muscled match was distempered and flushed from hard riding. Dark brown hair laced into a traditional clan braid no longer acknowledged the pattern awarded by paternal birthright. Arithon had time to notice that much, as the young man just thrashed through the screening willow fronds slammed to a panting stop.

'Shame hasn't died. She's been at you again,' Kyrialt said, shedding all decorous royal courtesy. Hot, fully armed, he dropped to one knee. The fist at his heart nonetheless gave his liege the welcome his sworn service demanded. 'Some wicked creatures don't take the hint. You have to give more than a scalding.'

'And some, like the salamander, find their piquant sport by taunting the temper of dragons. Which are you?' Arithon reached out and raised Kyrialt. Then, his bright glance amused, he seized Glendien's wrist. His sudden yank toppled her forward. Now wickedly smiling, he stepped clear and watched the salvage as the bride stumbled into her husband's embrace.

'Best leave us,' quipped Kyrialt, 'since this wench seems to want her clothes wrestled off for a dousing.'

Glendien nipped his ear, tossed back her flame hair, and ducked her shirt off one nubile shoulder. 'Why struggle at all? I mean to bathe, anyhow.'

She had pearlescent skin, spangled with sun, and a ripe swell of breast, tipped a delicate, rose-petal pink. Yet if Glendien intended to gripe Rathain's prince, or inflame him red with embarrassment, she failed.

Her sidelong glance met no stunned or admiring eyes. The cool canopy of the old willow was empty. Only her husband succumbed to the lure, which was as she had intended. The game had been about taking the Teir's'Ffalenn down a peg. She would not bide content. Not until he acknowledged to her satisfaction that he was male, and no better than fallibly human.

Greenwood and running water had recharged the loss of vitality. Restored to the scouts' camp, reclad in borrowed leathers trimmed down for his slighter frame, Arithon shared their plain meal. Trail fare consisted of hardened bread, spread with a salt paste made from raisins, split nuts, and smoked meat. Loose talk caught him up on the news as he ate, terse phrases reporting the erratic progress of the Alliance's southcoast muster.

'No sense to the plan,' remarked the female scout, her toughened fingers twisting strands of deer gut into a new bow-string. 'Last week, we nabbed a requisition dispatch under the Lord Commander's own seal that turned galleys back to Innish for transport. No sense,' she repeated. 'At slack season, the trade there sends its hulls east to the shipyards for refit and careening. No reason they shouldn't be crammed full of troops. Unless some slick official's lining his pockets.'

'Not Sulfin Evend,' another scout quipped. 'That one's got hawk's eyes and a nose for corruption to make an exciseman bleed on his silk.'

'How many armed companies have embarked round Scimlade Tip?' Arithon asked.

'None, yet. An incompetence even a man without brains would find worrisome.' The boisterous opinion was Kyrialt's, carried uphill from the streamside. Next moment, the young man hove into view, soaked and covered by nothing but shirttails. By unself-conscious clan habit, he flopped his shed leathers and weaponry over a branch, then wrung out his dripping clan braid. All the while, his tight survey tracked Rathain's prince. A pleased grin emerged. 'Your escort short-changed their report, busy man. Fit or not, you've leashed Lysaer's southcoast officers up by their short hairs.'

'Fiark's agents did, mostly,' Arithon amended. 'They retired on orders after my personal interview with the Alliance Lord Commander.'

'You came face-to-face and let that one live?' Kyrialt snapped, surprised. His direct stare unbroken, he reached behind and fished for his small-clothes, smartly followed by his hide breeches.

Arithon watched, also unblinking. 'Since the man was the guest of the Sanpashir tribesmen, neither one of us carried a dagger.'

'That shouldn't have stopped you.' Kyrialt stuck his sheathed blades through his belt, then slung on the bossed baldric that hung his plain sword. 'Am I wrong, then? This was the same dog who caused Jieret s'Valerient's torture, followed up by the ignominy of a sorcerer's execution.'

'I deemed Sulfin Evend more helpful, alive.' Still without armament, Arithon stood. He should have lost forceful ground, since the strapping young liegeman topped his height by six fingers, and outmatched him in muscle and strength. His phrasing seemed too mild, as well, for the fact he delivered a warning. 'If you meet the man, you'll acknowledge my thanks. His orders alone have bought Alland its margin of safety.'

That shocked the scouts.

Amid their stiff silence, Glendien reappeared, wet and thankfully already dressed. Without a glance towards her, the Prince of Rathain briskly addressed the scout who managed the horse relays. 'The rest must wait for the ear of

Shand's *caithdein*. Might we ride, and spare your High Earl a night in the saddle to cover the distance?'

Rest by the stream-bank had wrought its strange alchemy. The Master of Shadow withstood the harsh pace that Kyrialt set in response. They covered rough ground through the afternoon heat, until even Glendien's sharp tongue lost its edge to the lathered press of necessity. Sundown's fire faded into a grey twilight. The pines moaned to the lash of a rain squall. Through biting insects, and sultry damp, the small cavalcade thrashed their steady way north-eastward.

By a tortuous route, marked by stones and faint game trails, they entered the heartland of Selkwood. One month had passed since last dark moon. The scouts crossed the forested hills under glimmer of starlight. Guided by woods lore, the party changed horses at speed and passed through a hidden series of check-points.

The country-side was more than just tightly guarded, with the clan women and children withdrawn deep inside protected territory. The precaution gave Arithon the comfort to breathe. Alland's ruling council of chieftains had not chanced their families' safety to the climate of pending war. When midnight came, he reined up in a clearing, nose to nose with another mounted company who had not spared their horseflesh to reach them.

Arithon awaited no man's formal leave. At the first sight of Lord Erlien's tall frame and imperious white head, amid the tight cluster of outriders, Rathain's prince dropped his reins and dismounted. He strode forward, leaving his horse unattended, and dropped to one knee: even in darkness, none could mistake the traditional bow of deference *offered by royal blood to caithdein*.

Kyrialt sprang from his saddle, remiss. The liegeman's courtesy that commanded his place at his prince's back came too late. Resentment nursed from the day's rebuke withered, as Arithon's greeting to the High Earl struck even the hardest scout silent.

'Lord Erlien s'Taleyn, I am not your crown prince. Yet my actions have drawn the adder to Shand, with none of the support I fore-promised. I will stand at your side for the reckoning. All that I have, with all that I am, I will do what I can to defend here.'

Witness

Sidir did not manage the down-river journey to Shipsport with anything near the aplomb that upheld his steadfast character. The wedged bone in the stark teeth of necessity became the fact he distrusted staking his life at long-term on the spells of an oath-bound Koriathain. Elaira's allegiance was not her own. A direct order from her Prime Matriarch could overrule her heart's love for Prince Arithon. Foremost a liegeman who chose courage before chance, Sidir rejected the risk. Should he fail in his charge to curb Jeynsa, he would not leave Feithan the legacy of a public maiming on a town scaffold. His unshakeable honour also denounced the enchantress, who would have raised blistering argument.

He slipped off while she slept. By morning, three leagues removed through dense brush, he left a flagged trail for the hounds. Small doing, from there, to permit the unthinkable and let a head-hunter tracker ensnare him. Hale as he was, bruised with fight, but not broken, the league's greed spared him as a living asset. Avenor's pledge of double bounty in gold saw him roped and turned in at Daenfal. Branded and chained, he was dispatched down-stream to be sold to the galleys at Shipsport.

The appalling tactic forced Elaira to follow his lead. She paid coin for deck passage and kept her anonymous distance.

No bargeman left such captive muscle to waste. Sidir suffered his first taste of the whip at the oar, crossing Daenfal Lake. At the far shore, he endured the cuffs and jeers of the rivermen, who steered their blunt craft on its white-water course past the southern spur of the Skyshiels. The torturous heat of the low country followed. The laden keel scraped and grounded on sand-bars where the slack current meandered through bulrush and marshland. As the river looped south, threading the mud channel that led towards the bay head, the tall Companion bore the harsh price.

Twenty-four days chained to the deck with a pole sweep left him sunburned to weeping blisters. He had cankers from leeches burned off with salt, after the hours spent waist deep in muck, dragging the barge with a tow-rope. If his raw palms grew callus, the festered scabs on his shoulders and back became scoured livid by the pitch slapped on him to ward off flies.

At nightfall, upon the first day of autumn, the choking heat had not broken. Sidir sat curled by the rail, eyes shut and tucked motionless. He was alone, except for one sentry, who paced out his irritable watch. The other bargemen lounged on the shore, just finished with roasting their supper. The scrape of tin plates travelled on the light breeze, and the pop of seared gristle, as chewed bones were tossed in the fire pit.

'Dice, boys? Winner to get his first pick of the strumpets?' Guffaws broke through another man's boastful rejoinder. The rough journey behind them, the rowdy crewmen were primed with jingling pockets and lust for the harbour-front dives crowding Shipsport.

While the forlorn sentry slouched at the stern, wistful to rejoin his fellows, Elaira crept from the willow brake lining the bank. She slipped without sound through the reeds in the shallows. As the black, open water lapped up to her chest, she ducked under, scarcely breaking a ripple. The current was not strong for a determined swimmer. She stroked at length alongside the barge, nearly silent except for quick breathing.

'No spells!' Sidir mouthed at a desperate whisper, the first exchanged word since his deceit had left her, asleep, by the Arwent.

Her eyes flashed, cold grey. Tight with stifled fury, she seized his manacled wrist: pressed into his palm the tinker's steel wire he needed to spring his locked irons. Since caution would lead him to silence the watchman, the enchantress dived back under and left the prisoner to make his escape.

Elaira pushed herself hard, stroking downstream beneath the inky water. She did not resurface until her cramped lungs screamed for air. The murky flow buoyed her on, after that. Better to float slowly than risk splashing noise. A half league from the delta, she overtook her wrapped bundle of baggage and remedies, set afloat and left drifting since sunset.

'Blessings for small favours,' she gasped, bleak-tempered after weeks of anxiety, and chills that set her teeth chattering.

The choked stands of reed on the bank finally thinned, where a willow grove shaded the verge. Elaira crawled out of the river. She masked herself in the dank gloom of the hummock, laced with dense brush and old roots. Forest-bred scout, Sidir could seek her out. No pity for his inconvenience: she could not bear to watch as he murdered. Companion to his fallen high earl, hatred for town-born would have marked him young. Since his kind preferred death to a life in captivity, he likely would vindicate his mishandling by strangling the luckless guard.

Elaira gritted her jaw, still annoyed as she surveyed her surroundings. One night after dark moon, the sky blazed with stars. Their reflections drizzled the face of the river, blurred where the black eddies ruffled. No pursuit seemed in evidence. The enchantress wrung out her sopped shirt and sat. She waited, arms clasped to her knees, while her braid ticked an erratic tattoo of droplets onto the moss at her back. *Twenty-four insufferable days, with her hands tied up by appearances*; the experience galled, quite as cruel as the iron set upon Arithon's prized liegeman!

'I'd rather have saddled myself with a donkey!' Elaira snapped under her breath.

A wavelet lapped against the mud shore-line. Then the waters parted, and Sidir emerged, furtive as a stalking lynx. He slipped through the undergrowth with scarcely a sound, then came on as though drawn by a beacon. Naked, emaciated, he had lost no strength. His hand was a vice from the barge pole. Elaira was inflexibly caught by her wrist, then jerked to her feet before protest. As she bristled, she felt his born talent sweep over her, a sensation like flushing heat. Too late for resentment: his lineage was gifted with truesight.

That stripping exposure slid past her shields, and his rushed whisper snapped in reproof. 'I didn't kill anyone! The wretch on deck got himself a dinged head. Nothing more. He'll wake back up howling and chew off the gag. For my kindness, we have to keep moving.'

'Arrogant beast!' She broke his taut grasp. Bent to her damp baggage, she yanked out the plain shirt and breeches inside, since all he had thought to retrieve from the barge was the rope coiled over his shoulder, and a riverman's knife, unsheathed in his opposite hand. She tossed the clothes at his feet. 'We could have sped south on a galley from here, but for your insane sense of caution!'

Sidir tilted his dark head, dropped the knife, caught her chin. Starlight brushed the white hair at his temples; and also silvered the tears, streaming hopelessly down her cheeks. '*Anyn'e ain s'teirdael*,' he murmured in musical Paravian, then translated the diminutive phrase. '*Handfast to my prince*, there's no more hurt than a brand for this.'

She could have slapped him, if not for the noise. 'Sting for your pride! *Atwood is closed to us*! A Fellowship Sorcerer has wakened the old centaur markers. For eight days, my scryings have shown nothing else. You'd have heard the song of the stones in your dreams, if you hadn't been hell-bent on slavery!'

Sidir caught his breath. He let go, touched her fingers to quell her alarm. Then he snatched on the shirt, which had been loosely cut to keep from binding his welted skin. His quick pause could be sensed, for that kindness. The enchantress held her tongue, grim, while he eased the breeches over the weals on his ankles. Yet wordless, she passed him a soft, calf-skin belt. He fastened the buckle, which chafed nonetheless. His strained breath said as much as he bent and retrieved the knife from the ground.

Before Sidir straightened, the enchantress delved into her satchel again. His cry was stifled ruthlessly silent: perhaps he wept, masked in darkness. His gratitude warmed her subliminal senses as she thrust upon him her gift of hide lacing and boots.

'Princess, Lady,' he murmured. 'The trade-road. Most swiftly. If Atwood is closed, the wise course is to raid. This country's no place to throw off the search those townsmen will launch for a fugitive. We'll have to go mounted if we're to escape.'

They set off at a run, with Elaira unable to match his long-strided sprint. Sidir slowed and flanked her. Through thicket and thorn brake, and forest-bound glades, he pushed on until she was winded. Forced back to her pace, he pressed towards the low ground, sloshing through streamlets to confound their scent for the dogs.

'They won't expect us to try the road, south,' said Elaira, first chance she could speak.

'I won't rely on that hunch.' Sidir laid bold hands on her waist. Before the enchantress exclaimed in surprise, he boosted her onto a tree branch. 'Stay here. Catch your breath. I'll find horses and come for you.'

Gone the next instant, he left her no choice but to mind his instructions. Elaira braced for an uncomfortable wait and a struggle to remain wakeful. Yet the Companion's return was swift. This time, past question, his knife was not clean: he carried two Sunwheel surcoats. The horses had messenger's seals on their saddle-cloths, and a dispatch case, tagged for Pellain.

'Irony's with us. Tight security's got the couriers riding in pairs.' Sidir tossed over the smaller of two man-sized garments. 'Put that on. Leave your braid tucked inside. If we gallop the check-points, we'll be waved straight past. Damned war's got the country-side stirred like a pot. Stay moving, we won't be questioned.'

Elaira took the reins of a fiery mare and mounted despite the beast's sidling. Sidir stowed her satchel inside the cerecloth cape the past rider had rolled at the cantle. Since her beardless face would draw notice, past daybreak, the clan liegeman vaulted astride and plied urgent heels to his horse.

The pair of them rammed ahead through the brush. Whipped by low branches and snagged by dense thorns, they broke through to the open road. Sidir spurred ahead, pressed beyond care for horseflesh. 'I strung a rope trap,' he explained when, reined back to ease their blown mounts, he flashed a glance over his shoulder. 'No way the bodies I left in the brush are not going to draw buzzards, as carrion.'

Now, every league of advantage was precious, covered by moonless darkness. Elaira rode with no word of complaint. Here, where the trade-route skirted the coast, the lights of southbound galleys could be seen, riding the sheltered waters towards Whitehold. They passed encampments of tents more than once. The smell of manure meant troops of light horse, and ox-drawn supply trains.

Elaira stroked the soaked neck of her mare, sorry for the hard usage, but too well aware of the risk to Sidir. A slacker's mistake would doom his survival. Though she ached, and her knees stung with saddle sores, she asked for no respite. Already, the stars in the east sky were paling. Dangerously soon, the first blush of rose brightened the low-lying cloud-banks.

By then, the horses were stumbling and spent. Sidir opted for mercy. He dismounted before letting them founder. The animals were stripped of their tack and set free, with the gear and the Sunwheel surcoats left sunk under rocks in a trout pool. The cerecloth, they kept, since the weather would turn, bringing the chill rain of autumn.

Since no rest was prudent within sight of the coast, Sidir stuffed the dispatches under his shirt and plunged westward into the undergrowth.

By noon, he found them a bed in a thicket, piled under the yellow drifts of shed ash leaves. Elaira fell asleep where she sat, sunk into dreamless exhaustion. She did not awaken through the afternoon. Sidir snatched the interval before she aroused to thumb through his stolen dispatches. Their content painted the picture he feared: of troops on the march from all points north, with conscript gangs sent out scouring for able young men to answer the Light's call to muster.

'Shipsport and Tharidor have served summons on the outlying villages,' Sidir disclosed, as the shadows lengthened towards sundown. His penetrating glance met Elaira's frown and prompted more irritable commentary. 'Sieges don't need every hand trained to fight. The officers will take farm-steaders for digging ditches and hard labour. They'll work every hand they can find to speed the construction of rams and assault engines. Grief will scarcely stop there. Women will be forced to serve with the cooks, and daughters for laundresses and camp-followers.'

His dire prediction encompassed the worst. The roadway would stay relentlessly jammed with the tramp of armed enemies. Rapacious horsemen also would sweep the hills, stripping the country-side of game and fodder.

'Then let me lay wardings,' Elaira insisted, a hand on Sidir's wrist as he bridled. 'I know other ways. Means that lie outside of Koriani doctrine. A hedge witch once taught me her bundle of skills as repayment for curing her grandchild.' When the clansman's tension failed to unwind, she was moved to rare anger. 'Then what would you do? You are not in hale shape! Or haven't you noticed you're sweating a fever, with leaking sores that have festered? We'll handle this here and keep you on your feet. Or else, of course, we'll move on as you wish, until you keel over from sepsis. Make your choice, stubborn man. Lie down for this, now, or wait like a fool, until you're raving and prostrate.'

Sidir's glower melted into a flush, followed up by his soft laughter. 'Did I say you're well matched for my prince's hot temper?' Reliably steady, he shrugged, contrite, and stripped off his shirt and breeches.

Elaira made a small, smokeless blaze and mixed her concoction of simples.

Though the remedies stung without use of her spells, her charge endured the full course of her treatment. By twilight, the deep-set infections were lanced. She wrapped up the scabbed flesh at ankles and wrists using salves that would draw down the swelling.

'I could not sleep, before,' Sidir confessed, his piercing glance fixed on Elaira's deft hands as she secured the last dressing. 'The pain was the goad that kept me alert. Now I fear I'll nod off standing watch.'

'Leave that part to me for tonight.' The enchantress arose, dusting leaves from her lap. She would fetch four rounded stones from the streamlet that wound through the gulch where they sheltered. Given rock that was willing, she could bind an entrainment that would turn away venturesome foragers. Darkness always lent force to such spells. Even dogs should move past without scenting their campsite.

By nightfall, the Companion was deeply asleep, likely his first sound rest since the harrowing choice to fare south in captivity. The wood kept its peace. Ripe with the tang of on-coming frost, alive with the rustles of field-mice, the thicket his instincts had chosen provided the semblance of a secure shelter.

For Elaira, the seclusion permitted the chance for another tranced scrying. Sidir did not rouse when she retired to the mossy bank of the stream. Afraid for Jeynsa, and anxiously fretting the hazards of the open road, the enchantress engaged her disciplined skill to open her inner awareness. Her mind settled, then stilled. The reactive nature of water enveloped her. She let herself flow with the grace of the element, poised between thought and intent.

The moment did not unfold without incident: wild as wind, subtle as the scent of a flower, a welcome arose and embraced her. Touched by a tenderness beyond all words, she immersed in sweet silence until her breath caught with ecstatic delight. At long last! The enchantress encountered the presence that answered her aching heart.

'*Elaira, beloved,*' Prince Arithon sent.

A flood of sensation enlivened his words: of fire-light, and camaraderie, and air that smelled of goose grease, tanned leather, and tallow smoke. He sat in the comfort of a clan lodge tent, where the warm, southern wind wafted the tang of pine resin. Struck through by a sweet bolt of joy in reunion, Elaira soaked in the details: the Teir s'Ffalenn was at large within the free wilds of Alland. His guarded chagrin meant he would be a guest of the hard-bitten High Earl, Lord Erlien s'Taleyn. That powerful, combatively capricious man served as *caithdein* to the Kingdom of Shand . . .

The roisterous gathering called in for his counsel included two Selkwood chieftains, a clan grandame whose talent was healing, and an aggressive company of scouts. The captain of Selkwood's war band presided, a slit-eyed panther hunched over a trestle, buried layers deep in maps. The discussion at hand was raid tactics, and the nascent fire riding the air meant divisive contention.

The High Earl watched the sparring like a satisfied bear, chaos being his element. His avid glance gleamed, eager to see how his visiting royalty would field the heckling debate.

Arithon perched to one side on a hassock, deceptively calm, while the argument flurried about him. He had changed his borrowed leathers for the grey robe and sash given by Sanpashir's tribesman. His hands were laced over his drawn-up knees, the nonchalant pose in striking contrast to the edgy young liegeman who stood at his back. Kyrialt carried both targe and sword, tense enough to pounce on all comers.

'*It's the mouse fallen into a den of stirred adders,*' Arithon agreed, sharing Elaira's dismayed assessment. '*Already, fangs have been sunk deep in fur. They're only stumped now out of contrary irony and an embarrassing conflict of honour.*'

The enchantress grinned, secure as observer, couched in her distant glen. '*They've forgotten the range of your initiate talents? Don't say they believe the stacked odds set by numbers makes their brash challenge unsporting?*'

'*Well, Erlien's not fooled.*' That statement came through with flint-edged delight as Selkwood's bearded war-captain banged a cantankerous fist on the planks, then assailed his lord nose to nose across the crimped maps.

'Dharkaron's black bollocks, we're not equipped! The southcoast is swarming with Sunwheel galleys. Give their hazed troops any reason to land, we'll see Alland's trees put to the torch with intent to smoke out our families like vermin.'

Still seated, the High Earl bit back. 'Then you might want to save your bristles and fight for trouncing Light-rabid fanatics!'

'They'll attack our north flank out of Atchaz, as well!' the hatchet-faced veteran snarled, embittered. 'We'll be overrun. Struck down in cold blood, and for what? By the point on Dharkaron Avenger's Black Spear! What brazen hope can be salvaged? If we're lucky, our seasoned ranks will be pressed to defend us at hundreds to one!'

Erlien rose to his towering height. His icy blue eyes raked the company. 'Yes. And we're scrapping to see how much of our war band should rush to the slaughter at first engagement?'

'Best to die free, if the compact's to fall,' a grizzled chieftain yelled from the side-lines. 'Pack up our children. March them north with all speed. Those who are fit to survive the journey must plead for the Fellowship's refuge with the spellbinder on guardwatch at Methisle.'

Shand's *caithdein* smiled, now primed to provoke. 'But the Prince of Rathain insists there's a recourse. He's given us his promise to lend help for the numbers we can keep living.'

The eldest veteran shoved through the press, a rumpled cock in a brigandine stitched out of boiled leather and elk bone. 'Royal or not, he brings us a flawed trust!'

A second dissenter expounded, 'I, too, bore witness the last time his Grace visited Alland from Merior. We heard him describe the geas that binds him.

The curse of Desh-thiere is not revoked! His Grace's own word once warned us to beware! The Mistwraith's foul working undermines his intent. It can sap his free will, even claim him. If he fights at our side, he might turn, or go mad. We can't sanction that danger. Only a fool would rely on his sword-arm among us!'

Linked into rapport, Elaira stopped breathing. Restraint veiled her distress: for that harsh accusation held only truth. The Mistwraith's curse might well awaken. If its raw drive subsumed Arithon's nature, his allies would be caught without recourse. The anguish of that incontrovertible flaw had almost shattered his spirit during his challenging passage through Kewar. Now braced to absorb his shamed recoil, Elaira extended her tactful support.

Yet Arithon did not flinch, even as Erlien's shark smile widened. 'By Ath, are we gone to the dogs like the town-born? Here, if I recall, we allow the condemned man to speak in defence before judgement!'

No comment, from Arithon. He failed to bridle. More startling still, his green eyes stayed wide-lashed. Elaira, who touched his bared heart, sensed his flicker of masked amusement.

If the High Earl suspected, he rose to the match, suave as honey spread over poison. 'You may test his royal mettle. Push hard as you wish. The stakes are not small: his Grace has granted my son a crown prince's oath and embraced him for Rathain as liegeman.' A gesture towards Kyrialt forced affirmation. The young man looked peaked. He knew his father's badgering ways: every circling feint would be closed without mercy upon the misfortunate victim.

'If that signal honour does not bear enough weight,' the High Earl ran on with relish, 'Rathain's prince has shared guest oath under my roof. Most who stand here saw him drain the cup that pledged amity! If, after all, his Grace dares to lie, as *caithdein*, under the law of this realm, I will be required to break him.'

The war-captain ruffled up like a falcon just hooded and leashed to the block. The chieftain beside him pursed sour lips, while a scout towards the rear hawked behind his closed fist, ready to spit at the feet of the effete royal among them.

The scarred tracker who tended the torch was first to try Erlien's challenge. 'We've got to sit through a nattering parley? Then have done! Let his Grace state his case on his merits.'

Least restrained of them all, the healer-trained grandame grumbled a withering phrase in old dialect. 'Who trusts a man who won't carry a weapon?'

A scout catcalled. 'Daelion Fatemaster's mark on my name! Should we follow a sniveller? There's no butty born with two bollocks who shrinks at blooding cold steel on his enemies.'

Lord Erlien turned, his hawk's profile tinged ruddy by flame-light. 'You do have a strategy,' he invited the prince, seated still, his laced fingers artful as sculpture. 'We'd like to hear out your plan of attack. You've already said you refuse to spin Darkness. Won't sow fear through our enemy's ranks by means of initiate talent. If the man is too proud, and the master too scrupulous, just how *do* you intend to participate?'

Arithon stirred, set his feet on the ground, his unruffled humour intact. 'I came to defend. Nor can I be badgered to raise Shadow, or cause injury for the least of your fatal offensives.'

'Cringing daisy, I said so!' the war-captain barked. 'Speak fast, ere we slice you to mincemeat!' His calloused fists fended off the two chieftains who surged to draw knives for the insult.

Savagely pleased by their bursting aggression, Lord Erlien towered over the diminutive prince on the hassock. 'Don't claim you'll spare Selkwood with naught but that jewelled bauble of a lyranthe?'

'Well, yes,' said Arithon, unperturbed. 'She's no pretty toy, but a master-bard's instrument.' Against the explosive muscle and shouts, he gave no ground, except to arise empty-handed before them. 'You can listen! Bear witness yourselves. See if my act of protection is binding. Or you can fight and send your strongest to die! Don't ask me, then, to applaud for the pride of walking blind in your forefathers' footsteps.'

While the uproar redoubled, and more roughnecks ploughed forward, Kyrialt's grip locked on his sword-hilt. Yet Lord Erlien's voice arrested the rush to thrash Rathain's prince for rank insolence. 'You'd lay a singer's warding on Selkwood?' His surprise swept the gathering, while the crowding insurgents exclaimed with stung disbelief.

'I'm proposing to try,' Rathain's crown prince appealed, then smiled with a grace to wrench heart-strings. 'My theory can be tested tonight. If I fail, then I promise you'll still have the time to fall back on armed force.'

'A stripling talent can shoulder this feat?' The war-captain's doubtful glance darted between his High Earl and the prince, whose fine build was eclipsed by Kyrialt's strapping prowess.

That able young liegeman refused to speak: not for a trained sorcerer whose unfathomable wiles blindsided his sire's ferocity. Shocked quiet, but not mollified, the High Earl of Alland had to accept that brash dare at face value. His order reddened the ears of the sceptical tracker, and sent the man scurrying to fetch the heirloom lyranthe . . .

'Stay with me, beloved.' The plea crossed the empathic link of the scrying. Elaira sighed as the intimate contact cradled her like a caress.

Such flooding tenderness melted her heart, but could not unstring her concern. *'Could I do less? The High Earl who pads at your heels is not tame. If you fail to satisfy, his wolfish following will rip you down like staked carrion. At least I'll know where to seek your remains. That's assuming a dismembered corpse is left to require a memorial.'*

Arithon's humour downplayed her fear. '*If Erlien gnashes his teeth any harder, there won't be a fang left intact for the ripe spree of slaughter.*'

'Well, Kyrialt's worried,' Elaira pointed out. '*Somebody ought to be holding his sword-hand. That's if you don't want to drive him berserk before he can sire hale offspring.*'

'You've seen Glendien,' Arithon quipped in response. '*She'll set him a clutch. That's the price of mating young oak with a fire-brand.*'

'*You say!*' Elaira felt her cheeks warm. '*Clear your business in Alland. I'll make you a blaze to torch down stars and moon.*'

'*You have, love. Already. I'm branded, soul deep. If your meddling Prime Matriarch values her life, she'll leap high and fast to dissolve every obstacle she's raised between us.*' Which framed his bald warning: Elaira could sense the shocking, grim force behind his bed-rock sincerity. Whether the trial ahead brought him triumph, or the bitterest, agonized failure, Arithon Teir's'Ffalenn desired her presence, spun through the weave of his heart's hope.

Just now, threat to Alland commanded priority. At one mind with her living awareness, as he had not dared to indulge since Etarra, he baited Lord Erlien's mettlesome scouts and lured them into the deeps of Selkwood forest. Throughout, he was chaffed for his frivolous errand. Others berated his untoward character with slangs and ribald aggression.

'If you wanted the evening to tomcat, why couldn't you tell us you itched for a wench?'

'No sweet pickings, there!' someone else quipped. 'Not since Kyrialt's hussy got her licks in first and declared he's got ice cubes for bollocks.'

Arithon laughed. 'This happened *after* her fingers got singed?'

'Try harder,' jabbed Kyrialt in his wife's defence. 'The lady's equipped to pick her own fights. She'd hammer Dharkaron himself, just for sport. You lot would be spurned to bay at the moon and gnaw the shat bones of the hindmost.'

Such boisterous by-play lasted until they reached the prince's obscure destination. Broken out of the velvety murk of the pines, Arithon entered a clearing rinsed under starlight. Hush fell over the crowd at his heels. On stopped breath, their jeering stayed silenced. Ahead rose one of the moss-capped, carved stones the Ilitharis Paravian guardians had laid down to demark the sanctity of Alland's free wilds.

Elaira divined Arithon's intent as he knelt to unwrap his fine instrument. '*You plan to awaken the old centaur wardings and raise the arcane defences of Selkwood Forest?*'

'*I will try*,' returned Arithon, while around him, the scouts recoiled in shock as they also guessed his brash strategy.

'Blessed Ath, you're not serious!' Kyrialt gasped, afraid to speak over a whisper. 'Your Grace, do you *know* what you dare? Is there language to chasten such arrogance?'

For the brazen endeavour just claimed was no trifle. A crowned high king rightfully oath-bound to Shand, and attuned to the cardinal elements, would be loath to disturb the coils of quiescent Paravian enchantment. Such a mystical working must rival the reach and strengths of a Fellowship Sorcerer.

The forces laid down here could ignite mortal flesh or burn out the mind with insanity.

The bard spoke no word. He gave no apology. A slight figure merged with the stone's looming shadow, he slipped the cover from his lyranthe. Silver strings flashed, needle-thin, as his deft fingers perfected the pitch.

'Stand back!' murmured Kyrialt to the awe-struck scouts. Dread set him trembling. 'We will observe from the verge of the wood, and woe betide us if tonight's work destroys us for your act of invasive meddling.'

'*Best beloved*,' sent Arithon. '*Withdraw or stay, as you wish.*'

Crime or folly, no warning might tear Elaira away, as he settled himself to begin.

Stillness reigned, and unbearable tension. Athera's Masterbard knelt with bent head, immersed into listening silence. The enchantress shared the moment of burning immersion, as his heightened awareness evoked his trained mage-sense. With him, she felt the night clearing dissolve, all sight and sensation of physical form redefined as a lacework of energy. Amid that sparkling lattice of light, form spoke as a singing vibration. The musician merged with that ripple of sound. His clear talent mapped the subtleties and embraced their ephemeral harmony.

Then he settled the strap of the lyranthe and stood. Erect, head thrown back, he set fingers to strings and opened the line of his melody.

One note sheared the air, aching with a stark purity that framed the essence of solitude. The bard came alone. His phrase began an appeal to a force that stood beyond mortal knowing. He showed no contrition for his brazen nerve. His intrusion was not masked in blandishment. He brought the living cry of his need in a tone that stung flesh for its vibrancy.

Against the single struck string, he built dissonance: a snarling, discordant plunge that enacted the ruinous fury of war. He played destruction, hatred, and hurt, that smashed like a breaker of fury and ebbed into desolate grief. To the shattering vista of sorrow, carved by howling chords of unreason, he added his voice, and shaped the savagery born out of geas-bent madness.

He sang Desh-thiere's curse. All who bore witness recoiled with shame. The watching clansmen cringed with betrayal. The storm he built raged on without quarter, until the glen's silence was made utterly violate. The bard did not relent. The brutalized horror of ruin was unveiled with unvarnished honesty.

'Ath wept, he'll be killed for this,' somebody gasped.

No others could bear to comment. They only wished the harsh moment undone. To a man, they wept in bitter remorse, that the bard they had brought used his gift to rape a peace they were sworn to hold sacrosanct.

Cold as struck iron, the musician who wielded the lyranthe did not recoil. His art refused pity. The face of cursed war was forged into a harrowing challenge: as the aimed sword might thrust for the viscera, he did not pull his stroke. With a brilliance past mercy, the discord he played shaped the very wreckage of hope.

The crescendo reprised the unbearable pain, bleak beyond reach of requital: except for the last line, which hung on a pause, with one note struck through as a question. One note, and one man, left the horror unfinished, a raging query demanding an answer.

The bard's voice rang out and sustained, *and then became partnered.*

But this time, not by his hand on the lyranthe. The dormant power in the Paravian marker stone aroused and shaped his response.

A shimmer of light appeared like a star. At first, little more than a gossamer flicker licked over the ancient, carved patterns. Then rock itself chimed. A swelling chord sounded. The tones met and meshed with the bard's strain of chaos, and matched him in straight opposition. Where his measures cried violence with barefaced appeal, the circle now became closed. Light brightened and blazed, as the guardian spells countermatched agonized ruin with the outpouring of unconditional tranquillity. Wholeness resulted. From horror and destruction came the exquisite freedom of unbridled peace, the harmonic dance as death was rebraided into the dazzling glory of rebirth. Grace resounded. The dark and the light were not separate, but *one*, reforged in dynamic balance. Where calm, of itself, must engender stagnation, the exuberant range of *all* possibility turned the symmetry of Ath's creation.

Power exploded. The stone lit, then burned, an exaltation that overwhelmed sight and creased the night sky as a beacon . . .

Far north, still wrapped in trance state in the brush, Elaira experienced the chord raised in Selkwood, at one with Arithon's mind and emotions. The bursting flare impelled her love beyond ecstasy. At his union with the Paravian magic, purity illumined *all that he was, and all that he held in connection.* Vision exposed her heart's tie to his being, and more: the lines of affection Arithon held for all his friends and associates. Elaira saw the blue steel of the attunement wrought on him by the Fellowship's oath of crown service. Above that eightfold pattern, scribed in binding fire, lay the promise once sworn in behalf of Earl Jieret's dying request: *the mage's vow, sealed in let blood, that granted his binding protection to Jeynsa s'Valerient until his last breath.*

Elaira's scrying through water showed where that oath led, terrible as a cry of despair in the darkness. The bolt of discovery brought Sidir's ruthless palm, smashing the delicate web of her trance as he stifled her agonized scream.

'Lady! Elaira! For mercy, be still!' The Companion's concerned glance pierced hers, as her shattered senses regained distraught focus upon her surroundings.

At once, the clansman's harsh grasp released. The arm that pinned her quivering shoulders gentled with sincere distress. 'I could not withhold,' he exclaimed in apology. 'The least noise will alert our enemies.'

'Jeynsa!' Elaira gasped with alarm. 'She's gone to Alestron. Joined her headstrong intent to back Bransian's ill-starred defence of the citadel.'

No fool, Sidir grasped the unconscionable gist. 'She'd dare twist her crown prince's oath, force his honour, and draw him into the conflict?' The liegeman shivered, unnerved by dismay. He had stood steadfast at Arithon's side through the horrific tactics that once brought Lysaer's war host to a stand down at Vastmark. One of a privileged few, he understood how desperately near the experience had come to destroying his crown prince.

'Dharkaron Avenger avert!' he wrung out. 'The girl must be stopped! She'll seed a disaster beyond all imagining. We must drag her clear, no matter the stakes. Until the hour we have her secure, his Grace must never discover her whereabouts!'

Elaira permitted Sidir's urgent grip to haul her onto her feet. Her trance was disrupted: she could not be certain. Yet the empathic link she held with her beloved could not mask her jagged unrest. Arithon owned the rogue Sight of his s'Ahelas forebears. Joined with her heart, the dictates of his talent meant *he probably already knew.*

Closure

The Masterbard in the night glen in Selkwood crumpled, then slid to his knees. A man, and still mortal, he could not sustain his aware consciousness as the dance of raised harmonies sang past the veil. Immersed as his engaged talent fired the grand chord, he was caught fully exposed. The exalted energies blazed through his being, eclipsed his senses, and whirled him into tingling vertigo.

His onlooking escort of scouts became shocked as well by the standing wave of potentized harmony. Weeping or laughing, rushed witless by ecstasy, they could never tame the unbearable moment. The strongest of them were swept off their feet. The singing, sweet deluge dropped them into a faint, overwhelmed and riven senseless. Then the blasting wave of peak resonance passed. First the light, then the piercing brilliance of sound subsided through the lower octaves. Only subliminal harmonics remained, a live charge laced amid the stilled air. The unseen force thrilled the nerves like a tonic, with the marker stone's blaze of raw glory reduced to a glimmer. The radiance shone like a pearl in the glen, pure as a star brought captive and spell-bound to earth.

Kyrialt s'Taleyn was ahead of his prostrate company to recoup his scattered wits. Born of the lineage that bred Shand's *caithdeinen*, his heritage granted the depth to withstand the grandeur of the Paravian presence. He marshalled himself, then determined his quivering legs could bear weight. He checked and ascertained the others still breathed; braced the dazed who stirred from blank stupor. His driving concern swung back to his liege as he grounded back into coherency.

The glen remained seized by a powerful hush. Past the range of natural hearing, the stone's active presence was felt. A quickened vibration raced through flesh and bone as Kyrialt stepped from the verge of the wood. Nearer, his vision became preternaturally heightened. Scent infused his stripped mind as *experience*, distinct as a physical touch. The dew-soaked air wore the change in the season with the sweet glory of vintage wine. In darkness spiked with the fragrance of pine, the gleam of the marker stone spattered the glade as though each living leaf had been dipped into mercury. The seed-heads of the grasses seemed graced in light. The autumnal tangle of nettle and weed breathed the majesty of Ath Creator.

The same pallid radiance traced Arithon s'Ffalenn, where he curled with his instrument couched in his arms.

Shivering, still awe-struck, Kyrialt knelt.

'*Alt,*' husked the bard, just barely aware. 'Done. Though I fear the presumption's unravelled the sinew required to stand.'

'My strength will bear you.' Kyrialt's touch was received without protest as he lifted the lyranthe away. To the soft inquiry voiced by a scout, he replied, 'His Grace is down, but not prostrate.'

The scour of back-lash already heated the flesh that he handled to fever. Initiate master, Arithon also recognized the draining onset of weakness as his physical body succumbed to release. He let Kyrialt raise him. The shift caused by his unshielded proximity to the mystery that commanded the elements was not sickness. Quiet and sleep would heal the imbalance. Clan lore yet maintained the old knowledge to steer him into a safe recovery.

Kyrialt shouldered the prince's limp weight. Then he called for the steadiest scout to retrieve the Masterbard's instrument. Not a man of them did not have stars in his eyes. None walked unmarked, from the touch of grace on their being. The stupefied company regrouped, dazed and stumbling, and surrounded the bard in retreat.

'Forgive the unseemly haste,' the young liegeman apologized to his prince. 'Best we get you away to less-sensitive ground, before the flux of the centaurs' warding wrings all of us into collapse.'

They settled at last in an open-air camp, where Kyrialt insisted his oathsworn place was to keep watch through his liege's recovery. Care kept him alert. He stayed at Prince Arithon's side until the fever broke prior to dawn. Rathain's prince slept then, a repose kept unbroken, even when the scout sentries reported the arrival of Selkwood's acting war-captain.

'Hilgreth himself? Whatever for?' Kyrialt scrambled erect, stopped by the placating fist of the messenger as he reached in alarm for his sword.

'No trouble's here,' the woman assured. 'Not even a muster. The old man's decked out. Full ceremonial, including his clan badge and Shand's chevron blazon.'

Which meant the occasion would involve a matter of state. Mystified, Kyrialt brushed the caught leaves from his hair. He slapped the stuck pine-needles off his breeches and strove to focus. The after-shock of the Paravian warding still hazed him to dizziness. Still, he managed to stay on his feet when his father's right-hand officer strode up and exchanged the wrist clasp salute of formality.

Hilgreth came fully armed, a resplendent figure in the belted surcoat once worn to honour Shand's ancient, initiate kingship. 'Your father's sent summons,' he opened, clipped brisk, his lined face pink in the dawn light. 'I was dispatched on Lord Erlien's order to stand in your place as relief.'

The veteran campaigner acknowledged the bard, still curled in vulnerable sleep under a scout's borrowed rain-cloak. The dark head pillowed upon the fleece-wrapped lyranthe exposed his over-fine features, stripped artlessly naked. But no more the brunt of the old man's contempt: the war-captain's gruffness showed awe. 'Go with a clear heart. Rest assured, I'll not shame the discharge of your duty.'

Which was near as that campaigner's outraged pride could bend, by way of apology. Kyrialt slapped Hilgreth's shoulder, and went.

Lord Erlien s'Taleyn, *Caithdein* of Shand, awaited his youngest son in the lodge tent maintained by the varied tastes of his mistresses. Clan ways saw a life vow of marriage as an affair of the heart, with the High Earl of Alland a law made unto himself. The five women who loved him held a single passion in common: they shared before giving him up.

Seldom had Kyrialt seen more than one in camp residence at the same time. The four who were not his birth mother had fostered him alongside their natural children since infancy, each of their lord's brood of stepsiblings cherished with even-handed affection. Whose son or daughter would shoulder the titles was never a source of contention: clan lineage bestowed the perils of inheritance strictly by merit. Fellowship Sorcerers could upset an assignment. A cousin or sister-in-law's issue might as readily bear the succession ahead of their own.

Therefore, the tempestuous style by which the High Earl sharpened his regency did not reign under his lodge-pole. To enter the home shaped by Erlien's women was to shelter inside the eye of the storm.

The lamplight was soft, and the earth floor spread over with a luxurious wool carpet soaked in oil of balsam. Throughout the extended warmth of Shand's seasons, the hassocks and dyed, deer-hide pillows exuded that resinous fragrance to discourage the night-biting insects. The lacquered wood chests and the loomed horsehair mats always gleamed under lavish care. Kyrialt ducked through the black-out felt flap. Always, he knew which foster-mother held residence: personalities spoke through their floral perfumes, or the herbal-ist's fust of drying medicinals, or the tang of the rosemary grease the lean huntress brewed to supple her trail gear.

Yet today, he walked in on the crowding presence of all five of the mistresses, his two full sisters, and those of his brawling pack of half-siblings within reach of the High Earl's summons. Most had found time to put on state dress. Come also, the wizened chieftess in Selkforest's green, whose Sighted talent at times tapped the future. She held the place at Lord Erlien's right hand, solemn and stilled at the forefront. Seated to his left, a slim form unfamiliarly hooded in Atchaz silk: Kyrialt started, this once unnerved to meet the proud glance of the scout who was his blood mother. Beyond her hawk's reserve, a stiff reticence suggested she might have been weeping. The earl's other mistresses stood at her back, their presence perhaps to support a sister in need.

Kyrialt bent to his knee. Still suffused by the lingering glow of the mysteries, he arose, hands crossed at his chest, as son to acknowledged *caithdein*. Although he was sworn to Rathain's crown service, he stood upon Shand's sovereign ground. Tradition commanded the time-honoured line, made in obligation to charter law. 'How may I best serve the land?'

His uncertainty showed, amid the dense hush. This session would be no inquiry over the Masterbard's commensurate bidding of Alland's deep mysteries: beside the report dispatched with his runner, the ripple evoked by the unfurled wardings had left no born talent in Selkwood untouched.

Pinned before all eyes, Kyrialt could not suppress the expectant glance, flicked towards the clan seeress. 'What untoward happening should call me away from my place at my liege's side?'

Though youngest, he once had been his line's heir apparent, yielded over to Rathain's crown as a gesture to balance clan honour. The sacrifice meant a half-sibling must inherit the titles. No felicitous appointment, to succeed Teir's'Taleyn, after the primary candidate. Kyrialt shivered. The hammered glint in his father's eyes now bespoke a grief to outmatch his disrupted inheritance.

Yet none ever claimed that the patriarch's fibre did not match his illustrious ancestry. 'My son, hear the course of tonight's augury, seared in white fire through the lane flux when the twelve centaur markers flared active.' An untoward precedent, Erlien's massive arm was unsteady when he raised the seeress to speak.

She bowed before Kyrialt. The taut atmosphere in the tent became forced as she told over her vision: that Rathain's sanctioned prince had joined his love with a Koriani enchantress whose talent spoke clearest through water. 'They are paired in communion, and inseparably mated. Heart and spirit spoke when the marker stones blazed, and the imprint rippled the flux. Far more than the Warden at Althain will have heard the cry that his Grace's beloved released.'

That young Jeynsa s'Valerient had gone to Alestron, and conspired to entangle the blood oath of protection granted by Arithon at Earl Jieret's bequest.

Against dumb-struck silence, the seeress pressed on. 'I shared the destiny to occur as the Teir's'Ffalenn answers that charge. He will leave for Alestron. The day must come soon. The binding he holds cannot be forsworn, and his trial, to spare the girl from the Light's immolation of the s'Brydion citadel.'

Here, his mother's hooded head lifted. She would not show weakness, though her bravery should unman him. Kyrialt could but match his sire's fixed stance, that straitly mastered a pressure that threatened to tear him asunder.

'Arithon Teir's'Ffalenn is not our rightful liege,' Lord Erlien acknowledged, not as father, but by the unflinching iron that commanded him as the realm's regent. 'Yet his Grace of Rathain bears the s'Ahelas lineage, endowed in full measure with the royal gifts. He has granted this kingdom a born prince's duty by his act of unparalleled courage. For last night's warding of Alland, we can do no less in return. When his Grace leaves in defence of Alestron, he will ask not to accept the full charge of the crown oath my son carries. Until now, the honour pledge bestowed in reprisal has only been kept as a matter of form.'

'As before, his command would constrain Kyrialt to stay. I've foreseen!' The old seeress acknowledged the young man, arrow-straight, come before them. 'His Grace would leave you with us here in Selkwood, and not take you north as his own.'

'Kyrialt, as your father, I bid you to refuse your liege's dismissal. At his side, this royal deserves the protection assigned to a crown heir of Shand. As the flower of our lineage, I ask you to go. Guard Arithon's life. Stand shadow for Rathain's principled ruler with my blessing, through whatever Daelion Fatemaster should hold in store for him.'

Kyrialt swallowed. He bent his dark head. Never to object, but in fact to veil his surging relief. The light in the glen had not left him unmarked: none who beheld his changed presence might deny the course of fate's choosing. Given the conflict between duty and kin, his father's grace spared him the cruelty of making his plea to go, anyway.

Yet regret was not painless. 'When I do this, you know my wife Glendien will insist she should not stay behind. There's no way under Ath's sky I can stop her.' Nor could anyone do so; not without breaking her spirit.

'Glendien knows, already.' This time, his mother's unswerving strength gave the kindness of understanding. 'Your commitment is not solitary, though we tried. Her own family could not dissuade her. Unless your prince can change her mind, your lady will serve Rathain as the woman beside you.' The strain upon those silk-veiled features stayed masked, upheld by more than state protocol.

'Who better to send?' Her pride rang before those who gathered to witness. 'You were to become our realm's next *caithdein*, and by appearance, the Teiren's'Valerient has fallen shamefully short!'

Kyrialt bowed. 'I will defend Arithon Teir's'Ffalenn, as required. Not just for the sake of kingdom and clan, but with the whole of my heart.'

His declaration closed the formalities. No one knew when the last summons would come. The seeress could not say whether the timing would permit a final leave-taking. Therefore, clan family seized on the moment to unburden its private sentiment. His mother swept forward. Silk hood thrown back, eyes wet, she embraced him. Her affection was followed by his full siblings, each one; then by his half-sisters and half-brothers, and their mothers, whose love also flowed without stint.

His father came last. Erlien s'Taleyn gave up his rank and delivered the accolade on his knees. 'Ath has gifted me with no better son. My blood is diminished, and my name in your shadow, to carry the debt to Rathain that our people can never repay.'

Deflections

Touched by the echo of Elaira's scried insight, Dakar bids the galley-man who gave him passage to put him ashore at the delta up-stream of Pellain; more sharp bargaining procures him three mounts and a stocked pack-horse, which he drives past the verges of Atwood with intent to join company with the enchantress and the Companion, Sidir . . .

Returned from his search of the vaults underneath the burned ruins at Avenor, Luhaine bears dire tidings back to Sethvir at Althain Tower: that the four hatchling dragon skulls once bound under the influence of Koriani jewels in fact have fallen casualty to the fires, with their shades freed and subject to rise . . .

The sun chases a blinding glitter of gold over the horse guard escorting Lysaer's Lord Seneschal, a shimmering form in the Sunwheel tabard of an Alliance ambassador; yet the Light's vested envoy meets Alestron's shut gates, and his scribed ultimatum is spurned by Duke Bransian's adamant silence . . .

Autumn 5671

IV. Feint and Assault

The looming spectre of war strained the days that followed the rebuff of Lysaer's sent envoy. That discordant, first note swelled into the overture that presaged the onslaught of siege. Both fortress towns at the mouth of the estuary dropped their posturing: Kalesh and Adruin launched ships for blockade and unleashed the advance of armed troops.

Parrien's war galleys still ranged at large. Yet even Duke Bransian's bellicose temper acknowledged the damaging fact: the massing deployment set under way defanged his fleet as a tactical asset. Oared ships could not breast the rough, autumn sea. No vessel under Alestron's flag might claim safe harbour in any port sworn to the Alliance. Cut off from access by blue-water sail, and the free territory under clan loyalties as his last source of provision, s'Brydion could only fume. His captains' rapacious prowess was reduced to the strike-and-flee raiding of harriers. Such engagements might nip at the flanks of enemy shipping. But resupply could no longer reach the citadel with impunity. Not without running the gamut: the narrow inlet, with its vicious tides and its forty leagues of ledged shore-line that daily became entrenched by the tents and banners of hostile encampments.

Each morning, Duke Bransian awoke to his wife, gauging his mood in sharp silence.

'Death and plague, woman!' he barked at last, distempered by too many quandaries. 'Why not just spit out your opinion? By the red spear of Dharkaron's vengeance, a man could watch his parts shrivel under your hag-ridden glowering!'

Liesse pushed her raw-boned frame upright in bed and eyed the bristling jut of the beard on the pillow. 'You would actually listen?'

'I always listen,' the duke said, annoyed. 'Just hang your silly, unnatural notion, that hearing means following your orders.'

His duchess snorted with peeling contempt. 'The day you take instruction from anyone else, we'll be torching your corpse at your funeral!'

'Don't tell me again that we should have tucked tail and not ripped with bared teeth for the jugular!' Unmoved, lounging flat amid crumpled sheets, the duke crossed his battle-scarred forearms. 'Prince Arithon chose to abandon us, first. He well deserves the whip-lash he'll get from that snip chosen as his *caithdein*.'

'You presume I would lose the same argument twice?' Liesse flounced from the mattress. Beyond the keep's floor-boards, scarred by hobnailed boots, an orange sunrise brightened the arrow-slit. The glare spat sullen glints off the bronze-cornered chests, and burnished the steel bosses of the duke's baldric, carelessly slung on a chair-back. 'It's not Rathain's feckless prince,' she admitted, 'but the warnings delivered by three Fellowship Sorcerers that set the cold into my liver.'

'My heir should be wearing tanned buckskins in Atwood? Ath, woman! You bleed me!' Bransian levered upright, to a groan from the bed-frame, which also bore scars, where an ancestor had stabbed his knives inside of arm's reach in the head-board. 'Sevrand's an adult. Let him choose for himself.'

The duke kicked off the blankets and snatched for the grimy gambeson that had padded yesterday's chainmail. 'You would shame me ahead of the Fatemaster himself! No fighting man on these walls will stand firm, believing I planned on defeat.'

To which Liesse bent her head. Face buried amid her uncombed brown hair and the clutch of exasperated fingers, she sighed.

Bransian's bunched fists released, as he realized she was trembling. 'Wife!' he barked, sucked hollow by tenderness. One barefoot stride and he gathered her close: her tears *would* bring him to his knees, if not wring him wretchedly gutless. 'You should fear a few enemies?'

'No,' Liesse gasped, muffled. She raised her chin from his chest, coughing back laughter. 'I should despair of the hope you could reach for clean clothes before letting the filth rot them to rags off your back!'

Yet no biting humour might stem the Alliance advance that surged in on them like flood-tide.

As the new morning brightened, the shore-side watch beacons relayed more damning reports. Alliance companies now mushroomed over the muddied acres left scorched by the reivers' torch. Hourly, more troop-laden warships hove in. Anchored hulls jammed the coves like teeth in a trap, until the expectant tension locked down, cranked as an overtaut drumhead.

Day followed day. From lookout tower, to battlement, to the eyrie vantage of the upper citadel, the sentries flashed mirrors in coded signal. Alestron watched

Lysaer's grand war host assemble, until the counters that burdened Bransian's maps swallowed all of the surrounding shore-line. Dawn followed dawn, while the town hunkered down behind fast-shut gates and denied egress to outbound civilians.

'I don't understand,' Fionn Areth complained from his leaned stance between the Sea Gate's battle-scarred merlons. Above him, the massive groan of the winches raised the hoist, bearing stone-shot and slopping, filled casks. Saltwater was being stockpiled ahead, for the flammable hidings that guarded the foundations under the ramparts.

As the platform's shadow scythed over his face, the goatherd sawed on in his Araethurian twang, 'Shouldn't the duke bless every tuck-tailed coward who wishes to leave? Why hang on to their chicken-shit mouths? They're just wasting his food stores and draining his cisterns.'

'Morale,' stated Jeynsa, as bitten as forest-bred manners could frame a response.

Fionn Areth slid his gaze sideward and studied her. A tall, freckled lynx, she lounged with her chin on her fist, while the wind fluttered through her knife-cropped brown hair. Her bitten-off nails were black-rimmed with tar. That would be the remnant of yesterday's toil, a longshoreman's morning spent loading the pitch barrels sent to the Wyntok Gate.

Engrossed, the grass-lander chafed to dissect the enigma she represented. Forestborn daughter of a former high earl, she wore bladed weapons as though bred to war. Though her woman's build could not outmatch a man's bulk, the fact never humbled her manner. Jeynsa's brazen promise to summon her crown prince gave even s'Brydion aggression a frost-ridden pause. If the duke and his brothers were wont to treat her tenderly for a move that bordered on treason, their citadel's matrons, with their clinging toddlers, applauded her as a saviour.

For Fionn Areth, the fascination stayed fresh: he wondered how Arithon was going to handle the chit, if and when he chose to arrive.

Until then, the arena became verbal prodding. 'Morale, so you say?' the grass-lander mused. 'Then you'd be the going expert on sieges, come from an even more back-country birthright than I?'

Jeynsa laughed. 'Rats leave sinking ships. The s'Brydion banner has never been struck.' Six hundred and fifty-three years to the day, all campaigns to rout charter rule from Alestron had been smashed at punishing cost. 'Clanblood doesn't shrink at long odds. Let the squeamish guilds bleed their wealth from this town, or pack off their wives and young children, there's too little left at stake to stem losses. Some panicked town turncoat might unlatch the back-postern, or take bribes to welcome the enemy.'

But no assault in Alestron's proud history carried the threat levelled now.

Fionn Areth had shared the look-outs' reports. He had heard the opinions of Vhandon and Talvish, and eavesdropped on grim talk in the barracks. If today's white-capped view from the Sea Gate embrasure did not show the invidious advance at the harbour mouth, the truth was not secret: their sea-bound supply line was thwarted. Kalesh and Adruin commanded the narrows. The massed counters stacked on the duke's tactical maps also stymied the citadel's access by trade-road. Just as likely, the outer gates had been barred to stop nervous deserters from joining the enemy.

The more telling point, to Fionn Areth's stark eye, was how the sorcerer known as the Spinner of Darkness would grapple the appalling scale of sheer numbers. If the Teir's'Ffalenn elected to bestir himself, and risk Jeynsa's bid for protection; the grass-lander felt qualified to weigh the question. His own reprieve, snatched from the scaffold, had not been the pitched target of three kingdoms' fanatical muster.

'Charter law would seem scarcely a boon,' he declared. 'Or why else should you lump those of us without lineage in arse-kissing terms with your foemen?'

That touched a nerve, finally. Jeynsa straightened and stared. Green as fire in opal, her glance raked him. 'Ask your royal double how my father died. Then remember. The price in bloodshed on Daon Ramon Barrens was the cost of your rescue from Jaelot's executioner.'

'I was not made party to your prince's choice,' Fionn Areth said, a piercing fact to strike wind from his victim.

But not Jeynsa Teiren's'Valerient, who backed down from no scrap: whose arms underneath her short-sleeved leather jerkin wore bruises gained sparring with Sevrand at quarterstaves. 'You dare to pass judgement on me? Or set me up for comparison?'

Fionn Areth sustained her blistering stare. 'I condemn nothing,' he pronounced without shame. 'Rather, I'd ask: are you Arithon's friend or his enemy?'

That touched a nerve, also. Fanned rage chilled to ice. Jeynsa sized up the goatherd's antagonism, then dismissed his bold query, unflinching. 'You've spent too much time under Talvish's heel, in quarters with rank-and-file fighting men. They measure by nothing else but brute force, which dangerously narrows your view-point.'

'Then show me,' Fionn Areth insisted.

Jeynsa snapped up his challenge and led him through the town. Not from the vantage of the inner citadel, whose lofty battlements had been raised by Paravians. Not over the chain-bridge to the middle town district, where the cast shadow of pending attack dimmed the air with stirred dust from lance drills on the practice field. Nor where the squads of sweating men laboured, refining the range of the trebuchets. Instead, Jeynsa marched him into the arched carriage-way that fronted the ducal residence.

A wagon was parked by the carved, granite steps, with their pillars of Highscarp marble. The four-in-hand team at the hub of activity wore gleaming harness, brasses studded with Alestron's bull blazon. There, Jeynsa prevailed upon Mearn's pregnant wife, and asked for the two of them to accompany her on the daily rounds shared between the ranking s'Brydion women.

'Someone must hear and respond to the people,' Lady Fianzia explained to the baffled Araethurian. Her piled, blond hair was wound with strung pearls, a delicate accent to her jade dress, trimmed at the hem with white ribbon. Blunt as flint, despite the kestrel's build that seemed overwhelmed by her ripened belly, she tipped her chin towards the servant who loaded a stacked pile of hampers. 'Lend a hand. We'll be away, soonest.'

'You've packed bread for the needy?' Fionn Areth inquired, hefting baskets that smelled of fresh baking.

Fianzia arched her eyebrows in signal offence. 'Shame on you, goatherd! Alestron's seat rules under charter law!'

The grass-lander scowled through his tumbled, black hair. When he failed to amend his insulting mistake with apology, the lady gathered up her full skirt. She declined Jeynsa's help; leaned on the armed man-servant, who assisted her gravid weight up to the driver's seat.

'Get in, young fool!' The instant her passengers clambered aboard, she took reins and whip into tiny, ringed hands and rousted the team out with tart vehemence. 'Jeynsa was right. Your presumptions are dangerous. Stuck as you are with the face of a prince, you'd better learn quick what sets us apart from the usurping mayors.'

The wagon rolled out of the carriage-way to the brisk jingle of harness bells. Past the arched gate with its charging bull finials, Fianzia steered the gleaming horses down-slope. No novice, she jockeyed between the drays that ground uphill with stockpiled supply for the warehouses. She threaded the steep, switched-back turns and showed crisp courtesy to the other drivers. Baled fodder, crated livestock and chickens, barrels of flour and beer, and sacks of hulled oats and barley vied for space with packs of shouting children. From the smithies came chests of crossbolts and arrows, and for the defenceworks, the reeking scraped hides, bundled up green from the stock-yard.

Few vehicles moved outbound. Fianzia's wagon seemed out of place, breasting the war-time bustle past the stone mansions and officers' homes in the merchant precinct. Her place on the whip's box commanded no deference. The ducal badge on the lead horses' bridles was scarcely imposing enough to draw notice.

Yet the way parted for her. Amid din and turmoil, through dust and smoke, acrid with the bite of quenched steel and the charcoal fumes from the armourers', she drove like a breath of spring sunshine. Irascible carters granted her precedence. The armed guards at the barbican saluted her through. By now sweated over their burnish of grooming, the horses clopped through the slatted lanes, bordered by wood-frame tenements; past the tiny, fenced yards with their pecking hens, and the shuttered sheds, where the journeymen's shacks butted into the shops of the craft quarter.

Mearn's lady reined up at length in a cramped, public courtyard, criss-crossed with string lines drying laundry. The cobbles were slicked with puddles and run-off, centred by a neighbourhood well. Hung linen snapped on the sea-breeze. The tin strips of *iyat* banes jangled. Children in motley peeped through potted herbs and leaned at the railings of the outdoor stairways. Women with crying babes and toddlers in tow gossiped over yoke buckets, or else pounded soiled clothes in hooped tubs.

No citizen was ill-fed. The matrons' stout arms gleamed with bracelets. Some wore gemstone beads and enamel, and others, fine rings of wrought wire. The garments they scrubbed for their households were plain: stout broadcloth biased with wool, but not ragged. As Fianzia invited, the hampers were shared, food and wine passed with cheerful camaraderie.

While Fionn Areth and Jeynsa did a groom's work, and steadied the draught team's bridles, Fianzia sat down on the lowered tail-board. Patient, she listened to whatever subject the women who gathered might broach. She answered their questions, no matter how difficult, making no effort to hide that the siege would draw Lysaer's might to attempt their destruction. Duke Bransian had set aside barracks space. All families were invited to shelter within the Paravian-built walls of the upper citadel. Folk need do no more than submit their names to be assigned to a billet.

Several voices protested.

'We can't leave our craft shop!'

'My husband's smithy is all of our livelihood!'

Fianzia set down her wine goblet. 'Whoever decides not to evacuate won't be left abandoned without due protection.' She qualified through the expectant silence, as molasses sweets quieted the fretful children, and the pearl cincture just unwound from her hair was dangled to distract a wailing infant. 'No less than the duke's immediate family are entrusted to shoulder your safety.'

While the baby burbled and sucked on the pearls, Mearn's lady backed up her assertion: besides Parrien's fleet, harrying the coast with the ferocity of a wolf pack, Sevrand commanded the garrison at the Sea Gate, and the sentinel turrets flanking the harbour mouth. Field divisions under Keldmar secured the outlying farm-steads for the crofters, who cured the winter's meat in the smoke-houses and gathered the last cutting of hay.

Fianzia asked Fionn Areth to verify fact: that the captains at large stood with the front ranks, backing Bransian's staunchest veterans. Through Talvish, the grass-lander knew the details of Vhandon's latest strike forays. He was urged to describe the rings of set traps, engineered to bloody the enemy advance.

Since clan custom required a father's presence at birth, Mearn was the brother kept closest. 'My husband has charge of the outermost walls.' A steady hand laid on her swollen stomach, Fianzia finished her reassurances.

'Why doesn't she mention the trebuchets, or the placement of the new ballista?' Fionn Areth demanded of Jeynsa at a spiked whisper.

'Because every citizen born under s'Brydion rule has studied the engines of war. Didn't you notice the crews at their drill? They're craftsfolk.' Jeynsa swiped off the flies that bothered the harness horse under her charge, then added, 'Defence of these homes will not be left to chance. Every one of these wives knows her archery. The young here learn sword-play as school-children.'

Yet arrows and stone-shot and skilled handling of weapons could not stop an avatar wielding raw light.

Fionn Areth cringed, gut-sick to recall the legitimate claims: accounts sworn by townsmen elsewhere, that insisted clan mothers in the wilds of Deshir raised their children to wage bloody war. Daring, impatient, he pressed for the truth, if only to silence his conscience. 'If Tal Quorin's slaughter was not a mistake, s'Ilessid justice will make a clean end to the lie that puts steel in the hands of the innocent.'

Jeynsa did not strike him. She stared him down, until the unquiet shadow that darkened her eyes hackled him to clamped teeth.

Then she said, 'I'd have you witness the head-hunters' league at their work. Before being spread-eagled for rapine, then butchered with my scalp cut as trophy fringe on a saddle-cloth, I will teach my daughters to use a sharp knife. Or my sons, that your false avatar's *mercy* would see cuffed in irons and branded for slavery.'

'Only the criminal condemned row the galleys,' Fionn Areth retorted. 'Do you clansfolk not also slaughter for lies? How many of these people have been told they'll raise arms for a turncoat spy's act of treason?'

Jeynsa's smile was savage. 'Listen and learn.'

For a ruddy laundress now broached the issue headlong. 'Has anyone in Alestron borne recent witness to the s'Ilessid's rogue powers of Light?'

'Since Vastmark? Mearn has, when he served the duke's wiles as ambassador sent to Avenor.' Fianzia delivered the harsh assessment, unflinching. 'He would urge you, each one, to value your lives before your possessions.'

The impact of her quiet statement turned heads, that her husband was not stationed above the Mathiell Gate, beyond risk of the front line of fire. As nothing else could, the poise of Mearn's lady defined the steely integrity upholding the s'Brydion defence.

Tensioned quiet remained, torn by a wail as an aunt reached to rescue the pearls from the infant, who stuffed the whole string in his drooling mouth. No untouched observer, the lady tousled the babe's curls, then graciously left him the gift of her mangled jewellery. 'Keep your nephew and all of your kinsfolk safe,' she said, and smiled, and retired to the driver's seat on the wagon. 'As you will, give your names to the quartermaster at the gatehouse garrison.'

'Never! Not while your husband's at risk,' the smith's raw-boned relative declared. 'Should our courage be any less than your own?'

Mearn's lady inclined her head. She gathered the reins of the team in firm hands, while her oddly rankled young escort clambered aboard to ride on.

Stop after stop, Fianzia heard questions and spoke, and consoled countless fretful children. Her rounds did not finish until the last hamper was emptied. By then, the late shadows bled the warmth and colour out of the teeming streets.

The wagon team climbed uphill towards home. Fionn Areth and Jeynsa sat elbow to elbow on the dropped tail-board, backs nestled against the stacked basketry, while the flies buzzed over the lees in the wine jugs. Barking dogs, the screams of scavenging gulls, and the horn-call that foreran the watch change carried through the grind of the wheels. Day fled, while the shingle roofs dropped away in stepped tiers to the patchwork of fields, far beneath.

Against the cries of a street vendor hawking two penny charms for young lovers, the goatherd laced into contention again. 'You don't believe that your crown prince is blameless.'

'Did you see nothing in front of your eyes?' Jeynsa shoved erect, cold fire in her jade eyes. 'Do you think those families don't deserve to survive? Or that the indulgence of one man's sensibilities should be gratified at their expense? Why not ask Fianzia what kind of legacy she would leave to her unborn child? Life's owed, for a life.'

Certainly, there, history spoke in support: the s'Brydion withdrawal from Lysaer's campaign had salvaged the Master of Shadow's entrenched fight in Vastmark. Because of Mearn's warning, rushed out of Avenor, Tysan's clansmen had sent the timely message that enabled Dakar to unmask the Koriani snare laid to trap Arithon at Riverton.

'I don't call my liege to account for the sake of position, or lineage,' said Jeynsa s'Valerient with unblinking candour. 'I came because I believe in defending the lives of civilians. One might ask, Fionn Areth: what besides rancour draws you?'

'Truth,' the mulish Araethurian insisted. 'Since I lost a misplayed challenge at arms, I was promised the chance to determine whether your prince is a criminal killer. He's already been condemned, by Alliance decree.' Passion flamed, in blind disregard. 'At heart, do you know? Is your Teir's'Ffalenn the minion of evil declared by Lysaer as Spinner of Darkness?'

To which sweeping mouthful, Fianzia interjected, 'Rathain's prince is a man. Human enough to rue his mistakes and to challenge his outworn assumptions. That's what Mearn said, when I put the question. Grandame Dawr's tart wisdom agrees. If Liesse held the influence to batter her duke off his bone-headed complacency, I would not be lending false comfort to matrons! Alone, without loyalty to my marriage, I'd give birth at old Tirans, secure in the wilds of Atwood!'

The pinnacle towers of the citadel were bathed in the fading light of the afterglow, while twilight deepened over the outlying fields. To the captains at arms who safeguarded the ground before the remorseless advance, the swish of the crofters' scythes through the hayfields kept time to the tramp of the Alliance troops who marched in to the boom of the drums. The enemy established their lines beyond bowshot. They raised the banners of East Halla's towns, and other, far-northern garrisons, inbound from the sea routes past Vaststrait.

Alestron's farm-hands set their sweating backs to their work. Strove to turn a blind eye, even while harried by the intermittent whine of an arrow, or the punching crack of loosed crossbolts as hostile archers tested their range. The grain shocks were gathered and tied. Fodder was roped onto carts under torch-light, while across the plain, more fires lit the enemy, swarming to close for the siege.

'They'll have us bottled within a few days,' observed the grizzled scout, arrived overdue with fresh blood on his hands to recite his dismal report. 'Time to leave them a singeing wee present and run, if you'll hear my considered opinion.'

Keldmar laughed. 'Soon enough, laddie! Get along. Clean your knives. Rest and grab a hot meal.' To Vhandon, who leaned with his back to a sheep-gate, taciturn as weathered teak, he mused, 'Damn well not soon enough to sow havoc!'

The craggy field-captain never minced words. 'You've planned your parting gift for these invaders?'

'Haven't we just!' Keldmar's raffish stubble split with delight. 'The cook's cobbled up a spiked broth to be left on the hobs in the farm-wives' kitchens. Tastes like your granny's savoury soup. Goes down slick as butter besides. Too late, the Light's dupes'll be gushing like gossips, but from the duff end, doubled at the latrines.'

'Ath wept!' Vhandon had always been sharp on his feet. 'He used unboiled swamp water?'

Keldmar's smile turned evil. 'Dysentery's no damned fun in the field. Make a few whimpering pansies bolt for home, once their bung-holes chap raw and start bleeding. And anyway, bowmen cramped up with the squirts will have a rough time taking aim.' His sideward squint narrowed. 'Are you frisky, tonight? I've an errand needs running inside enemy lines.'

'Never ask,' Vhandon stated. 'My troop's at the ready.'

They would be more than keen; Keldmar's sibling had once loaned this war-captain to Arithon to clear a debt for mishandling. The veteran campaigner had been returned, but resharpened: depth now ran beneath that straight-thinking intelligence.

Though Keldmar shared the s'Brydion penchant for armed force, he was not the brainless brawn he appeared, to blindside his opponents. As he realized the older man measured his mood, he looked away.

'I want you to go in yourself,' he declared. 'Have the villagers' hedge witch fashion some talismans to muddle Lysaer's sighted priests. Then pick ten from your company and find out when the false avatar plans to arrive.'

Vhandon took pause. Then he said, gently blunt, 'Since my presence should not be required for that mission, what do you fear to expose?'

Keldmar's frown tightened. He was never easy with intimate questions. Vhandon was his elder by more than ten years; had been the mentor he had stretched to match in callow youth as example. Never Bransian's prized field officer by accident, all but a part of the family, now Vhandon was given the role of a scout whose assignment ran beyond dangerous.

'Why?' Vhandon prompted, as silence extended, thick with the tang of banked cookfires, and the musty scent after hard frost. 'What do you dread for me, or yourself?'

'Avenger's own death!' Keldmar swore. 'I'd not send you to a sure end as a suicide!'

'No,' Vhandon agreed. Tonight, against his natural grain, he let down his granite mask. 'But both of us have too much seasoned experience. Survival may force me to return your answer by signal arrow, then stage my escape through the far side of the lines. If you want me shut safely out of this war, I deserve to know what you're thinking.'

Keldmar recoiled, then curbed his venomous retreat. 'Ath, I can't hide this! We've fought at each other's shoulder for too long.' How he hated to grapple the emotions he preferred to vent, picking blustering fights. 'You realize Jeynsa's decision must break Prince Arithon's ultimatum. With his Grace gone, you freely gave your loyalty back to Alestron. But sitting here, I don't know how to ask what you feel.' Anguished, he clenched the fists crossed at his knee. 'Are you fighting because Bransian gave no other choice? Or do you honestly think we can win this?'

Before Vhandon's response, Keldmar smashed on, 'If the Master of Shadow returns to spare Jeynsa, how will you reconcile your split allegiance?' Then, 'No!' he snapped, over stripped nerves and hurt, 'No, don't speak! I've granted you space to choose your own fate because I don't want to hear how you'll answer!'

'I'll tell you, anyway,' Vhandon persisted. 'Doubt packs more damage, kept secret.' His stalwart manner ploughed on with an eloquent care that was new. 'I don't know what the future will bring us, or what fate may befall your brothers. But my birthright lies here. This is my home ground. I won't be dusting my hands of our friendship, or bolting for Atwood.' Through a tensioned breath, he regarded the sky, pricked by cold stars and a rising moon through the gathering sea-mist. His form was a statement of unshattered strength, from the trim of his officer's surcoat, to the competent hang of his sword and his matched brace of knives.

That self-possession lent Vhandon the vulnerable daring to hazard the rest. 'There are depths to Prince Arithon few understand. I've lost my temper with him often enough. And bled from the heart every time I've encountered the mercy he shields behind satire. That hurt made me change. I had to drop every rigid concept I held over the meaning of honour. Though I don't see your duke's act of war the same way, I won't disown my roots. If your citadel stands, it will be for right reasons. If it falls, what survives will be raised out of ruin, reforged with more flexible temper.'

Though Keldmar's casual posture was forced, and the grip on his knee now was shaking, Vhandon finished off with a love that exposed without flinching.

'My commitment is made to serve Alestron. Lean on the fact I will stay here. Our needs have never been separate, my friend. Brought against his free will, his Grace of Rathain is going to be savaged by pressures no one can foresee. You will need a bridge. If your family name can survive this unscathed, you'll have Talvish and me at your side to stand as liaison.'

Keldmar pushed erect, too embarrassed to bare his own spirit. 'You don't need to go, personally,' he allowed, cringing red. 'Any ten trusted scouts are sufficient to handle this foray instead.'

'No, friend, they're not.' Vhandon surveyed the man who had grown in his shadow, since their earliest days wielding practice sticks. They had shared the joy. The same punishment, too, nursing the bruises and triumphs that raised them to mastery-at-arms. For all Keldmar's juggernaut muscle and will, despite the courage that wedded his life to s'Brydion defence, he nursed a bitter uncertainty. Tonight, no sharpened sword or soft word could assuage the storm raging inside him.

His blood heritage had been hounded by enemies for too long. Survival came at too high a cost for a blindfolded leap on another man's faith.

As darkness fell, marred by the fires and smoke of the enemy war host, the field-captain longest in active service held his peace. He knew not to try his titled commander with a comforting clasp on the shoulder. 'I will go in myself,' he insisted, flat calm. 'But only to prove my conviction as truth to rely on, when I return.'

The second Alliance entourage was dispatched to confront the s'Brydion stronghold at daybreak, well after Vhandon's picked squad had departed.

This pass, the approach to Alestron's barred gate was attempted by the Alliance's gaunt Lord Justiciar. That worthy proposed no amicable settlement. Clad in arrogance and finery, he bore the Light's sealed arraignment against the recalcitrant duke and his blood family. No one spared time for his pompous town document, sent by a posturing upstart. Since his glittering cavalcade never asked leave, Bransian also declined every civil respect. No safe conduct was granted.

Lysaer's polished state overture encountered, instead, Keldmar's entrenched field troop, and one arrow, shot dead-centre through the cloth-of-gold blazon worn by its delegate.

The corpse was packed off at an indecorous gallop. Pounding after the caparisoned horse, the Light's ceremonial escort took panicked flight, spurred ragged by more hostile volleys released by Alestron's crack marksmen. Sunwheel banners made irresistible targets, flushed into routing retreat. Cocky defenders leaped at the excuse to display their frustrated prowess. The exercise inspired Keldmar's outlying companies to skilled contest and spirited wagers. No one else died. But the avatar's stainless, white standard returned, sliced to fluttering rags in the hands of the rattled bearer.

The savaged procession reached friendly lines. Too hot to rein up, they belted in lathered disorder through the troop tents of the central encampment. If they dressed their torn ranks before they slowed down, nothing could mend their decorum. The murdered corpse of Lysaer's titled emissary woke turmoil and rage in its wake. Camp-followers shouted. Wash women and cooks broke away from their wagons to scream with indignation. Dedicates and new recruits faltered at arms drill, then jumped as their sergeants barked to upbraid their strayed focus.

Through the tolling bells of alarm, and the outcries of furious priests, the officers bugled for order. The sharpened swords, and the honed sinew of men might be promised for war against Shadow. But not before the Light's avatar chose to unsheathe the aimed spear of his vengeance.

Therefore, the horse with its blood-stained burden was passed through the innermost check-point. The mauled cavalcade crossed the gamut of garrison flags and filed past the officers' quarters. Now trailed by an irate mob of captains, they came to a stop at the white-and-gold canopy that fronted the Sunwheel pavilion.

The experienced strategist from new Tirans held charge of the Alliance command, ranked second beneath the Lord Sulfin Evend, still absent to levy troops on the southcoast. A blustery man not given to patience, he burst from the tent in a spatter of shaving soap to dress down the tumultuous intrusion. His balding servant chased after, in vain: the offered towel was hammered aside by the livid standard-bearer, who brandished his shredded banner and howled in shame for the injury.

'By Dharkaron's Spear, I haven't gone blind!' The lather was swiped off with an immaculate bracer, while the displaced equerry winced. 'We're not here to mince words over etiquette! Nor is an enemy who won't negotiate any cause for hysterics!'

The field-captain advanced on the clustered horsemen. A hulking tyrant, he silenced their clamouring and issued brisk orders for the slaughtered envoy. 'Bear our casualty inside. Then bring the women who work for the healers. I want the Lord Justiciar's body laid out straightaway. He'll be honoured in state with new robes and candles. Move to it! Clean him up before the Blessed Prince and his retinue arrive with the Mayor of Kalesh!'

Two liveried servants left at a sprint, while the armed hotheads set hands to drawn swords, prepared to rally the ranks.

'Stand down!' barked the captain. 'No one *moves* without leave! Damn you, those horses are too hot to be standing. Where are the boys to attend them?'

The chastised riders dismounted, while the idle grooms jumped to take charge of their blowing mounts.

Engulfed by that bottled-up swirl of banked rage were two onlooking bumpkin recruits. They still wore the sunburn of toil in the field, rough-clad in the stained boots and coarse cloth of crofters.

'You there!' bawled the thick-set master of horse, too overburdened not to collar the available by-standers. 'Hop to! We've got bridles to clean and soiled brass that needs polish!'

The pair were shoved forward by one of the sergeants and heaped with armloads of stripped harness. The older one tugged his grey forelock and bent to unbuckle stained bits, while his freckled companion fetched a bucket and rag, and crouched over the task foisted on them.

'We're hooked, now,' the younger one fretted, as pandemonium continued to inflame the surrounding Alliance encampment. 'We've got to reach Keldmar. Dharkaron's black bollocks, he's got to be warned the false avatar's due on the front lines in an hour!'

Vhandon buffed the rimed dirt from a curb chain and frowned. 'Be still! Mind your tongue. Slouch your posture, and damned well stop acting desperate. We've got to wait for a safe opening to slip out.'

The impatient scout with him snatched up the next head-stall. 'What if the moment fails to present?'

Vhandon shrugged, absorbed. 'Then we do our best to create one. If we fail, there's no gain in suicide. We bide on the hope that someone from our party finds his chance and wins through.'

Climbing sun burned off the last wisp of sea-mist. The camp hummed, set in ominous order, with too many sentries left sharp at their posts in the atmosphere of agitation. The two covert observers cleaned bridles with lowered heads, while Tirans' abrasive captain at arms convened a council of war. He could not give the order to deploy the Light's troops. But zeal could ensure the men were prepared to fight at a moment's notice.

The shed pile of harness was only half-cleaned, when Lysaer s'Ilessid arrived on his dappled charger. He reined in, a white cloud against storm amid the mounted guard wearing the silver-and-sable surcoats of Kalesh. From shining blond hair to immaculate appointments, to eyes glinting blue as cut sapphire, the avatar's presence seared sight to witness. Men in his shadow were reduced to servants, but never so callously disregarded. Lysaer's smile of welcome to his least groom made the bearded, blunt mayor in his gaudy wealth an over-stuffed caricature.

Both men dismounted. For an instant, the attentive descent of trained staff obscured the immediate view.

Then the acting captain at arms shoved from the shaded pavilion. Massive and rumpled, he forced his way through. Man and horse, groom and equerry, the tableau before the staked standards and awnings crystallized to expectation.

Sunlight shone down on snowy silk and cold majesty as the dawn's urgent news reached the Blessed Prince.

'Ath above, show us mercy and sense!' murmured Vhandon, unwittingly stunned. No thought had prepared him as his lungs stopped with awe. He had never expected such beauty and strength, or the *impact* of Lysaer s'Ilessid's innate charisma.

Every retainer's rapt face showed that grace. His brief smile to the least, insignificant page could have fuelled a torch by sheer caring.

Before *this*, the patient years spent unravelling Arithon's reticent quiet became as a dream, scoured off by noon heat.

Then the moment passed. The pavilion's flap was thrust open again. More ranking officers rushed out in a pack, declaiming Keldmar's brute ferocity. Lysaer asked them for calm. Against abashed silence, he demanded the recount of his Lord Justiciar's murder.

There came no self-righteous cry to raise arms. No flourish of trumpets to strike in retaliation. Lysaer stood firm. Upright as the poised spear-shaft, he heard through his officers' riled account with focused attention. That stillness gripped him for one second more. Not a diamond stud on his gold-braided collar flashed in the flood of the morning.

Then he said, 'Fetch the banner-bearer who carried the Light's abused standard. I want a front-rank witness to corroborate.'

'But of course!' Flushed by self-conscious embarrassment, the subordinate captain from Tirans backed down. Movement ruffled the packed horsemen as he sent an equerry, bearing the summons. Liveried grooms crept on with their chores, apologetically gathering reins and running up dangling stirrup-irons. Inert in their midst, Kalesh's flummoxed mayor watched the proceedings like dead wood.

'Carry on,' murmured Lysaer. His wave dismissed the hovering escort. Sun burned through his jewels, as he raised taut fingers and raked back his sweat-damp blond hair. For that brief moment, he averted his face, a seamless pause, apparently made to ease his overwrought company. The wise leader with setbacks allowed his fraught men to vent their unconstrained reactions.

Yet the perfect, staged move granted Vhandon full view, as the impact touched Lysaer's expression.

He looked tortured with pain. Sorrow transformed his face. Given his stance, he now had to act, regardless of personal preference. *He was no born killer*. Only a man, dedicated to courage, who carried a steadfast commitment. He commanded selflessly, and without stint. But never without thought: *and not without feeling the hideous cost for the retribution he must now carry forward.*

Soul spoke, in that instant of scalding agony, torn down to honest revulsion. For Lysaer's sworn covenant to stay unbroken, he would bear the weight of the service he had pledged all his resource to defend.

Then the distraught standard-bearer arrived. Lysaer straightened to meet him; reforged the façade that claimed to be avatar, and with the purity of his conviction, requested the spoken truth.

Hush fell over the officers gathered for council. Their advice was not asked. None ventured to speak, while the barbaric fate of the Light's dead ambassador became repeated in full. Lysaer s'Ilessid did not interrupt. Every inch of him royal, he listened as though each stammered word was the last sound in the world.

Then, as fresh anger savaged the ranks, shouting for blood in redress, Lysaer raised his fist.

Silence descended. 'Fetch another white stallion,' he bade. 'Bridle and saddle him in full state panoply.'

As his dismounted lancers crowded and begged for the chance to bear arms as his vanguard, Lysaer turned them down. 'I have no need for protection! No call to risk you, or rely on your bravery. Not for this, the opening hour that the Light is called to scour this land of hypocrisy.'

'You will burn them out!' exclaimed the war-captain from Tirans. 'Rout the enemy with fire until the citadel boils to magma!'

'I support no such cruelty!' Lysaer pealed back. His cool purpose was unassailable, a chiselled display that cowed those men closest, and pressed the faint-hearted to unwitting retreat. Justice enforced the gap between the aroused dedicates and their hailed idol.

'The enemy captain of Alestron's field defences was the man who delivered the honourless order to fire. His archers enacted this uncivilized death. The farm-hands they defended condoned the crime. These are the guilty. I shall not tear down walls! Or destroy innocent town citizens over an action they did not commit!'

The crestfallen officer flushed. Around him, his fellows shifted, abashed, as though the ground trembled beneath them.

Against that crushed pause, where none dared opinion, the Mayor of Kalesh cleared his throat and clapped the shoulder of Lysaer's white surcoat. 'My Blessed Lord! That's ingenious strategy! Of course, if you raze the field troops alone, those trapped inside the citadel will mew themselves up. They'll crowd in panic and stress their own garrison, while we set our leisurely course for a siege.' His shark's smile widened. 'We can watch in comfort as the s'Brydion fortress becomes overburdened, then starved to submission.'

Lysaer s'Ilessid's smile curdled with frosty politeness. 'Quite, as you say.' He sucked a sharp breath. 'Except, for civility, I will deliver their barbaric duke his due warning.'

His poised fist stirred. Lean fingers snapped, once. Out of clear air rose a pillar of light. The beacon pierced like a needle towards heaven, dazzling unshielded sight. The self-proclaimed avatar shone for the masses. He became as the blade of the unsheathed sword, crowned in white fire and diamonds.

'Mercy!' gasped Vhandon, forgetting the young scout, who shared equal danger beside him.

How could any man bear to witness such splendour? How not to become bedazzled by triumph? Could any mortal mind fail to be stirred by the clarion cry to honour the moral high ground?

'Mercy alive!' Vhandon wept, torn in pieces, and all but seduced by the lure of sheer fascination. Such glory could not do other than blaze. Every last blinded follower would marry their efforts to what seemed a lofty ideal. Those who cheered with their dazed eyesight sealed would hurl themselves into a life-and-death struggle. By sheer mass and numbers, they would kill every standing troop caught in their path.

Vhandon ached for hope's loss. He was alone, clenched fast in the breach. His hand was not other than human. No field-captain possessed a sorcerer's wisdom. To denounce the false avatar in the enemy camp could only bring swift self-destruction. The horrific thought chilled him: *that he was informed.* Had he not held an intimate association with Arithon, he would not have escaped the insanity. Would not have grasped what these followers never had grace to perceive: that this war had been seeded by Desh-thiere's curse. If not for the memory of a clearer music, called forth from a Paravian-made sword, Vhandon realized he could have been swept off his feet. Too easily, ignorance swayed decent men to cast their lot with the Light's mustered soldiers.

Yet he *had* heard. His vision saw past ennobled passion as the bridled white stallion arrived, and its blond rider accepted the reins. Lysaer received the dazzled salutes of his officers, then strode forward to mount.

Which left ten s'Brydion liegemen still masked under cover inside the enemy's camp. They could send no word, before the forces unleashed. Make no move, lest they risk their companions. Alone, they held out on the rags of torn will. For they knew, beyond doubt: their duke's brash defiance was futile.

Such rage masked under self-righteous nobility would spark the irrevocable fire and not rest until the citadel was reduced to ashes.

Autumn 5671

Strike

The first blow unleashed by the white rider exploded, an eruption of light that burst like a scream from the eye of a malevolent sunrise. The conflagration roared forth as a wave, storming across the hedged pastures, and breaking the outlying farm-steads under a blast of annihilating heat. The flash-point lasted but a fleeting instant. Yet amid the booming report of shocked air, the fields and hayricks surrounding the s'Brydion citadel were engulfed by scouring flame. The scourge destroyed everything: devoured all in its path without any breath of resistance.

No hamlet escaped the sweeping assault. No farm-wife or miller or child was spared, no matter that they were innocents. The thatch and timber over their heads became torched at one hammering stroke. Chimney stones were reduced to slag, tumbled over the carbon scorched earth, where all life was stripped of animal industry and autumn-rich foliage.

Smoke drifted, stinking, where moments before, crofters had scythed the last cutting of straw and raked the cured stalks into windrows. The drays and ox teams were immolated also, bone and carcasses scattered to ash; undone alongside them, the steadfast, armed guard of Keldmar's veteran troops. No man in the open lived to report. Lumped metal remained of wrought weapons and wheel rims, glowing dull cherry upon the sere ground.

Inside the burst barns, where the bulwarks of revetted stone had been melted, the shrieks of a handful of light-scalded sentries shattered the morning quiet. They were the misfortunate few, roasted to agony until death could relieve their wracked suffering.

Vhandon and his picked company of scouts witnessed the horrific flare of the assault while set on the run. Half a league to the north, miserably huddled in a marshy covert that verged the enemy camp, they had never dispatched the warning to spare their commander. In flight for their lives, they had hoped to swing wide and cross the far side of the lines.

As the rumbling report shook the earth, and pummelled wind through the frost-killed hummocks, Vhandon needed force to restrain his young men.

'Hold fast where we stand!' While an unhinged scout surged to avenge his dead family, Vhandon tripped the man's rush, then clouted his nape and dropped him sprawling. 'D'you think you're the only one that's bereaved?' A stiff swallow, to jam back the upsurge of grief none could afford at the battle-front. Vhandon snapped, emptied, 'I just lost a son! His wife bore my grand-children, four of them, gone! By Ath, you'll keep courage, if I can!'

He helped the weeping man to his feet. 'Steady on. Bear this! Believe what I know of the wars fought before! None of us can outface Lysaer's powers. Nor can we salvage what's wrecked, or snatch back one life delivered to Daelion's judgement!'

'If the field troop's razed down, we're now cut off, here!' a rattled veteran argued, afraid. Parching gusts raked from the blast site in back-lash, hard enough to suck tears from dry eyes, and wilt the brush that provided inadequate cover.

'Down!' Vhandon ordered. 'Smear your faces with mud!'

But no skulking tactic allayed his dread: that no defence at arms might mount a counter-strike against the baleful fires of the s'Illessid gift. With Keldmar's field troops lost, the cruel fact wrecked morale: that the citadel's lower walls lacked the shielding grace of the ancient Paravian craftwork. Every man nursed the horrific pain. Caught in hiding, they seethed to act before abject destruction should slaughter their fellows on guard at the trade gate.

As a second fool moved to draw steel, Vhandon clamped a harsh fist. 'No! Stay your hand! You'd bring death upon us, and for what? A martyr's end here will serve nothing!'

'Merciful Ath!' The man shook with rage. 'My wife and kinsfolk are still alive inside the lower citadel.' Over dry coughs, as another man vomited, he vented his raging despair. 'This false avatar can destroy us all on a whim. I can't skulk here and suffer the ruin of all I hold dear in this life!'

'You've forgotten!' Vhandon slashed back. By ice-water nerves, he *would* pull these men clear, wrestle their poisoned stew of emotions until they could be steered from lethal danger. 'Keldmar s'Brydion had the savagery to murder an accredited ambassador!' Feet braced, his callused fist locked in restraint, the field-captain crushed sapping distress; forced reason above shock and heart-break. 'We can't measure the toll of destruction from here! Can't know the full story, until we make our way beyond the direct line of fire.'

While the screaming winds lashed the turned leaves from scrub maples, and whipped smoke hazed the pristine morning, the ranked sergeant among them responded. 'Our innermost walls were designed to stop drakefire. Surely the heart of the citadel stands secure!'

Yet even if their duke's banner still flew, the experienced eye must acknowledge that their straits had gone from dire to desperate. Fellowship intervention might preserve Atwood's timber inside of East Halla's free wilds. But the shipworks at Kalesh and Adruin stayed supplied by the zeal of the Sunwheel Alliance. Their galleys would import cut lumber from elsewhere. Cordwainers and craftsmen pressed by the campaign would labour to erect siege engines. With Alestron stripped at one stroke of her field troops, the duke's superbly trained men-at-arms were left in no position to stop the advance.

Construction could start within range of the outside walls. Lysaer's ruthless gift could burn down the defensive board hoardings. Clearly, the first line of fortifications was useless.

'Depend on this much!' Vhandon cracked with brute honesty. 'We'll see sappers mining our last unbreached wall before the full onset of winter.'

Thrown back on resolve, he jammed on his helm. 'Talk will not save us! Nor can retreat serve a thing but add our hungry mouths to the strapped needs of our countrymen.' Grim as carved oak, Vhandon turned his back on the smoke-hazed wrack of the farm-steads. 'Stand firm with me! Use our loyalty wisely. Outside, as free agents, we can best serve our duke through covert raids and harassment.'

The blast that scorched Alestron's pastures and fields outstripped any word for destruction. Inside the s'Brydion citadel, the explosion enacted stunned shock, an inbreath before pandemonium: the painstaking lists with the garrison's scribes were no longer going to matter; detailed inventories of food stocks and barrels of preserved rations were thrown into eclipse by the staring shadow of crisis.

Panic struck every man, woman, and child as the city's craft quarter was confronted by the stark scope of the wreckage. The false avatar's ultimatum had been served upon the ashes of competent troops, loyal officers, and bystanding innocents. The act shattered morale. Unless every member of the duke's family should be delivered to Lysaer's justice in chains, today's rain of fire and light would not end. Not before the Fatemaster's Wheel had turned, and the last life was reaped out of havoc. Hold fast to their own, and the folk of Alestron were foredoomed, with all ties to diplomacy forfeit.

The crushing aftermath fell hardest of all on the defending companies posted at the outer walls. Mearn s'Brydion suffered the brunt, as their commander at arms.

The cocky dandy in him was no longer recognizable. Ripped haggard, his neat surcoat singed by the cinders that swirled as the scorched air recoiled, he retched on his knees, gagged by the reek of singed meat. His equerry, his officers, and the fleet-footed boy who ran his messages were wrung just as wretched beside him. They all fought to breathe, as the poisonous pall of hot smoke rolled off the surrounding, raped acres.

Mearn dared not languish. He choked down rank nausea and his cry of grief, for the death of a feckless brother. Though loss savaged his heart, and his sword-arm was burned, he straightened, then moved: grabbed the nearest of his shaken captains, and yanked him onto his feet. 'Jervald! Now! I need you to find Talvish! We have people to help. Whole families and tradesmen. They aren't safe until they're secured inside of the upper citadel!'

Emergency gave them no time to organize. Every war-hardened veteran Mearn could haze must salvage the grit to respond. 'Halve the numbers who were standing watch on the walls! Draw lots for the duty. The rest will retire at once to the streets! Get the populace out! Brandish arms, threaten bodily harm if you must! Damn your eyes! *Rouse yourselves*! To Dharkaron, the slackers who falter to stare! Surmount this, or die! Every second we crumble to terror hurts our chances of long-term survival!'

Mearn kicked the prostrate weepers. He slapped men's slumped shoulders, then snatched up a dropped halberd to prod on the stunned, all the while shouting in vicious language to roust the numbed and immobile. 'You louses, get *up*! We cannot mend today's blast of destruction. *All* of our safety depends on swift action! You and you! Pick ten others. Commandeer every hand-cart and wagon! Seize any transport to shift the infirm.'

For no grace was given: already the screaming and cries in the streets surged towards riot. Worse, Mearn tripped over a man on his knees. The fellow moaned with inconsolable pain. Both sticky hands were pressed to raw burns, his blistered face utterly ravaged.

'Ath's pity,' Mearn gasped, jolted sick. Hapless men on the walls had been struck blind. Trusty sentries, caught wide-eyed in the breach, in the moment the light burst before them. Already, their scorched sockets and agonized torment gutted the nerves of their fellows.

'Hold on, man! Bear up! We'll get you a healer.' Mearn's biting grip on the stricken man's shoulder was no less than brutally desperate. He must restore reason, no matter the cost. Or else terrified confusion was going to claim more than the slain caught outside the defences.

Spurred by necessity, Mearn handed the wounded man off to his comrades. Then he sprinted through the disarray on the battlements, yelling sharp orders to rally. 'You! Lieutenant! Get the injured together. Have one sighted man keep them calm. Send a sensible sergeant to commandeer someone skilled to treat them! You there, no snivelling! March your squad through the streets. Man, woman, and child, everybody moves out of here! I will have no stragglers. No one gets left behind! The least grandame and elder must not be overlooked in the crush! I want the craft quarter emptied by sundown, with no one's excuses for failure!'

The task lying ahead was enough to crush dauntless spirits, beforetime: not only were the non-combatants unsafe. Now unbridled fear posed the s'Brydion clan holding a lethal liability. In dread for their lives, or the well-being of their children, what forthright citizen or threatened merchant might not sell out to appease Lysaer's ruthless ferocity?

Then Talvish arrived, a rock in a storm, in the soot-blackened rags of his surcoat. A rash of blisters disfigured his cheek where the light's strike had glancingly brushed him. Though his fair hair was singed, and his jade eyes, struck numb by awareness that Vhandon had been caught outside with Keldmar's slaughtered field troop, he needed no part of Mearn's hoarse entreaties to grasp the huge scope of disaster.

'I've got teams of men working through house to house.' Rasped raw, he coughed; swiped let blood from his brow, laid open by fragmented debris. 'Jeynsa and Fionn Areth were packed off straightaway. They suffered no harm!' he reassured, fast, before Mearn recoiled to worry. The ghost of a rueful shrug, as he added, 'Though Daelion Fatemaster's judgement bear witness! The goatherding idiot wears a bruise on the jaw for the privilege. Nothing would make him stop yammering but my fist.'

Mearn swallowed. He had no stomach left. Only the jagged ache of despair, which found no direction to lean for reassurance. 'You know the s'Ilessid will strike us again. How we can possibly move to secure the bone and marrow of our skilled tradesmen?'

Talvish shook his head. He could offer nothing beyond the tact he had learned the hard way, serving Arithon. 'You were never the fool, Mearn,' he prodded, most gently. 'As the ambassador sent to Avenor, what do you think from experience?'

And the brutalized, youngest s'Brydion brother shivered, as the pain stared him down. Wreathed in stinking smoke, he allowed, 'Lysaer will serve justice. You think we were spared to be offered reprieve? Then woe betide us when we turn a blind eye. For as I stand here, I already know. My brother Bransian will be crazed with rage. Family pride will not let him surrender.'

'Best pray that you're wrong,' Talvish stated then, sorrow braced by war-hardened tenacity. 'But should you be right, I think we'll be given as much time as we need. If only to set the hook in the fish. Lysaer's a strategist. He'll hang back. Allow us to stew, until we're worn-out by our agony.'

Few could match Mearn for bravado. He nodded once; swiped back his soaked hair. Amid ugly shouts risen from the clogged streets, through the echoes slapped off the stone revetments, he clapped Talvish's back. 'You're cruel as Dharkaron's Chariot, my friend.' Reckless causes sparked off his penchant for gambling. 'We can't give way, now. Just spike the odds higher. Upset the presumption, that more mouths in the citadel will starve us to submission the faster.'

Talvish rubbed his temples to ease his pounding head, then reset his helm with grim purpose. 'Nobody's fooled. But the trust of the populace has to be kept.'

Mearn's hollowed face tightened. 'Well at least we won't be afflicted by troops gripped in the throes of vile practice!' Since Arithon had raised the grand chord at Etarra, the hideous threat posed by the Kralovir's meddling had been unequivocally routed.

Yet on that reprieve, Talvish spoke no word of false platitude. Unlike the high-strung intelligence before him, he had witnessed Prince Arithon's personal torment, just after the Fellowship's charge was accepted. For the dread future, who but a Sorcerer dared measure the price of the miscast blame that now impelled Lysaer's Alliance to war?

Alestron might yet bear the terrible cost of that shining victory.

Yet a self-possessed man with Mearn's sensitive character, who had also just lost a brother, was no spirit to be forced to reckon with future intangibles.

'Let us do what we can for your people.' Hard-set, dedicated to practical mercy, Talvish shouldered his captaincy. He was no sorcerer, no musician, no blood-born seer stung by the vista of far-sighted consequence. He accepted that he had naught else to give but the conviction of human resolve.

Consequence

Night followed night, while the townsfolk of Alestron held their collective breath. Under confusion and back-breaking labour, the lower citadel accomplished its evacuation. The winds stank of ash. The drays that stripped the emptied homes of their blankets and food stores moved through air clogged like tarnish, with each breath men took made harsh with silted dust and the scorched taint of debris. Keldmar's distraught widow could not be consoled. At Dame Dawr's behest, Parrien's wife shouldered the burden of loss, making rounds to acknowledge the field garrison's bereft families.

Pitched sleepless by Duke Bransian's white-heated rage, the elite guard held their posts on the innermost walls, while Mearn's captains oversaw the chaotic influx of distraught refugees without faltering. The looming spectre of siege was not new. Behind the massive keeps that guarded the Mathiell Gate, amid starlit dark, Alestron's stalwart companies imposed order. They kept watch, while the inner citadel's burdened resources became strained, then overwhelmed by the crush of displaced families and craftsfolk. Through the night hours, when torches were doused to sharpen the night-vision of the sentries, the storytellers spoke in the overcrowded encampments jammed into the open baileys. They recited the course of bygone history, passed down through each generation.

The citadel's inhabitants were reminded again: they were a proud people, descended from the deeds of high hearts and war heroes . . .

The first flame of the uprising remained unforgotten, when insurgent townsmen had crept through the houses and halls, slaughtering resident clanborn. On that dread night, the reigning s'Brydion duke and his family had died in their beds, betrayed by their own merchants' henchmen. The clan heir who survived to stand off the assault had escaped execution because he had jilted his wife to indulge himself with a mistress. Naked, sprung from bed by a panicked page, he had rallied the Mathiell garrison. Alongside the watch captain, he and the skeleton company on duty had barricaded themselves inside the flanking drumkeeps. They had cocked the catapults. Hurled flaming bladders of oil into the rioters sweeping the streets.

To the screams of the dying, friend, family, and foeman, they had hardened their nerves. In cold desperation, to foil snipers with cross-bows, they had loaded the massive arbalests with fire-bolts and torched the wood span to the Wyntok Gate.

Even after six and a half centuries, the echo of horror still lingered: of the hour that the floors in the ducal palace ran wet with the blood of the slain. As the cries of their murdered kinsmen and children shrilled under winter starlight, the trapped guard, who were fathers lashed insane by grief, had forced through a suicidal sortie. Their berserk rage had burst from the barricaded keeps, leading the charge that smashed through the insurgent force holding the palace gate. A few knots of fighting survivors rallied to their initiative. Half-clad, or armed, or bearing the stubs of smashed furnishings, they cleared the streets of the inner citadel by killing all comers who failed to fall in at their side through the melee.

By dawn, the flag with the s'Brydion bull blazon still streamed from the height of Watch Keep. While angry factions denouncing the Paravian presence still ravaged the craft district down-slope, the assault that had murdered the reigning duke was repulsed, and its backing ringleaders faced with a siege . . .

The legacy inherent in Alestron's oldest revetments had withstood far more than the savagery of human rebellion: the innermost walls had been crafted by Paravians, centuries before the Fellowship's compact had granted surety for mankind's refuge on Athera. History spoke, in sealed stones: the mysteries of centaur masons and the flutes of the Athlien singers had laid down defences against concerted attacks by Khadrim, themselves errant offspring spun into form by the dreams of grief-maddened dragons. The sea-tides that ripped through the sluice from the inlet had flushed the let blood of besiegers, even before the Third Age insurgents cast down the high kings enthroned by the Sorcerers.

Alestron guarded her freedom, this day, by the gift of her forebears' resiliency.

So the spinners of tales and the bards reassured the frightened mothers and their clinging children. Brave epics were offered to bolster the uprooted families who faced horror, and certain privation . . .

When the next traitorous assault tried to storm the high citadel from beyond the burned span of the bridge, the attackers had been shattered by archers and sliced to ribbons in routed defeat. Starvation served as the enemy's weapon, then. The innermost defences were forced to endure a dreadful four months, spent besieged. Children were taught to overset scaling ladders. Grandames boiled oil to flush out the sewers encroached on by enemy sappers. As supplies failed, the populace ate the garrison's horses, then turned to trapping the rats in the culverts. The hale learned to wield weapons, regardless of age. Dress-makers used their thread to wind fletching and refurbish arrow shafts. Each wave of attack had been broken at harrowing cost, in the tidal chasm under the cliffs of the Mathiell Gate. Names were remembered, and acts of selfless sacrifice, until the town rebels' resources were mangled, and finally worn to exhaustion . . .

The duke's restored banner had never been struck. Men on the embrasures, and grandsires making shift to watch toddlers were told over the fact as a litany.

Yet where yester-year's brutal rising against charter law had accosted the s'Brydion by stealth, the offensive waged now by Lysaer's Alliance resumed the ominous massing of troops. From the upper walls and the sea-misted battlements, Alestron's penned citizens watched their industrious enemy, unlading timbers from galleys. They heard the chants, as the work crews dragged lumber over the blackened earth of their wrecked farm-steads. Wind carried the groaning of the log carriages that fed the insatiable saws of the carpenters. Hammers banged, to the shouts of the engineers' overseers. Just out of weapons' range, swarms of conscript labourers constructed the wheeled shelters for sappers; the frame slings for the rams; and the squat, spring-cocked arbalests, that would fire pronged grapples or incendiary arrows over the crenels and walls.

Such activity was not reserved to the ground scorched lifeless by Lysaer's first overture.

Wooden structures notched the hills, where no timber grew: a leafless frame-work of scaling towers, the throwing arms of wheeled trebuchets, and the squatter beams that would mount the notched winches that cocked back the mangonels.

The Light's forces closed by the muscle of ox teams. Their inexorable, creeping pace advanced less than a league, in a day. Soon, only hours remained, before the duke's stronghold became surrounded.

At the last moment, three furtive, cloaked figures ran the Alliance gauntlet. Their desperate mission aimed to enter the citadel, before the poised war host established position. They skulked by the eyes of the enemy; slipped under the arcane vigilance of Lysaer's initiate priesthood by crawling through middens. They slunk, heads down, where the rank-and-file recruits sweated in drill with the shock troops.

Petty officers waved the intruders along.

Masked by Dakar's knowledge of Fellowship wardings, and Elaira's skilled use of hedge glamouries, the trio traversed the naked acres scorched sterile by Lysaer's assault. They threaded the gamut of unquiet haunts, disoriented still by the horror of life's savage ending.

The shut, unmanned gates at the lower wall posed the arrivals a strategic difficulty: the singed timbers and stout grille-work had been left secured, too massive for Dakar's light fingers. That forced a return visit to raid Lysaer's encampment, where Sidir's forest-bred stealth purloined a stout rope, some twine, and a bow. Better prepared, they waited for nightfall, crouched near the stripped bones of dead sentries. Dakar whispered cantrips to settle the shades, while Sidir kept sharp watch. Darkness did not relax their protections, as they poised to slip over the barbican.

'I don't fancy being done like a seamstress's pincushion,' Dakar grumped, nursing a heel with burst blisters. He distrusted the duke's archers. Year upon year spent in hair-trigger drills made them shoot at the first sight of movement.

'The s'Brydion won't have winched in the span bridge,' he argued, against Sidir's doubt. 'That precaution will be held until the last moment, since they hope to draw in the Prince of Rathain.'

'Over the stinking meat of my carcass,' Sidir snapped under his breath. The murderous glint that sparked his pale eyes did not bode well for Jeynsa. 'I would be done here. Soonest is better, that my liege should never behold this sorrowful place.'

Still thin from captivity, the tall clansman shouldered his work with bow and arrow and unreeled the twine after the shot used to thread their rope through the battlement. Once the knots were secured, Dakar kept his counsel. While Sidir lent his strength to assist Elaira through the arduous effort of scaling the outer grille, they climbed, breathless, and breasted the gate arch.

Then reached the far side, scraped by rough stone, with tough leathers snagged by the slice of embedded glass. No sentry emerged to call challenge.

'Learned their lesson,' wheezed Dakar, overcome by exertion, and starting to sicken from excessive use of fine spellcraft.

'Is that blessing or curse?' Sidir whispered back, through the sea-mist that curled through the lanes. The full moon was rising, a set-back beyond any forest-bred skill. Since the Mad Prophet looked ready to snooze where he sat, the Companion extended a firm hand and raised him.

'Why haven't they burned this place down?' he snapped, fretful. 'These houses can only shelter the enemy.'

'Don't ask,' murmured Dakar, braced on a yard gate, and white as rolled dough.

The three of them slunk through a craft quarter emptied of people. Nothing moved but the foraging rats and a gaunt cat, stalking for vermin. They climbed, while the incoming fog lapped the shop-fronts, and moonlight carved shadows deep as Sithaer's pits, and glanced in mercury ripples off the roundels of the unlit windows. S'Brydion reigned with an iron-clad fist: no looters had rifled the deserted craft shops. Doors and shutters remained locked, while strained silence hung in the streets.

'Ath's own grace, don't ask,' Dakar repeated at a mumble.

Sidir voiced his rattled thoughts anyhow. 'Be seen here, we're apt to be cut down for thieves.'

'Dakar's spent out,' Elaira protested. 'After settling the dead, he's left unfit to weave wardings.' She raked a wisp of hair from her face, forced to quell the clansman's raw nerves on her own. 'I don't sense any presence. Since Bransian's men trust main strength before talismans, my old hedge wife's skills ought to serve.'

Cloaked against stabbing chill, touched by a desolation that bit to the bone, the three skulked under the ephemeral veil of Elaira's suggestive illusion. Stray sound was less biddable. Dakar's staggered footfalls cast echoes before them, up the zigzagged streets, and through closes, past the dead chimneys of the forges and the vacated barracks that loomed still as the sealed vault of a tomb.

The pervasive quiet unnerved, even words an unnatural intrusion.

Ahead, carved in jet silhouette, the lead roofs of the upper citadel drum-keeps notched the indigo sky. No watch lamps burned, there. If candles lit the alcoves for healers, attending to births and infirmities, not a gleam pierced the pervasive black-out. Only moonlight painted the empty lanes. The air smelled of oil, perhaps leaked from stores at the gatekeep, though the oddity grated, with no imminent sign of attack yet in evidence. Nor did the saving blanket of sea-mist wreathe the height of the promontory. The clear night exposed knife-edged shapes without mercy: in fraught stealth, the party of three crept upward to the gap at the Wyntok Gate. Under its inky shadow, Elaira came forward with her woman's voice to approach the sentries.

'Hello, the watch!' she called out. 'You have friends, come in peace to the citadel on behalf of the Crown of Rathain. With your duke's leave, we ask to treat directly with Jeynsa s'Valerient.'

Which opening was honest, if not what Alestron's overstrained guardsmen were disposed to hear. The response came back surly. 'Stand forth! Show your-selves and disarm!'

'Obey!' Dakar cautioned, as Sidir bridled to protest. 'Now they know we're here, Bransian's archers will have us skewered at the least hesitation.'

'In the dark?' Sidir snarled. 'You claim they're that good?'

'Skilled as your best forest clansmen. Incompetents don't serve the watch at *this* bridge.' Dakar gritted his jaw, shoved away from the door-sill that shel-tered them. 'Disarm, as they ask. We'll be shown to the duke under surety, once they've recognized me for a Fellowship spellbinder.' Then, as six armoured men blocked the lane, with more cross-bowmen positioned at vantages in the battlements over their heads, Dakar gave rushed advice to Elaira. 'For today, you're no crystal-bearing Koriathain, but a healer trained by Ath's adepts who's chosen to side with the clans.'

'I won't lie to them,' Elaira warned, a freezing reprimand.

Dakar rolled his eyes, caught a fist in his beard as though to yank hair in frustration. 'For love of your prince, then! Try to limit yourself to the strategic truth that's least likely to rile s'Brydion temper.' He added, wrung nauseous, 'I have faced the whip, here, only spared by a Sorcerer's intervention. These men never compromise. They'll kill without thought. If they're shown cause to believe they've been cornered, even your Teir's'Ffalenn cannot handle them.'

Then the moment for breathless precautions was past, as the men down the lane advanced to take charge of them. Sidir was given their blunt command to drop his bow. No one cared that he possessed no quiver or arrows. Surrounded at weapon-point, inspected and frisked, the arrivals were made to stand, half-clad and shivering, while torches were fetched. The flaming brands were thrust into their faces, within a whisker of blinding them.

The splintering light made Dakar's head spin. He wrestled back dizziness, given no choice but to suffer rough handling.

'Disapprove as you like,' snapped the burly captain at arms, unfazed by Sidir's hackled dignity. 'The last ambassador here got an arrow through him. You haven't, because Dakar is known to us.'

The torches were snuffed, then, perhaps not a mercy. Held captive, the three were prodded forward, stumbling in their state of rifled undress, and scrambling to snatch loosened laces.

Sidir set his chin, large enough to balk at the shove that would spill a lesser man to his knees. 'The lady,' he said, 'is deserving of courtesy. You treat with her no better than ruffians.'

The protest met laughter, followed up by the clap of a gauntleted fist. 'You'll not get your weapons back yet, feral scout. Peace with you, for now, since there can't be honour between us until you've survived your coming interview with our duke.'

The hour was uncivilized to question intruders who might be spies sent by the enemy. Yet Alestron's ruling duke was awakened from sleep no matter the time was past midnight. He would interrogate all surprise guests, and without the amenities of state courtesy. Bransian rolled from bed, slit-eyed, while the report still tumbled from the lips of the runner sent in by his vigilant sentries.

'Not that filthy gambeson!' snapped Liesse, still blinking.

The duke glowered. He settled for the scarlet dressing-robe. Let the scuttling servant throw the garment over his shoulders, roped with surly scars and hard muscle, and skinned by the chafe of his chainmail. 'I look like a floor mop,' he groused, and shook off the wife's urgent plea for a comb. 'Beard tangles be damned! And forget boots, as well.'

He stalked for the door, while the extravagant gold tassels sewn at his hem tapped and glittered against his bare ankles. He paused at the threshold to snatch his sheathed broadsword, belting on the steel-bossed baldric.

Concerned that such driven haste boded ill, Liesse kicked free of the sheets. She grabbed the nearest dress in her wardrobe and slapped off the dithering servant. 'Fetch up Keldmar's widow. Run, do you hear? If my husband holds this interview by himself, we'll be mopping up someone's let blood off the carpet!'

Liesse hurried, yanking at laces. Already, the duke's voice boomed up from below, directing the session to the closet room he used for hostile receptions.

That tiny, cramped chamber was airlessly hot, sealed by felt curtains for black-out. Only two of the available wicks were alight, thin flame struggling in the tall candelabra that flanked the duke's raised chair. Mearn was not present; as the only other sibling in residence, he stood active watch on the walls. But Sevrand sat as the s'Brydion heir apparent, clad in his silver-trimmed captain's breeches and sartorial, bare-chested splendour. The two wives called at short notice showed their unfinished dress, lacking state jewels, and in hair falling uncoiffed to the waist. Their tight faces redoubled the ominous weight, imposed by the row of heraldic chairs with Alestron's bull motif worked into the cushions, and stamped in chased gold on the finials.

The presence the women commanded instructed the captain at arms: the petitioners just prodded in from the stairwell were offered a seat before the raised table. Dakar accepted at once, of necessity. Red-faced and puffing, he leaned back, straitly desperate and battling dizziness.

Elaira perched also, rough in her scout's buckskins. If her level stare did not disclose the focus of her order's training, she would seem ordinary, with her bronze hair tied back in a farm-wife's plait. Sidir declined to sit. His insistent presence kept a liegeman's stance, on his feet at her right shoulder.

Which mannered defiance bespoke her importance, and also proclaimed the ritual warning that Rathain's crown interests would not yield the s'Brydion cause undue deference.

Bransian's eyes glittered: tight as cranked wire by threat at his gates, he came stoked for explosive contention. He introduced the raw-boned, brown-haired matron as his wife, gave the name of his heir, then nodded his greying, leonine head in salute towards the more fragile woman in mourning. 'Lady Sindelle, my late brother Keldmar's widow.'

Despite the late hour, Bransian's expectation burned incandescent as he addressed the captive delegation. 'Do you bring us news of Prince Arithon? Has he changed heart? By Dharkaron's thrown Spear, if he has, we have a need that commands our survival.'

Dakar broke that hope quickly. 'No change, my lord. I am Fellowship-sent, bearing a mandate from Melhalla's *caithdein*. Rathain's crown must stay clear of your personal blood-bath. We have come instead to pull Jeynsa out of here.'

'Did you, by Ath?' Liesse tucked worn fingers to a gleam of pearl rings. 'And how will you propose to do this against the young lady's free will?'

Sidir folded his arms, the fresh scars on his wrists shining baleful under the flame-light. 'You're going to back her against us?' He skirted the indelicate brunt, that to try would defy charter law, by disregard of a crown steward's edict.

'It's our children's lives and s'Brydion heritage,' Liesse stated, blunt, while the red-rimmed, dark eyes of Sindelle observed with a glass-brittle calm that would shatter reason.

'You can't stop us,' the bereaved woman attacked. 'Nor can Melhalla's long arm reach us, now. Dare you break your own code, and censure us with the use of unbridled spellcraft?'

'Won't, rather,' snapped Dakar, looking rumpled and flustered, the grey streaks grown prominent in his cinnamon hair. Strong spells and prolonged use of mage-sight had drained him. The appalling effort he required to think fast undid his remaining resource. 'There are limits. The ethics I follow mean something more than your use, for political convenience.'

'Expediency,' Sevrand drawled, insolent. He lounged back, his main gauche drawn to rout dirt from beneath a ripped thumb-nail. 'Tear us down from within, you'll just feed the lunatic madness of Lysaer's forsaken Alliance.' A shark's grin split his beard as he snicked his steel back into its well-oiled sheath. 'Jeynsa's dug in her heels. That point's uncontested. How can you think you'll stop Arithon?'

Which *was* the bone in the meat of the unwelcome challenge to start with. Duke Bransian watched, alert as the coiled adder, to see who would choose to flinch first.

There, tension hung, to Elaira's wise silence, and Sidir's *almost* seamlessly self-contained rage.

The candles streamed, choked by untrimmed wicks, while the curtains hung limp in the stillness. Everyone sweated, while the freshened breeze off the harbour whined and buffeted at the latched casements.

Dakar fought to stay upright. The airless room had started to spin. He swayed, bedazzled by heraldic bulls, heads lowered to charge in rash fury.

Sidir spoke, finally, with the stark dignity that had snap-frozen fights between Halwythwood's proud chieftains. 'One can hope, with a Fellowship spellbinder present, that Arithon Teir's'Ffalenn might not choose to stoop to the part of a nose-led sacrifice.'

Bransian leaned forward. 'And the woman, Elaira? What is her interest?'

'She's a schooled healer,' Sidir said without blinking. 'I'm amazed that you'd brush off three Sorcerers' counsel. Stay this course through, and you'll need to beg Arithon's good graces! Though as his liegeman, I'd venture to caution. Your space for apology rests on thin ice.'

'We should run like a forest-born squirrel for a tree?' Sevrand grinned in contempt. 'Clansman, for shame! You've sent your cowardly mind ahead of your carcass to Sithaer!'

Liesse interrupted, to stop slanging abuse. 'Do we even know where among Dharkaron's damned your Master of Shadow happens to be?'

'Dakar does,' Sindelle reminded with fixated focus.

Sevrand slapped the boards, rocked by cynical laughter. 'Well in that case, we're sunk! Did you look at your prophet? He's sloshed in his chair. How much liquor did you have to slug into him to raise the guts for this interview? By the list to his posture, I'd give him an hour before he keels over comatose.'

Sidir's pale eyes narrowed. He dared make no move: not since a chopped signal from Duke Bransian had summoned the men-at-arms in from the wardroom. Weaponless, the Companion had no leverage to argue, as Dakar was dragged from his chair.

Nor could the spellbinder help himself. His overtaxed faculties slid him towards collapse. The fevered skin and reeling faintness of back-lash left him saucer-eyed as an owl, dazzled half-blind in the candlelight.

'Sober him, then!' Elaira jabbed back. 'Find out what you've earned, by your efforts.'

Yet even that withering satire failed. The duchess gave the barest shake of her head: in warning, Liesse set the urgent example. Bale-fire burned behind her duke's eyes. Since Keldmar's death, her husband's temper had frayed beyond reach of appeasement.

'Stay, Sidir!' Dakar mumbled. Manhandled upright, he raised no fight as he was dragged to the centre of the carpet. His legs failed him at once. He sat there, unstrung, a mound of limp russet, eyes shut and round features slackened. His brosy, alcoholic's complexion completed the picture of witless beatitude.

Bransian shouted. 'Daelion forfend! You're a barrel of sops! Left to yourself, I doubt you'd be competent shoved up against the eighth gate of Sithaer!'

Patience was absent. The garrison remedy to shake a drunk out of stupor sent a man to the spring cellar for a filled bucket. The rich carpet was soon puddled with ice melt. Dakar dripped, curled up in a shivering lump. Pink and coughing, he glared daggers at his tormentors.

The s'Brydion paused for no civilized apology; no solicitous offer of blankets.

The moment the water ran out of his ears, Dakar was accosted by Bransian's demand for Prince Arithon's location.

'How should I know?' The spellbinder screwed his eyes shut, trusting Sidir to keep sense and curb the justified outrage that could only spur on the duke's cruelty. In tried forbearance, the Mad Prophet mocked, 'Who trusts a libertine? By the time the Master of Shadow confides in me, everyone else has forgotten.'

Sevrand stood and up-ended the sloshing dregs over his victim's soaked head. 'If you don't know, you wallowing skinful, then find him. We have no clue where to look, and no liberty! Nobody's heard from your ingrate liege since the hour he walked out of our hall and abandoned us.'

'Well, you wouldn't,' Dakar said, sulky. A swipe of numbed fingers scattered the droplets fringing his beard. 'Since his Grace as a rule keeps to his spoken word, I suggest you apply to the Fellowship, the Koriathain, or else bend your iron-clad knees, begging Ath's everlasting mercy!'

The sullen frown on the duke's livid face, now mirrored by his subordinates, raised unpleasantly brutal memories. Dakar set his jaw. 'Damn you all to Dharkaron!' he cracked to Liesse. 'Since when has the province of charter law become the mouthed word of convenience?'

'He's sober!' the enchantress pealed into the shocking breach. 'And telling the truth!' Before the armed men were unleashed for bloodshed, Elaira snapped the deadlocked inquiry forthwith. 'I know how to reach Arithon! Be very sure, before you ask, that you are prepared for the consequence.'

Her courage stopped breath.

As the duke shifted focus, Dakar heaved his dripping bulk to his feet. 'My lady, Lord Bransian, here are your terms laid down by Melhalla's crown steward: we must be granted our appeal to turn Jeynsa.' Upright in a puddle, pushed to near dissolution, he showed steel beneath his wrecked dignity. '*I am Fellowship-sent*! If the Teiren s'Valerient refuses, if she won't answer my charge as the Sorcerers' agent, then no one can turn back the ruin that has stubbornly been set in motion. Elaira will find his Grace. She *does* hold that power. If, pray Dharkaron, his mage-taught shields are let down, and if in the binding heat of the moment, he's inclined to toss reason and listen.'

Duke Bransian smiled, a show of bared teeth that defied Elaira's drawn presence. 'Fetch the girl,' he commanded. To Sidir, who had moved no muscle throughout, he added with provocation, 'I don't care why this woman's come, or why she's placed under your charge. You are all deaf as rock if you don't already see that we're leading a dance of formalities.'

The steadfast Companion needed no words. He had not been fooled. In blighted fact, they had cut their timing too fine: Lysaer's war host would have the citadel tightened down and surrounded by morning.

'If Jeynsa refuses, I can't let you go.' The duke's glance raked his three captive adversaries. 'Alestron won't take the risk you might spill what you know of our straits to the enemy.'

Now, Sidir spoke. 'Depend on this: if Jeynsa refuses, we will never leave Prince Arithon's interests so nakedly unsupported. Nor are you above the law of the realm. In the name of Alestron's people, every move that you make will be witnessed and sealed by the eyes of a Fellowship agent.'

'You'll have to survive, first!' Duke Bransian agreed, a poisonous jab of black humour. 'The Sorcerers aren't much threat. I daresay they're strapped helpless. Or why else would they send in a spellbinder who lacks teeth to back up their vaunted authority? Your fate's now joined to Alestron's, and mine. Who else is left, except Rathain's prince, with the brute power of Shadow to save you?'

Autumn 5671

Glimpses

As the duke's runner leaves to summon Jeynsa s'Valerient, one of Dame Dawr's watching servants observes, and through a ruthless tussle of back-corridor politics, the errand is made to change hands: Talvish is plucked from Mearn's watch on the walls, then charged with the order to escort the young clanswoman throughout her pending audience . . .

In the central command tent, under mist that drenches the Sunwheel emblems, the false avatar tosses amid his damp sheets, under guard by Ranne and Fennick; and when the cold horror of dreams snaps his rest, they witness his tormented pain, as he paces, awaiting the comfort of dawn-light to scatter his haunting burden of ghosts . . .

Amid Elssine's harbour, while autumn winds toss the Alliance flag galley's unsettled anchorage, Sulfin Evend rubs tired eyes with his fists, elbows braced on the lists, piled up through his long-deferred muster; then he speaks, to his hovering captain's relief, 'Our work is complete. Tomorrow, we row north to rejoin the Light's entrenched troops at Alestron . . .'

Autumn 5671

V. Blood Debt

The gleam of the full moon sank to the west, slanting shadow through the heart of Selkwood. Since the waking of the old centaur wardings, Lord Erlien s'Taleyn had moved his lodge tent. His chieftains' encampment retired far inside the free wilds, where the roused song of the marker stones did not fray the sharp minds of his scouts into the mesmerized fever of backlash.

Steeped in the old way, the shadowed depths of the forest were no place to wander at large. Even scouts did not fare without guidance. Here lay the core of the land's silent power, and the sites where the mysteries flourished. Here also, the trust preserved by clan heritage in the absence of the Paravians: paths where no human being might walk without due permission. The hushed glades stayed undisturbed, and the most ancient groves, where the moss-hoary crowns of the patriarch pines combed the restless winds risen with autumn. Trees spoke, in the moaning whisper of needles, and through the tap-roots struck deep in black soil. No two-legged intelligence might fathom the hidden tracks under their branches. None ventured the fringes so near sacred ground without the grace of true talent, bred across generations of recorded lineage.

Even to risk guarded sleep in this place, human faculties brushed the bounds of the veil. Danger lurked for the untrained and stalked the unwary, where a strayed thought could unseal the grand portals. Lord Erlien's chieftains gathered their people in refuge, where *no* mortal footstep went lightly. Not every hunter dared to stalk the game, or presumed to forage and set cookfires. Ones without subtle perception left such tasks to the gifted among them. Here, to act out of harmony with the land might carry irrevocable forfeit.

At full moon, when the lane tides peaked, sleepers rode the driving swirl of raised flux, sunk in the meteoric splendour of dreams. Athera's web of active consciousness beguiled them, entwined with the seasonal currents, until even waking thought sailed through the life-quickened stream, where vivid colours and sound ran outside of the familiar senses.

The initiate mage, and those who were seer-gifted, did not rest at all, as the bore of the mysteries ran through them. Some anchored themselves in the comfort of groups. Others took solace in solitude.

In the hours before dawn, while the moon's silvered face laced the forest in velvet shadows, Arithon Teir's'Ffalenn sat tucked with his back braced against a mossy boulder. His bare feet were rinsed by a streamlet, run chill since the passing of summer. The air smelled of frost, although Selkwood never saw ice and hard freeze, or the snow, soon to blanket the north. Tonight, his lyranthe was not at hand. He carried no steel, and no knife. Stripped of all things but his leathers and shirt, he held quiet, while the burning, rogue gift of his s'Ahelas heritage traced the land's untamed concourse, listening.

His beloved's call touched him most easily, there, a contact dispatched from Alestron. Trained master, he curbed his distress for her danger. Right choice, founded by her conviction as healer, had sent her inside harm's reach. Love did not confine her. Nor could Arithon's sovereign straits argue the need that had brought her: to pursue Feithan's headstrong, s'Valerient daughter, and circumvent a disaster.

Wide open, beyond censure, Arithon gave his enchantress the spark of his joy, alive with the trust of his confidence. *'Best Beloved. Elaira.'*

'I would have you bear witness,' she sent in return. Beyond words, the warm invitation extended to share her immediate presence, as Jieret's daughter was brought in for interview. He would see precisely what drove the girl's motives; could measure what childish ideal shoved her into the ugly, cross-chop of politics. The gravity of his decision from Alland would be enabled by first-hand perception.

Arithon closed his eyes against the seductive allure of the moonlight. Held secure by the trickling flow of the stream, and by the pines standing over him, he let go and sank into the contact. His link with Elaira drew him away, to a closed chamber, clogged with the scents of wax candles and musty travel-stained wool. He experienced the worry that freighted the air, inside the shut gates of Alestron . . .

Elaira was not complaisant. Through Arithon, she discovered that state meetings in the citadel were seldom conducted in privacy. Duke Bransian was likely to post his own listeners, or lurk at a spy-hole behind the carved panelling. Yet Jeynsa was given the semblance of dignity for her encounter with Rathain's delegation. The chamber was cleared of by-standing men-at-arms. Hurried servants removed the splashed carpet. The tall chairs with their heraldic trappings stood empty as the waiting crown spokesmen were brought a carafe of wine.

Head clamped in pained hands, Dakar could not respond. Since Sidir stayed walled behind his compressed anger, Elaira received the servant's request and declined the offer of drink. Unimpressed by the pretence, she stayed on the backless chair taken first, at the foot of the vacated dais. In travel-stained leathers, hardened fit by her rigorous journey from Halwythwood, she displayed an unbroken composure. Sidir stood at her back. The shadow about his gaunt face and grey eyes ran beyond the shorn loss of his clan braid. Nascent horror still marked him, the iron set of his shoulders reflecting his recent mishandling.

Dakar slumped on a stool in wet clothing. Huddled under a blanket the serving-man tossed him, he wore his stout flesh like a wad of soaked pulp, sunk to the eyeballs in misery. His aura bled off wisps of shuddering light, sure sign to the refined perception of mage-sense that he had stressed his arcane faculties. Yet Elaira's finesse gave the crown prince in Alland no time to plumb surface appearances. The outer door crashed back and admitted Jeynsa s'Valerient. An unlooked-for grace: Talvish served as her escort. His lithe footstep shadowed her heels, a warning to any that knew him. He bore full arms, the fist riding his sword-hilt bespeaking annoyance that he had been pulled off his watch-post.

Jeynsa was herself, a bristling young wildcat who tested authority through roughshod defiance. Hauled barefoot from bed, *she had dared to wear black*!

Uninvested *caithdein*, the brazen nerve shocked: even Dakar vented outrage. 'You have *no* right!' But his cry was snapped short by Sidir's clamped grip on his forearm.

The Companion knew how to handle her best; had been Feithan's choice to check-rein her daughter's rank insolence. 'Who gave you the clothing?' he said, scarcely nettled.

For, of course, the affront would not have political backing. Dame Dawr's seamstresses were never such fools.

Jeynsa flushed. She marched into the breach with a rattle of steel, bearing her load of scout's weaponry. 'Who else here would call our crown prince to task? I refuse to condone his Grace's desertion.' Candle-flames whipped as she stopped to rebut Sidir's nerveless interrogation. 'Our clan code does not strand a loyal ally!'

Up close, the ruse showed: her robe had been filched second hand from a heavy-set scholar. The fabric was streaked by unfinished dye. Sleeves and hem had been hacked down to size with a knife.

'You're a sight to shame your s'Valerient ancestry,' Sidir observed in cool quiet. 'Be glad you face us and not Asandir. Though you will, in due time.

Never question the certainty. You may have been one month old at your choosing. But now, you are quite grown enough to speak your own mind and reap the sour fruit on your merits! We're not your authorities. This is not a reprimand. Beware of your mouth, girl! Lives ride on your drama. A Sorcerer might call the account for your actions, and where can your mother appeal for relief?'

'Feithan does not command me,' Jeynsa replied. 'You might share her bed, but don't speak for her!'

Only Sidir could withstand that cruel barb. No raw venom could unseat his dignity. Throughout, he stayed as sure of his own mind as ever he had been during his hard stint in Vastmark. 'Jeynsa. Sit down. Let go of your anger.' With the same, unimpeachable gentleness, he added, 'If anything *could* have turned Jieret for home, our liege would have paid any price that was his. He'd have risked his own life before losing your father.'

'We aren't discussing my sire,' the girl snapped. Unappeased, she accepted the chair that was offered.

Talvish remained by the door, taut with nerves. His worried, jade eyes sought Elaira, who had not stirred. Dakar kept his own counsel, raw yet with exhaustion. Exquisitely practised at cozening whores, he had never owned this Companion's born skill, to sort human needs and negotiate.

'I will ask, as a liegeman,' Sidir appealed. 'Leave this place in our company, Jeynsa. Set your sovereign prince free. Duke Bransian's people are fit to handle the fate they have flaunted before Lysaer's war host.'

Jeynsa lifted her chin. 'I don't promise false hope to the mothers I've seen. Or desert my Named word. I would die by the sword, in this room, before I allow you to force these folks' deaths on my conscience.'

'My weapons lie in the hands of the duke,' Sidir declared in strait scorn. 'Nor would your feal escort strike an under-age child in the back! You insult us, as a galling snip of a girl. The adult would step in with bare hands and disarm you. Bend you over a knee, for the strapping your bluster deserves!'

Jeynsa pulled a riled breath. 'Just you try –' she began.

Sidir overrode her. 'Act your age! I wouldn't soil my hands, *or my Name*! In this, I am not Feithan's ally!'

That icy wording slapped Jeynsa white. She was shivering, though protocol spared her: as the welcomed guest of Duke Bransian s'Brydion, nobody present could touch her. 'I will not release Arithon,' she announced, sounding plaintive, though her manner gave not an inch. Afraid she might be, wrung to sweating disgrace, still, no doubt assailed her fixed purpose.

Sidir bent his head, his sudden tears masked as he ceded his lead to Elaira.

Who still did not move: Koriani, and dangerous, her cold regard held the surgical edge of her training. At a word, she could lay open a soul to the bone or drive a wrought spell for the viscera. Had that been her way, the girl would be dead, before Talvish's reflex could unsheathe his steel.

'You will not bear the cost,' warned Elaira, point-blank. 'His Grace will, to the agonized depths of a spirit not made to divide you from your poisoned claim to integrity. This is no longer grief, but a back-stab done only for pain, and self-punishing, vicious contention. The exchange, if you stay, will not be one-sided. You will lose your light heart. I would suggest, Jeynsa, that if you fail to listen, you will hurt Arithon. Wound him this way, and you could destroy the last shred of your true peace of mind in this life.'

Jeynsa glared, fighting tears. 'Will the children who die care a jot for my pride?'

'*Arithon does!*' Elaira attacked. 'Not even a blood-binding can halter his being! His Grace can break his pledged oath through bare will! You left that knot incomplete and unreciprocal. The option's still open. Your crown prince may well choose the personal penalty, before being drawn to self-sacrifice.'

'He will not,' stated Jeynsa. 'For Jieret, he won't.'

The truth rang incontrovertible. After all, the young upstart had taken her crown prince's measure in Halwythwood. The gift of his presence, bestowed without strings, had exposed his core self beyond salvage. The girl knew her quarry. Birth talent had driven her insight too far and too desperately deep.

'Then woe betide you, we are done.' Dakar heaved himself upright. 'This has all gone wrong. Far more than this citadel is going to burn, if the Master of Shadow takes up your brash challenge.'

'He already has. He is here,' Jeynsa stated, made wild by salacious relish. 'You don't see? Elaira has brought his Grace's awareness. *Arithon* doesn't intend to back down. Or his woman would have withdrawn from this room and abandoned my case without pleading.'

Sidir lifted his head. Helpless, beyond weeping, his features were haggard. Beside him, Dakar recoiled in disgust from the girl's overblown histrionics. 'Ath's mercy, your crown prince was made party to *this*?'

When Elaira returned no word of denial, Talvish stirred fast and moved in.

'I'll take her!' he cracked, to spare Sidir's stunned grief. His mailed grasp caught Jeynsa's wrist from behind, spun her headlong toward the doorway. 'We're off to your room! Believe this, girl. If you spurn Bransian's guest oath and fight, I'll break your damned neck, and crow to Dharkaron Avenger for seizing the privilege.'

The instant the door slammed, Dakar found his wits and rousted Sidir with hard urgency, 'Out. Let the enchantress have her time, alone. This has been a raw set-back. If Elaira's still in rapport with your prince, *they should be left in communion.*'

Sidir rallied his poise. But before he took Dakar's advice and stepped out, he went down on his knee. His considered clasp gathered the lady's chilled hands and lent her the solace of his warm fingers.

'*Mi a'daelient,*' he murmured in cadenced Paravian. Before he arose, he touched Elaira's palms to his bent forehead in the formal salute only given to the realm's queen . . .

In the foil-and-felt tableau of moonlight and shade, Arithon held to the peace of the greenwood. The strength of his calm met the brute storm of heart-ache, and clung to grim balance, unflinching. Through the tearing interval, as Elaira wept, nothing moved through his linking presence beyond the cosseting flow of affection.

Her sore disappointment could not be assuaged. *'I've failed you,'* she sent. *'Feithan, as well, and not least, Sidir. You know what he suffered to come here.'*

Whip scars and shackles, and the ignominy of a branding that would gall him, lifelong; Arithon was experienced enough not to bury the black rage under platitudes. Since he had no avenue to console Sidir, he tempered his touch, for Elaira. He let the held cup of her being fill all that he owned in the world.

'I know Jeynsa,' he stated aloud, that the site he had chosen to greet the full moon could transmute his burden to sorrow. 'She is Jieret's daughter, with her mother's more-quiet resiliency latent. I think that her father foresaw her rebellion when he asked for my vow, by the Aiyenne. Don't ache for the spirit that girl can't deny. I don't *need* to come north to protect her.'

That he would leave his warded haven in Alland was never in doubt. Embraced by his care, Elaira was given the question that stabbed like cut glass.

'Why should I rise to a stroke of foul play?' Arithon grounded his naked feet into the stream bottom. While the water purled over mossy rock, and the breeze riffled the surrounding evergreens, he leaned upon calm, soothed down Elaira's rife hurt and from somewhere bought courage to answer. 'I will come because Jeynsa will not be left to her scars. She shall have one more chance. This much, I can grant her. To take charge and learn that pain and loss are not life. That her will is no weapon, to forge betrayed love into a shackle of tyranny.' He added, still settled, 'I promised Earl Jieret not to abandon her.'

At which point, Elaira's linked sensing could snatch the silk from the dross: see just *how much* of his poised equilibrium had been borrowed at need from the forest.

Arithon changed the subject. 'I've a sovereign charge to lay on Sidir, though Ath knows, he doesn't deserve the rough burden after tonight.'

'Fionn Areth?' sent Elaira, acquiescence not fooled. At one with his thought, she knew not to ruffle the vessel that rode such stilled waters.

Rueful equilibrium met her, gratefully warmed by her tactful understanding. 'I gave my word, once. The grass-lander was to have an eye-witness to sort out the criminal evidence listed against me. Please ask Sidir to stand as my spokesman. Let him deliver his honest testament, even to the most damaging questions. This is no time to shelter my dignity. I want that young herdsman kept *safe*. Or he will be destroyed, run under by Desh-thiere's machinations and the strife between me and my half-brother. Expose me, and Lysaer, for what we are, when the curse drives us outside all mercy.'

'Burn away the false dross of idealism?' Elaira's wry amusement uplifted him. *'That's a signal task, while mewed up with s'Brydion, who live by the skin that hangs their brass bollocks, and breathe on the passion of brimstone heroics!'*

Arithon laughed. 'They thrive in a fight. Even my brother's mad pack of fanatics are going to be vexed by the reckoning. Your stirred nest of hornets will not crumple without sting! I am not worried, yet.' The assessment was sincere: he owned the rogue gifts of the s'Ahelas blood-line, once crossed with the seers of s'Dieneval. Yet the shadowy offshoots of probable futures posed an abyss he was forced to skim lightly. 'Bereaved mothers and widows won't embellish the Alliance's grand cause. And Duke Bransian's wicked bent for dark strategy should secure the gates until the hour I can rejoin you.'

'I'd hoped to be left to my own devices,' Elaira said, tart. As the warmth of his smile dissolved, she thrust again, in stripped wording: 'not least for the sake of the script that drives my Prime Matriarch's grasping agenda.'

'At her own peril!' Arithon snapped, not offended. No brazen threat from the order could move him. 'I'll come in my own time,' said the Teir's'Ffalenn, 'and by my own terms, which won't be entirely for the sake of my binding oath to Earl Jieret.'

'It's Feithan's debt on you,' Elaira accused, also aware that her phrasing encompassed all of Sidir's future happiness.

'Some gifts of friendship cannot be earned, no matter how hard we try to live up to them.' Recognition leaked through, of the grief lately cleansed by the cautery of remorse. 'Rathain's clan families have suffered too much. All I have, I would give for s'Valerient.'

There was more – too much more, walled behind that stripped statement. Yet Elaira chose not to encroach. However the Prince of Rathain met his debts, the man who was Masterbard needed to lay his own course through the obstacles at the s'Brydion citadel. When Arithon plunged into the hotbed of jeopardy to confront Jieret's wayward daughter, he would act by a strategy to shatter all precedents.

'Beloved, don't weep.' The flood of aimed strength that came through in parting, this time was not taken from Selkwood. Arithon's surety was as honed steel, forged by a conviction in the fullest command of all his protective male instincts . . .

Elaira shivered, chilled and apprehensive as the contact came to an end. Even she dared not try to fathom how Arithon might reclaim the slipped reins of his fate. Cold, though she sweated within a closed chamber inside of a threatened citadel, she dried her last tears with the back of her wrist.

'Merciful grace, Jeynsa!' she swore at due length, when composure returned and sparked anger.

The girl was a fool – no, all the worse – a naive, callow spirit, to believe she could confound Arithon Teir's'Ffalenn or tie up a man with initiate stature in the strings of a sworn obligation.

While the Alliance war host surrounded the s'Brydion citadel and dug in for an entrenched siege, the full moon waned and the forest of Selkwood tossed under a whipping cold rain. The soaked canvas of the *caithdein*'s lodge billowed, punched by buffeting gusts, until Lord Erlien called for torches to relieve the gloom behind the laced door flap. The sumptuous, dyed carpets had been rolled aside, with a mat of pine-needles laid down to blanket the sodden ground. The scouts came in drenched to make their reports, while the fire pit fluttered and smoked, and delivered no warmth to offset their damp misery.

The afternoon brought Arithon Teir's'Ffalenn, politely requesting an audience.

The scouts caught lounging off duty ceased their horse-play. They retrieved their oiled cloaks and filed outside without grumbling. The bard who had wakened the old centaur wardings had earned their uneasy respect. Only Kyrialt walked without nerves in his presence. If this prince preferred to evade crown formalities, his liegeman would not let his entrance pass unremarked.

Given privacy, Arithon came forward, skin wet. He offered due courtesy to the reigning high earl with no trace of needling irony.

Lord Erlien did not rise. He laid down the strips of oiled leather in his hand and raked his diminutive royal guest over with his usual aggressive inspection. 'My sentries are all dripping like drowned foxes, too. Why aren't you singing for one of my women, being plied with mulled wine in comfort?'

Arithon flipped back his streaming black hair and showed his teeth in delighted affront. 'Because wet fingernails tear, on a lyranthe's wound string. And because your huntress in residence likes to use darts before words to nail down my wool-gathering attention.' He added, across the pervasive ambience of goose grease and freshly honed weapons, 'I've brought a wine-skin. The vintage is an exquisite year, from the vineyards of West Halla.'

'The prize you won over a contest with bows? I heard about that. My scouts don't, as a rule, lose their bouts to outsiders. They're never going to settle your triumph without demanding a rematch.' Lord Erlien leaned forward, his folded arms braced on the boards, where he had been wrapping new grips on his knives. 'What's my woman guessed that you haven't told us, your Grace?'

'Am telling you.' Arithon uncorked the shoulder-slung flask, pulled a neat swallow, and passed the choice red across the razor array of bared steel on the trestle. 'I need to ask a boon of the land's steward.' He did not take a seat on the vacated bench, plain enough indication that his request would be other than commonplace.

Erlien belted back a stiff slug, though the fine wine deserved a more-delicate appreciation. 'You drink like a milk-nosed virgin,' he accused, his frosty eyes kindled to warning. 'Did you come bearing sops as bribe to appease me? Or did you think to bolster your courage before asking for something unreasonable?'

'Merely unreasonable? Why not outrageous?' Arithon accepted the gurgling skin. He sipped without hurry, and smiled with a candour that would have pitched Dakar to jangling anxiety. 'After all, I bear the lineage of Shand's ancient kings, along with the mettlesome brew sprung from Dari s'Ahelas's rogue talent.' Before the realm's *caithdein* could bridle, Rathain's prince attacked without blinking. 'I want no authority, but only permission to visit the King's Glade in Selkwood.'

Steel rattled, as Erlien slammed to his feet. 'Dharkaron Avenge! Your gall has no limits! You may have blood heritage, but no rightful claim! Don't cite me Rathain! Your legitimate inheritance remains incomplete. As an affirmed prince, you have yet to receive the attunements that finish a royal coronation.' To the son, whose steadfast bulk guarded the shut door flap, Erlien snapped, 'Kyrialt! Did you know his Grace meant to ask this?'

'I didn't consult,' Arithon broke in, tart. He recorked the flask, tossed the last of its exquisite joy to his liegeman. Throughout, he regarded his outraged antagonist with maddening, unruffled sobriety. 'Do I have your blessing? Or will I have to play games and win my way past the ornery knives of your war-captain?'

'We should stand aside while you take such a risk? Ath's blinding glory! You could shred your mind! Lose yourself, until you forget every tie that preserves your earthly identity.' Erlien peeled off his fringed jacket and paced. 'Sky above, prince! What wretched point are you trying to prove? Selkwood lies under sufficient protection to weather this rising of town-based fanatics.'

'This is not about adding to Alland's defences.' No longer reticent, Arithon stepped into the light. Haunted tension sharpened his face. Even within the wood's guarded preserve, his aroused gift of far-sight entrained disturbed dreams: the overlaid patterns of violence spun off by the s'Ilessid assault on Alestron that *would* come to abrade his held mastery of Desh-thiere's curse. 'If I'm to surmount what awaits in the north, I'll need more than commitment and courage. Bound by oath alone, I can't stand off disaster. Dangerous measures are called for, I think! I would go to the King's Grove to invoke higher wisdom. Beg for the strength to lay claim to this task with more than my own human grace. There are risks,' he agreed. 'But where's the alternative? Who am I, to shoulder the perils of a geas-cursed war on the faults of my blind limitations?'

Chill truth gripped the stillness. Even Lord Erlien's contentious nature could not deny this appeal had true cause. The depths of those green eyes upon him retained the unquiet imprint of nightmare. When Arithon chose to expose his defences, the ugly reminder shocked thought: that little more than three fort-nights ago, his horrific travail with the Kralovir's witcheries had all but torn the spirit out of his breathing flesh.

Arithon pitched his case now, unswerving. 'No man might ask this permission of you. But I am a high kingship's sanctioned heir, and also a titled masterbard. Even without the fulfilled powers of Rathain, a liaison with the force that quickens the groves is a claimed part of initiate heritage.'

Erlien dared not reject this request. Yet neither could the titled ruler of Shand turn a blind eye to such scalding presumption. He had been asked to bless an unguided encounter with the perils that guarded the sacrosanct mysteries. No light matter, to be dismissed without fear. 'If you do this, your Grace, you will take my son Kyrialt with you. He will watch your back at every step.'

Arithon knelt. 'My lord, no. I implore you. Allow me to court this particular danger in solitude.'

But under his ironclad oath as *caithdein*, the High Earl of Alland planted his feet. 'Set-backs are life, and my heir is the realm's pledge. He will be there to safeguard your welfare for as long as his strength can give service. You have earned that regard from my people, your Grace. If Kyrialt comes to harm as your man, another of my lineage will supplant him. We are the ones transient. Shand's legacy will survive all of us.'

'Kyrialt,' said Arithon, still on bent knee amid the soaked scatter of pine-needles, 'I would reject the choice that demands your feal company.'

'Never.' Kyrialt strode forward, caught his liege by the elbow, and raised him. 'You would go in the morning? Then I will be ready.' At the slight shudder of recoil, he added, 'Say nothing! Abide. Selkwood's seeress has already joined my fate to yours. Nothing you try will gainsay this. Beyond argument, you can't deny that you'll need a s'Taleyn to show you the hidden way.'

Naught could be done. No protest might sunder the bond with the self-contained swordsman who braced him. Arithon tried anyway. The taut moment hung, while he sorted the tissue of prismatic far-sight that razed him through like a fire-storm. *Some lines converged with too cruel a clarity.* Arithon was forced to acknowledge the shimmering knot that twisted the threads of paired destiny. Regret remained: that Lady Glendien had once entrained a bold bid to turn her husband away from a loyalty that might rob the fruits of her marriage bed. Her brazen tactics had failed, the opportune victory ceded in spring when her stubborn courage had faltered. Now, while a rampaging autumnal storm battered the peace of the lodge tent, the double-edged gift of joined fellowship with s'Taleyn could never again be dismissed.

'I stay at your side,' Kyrialt insisted, 'no matter where you dare to tread.'

Prince Arithon bowed his dark head in surrender. He accepted the wrist clasp. 'Then let us not live to regret.' His rare smile burst through, alive with the sudden, shattering warmth that stopped the breath for its heart-felt sincerity.

The gale broke, before daybreak. Its moist cover of cloud flayed away in brisk winds that scattered the wet like flung diamonds. The wood smelled of resin and fresh, rain-soaked earth, and Kyrialt awaited, as promised. He had dressed in tradition for the occasion. His leathers were masked by a heraldic surcoat, and the sword at his hip was an heirloom. Silver wire wrapped the shining, black grip. The pommel was inset with the chevrons of Shand, inlaid in fine amethyst and citrine. On the hour he presented himself before Arithon, his dark hair was rebraided in the s'Taleyn clan pattern, and his blue eyes were clouded to smoke. Apprehensive concern for his liege undercut the gravity of formal trappings.

'I have no intention of playing the fool,' Arithon reassured as he gestured his readiness to depart. 'I promise I'm not going to shame you.'

'Your Grace,' said Kyrialt. Nothing more. Though his swift, sidelong glance as they left the encampment reflected a tacit approval.

The prince he escorted showed proper humility, and came in accord with ancestral customs. Arithon had done away with scout's leathers and boots. Today, he wore only the sashed robe from Sanpashir, and thonged sandals, woven from sweet-grass. Those would be discarded, as morning wore on, and the threshold that demarked the subtle boundary between the free wilds and Selkwood's pristine, inner sanctum was crossed. Arithon walked empty-handed, as well. His lyranthe remained in the guest-quarters. Where Shand's ancient high kings would have shone with the circlet and crown jewels bestowed at their ritual coronation, Arithon wore no adornment at all, nor carried so much as a talisman. Unarmed and unheralded, he came with only the cloth on his back and the grace of hard-won self-awareness.

His slighter build seemed an unfinished child's, in the shadow of Kyrialt's muscle. Even so, his quiet presence turned heads. The stillness inside him towered. The light stride that ventured into the deep wood held the poise of the initiate sorcerer.

'You know we can't stop to forage at noon,' Kyrialt warned as they passed through the check-point, waved on by the scouts.

'I am meant to be fasting, though I may drink running water from any stream we may cross on the way.' Arithon smiled. 'Sethvir and Halliron between them made certain that I was well versed. Since I may not know everything that applies, here in Shand, your instructions aren't taken amiss.'

Kyrialt pointed towards the left fork in the trail. 'That way, liege.' His reluctance was palpable: plainly, he would give anything to avoid that particular turn in their pathway.

Yet the fickle fall weather gave him no excuse. The new day was a jewel, around them. Sunlight spun slanting beams through foliage lit like a riot of cut silk. Still sheltered from frost, the last, blooming asters flecked the clearings where deer had grazed off the underbrush. Tree branches rustled to the wing-beats of birds and squirrels at their nesting. The mud at the verges bore the flurried prints of mice, the pug marks of bobcats, and in velvet shade, the more secretive, southern lynx.

'Leftwards, again, by the leaning maple,' said Kyrialt. Speech seemed an intrusion against the hush, which gathered and built at each step. The path to the King's Glade did not lead them straight but bent into a spiralling curve, that closed with impeccable gentleness. The approach was a kindness. The slow, upward shift in the resonant flux allowed body and mind to acclimatize to the range of exhilarated sensation.

The expanded state of awareness caused thirst. Both men paused to drink at the rock-springs and streamlets. Their breathing deepened, although the terrain underfoot was not arduous. They walked steadily on, while the energies sang in ever-tightening bands, which thrummed solid bones and stretched ear-drums. Oppressed by the mantle of their human flesh, the two travellers exchanged no conversation. Shortly, without warning, Arithon bent. He unlaced his simple grass sandals. Though the morning was brisk, and the sky stretched above, wind-swept to a cold, cloudless azure, he must walk barefoot, henceforward.

Arithon Teir's'Ffalenn trod in the same steps, as those of Shand's ancestry had, before him.

Soon enough, the path led to the pair of live oaks, that Paravian hands had braided into an archway as saplings. Ancient now, streaming moss and speckled with lichens, the twined trees carried living awareness as sentinels.

Through their wakened gateway, no man might pass, except by rightful purpose and with due permission.

Arithon touched Kyrialt's forearm and stopped. He had sworn not to spurn the old ritual. Committed, still steady, he loosened his sash, then slipped his robe free, and left the cloth in the trembling grasp of his liegeman. Naked as birth, he must enter the glade, as every crowned sovereign before him. Yet where those past supplicants had held the jewels of s'Ahelas heritage to protect, and act as a beacon before them, Arithon brought nothing else but his voice, and the frame of his human intention.

He advanced, flushed to sweat, but not frightened. His step made little sound in the carpet of leaf mulch. Up to the knotted, black portal of branches, he made his way without flinching. There, on his feet, his hands loose at his sides, he looked upwards. Dwarfed by the boughs of centuries-old oaks, he drew breath and uttered his Name.

Wind arose, on a breath. The first, breezy overture built, then screamed, wrapping his form in a whipping, tight gyre, until his exposed flesh became scoured. The force could have hurled him onto his knees, thrown him down and smashed bones in reprisal. Arithon braced his stance. Eyes shut, determined, he held his footing. The gale slashed his hair, stung his skin to red gooseflesh. Upright, though the buffeting shoved him left and right, he staggered a step, and recovered. He did not give way, though his frail body shivered, ripped through by a chill that could kill if he stayed without respite.

Then the tempest parted. The twisting, last gust chased leaves down the trail. The dry grasses rippled beyond the oaks' arch in a capriciously mild invitation.

Arithon had received leave: the way to the King's Glade lay open before him. Kyrialt took the liegeman's place at his back. As the Teir's'Ffalenn crossed through the portal, the youngest son of s'Taleyn followed, remarked by no more than a whisper of air through the rustling leaves overhead.

Whether or not the cold posed a hindrance, Arithon showed no hesitation. He walked upon ground that had known no man's step since the death of the last King of Shand: a boy crowned one generation after the uprising, at the tender age of eighteen.

The ancient path meandered. It traced the earth as the barest, single-file indent, overgrown with flowers and myrtle, and bird-scavenged stands of wild oats. The ivied trunks of the pines and the spreading, grand crowns of the oaks cast their shade, dusted by motes of sunshine. Breeze frisked the foliage and scattered the seed down of paint-brush and late-blooming hawk's eye. Midday had passed. The air was alive with the chatter of sparrows and the lilting cry of a falcon. Kyrialt moved as though wrapped in a dream, sucked into light-headed vertigo. What Arithon experienced could not be guessed, exposed as he was to the land's direct energies, barefoot upon the warmed soil. Here, where the tides flowed as a palpable force, the mind and the heart sensed the pulse of the flux. Mortal flesh shuddered, wrung into ecstasy by the effervescent cascade.

The pervasive presence that rang through this place was not fashioned for breathing humanity. Kyrialt walked at Prince Arithon's heels, his unstrung nerves lulled beyond sense. The danger stayed real: madness, addiction, or unrequited longing afflicted those who experienced the wakened mysteries for too long.

Sundown approached, a lit glory of gold, when the path reached its end, and the King's Glade lay unveiled before them.

The hollow encompassed a gently sloped mound, ringed by the hoary crowns of twelve live oaks. The trees were old, their twined roots overgrown by dry grass. The tipped seed-heads lapped at a weathered stone slab, where the bared bones of the rise jutted through. The rock was laced round by a tangle of wild rose, still bearing the reddened hips of the late blossoms. Kyrialt trailed Arithon up to the crest. No spoken word passed, between them. In time-honoured custom, he spread the shed cloth of Arithon's mantle over the mossy face of the granite. Here, where Shand's former high kings had petitioned the Paravians to answer the needs of the realm, a prince who was not the land's titled sovereign presented himself, just as naked in supplication.

The sentinel oaks that had granted him entrance made no guarantee for his safety. Unattuned to the role of his Shandian ancestors, Arithon dared to invoke the wild powers, for a consequence beyond precedent.

Here, at the crux, Kyrialt forced speech through the blaze of his scattered senses. 'Nothing I say can dissuade you from this?'

'No harm dwells here,' Arithon replied at a whisper. 'Sleep, if you can. The dream-state will lift the stress from your mind, and protect you from suffering withdrawal.' As the young man took issue, he added, most firm, 'There's no need for you to stand watch, in this place. The initial danger is already past. Or I would have been flensed skin from bone on the moment I queried the trees at the gateway.'

'You addressed the sentinels?' Kyrialt asked in surprise.

Arithon drew in a bracing, quick breath. 'No. I gave myself over. As I will again. If I live to return, and the forces that quicken their being decide to let go and release me.'

His bid had been cast. He could not turn back. No matter what fate should await him by night, Arithon stayed resolute. He climbed onto the slab. Though the breeze that riffled across his stripped skin fore-promised a vigil of misery, he prepared to lie down for the consequence.

Kyrialt wrestled the salt prick of tears. 'My liege,' he gasped, helpless.

But naught could be done. Words of disharmony lost their edge, where the flux burned flesh and blood with the volatile fire of unworldly majesty. Kyrialt assumed the *caithdein*'s post at the feet of his sovereign lord. He seated himself on the ground by the slab, torn by the shame of frank cowardice.

After all, he could not bear to watch, as this uncrowned descendant of Shandian royalty surrendered himself to the glade. Arithon would be at the mercy of who *knew* what powers, with the Paravians gone from the land, and the old ways all but lost to the discord of strife, desperation, and short-handed neglect.

Sunset came and went, a raw glory of scarlet that faded away through the black silhouette of the oaks. The breezes stilled. Dew fell, moist and cold as beaded quartz on the lichened face of the slab. Arithon lay on his back. The desert robe gave no more than a thread's width of comfort, beneath him. He had been trained. Rauven's schooling let him abide in deep stillness and sustain the relentless chill temperature. He could not withstand such cold for too long. Not without taking sustenance, after the day's rite of fasting depleted his reserves. He settled the unquiet fields of his aura and held on to the calm of deep centring. Mage-taught discipline must see him through until sunrise if he was not to burden his trustworthy liegeman with arranging a funeral.

Stars burned in the cobalt sky, their magnificence only slightly dimmed by the ascent of the last quarter's moon. Arithon had chosen his timing with purpose: the flux lines ran thinnest, poised between the nadir at dark face, and the white tides that blazed highest, at the full. Even still, the scald of the currents by night laced his nerves with the rush of their passage. The memory still hurt, of past crisis at Rockfell, when the surfeit of lane flow he had sustained had all but torched his breathing flesh.

Arithon viced his errant thoughts still. Whether he left his eyes open or shut, mage-sight unveiled the King's Glade about him, ablaze with the glory of life. Here, the whisper of grasses spoke out loud. The chorused chord of the trees formed the bass notes that anchored the harmony of the risen stars: voices that presaged the onset of winter, and that stone recorded, eternal.

Wide open to nuance, Arithon lay quiet, every part of him listening. His masterbard's ear for subtlety plumbed the glade's stillness to fathom its pulse and gather its rich lines of melody. Time passed. The heavens spun. While the pole-star glimmered above the north axis, the icy half-moon passed the zenith and sank towards the west. The trees spilled their plinking mantles of dew. An owl called, hunting mice. Deer crossed the glade, twice. Antlered bucks sniffed the air and stood guard, while the does and weaned fawns grazed the grasses.

Arithon poised, suspended in mage-sight, *waiting* for song amid silence.

On the far side of midnight, the whisper of mystery plucked his poised mind like a quivering string. He experienced, past sound, what ears could not translate: the swell of the grand chord that ranged the realms past the veil. He saw beyond vision, engulfed by the scalding light struck through the unseen deep. Shuddered to ecstasy, Arithon fought the pull of sublime desire. *He had to hang on*, stay grounded to the stone that supported his prostrate frame. Gently still, he regarded the forest, and looked for what eyes could not see: the path, that would leave its etched imprint in time. He sought the way that the centaur guardians had used, when their grace was petitioned to act in behalf of the realm.

The place where the majesty of Ath's living gift had stepped from the deep wood, and communed with the waiting, crowned kings.

And there, to the south, like a wisp of caught flame that shimmered indigo in the darkness, Arithon read the trace that he sought. The remembrance, where an exalted presence had walked, the brush of its passage etched like hazed phosphor beneath the shadow of the eldest oaks. Memory remained, stamped in pebble and earth: the key to the mysteries lay open before him, who had asked without raising his voice.

Arithon arose. Weak at the knees, he swayed and stood upright. Leaving the mantle on cold stone behind him, and skirting Kyrialt's tucked form, he strode from the low mound and ventured the forbidden deeps of the night forest. Where no man had gone, this one dared to tread. Bare-skinned, on naked feet, he entered the path towards the heart-wood that was the sole provenance of the Paravians: once sent to Athera as Ath's living gift, in flesh-and-bone congress with powers beyond the pale of mortal imagining.

Where, behind, the flux had surged like live flame, now the currents roared through like a tidal bore. Arithon moved, lashed and winnowed by storm. As though lifted by tienelle, he fought the flare of his initiate sensitivity, reamed wide open and drowned to immersion. Yet where the drug's nonselective effects hurled the mind to explosive, raw chaos, this shift was ordered, a ripple of subtlety fit to unstring the frail bounds of the flesh.

Arithon reeled. Scarcely able to set one tender footstep after the next, he had no choice but to lean on the trees to stay upright. Light and sound swelled into a bone-shaking chord. Mage-sight unravelled to wonder. Ripped ragged by overlaid layers of perception, he went with closed eyes, and *sensed* his way forward. The play of the mysteries scalded his heart. Desperate, but not frightened, he held on to his boundaries. Used discipline to keep his aura in place, with the utmost, aware care and tenderness. He battled to hold to his human separation, as the stones and the plants and the teeming of *life* threatened to unstring his whole being with welcome.

As he moved, one fraught pace to the next, he understood that the sacred glade was not passable to flesh-and-blood form. For his kind, the place would react as a portal, that led to the realms past the veil. Long before he reached the heart-wood's surrounds, his firm substance would sublimate, absorbed by the greater chord of Ath's mystery into spirit, then streaming consciousness. The thought seemed detached, and the peril, unreal, that he might pass too far to return.

Only mage-taught purpose sustained him, a ghost pattern of embedded reason. To survive in this place, all thought must be leashed. The chance slip, and the unbridled fire of mind would react like volatile flame. Here, the least inclination of will could ignite the live flux to explosion. The tiniest whisper of wrongful intent could seed discord, and touch off unravelling damage and shattering harm.

Arithon went forward, too aware of the penalty he might invoke, inadvertently. His brash, human trespass could blight the clean flow of Selkwood's inviolate balance. He inched onward. Another step, trembling, until his overstrung mind and assaulted senses dissolved at the boundaries of dream. Neither waking, nor sleeping, he stopped at that point. Gently, he moved to the verge of the path and set his back to the first mature tree. Stilled once again, he held, poised as silk, his masterbard's heritage open and waiting.

Black-out claimed him, perhaps. He could not track time. The white burn of the flux, and the shattered rainbows of energy that strung the web-work of all solid form lured the mind, and wore the will towards an unwary peace. Glassy-eyed, sated, enraptured past thought by the ringing chime of the mysteries, Arithon drifted. He sat finally, unmoored, the plumes of his breath silvered by the last glow of the moon's light.

There, like the gossamer cascade of sweet harmony, he heard the first notes of a crystalline flute.

The sound tore his heart. Brought tears to his eyes, for its exquisite tones of enchantment. The pure melody rushed his nerves and blazed through his bones, and rocked through his quivering viscera. He listened, struck helpless by cascading joy, as the sunchild stepped from the wood.

She was delicate, *tiny*, a sprite no more than a cloth yard in height. Her lucent skin seemed fashioned of mother of pearl, agleam in the soft, phosphor moonlight. Her step made no sound. Her least movement suggested the grace of a dance, spun from the moving breath of the wind and alive as the sparkle of gemstones. She had small, song-birds' feathers caught in her long hair; slanted eyes, porcelain ears, with cheeks and fingertips brushed with the delicate tint of blush coral. She approached through the trees, ablaze with her own light, while the quartz flute rang and trilled an exalted response from the ether.

Then she lifted the instrument from her lips.

The cessation of her sublime melody scalded a musician's spirit like a whip-lash of pain. Arithon felt the air stop in his throat. Hurled into blind dark, he fought to exist, through a weight like a fist at his heart-strings. Numbness threatened to sweep him away, run him through, and unravel his being. The howling void beckoned.

Arithon yanked back his slipped discipline. *Barely in time!* he stilled the raw cry that burst to escape his locked throat. Into silence that hung fragile as the symmetry in a snowflake, he bowed his head in hushed shame.

The sunchild paused.

Sight recovered, with her not a pace from his feet. The lit warmth of her aura caressed the stilled wood and soothed his wracked nerves like a tonic. Arithon still reeled. Unmoored, and flat helpless, he fixed on the jewels caught like stars in her midnight hair. The perfume of her presence overwhelmed sense, a blend of sweet summer that hung between sun-drenched meadow grass and evening rose.

'*Are you real, Exalted?*' he asked, not in words. His tears fell, that the coarse grain of his reverent thought slapped the flux as a shouted intrusion.

The Athlien Paravian cocked her pert head. Eyes bright as green opal regarded him. Since her stillness *inquired*, he gave her his Name. Her percep-tion, which unravelled his being past form, already welcomed the purpose that brought him. She would see the raw coils of Desh-thiere's curse and know the flawed turmoil that rode him. 'I am your sent answer,' she told him at last. 'You have asked to be freed?'

His tears fell and fell. He turned his scarred palm, knotted, long past, by a light-bolt unleashed by a half-brother's entangled malice. '*With all my heart, Blessed. I rest in your care.*'

She lifted her flute, breathed one note on the air. Yet the charge in the sound loosed a levin bolt. Light burned, then burgeoned, and smashed like the sun through the held focus of initiate mage-sight. Arithon Teir's'Ffalenn did not see her move. Only felt her brief touch, that cleared the raging heat from his brow with a caress of insatiable tenderness.

More of her kind must have joined her, although by then, he was hurled beyond seeing. He felt other small fingers trace over his skin, then many hands, insistently lifting him. More flute song arose and joined hers in the night. A music beyond sound wove a net of wild harmony. The sweet tones spun a magic that drew down the dark, and dropped a veil like a nimbus about him . . .

Arithon awoke to the first blush of dawn. He lay on the stone slab, with the desertman's robe wrapped over his shivering nakedness. The gift of the sunchild had been no figment of promise, or wistful remnant of his unhinged senses. His breath flowed in and out, as though his lungs filled his flesh to the soles of his feet. Beyond the miracle that had scoured his aura clean of the Mistwraith's entanglement, he noticed the second gift, rested beneath his crossed arms.

He cradled no less than the Paravian blade, Alithiel, that he had left secure, back in Halwythwood. The scabbard that covered the steel was the same: a sturdy sheath of black leather, fashioned by the Fellowship Sorcerer, Davien.

Arithon clutched the sword. He gasped, wrung to dizziness. As the world brightened around him, and brushed the King's Glade in Shand with the blaze of new day, he mustered the shattered rags of his will. Trembling, he stirred and sat up. Before Kyrialt roused from oblivious sleep, Arithon Teir's'Ffalenn lost his poise. Overwhelmed by a gratitude beyond words, he gave way, then shuddered, riven through by an unutterable loss that now left him in desolate separation.

He bent his dark head. With the Paravian weapon braced across his knees, he broke down and wept like a new-born.

Response

The ripple unleashed by the event within Selkwood resounded bright echoes the length of the seventh lane. The stone ruins at Ithilt and Athir rang like a bell to the tones of grand harmony. Ath's adepts in their hostel north of Shaddorn were rocked to their knees by a wave of blind ecstasy. In sheltered anchorage under the walls of Ishlir, the Prime Matriarch shouted to summon her seers, then embarked on a fierce course of augury that extended well into the day.

Farther afield, other factions took note of the cascading impact. In Atwood, within the seclusion of a tumbled keep set amid the old ruin of Tirans, a raven fluffed up black feathers. Crest raised, the jet bead of his left eye cocked upward, he sounded a note like a struck bronze chime.

Traithe stirred in amazement. Caught in conference with the crown council of Melhalla, he raised his silver head, listening through his bird, while the brisk wind outside flapped the canvas securing the gap where the roof-beams had rotted.

'Are we endangered? What more's gone amiss?' asked the commodious, fair woman who wore the realm's blazon as steward. Her generous heart melted: too quickly, the Sorcerer's kindly brown eyes had widened with shock. 'Can my people lend help?'

'Ath's presence on earth!' Traithe exclaimed, while around him, the chieftains attending their *caithdein* stopped speaking, alarmed.

Caught in midtirade, the distinguished High Earl of Atwood shoved straight. 'You've received more bad news?' he snapped across the sap-sticky boards, cut in haste to enlarge the main trestle. A competent man tasked by fraught crisis, he snatched for his field-worn weaponry.

Around him, the clan elders displaced by armed invasion dropped their on-going concerns. Strapped without supply, they foresaw that their cloth goods and food stores were too scanty to last out the winter. The desperation that heated their arguments died, rendered grim before the Fellowship Sorcerer's stretched silence.

The dank, mossy keep contained their stark quiet. Another set-back could unstring morale, if not press shortened tempers to outright explosion. The scourge of Lysaer's war host blighted the country-side beyond their protected forest. A nightmare invasion, come after a decade of fear: when too many strained families who guarded the realm's blood-lines had become relentlessly threat-ened as Alliance gold spurred on the head-hunters' leagues.

Anxious built, until a smile of wonder lit Traithe's features like sunlight burst through a cloud-bank. Shaken to laughter and confounded joy, he spoke in quick reassurance. 'It's Arithon, blast his nerveless s'Ffalenn effrontery! He's just gone and torched the rule-book, again. Where our Fellowship's arts were not sanctioned to act, he has dared the razor's edge and won triumph.'

Tension broke. The *caithdein* masked her pale face in plump hands. The earl, who had stood for years as her consort, touched her shoulder in shattered relief. He folded his lean frame back onto the bench, while speculation buzzed through the gathering. Heads turned, most of them bitter and scarred, or turned dour by recent hardship.

Traithe rose, dark as shadow stamped into gloom; but not his announce-ment, which rang off the ruined walls. 'Here is hope to lighten your hearts! The crown heir of Rathain has broken the hold of the curse that Desh-thiere laid upon him.'

Through surging uproar and somebody's wild applause, Traithe found himself importuned.

'How has this happened?'

'What custom's been flouted?'

'Can the s'Ilessid half-brother also escape the horror of cursed domination?'

Traithe related particulars, to more shouts of stunned disbelief, underrun by elated excitement. The Teiren's'Callient was the first to steady rocked nerves. The earl at her side matched her startled glance. She met the round of shat-tering news with a *caithdein's* due consternation.

Her insistent grasp touched the Sorcerer's sleeve. 'You say that Prince Arithon called a Paravian presence to step from seclusion *in Alland*?'

That precedent rocked, for its arrogance. Still smiling, Traithe turned his wrist and clasped the soft hands of Melhalla's crown steward. 'His Grace raised an Athlien circle of dancers, but they've gone. We were blessed by their singing for only a moment, as their healing invoked divine balance.'

Yet the acting authority for a kingless realm was not to be swerved from tight inquiry. 'His Grace did this, you say, for the sake of the headstrong s'Valerient daughter who has placed herself at risk in Alestron?'

No fool, she had grasped the mad implication: Arithon Teir's'Ffalenn now would be bound north. The woman who bore reigning title for s'Callient had met his Grace only once, an uneasy encounter that stayed acid-etched in her memory. Her canny perception had measured the man, and seen a fated spirit whose determined character would brook no traditional constraint.

Rathain's prince meant to plunge into the scene of armed conflict. He would come, despite the might of Lysaer's war host, and the insane risk posed by fifty thousand spouting fanatics, swayed by the directive of Desh-thiere's curse. The shrewd mind never rested, behind the munificent warmth that the Teiren's'Callient poured from her tender heart.

She appealed to the Sorcerer, while the bird on his shoulder observed through unswerving jet eyes, 'Just how much did your colleague foresee, back in Daon Ramon Barrens seventeen years ago? Did Asandir read today's outcome when he chose Jeynsa as a *caithdein's* successor in her infancy?'

'Did he or Sethvir forecast these straits?' Which *had* brewed a dilemma of such daunting scope to force Arithon's reckless hand; *and launched this monumental, extreme bid to escape from the Mistwraith's binding.*

Against the posited risk, that *might have* disrupted Athera's sacrosanct mysteries, even unravelled the stability of Alland, Traithe looked bemused. 'In truth, I can't say.' While the raven fixed his disconcerted review with a gimlet stare, the Sorcerer admitted, 'If such an exchange passed between Asandir and the Warden of Althain, they never discussed the outcome.'

Traithe refused to qualify further. Too many crises still jeopardized his Fellowship's resource: looming troubles that today's stunning triumph could not hope to alleviate. At Althain Tower, Sethvir was still sinking. The adepts at his bedside reported that he had not aroused: only wept in his sleep, when the flowering resonance of Arithon's victory had streamed through his earth-sense. If the flutes of the Athlien dancers could not lift him to partial recovery, some other relentless draw on his reserves pressed him into dangerous depletion. Little else could be done to relieve his blanketing lethargy.

Luhaine and Kharadmon were too far away, rushed offworld to reweave the mazing spellcraft that thwarted a deadly incursion of free wraiths. Asandir's peril remained unresolved, obscured inside Scarpdale's grimward. He would be beset: the drifters had lately weaned a black colt, spring's get of the field Sorcerer's trustworthy stallion, and surely sired to serve as successor.

Traithe stood firm, while the raven dug uneasy claws into his threadbare mantle. The unsettled projection fuelled concern, that the Master of Shadow might wield too much influence. For best or worst, Arithon's fate already held the indispensable linch-pin: the hope that fore-promised the Fellowship's reunification, and also the adamant cipher that threatened the downfall of the Koriathain. Today's repercussions could only inflame the Prime Matriarch's grasping agenda. Selidie would redouble her efforts with even more wily diligence. Traithe ached, as he numbered the threads of entanglement: the ancient prophecy of Sanpashir's Biedar, that predated mankind's settlement on Athera, and never least, the precocious Masterbard's talent, that opened the chance of redeeming the ravening spirits that languished upon Marak.

The towering stakes riding *just that one life* smashed the frames of reliable augury.

Brought to bear on the volatile crux at Alestron, none could guess how the balance of power might shift. Traithe surveyed the mismatched assembly lined up at the keep's ill-made trestle: the eyes looking to him, both grim and exhilarated; old and young; expectant, and begging clear guidance. The Sorcerer felt unfit for the task of advising Melhalla's council.

Consumed as he was by foreboding, Traithe quieted his fretful raven. No Fellowship colleague could forsake his post, or shed the responsibility imposed by the dragons.

To that end, a smaller disaster-in-waiting must be nipped off in the bud. Traithe measured the shining eyes of the clan heir, a fair-haired young talent who was the High Earl's importunate issue. 'You will dismiss that thought!' he cracked in rebuke. 'Make no mistake, son. You lack the strength to try Arithon's path, or seek the Queen's Grove here in Atwood. No plea you might raise could brave that dire peril, or raise the powers to unkey a grand portal. Never mistake altruistic intent for the tempered awareness born out of initiate training! Without such wisdom, you would meet your death, and bring no Paravian presence back to the realm to succour the need of your people!'

As the cringing boy bowed his tow-head , the Sorcerer's gruff manner eased. 'Your *caithdein* needs you exactly as you are, young man. Even my Fellowship cannot solve the great mysteries, or force the old races out of withdrawal. We abide, man and woman, on our combined merits, though the future presents us with shadowed uncertainty.'

'Should we fear, do you think?' asked Melhalla's *caithdein*. 'Lysaer's war host is mustered.' The daily influx of additional troops ravaged the bounds of her territory. 'If Arithon succeeds in weaning s'Brydion interests away from destruction, what will happen? Can we dare to lower Atwood's defences and absorb the burden of Alestron's refugees? At the ninth hour, how could our clan enclaves hope to sustain them, when we are hard-pressed ourselves? The old hatreds from outside are bound to prevail. What if the town garrisons unleash their armed might against us in concerted attack?'

The old earl cut in, determined to keep the realm's peace at his consort's right hand. 'Surely the false avatar's combined horde could expand the siege and surround East Halla's free wilds.'

His point was not empty. The Alliance war host was massive enough to pose such a wide-ranging threat. All of the eastshore's trade towns were involved, with too many ignorant factions aligned in support of Lysaer's fanatical doctrine.

Traithe sighed and sat down, harried by more than the pain that plagued his twisted leg. He had no long-term comfort to give. No sound planning to shape a solution. He could not back the promise, that another Sorcerer's help could reach Atwood in time to avert disaster.

The raven shifted clawed feet, too subdued for an aspect of the mysteries, enfleshed as a bird.

'*I grieve, as well, brother,*' Traithe sent without speaking.

He stood alone, here, with the well-being of Melhalla's clan presence left in his hands. He had no words to tell these proud people they were thrown at the mercy of whatever back-lash Arithon's next actions might stir. With his Fellowship colleagues engaged beyond recourse, Traithe had no more than inadequate strength: such limited power as he could raise through the impairment of his crippled flesh.

Surely worse, Asandir's absence and Sethvir's strapped resources left the unpredictable bent of Davien's interests an open arena and total free rein.

Storm

When Duke Bransian confronted his frothing suspicion that Elaira was Koriathain, his outspoken impulse stung the ears of his wife straightaway. 'Toss the chit out on her meddling arse and let the false avatar's priests have their field-day.'

Liesse glared back at her husband over his spurned bowl of oatmeal. Shortened days stopped the chickens from laying. The dwindling hoard of eggs cold-stored in the spring-house for baking meant meagre breakfasts, which always fanned the ducal temper. 'That enchantress snuck in here straight under the pack, with their wall-eyed talent and snooping noses. Raging hot as they are to burn hedge talent, they're not stupid. Tweak the tail of the Koriani Order, and they'll earn a catfight even their simpering avatar can't win.'

'I'd risk that and grin.' The s'Brydion lord stabbed his spoon upright in his cold mush, both wrists chapped by the bite of his bracers, and his carping mood unabated. 'Except the confounded witch might stir up who knows what vexing mischief to slap us in retaliation.' His next sober thought was to order the problem set into irons and placed under locked confinement. 'That way, we'll keep any spell-driven wiles under our thumb in surveillance.'

'You've abandoned sense!' Liesse shrieked. 'Like the dumb ox pricked on by the thorn goad, you'd back your shambling butt straight into the shafts and haul the dung cart for your enemies!'

The duke barked out orders. His summary dispatch for arrest became stalled, because the wife hiked up her skirts and moved first. She kicked over her carved chair with a bang. Aflutter in layers of lace petticoats, she placed herself in the doorway and stymied the burly captain just given the ducal command.

'You catty-whomping bitch!' Bransian thrashed to his feet. 'Interfere further, I'll skin you for the grease to quiet the squeal in the gate winch!'

'And does your drum windlass make such a noise? Who'd hear it?' his wife cried. 'Not the Mathiell Gate sentries! With you reared up on both your hind legs, and braying like a smacked jackass, it's a wonder that anyone else gets the chance for two words and a simple answer!'

The match burgeoned to shouting, overheard two floors down by Dame Dawr's ubiquitous servants. The dowager's sent runner short-cut through the back corridors and applied astute influence, which double salvo arrived just in time.

Talvish strode up in his polished appointments, touched Liesse aside, and leaned an armoured shoulder against the door-jamb under dispute. With lazy provocation, he said, 'Did you realize this Koriathain is Prince Arithon's woman?'

Politically sensitive as an explosion, *that* name pocked a gap in the argument.

'Imprison her,' said Talvish, 'or show her the least gesture of discourtesy, and I can promise, as I know his Grace, that we'll have a round of vindictive offence to smoke our hides pink with embarrassment. Worse yet, the woman's a power in her own right. She spent a year with Ath's adepts, Sidir says. Earn her enmity, you might have to beg for relief that's as wishful as a cold bath in Sithaer.'

'Piss on Dharkaron Avenger himself! I don't simper and scrape before threats.' Duke Bransian jerked his chin at his captain, fist laid on his sword to back up his bluster. 'The woman's live trouble and damned lucky at that, to bide in a cell as my prisoner.'

Except Mearn sauntered up to the doorway outside, slit-eyed as a prowling tiger. He was roguishly clad in a red velvet doublet. The empty, right sleeve had been pinned, with his burned sword-arm done up in strapping. 'Evidently I'm missing out on a fight?'

He slipped like a marsh wisp past Talvish, side-stepped the impasse on-going between Liesse and the armoured officer, and confronted his brother's cocked rage. 'You fish-brained mule! Crap into a gale, whose arse wears the stink?'

'He's grieving,' warned Liesse. 'It's Keldmar's loss hurting. He strikes out because inside, he's bleeding.'

'Ath, who isn't?' Mearn sucked a fast breath. 'I pity the man who can't cry.' He snatched for the duke's chair, poked his brother, and snapped, 'Sit! You've gone dumb and blind to current events! Dakar's in recovery, and likely to block any effort you make to upset the Fellowship's assets. We need allies, you idiot. These are Arithon's people, here to help hold our gates if they want to live long enough to spare Jeynsa.'

Bransian snapped a signal for his officer to stand down. While Talvish looked on with glacial eyes, and Mearn held his ground like poised flame, the pause stretched. For a second, the rising sun through the casements streamed across the laid table and sparked stinging high lights off crystal and cutlery.

'We won't see attack till the dark of the moon,' the duke stated at unpleasant length. He spun the oak seat. Kicked back the jut of his scabbard and perched, his regard tracking his younger brother as he folded his arms on the chair-back to brangle. 'You actually have your eye trained on Sidir.'

'I do, at that.' Mearn's sly grin emerged. 'My men need his touch, setting spring traps.'

No paltry asset, the skilled ingenuity that had made Rathain's clansmen feared far and wide for their viciousness. Despite raging loss, the Duke of Alestron had not jettisoned reason for stubborn insanity. 'You think you'll wheedle that spellbinder's assistance, and engage his talent as well? A gambler's thrill, Mearn. This nest of vipers we've harboured for Arithon's interests is dangerous! Nary a one owes their loyalty to me, or this town, which stresses my liver. I feel like the gaffed frog who doesn't yet know that his legs will get fried up for dinner!'

'Have the lot watched,' Mearn agreed. 'Who's better than family? Though how anyone around here can get a damned thing past Dawr's perked-up ears is a nuisance I'd give up the cards to eliminate.'

'Old besom was born with two sleepless eyes set into the back of her head,' agreed Bransian. 'Got a nose long enough to stick crosswise into whatever's been stowed behind a locked keyhole, besides.'

He snapped up a cold piece of toast and bit down, which signalled to Liesse and the disgruntled officer that the air had cooled enough for intelligent discussion. The grandame's usurping decision would stand, over Talvish's reassignment. The troublesome goatherd and the s'Valerient daughter would stay curtailed by the blond captain's aggressive attendance.

'We've got a war, outside, poised to rip out our guts,' Alestron's lord groused through his beard. 'Can't afford trouble stirred up inside, fit to raise spellcraft against us.' He waved Mearn off. 'Let the weasel kiss the bared fangs of the serpent. Find out if yon pack of initiate talent can be tamed enough to recruit.'

Mearn s'Brydion wasted no time. First breath, his low-voiced instruction to Talvish ordered Sidir's blades and recurve returned. 'Clan honour won't let him strike at our backs. Not with the might of the towns set to flatten us.' Belting down stairwells two steps at a stride, the pale swordsman's longer legs an effortless match for his quickness, the duke's youngest brother broached the stickier problem. 'We've got to roust the Mad Prophet out of bed.'

Talvish laughed. 'You don't. He's already immersed his sore head in a hot tub. Suds up to the chin, and for the next hour, sweating out toxins, flat help-less.' He added, serious, 'You've got time to change clothes, well enough.'

'Good.' Mearn grinned back. 'My singed surcoat's waiting.' Which was shrewd good sense: ball-room rags were pure genius to quell Bransian. But no forestborn scout with a Companion's grim history would respect affectation, wrapped up in silk cuffs and braid trim.

'I can't stay to advise you,' Talvish apologized. 'Jeynsa's shooting the butts into straw chaff with war points, and the nit-brained double's too eager to brangle himself into mince. He's already twitching to pick a ripe fight with yon fettlesome northern barbarian.'

Mearn knew that chill tone. His keen glance flicked sidewards. 'A warning?'

Talvish nodded. 'Walk softly with that one. He's seen the rough side of Tal Quorin, the Havens, and Vastmark, and came through with a fist that once knocked Arithon onto his backside, cold senseless.'

Mearn gave a near-soundless whistle. 'By Dharkaron's Black Chariot, did he so!' Beyond jokes, the youngest brother s'Brydion was too canny to play-act, or press the martyr's role, nursing an injury. With Talvish's counsel still tumbling his thoughts, he presented himself at the shut door of Dakar's bath chamber with a polite knock.

A peeling curse arose in rebuff. 'If you're a man-servant with a razor, take off and stick it!' Dakar added, 'I'll have no duke's lackey with bloodthirsty fingers plying stropped steel at my windpipe!'

Mearn let himself in. 'And good morrow to you, also.' Without invitation, he minced past the puddles slicked over the white marble floor-tiles. His singed surcoat, in fact, had been torn up for rags, as flammable lint to tip fire-arrows. Now dressed in serviceable leathers and plain steel, with his poulticed arm free of the sling, he paused by the towel-rack and rested a nonchalant elbow on Liesse's best folded linen. 'I should send you a maid with lascivious hands and a drink?'

Dakar glared. His affront lost its edge, muffled through clouding steam lifted off the hot water by the chill breeze through the arrow-slits. His round face was scarlet. Though his eyes were bloodshot as a cut of raw beef, his contempt sliced back without quarter. 'You presume I'd loll back and pant in sweet dalliance, while Lysaer's pack of minions hammers down your front gates? Think again.'

Mearn licked his lips; smiled. 'By the nitpicking pen of the Fatemaster's judgement! Then you weren't so far gone that you missed what we left out for welcome down in the trade precinct?'

'Inside the closed homes, and behind the craft shops' locked shutters?' The Mad Prophet huffed, his greying head sunk to the ear-lobes, and his breath scattering strayed bubbles through his moustache. 'I saw enough to show you a hedge witch's way of striking a spark inside a clay fire-pot.'

Mearn tapped the plain hilt of his weapon, left-handed. He said in testing overture, 'I did not want this war.'

'Neither did Elaira.' Dakar's bedraggled beard lifted clear of the soap scum. 'Don't comment. You'll regret the effrontery, since she's come through the doorway behind you.'

Blindsided, Mearn spun like a flicked snake. The taunt was no feint: the enchantress stood, not a pace from his back. As slender as he, though a handspan shorter, she regarded him with eyes like dawn mist, and the braid of her deep auburn hair draped, unadorned, down her shoulder.

'Are you the ambassador, come pleading for peace after last night's appalling reception?' Unsmiling, she added, as though her thought snatched the thread of intent from his mind, 'The citadel may call on my skills as a healer. Payment will be met in straight trade for my upkeep, with no debt incurred by my order.' Before Mearn could voice his nettled rejoinder, she cut in with commanding expediency. 'Yes, you did see the banners of Koriani pavilions pitched by the enemy camp, past your walls. They are not in conflict. The sisters who've come are in charitable service, equipped to succour the wounded and assist with the dying.'

'Never ours,' Mearn snapped, cautious. He was thinking of blind men.

'You've got sentries in agony, and case in point, your arm needs something more than a burn salve?' Elaira laughed outright, unintimidated by the hackles of upset male authority. 'Ath above, I won't bite!' Her tartness had vanished. 'Come into the lair of the spider and sit. Sidir's drawn his teeth also, since you gave your trust, and sent Talvish back with his weapons.'

The tall Companion from Halwythwood was not hard to convince to contribute his skills to Mearn's day-time forays. 'Slavers and locusts that strip growing trees? I would see that sort of two-legged parasite across Fate's Wheel without breeding.'

Sidir asked for twine, sharpened stakes, flint strikers, and shaved birch, his spare requests clothed in glass-crisp forest accents. 'I work alone,' he declared with finality. 'No one hangs over my shoulder.'

Allowed his strict solitude, he applied his skilled knowledge from dawn to dusk without stint. Perhaps as a foil to thwart Fionn Areth, past doubt disdainful of living pent-up inside of stonewalls, he came and went with a reserve to confound even Talvish's secretive nature. He would simply appear, when Mearn's company moved out. Though his high-strung, tuned instincts made him start, in close quarters, his flickering glance absorbed everything. Sidir never needed to ask for directions. His scout's footfall made not a sound. Once the squads crossed the bridge by the Wyntok Gate, he would melt away, unseen in their midst, as they fanned out and flitted like ghosts between the steep lanes and shut houses.

Their tasks were done quickly, in silence. Sweating in the cold air, flinching from the sudden scramble of rats and the yowl of feral alley cats, they worked their way through the attics and crawled through the darkened root-cellars. Length and breadth across the lower precinct, they strung ropes and tackles, and used sharpened chain under muffling rags to saw through strategic support beams.

Peril hung over their furtive efforts. At any moment, the hammer might fall: unwarned, unprotected, they might burn to ashes beneath the surprise fury, if Lysaer raised Light and attacked.

The false religion's self-proclaimed avatar remained with his field-troops, now entrenched outside the shut gates. Beyond the vacated battlements, he could be observed, a toy figure trotting his caparisoned charger up and down his poised lines. Such glittering prominence maddened the eye; served as flaunting reminder, that his gift of elemental power could unleash destruction and slaughter at whim. Under noon sun, in parade-drill order, his captains in their Sunwheel surcoats faced their war host against the lowest tier of the citadel.

No movement was hidden. The chopped turf saw no contest. The gables built to shelter the sappers creaked across the burned ground, dragged by the lashed muscle of ox teams. The scaling towers and trebuchets inched into position, brought to bear on the outermost walls. Streaked by the pervasive, soot-laden dust and the rust stains leaked from spiked iron, the log rams in their slings were lined up on the studded, barred gates. Pressed by the overseers, the ant streams of labourers with their levers and ropes warped the engines of siege into place.

Duke Bransian's men-at-arms might grind their frustrated teeth, while Mearn's skulking companies set furtive traps in the emptied mansions. They dared not mount any open resistance. Sunrise to sunset, the air boomed to the ominous beat of the enemy drums. Each passing hour, growing dread choked the crowded baileys of the upper citadel. Under flapping, sagged awnings, and on blankets spread over rough cobbles, the refugees endured their pent-up misery beyond relief. Crammed into barracks, or waiting foot-sore, in ration lines that snaked past the ramshackle cook-shacks, Alestron's folk settled their crying infants and broke up the disputes that unravelled to fisticuffs. Anxiety already pinched the colour from their haggard cheeks.

No able hands could be spared. All day, teams of soldiers hauled jakes to the slop carts. They boiled wash water, and scoured the latrine drains with lye, or scrubbed the bath houses with brine, winched up from the Sea Gate.

Talvish was not exempt from such duties, despite his nuisance assignment: he set Fionn Areth and Jeynsa to hauling fresh water from the spring-house well.

All hours, every day, they trudged with yoke buckets to fill the outdoor stock troughs and catch barrels. The stiff-necked pair were too proud to complain of aching shoulders and chapped hands. With each sloshing load carried up the steep stair, then hauled breathless through the windy sunlight, they vied with bets to lift their dull spirits and relieve the back-breaking tedium.

Fionn Areth lost his stake for the second time running. Not, in this case, by fair contest, since he had delayed to return a strayed child to her mother. The pause left him filling the last trough at twilight, too tired to care if he stumbled.

The wind had risen. Icy gusts flapped the soaked knees of his trousers and whined over the darkened dormers. No lamps burned in the pewter grey street, and no squabbling gulls roosted on the bleak cornices.

A hurrying matron bundled up in a shawl chided him for leaving his jacket. 'Storm's coming in. Cotton fog and cold rain. You'll see ice on the puddles, come morning.'

'Last trip,' Fionn Areth assured her. He leaned into the howling teeth of a gust, and passed through the narrow wrought-iron gate that led to the yard where the duke's couriers watered their horses.

Because of the wind, his approach went unheard. And because the stripped man at the trough had his back turned, Fionn Areth had warning in time to stop short. No guess, that a veteran fighter with such livid scars ever chose to be caught, sluicing down in an alley at curfew.

The buckets were too full to set down without spilling, upon the sloped cobbles. Hard-breathing, unsure, the goatherd surveyed the man's sable hair, streaked with silver, tied tight at the nape, but too short for a clan braid. The old scars, left by blades, and the new, cut by whips, that marred the taut muscu-lature of a wild animal: *this would be the forest-bred clansman from Halwythwood, whose mission had failed to curb Jeynsa.*

Now absorbed by unwise curiosity, the grass-lander regarded the bracing, left forearm, and confirmed: the Sunwheel imprint found there was a recent brand.

He had made no sound, no slight move to betray his fascination.

Yet, without warning, the man at the horse-trough exploded into a spin. A flash of silver sped from his hand: a thrown knife! The blinding speed of such reflex left Fionn Areth no instant to duck; no chance to take panicked flight, as the whistling steel flicked past his neck and shaved skin in a burning cut.

He shouted with shock. Would have hit the cobbles on his knees, except that the uncanny hunter was on him. Harsh fingers gripped his yoked shoul-ders and pinned him, while stripping grey eyes raked him over.

'*Sliesheng dhavi! Aykrauk i'en kiel'd'maer tiend!*' snapped Sidir in a torrent of outraged Paravian. He shook his prey, hard. 'Stand up on two feet! You are not worse than scratched, though by Ath! for rude presumption alone, you deserve to be more than just bleeding!'

'Because you might have killed your sworn liege? That's if your thrown blade had not missed!' Fionn Areth retorted with injury.

The clansman's hold shifted. The bucket yoke lifted away in his grasp, while his left-handed cuff slapped the goatherd aside. 'Fool puppy, to think I'd make such a mistake.'

As the Araethurian reeled against the stone plinth that supported the gate hinge, Sidir brushed past. He retrieved his cast dagger. His victim dismissed as beneath his contempt, he returned for the full buckets. Their contents were dumped without splash in the horse-trough. Each coiled move precisely deliberate, he set the yoke down without anger. Then he rinsed his fouled knife. He wiped the blade dry on his cast-off shirt before he redressed his soaked skin, or his nakedness.

Fionn Areth shivered. Chilled and bruised, with his palm pressed to stanch his let blood, he realized: *the dead accuracy of that thrown knife had been pulled!* The rumour was true, then. Forestborn clansmen were trained from infancy to track and fight by their arcane instincts. Nor did they seem to be bothered with modesty.

'What crime saw you branded?' the grass-lander inquired, point-blank.

Already reclad in his breeches and belt, Sidir sheathed his cleaned steel. He granted his observer no second glance. 'I was born.'

Fionn Areth bridled. 'Didn't your vaunted prince leave instructions that you were to answer my questions?'

Sidir straightened. The cold wind between them ran beyond chill, and yet, he displayed no discomfort. The soiled linen he refused to wear had been tossed, without shame, over his disfigured forearm. 'I don't answer to insult. Or stoop to the sick curiosity that itches to pry into a man's private history. You may ask of things that bear on such subjects *only* where royal will binds me. But I think, not tonight. Your appalling discourtesy owes nothing less than an honest and heart-felt apology.'

Regretful or not, Fionn Areth received no opportunity to redress his affront to Sidir. For three days, a salt-laden wind whipped the citadel, lashing in sudden downpours laced with the needling rattle of sleet. Such weather was untimely, Duke Bransian declared, pacing in angst from his draughty vantage atop of Watch Keep.

While Mearn's companies swore over clogged drains and drenched thatch, the distress of the families in the baileys burdened down the benighted garrison. Their crowded misery rose to fresh heights, as men laboured to secure frayed canvas and tarps, and keep mothers with children in shelter. Outside the walls, thickened mist masked the view, a trial that fretted the ranks of attacker and defender alike.

Lysaer's war host stood, mired. The last of the siege engines loomed, sunk in mud to the axles, while shivering squads laboured with shovels and boards to free the stuck wheels. The assault staged to launch at the dark of the moon was deferred for three wretched days. While the roped field pavilions shuddered and swayed, the readied war host languished. Men hunched, grumbling in their rust-stained cloaks and soaked gear. They chafed their cold hands around spitting fire pits and endured the stink, as icy torrents sluiced through the horse pickets and brimmed the latrines.

Disease posed a threat that could not be ignored. Alestron's citadel was not sited within the free wilds, where the surge of the flux lines ran strong enough to stabilize robust health. Stored food and crammed quarters bred vermin.

Sickness could blunt the campaign, while sinking morale could attract storm-charged *iyats*, their pranks to cause accidents and misfortune.

Since the Light's priesthood did not wish its faithful seeking remedies from Koriathain, the houses abandoned in Alestron's lower citadel became a strategic necessity.

If their fair avatar might have preferred to attack after the return of his first Lord Commander, high seas off the Cildein stalled all inbound galleys. Quarrels rode the disparate contingents of garrison troops, until their hag-ridden captains sweated the hours and cursed, awaiting a break in the weather.

And the day came, when the shrouding mist lifted.

The sharp winds backed and changed, shredding the cloud cover to racing scud, then tatters. Sunlight sheared like spilled brass through the rifts, and the puddles steamed and dried to pocked dirt. The last scaling towers nosed up to the wall, with the furtive squads of Mearn's saboteurs forced to dash in last-minute retreat. They left the lower town emptied behind them; bolted at a breathless, single-file sprint across the span bridge at the Wyntok Gate. Once the stragglers crossed, a distant s'Brydion cousin, and three older veterans with war injuries removed the board treads that planked the stone gap. They oiled the steep cobbles and unshackled the massive chains that secured the narrow, wood causeway. A sparkling flash, their mirror-sent signal leaped across the rock chasm that funnelled the tidal race.

The duty watch at the Mathiell Gate returned a horn blast in salute. The traditional flourish, repeated three times, that denoted full honours for heroes.

Then dreadful, uneasy quiet descended, filled by the croaks of the wheeling ravens, and the rattle of chain, as the drum winches were turned to draw in the span bridge. More men dismantled the cross-links that supported the board-walk. When its length wrapped the drum, and the slender thread of the stay-chain was left rocking over the chasm, the stalwart volunteers at the Wyntok Gate sawed the anchor pin at the stanchion.

The chain fell with a mournful whistle of air; splashed into the white flood in the channel under the cliff.

The town was cut off from the ancient keeps that crowned the island promontory. Four men, now alone, made the last preparations: lowered the grilles and barred the armoured gates at the Wyntok gap. A rushed word of parting, a wrist shake for luck: split into pairs, they retired atop the flanking towers to stare down the face of death.

For the mournful clang of the steel grilles that secured the Mathiell towers was no longer the only sound of men's industry. Above the cutting rush of the wind, the war-drums of the Alliance infantry boomed out the rhythm to march. The din rolled upslope, shattering echoes off the deserted house-fronts. A roar like surf answered: shouts from poised ranks, shaved by the throaty bray of bronze horns to signal the fleet in the estuary. More trumpets blared. The quavering note hung on the tissue of air, until a bass roar welled up from beneath: a crescendo wrung from the throats of tens of thousands of armoured men, as a thin line of gold creased the sky.

Lysaer engaged the Light's signal, calling his front-line officers to engage the advance.

The seething blocks of troops charged in step. No arrows sleeted to meet them; no burning wads of oil-soaked rags, bound over rocks hurled from mangonels. The arbalests of the attackers spoke first, launching the grapples with their unreeling tails of rope. The positioned siege towers shuddered beneath their layers of soaked hide, and lowered their wooden traps. Hobnailed wood clanged and bit glass-studded stone; snagged and lodged fast, while the yelling, steel figures streamed forth in storming assault. They poured over the unmanned, outer battlements. From the heights' vantage, they came on, a teeming wave flecked with glittering steel, and the stainless flash of white surcoats.

The land-based attack on Alestron's defences began as a triumph, unopposed by a murmur of aggressive response from her s'Brydion defenders.

Vantages

As the ram manned by the Alliance attackers reduces the triple gate of Alestron's outer wall to burst wreckage, a Sorcerer in the form of a golden eagle turns from its circling flight and wings steadily southward . . .

Sequestered in Selkwood, and recovering mazed wits from the healing bestowed by the Paravian presence, Arithon traces the left scar from the light-bolt that subjected him to Desh-thiere's curse; and awareness brings thought, that the mark stayed untouched to remind of the horrors of suborning enslavement, an experience he must bear throughout life . . .

In port at Vhalzein to off-load the prized wines from Carithwyr, and accept a shipment of lacquer furnishings bound in trade for the silk guild in Atchaz, Captain Feylind of the merchant brig, *Evenstar,* first hears of Lysaer s'Ilessid's whirlwind campaign to destroy the s'Brydion seat at Alestron . . .

VI. Counterstrokes

The eagle who was the live construct of a Sorcerer soared over the plain of Orvandir. Each flap of broad wings engaged powerful spellcraft that shifted both air and earth. Gliding on thermals, the bird passed over the town of Six Towers. His flight flickered a shadow across the beaten track of the trade-road, where the creeping industry of commerce goaded the caravans southbound towards Atchaz.

He skimmed by that town's baked, saffron walls, then the angular sprawl of its compounds and silk sheds to a hiss of knifed wind, parted by razor-edged primaries. The eagle banked into a lazy circle. His lofty presence scattered the mayor's outbound messenger pigeons into fluttering panic, before his yellow beak turned to the east. His course bent to follow the watercourse that gleamed like kinked ribbon, and whose stepped, silver waterfalls snagged the shaded channel of the River Lienriel, which crossed into the free wilds of Alland.

The raised wardings of the Paravian marker stones acknowledged the eagle's request. His presence crossed their ranging protections and ignited a brief shimmer of golden light. The display passed unseen by the party of scouts hunting for game on the river-bank. Unchallenged, the avian predator swooped inside the guarded borders of Selkwood.

His strafing descent set him down in a clearing, a stone's throw from the secluded encampment surrounding Lord Erlien's lodge tent. There, the black-haired subject he sought did not fail to mark the intrusion.

Arithon Teir's'Ffalenn laid down the strap leather his lock-stitches were fashioning into a shoulder sling for Alithiel's scabbard. 'You don't need to perch in a tree to intimidate. Why not converse from the ground? Let Kyrialt adjust to unannounced harbingers without thinking I talk to myself for no reason.'

To the liegeman, whose scout's instincts were already ruffled, and whose hand had snapped to his sword-hilt, Arithon explained, 'The day Davien alighted upon the *Evenstar*'s taffrail, his surprise visit stunned the wits out of Feylind's deck-hands.'

That statement as warning, the eagle unfolded its majestic wing-span and glided down from the limb overhead.

Unsmiling, Arithon watched the descent, still musing in piquant after-thought. 'You *haven't* come here to recoup your loaned cloak?'

'Which won't be found where Feylind's ship's steward last stored it!' came the acerbic reply. 'You are criminally careless with gifts, Teir's'Ffalenn.'

What alighted was no longer a bird, but two-legged. The Sorcerer's trim height wore a tailored jerkin and hose, flame-coloured in orange and russet. He had a narrow, intelligent face, with greying, fox hair tumbled over straight shoulders. One tapered hand bore a citrine ring, and the boots fitted over his elegant calves were cuffed in costly black lynx. His striking mantle was loomed from jet wool, bordered with chased-silver bosses and gleaming embroidery: unmistakably the same garment just mentioned to open a sparring exchange.

'You wanted news?' Davien the Betrayer provoked. 'Your siege has begun, at Alestron.'

Unlike Kyrialt, blanched by startled shock, the Sorcerer regarded the crown prince before him with avid, dark eyes and flushed interest.

'*My siege?*' Arithon's lifted eyebrows shrugged off that hurled challenge. Seated with what had been cross-legged indolence, he showed no concern, despite the shadow his visitor cast over him.

Kyrialt stayed on guarded edge, helpless to warn off a maverick Sorcerer whose unsavoury reputation and long exile had done nothing to reconcile a past fraught with murderous acts.

Neither was Arithon back in trim form, since return from his trial in the King's Grove. Ten days after his unshielded encounter, the mark of Paravian presence rode him still. A haunting, near sorrow, distanced his manner – as though yearning change left his spirit bereft. Former high kings had wasted and died of such loss. The histories recounted their trials: the searing experience of an unworldly grace that could not be retained, or reconciled. Yet where other crown forebears had languished from that relentless, invisible wounding, this s'Ffalenn prince fought his way back. As the after-shock of tranced vision and dreams brought intervals of silenced weeping, he turned the adamance of initiate discipline to rebuild his shocked equilibrium.

For this morning's fresh onslaught, to Kyrialt's relief, the royal wits seemed resharpened.

'What tedious news can you bring, if Alestron's inner citadel is secure?'

Arithon pressed the rogue Sorcerer. 'More to the point, I'd planned to call you. But not within the next fortnight, and only concerning a favour to balance the uncivilized service I was just asked to render.'

'The affray with the Kralovir at Etarra?' Davien's grin would have shamed a weasel. 'A pit fight that you were well suited to win. Are you bitter?' His riposte turned sardonic. 'It was *Traithe* who delivered your bleak course of training. Not my frank invitation to unlock the black grimoires stored within Kewar's library.'

'Ciladis's notes were too riveting,' said Arithon.

And Kyrialt, watching, sucked back a stunned breath, as the *Sorcerer* recoiled from the hidden barb within that nettled rejoinder.

Dangerous in recovery, Davien rebounded to delight. *'Nai ffiosh e'elen slieth'i,* my wild falcon! Wings such as yours are more suited for soaring. Strike and snap as you will, the hot nerves of your ancestry have never ruled your decisions. You *are* wise enough not to slaughter your messengers?'

'Over Alestron's debacle?' Arithon shrugged.

Kyrialt endured the unpleasant, stretched interval. While the breeze through the pines kissed a sun-mote across his liege's *too carefully* expressionless face, he realized: there would be more than one resource at play. If Lysaer's war host assaulted the s'Brydion citadel, his Grace's on-going link with Elaira would deliver the tensioned gist. Behind the mask, Arithon would be aware of the Alliance engagement already.

Outwardly unruffled, the sitting prince qualified, 'I could as easily scry the particular event on the lane tide.'

Yet the nuance was evident before Davien pounced: the Master of Shadow did not resume his lapsed handiwork.

'But the news won't be vivid at second hand!' Volatile flame poised for *who knew what purpose,* the renegade Sorcerer bowed to his quarry.

Arithon did not rise.

Therefore Davien presumed, and retrieved the dropped awl. Too direct to gainsay, or else moved by gadding caprice, he scribed a circle into the ground beside the abandoned strap work. 'See for yourselves?'

And his mortal observers became drawn in: by the flash of his ring, or perhaps snatched into rapport by the flourish that demarked his spellcrafted figure.

Enthralled past resistance, too gently surrounded, Kyrialt experienced the shift in perception that also claimed Arithon s'Ffalenn. All grounded awareness of the forest dissolved, replaced by an eagle's preternatural focus, from the wheeling vantage of flight. Kyrialt shared the panoramic view as the Light's forces breached Alestron's first wall and invaded the lower town . . .

The citadel's outer defences were decisively overrun. Alliance captains from fifteen allied garrisons strutted on the high ramparts. Already, they prepared to extend their advance into the trade precinct, laid open before them. The triple gates with their steel grilles were smashed down, the flanking keeps stormed and occupied. If the Sunwheel standard did not yet acknowledge their easy conquest, the oversight was being remedied. The duke's empty flagstaff had been abandoned with the halyard cut down. An eager boy now shinnied up to thread a replacement line.

The contest had yielded no other resistance. Men stood on their hollow victory. No drawn sword was blooded. The handful of injuries had been caused by falls, the penalty of a careless ascent, or raw luck, when an ill-set grapple had failed to support an over-zealous campaigner. Troops milled on the ramparts with no task at hand. The absence of crowing triumph all but stung, while the taintless sunlight rinsed barren stone, and mild winds fanned sweaty faces.

The flush that expected a battle held on: a froth that was granted no action to dissipate, upon tempers unfit to be tamed.

The Alliance captains needed direction to muzzle their manic troops. Handed a town that seemed emptied before them, they knew little of value would be left to loot. If their green recruits swaggered, the veterans viewed the tranquillity with foreboding. The houses with their locked shutters and doors, and the barred gates on the idle craft yards, yet posed them an unknown risk.

Alestron's aggressive resistance was legend. The vindictive citizen who might have stayed mewed up inside; the hidden squad of defiant archers; or the sharp probability that enemy snipers might lurk in sly cunning with cross-bows could not be discounted. Against such surprises, the attackers had profligate numbers to spare: too many restive troops to keep penned without laying claim to their due reward.

Lysaer s'Ilessid sat his splendid white horse before the mounted lancers holding rear-guard on the field outside. He raised his right arm. His sent beacon speared the heavens and signalled the horns of the priests. The readied columns of mailed infantry tramped forward and funnelled in columns through the flattened gate. Smart companies re-formed atop the secured battlement. Yelling, they poured into the lightless stone stairwells that accessed the ward-rooms and barracks. Other squads formed up at the crenels and lowered their scaling ladders to storm into the vacated streets.

The second wave of the advance surged in to occupy their breached prize.

Pikemen charged down the thoroughfares and flooded the shaded byways. The roar of their incursion echoed off the shop-fronts and emptied houses. Sloped lanes split their forces into small groups and isolated their wary commanders. The eager, dense packs of front-running skirmishers plunged ahead, and the narrow streets hemmed them. They could not swerve when the first mishaps struck; as the waiting, cocked trip-wires unleashed concealed deadfalls, or the crudely set barrier that blocked a steep lane, trampled down, freed a rumbling avalanche of propped barrels. Such rolling bludgeons mowed through screaming troops. Staves struck and burst, disgorging chipped stone that smashed bones, and clubbed armoured men senseless.

High over the roof peaks, the eagle's eye view exposed the unravelling disaster: the snares that erupted one after the next in diabolical timing. The ropes that dropped nooses and snapped men by the neck, or spilled hammering cascades of loose tiles; the hammering falls of knife-edged slate that sliced through boiled leather and stabbed flesh, or else viciously blinded. The darkened houses provided no haven. Plank floors caved into root-cellars planted with stakes. Sawn beams in the attics became jerked awry by blocks and tackles nailed to the forced doors. Invaders were crushed under lintels that fell. They died without screaming as cleavers whumped down from rigged traps in the overhead balconies. Wounds took them as quarrels hissed from cocked crossbows, set off as barred shutters were bashed open.

The boisterous shouts changed to a wounded roar as the Alliance forces jammed into bloodied recoil. Rank chaos, and the sprawl of the maimed fouled their efforts to stage a retreat. Reverse movement snarled into the press of the rear-guard, who came on, unaware of disaster. While the gutters ran red, the deadly havoc continued. Horns wailed. Captains harangued to rally their men and dispatch help for the injured, when a revetted wall tumbled into collapse. Rolling logs scythed down parties of rescuers, and pummelled the already prostrate. Screams shrilled over men's furious shouts. Frantic sergeants snatched bugles off their fallen officers and struggled to withdraw their lacerated ranks and regroup in the deserted markets.

The harried troops lifted their groaning casualties. They bunched into knots, driven into a wary rout by trapped ground and treacherous mishap.

Even in escape, they found themselves beset. In the sills of the dormers, nestled amid oiled thatch and board kindling, the clay pots with their crafted witcheries sparked vicious explosions. Flame and clouds of unnatural smoke hazed the soldiers to panicked flight.

Pelting downhill, the confused lost their way. They stumbled and crashed on oiled cobbles, or blundered, yelling, into blind alleys, where Sidir's ugly handiwork waited. Victims died disembowelled, or stabbed through the viscera. They fell, choking on their spilled brains, with shattered skulls crushed to fragments.

In shocked disarray, the Light's war host pulled back, without a s'Brydion casualty.

There would be redress. No life-dedicate officer in his sullied white surcoat harboured doubt. While the survivors consoled their dazed comrades, and bound up the lucklessly broken, that sullen promise sustained them. Their blessed avatar would unleash his god-sent gift. Grim-faced, the troops kept their pride in defeat. For the cold-blooded slaughter laced through the craft quarter, Lysaer could raise a cleansing by Light fit to scour Alestron to the foundations.

Yet by righteous mercy, not before every live soldier marched out, and the litter-borne wounded were packed off to safety beyond the trampled front gate.

A semblance of efficient handling returned as the sea-wind cleared off the thick smoke. Midday glare unveiled horror's wake. Every man limping, every man bloodied, and every one of the prostrate too mangled to walk passed beneath the Blessed Lord's view. His steadfast gaze did not flinch from their suffering. His calm acknowledged, but did not deride their shamed tears. The dead, by strict orders, would stay where they fell. A shattered city would become their monument.

The living who filed by walked assured of Lysaer's punitive judgement. Their suffering would be answered measure for measure, to the last atrocity served upon their hapless flesh by vile tricks fit to snare wild animals. When the rear ranks had passed, and the last, moaning casualty, the avatar sat his white horse. He regarded the rammed maw of Alestron's front gate. Then he spurred his mount face about. His raised fist was offered in lordly salute to honour his standing war host.

His other hand tightened upon his held rein. The rowel at his heel moved and flashed. Gilt in sunlight, he wheeled his stallion again; gold on snow, the wind-ruffled flutter of silk, and the bullion tassels adorning the magnificent animal's caparisons. Lysaer's arm, still upraised, held poised for the strike to enact divine justice.

High above, an eagle's eye, circling, noted the flash of a mirror from inside the keep by the Wyntok Gate. The signal was dispatched by one of four men, doomed as they held to their station. Their unobscured vantage exposed Lysaer's move, which could not be observed from the promontory. The winking flare was caught by the Mathiell Gate's watch, and passed onward the instant before the Light's retribution unleashed.

Then the bolt crackled and burst from the avatar's fist and bloomed into howling vengeance. Hurled power roared out, an unstoppable wave that consumed sky and earth without quarter. Shattering, bright heat and destruction unfurled with the force of a whirlwind. Walls and buildings exploded. Air shrieked with blinding flame. Stone screamed, flared to ruby, and boiled to slag. The conflagration crested and burned every structure that stood in its path.

Farthest up on the rise, the Wyntok keeps torched and crumpled. The insatiable holocaust hissed over the tidal chasm, while the eagle that circled the ripple of fumes beheld what no living mortal had witnessed: the protective response evoked by warded stone, raised to strength by Paravian builders.

Lysaer's raw power clashed against Alestron's innermost bastions. A quartz-bearing granite laid down and fused by the endurance of Name, the conscious grace holding the citadel's heart spanned the veil and invoked the spiralling arc of eternity. The presence that answered knew itself *as itself*, a foundation of being, inviolate.

The howl of light element fashioned to harm was turned in midstrike and deflected. The back-lash whipped skywards. Raging curtains of flame shrieked into a towering ring, slammed against arcane shielding. The pillar knifed towards the zenith, a perfect, drilled vortex, with the citadel left untouched at its centre. The roar of its passage trampled all sound; ate the wind; consumed by thunder the cries of men's voices.

Yet the mirror-flash from the Wyntok Gate, last dispatch from a captain scorched dead at his post *had been sent in time.* The critical signal already unleashed the poised line of s'Brydion defence.

Trained troops responded. Trigger lines were cut free as the light flared, a murderous act of drilled timing: from their bedded platforms set high on the cliffs, the massive trebuchets tripped into release. One after the next, their slung missiles were launched, to the ponderous creak of their throwing arms. Load upon load of hurled boulders sliced into the dazzling sheets of the false avatar's unnatural assault. Their whistling passage creased the stressed air, shot into torched light that obscured the view.

The hard-bitten captains howled against pummelling winds, and spurred on their sweating crews. 'Reload and fire!'

Even deafened by the unbearable noise; even with their watering eyes masked with wet rag, the trained squads cocked back the huge engines. They shot by rote, well-primed to seize their moment to enact their duke's desperate strategy.

Only the eagle observed the course of the missiles' trajectory. Mage-sight sensed the moment, as hissing, flung rock dissolved into spattering magma. The oblivious ranks of the Alliance war host received no second of warning. No moment in which to pull back. The barrage from the promontory burst through the white sear of Lysaer's light and sliced havoc across their drawn lines.

S'Brydion were unparalleled masters of warfare. Ruthless practice perfected their tactics. The first impacts struck down their standing marks with diabolical accuracy.

The molten splashes set fire to scaling towers; whumped into the squat frames of the mangonels and shattered the poised rams. Others whipped like a scourge into rows of armed men and dropped them screaming, aflame. Order dissolved. Shocked devotees scattered. The planked frames for the sappers and the piled oil casks for the fire-arrows splintered and ignited, and sowed mayhem. Phalanxes unravelled in panic as their officers fled for their lives. Underfoot and around them, the fallen still thrashed, scalded to agony inside their heated armour: and still, without cease, the impacts hissed down. Death slammed in their wake, stones melted to slag by the intensity of Lysaer's raised offensive. Other loads became fire-balls that streamed poisoned fumes and volcanic cinders.

The false avatar doused the white blast of his gift, but too late. His elite honour guard were already broken, half their number cut down. His priest acolytes pelted and scattered. While the white charger bucked, singed mad by flung slag, its rider was forced to take charge to avoid being tossed from the saddle. If his elemental strike left a vista of ruin, and the smoking shells of wracked buildings, the retort from the citadel did not let up.

The hail of flung boulders continued to fall, ripping down camp tents and tearing through horseflesh and men, and smashing the stragglers who carried the wounded. No retaliation could answer, uphill. The high keeps of the citadel lay beyond range. Red bull banners still streamed from the watchtower.

No rag remained of the Sunwheel blazon strung up in premature triumph. No man strutted, before gutted walls. No horns blew, and no trumpet flourished. Only the cries of the wounded and dying lifted above drifting smoke. For the wreck of their craft precinct, Alestron's defenders exacted their bitter price: a rout in let blood that might force back the lines, but that could never concede them a victory.

Far overhead, a circling speck untouched by the reek and the slaughter, a lone eagle folded its wings and vanished.

The appalling shock of a spinning descent dropped away into *nothing*. The mind reeled, disembodied. Then the pine-scented greenery of Selkwood returned with a wrenching rush. Stunned breathing resumed. Shocked nerves recoiled as the unmoored spirit snapped back into cognizant flesh.

Kyrialt shuddered. His senses felt painfully magnified. Sound hurt and sight stung, so much colour and noise, as he swayed on his feet. When his spinning head cleared, he noted the renegade Sorcerer, *still present.*

Davien remained standing, arms folded, his flamboyant dress like a shout against the undisturbed forest. He watched the crown prince at his feet through unblinking, relentless black eyes.

There, the moment hung, burning. Shand's guarding liegeman rejected the reflex to unsheathe his sword. No fight could prevail, here. Davien's errant interests were too deep to fathom, and his motives, unimaginably perilous. Kyrialt was not given the opening to challenge. At his feet, his prince had emerged from the scrying, utterly shattered from peace.

Arithon's outcry was stifled, just barely, his muffling palms locked over his lips as he choked. His skin had gone bloodless. Tortured eyes were pinched shut, while the tears he could not repress welled and spilled through his lashes.

Kyrialt dropped to his knees in blind shock. 'Your Grace!'

He reached out, afraid. Would have braced up his liege's bowed shoulders, had his touch not been rammed aside by Davien.

'He's seen everything you did, but opened through mage-sight.' The Sorcerer knelt himself. He captured Arithon's wrists. 'I am here! Let me help.'

As though no incensed liegeman scrambled to rally, murderous with outrage beside him, the Sorcerer stayed riveted. 'Arithon.'

Rathain's prince hung on, his face pressed behind his clenched fingers.

Davien laid his brow against Arithon's untidy black hair. '*I'tishealdient*, Teir's'Ffalenn. *Blessed peace.* You heard the outspoken chord laid into Alestron's white stone by the grace of the Ilitharis Paravian wardings?'

A shudder raked the overstrung frame he supported. 'That.'

While Kyrialt watched, distressed, Arithon forced his stopped lungs into motion. He husked, 'More.'

Davien murmured in Paravian. If he had been sharply commanding before, now his tone held melting compassion.

Arithon shivered. He tried to move, to reject, but could not recover the will to stay private. Contained by an embrace too tender to break, he let go. His shuttered hands moved. Green eyes flicked open and let in the sight of the Sorcerer's face.

Kyrialt lost his wind; averted his sight, but not fast enough. The suffering clarity had been unmasked: pain and pity exposed beyond even a Fellowship Sorcerer's redress.

'Ath have mercy,' Arithon whispered, bereft. 'My brother. I saw how he's –'

As language failed him, the Sorcerer did not: the swift weave of his spell-craft unfolded and dropped the Teir's'Ffalenn into sleep. As Kyrialt moved, Davien shook his head.

'No. Let me.' His deft hands gathered the prince's limp form, then bundled him under the sable cloak that still mantled his shoulders. The Sorcerer arose as though his burden posed less inconvenience than a sick child. 'Where are his Grace's quarters? Gather his things. I will take him.'

'Was this necessary?' Kyrialt snapped, on edge for the affront to his liege's dignity.

Davien glanced sidewards. 'Would I trifle? Your prince can assimilate what he's learned with less trauma through his initiate use of the dream-state.'

Rather than test the Sorcerer's censure, Kyrialt retrieved the dropped awl. He scooped up the lacing and unfinished strap leather, in haste to keep pace with a creature whose reputation frightened him beyond sense. 'If you knew that his Grace would suffer this way, why did you come here to bedevil him?'

'Is your loyalty true enough to find out?' Davien turned his back and strode directly toward the scout's tent appointed to Arithon. As the flustered liegeman stayed in flanking step, the Sorcerer said quickly, 'Don't try to speak here! Not if you don't like unwarranted notice, since I won't respond to anyone's bothersome questions.'

They passed the s'Taleyn lodge tent, where no sharp-eyed scout raised the alarm. Bore on across the central encampment, where two younger women scraping raw hides failed to look up, as Davien's moving shadow flicked over them. No laughing children broke off from their play. The elderly man who heated pine resin for torches said nothing. Another, who split grouse feathers to fletch damaged arrows, kept on telling jokes to a neighbour, as though no untoward apparition circled the cookfire or passed in front of him.

Kyrialt followed. Jaw clenched, he bore uncivil witness as his father's security was invaded with high-handed effrontery.

Davien paid no mind. Whatever dire warding allowed him to pass, even the seer-gifted hunters who read flux lines did not notice his passage. Unerring, the Sorcerer ducked into the guest tent, with the clan liegeman stalking behind.

The door flap slapped shut, leaving gloom. If Kyrialt bristled, thrown back on scout's instincts, the darkness afforded the Sorcerer no inconvenience.

Davien flipped back his mantle and laid Arithon down on the pine-stuffed pallet. 'Your Grace,' he pronounced, as respectful, his touch straightened out tumbled limbs and arranged the pillow. 'I will not leave your side until you can rest without reliving the carnage through nightmares.' Though his unconscious charge seemed unfit to be listening, Davien finished off with a tart remonstrance. 'One thing further, I don't fancy repeating myself.'

He unpinned his rich mantle, that once had been gifted and left, overlooked in the leave-taking from Feylind's brig. The jet cloth tumbled over the motionless prince. Davien smoothed the fine wool, with its pearl satin lining and exceptional silver embroidery. Then he dragged up a hassock and perched with intent to honour his promise.

The liegeman who witnessed was left at a loss. Aware of the Sorcerer's black eyes upon him, bright with irony and obtuse humour, Kyrialt set Arithon's unfinished handiwork down on the empty trestle. If every protective line of his carriage screamed to stay standing at sword's reach, he had the courage not to act foolishly. Kyrialt dragged out the pine bench. He sat. Leashed his riled nerves through a quiet that pricked like a knife's point.

Davien chose to relent in due course. 'I will say what should be put in words only once, to spare Arithon's need to explain himself. He thought to leave for Alestron in ten days. My lesson has shown him, by graphic example, that he is ill prepared to support the experience.'

Kyrialt released a pent breath. 'What occurred in the King's Glade has laid him wide open. Our healer can't help. She says he's not ailing. Yet at times, his Grace can't bear the sound of his own voice. He won't touch the strings of his lyranthe.'

'That acute state of sensitivity will pass.' Davien folded his artisan's hands. Under spilled light from a tear in the canvas, his sculpted knuckles wore the spark of a trefoil ring, silver inset with citrine. 'You must understand. To break Desh-thiere's curse, your liege extended himself to the verge of dissolution. He carried the scourge of the geas, *self-contained,* and went far enough to surrender himself to the mysteries. Throughout, he had to stay in command. Fully conscious, he held what could never be balanced, until the interlocked layers of his aura refined and all but sheared away. He did not die, because he willed to live, free. The healing he asked for respun his whole pattern, set under exalted influence. The gift of the Athlien Paravians will not fail him. *He is still himself.* Yet he needs to discover his natural balance. He battled the Mistwraith's drive for so long, he can scarcely recognize his own spirit. Despite what he presumed, now he knows: he is not ready to withstand what awaits on the field at Alestron.'

Kyrialt frowned. 'The Paravian warding set in the old wall, can you understand what it did to him? Ilitharis would not work in disharmony. What note could Arithon hear that was damaging?'

Against waiting stillness, perhaps reluctant, Davien decided to answer. 'He heard joy.'

Unbidden, Kyrialt recalled the sheer *force* that had seized and turned the wild fires of Lysaer's assault. Before a truth that demolished resistance, his naked intellect faltered. *All of his presupposed thoughts lay in error!* Wrenched into humility, he shivered. 'I see that I lack the experience upon which to base understanding.'

Profound silence answered, conclusion suspended. Where wisdom was lacking, courage remained. Kyrialt dared. He tested the Sorcerer, whose name walked hand in glove with contention, and whose ascetic, intelligent features showed nothing at all in deep shadow. 'You've implied something other than time may be needed?'

Davien's smile was sudden and bright. 'You are worthy enough not to make a mistake. Yes, there is more. The s'Ilessid still suffers. No recourse exists, yet. Desh-thiere's geas still grips Lysaer in wilful blindness. All of his choices are clouded. That madness can't help but turn for the worse if Arithon comes into close contact. The half-brother will strive to murder his nemesis. To survive unscathed, your Master of Shadow may require Dakar's help, or Elaira's assistance to shield him.'

Now Kyrialt did use the striker to brighten the tallow dip, the trembling move in defiance of the Sorcerer's piercing regard. 'Then stop him,' he pleaded. 'Let his Grace never enter the s'Brydion citadel. As his sworn protector, for the honour due him by this realm, I will have the Teir's'Taleyn, Lord Erlien, take action to back your decision.'

'You can all try, and fail.' Davien seemed amused. 'Be sure this prince will reject every effort to override his free will.' An impatient gesture foreran the venom drilled through the last line. 'Dharkaron Avenge! Did you actually think I arranged today's scrying merely for petty cruelty?'

Kyrialt's anger was damning. 'Could any survivor of Shand's royal lineage have a sound reason to trust you?'

'This is not Shand's sovereign,' Davien stated, precise. Irritation gave way to fury that cut, the more dangerous under distrust. 'Tell me, what other means, fair or foul, could have deferred your liege's *unwise* planned departure from Alland? I never came for the sake of his s'Ahelas ancestry! Don't make that assumption again.'

So began the long and uneasy vigil, which ended before dawn the next morning. Kyrialt did not recall that he drowsed at his post. Yet through the night, as the tallow dip burned, Davien arose, undetected. All that remained of his high-handed visit was the magnificent black cloak, draped over a prince who rested past reach of harsh dreams; and the shoulder-strap, meant to hang Alithiel's scabbard, that was left neatly finished, spread out on the trestle table.

A man in no hurry to fare northward by galley never lacked for excuses to stall on a midautumn passage. Avenor's state flagship might boast a superb crew, with spars and bright-work kept trim. Yet the stiff winds and high seas off the Cildein could still overmatch an oared vessel's flat keel and low free-board. Sulfin Evend, Lord Commander of the Alliance war host, also sailed escort for the unwieldy flotilla bound for the siege of Alestron.

The two dozen hulls straggled in his warship's wake flew the banners of seven towns' registries. They wallowed, as well, packed belowdecks with gear, and jammed by the ranks of the disparate companies culled to fight by the southcoast muster. The arguments thrashed between the ships' pursers and their equally contrary captains made each day's logged course a predicament. Two severe storms had furthered delays. Once, the fleet sheltered at Ishlir's sea-walled harbour. A second, more maddening hold-over was spent pitching at anchor, tucked inside a cove above Durn. By then, the new recruits were green-faced. Oarsmen and deck-hands turned rank as caged bears from dull food and over-tight quarters.

Worse than the trials of weather and supply, Parrien s'Brydion's packs of armed warships roved the sea-ways like nipping wolves. Their furtive night raids and gadding strikes at the laggards were no use to keep fighting men in trim form. Land troops were unwieldy, crammed on a ship's deck. Infantry weapons at sea carved blundering wounds and made accidents caused by slashed rigging. Two galleys were sunk, over one lost to Parrien. The archers evened the stakes, launching fire-arrows. Three of Alestron's ships were set flying, aflame. Yet no paltry victory might satisfy injuries. Each surprise engagement resharpened short tempers, and unravelled the confidence of drilled training.

By the hour Sulfin Evend's force hailed into Adruin, the contrary current hissed to sea in full ebb. Crossing to Kalesh must wait until the slack-water past sundown to avoid being swept offshore. The galley-men refused to make the anchorage temporary, demanding their pay packets for hired transport to East Halla's war straightaway. No passage, they claimed, should have taken so long. Choleric captains were determined to clear the Light's brawling army out of their cabins and off their packed cargo decks.

'Hit port, and the rankers will scarper like mice,' grumped Sulfin Evend's barrel-chested first officer, parked with ill grace at the flagship's stern-rail. The tide surged in black eddies, beneath his bristled stance. 'The troop sergeants are frothing. Makes for a bad mix. Set a sorry impression on Adruin's town council, if the rushed landing won't let us keep discipline.' He scarcely dared to belabour the rest: that Avenor's flag galley should demand a mooring. In the lull at slack-water, she should pull into the wharf with dignified ceremonial honours, and not wrestle their arrival by swearing and sweat, while the white rip raced through the estuary.

Dark hair clipped short, his shaven jaw brooding, Sulfin Evend chose not to hear sense.

Whorled chop swirled below, as the breathless rowers strained and backed oars. Under the harried eye of the master, the flagship's mate bellowed, while crewmen, crammed into their white livery at speed, set fenders, and tossed off the docklines.

Sulfin Evend's spiked posture did not relent.

The troop officer knew that vicious quiet too well. His shrug was resigned. 'The town better have enough beer in the taps, and trollops prepared to appease twoscore's worth of ships' rowdy companies.'

'Your problem,' dismissed Sulfin Evend. His whipcord fitness was turned out for parade, the helm he shoved on with curt irritation buffed to a dazzling finish. His mail shirt chinked under a Sunwheel surcoat, agleam with gold thread and dress accoutrements. 'I'll be ashore without any pause for Adruin's foppish amenities.' He snapped to drive off the persistent equerry, who had chased him topside to fuss. 'Damn the forsaken braid on my finery! I'm not dawdling through the welcome reception. Get the boatswain's attention! Tell him to ready his crewmen to run down the gangway at once.'

Wavelets slapped against the hull's planking. Riffling current shuddered the keel as the galley's bulk was warped in and turned to by the muscle of two dozen longshoremen. Sulfin Evend fumed like the hungry, jessed hawk, too long teased by the lure.

Electrified tension also gripped the crew, as fishermen mending their nets at the harbour-side shouted the most recent news: the siege of Alestron had started in earnest. Before the return of the Light's first commander, Keldmar s'Brydion and his field company had been burned alive by Lysaer's retribution. Worse, a determined assault on the wall had ended in chaotic set-back.

'Scorch all to Dharkaron!' Sulfin Evend cursed under his breath.

'Well, you had to expect this!' the troop officer cracked, prodded to slit-eyed frustration. 'All this time, spent dallying through the southern ports, fiddling with lists and dickering with roomsful of pinch-fisted merchants. Why, in the Light's name? While the men ploughed the whores long enough to sow bastards, we could've saved a month's fees for wharfage! What weasel-faced supplier couldn't we have slapped into line with an Alliance writ of requisition?'

'Are *we* the fools?' Sulfin Evend shot back. 'Or do we scrape, nose to dirt, for a delusional icon who's become a magnet for rabid fanatics? Vainglorious tactics against the s'Brydion will only slaughter my troops like hazed game! Lysaer s'Ilessid won't have my applause. Not for the making of martyrs.'

'Well tread carefully, Lord,' the captain replied, his sunburned brow creased with concern. 'Fifty thousand armed zealots aren't here to make peace. Fly in and accuse their idol of foolishness, the priests might be moved to cry blasphemy.'

'Flip the lot straight to Sithaer! I don't kiss their pink arses. Or bow to their simpering theology!'

A string of flag-signals snapped at the masthead, the request to assemble a courier's horse and swift escort already in motion. Sulfin Evend planned to ride post until the tide changed, then catch a fast boat on the flood. In scorching haste, he could close the last fifty leagues of his journey by sunrise.

'Billet the troops, get them rested and fed,' he belted off in last-minute instruction. While the gold-and-white galley nestled into her berth, and the gangway rumbled into position, he called over his shoulder, 'The men can be marched to Alestron in stages. No need to rush them to the front lines unless I send word they are needed.'

The veteran officer snapped off a salute. Wasted motion, since his senior commander already strode down to the dock. Sultry gold amid the drab press on the wharf, Sulfin Evend shoved shoreward with an urgency fit to clip the god-sent wings of the avatar himself.

Stand-off

The afternoon following the ungainly rout at Alestron, the reek of char and corrupted, burned flesh lingered on, laced by the mineral taint of glazed slag and the tang of smelted metal. The pall spread on the sea-breeze, razed off the husks of slagged buildings and the tumble-down walls left by Lysaer's first strike. The poisoned gusts riffled the lists of the bursars, who plied pen and ink upon makeshift trestles to tally the rout's mounting toll of tactical embarrassments. The high temper of after-shock quickly sunk into gloom, then progressed to dour grumbling as reeling captains measured their damages. The loss lists crept upward: a laboured assessment attempted to catalogue which critical short-falls demanded the Light's requisition for resupply at short notice.

Those ranking officers who nursed complaints were granted short shrift by their avatar. Their clamour for an audience chased a moving target, since the Blessed Prince still pursued his unswerving tour of inspection. Lysaer turned a deaf ear on disgruntled petitioners. Done with the strings of burned horses that languished in the care of the grooms on the picket lines, and moving apace towards the camp's outer fringes, he snapped, 'Did you think you would not become tested and tried?'

When no one answered, he spun sharply about; faced down the whiners with scourging amazement. 'Our cause is not changed by a minor defeat! We fight traitors who seek an evasion of reckoning behind walls defended by sorcery. They will be taught otherwise. But not by the weak! Do you mope at my heels like whipped dogs, cowed as the chase draws first blood?'

The stout captain from Jaelot, who mourned a close cousin, exploded with indignant injury. 'Blessed Lord, even your god-sent power –'

'Is only as strong as the faith that stands in the breach!' Lysaer's blue eyes flashed in searing rebuke. 'Have you come here to resign from your post?'

The stonewalled officer blinked. 'Light's mercy! No.'

'That's good to hear. For I haven't the time.' The shamed man and his shrinking companions received the Divine Prince's relentless dismissal. 'For anyone else who brings a faint heart, my seneschal would be the proper authority to strike unworthy names from the roster.' Lysaer surged on his way, his profile keen as an axe.

The tongue-lashed party stared after him, speechless, while late comers bearing legitimate grievances scrambled to assay the next bitter salvo.

Lysaer paid their chorused objections no mind. Light glanced on blond hair, trimmed free of scorched ends, although no one had seen the avatar retire for sleep, far less pause for grooming. Throughout the disaster, and during the long night, he had stayed with his troops, making dispositions and speeding the orders to clear stunned inaction and debris. His voice restored calm, soothed nerves, and brought reason wherever confusion was thickest. While the wounded were shifted and salvaged tents were reset, his exalted person had worn the same grime as the meanest recruit.

Every trace of shared suffering seemed vanished by afternoon. Of yesterday's burns, no discomfort showed. Lysaer's trim frame displayed no suggestion of bandages. His fresh surcoat and gold braid shone pristine as new snow, clothed over in icy composure. 'I have no use for men who fall victim to hardship,' he cracked through the tirades without breaking stride. 'You'll leave my ranks now if you fold under pressure. The Light's work will be finished by more-steadfast hands, and by men who will not abandon this field before the hour of victory.'

The balked officers choked back their seething excuses. Invalidated, disowned, they bristled to realize: their avatar crossed the perimeter set by his sentries. Now, his insolent daring approached the pavilions that housed the Order of the Koriathain.

The collective cries of dismay raised Lysaer's redoubled contempt. 'Have you nothing better to do?'

No hale officer could afford to stay idle, in fact. The sprawled factions of the Alliance war host struggled yet to treat their wounded. They still faced the rows of their unburied dead and a crippling morass of ruined equipment: holed tents, splintered siege engines and burned harness that could not be replaced. Stocks of food stores, weapons, and fodder lay in wreckage beneath the slagged walls.

The unwieldy piles in process of salvage teemed like a hill of kicked ants. Whole companies languished to lick bleeding injuries while some rank-and-file dedicates sought to desert, and others affirmed their raucous survival on the hot flesh of the camp-followers.

Faced by trauma on one hand, and the uncanny power wielded by Koriani, the distempered troop captains stifled their badgering. Far safer to redress their own human troubles than risk the affairs of the initiate sisterhood. If their avatar would tread on the Matriarch's turf, he must go forward alone.

Lysaer spared no glance at the retreating stragglers. His formal dress proclaimed his approach, a shout of authority that required no herald's flourish. He passed the rampant swan banner, with its gold fringe and amethyst field. His direct step assailed the rush mat, then the runner of carpet before the canopied entry to the central hospice.

A sister with coiled wheat hair and the grey robe of charitable service intercepted him at the threshold. A band of white ribbon bordered her cuffs, badge of her lowly rank as a first-level initiate. Despite common stature, she showed no deference to honour a state arrival.

'How may my order grant service?' The same address met every supplicant, or petitioners who bargained for talismans.

Lysaer's level survey matched youthful, clear eyes that overlooked magisterial splendour. His testing regard did not ruffle her poise. Patient as she seemed, she must be unaware of his past confrontations with the order's senior authority.

Therefore, his request was well-spoken and genuine. 'Since your healers are consoling my critically wounded, and also attending my dead, I have come to express the Light's gratitude. More, please offer your colleagues my help if there's aught I can do to assist them.'

'A worthy intent.' The sister inclined her head, smiled, then blushed under his regard. 'You are permitted to enter.'

Lysaer followed her lead. A thicker, spread carpet absorbed his firm step. Softer lighting gentled his eyesight: not coarse candle-flame, but a steady glow that issued from crystals in gold-wire cages. The air smelled of herbals, and also the sharp, ozone tang that discharged with the use of strong spells.

'You have asked to serve?' This polite challenge arose from the left, the new speaker's approach gone unnoticed.

Lysaer paused. 'Where need will allow, yes.' His cool glance appraised the older initiate, seamed with years, and yet still supple in movement. Her austere robe bore three bands of rank, the glint of ribbon like moon-caught silver at sleeves and hood. 'You are the sister in authority here?'

'I am the ranking peeress, directing our mission to ease the afflicted.' Her eyes were kindly brown, and her welcome, graciously honest. 'Follow me, if you will?'

She ushered him into a small, curtained alcove, where an injured man sprawled on a pallet. Two healers attended him: the first clasped his unconscious head between gentle hands, while the other probed an ugly wound on his thigh, the swollen flesh purpled around an embedded splinter of wood. Lysaer recognized one of yesterday's casualties, dragged from the wreck of a siege engine.

The peeress presumed, touched his wrist, and inquired, 'We know you can manifest large-scale destruction. How finely can you control your given gift to raise light?'

Lysaer searched her face but encountered no arrogance. 'What are your needs?' Gravely still, while only his diamond studs shimmered, he added, 'I could illuminate your surgery, or provide warmth. Perhaps boil a cauldron of water, or ignite a lamp's wick.'

The peeress nodded, then invited the enchantress who frowned over the maimed leg to speak.

The kneeling initiate never glanced up to acknowledge the imposing state visitor. 'What about cautery?'

'I don't know.' Lysaer lifted his opened, ringed hands. 'I never tried. The skills of your trade could be learned?' A touch on his shoulder, and the elder peeress departed, leaving him with the pair who tended the stricken soldier. Lysaer bent his knee and smoothed the prostrate man's arm without squeamish hesitation. 'Perhaps,' he suggested, 'you could explain how my gift might improve your prognosis?'

The healer beside him owned three bands of rank, though her rolled sleeves were damp and her pink wrists flecked with blood. She had rich brown hair, but pulled back and pinned with an unbecoming severity. When at length she looked away from the leg wound, she lost her breath, as most did in Lysaer's close presence. His fair-skinned, male beauty was not contrived but a natural force to stun thought.

She shut her eyes, shivered, then rallied her discipline. 'The sliver has split.' More effort still, and she steadied her voice. 'If we try to draw it, the fragment will tear the artery. Removal by surgery could damage the nerves. Blood loss stays problematic. Hot steel to stop haemorrhage will leave intractable scars. At best, if he lives, your soldier will limp for the rest of his days.' Regret raised a tired shrug. 'If only we could have attended him yesterday, before the tissue became congested –'

'Others you saved had more critical injuries?' Lysaer clasped her stained fingers. 'Wars force hard choices.' His comforting squeeze flared to a dazzle of rings, then withdrew. 'How may I help?'

The healer lifted her chin, now determined. 'If you sourced us your light, subject to our sigils, I could burn that wood out. A stay spell could contain the applied energy to the torn muscle that's in direct contact. The cauterized wound might then cleanse itself. We can induce a select amplification to spur the body's reflex to regenerate. Could you grant us the bale-fire use of your gift and entrust us to channel by spellcraft to achieve what's necessary?'

Lysaer smiled like sunrise. 'Lead on, enchantress. My talent is yours to be guided.'

All business, despite her embarrassed blush, the Koriani sister directed the initiate who cradled the prostrate man's head. 'Hold your trance, keep him

under. I'll need the small copper coil, and a few minutes to align the appro-
priate crystals. If this should work –'

The hope that blazed after her unfinished sentence flushed indelicate heat
to her cheeks.

'You have other cases as difficult as this one?' Lysaer asked, despite himself
moved.

'Many.' The healer delved into the satchel at her hip. 'Some who are worse
off.' Despite discouragement, her movements stayed crisp as she handled the
tools of her trade. 'I'm called Samaura, and if you are willing, we could keep
you busy all night.'

'Then we have all night.' Lysaer fielded the woman's surprised glance,
amused.

She pursed her lips and tried not to grin back. 'Why are the Koriathain led
to believe that Avenor's state policy condemns the practice of spellcraft?'

All white elegance blazoned in Sunwheel gold, Lysaer s'Ilessid stayed
unoffended. 'My examiners burn rogue talent that defies a just law. To that
end, I will bear no exceptions.' Against ultimatum, he added, precise, 'This
man fell at war against Shadow. Any who act for his benefit will receive the
Light's gratitude and support.'

'Will you recognize the possibility, yet, that such cause may pose the common
ground to extend your alliance?' The intrusive, cultured voice that observed
arose from the main tent behind.

Although taken aback, Lysaer kept his poise. The two healer initiates owned
no such grace: without regard for the fact he stood witness, they abandoned
the hurt soldier and bent prostrate in supplication.

'Your will, Matriarch,' they declared, unimpeachably obedient, and prepared
to forsake their suffering charge on the instant.

Prime Selidie enforced her due claim to such service. 'Carry on as you are
by my will, and none other!'

Despite the sudden, electrified atmosphere, Lysaer turned not a hair. 'My
pledged word is never subject to interdict.' He did not turn from the soldier
before him, but with calm disdain, ignored the haughty authority crowding
his back.

His comment raised no disturbed rustle of cloth; no hiss of breath, or rebuttal.
Yet the enchantress who minded the wounded man's trance blanched with
near-paralyzed fright. Her sister initiate trembled, bobbed her head, and
murmured, 'Prime Selidie, forgive this man's ignorance.'

Yet the white-clad avatar brushed off her plea. 'I am no supplicant!' he
chided, his goodwill toward the attending sisters still without due regard for
the peremptory presence behind him. 'Nor shall I take pause for your Prime's
dispensation, if my loyal men become compromised. Their lives are not tossed
as bargaining chips into the arena of politics. My wounded have come seeking
help in good faith. Your order chose to admit them. If my offered talent can

spare even one, or renew the least hope of hale function, then your Matriarch had best heed the judgement I laid upon each of her two former messengers.'

'And that would be?' The slim figure swathed in the Matriarch's purple mantle sounded no more than amused. Yet the avid peeresses arrived with her presence caught their collective breath: they were of the order's Prime Circle, invested with the red bands of senior rank.

Lysaer inclined his head, and said, frosty, 'Honour the dignity given in trust. These men are under my oath-bound charge. Fail their genuine need at your peril.'

Prime Selidie smiled, only the curve of her coral lips visible under the shadow of her hooded cloak. 'You presume. In your arrogance, did you believe I had come to brangle over the sick? Our order has provided charitable service for millennia before your first forebear set foot on Athera. Royals leave guildsmen to oversee trade. While you might play at slumming alongside my healers, I am no shopkeeping merchant. Should I trifle with you as you kneel in the dirt? Or fiddle with verbal contests of power concerning the devotion you wield through your followers? You are mistaken, son of s'Ilessid. I am not to be measured, based on your encounters with underlings.'

Lysaer's quiet pause gained a spark of grim irony. 'You've come to defeat the Master of Shadow for the greater good of humanity?'

Yet if his challenge matched the Matriarch's intent, the overture was refused. The hanging ruffled. A rustle of withdrawal, as silk slid on silk, and the Prime's haughty entourage had departed. The man hailed as the Light's avatar was abandoned to fulfil his proud promise and soil his hands with the infirm.

For a suspended instant, Lysaer s'Ilessid regarded his clenched knuckles, lined in the merciless sparkle of rings. Then his poise broke. The untoward explosion arose from his belly, and swelled into full-throated laughter. He clasped his gold head, disarmingly helpless. 'Blinding glory!' he gasped. 'By all means! Let us keep our caring for others off the administrative chess-board, and past the reach of such bitter authority!'

Lysaer flashed a dazzling grin to the pair of enchantresses, left at a loss by uncertainty. 'Proceed. I'm not leaving until your last needs are met, and no stricken casualty inside your hospice requires the light of my gift.'

Haplessly trapped in the wake of her Prime, the enchantress deposed from past rank as First Senior also pondered the barbed sally just exchanged with Lysaer s'Ilessid. Lirenda remained forbidden to speak unless she received dispensation. Her spell-bound will still stayed subject to the extreme punishment that tied her in mute subjugation. She held no authority beyond the pawn's chores, tasked to her from moment to moment.

Today, she was handed the menial assignment of unpacking the sea chests brought by cart from the wharves of Kalesh. Lirenda curtseyed in slaved acquiescence. The wisp of black hair that tickled her cheek could not be shoved back, without leave. Sealed in silenced rage, she could not spare her wretched, plain hems from picking up stains from the trampled earth floor of the half-pitched pavilion. The unkempt state of her person and dress ground her down in humiliation.

She retired to refresh the Prime's wardrobe, all but colliding with the two boy wards unfurling the lavish carpets. More unsworn novices scurried to heat mulled wine and tea and arrange for the Matriarch's bath. Lirenda turned her hands to a maidservant's duty and unlocked the sea trunks. She shook out and aired the Prime's jewelled robes and lace finery. Once the filled buckets and coals for the hot iron arrived, she finished off with a laundress's work and pressed the wrinkles from the ceremonial gauze veils.

Those lavish trappings should have been hers, had she not been cast out of favour as the Prime's hand-picked successor. Lirenda fumed, beyond consolation. Selidie would never restore her to liberty within the foreseeable future.

The twelve ranking seniors still rumpled from travel, also stayed unexcused from their Matriarch's presence. They flocked like ruffled hens around her great chair by the brazier, crowding to warm out the miserable damp inflicted by salt-fusty clothing. Unlike Lirenda, whose lips remained sealed, the inner circle lived unaware of the terrifying fact that the woman who ruled the Order of the Koriathain was a spirit locked under possession. To escape death in office, the former Prime had invasively supplanted a younger protégé as her living vessel. Now, above all suspicion, the creature walked obscenely clothed in an innocent's purloined flesh.

While Prime Selidie perched in cosseted comfort, her train fussed over the testing by-play just exchanged with Tysan's regent pretender.

'. . . such cheeky nerve!' huffed a withered seeress, nursing her aching joints. She could not sit down: the hastily erected pavilion was not yet furnished, beyond the appointments to honour the Matriarch. 'An upstart, and a supplicant under our roof! To have addressed our Prime with his royal back turned! He asks to be served a sharp lesson!'

Another senior with five bands of rank laced her fingers in superior censure. 'Your predecessor would never have stood for such insolence!'

Selidie Prime tossed back her hood. The imperious lift of her chin raised a stinging glitter of gemstones: pins set with rubies and amethyst tamed her netted coil of blond hair. Yet no finery could ease the deformity of her ruined hands, mittened in fur in her lap. 'Lysaer is no supplicant,' she corrected, while a hustling page unclipped her frogged fastenings and slipped off the weight of her mantle.

She was not perturbed. As Lirenda accepted the cast-off garment to be brushed out and retired, the Prime's unflushed skin and pale eyes displayed no rancour.

When the prim senior bristled to argue, Selidie snapped her off short. 'No Prime of our order would sink so low, trading slangs in a public display.'

'The charitable sisters won't grant proper respect for such tolerance,' another enchantress felt moved to point out.

Selidie said nothing. The refreshment tray arrived in the hands of an awe-struck child. Rather than risk her gown to a spill, the Matriarch beckoned to Lirenda.

The debased enchantress was forced to step down from the wardrobe and wait the Prime's table. Lirenda filled the cups, as though she had never possessed a true talent, or been born to a moneyed family. She dispensed spice and sugar to the Senior Circle, mocked by their gloating, ambitious eyes, and snatched what sour comfort she could by tracking the close conversation.

'I will have what I wished through my scryer,' Selidie declared in due course. Where her predecessor would have snapped fingers, she must exert command through commonplace speech. 'Saysha? You engaged a sigil of rapport over Lysaer and carried out my instructions?'

The slender initiate bearing one scarlet band stepped forward and gracefully curtseyed. 'My Prime, yes, indeed. Your quarry was most easy to read, his stead-fast nature all but transparent. Bank on the fact he will stay the course and not lift his siege under pressure. He may guess at our motive to break his half-brother. Yet he does not suspect we have an enchantress already placed in the citadel.'

Elaira, cast into the fray as the irresistible lure to draw Arithon, and whose tender love would deliver him into the Prime Matriarch's grasping hands.

Sunk in turbulent thought, Lirenda lifted the heated pot. She dispensed tea and spooned honey in dutiful servitude. Amid the taut quiet, civilized by the sweet plink of spoons and fine porcelain, she veiled the blaze of anticipation in her tawny eyes, as she considered the upstart sorcerer and masterbard whose interference had seeded her shameful downfall. She, more than any, awaited the day Arithon's captivity became the wedge used to drive the Fellowship Sorcerers onto their knees.

'Our hook is well-set,' said Prime Selidie, well content to shrug off impro-prieties. 'Lysaer's grating manners are not worth correction. Let our sisters in grey treat his grievously wounded. Embrace him and smile, knowing his pompous cause and his war host will be played as the pawns to corner our prize for the taking.' From Lirenda's hand, the Prime accepted the mulled wine her maimed grasp could never manipulate. 'To the ruination of the compact, and to Davien's defeat!'

While the Senior Circle shared her spirited toast, the Koriani Prime Matriarch sipped her spiced drink, replete with satisfaction. 'Where my predecessor failed, I will force the victory and raise our order back to due prominence.'

She had but to wait for Arithon Teir's'Ffalenn to take her laid bait, then jerk the puppet strings tight at the opportune moment.

Lysaer s'Ilessid did not finish his work with the injured, or leave the Koriathain until almost noon the next day. His rich surcoat and poised elegance were no longer faultless when he finally emerged. Paused just outside the dimmed quiet of the hospice tent, he snatched a moment to straighten his shoulders. His rumpled white silk was marred by flecked blood and water-stains. A tarnish of stubble roughened his chin. Except for gold trim, which the sunlight burnished bright as his fair hair, he could have been mistaken for one of his war-harried senior officers.

An escort he failed to expect had apparently ridden to meet him. The snap to his posture as he sighted the party evinced his stifled displeasure: two mounted guards and an apprehensive young equerry, holding the reins of his second-string horse.

Up close, his pallor betrayed lack of sleep. Another night, after the disastrous assault, was unlikely to sweeten his temperament. Ranne and Fennick stayed straight-faced and dared not try to fathom his current, vexed mood.

The Light's avatar accepted the horse. He mounted without a word. His silence beat at his escort's taut nerves, while the equerry wheeled the odd, lop-eared mare, kept on string for unskilled riders to run errands. Still ungreeted, the small party began its unhurried course towards the Sunwheel command tent. Lysaer rode ahead. Whatever thoughts lurked behind his fatigue, the stamped lines around his blue eyes did not welcome the company.

The foursome crossed the posted ring of camp sentries, passed the new horse picket, and cut an oblique course around a latrine trench, which had not existed at sundown. More men with shovels dug a fire pit to burn the carcasses of two destriers, while the distant thunder of hammers bespoke a labour team's effort. Lysaer did not pause, or acknowledge salutes, or praise the brisk industry found in his path.

The supply tents were standing with rolled-up flaps. Within their pooled shade, the dry goods had been organized: the filled casks sorted out by their brands, the sealed barrels of flour separated from the boxes of oiled weaponry nested in straw. A squad of men under someone's crisp orders muscled the inventoried items into neat stacks. More boys rolled and tied salvaged hides. Additional space had been cleared for a practise field. There, squads of recruits with pikes drilled under the squinting review of an officer. Others, between duty, slept in shifts under blankets, while their fellows plied needles and twine, patching tents, or cleaning the singed gear stripped off yesterday's dead.

Lysaer measured the stamp of brisk purpose in place since his visit to the enchantresses. 'Who ordered you out, and how long were you waiting?'

Taciturn Ranne raised his eyebrows, while Fennick coughed behind a mailed fist. Neither man rushed to answer. The fury leashed behind that bland tone meant the avatar already guessed the sore point under question.

The inexperienced equerry plunged ahead anyway, pink with cheerful enthusiasm. 'Our Lord Commander, Sulfin Evend's returned. He arrived by fast boat before dawn.'

'He's late,' Lysaer answered, and dug in his spurs. The horse underneath him grunted and pelted ahead at a gallop.

When the naive boy kicked his mount to keep up, Ranne clamped a stout fist on the bridle and hauled the boy's mare to a plunging halt. 'Don't think to follow your Blessed Lord now.'

Fennick spoke just as fast. 'Trust us, you don't want to be anywhere near when that pair squares off for their reckoning.'

Sulfin Evend's presence continued to make itself felt when Lysaer reined in at the lavish command tent that also served as his personal quarters. Met by deserted quiet, he dismounted without need to fend off any rush of fawning attendants. No pestering cluster of petitioners milled under the awning to beg for his audience. Only a single, liveried groom appeared to lead off his hot horse.

A high-handed precedent, the ceremonial guards that flanked the front entry had been summarily dismissed from their post.

Had Lysaer not been worn flat, he might have laughed for the irony. Plain as shouted warning, his wayward commander had ascertained their meeting would take place in privacy. The front flap, tied open, displayed shaded gloom sparked by the vacated sheen of lacquer and mother-of-pearl furnishings. As Lysaer stepped inside, someone unobtrusive stepped forward: his long-faced valet, for the gentleman's service of taking his soiled mantle.

'His Lordship Sulfin Evend awaits in your map room,' the servant disclosed, then retired with faultless courtesy.

As the storm broke, there would be no witnesses; if, in fact, anyone sworn to the Light owned the courage to stand in the breach.

Lysaer crossed the lavish carpets. He slipped through the curtain that masked the long trestle used for war counsel and troop assignments. Candles burned there. A pool of light set off the tactical maps with their array of pinned banners and coloured counters. The deployment had changed, the emphasis shifted from offensive lines to a tight ring for impenetrable containment. Not only in symbol: the troops on the field would be re-formed as well. Sulfin Evend's crisp style chose action before consultation.

Tireless strategist, the man himself spoke out from the darkest corner. 'I put the heart back into the men with a promise: there will be no more extravagant gestures, and no other messy, headlong assaults.' The accent of the Hanshire aristocrat continued with stripping sting. 'I will give you the victory your allies demand, but not as an epic display soaked in bloodshed. This siege will be won by conventional means. The defenders will die of their own stubborn will, or else lay down their arms, starved into surrender.'

'I should value such counsel, in hindsight?' Lysaer replied, his indifferent tone a reproach. 'You took your time mooning about on the southcoast. So long, in fact, filling my *straightforward* muster, it's a wonder you didn't grow roots there.'

Neither was Sulfin Evend inclined to shy from attacking engagement. 'Good men were burned alive for stupidity. Not over my delay.'

The Alliance Lord Commander had bathed, since arrival, but had declined the entitled splendor of his formal post. Within masking gloom, the detail of his person emerged under aggressive survey: the plain hose and the common-place jerkin that embraced comfort, before authority. Then the straight, dark brown hair that was expertly barbered, a sharp reverse: today, his liege was the one on his feet, unkempt and jaggedly sleepless.

Past question, such uncharacteristic, sleek grooming would be the perfidious touch of the royal valet. That overly fussy, devoted servant bestowed the attention reserved only for his chosen master. Against form, he acknowledged Sulfin Evend as equal. Such care acknowledged the exemplary courage that had once steered the avatar's life clear of jeopardy.

Sulfin Evend bestirred one polished, black boot, and shoved a padded chair forward. 'Sit down, man. You look eaten hollow. I've taken the liberty of sending for wine.'

Which amenity had already arrived on the soundless feet of a servant. Lysaer let his aching frame sink into the cushions, and clasped the filled goblet pressed into his hand. As he sipped, he regarded his prodigal officer: lean as a prized hound, and burned ruddy from weeks in the harsh southern sun. As the drink hit his belly, a slow thaw began. 'You took the time starting the pressed men in training?'

'So you'll see.' Sulfin Evend lifted his glass in salute. 'Your health.'

Those eyes, level grey, were relentlessly keen. The straight brows and cleft chin could intimidate also, when coupled with acid silence. Lysaer had not forgotten the intractable will, which refused to bow as an underling. Bone-tired, he also regretted the fact he had missed this hard man as a friend. Anger and hurt for the extended absence became much too difficult to sustain. 'Your hatred will never relent, for the witches.'

'I don't trust them,' Sulfin Evend replied. 'There's a difference.' He never blinked, before he attacked. 'How did you fare with the Koriani Prime? Was the interview your choice, or hers?'

Lysaer hissed and sat up, catching a dollop of spilled wine in his lap. 'Demon!' he snapped. 'Has it escaped your notice? We have wounded men under charitable care by the auspices of her order. Some are your finest. They won't arise hale, if you haven't heard, without somebody's spellcrafted surgery.'

'Then we're haunted by piteous visions of invalids, done up in unguents and bandages?' Sulfin Evend's teeth flashed as he tasted the fine vintage, then set the goblet aside with an irritable click on the map trestle. 'No. The grey robes and the novices do such menial work. Never, the Prime Matriarch or her secretive clutch of scarlet-ranked seniors! Don't pretend that's not Selidie's pavilion pitched in the midst of their camp. What did she ask of you, Lysaer? Don't hedge!'

'Nothing.' A drawn second passed, while the wine spill soaked in, and the rumpled blond hair shimmered to a run of fine trembling. Lysaer shut bruised eyes. 'The Matriarch asked for nothing. I was there to attend to my casualties. No more and no less.'

Disadvantaged, Lysaer reopened pinched lids. This was Sulfin Evend, who mauled every pretence at subterfuge. The man deserved an honest hearing; had earned the right, since his heroic role at Avenor, which defeated a deadly incursion by necromancers. Against the last campaign's legions of dead, and the nightmare whispers that tormented his dreams, Lysaer had no bastion left. Distrust of this man became a barrier too high for fraught strength to maintain.

'The Matriarch passed through,' he admitted. 'She tried conversation, perhaps even tested the tentative grounds for an overture of alliance. I gave my refusal without ever showing her anything more than my back.'

'Then be assured, we are her acting tools in this game,' Sulfin Evend declared in soft venom. He thrust to his feet. Gave way and paced, and at last the candle-light caught him: more haggard than lean, and fretted inside by unease that spurred him to restlessness. 'Don't underplay that woman's power, or underestimate her long reach. Her initiates act, never knowing her reasons. The arcane trickery wielded by her nest of harpies surpasses the meaning of dangerous. I want the Prime's motive for showing her face, here. Because as things stand, I don't like the taste of knowing we're used as her game pawns.'

'Are we?' Lysaer regarded his Lord Commander, astonished to realize: the man was needled by more than gruff nerves and exhaustion. The concern that reordered the war camp at speed was lashed on by the Matriarch's presence.

'If not for testing the climate for friendship,' Lysaer pressed, 'the Koriani Prime might be here because my half-brother's made the sisterhood his inveterate enemy.'

Sulfin Evend returned a sharp head-shake. 'No. That's too simple. We are holding Prime Selidie's line and doing precisely as she requires, without any clue to the stakes before we get caught in the end-play.' He leaned on the trestle to survey the map, in fact soothed by the inward relief: that Lysaer s'Ilessid *this once* was too tired to unmask the core dread beneath ragged anxiety.

The darkest fear could never be spoken. Lysaer fought this war under the latent pressure of Desh-thiere's cursed influence. Not a fool, the s'Ilessid was strong, and insightful. The values he honoured at heart should have been unimpeachable. Yet he was no avatar; only a man, all too human and desperately vulnerable. Subject to the Mistwraith's warped influence, he posed an ungovernable force for destruction.

Koriathain *owned* that power. The horror stopped thought, that they could, *and they had* instilled such rife madness for their own ends: once, in Lysaer's absence, Sulfin Evend had witnessed such a vile machination. Years ago, the former First Senior had tried to trap Arithon at Riverton, using a conjured fetch to invoke the Mistwraith's geas. Unscrupulous schemers, Koriathain had unleashed that mad drive in cold blood, then used its force to goad their quarry to hapless flight. As a trained mage and initiate master, Arithon survived the experience.

Yet Lysaer owned no such defensive protection. Here on the field, he stood as the poised spear-head of a fanatical war host. When Etarra's troops joined, the numbers that answered his cause soon would swell to seventy-five thousand strong. The frightful potential existed for Prime Selidie to play the Light's Blessed Prince as her personal weapon to launch a disaster.

Autumn 5671

Brangle

Two weeks out of Vhalzein, and hag-ridden by news that the siege had closed in at Alestron, the merchant brig *Evenstar* hove into the trade port of Thirdmark. There, her three-masted rig and furled canvas made her a looming albatross set down among bobbing gulls. Her ocean-going keel forced her to anchor outside of the jumbled stone breakwater that enclosed the town wharves, since the Mistwraith's invasion reshaped the ancient patterns of commerce. The placid, cove harbour now catered to trade fleets of shallow-draught galleys. Even three decades after clear sky restored accurate navigation, the shoal-ridden narrows within Rockbay Harbor continued to favour oared vessels. Tight inlets and jagged shore-lines, compounded by swift-running currents, posed hazards few blue-water captains cared to attempt, under sail.

Evenstar's master prided herself on being the glaring exception.

From Vhalzein, she had run the estuary to Redburn to take on dispatch packets from Quaid, and to onload the spruce lumber preferred by the Southshire shipyards. Her next call, at Spire, picked up casks of beer, flour, and soda ash to be resold to the glassworks at Ithish. Outbound, and riding low on her marks, she had rounded the north point off the Isle of Myrkavia, a trial of seamanship that had snagged many lesser ships on a reef. At Firstmark, upcoast, she laid in wine and hides for the milk-run that fetched her this rolling, second-rate anchorage.

The charts of those treacherous waters were presently furled and shelved. Now, as the exhilaration of dicey handling subsided to restive fatigue, the news came in by pigeon from other points east that the Light's vengeful war host had claimed its first casualties.

Worse, to Captain Feylind's jaundiced eye, the *Evenstar's* chart desk lay

206

mired by mercantile trade. Landlubber's paper-work, bruised by the officious ink stamps of the harbour-masters, and the fussier parchments, crusted with the seals and ribbons, preferred by the excisemen.

While the ship creaked and swung to the outbound tide, *Evenstar's* master jammed her taut fingers through the straw hair at her temples. 'Fatemaster *crap* on the scribblings of clerks!' *Lading lists!* She hated them. Almost as much as the blow-hard authorities who imposed their port taxes and wharfage. Far-sighted, she squinted at the miserable squiggles that valued the brig's current cargo.

'Pirating bastards,' she muttered, irked by the inflated assessment placed on the spruce.

A shadow loomed overhead: the first mate, peering down through the quarter-deck hatchway. 'That's better. You've been much too quiet since hearing the scuttlebutt ashore.'

Feylind's return tirade would have shamed a fishwife. She added, 'I don't like the news, and you didn't, either. Is that why you've made sure every-thing's planned to a fare-thee-well in advance?'

At Thirdmark, said the lists, she would take on goat cheese, and bone meal for the porcelain guild at Sanshevas. Ahead, the bursar's needs were detailed for reprovisioning at Shandor. To make the stop pay, the brig would swap the cheese and some of the beer for board lengths of West Shandian oak. At Ithish, she would exchange her flour for baled wool bought raw from the shepherds of Vastmark, then that reeking load was bound on to the auctions that supplied the dyers at Innish.

'We're scheduled tight as the gears in a pinch-fisted shore factor's clock!' Feylind groused.

The shadow solidified into a breathing, warm presence as the mate slung himself downwards into the stern cabin. 'Damned right.' Teive approached from behind and folded her into a consuming embrace. 'We've chased our own tail in these forsaken cold waters for too long.' His salt-crusted chin parked on top of her head, he added in gentle remonstrance, 'In case you've forgotten? Our children are at Innish. Probably banging holes in the tiles of Fiark's wife's pretty kitchen. They miss you, too.'

Which stinging line inferred her past night, spent pacing the deck under starlight.

Feylind swatted him off. 'Your damned stubble itches.' She tipped up her head, accepted his kiss, then grabbed him, hard, and held on. Wrapped in the fusty smell of his sea jacket, she strove to subdue raw anxiety.

'You don't know that Prince Arithon will be drawn to Alestron,' Teive stated with maddening calm.

Feylind shivered. 'We don't know that he won't.' She pursued, 'He came for us when this ship was threatened, and s'Brydion have stood as his allies for years. You think his soft heart can deny them?'

Something bumped, abovedeck. By the quartermaster's haranguing tirade, the disturbance involved an inept longshoreman and the cask of grain alcohol just slung aboard for treatment of salt-water lesions.

'You'd better go topside,' Feylind said, resigned. 'Before some slacker thinks to straw-tap that barrel and suck himself rip-roaring prostrate.'

Yet Teive was not diverted so easily. 'The crew can look after itself for the moment.'

Feylind stirred for sharp protest. He forestalled the attempt, cupped a weathered hand against her turned cheek, and captured her shove to release him. Then he tightened his hold, appalled as he sighted the paper-work on the desk-top. 'You're planning to contract our cargo out on consignment to another vessel bound into Innish? Feylind, why? If I allow this, your brother is certain to dice both my bollocks!'

'If you don't agree, I'll claw first,' threatened *Evenstar*'s captain, her tigerish mood turned defensive.

Teive had the experience to hear her distress. He fished the snagged loop of blond hair from his callus but did not release his embrace. 'I won't let you go until you tell everything.'

'When bulls give fresh milk and lay hen's eggs!' Feylind wrenched herself free. Ever and always, Teive's deep concern cracked her nettled rage and undid her. She leaned back, elbows braced on the traitorous documents.

'We'll provision at Shandor, well enough,' she relented. 'But not keep this cargo. I'll have nothing else loaded into our hold that's not westbound round the cape.'

The mate perched his sturdy frame on the chart locker, his grey eyes agleam with challenge. 'You'd run back to Havish?' He caught the flicker of determination before she broke off his glance. 'Telmandir!' he corrected, appalled, as intuition unveiled her conniving. 'You want to petition High King Eldir to send relief to the s'Brydion citadel?'

'Someone must.' Feylind was never frivolous. Her radical decisions always were framed by the logic of an off-shore navigator.

Teive tried and failed to suppress his sharp qualm. Practical, first, he shouted topside to clear off the *Evenstar*'s quarterdeck. 'We don't need to perk up the ears of the crew,' he told Feylind. 'Yes, lady! We're going to discuss this.'

She folded her arms and glared back at him.

Which only moved Teive's good nature to laughter. 'You never bite half so well as you bristle. If you're going to clam up, I'll toss you in bed. That's easier than sweating over the clues to your hare-brained habit of thinking.'

'No,' Feylind said.

The cabin between them seemed suddenly cold, beyond what the season should warrant. As the quiet stretched, loud with the creak of worked wood, and the wind-driven slap of snugged halyards, Teive sighed. He could be quite as stubborn.

'What if I agree with you?' he suggested, dead calm. 'That Arithon is a friend, and his s'Brydion allies might be in need of us. Why should *Evenstar* put in to Havish?'

Feylind exploded and stood, as trust smashed her reticence. 'Who else could go?' she exclaimed, her voice cracking. 'If we're going to smuggle supplies for Alestron, we can't involve Fiark! The Light's influence over the southshore towns would have priestly noses poked straight up our backside! Any one of a dozen corrupted officials could tip off the vengeance of the Alliance. King Eldir owes us twice over, after our help throughout last year's famine. And unlike the other ships loyal to Arithon, *Evenstar*'s neutral registry can slip us past the curs at Kalesh and Adruin that watchdog the blockaded estuary.'

Teive scraped his rough chin. 'You think we could carry the pretence of bearing provender to Lysaer's camped troops? Then signal, once we're close enough to be recognized, and our hold's contents to be overtaken by Alestron's defenders?'

'Ath!' Feylind fetched him a cuff on the shoulder, then let him snag her back into his arms. 'You know my mind much too well for a man who's never been wed as a husband.'

'And whose fault is that?' Teive chuckled. 'Not mine, wild woman.' Then he sobered. 'You know by now that wherever you go, I intend to stick like a lamprey.'

'Including the teeth,' declared Feylind, unmoved. 'I take it you're crewing this tub west to Havish?'

'Especially with the teeth.' The mate bent his neck and nipped at her ear until she shrieked with ticklish outrage. 'I am going to Havish,' he added, smug. 'If only to see what High King Eldir will do when you land this whopper in his royal lap. That's if his majesty will agree to allow a tramp captain the daylight for a crown audience.'

Feylind grinned, then kissed Teive's lips with a will to disrupt the dastardly paper-work. 'King Eldir will hear me. It's Fiark,' she murmured, 'who's going to need the threat of Dharkaron's Black Chariot for softening.'

And Tharrick, and Jinesse, and Fiark's wife, prayed the mate, alongside the lunatic, outside hope, that time with the children might prevail against his beloved's bed-rock sense of loyalty.

Stirrings

In the Kingdom of Tysan, buried under the ruin that once housed Avenor's state treasury, a wrecked coffer enclosing the skulls of four hatchling dragons settles in the debris; and as their singed silk covering crumbles, a wakened flicker of energy spins out a tendril that is *almost* a thought . . .

The same hour that a drifter gifts a weanling colt sired by Isfarenn to Althain Tower, Asandir struggles against driving sleet inside of Scarpdale's grimward; he still holds the shade of his stallion secured between his cupped palms, though he slips as the footing shifts to glare ice, and a lightning flare blinds his bearings . . .

While onloading contraband provisions from a fishing lugger, Alestron's roving war fleet hears rumours of the Alliance assault, with Keldmar s'Brydion burned alive with his field-troops amid Lysaer's first onslaught, and through raging grief, Parrien swears to wreak a revenge that will grant the invaders no quarter . . .

VII. Siege

A fortnight beyond the initial assault, the entrenched siege gripped Alestron in deadly earnest. Lysaer was not making a second mistake. His troops maintained their fall-back position, past reach of an offensive strike. The duke's massive trebuchets poised, unused, while their idle crews huddled against biting sea-wind, under the diligent eyes of the garrison. Sentries and armed companies stayed alert at the crenels. They held their posts, watch upon watch, prepared for assault, but offered no useful target. Day upon day, the white-and-gold standards flapped over the Alliance war camp, a view that mocked them with immobile serenity, and a drawn line that enforced their captivity.

No forays occurred, night after stilled night. Upon the stripped earth, the enemy drilled troops and exercised fractious horses. They sprawled and caroused in their invasive pavilions, while the mewed-up defenders watched their manoeuvres from the cold, distant height of the parapets. To stand down was to risk being taken off guard. Any dark, cloudy night, the Light's Lord Commander might launch a sneak attack against the watch turrets at the harbour-front. To endure each patrol, hung in fraught expectation, became an agony in itself. The empty hours sawed at the nerves, until the misery of endless inaction blunted the senses like a dull knife.

Routine begat the worse poison of boredom. Time was the weapon to break steadfast will, while the stockpiled food in the warehouses dwindled, and tight rationing eroded resolve.

The wait bore hardest of all on Sidir. Not the shrinking portions, which ended each meal on the pinch of unsatisfied hunger. Hard winters had shown him gaunt seasons before. His experience weathered such short-falls in step, and his touch with the fretful and crying children could rival a mystical healer's. But his lifelong venue had been the free wilds. The enclosure of walls and stone-paved streets wore down his forest-bred spirit: first to short words, then to deep silences, which extended into reclusive retreat atop the swept crags overlooking the bay-side defences. He was not wont to brood. Since the bow stolen from Lysaer's camp was sub-standard, and the offered replacement from Alestron's armoury never suited his exacting taste, Elaira found him stirring a glue-pot over a frugal fire. Beside him, spread out on a dry wrap of leather, he had laid out the composite laminates: sinew and shaved strips of ox-horn to bond with the frame for a recurve bow.

'Where's Fionn Areth?' the enchantress inquired.

Sidir looked up, his metallic eyes piercing. 'Should I care?'

'Yes,' said Elaira. 'You've been avoiding him.' Against a sovereign imperative, she did not have to add: *this* clansman's expression of polite reserve was as good as a spoken rebuff. 'Why?'

Sidir's eyebrows lowered in bristled offence. 'You have to ask that?'

'I shouldn't,' Elaira agreed. 'Which is the reason I must.'

Gusting wind streamered the bronze braid she had tied with plain cord and blushed cheekbones that showed the first edge of privation. Despite the pervasive stench of hot glue, she sat on a mossy rock by the verge, where the cliffs dropped sheer to the closed defences that sheltered Alestron's cove harbour.

Sidir's obstinacy kept him stirring his pot, while the rudely hacked ends of his greying, dark hair lashed at his weathered face. 'Did you think an encounter should be so easy?'

Direct to the point of brutality, he inferred the raw pain left from Daon Ramon Barrens, and the horrific cost of the Araethurian's royal rescue. Earl Jieret had died to draw Arithon clear, as well as eight of the remaining Companions, adult survivors of Tal Quorin's massacre, who had seen a generation of children put to slaughter by Lysaer's troops.

Yet the astute awareness of Koriani training saw past the convenient – *the obvious* – shield spun from grief: this clansman's hands were too steady, immersed in his work.

Elaira shivered. 'You aren't that squeamish, concerning your dead.'

Sidir's jaw tightened. He looked away then, his spare, rugged profile stamped against sky. His reluctance ran deeper than recent resentment; was no wounding due to Tal Quorin, or Daon Ramon, after all. He braced before speaking. 'You weren't at Vastmark when –'

But she had been. 'Look at me, Sidir!' Exposed to his searching regard, Elaira incited his birth-gifted insight for truth: that she *had* been made witness to the horrors that Arithon's hand had unleashed in that mountain campaign. She also knew every twist that occurred in his Grace's deadly, flawed reasoning. 'I shared my beloved's traverse of the maze under Kewar.'

The clansman unlocked his penetrating stare in discomfort. 'You saw most. But not everything.' Attention fixed back on his task, he added, 'Not what was done to keep your man sane, through the back-lash and during the aftermath.'

The soft phrase stayed dangling, a warning that failed. Elaira leaned forward, flipped the hide over the fitted bow frame. 'You will answer this!' Shown his taut offence, she shoved to her feet and rode over clan stubbornness. 'Sidir! Without distractions.'

'This weapon can't equal the ones that are shaped, lashed onto forms for a year,' the Companion disparaged. Never inclined to swear over set-backs, he relinquished his glue stick and swung his bubbling pot off the fire. 'That boy's an errant, wild spark,' he declared. 'Sets his stormy, emotional blazes without care for anyone's dignity.'

'Perhaps that's why Arithon wants his loyalty grounded,' Elaira allowed without compromise. 'Volatile, he's a danger to all of us. The weak link too likely to fracture.'

Sidir surveyed her. 'Fionn's not so foolish as that, or so angry he won't listen to Talvish. And yet, to hand such a one my prince's deepest vulnerabilities feels like a stark breach of trust.'

Elaira had no grounds to argue that point. Faced by the livid, disfiguring weals on the wrists of a man who was already war-scarred, she said gently, 'Do you know of another way?'

Sidir's recoil was instant. 'Arithon didn't,' he snapped, now annoyed. 'I protest because I don't like it.'

The root reason *would be* some uncanny awareness garnered through his gift of Sight. Patience might coax his disclosure; or not. Sidir was a tiger, for principles. Elaira gave him space. Further speech was not needed. Sound carried, even to these wind-swept heights: the relentless clash of practise engagement, and the boom of the drums, as the Light drilled its troops through the boredom of deadlocked warfare.

'I don't trust the heart of that young man,' Sidir relented at last. 'He has never been sure of himself, even at home with his herding family. He does not know, at his core, who he is. Which drives him to count coup, and hold grudges. To look outside, seeking for positive proof that his loyalties are not misguided.' Now came the tortured admission: 'If I answer his questions, Fionn Areth will use what he knows. Not to stand firm on his chosen ground but to hurt and tear down for advantage.'

Elaira faced away, watching the eastern sun scatter chipped-diamond reflections across the water below: a view, in these days, unendingly smudged by the smoke from Sevrand's troops, manning the signal turrets. Into the punishing pause, she said carefully, 'Fionn's potential betrayal of Arithon feels altogether too much like disloyalty.'

'To all that I stand for!' Sidir had not stopped listening after all. Though her calm tone stayed flawless, he unfolded his tall frame. Hands set on her shoulders, quite firmly, he spun her around.

Her vivid tears streamed. His callused touch a contrite apology, he brushed her wet cheeks with a finger. 'You feel responsible.'

Which was too accurate. 'I helped change that boy's features,' Elaira said, bleak. 'By my Prime's directive, I laid that fate on to a child just barely six years of age.' And burning, unspoken: *should anyone wonder why this Araethurian does not understand who he is?*

She permitted Sidir's stringent grip. Let him bundle her into a chaste embrace that did little but break the harsh wind.

'I will meet with your goatherd,' the clansman allowed. 'Not so much for my liege's royal command, but as your service, done without asking.'

Sidir's glue-pot, perforce, became relocated to a cramped, barracks fire-place inside the chamber most often used to hear officers' complaints. The day-to-day grinding of dray wheels, and the tramp of patrols at the watch change did not penetrate the thick walls of the Mathiell Gate keep. The sealed silence kept by old, wakened stone at times seemed to whisper, alive by Paravian magic. Notes or words past hearing, the quickened strain weaved through the echoes of rough conversation that bounced up the steep stair from the ward-room.

Not every man who lived by the sword could abide that deep presence in comfort.

A forest-bred clansman would be the exception. Present as well, just come off active duty, Talvish sprawled in a battered, slat seat, one idle knee hooked on the chair arm. Shown the deft expertise of a Halwythwood bowyer, he watched, green eyes never fooled by the quiet skill that affixed the shaved horn to the wood frame. The blond war-captain opened, 'This place poses no refuge, except from the troops. If they haven't themselves been dressed down at this trestle, they'll shun the place where their fellows are cited for punishment.'

Sidir's lips flexed. 'I should be concerned that we might not stay private?'

'Fionn Areth's likely as not to show up here.' Talvish tested the murkier waters. 'If you meet, I presume that can't be by mistake?'

Sidir hooked a soaked thong from the nearby bucket and began winding the glued strip for bonding. 'No need to circle.' He did not look up. 'I am prepared to hear out the whelp's brazen questions.'

Talvish's lazy silence extended: a lynx might display such bone stillness. For the duke's ranking officers, days began before dawn. The wear showed in his pale hair, crimped from his steel helm, and in knuckles grazed red from some bare-fisted labour, performed in salt water below the Sea Gate. Tired or not, the field veteran perceived clearly.

For his own reason, this well-guarded clansman wanted the coming scene public.

Sidir knotted off the wet thong with his teeth, just past the splice that stiffened the end that would notch the finished silk bow-string. He stretched his shoulders, then extended the strapped limb of the bow frame into the fireplace. As the thongs shrank themselves dry in the smoke, he broached in soft-spoken reluctance, 'I am the last left alive, who endured both the reiving at the River Tal Quorin, and the campaign against Lysaer at Vastmark. Twice, I've wrestled to subdue the hard aftermath when my liege was forced to fight under Desh-thiere's directive.'

Across the dimmed closet, Sidir confronted the most subtle of the duke's war-captains. 'I have sensed that your loyalty serves my liege from the heart.'

Talvish paused. Against a muffled contention in the ward-room below-stairs, he chose not to gainsay, though Sidir's piercing statement effectively split his allegiances.

'Without pride,' the clansman laboured on with distaste, 'some things may be needful to know from inside my store of experience.'

Talvish resisted his impulse to straighten from informal posture. Against knifing grief, that Vhandon was not the accustomed rock at his side, he scoffed gently, 'Here I thought you wanted a yapping dog leashed, and no suicide leaps by the idiot hare, thinking to rip the wolf's jugular.'

Sidir laughed. 'That too! The Araethurian pays your soldier's discipline lip service, at least. Some pitfalls of personal embarrassment might be disarmed by your presence.'

'As Arithon's won't be,' Talvish closed without flinching.

Humour died. 'A man's strengths can break,' Sidir allowed. 'During the bad times, three of us at full strength could scarcely contain the set-backs brought on by his nightmares of self-condemnation.' And those bulwarks were gone. The irascible clan war-captain, Caolle, and the Companion, Eafinn, both years dead; Sidir kept the clenched pain of their memories locked fast.

'We've got Dakar and Elaira,' Talvish pointed out. Their advantage *might* balance the powerful changes wrought by the maze under Kewar; or might not, which spurred the ongoing concern. He risked the hard question against the creak of thongs, drying in flame. 'What do you fear, liegeman?'

This time, Sidir replied at sharp speed. 'A knife in his Grace's back.'

'The one he'll invite out of sheer provocation? Then rest content. We see eye to eye.' Talvish shoved straight. 'For now, your royal debt has come due.'

But forest-bred senses had already flagged the steps from the passage. '*I'taer chya strieka'an am'jiere,*' Sidir snapped in Paravian under his breath.

Then 'the calm that bred chaos' banged open the door. Fionn Areth bounced in, bringing the reek of hot horse and oiled steel along with the sweat-ragged fleece of his gambeson. 'You should see the uproar over today's wager!' he blurted. 'Jeynsa's thrashed Sevrand at lances, thrown from ambush at moving targets.' His belated notice encompassed Sidir, which first widened his eyes, then silenced him.

'Today, my knives are for carving dead wood,' the clansman declared, accent cracking. 'Take care with your manners, young sprig.'

'Which implies that he's ready to answer your questions,' Talvish suggested with sly provocation.

'I would sooner converse with a snake!' Fionn Areth side-stepped the clutter. Arrived at the trestle, he camped on the bench beside Talvish's chair and eyed the unfinished staff being cured in the hearth. 'That's a bow?'

'Half of one.' Satisfied with the tension set up by damp leather, Sidir laid the baked frame across his thigh and began daubing glue on the opposite limb. 'Speak and have done. Even snakes prefer their choice of company.'

Fionn Areth regarded the clansman's bent head, dark hair threaded white at the temples; the hunter's hands confident, as the shaped strip of horn was warped into place with another soaked thong from the bucket. Whether or not such calm should be disturbed, the Araethurian dared the first hurdle. 'You saw the horrors at Tal Quorin and Vastmark. Endured the brunt of the losses. I wanted to ask of your prince's intent. Why don't you believe he's a criminal sorcerer, shedding the blood of the innocent?'

'Because there's no truth to the claim,' Sidir said, twining thong with near-mystical patience. 'Otherwise, I would be dead, and all of my people along with me. Arithon's acts spared our clans at Tal Quorin. Etarra's attackers fell in harsh numbers, but the same terms that killed them granted survival for two hundred lives on our side. Town-born will overlook that accomplishment. Yet a fact ignored by the cause of the victor cannot be refuted for convenience.'

'Why not?' challenged Fionn. 'A death is a death. A thousand cut down to save one is too steep a price, no matter whose sons filled the grave-sites.'

Sidir yanked his knots tight, in no hurry. But his eyes were steel as he glanced up. 'Should such townsmen have invaded the free wilds to start with? Whose warmongering choice brought them on us, but Lysaer's? Why raise Etarra to arms against the pledged terms of the compact? There are boundaries set to curb merchant trade, and town factions who desire them broken.'

'Your old ways, maintained at what cost to humanity?' pressed Fionn Areth, unsatisfied. 'Should anyone die for a law that's defunct? Your people prey on the roadways as thieves, and no more Paravians inhabit Athera!'

'I can guarantee that they do,' Sidir said. 'Or I would not be here, engaged in a theoretical debate over a justice our royal lineages have pledged to protect.'

Fionn Areth hooted, and pounced. 'You can't know for certain!'

'I haven't the vision,' Sidir agreed. 'Not to gainsay the Fellowship Sorcerers, whose binding purpose preserves the old races' line of survival. The crown our Teir's'Ffalenn must uphold *is* the fulcrum that maintains the care-taking balance between human need and the mystery that nurtures a living Paravian awareness. The trade-guilds have long overstepped charter rights! Clan heritage serves the free wilds, and the high kingship is the marriage of human flesh with the creative matrix of Athera's existence. For this, Prince Arithon was acknowledged by Fellowship hands to carry the terms of our fealty.'

'His defence claimed your family,' Fionn Areth bore in. 'For the sake of an abstract you've never experienced, I want to know why don't you hate him.'

'But I do,' Sidir contradicted. Raw flame licked the bowstaff. The heat-dried sinew popped and crackled, cranked under the stresses of tightening.

Through the shocked pause, Fionn Areth should have crowed. Instead, he gaped beyond speech.

Sidir turned the bow. The fresh weals on his wrists shining with scar tissue, he stated, 'I hate his Grace for each of my beloved kinsfolk, gone from this life for his defence. For all of the times he deserted our clans. Left us on the run from the knives of the scalpers, who feed on trade greed and Alliance corruption. Who despoil our clan women and innocent girls under the dog-pack brutality that infests the head-hunters' leagues.'

'But –'

'Such events are not myth!' Sidir interrupted. Into Fionn Areth's disbelieving, set teeth, he said more. 'My sister was gutted and raped, at Tal Quorin. My aunt in Fallowmere, staked out on cold ground, while eight men with league badges took turns forcing her till she died, bleeding. My mother, I won't further defile.' He added, 'I don't weep in your presence! Those I loved dearest are quite beyond pain. Now, their justice relies on the *merciful* rule of my prince, who ought to be crowned at Ithamon.'

Fionn Areth fired back, his frustration ringing within the closed chamber. 'And was his Grace's *mercy* what brought down the mountain upon twenty-five thousand, at Dier Kenton Vale?'

'His sore desperation, entrapped by the geas of Desh-thiere,' Sidir responded, unmoved. 'I lived that horror. It still threads my dreams, for the dread power contained by that one, fragile vessel. How fragile, I realized. My hand was one that helped shore up the cracks.'

'Then you acknowledge a crime was committed against nature, and for naught but cold-blooded mass murder,' accused Fionn Areth, while Talvish, cat still, attended the scene in braced stillness. 'What cause can justify cruelty on that scale?'

'No cause. Ever. And for Vastmark, no false cloth of reason at all! Both parties were cursed. They engaged by consent. Arithon, to defang a war host that had nowhere to turn, except to target his friends. Lysaer, to destroy *one man* that a geas-borne belief posed as his arch-enemy. In defeat, the s'Ilessid salved his losses through conceit. He claimed to speak for Ath Creator. In victory, my Teir's'Ffalenn wept for the wounding, arisen from the flawed nature of his convictions.' Sidir lifted the bow frame away from the fire and tested the wrap with quick fingers. 'Our hatred is easy, for each time his Grace's strength lets us down, and for the clay that reminds us he shares our humanity.'

Fionn Areth stared, speechless, though always with him, such deflated pauses were brief. 'If you knew Arithon might commit such atrocities again, why didn't you kill him?'

'Best ask why I love him,' Sidir answered back, and looked up with his features stripped naked.

The sheer, caring depth of adult vulnerability caught Talvish's breath in his throat. He resisted the raw urge, to grab the glib grass-lander's shoulder and shake him. Though his swordsman's instincts cried out to act, before lancing such pain caused explosion, he understood why Arithon had picked this stead-fast clansman as his personal spokesman. Fionn Areth must decide for himself: whether to sort out his conflicted loyalties, standing upon his own merits. Or whether to cashier respect and ask Sidir to lay bare his soul in a way that must open him down to the viscera.

'I see that I can't lean on another man's values,' the Araethurian declared, sounding shaken. The Companion's raw courage, exposed at close quarters, had seared off his protective bluster. 'Direct principles count,' he finished, subdued. 'Since the features I wear weren't ever my own, I'm caught in the turbulence sown by your crown prince.'

'That's why Arithon insists that you matter,' Sidir agreed. 'And why he fears most for your safety. Do you find his wish to safeguard you so hard?'

'Yes, since the price is my freedom!' The Araethurian slammed to his feet. 'I don't have the option of choosing my way! Even if, s'Brydion tempers forbid, my sympathies lie with your enemies.'

'And do they, in fact?' Sidir asked, tautly poised. 'Is self-honesty what you're afraid of? *Are we thrashing out Arithon's short-falls, or yours?*'

'Mine, of course,' snapped Fionn Areth with venom. 'The duke runs a clan stronghold. Should I invite another six months, shut in with the rats in Alestron's dungeon?' The goatherd stomped out. Shed fleece from his gambeson whirled on the disturbed air, sucked in by the draw of the hearth and lit to sparks in the updraft.

'Volatile,' said Talvish. 'But too right.' He stretched, unkinking the knots in his shoulders. 'If Arithon's the criminal posed by the Alliance, that young man can't leave without losing his neck over principle.'

'Well, he has got a spine underneath all the muddle.' Sidir covered the pannikin of hot glue. Thoughtfully fatalist, he hefted his afternoon's handi-work under his critical eye. 'Like this bow, and choice wood, we won't know if yon goatherd shoots straight or contrary until the moment he's strung and tested against the mark.'

Talvish himself did not relish patience. 'Then let us all hope that the moment occurs when no one around him is caught under pressure.'

The clansman gathered his lean frame and stood. Across the reddish glow of the flames, grey eyes met green in a moment of locked understanding. 'You'll keep the watch with me?'

'Always,' said Talvish, quite aware that the subject was no longer the double, but the unbroached burden of confidence this liegeman had carried since Vastmark. 'You know Arithon's coming?'

Sidir nodded. 'In that way, Elaira's infallible.' He offered his arm for the wrist clasp that sealed amity. 'Heed my fair warning, once my liege arrives. If he loses the nasty edge on his tongue, by that sign you'll know he's endangered.'

The new moon came and went, which heralded the month of late autumn. And as Selkwood's wizened seeress had foretold, the hour arrived for departure. Informed by the uncanny tingle that raked through his bones and warm flesh, Kyrialt s'Taleyn tossed off his sleeping furs. He sat up, aware that Glendien had arisen ahead of him. No secret escaped her. The innate talent of her clan lineage sensed pending change like a weathercock.

'I've packed already,' she declared from the dark, her voice charged to vibrant excitement.

'Packed?' Kyrialt stood, the bite of cold air heightening his jangled nerve ends. 'Woman, what on Ath's earth does a man take to war, beyond his trained skill and his weapons?'

'Medicinal herbs, salts for physics, willow bark, and wild rose hips,' Glendien retorted. 'My bundles will ease hurt and spare lives, while you clean your sheathed weapons more often for rust in a siege.' She sounded too smug, that sickness from crowding was more likely than steel to bring the duke's troops to their knees.

'That's presuming without Bransian's hot-headed temper, to sit when he'd rather be fighting.' Kyrialt padded across the chill lodge tent and began dressing at speed, as a scout would do, by rote touch.

'That's presuming,' Glendien retorted, dead crisp, 'that your Teir's'Ffalenn's not a fit match for bullish entitlement.'

Kyrialt laughed. 'The pair are hell-bound to lock horns. Shall we wager how soon?'

'Rough sport,' said his wife. 'You're actually guessing how long it takes for s'Brydion wit to learn how to corner the gad-fly.'

'Or us, for that matter.' For everything had changed, since the night in the King's Grove. Kyrialt belted on the boiled-hide tunic he kept for hunting amid winter briar. As he reached for his arms, he found Glendien's hands there, ahead of him.

'Mine, the wife's honour, husband.' She did not have to ask which blade to gird on him. The sword with the ancestral inset of Shand would not be carried afield to Alestron. The plain steel would go, and the baldric with the carved bosses. As Shand's gift of honour, the High Earl's son went, pledged under the Crown of Rathain. The farewells to friends and kinsfolk had been said, in private tears and bitter-sweet celebration. Kyrialt sat on a stool made of stag's horns, while the agile fingers of the woman he loved bound his dark hair into the pattern of the s'Taleyn clan braid. After, he arose and threw on his cloak, then snatched the moment, while she handled the fastenings of hers, to steal the kiss he preferred to welcome the morning.

They left his lodge tent together and stepped into the windless dark. Fuzzed stars shone through the scudding clouds that would bring drizzling rain before dawn-light. Kyrialt followed Glendien, past the banked ash of the camp's central fire and the skeletal frames of the drying racks. They slipped through the bounds observed by the sentries, and exchanged wrist clasps with the outlying scouts. No one asked awkward questions. Everyone accepted that Kyrialt's destiny took him from Shand. The chosen path led away from the picket lines, since he and Glendien would not be travelling mounted. A departure from Selkwood, with the marker stones roused, bespoke the power of a Fellowship Sorcerer.

'He'll call on Davien,' Kyrialt surmised, the saw-tooth edge of his trepidation passed beyond onlooking earshot.

Glendien's anticipation did not abate, or the hamper of herbs slow down her electrified eagerness. Sure of foot, and winding down-slope towards the willow groves flanking the river-bank, she admitted what her hunter's gift told her. 'The Sorcerer's already waiting.'

Kyrialt frowned. 'You trust him too easily, not knowing his motives.'

Yet the wife always relished encounters that promised uncertain danger. 'Predictability's boring.' Glendien slid through the last, screening trees, and bent to unlace her soft boots. 'Best strip if you don't want wet clothing.'

'Might have warned me we'd wade before I was clad,' Kyrialt groused, unhooking a thorn from his sleeve.

Glendien snorted. 'If I'd done that, we'd still be abed, gorgeous man, with no cold water to pucker your bollocks.'

'I'll watch what else puckers and take full advantage,' he threatened, peeled down to the skin. Roughened with gooseflesh, he wrapped his shed mantle over his weapons and tossed leathers and shirt across his powerful shoulders.

Then, for her insolence, he reached out and snatched, piled bundles and all, and hauled his wife backwards and kissed her. Glendien elbowed him off, spluttering with laugher. 'Randy young spike!'

They plunged into the river side by side. Gasped as the chill slapped into warm flesh and swirled without mercy, waist deep. Selkwood was not touched by frosts before winter. Still, the brisk nights braced the current that eddied and lapped at their groins. Over mud bottom and slippery stones, the couple breasted the channel. Their shuddering breaths hissed through their clamped teeth and cooled all merry impulse for dalliance.

They emerged from the shallows onto Stag's Islet, a narrow spit snagged with flowering weeds that flooded in the lush spring. Through autumn's low water, the herds of dun deer grazed the verges and locked horns in clattering rut. A confluence of flux lines crossed the low rise, magnified by the watercourse. There, on the snag of a lightning-struck pine, the silhouette of an eagle hunched against star-silvered mist.

'Davien. I told you.' More thrilled than afraid, Glendien pushed through the summer's dried reeds and melted into the shoreside coverts. 'Hurry,' she whispered. 'His Grace won't be far behind us.'

'He won't like your wanton eyes, spying,' Kyrialt chided. Yet he followed her into the brush to dry off out of sight in the darkness.

To Glendien's disappointment, Prince Arithon did not wade, half-naked, across the black water. He approached from the north, dark hair soaked from a swim, and in stinging command of his dignity. He wore briar-scarred leathers: the same ones used for the hunting excursions that had provided fresh game for two fortnights. The chase had hardened him. His fit tread made no sound. If his grooming was raffish, his linen was clean, the bow at his shoulder replaced by Alithiel's hung sheath, and the fleece bundle of his lyranthe. He also carried the gifted black cloak, draped over the crook of his forearm. Starlight glinted, thin as flecked ice, over silver-thread borders and fastenings.

As his light step brought him under the pine snag, the eagle unfurled massive wings. Form and feathers dissolved as the Sorcerer alighted, erect on two legs as a man. His very presence diminished the night. Taller than Arithon, and mantled in velvet trimmed with edging of spotted lynx, Davien towered. Tumbled hair licked over his shoulders, and his chiselled demeanour showed laughter.

'What does the cat do, but land on its feet?' he opened as informal greeting. 'I see that you've mustered the strength for the challenge you've chosen to face at Alestron.'

Arithon sustained the subsequent, measuring stare. 'The time's come to ask. I need help with the crossing.'

'Said is given,' Davien agreed, 'provided you know that your passage comes at a price.'

Amid the streaming tissue of mist, Arithon stood without flinching. 'The lesson that dogs every choice in this life?'

'Until you receive the clear joy in the gift, with the spirit in which birth was rendered.' Davien sobered, his moods ever volatile. 'I can get you inside of the citadel's walls. Don't depend on me, afterwards. I can't promise to be available on the fraught hour you need to escape.'

'Fair enough.' Arithon cocked his head to one side. Through the lisping rush of the Hanhaffin's current, he sounded the Sorcerer's abrasive presence. 'And the rest? You're too quiet.'

Davien's tigerish smile could all but be felt. 'You won't be alone on this journey.'

The embroidery on the folded cloak flared, to the catch in Arithon's breathing. 'I've lost my argument with Lord Erlien already. We don't agree that the best of his sons should be asked to come as my liegeman.'

'His first heir, and one more.' Davien's humour met s'Ffalenn temper head-long, and the silence turned suddenly caustic. 'You object?' The Sorcerer chuckled, then lifted his narrow ringed hand and beckoned the two lurkers out of the thicket.

'So does the lone wolf howl at the moon,' snapped Arithon, run out of patience. If he expected Kyrialt's battle-firm tread, nothing prepared him for Glendien.

She swayed up, insouciant, and kissed his cold lips, then mocked his stiff posture, against her. 'Ever the bane in the blessing,' she teased without an apology. 'Kyrialt's speechless. We can't wait to meet your enchantress.'

That woke Arithon's hilarity. 'I won't ask how you know, since her name's not been bandied as gossip.' To the fragrance wafted off her bundles, he gouged, 'You've brought simples? The tactic's unsporting, if there are sick babes, and you hoped such a bribe might wheedle Elaira's trust.' Before Glendien's flaming tongue could retort, or her irascible nails raked his cheek, he accosted the by-standing Sorcerer. 'Shall we relocate the catfight and show the watch at Alestron a surprise fit to startle them silly?'

'That's madness fit for a man with a death-wish,' Kyrialt interjected. 'Since I'm the damnfool guarding your back, I'd prefer a more decorous entry.'

'We aren't decorous,' said Arithon, still entrained on Davien, who stared back with sardonic, raised eyebrows. 'Nor do I think we'll be given the choice as we make our explosive appearance.'

'I would send a harbinger,' the Sorcerer corrected, 'but in fact, your arrival's expected.'

'The enchantress?' quipped Kyrialt, as entranced as his wife by the triumph, as the Prince of Rathain swore aloud.

Then the badinage ended. Davien offered his opened palms and commanded, 'Take hold of my hands.'

The instant went strange. As though perception split off from rational cred-ibility, each of the three saw and felt no one else in the world but themselves, and the Fellowship Sorcerer, positioned opposite. As each, individually, received Davien's clasp, the misted night quiet of Stag's Islet up-ended.

Awareness shattered into a blaze of incandescent colour. Scalded, consumed, hurled into a current that unravelled logic, the mind stumbled. For Glendien and Kyrialt, the whirling dissolution hurled them into black-out oblivion.

Arithon, mage-trained, retained his centred balance. He was braced for the absence of bodily sensation, having travelled by transfer with Davien before this. The explosive vertigo took him, self-aware. Sustained by his *knowing*, innate right to be, Arithon rode, awake, upon the clear thread of his consciousness. He experi-enced the stretched moment that looped over what seemed the unshuttered eye of eternity: when a parabolic chamber of stone sealed him into the womb of the mountain that seated the Sorcerer's overarching access to power. A spark of light, falling, from Davien's turned palm, he sensed the spring of virgin water, rushing to meet the naked point of his spirit. That welling flow slid across a carved ring, sheeting over the intricate ciphers that freed the pulsed surge of lane energy.

For that fleeting instant, the mote of his being perceived more: the stark, yellow eye of a living awareness, coiled within the stilled earth. The bottomless black pupil lurked under the pool, enclosed by a shimmering iris.

Then the descending spark of himself splashed into the unruffled water. The impression *that something watched* fled away. While the chamber dissolved into rainbows and the high, singing stream of the flux, Davien's mastery, unerring, transformed to an eagle and steered a swift passage onwards to the citadel.

The meadow of Alestron's high commons was empty, except for three cows, and a few grazing sheep, whose bells clanked in dissonance. Weather had scattered the ashes where Sidir had boiled his glue-pot. The dark hours past midnight were slipping towards dawn, while the low, scudding clouds that fore-promised rain dodged past winter stars, whose names were as music in spoken Paravian. Brisk wind off the Cildein flattened the grasses and sang over the cliff-walls fronting the estuary. The lone figure who waited braced against the gusts that streamered her braid and cloak. The glamour that brought her past the sentries, unseen, had dispersed like the dew on a cobweb.

Elaira steadied the frisson that ruffled her nerves. Primed as she was with informed excitement, keen as talent could sharpen her senses, the moment still caught her, surprised. One second the darkened terrain was unoccupied. The next, a magnificent eagle swooped down and alighted before her. Then that form erased, and another replaced it, tall and straight and sardonically smiling. The fox-brush hair, with streaked white at the temples, tossed and tangled and snapped, in the breeze.

'Elaira, *anient*,' Davien greeted, his smoky baritone and peculiar address unchanged from their former encounter. 'I deliver your prince, and with him, two others. You'll be given your moment to greet him, alone. His escort will follow, though you'll need to wake them. The journey will leave them unconscious.'

The enchantress had no chance for a response.

'Take my hands,' said Davien.

As she reached, his form *shimmered*. Not in any way that the senses could follow. Yet the fingers that closed over hers were not the peremptory grip of the Sorcerer's.

These hands, she knew, lean and beautifully slender.

She had but an instant to focus on Arithon's face: level with hers, and untamed by the sudden infusion back into warm flesh. No grace was given to savour the sight, or measure his new-found serenity.

His urgency swept her off balance, headlong. Despite sword and lyranthe, slung at his shoulder, he bundled her into his arms. His hair was still damp from his wash in a stream. His weathered clothes yet smelled of pine from Selkwood's majestic glades. The muscle beneath was coiled and fit, beyond her last memory from Halwythwood.

Elaira gasped, overcome by sheer pleasure. Made safe from the wind, she felt his fists lock amid the spilled warmth of her hair. The silver-and-black mantle draped over his forearm slipped from his grasp and fell free.

Arithon left the rich cloth in a heap. 'Beloved.' His kiss was all fire and longing and joy, exquisite with tender reunion.

She returned the greeting in cherished trust, held him close till his presence drowned reason. Stinging cold was forgotten. The rushed blood in her thundered, aroused to white flame. *Nothing within the world's compass should spoil that.* Not the fact that their love dared not be made consummate, nor the ominous truth, that his arrival must bring lethal mayhem. The sacrosanct promise he kept, for Earl Jieret, meant that other, more personal oaths were going to be rent without shame.

Late Autumn 5671

First Audience

Dakar chose not to frequent the whores, despite the dragging idle hours caused by the Alliance campaign. The marked change was noticed. Gossip spread the sulky complaint from the rouged lips of an abandoned favourite, that he was grown inept. Others, more kindly, sighed and supposed that last year's bout of bingeing, to mislead Koriathain, had soured his taste for the flesh-pots.

A more sombre truth chained him: the torrid comfort of doxies no longer thwarted his errant talent. The dismal change stayed, since two Fellowship Sorcerers had commandeered him to share the ward-sealing at Rockfell. Dakar snatched what indolent ease he still could; grumbled and drank, since Alestron's old fortress was cheerlessly grim while besieged. The tension afflicting the beleaguered populace and the latent charge guarding the ancient stonewalls sparked the wild surge of his talents. Too often he wakened, reeling sick, his senses burned by impending prescience.

'Mayhem like that fairly wrecks a man's peace,' he groused to the available barmaids.

Alcohol haze bought him a forgetful peace, until short-falls in the citadel put an end to all sotted carousing. Sobriety risked him to an uncontrolled plunge into the tides of precognizant vision. The Mad Prophet fought to stay wakeful. Night after night, he crammed himself into the company of Bransian's off-duty soldiers.

Often, the hour before dawn found him dicing in a cramped, corner tavern, loud with the coming and going of men. They came in from their watch-posts to warm out the cold, or for camaraderie before turning in to their barracks. Lean as scarred wolves, and jingling with weaponry, they elbowed for space on the benches, with Dakar's bulk a wadded, brown bolster wedged between broad shoulders armoured in chainmail.

That morning also, Mearn slipped in for the cards, a habit he used to sharpen his mind before assuming duty at sunrise. The siege had stripped off his fine cloth and lace cuffs. He came bearing full arms, belted over the oiled wool of a field surcoat. A long sword replaced his favoured rapier. Fitness pared his quick slenderness to vital flame, before which larger men cleared him a place at the trestle.

Rainy weather made the tap-room a dim cave. Candle-lamps on their chains flickered low. The windows were dark, still, filmed by the clogged air, redolent of sweaty fleece and damp steel. Dice rattled, and cards slapped and slid on worn wood, while the men soaked their hard, war-time biscuits in the onion broth that simmered the salted, jerked meat into palatable gruel. Noise reigned, but no drunkenness. The muscular bar-keeper rationed the beer, and defended his tap like a jackal.

As the hand-picked messenger lately arrived, Talvish shoved through the press. He dodged offers from friends to share a hot meal and declined the ale jack allotted to serving troops. His refusal drew notice: day on day of tight rations never quite eased the growl pinching anyone's belly. Urgency brought him to Dakar's hunched shoulder as the cast dice clattered across the nicked trestle. The veteran opposite whooped in triumph, while Mearn, grey eyes sharpened, peered over his card hand with inquiry.

Dakar's immersed concentration stayed deaf. He huffed over his losing throw like a walrus, his pungent curses unveiling the fact that his gambling stake involved forfeiting two chits for beer.

Talvish bent and spoke into the frizzle of hair at the Mad Prophet's ear. 'Your Koriani enchantress has guests!'

The swearing intensified, changed target to malign a black-headed feather-wit, whose folly should favour the Fatemaster's list as a suicide.

Mearn's rapacious interest perked up. 'Is the news made official?' he called through the racket.

Blond hair rinsed by the sultry spill of the lamps, Talvish turned his bare head. 'Not yet. Just till I go on watch and report. You'll have that much delay, and no more. That's if you're minded to act, and not scramble to keep your safe distance.'

Mearn would outrace that storm, either way. His shyster's instincts disposed of his game. Before the cup passed to collect his due winnings, he rounded the trestle, slick as an eel through the pack of rough men and the inveigling of the loose women. He reached Talvish as Dakar heaved to his feet, disrupting the patrons on either side like the rolling surge of an earthquake.

Through the hubbub of oaths, ducking fists from those jostled, Mearn broached, 'Where's the forest-bred liegeman?'

Talvish fended off a hothead's rash knife. A wedged knot in the swirl, hell-bent on a mission, he breasted the crowd towards the doorway. 'Sidir's off keeping young Jeynsa in check.'

'She's not been informed?' Dakar said, his flush anxious.

'Won't be,' Talvish answered, and banged into the street, with the pair, fat and thin, at his heels in matched haste.

Outside, the raw wet cast a pall over pending daybreak. Rain slapped, wind-driven, to sting exposed flesh. Talvish finished his statement through clenched teeth. 'Not first thing, at least.' He grinned, too aware that the spirited girl would rebel once she found herself leashed. 'I'll keep the lid on Fionn Areth, as I can. Catch him up and assign him down to the Sea Gate on my way past the barracks.'

Mearn applauded the foresight. 'If Bransian doesn't get his muscle in first, he'll be keen to chop royal bollocks for treason.'

Dakar puffed a warning, hunched against the gusts that pummelled the cobbles in torrents. 'Don't expect his Grace will give ground for protocol, or bow before Bransian's authority.'

'We're kites at that blood-bath, useless except to clean up the carrion after-ward,' Talvish said, grim. They had reached the cross-roads, where he must part company.

Mearn dared not stall, even to accommodate Dakar. Irked as a cat as the wet soaked him through, the duke's youngest brother stretched his lean legs, and sprinted.

Practised at suspicion, the s'Brydion lodged inauspicious state visitors in a defen-sible drumkeep with one narrow entry. The access bridge overhung a ravine. Rain transformed the spring-fed sluice in the moat to a torrent that jetted seaward as an air-borne waterfall. Who came and went passed the eyes of four sentries, on routine watch at the wall. If, by Talvish's tactful phrasing, the enchantress Elaira *had guests*, and the duke's men were left none the wiser, then *someone* had used arcane means on arrival to blindside Alestron's security.

'That's sure to bristle Bransian's hackles!' snapped Mearn, surprised to discover the stout prophet had matched the pace and kept up. 'If Talvish delays his report, he's a dead man. Which means your prince better have something besides talk to launch this citadel off the defensive.'

The spellbinder was too desperately winded to answer. Soaked through his woollens, wheezing under his streaming moustache, he crossed the plank span in a reeling rush. Mearn tripped the latch and let him pass, as a Fellowship agent. Dakar blundered off balance through the iron-strapped door.

A forest clansman Mearn did not recognize caught the spellbinder's panting bulk up short. No ninny for strength, to outmuscle that load, the creature's quick reflex recovered.

'Kyrialt!' gasped Dakar. 'Where's his Grace?'

The edgy young liegeman forbore to answer. Distraught as Sidir to be boxed by stonewalls, he clung to his poise as if drowning. His wary grip clenched to his sheathed sword, while his glacial stare fixed in challenge past the floundering spellbinder's shoulder.

Storm-lit in the doorway, the leaner arrival spoke fast. 'Mearn s'Brydion, brother to the reigning duke. Should I know you?'

'As a son of s'Taleyn, sworn to Rathain's crown service,' Kyrialt responded with correct apology. He extended his freed hand and offered the wrist clasp for amity. He did not lack manners: the Sorcerer's conjury that brought him from Selkwood had upended proper diplomacy.

As the fox would size up the dog caught in its territory, Mearn acknowledged that caustic embarrassment. 'Your prince isn't known to stand upon ceremony.' When the clansman's rapt guard was not bluffed into lowering, he added, 'Twice before this, his Grace crashed through our gates. He came in disguise as a mountebank. Should I expect the third pass to be different?'

'He's not in disguise, this time,' Kyrialt declared, cheerful. 'There's your fair warning, if you plan to walk in without pressing a host's claim against royal rank.'

Mearn showed his teeth in spontaneous approval, then unveiled all his knives as he shed his wet cloak. 'One doesn't wrest the advantage from your Teir's'Ffalenn on the limping excuse of propriety.'

'Well, the predator's rip for the vitals won't work.' Still amused, masking laughter, Kyrialt gave ground and permitted free passage. 'The prince is quite testily blooded, already. My wife Glendien's nipped in ahead of you.'

Dakar found his breath. His roaring disapproval all but shocked cracks in Paravian masonry.

While Mearn stared, intrigued, Shand's young liegeman endured being reviled as a frivolous idiot in epithets, piled one on top of the next.

Kyrialt's humour outlasted the tirade. 'I've come as my father's gift, done for clan honour,' he interjected through the first pause. 'Glendien's here by the whim of Davien. Without her, the Sorcerer refused to grant passage, and even your prince doesn't argue with the Betrayer.'

'More the fool he!' Dakar snapped, his eyes bloodshot. Chin out-thrust and dripping beard kinked into ringlets, he ploughed on towards the stairwell. Anxiety drove him. At first hand, he would gauge whether damaging scars still unstrung Arithon's subtle aura, and whether the dread rites of necromancers had unbalanced him, since Etarra.

Mearn launched after, a snap to his tread like the weasel set loose in a chicken-coop.

The siege restricted the usage of fuel. No oil-lamps burned on the upstairs landing. Dimness shrouded the chamber beyond, presently burnished by the hectic glow thrown off a pot of live coals: the enterprising enchantress had filched a brazier from the citadel's grumpy apothecary. Not for her own comfort: Elaira had set up a still-room. A glass boiler burbled on a squat tripod, heating a mash of crushed kelp.

The daunting reek of fresh iodine met the arrivals crowding the threshold. 'We haven't got cots, yet, to house the infirm,' Dakar huffed in humiliation.

Mearn, just behind, was scarcely prepared for the sweeping change imposed on the guest-quarters.

The once-naked stonewalls held a bright weaving from Narms, and the floor, a pretty, fringed carpet: loans from Dame Dawr, in antique good taste, and matched to the scarlet bed coverlet. The bronze tub, with its lion's head ring handles, currently soaked rags for bandages in a bleaching mixture of lye. The weapons rack had been commandeered to dry herbs, as well as the towel stand next to the wash-basin. More bundles of medicinal root-stock were strung from a line between two empty wall sconces. The armoire gaped open, jammed with bottles and packets, while the ousted clothes were piled with the linens on the sill, against the latched casement. A trestle set up in midfloor held pestles and stoppered glass jars, bees-wax for seals, and an ink-well, rested atop the rice-paper sheets used to package the powders for tinctures. Across the melange, two heads bent together, one fiery red, and the other, deep auburn, touched with a chestnut highlight.

Yet Mearn's avid glance scoured through the deep shadows and noted the wrapped lyranthe leaned against the far bedstead. The instrument's master sat by the hearth, unobtrusive against the brass andirons. To that slight figure, perched on a stool with tucked knees nestled into clasped hands, he observed, 'You've acquired an entourage fit to outrank a blow-hard Tirans ambassador.'

Teeth flashed in the gloom. 'That's presuming a bit,' returned Arithon, smiling. 'Talvish was discharged and sent back to your duke. Prime Selidie's tyrannical fist rules Elaira, and Glendien curtseys for nobody's rank, far less minds an order that won't put a shine to whatever whim's hooked her fancy. Right now, that's herb simples, and before you object, we don't plan to open an infirmary.'

'You may have to!' snapped Mearn, around Dakar's bulk. 'If you don't bow to sense, you'll have bloodshed before sunrise. Once Talvish reports, my brother will send an armed company to collect you. *Your Grace!*'

'If you've come to replace them as my advance escort, I'm reasonable. You suggest we leave now?' Arithon unlaced his linked fingers and arose.

The movement brought him into full view, with Dakar immersed in deep mage-sight. The sweeping, bright shift in the Teir's'Ffalenn's aura jerked him up short with a gasp.

Mearn, hard behind, slammed into collision. His nettled curse tangled with Dakar's awe-struck shout, 'Ath on earth, *how did this triumph happen?*'

Elaira was smiling, tears brimming her eyes, as Arithon stepped out of shadow.

'I'll explain that part later,' said the Prince of Rathain, also lit with exultant happiness. 'For my botched score in the present, I've got to mend my relations with Duke Bransian, first.' To Mearn's blazing annoyance at being shut out, he admitted with shattering brevity, 'I no longer bear the scourge of Desh-thiere's laid curse.'

To everyone's shock, the youngest brother s'Brydion slapped his thigh and exclaimed aloud. 'Don't you! By the balked Spear of Dharkaron's vengeance! I've just won a smart stake from Parrien, for that. When we argued the point, he stuck in his toes. Claimed that your half-brother's fanatics would toss you to perdition, beforehand!'

Arithon absorbed this, undaunted. 'Was that before, or after, he needed four guardsmen as backup to thrash me aboard your state galley?'

Mearn looked affronted. 'We're all sore losers. That's an inbred tradition, with Bransian frothing at full cry ahead of the family wolf pack.' That exigent point made, he shoved Dakar's obstructive person aside. 'I can't claim my winnings before I've thwarted the ducal order that's hell-bound to skewer your royal embassy. If we don't leave *now,* my brother's henchmen could stick their butchering swords in ahead of me.'

The fore-promised armed escort rammed into Mearn, who brazened through his insistence on blood precedence. Peeled down to rank-and-file skin by sharp insolence, the guardsman who led the troop of twenty fell into grim step behind. His men did not disperse, a forceful assurance the prince they had summoned would not evade his formal audience.

The knowledge their charge was both Master of Shadow and fully initiate sorcerer chafed their already ragged nerves. Troops elsewhere might see their edge dulled by the storm. But not these: Arithon's passage through the grey, windy streets was briskly staged inside a tight phalanx. Too many unsettled fists fingered weapons for anyone's peace of mind.

The matched tramp of feet in hobnailed boots cleared the way and scattered the bread-carts and maidservants. Awnings flapped, and signs creaked, spilling fringes of water, with the puddles brimmed over to frothing currents that gushed down-slope, and spouted out of the culverts. Beyond ominous weather, the hearing would not occur in the genteel hall, built above the upper citadel's practice floor. Instead, the duke waited in the high keep commandeered as his war room.

'No good sign,' Mearn related amid breathless haste, 'though he can't throw you out. The top floor has only loop-holes for arrow-slits.'

'*That* chamber?' Dakar spat through his soggy moustache.

'You remember the place?' Mearn flashed his most wicked, triangular grin. 'Where Bransian likes to interrogate spies, and once put the lash to a watch captain whose faulted duty was later proved innocent?'

Dakar planted his feet and rolled brown eyes in desperate appeal towards Arithon. 'Avoid this! I don't care what powers you think you can wield. You're stark mad if you face off against Bransian, four stories up in a guarded tower.'

Arithon said, too reasonable for a man being pummelled by ice-water, 'If I press your obstinacy with this escort, we'll have drawn steel in the street. The duke's owed the courtesy,' he added to Mearn, who let the balked captain resume the forced march.

The downpour at least deterred needless onlookers. Past the storm-shuttered forge, and the fletcher's, where a shivering boot-black hunkered beneath a niche doorway, the spellbinder lapsed into moribund silence.

The keep loomed ahead. Its slot-narrow archway funnelled the front ranks into single file. Arithon was herded behind, with Mearn weasel-quick at his heels. Dakar had to pause to twist his bulk sideways, to clear the opening without losing his buttons. The lag let the near men-at-arms close in step and deny his free passage.

'Duke's orders!' one snapped, an ornery bear who was stupid enough not to cringe from a Fellowship spellbinder's arcane abilities.

Before trouble erupted, Arithon flung back his demand to stand down. 'Dakar, not here! If I can't hold my ground before Bransian s'Brydion, no power you carry will signify.'

Ever since Talvish released his report, Duke Bransian had been pacing. His volatile nerves meant his wary retainers had twitched themselves dizzy, tracking his circles. The only man spared kept his poised watch at the arrow-slit, one eye trained against the damp wind. He currently peered down at the helms of the escort, clustered four stories below. As planned, the corpulent Fellowship spellbinder was being detained: abusive language from the stews of five kingdoms knifed upward through the pounding rain.

Impressed, the man-at-arms signalled his duke, that, per dispatched orders, the Mad Prophet had been shut outside. He withdrew from the draught, which spat beaded moisture on his greased mail, and reported, 'The Teir's'Ffalenn's coming alone, but for the one snag: he's brought Mearn.'

Bransian rounded. Gauntleted fists braced upon the oak table, with its tactical map and stacked counters, he declared, 'Mearn's a rank busybody. Got himself born with his sniping nose poked in the dark end of everyone's business.' The carping was cheerful, an ominous sign: since the day of Arithon's blistering leave, served in brutally stark ultimatum, the duke had fumed, between prayers to Dharkaron, awaiting his chance for a rematch.

'Has the chirping cockerel dared to come armed?' Granted a nod from his posted observer, Bransian laughed. 'Then bring his Grace on! The hour is mine, for the field-day.'

The Masterbard would rankle nobody with his silver-tongued liberties, now. He could not claim a free singer's courtesy. No women were present to foster his cause, and Dame Dawr's unimpeachable patronage did not shield his caustically elegant back. Arithon trod on s'Brydion turf, without the due grace of an invitation or the decency of an apology.

The brisk pace of the entourage echoed up the stone stair. Duke Bransian rubbed his palms to a rasp of plate gauntlets. 'Bring him on,' he repeated, and smiled, a scarred lion licking his teeth.

When the Prince of Rathain topped the landing, Alestron's duke sat in his formal chair, not astraddle the back-facing seat, his preference for mild confrontation. He wore a state surcoat. On his chest, against scarlet, the rampant bull of the s'Brydion blazon glittered in warning gold thread.

By contrast, Arithon eschewed formal dress: an unbleached shirt and the weathered, black leathers acquired for hunting in Selkwood. He was as soaked by the rain as the rest. Davien's gifted cloak remained with Elaira, the better to free the swept hilt of his sword: not hung at his hip, but borne in a shoulder-slung scabbard. Against his woods tan, flushed by the sharp wind, his eyes seemed too vividly green as his step passed over the threshold.

He crossed the close chamber. Paused before the table, with Mearn at his heels, and the four armoured men, positioned to cut off the doorway. The aggressive show twitched a slight curve to his lips that might have strangled amusement.

Or not; his demeanour suggested a watchful sobriety that eschewed the impulse to speak.

Bransian also was loath to break the unsubtle silence. He did not rise but allowed the savage pause to leach away self-assurance. If not Arithon's, then at least Mearn and the guardsmen might succumb to the pressured unease. Any small upset to whet the taut atmosphere and chafe at his visitor's poise. The keep was kept cold, which left the petitioning party immersed in a drenched state of misery. The duke and his stationed guards lounged at ease, prepared to let patience work for them.

A minute passed, two, while the wind outside breathed inclement gusts through the arrow-slits. Mearn ground his teeth, since his brother's crass tactics were not apt to rattle an initiate sorcerer's dignity.

Yet Arithon had no reason to prove his aplomb. He inclined his head, hands clasped in plain sight, and opened the fraught conversation. 'Make no mistake, I'm not here for your city's aggressive defence, but only for my oath to Jeynsa.'

Eyes half-lidded, Bransian kept his snake's poise. 'Need those goals lie at odds? You can't spirit the girl out through the enemy's lines. Along with my people, she lies at hazard to the violence posed by Desh-thiere's curse. How will you spare her, when Lysaer's close presence breaks down the restraint of your sanity?'

If he had hoped *that name* would snap Arithon's resistance, the laced fingers maintained their composure. 'My half-brother may throw himself at your walls. He can hammer your gates until he breaks the back of his allied town war host. His battle frenzy will not turn my mind.' As the duke stiffened for argument, Arithon Teir's'Ffalenn smiled. 'Then, or ever.'

The statement took a stunned moment to register. 'Say *again*?' Bransian's winter-ice glance flashed to Mearn but received no response.

Arithon stated, 'I've recovered my born right to autonomy.'

'And your half-brother, s'Ilessid?' Bransian snapped, caught aback and snatching for leverage.

'I could not speak in petition for him before the powers that graced me with healing.' The admission held sorrow. 'Which is why I won't raise my hand in this war. Already, my presence inflames his awareness.'

'Dharkaron's sweet vengeance!' Bransian shot back his state chair and pounced. 'The vaunted false avatar has to attack!'

For the first time, Arithon looked faintly tried. 'If I linger, even inactive, he must.'

'Daelion Fatemaster grant me that sweet kiss of judgement!' Bransian's rage softened into a glower. 'If you've broken us out of this forsaken stand-off, I might be convinced to grant you a pardon when we seize the honours of victory.'

'I will not be here, or care to collect. Which is why you will not obstruct my urgent intent to remove Jeynsa.' Knife sharp, the Masterbard's tone slashed across the duke's outraged objection. 'You are not defending your citizens, my friend! Only your pride, which is stubbornly tied to a cock-fight over a pile of rock in an estuary!'

'My ancestral home ground!' Duke Bransian pealed.

'Yes,' Arithon said. 'But a parcel of walled soil does not make the heart of a ruler or define the nobility of a people!'

The duke balled his mailed fists. His walloping blow struck the table-top, scattering troop counters hither and yon, and cracking stout oak. 'Your insolence galls, prince! As you're fit to bear arms, we'll settle this now! Over bared steel, until one or the other of us scores first blood.'

'Do you think so?' Arithon's quelling gesture failed to stay Mearn, who leaped forward, intent upon blocking his brother's rash charge. His interposed body was not going to shield. From behind, the guards snapped to clear weapons as well, while Bransian's murderous, two-handed sword screamed from the sheath, gripped in fury.

'Stand off, stripling!' he snapped to his sibling. 'I will not be mocked beneath my own roof by a nattering royal-born coward!'

'No more will I brook your rock-headed attack!' Arithon back-stepped, palms upraised as though to ward off the swung steel with only his naked flesh. The guardsmen stopped his hopeful retreat, a deadly prickle of points at his back, with Mearn, shocked to a pale standstill, beside him.

'You won't escape fighting,' the youngest s'Brydion advised. 'Nip in, quick. Try to land your wee nick in him first!' As his brother's rush vaulted over the wreck of the tactical map on the table, Mearn leaped to safety, still talking. 'I don't plan to tell Kyrialt how your liver got minced.'

'Not on this day!' One forgot how fast Arithon moved, when provoked.

He lunged to the floor, his weight caught on his hands, as Bransian's stop thrust ripped overhead and clashed into the guards' brandished weapons. A clangour of metal and curses exploded. Surprised men recoiled in a manic scramble to disentangle themselves from the misspent assault of their duke.

Arithon twisted and rolled, a dropped cat underneath. While the snarl of swords unravelled above, his sinuous scuttle carried him through spilled counters and under the table. There, sliding flat, he flipped on his side: the sheathed hilt at his shoulder escaped getting snagged on the hedging struts of the trestle. Before his inspired reaction was countered, he was out the far side and back on his feet, with Bransian turned roaring, to meet him.

At by-standing distance, irreverent with glee, Mearn watched to see which combatant would survive the fracas, uncut.

'Draw!' howled Bransian. 'Prove you're a man and no scampering rabbit! Or are you fit for nothing but flight, and cowering under my furniture?'

'Quite fit!' rebuked Arithon. His wide-lashed glance was a child's, *bemused,* while the Duke of Alestron tensed his ox frame to plough aside the riven table.

The Master of Shadow squared his shoulders, as much to resettle his untouched weapon, as a shrug to acknowledge obsessive ferocity.

Mearn suddenly found himself holding his breath.

Then Arithon s'Ffalenn set hand to his sword and cleared the black blade from the scabbard.

Alithiel spoke!

Light bloomed, and sound, a swell of wild harmony that smashed reason and hurled Duke Bransian's pitched might to its knees. Glued into glass air, every human awareness abandoned willed thought and let go: into sweetness like spring, and dark mystery like moonlight, scribed silver across restless ocean. Mortal existence lost every fixed boundary. No flesh-quickened memory could ever hold the moment's shattering fullness. The trembling heart ached to be *free,* unfolded into exaltation. The peace in the cry of the sword *was not passive,* but the flow of inspired creation. A note that sustained, then beckoned the leap: to vault consciousness into the limitless vista of imaginative invention.

Through the unbearable, ecstatic crescendo, a masterbard's speech emerged clearly. *'I will fight, but not to take lives in this war!'* Arithon spun the charged length of Alithiel. Before Bransian's dropped jaw and unstrung aggression, against Mearn's and the soldiers' astonishment, he impaled the sword through the tactical map, with its disarrayed scatter of counters.

There, in a not-quite-quenched ring of sound, the blade stood upright and quivering. The rune inlay shimmered, still active, a sheen of opalescent illumination playing down the length of the steel.

'A'liessiad,' said Arithon Teir's'Ffalenn in lyric Paravian. 'Let peace bide between us, regardless of differences.'

He stirred then, recovered the uncanny sword from the table-top. Alone in the room, he seemed able to move as he sheathed the blade and silenced its uncanny vibration. The will in that choice shook the air like scribed fire and left behind shocking, dimmed silence.

Loss swept the onlookers, which wrenched like blind pain; pitched them reeling across an abyss of dark separation. Through their helpless tears, they watched Arithon walk out with no hand in the room raised to stop him.

Refuge

Parrien s'Brydion was fed up with fighting heated engagements to seize a safe harbour to shelter his fleet. The deadly bother was not going to ease, while the autumn squalls built towards winter. Each storm that roared in off the Cildein crammed the coves that pocketed the coast of Melhalla. Oared ships were forced to jockey for space, or else battle outright for anchorage. Unlike peaceful years, the seafaring captains abroad were not mercantile, eastshore galley-men.

Today, the blazons that streamed from their mastheads might hail from the northernmost ports. Crews used to rough waters, and determined fishers whose encounters with icebergs and rock shoals bred iron resolve and an unflinching stare. The stout vessels beneath their commands braved the chop that broke hissing in whitecaps. They rode the stiff winds that foreran the wrecks which claimed human lives in gale season.

'Rot their confounded hardihood, timbers and flesh!' the duke's brother fumed in the lamp-lit darkness. He peeled off his oilskins. Tossed their soaked bulk to his hovering steward, while his flustered arrival fogged the latched casements, and rove the taint of wet wool through the warmth belowdecks. 'Every damned bolt-hole we've picked to snug down in is stuffed full of their wallowing tubs!'

Oared hulls as viciously guarded as a silk guildsman's prime bales, and as handsomely paid, to move the resupply for the enemy war host.

'Opportunistic toadies,' Parrien ran on in distemper, 'the lot of them teeming like curs with the lice, and burdened a yard past their load lines.' To the steward's prim silence, he jabbed, 'One gets tired of sticking a sword in the guts of their wall-eyed, fanatical officers. Not to mention the cowering, Light-blinded dupes just rounded up green from the ale shops!'

Paused frowning, Parrien shook like a bear. More wet showered off him, hissing against the hot panes of the gimballed lamp, and spattering over the tally-sheets spread on the chart desk. 'Dharkaron wept! We'd find cleaner sport chopping rabbits!'

To the clamped mug of his long-suffering purser, he snapped, 'You aren't sick of the screams? Here's a fresh blow, and no haven in sight without another bitch-bred stint of slaughter.'

The prospect rankled, beyond hope of let-up. For months to come, the open coast would stay lashed to rampaging spindrift. Amid heaving seas, pebbled grey with cold rain, the fleet's hard-bitten oarsmen were suffering. Too many had salt-water sores from the benches. Galls that swelled into festering malady.

Still snarling, Parrien heaved onto a locker, pried off his boots, and dumped out a brown stream of run-off. 'It's a goat-humping lash-up! Beats my good sense, why the mayors and their gabbling excisemen don't levy new fines for stupidity. Like whoresons with clap, they're all bent arse up for Lysaer's milk-sucking religion!'

The steward dutifully stowed the sopped oilskins, while the purser glowered in silence. Both men stayed loath to cross Parrien's temper. The siege at Alestron left his fleet stranded outside of the blockaded estuary. His crews had no choice but to shoulder their forced tour of duty without respite.

Stalled at last by his officer's jaundiced stare, Parrien exclaimed, 'Well, spit out the sour news, man! We're caught lean on stores again, aren't we?'

'Not well-set, at all,' the purser admitted. He scratched beneath his fusty jacket, upset by his harried assessment. 'Provisions are critical. The weakling ship's boy's got bleeding gums. We're facing a spreading case of the cough. Our rowers can't stay in fit strength on hard biscuit, and the village fishermen are learning to run before selling us contraband barrels of salt meat.'

'All right!' Eyes red from exhaustion, and chapped by harsh wear, Parrien embraced the inevitable. 'We'll assault the bolt-hole in the crab shallows to the leeside of Lugger's Islet. If we strike fast, and risk a few casualties, we can board what's afloat. Take a few officers hostage for ransom and ransack their holds for provender.'

The purser gaped over his pen in astonishment. 'Have we sunk to the morals of forest-bred clansmen? Or fallen to justified piracy?'

'Yes!' Parrien shot off the locker. Shivering in his stockings, he slammed back the lid and fetched out his helm and bracers, and the cutlass preferred for close combat. 'Because if Alestron's citadel falls, and my brother is forced to defeat, we'll be stuck begging for sanctuary with our barbaric cousins in Atwood! Or would you rather kiss arse with their sea-going brethren, and prey on the slave-trade that's poisoning Tysan?'

No seasoned retainer stuck out his neck with a s'Brydion hell-bent on battle. The steward scuttled to oil his master's dropped boots. The purser ducked fast and rolled up his accounts, while Parrien's bellow to the ship's mate ordered the desperate course change.

If Alestron's crack seamen were taxed by privation, their discipline remained as adamant as iron. The five galleys formed up on his relayed command and struck their last stitch of reefed canvas. Under oar, they sheared into the teeth of the storm, against gusts that ripped the seas into spume and hurled opaque sheets of rain. Four helmsmen muscled the buck of the rudder, their corded wrists cuffed to the whipstaff. The steersman called off the bearing from below, his compass dial lit by a candle-lamp, while the quartermaster howled over the gale and verified the new headings.

Parrien rode the toss of the deck, tied in to the flagship's stern-rail. Every man not streaming sweat at the bench worked the pumps, battling the green gush let in as each thudding wave deluged the oar-ports.

No ship's hand was fooled. Their hard labour could not subdue the raw elements. Above, the stripped yard reeled against tattered scud. Shrieking wind punched through the rigging. No galley could withstand the relentless punishment. She might pound and roll against such a sea until her crew dropped from exhaustion, or until the working strain burst a seam, or a crest broke over and broached her. The weather might snap the men's courage before they reached land, or drew steel on the enemy.

No use to pretend that their straits were not dire. Hungry, storm-battered, and shivering, they rounded the north point of Lugger's Islet and threaded the narrows that guarded the anchorage. Drove in at attack speed, despite wallowing hulls and sinews nigh crippled by weariness. They prepared to do battle against suicide odds, with frozen fingers clenched numb to their weapon hilts.

Parrien braced his stance at the stern, moved to pride by the fight in the men. None would be starving at sea like chased wolves. Battle would meet them, unvanquished. If the sousing rain spoiled the aim of his archers, the surprise shock would do damage, ram a few Sunwheel hulls to the bottom on the sheer force of momentum.

The five galleys rounded the spit at the headland. They shot into the lee side, beaked prows knifing into the billow of shoaling waters. The steersmen squinted through short visibility. Storm in their eyes, they saw little beyond the flare of the lanterns, pocked amid the blurred shadows of anchored ships.

'Stroke, you weasels!' screamed Parrien. 'No one's belly gets filled till we've torn out the throats of the pullets before us!'

Oars bit and spray flew. Iron-shod prows sheared down on their prey, primed for ruin and havoc. Leading the wedge, the flagship struck first. The ram crushed into timber. Water gouted and splinters exploded. The rocking, hard impacts slammed at each side, as the s'Brydion ships pounded into their targets. Men loosed their grip upon rigging and rails. They swarmed over the bows in a berserk attack, steel raised to grapple the enemy.

No blade met their rush. No yelling watch officers or armed defenders. Over the surging heave of the deck, and the judder of rain-wet, shocked planking, the oar benches yawned, dark and empty of life. No voices called, and no bells clanged alarm. No boatswain's whistle shrilled to roust up laggards from berths belowdecks. Right and left, as the adjacent hulls shuddered under the brunt of invasion, the s'Brydion rush met no resistance.

The Light's galleys wallowed on pebbled grey waters, deserted of human life.

Parrien snapped out of stunned incredulity. He bellowed for caution, too late. His first mate sounded an instant retreat, every nerve jabbed by suspicion. This unlucky foray surely had run them into an Alliance trap. Fallen back, shrill with panic, men stumbled in recoil. They crowded in distraught confusion. Frayed edgy by danger, they milled to regroup, while the overhead look-outs peered into the murk.

The storm yielded its secrets with eerie reluctance. Ahead, past the anchored hulls they had rammed, the harbour held flotsam and splintered timber. Here, floated the gleam of an overturned tender, and there, a smashed spar, or sunk wreck, with its canted mast pricked through heaving, black waters. The dotted flare of lit lanterns still blazed from the wrack of uncounted, smashed hulks.

'Dharkaron Avenger!' Parrien swore. 'Looks like the hammer of Sithaer has fallen and kicked the Light's faithful ahead of us.'

That discovery barely sank in, when another light flashed from the wooded shore-line.

The look-out's confounded cry from the crow's nest exclaimed, 'That's our own coded signal!'

Translation was swift, that s'Brydion forces occupied the inlet and anchorage.

Parrien shuddered, nipped into awed gooseflesh, as the next winking sequence identified the field-captain whose prowess commanded the beach. 'Vhandon! Come here? Sweet tits on a bull! How did he know that our straits were pressed beyond desperate?'

The bellow to sway out the flagship's tender was belayed over the pound of the rainfall. Apparently the empty, rammed hulls had been secured by ropes to barricade the hazards that had beset their Alliance counterparts.

'Take a close look!' The boatswain's excitable shout cut through Parrien's roaring displeasure. 'Past the rafted vessels blocking our bow, everything else in the water has been either stove in or sunk!'

The vicious truth registered, with the stalled oarsmen wretchedly shivering. Men and ship's boy shared the strain of delay as Parrien snatched out the ship's glass. His survey swept the shadowed curves of holed keels, then the glints of reflection nicked off burst timbers and snarls of drifting cordage. Ruin had left no vessel afloat, nor any living survivor.

Voices died, as battle-brash courage went cold. One man, then another sheathed weapons before the impact of utter catastrophe. Mollified, stunned, or subdued by bone chill, they shrank to grapple the vista unveiled through the sheeting rainfall.

'We're being hailed,' the sobered boatswain observed.

Parrien swung the ship's glass. He picked out the small boat on approach, then the upright, soaked form, draped in a field officer's surcoat. 'Have a welcoming party at the rail, amidships, and ascertain a loyal identity before you take on any boarders.'

Inside a short interval, Vhandon drew alongside. His square-cut face had grown chiselled and gaunt, and his chin bristled silver with stubble. His greeting no more than a curt nod to Parrien, he said, 'We've staked the harbour bed with cribs of stone and sharp logs to kill ships.' Beyond terse, he added, 'We had no other way to send warning, except to lash these few prizes in place as a barrier. Stand down your armed crews. I've come to guide you into safe waters.'

Too exhausted to cheer, and worn ragged by hunger, the battered war fleet regrouped, then rowed limping towards shelter.

Two hours passed. Sated on hot stew, with a draught of Sanshevas rum now warming the chill from his blood, Parrien s'Brydion sat in his steaming clothes inside the flagship's stern cabin. Outside that haven, with its desk of spread charts and its lockers of varnished bright-work, the gale still lashed, unabated. It howled through the galley's stripped masts, and rattled the winter-bare trees on the mainland.

Amid the fusty glue of close air, with his clan braid crusted with salt, Parrien lacked the words to measure his gratitude. His weary crews were sheltered and fed. After a night of unbroken sleep, the damage to worn lines, and worked seams, and torn sail could be assessed and mended.

Of the eighteen Alliance ships ambushed to grant his five galleys survival, Vhandon's statement was bitter and brief.

'We've been fugitives ourselves. Set too hot on the run from Lysaer's foot-troops not to guess how sorely your fleet needed respite.' He paused, his competent, blunt fingers clenched on his mug.

Parrien weathered the interval, silent. Vhandon's clipped speech and lined features often lent the misleading impression of gruffness. Without Talvish's banter to strike the hidden spark, his taciturn humour and sensitive insight eluded most casual eyes. Yet Parrien s'Brydion had learned his every trick from the mentor, seated before him.

Yet tonight, the veteran officer's ferocious stillness was utterly new.

'You've met him?' Parrien pressed at last on brash impulse. No need to mention the name of s'Ilessid, self-styled as Prince of the Light.

Vhandon's flint regard flicked away, loath as he was to answer. 'I did not understand the dynamic charisma that walks in the man's living presence.' A shiver raked him, not due to the cold. 'What chance do those lost, blinded followers have? The logical fire of Lysaer's convictions will admit to no creeping doubt. Mankind is born craving such absolute stability. Our mortal nature strives for a known order, though we tend to forget structured limits deliver stagnation that leads to sterility. Had we not met the s'Ffalenn half-brother first, would we ever have questioned? Dare we judge others who have fallen prey to the weakness that begs for a saviour?'

'You don't like killing men who flock to die like tame sheep,' Parrien said with cut-glass acuity.

'No.' Vhandon looked up. 'That's too dangerously simple.' The horror had eaten him down to the viscera. 'The slaughter is ugly, but what lives is worse. I cannot stand by and allow this infectious dogma to grow entrenched. These are men, made as weapons that kill without conscience! Like the farmer who harvests his croft with the scythe, they raze down all that stands without quarter. Nothing is left to give voice to diversity. True freedom can't thrive under one creed in conformity.' Now shaking, he set down his mug before he slopped the hot contents. 'Did you never see Lysaer unleash his royal gift?'

'Not in his element,' Parrien admitted. 'Years ago, he once ventured out hunting with us. He'd arrived in petition for an alliance of war, which required my brother's good graces. His silken tongue wooed us with reason, then caught us short by the fears underlying our drive for security.' His mouth tightened, strained by a memory no belt of rum could erase.

'Bransian swallowed the strategy, head first,' Vhandon murmured, not without sympathy.

'We all did!' Parrien shot to his feet, jabbed to shame. 'How do you withstand a statesman who leads his game with the cards of your wishful, self-serving agenda? You kiss his boots for saying what you'd like to hear, and before you think to examine the motive, you've sold yourself out! Bransian's not wont to forgive that mistake. The humility's not in him, to just walk away from the sting of being played by our whimpering short-falls!'

Yet Vhandon's rooted disquiet intensified. He covered his face, forced to stifle his impulse to weep. 'You've never witnessed Lysaer's destructive powers under sway of the Mistwraith's directive.'

Parrien sat. Tired frown and cold eyes, he measured the crisis that wracked his family's most dependable field-captain. Vhandon was worse than shaken. *The grief that distressed him, somewhere, somehow, had caused his matchless character to falter in stride.* No care could approach what had crumbled his poise; yet the friend who observed had to try.

'I've already heard the most damaging news,' Parrien opened with heart-sore reluctance. 'That Lysaer immolated our outlying troop, and that Keldmar died at the forefront.' Since the hurt was too brutal, he asked the steward to fetch in the vintage brandy.

'We stood witness to everything,' Vhandon said through shut hands. 'All ten of us, trapped on reconnaissance inside the s'Ilessid field camp. Keldmar sent us, I think, as a misguided effort to keep us this side of Fate's Wheel.'

The rocked swing of the gimballed lamp was not kind, as the tears escaped those clamped fingers. Vhandon held on through the loss of his privacy, while

Parrien poured two restorative glasses. Yet alike as he seemed to the brother now dead, his vulnerability was not as Keldmar's, which once had groped to find understanding through inept, but sincere camaraderie.

'You'll tell me exactly what happened,' said Parrien s'Brydion with fixated attentiveness.

No word, no touch, and no quickened breath moved his stillness throughout the dreadful report. By the end, he had heard every searing detail of Lysaer's first assault on the citadel. Not to console for the ruin and lost lives, or to bolster shocked nerves, never that; presented the face of a curse-bound disaster, Parrien's patience was as the adder's, that coiled to strike back in cold blood.

Late Autumn 5671

Responses

'1 acknowledge our debt to Rathain and Alestron,' King Eldir declares as he hands his horse off to a groom; then makes disposition to the sea-captain, braving her distrust of stable-yards to petition for aid: 'The Crown of Havish will grant supply for the besieged citadel, on condition that you and your crew on the *Evenstar* will arrange the delivery on your own merits . . .'

Caught while detailing the drills for green troops, Sulfin Evend stands frowning, as Lysaer's hound-faced valet reports that the Divine Prince's sleep has been broken by a feverish dream that carried the name of the Spinner of Darkness . . .

Suffering a headache following his late rebuff by the Prince of Rathain, Bransian s'Brydion grinds frustrated teeth, until his overstrung duchess snaps first, and suggests the coercive option, 'If his Grace has come here to safeguard Jeynsa s'Valerient, then she is the pawn in your fist, and your leverage to bring him to heel . . .'

VIII. First Turning

T he gale broke by sundown, blown out to feathered clouds, and a brisk change of wind that fore-promised new ice on the rain barrels. Cold to the bone, with her hands scoured raw from the handling of quicklime and mortar, Jeynsa left her mixing paddle and hand-cart to the relief at the change of the watch.

'Enjoy your turn, butty,' she said to the breathless boy arrived for his shift on the sea-wall. 'No question, I've sanded my finger-tips raw!'

Daylong, she had not questioned Talvish's orders, or the call for brute labour that annexed her to his company. If the duke's thwarted temper made him declare that the wharf-side embrasure required reinforcement, every hale person under s'Brydion protection was pressed forthwith to lay stone. Men cranked the winches and levered the cut blocks, while boys and strong women chipped facings and hauled in water and sand for the mixing troughs.

Jeynsa never minded the rough, outdoor work. Despite sore hands, she would have stayed on, even welcomed the diversion to thwart Sidir's over-bearing attention. Public presence alone averted the brangles that sparked, as she clashed with his tender authority.

Fionn Areth had less reason to make himself scarce, and no reservation against mouthing off his latest inflaming opinion. Crammed onto the lift with chilled sentries and bone-weary citizens, he declared, 'I don't see how more masonry can stave off the hour we die of starvation.'

Talvish heard, slit-eyed, from his place by the seaward blocks. This pass, he

245

chose not to silence the fool, but stood back and let his grizzled campaign sergeant slap down the offence.

'That's your grass-lander's ignorance speaking!' challenged Cortend, who still wore his gauntlets. 'If directed activity gives anyone hope, we are all better off.'

'Break our backs for a lie?' Fionn Areth shot off, while the turn of the winches caught up the slack, and the freight lift crawled under load up the cliff-face. The Araethurian stayed undeterred by the rancourous stir on the crowded platform. He shouted over the grind of taut chains, 'That's the same hypocrisy played against the Light's victims. Or so you lay claim as the cause for this war!'

Now, more than one tired veteran bristled. Several muscular townsfolk rocked onto their toes, incensed enough to start fisticuffs. Talvish's bark could have stalled the fresh fight.

Yet the sergeant laced in, ahead of him. 'Let our honest craftsman find their sound sleep in the belief they've protected their families. Keep everyone busy, we won't get betrayed by some man's helpless rage, as he tries for relief by defection!'

'Defection?' scoffed Fionn, 'Or just honest good sense, to dump pride and admit our position's untenable.'

The sergeant settled by cocking his fist. His battering right hook clipped Fionn Areth on the jaw, snapped his head back, and reeled him into Jeynsa's startled embrace.

'Serves the damned idiot right!' The sergeant flushed, unrepentant for blatant misconduct.

Talvish chose to laugh off the infraction. 'Spared my knuckles a bruising against Araethurian flint, though you won't win my praise for the effort.' Subjected to Jeynsa's infuriated glower, he shrugged. Unsurprisingly, no one else moved to help her prop up the felled victim. The girl was left on her merits to choose whether to drop her unwitting charge in a half-conscious heap.

Perversity won. Jeynsa elected to shoulder the load, if only to champion the brash underdog. Now hazed by the surly regard of the onlookers, she denounced, 'Even the stupidest gripe deserves kindness.'

The scapegrace sergeant averted his glance, intent to avoid further trouble. The men-at-arms pinned under Talvish's eye also kept buttoned lips out of prudence. But pinched hunger and exhaustion goaded the displaced craftsfolk to lash back.

'Ought to chuck out that one's whining carcass and give some joy to the feeding crabs.'

A matron brandished an indignant fist. 'I've a hog in farrow that's much too thin to be tossing fresh meat off for carrion!'

'Bait's a better idea,' yelled the gangling lad whose cousin walked rope for the chandler. 'Rot the choice bits and set a few traps! We'd be better off dicing the free-loader's liver to catch ourselves a fresh dinner.'

Jeynsa shrugged. 'I say the victim can level his own scores.'

For already, the icy gusts nipped the grass-lander back towards groggy awareness. He moaned, eyelids fluttering, then struggled against the locked grip that propped up his half-buckled knees.

Wise enough for her years, Jeynsa clamped his weight, hard. 'Stay still, you numb nuts!' she snapped into his ear. 'Or get beaten silly. Sure's fire, you'd be less of a threat to yourself, triced in chains in the citadel's dungeon.'

'Except the duke's puling justice just let the louse go!' a sharp-eared cooper denounced from the side-lines.

Jeynsa's eyes widened. *'When?'*

Her darted glance caught Talvish off guard and swearing. Since he would not answer, she spun and accosted the burly man who had gossiped.

'What happened?' she demanded, while the rising lift jolted, and plunged Fionn Areth from sheet white to the green of incipient nausea. 'What did I miss?'

The loose-tongued cooper found himself cornered as the stopped hoist ground against the lift's block and tackle, and now rocked, suspended. Since no one could debark till the hands on the ledge swayed the davit over firm ground, the fellow caved in to appease the clan huntress's singeing attention. 'Well, lass, the snippet's no secret. Before dawn this morning, an armed escort wearing state dress was seen marching your pet through the public street. Looked like an arrest for a formal hearing. Since the bleating billy-goat's here, yapping off, the duke must've suspended his sentence.'

'You say!' Jeynsa's riveted interest transformed, an epiphany cut short as the Araethurian raised protest, that no such arraignment had happened.

'Ath above, do you never know when to shut up!' Jeynsa spun the grass-lander face about and shoved his jelly-legged bulk to the rail.

Fionn Areth groaned, folded double and retching.

'Heave up fast and be done!' Jeynsa hissed at a whisper. 'My plan worked! His Grace of Rathain's in Alestron, and I won't waste the moment playing your nurse-maid.'

The platform jerked as the team at the winch locked the drum. More sweating stevedores heaved on the lines and swung in the massive oak boom. Fionn Areth endured, grumbling. 'Of course your dastardly prince would show up. He times his appearances for sensation, then leaves his friends to smooth over the ripe inconvenience.'

'And you don't do the same?' Jeynsa crowed.

Fionn Areth paused, working his swollen jaw. 'My front tooth's chipped! Damn all to somebody's sourpuss fist. Have you also lost your sense of humour?'

But Jeynsa had no more patience. On one count, at least, the goatherd was right: the loyal band of Arithon's allies already tightened their ranks.

Tall and dark as a scowling post, Sidir stood waiting to meet her. Before Talvish joined forces against her, she grabbed Fionn Areth's fleece jacket and jerked his groggy frame upright. 'Come on, buffle-head! We can't dawdle, even for you to be sick. Or we'll both lose the bid for our destiny.'

Yet as rudely fast as she elbowed her way down the lowered gangway, Sidir breasted the outbound shove of bodies and blocked her.

Nor was the Companion any less wind-burned from his thankless wait, standing vigil. 'You can't find him without me,' he declared forthwith. As Jeynsa took issue, he crushed her tirade. 'Give way. Now! Take my offer of backing. In hindsight, you're likely to thank me.'

Talvish arrived. Prepared to use muscle, his jade eyes took the girl's measure, then Sidir's flint glance of warning. 'Where is your liege waiting?' he asked with clipped tact. Never a glance, from those steel-sharp, cold eyes, as his reflex shot out a lightning fist and saved Fionn Areth from crumpling under the shock of his bruise.

Sidir held his tongue for an irritable moment, while the gusts lashed his shorn hair against his gaunt cheek. 'Dame Dawr's,' he revealed, and even for him, the admission was savagely brief.

Talvish stared, poleaxed. 'Well,' he remarked with a lift of arched eyebrows, 'we're forewarned, if caught disadvantaged.' As the tired, impatient folk on the hoist rammed against his obstructive presence, he moved on, herding Jeynsa ahead of him. 'Ill-dressed and unwashed as we are, it won't matter. The field's hand-picked and laid for the blood-bath.'

Lest Fionn Areth try to duck out, the field-captain firmed his grip as he matched Sidir's lead. 'Since when has this Teir's'Ffalenn *ever* welcomed an encroachment upon his kept privacy? We may as well march in there, shame-faced, and see whether the s'Brydion dowager's leveraged the bollocks to handle him.'

The person was an idiot, who voluntarily paraded hurt flesh or bruised pride, or unkempt attire before Dawr s'Brydion. Talvish knew as much; had watched seasoned fighting men lashed to boy's tears by the old woman's caustic style. Yet as the party bound for a crown audience passed through her wrought-iron gate, his nerve stayed resolute. He unstrapped his steel helm. Paused in the windy twilight, he laced dirt-rimed fingers through his rumpled blond hair. That laughable gesture complete, he tapped on the door to the apartment that housed Bransian's grandame in time of siege.

Both he and Sidir stayed deaf to pity. The young pair under their escort were not to be offered the chance for a slinking retreat. Sidir blocked the narrow, arched portal behind. He would keep the royal charge and bring Jeynsa with drawn knives, to judge by his death's-head expression.

Desperation failed to invoke mercy. The pretty carved door with its paned, amber glass already swung wide to admit them.

'Dawr doesn't nurse wounds,' Mearn s'Brydion warned, before words of greeting or welcome.

Poised in the lit entry, his avid regard had already fixed on the ice shard Fionn Areth held pressed to his jaw.

'You don't say!' Fionn Areth mumbled past his crude remedy. 'The old besom expects us to be decked out like bawds, in gewgaws and fripperies for dancing?'

'Ah! Did we neglect the engraved invitation?' Mearn flourished the neat, feathered cap on his head. 'So sorry, stripling. You *have* learned to read?'

Mearn flitted aside before a victimized hamfist could swipe at him. Jewels flared under the single sconce candle that burned on the lower landing: in fact, the youngest brother s'Brydion was groomed for the ball-room, silk-shod and clad in a red velvet doublet. The facing was edged with black ribbon and fire opal studs. By contrast, his dark hose and white shirt were both plain, the lace cuffs that should accent such finery spared from snags on his warfaring calluses.

At total ease, Mearn struck off up the stairway, still chattering in cool sympathy to Fionn Areth. 'By Dawr's parlour creed, any injury gotten by fighting amounts to a stupid mistake. *"Lick your own hurts, and learn how to think so that next time, you watch where you step!"* She said that to Parrien once, when he crawled in bawling and expected her help to dry his snotty tears during boyhood.'

Talvish snorted. 'You refer to the time he broke both his hands, picking brawls with the blacksmith's apprentice?'

'My brother was always a bullying ox,' Mearn agreed. To the Araethurian, he resumed, 'Dawr refused to call her private physician. She left the lame duck to drive himself across town to seek ease at the garrison bone-setter's. An awkward predicament, since no one but me dared her wrath to help harness the cart-horse.' Arrived at the stair-head, Mearn never paused, but pushed open another carved door. 'I was four.' Across the tight-shuttered, unlit ante-room, he resumed his grim reminiscence. 'The blighted chestnut cob mashed my finger, inept as I was with the bit. I chose to soak the crushed knuckle in the horse-trough, then arranged to fall in, head first.'

He paused and glanced backwards. 'That part was to hide the fact *I* was crying.' His smile was a crocodile's. 'Not much you can do for that bruising you've earned. The raw beef's all been smoked into jerky.' As he finished, his strong, narrow hand turned the knob and flung open the last double panel.

'You've arrived,' he declared. 'There's the dowager's sitting-room. You're to go in directly, and may Dharkaron Avenger himself show you lot the swift spear of mercy.'

Light and warmth spilled through the widening doorway, made mellow by a melting peal of plucked strings: Arithon, inside, was tuning the lyranthe inherited from Halliron Masterbard.

'Ath love the tail-wagging arse of a goat, here's a farce!' Fionn Areth threw down his ice-and-rag compress and balked.

Touched thoughtful, Talvish stopped short of collision and shot off a glance of calm inquiry.

Mearn shrugged in return. Before the battery of Jeynsa's corked fury, and Sidir's testy stare, ranged behind her, he said, 'Arithon's granted a concert for Dame Dawr. By his royal preference, you're asked to attend.' He gestured, polite, for his guests to precede him. 'Mind your manners. Piss and vinegar aside, my grandmother hasn't been well.'

'The great lady's not ill,' contradicted a quiet voice from within, each silken word stamped by edged consonants. 'Not yet. Though she will be, if she continues to lose the core value that drives her to live.'

'He's alone!' Jeynsa knew her antagonist. The prince who had thrashed her defences in Halwythwood always would speak his true mind. Yet the blunt words just let fly were not aimed in the old woman's presence. Primed to rage, the young clanswoman shoved towards the doorway to challenge her nemesis.

Sidir might have stopped her. Since he made no move, Talvish followed suit, in no mood to be caught up in the fierce confrontation. 'Let her go!' he urged Fionn Areth, who also, unwisely, surged past and crossed the lit threshold.

Mearn grinned like a fox. 'But we've all been invited.' His step at the grass-lander's heels was not brash. 'If the promised performance springs for the throat, my coin's on Dame Dawr. Hale or not, she'll draw the first blood.'

Inside, the small chamber was curtained and still, gently washed in the glow of an oil-lamp. Stuffed chairs faced a table arranged with a tray, and a low divan with lion's claw legs. The birch logs ablaze on the merled, marble hearth shed a comfort not seen since the siege tightened grip on the citadel. The décor was tasteful, resplendent, restrained. Amid the gleam of bronze finials, upon damask upholstery flourished with tassels, the graceful, Paravian-made lyranthe commanded the room. The scintillant glints thrown off abalone-shell inlay framed a living grace, captured in light.

In fact, the bard was alone with his instrument. His uncut jet hair had been tied at the nape, a harsh style not meant to mask the expression just now obscured by his bent head.

The adornment of jewels would have been wasted. His fine build was exquis-itely set off by the severity of his attire. These clothes were not borrowed: the lustrous pearl silk of the shirt-sleeves, and the dense, emerald doublet had been finished to the highest standard. The jet studs set in silver that pinned his cuffs flared and died, to the snapping strike of quick fingers. He said nothing more, but tested each string in a sequence of bell-tone harmonics.

'I should have guessed,' Jeynsa stated, her scornful tone charged for mayhem.

The lyranthe cut her off. Notes showered and cascaded through falling arpeggios, through which lyric space, Arithon finished her vicious denounce-ment. 'That I would be found cosseted in the shelter of a woman, idle enough to solicit a warmed niche and expensive new clothing? How insightful of you to presume that your hostess tonight has nothing but frivolous preferences.'

'Dame Dawr's seamstresses took his Grace's measure, last summer,' Mearn's tart assault interjected. 'The old bat's always been an insatiable tyrant on issues concerning propriety.'

'In her presence, alas, even renegade royalty is obliged to dress to crown rank.' Arithon glanced up. His impervious eyes were bright, even dancing. Neat hands, still busy, refused interruption. 'The lady's writ ordered the pretty cloth, Jeynsa. I understand that her seamstress was commissioned on the hour that Duke Bransian joined your conspiracy.' The observation delivered no sting. Behind razored words, he was smiling.

Jeynsa sucked in a breath. One forgot at one's peril, after months in the artless company of Fionn Areth: *this* face, and this man, with his rapacious intellect, could never be mimicked in counterfeit. Caught in grimed clogs, with her boy's woollen breeches crusted with quicklime, she dared not sit down on Dame Dawr's heirloom furniture. Cold to the bone, she resisted the sweet lure of the fire: fought not to fall to the *presence* that towered behind this show of disarming humour.

Direct as a lance thrust, she launched her complaint. 'If the duke's close relations are among your Grace's friends, you would have served them with cowardice.'

'I've shirked the sword *you say* I owe to their defence?' Arithon tightened a drone string. The bass note slid, gliding to melting, true pitch. 'There's an alternate view. That no man or woman alive is the disempowered victim of another's degrading circumstance. Each is equipped to pursue their own fate. No one needs saving. Any hale person who yearns to be free could ignore Duke Bransian's ultimatum.'

Jeynsa made her return sally brief, a cruel shot straight from the heart. 'By betraying their families?'

Arithon did not rise. 'Never betrayal.' His imperative glance shifted, shutting her out as he changed strings and addressed the next tuning peg. 'Man or woman, they had only to claim their firm footing and act for harmony by walking away.'

Rage flowered then, a storm that burned to strike down such impervious autonomy. Jeynsa leashed that primal surge to attack. Just *barely* curbed the impulse to wrest the distracting instrument away from those clever hands. 'Your Grace of Rathain, as my father's daughter, I must question your charge! The s'Brydion cheated the Alliance for you! Served as your spies and informed for your purposes. Now Lysaer is here to wreak punitive damage. You expected to *just walk away*? Let fathers and matrons with dependent, young children burden the free wilds of Atwood? As *caithdein*'s successor, I'm supposed to ignore the stain on your lineage's name and toss off the grief of their rescue onto your freebooter's *conscience*?'

'I did not reject loyalty!' Vengeance-quick, supple fingers slapped off singing strings. 'I offered change,' stated Arithon Teir's'Ffalenn against a nerve-shocking silence. 'I asked the s'Brydion to abandon a structure of stone. Not the flexible spirit that imbues human life!'

As Jeynsa bridled, he quelled her with a glance. 'These people you presume to champion are, of *themselves*, whole beings graced under Ath's mercy. They'd create a new home. One built without walls, upon clearer vision, with intention towards dissolving the distrust that rends our feuding society. Townsmen must share in responsibility for the world they inhabit. Let them learn to thrive without leaning on fear-based control, which constricts the free play of the mysteries! This has been the Fellowship's long-term commitment. Now, even Sethvir's strength has been compromised. The compact the Sorcerers designed as our guide-line has been undermined by connivance and greed. The driving roots are not wicked or evil, but only self-blinded ignorance. I asked nothing more than to dismantle the old bitterness that all factions use to fuel their hatred. Abandon the divisiveness between clans and towns. For that cause, Dame Dawr could stand as my witness! Before walking away, I offered to bear the weight of a crown to underwrite peace.'

Through the stunned pause, imposed by a masterbard's eloquence, Arithon struck the A string on his lyranthe. He brushed off a sweet note, then added a full chord, building his case over the intricate dance of his fingering. 'This choice was given to s'Brydion, then. It is still a choice, now. On no other terms would I be present. You cannot speak for Alestron's lives, Jeynsa! Only yours. And mine, perhaps, on the day that you shoulder the long view with wisdom, and claim your *caithdein*'s investiture.'

'Jieret did not abandon his people to die!' Observers forgotten, Jeynsa stood tall, her brave appeal as true as the father, who had been as immovable oak. 'Should I tie my life-sworn word to a charlatan? Where would you be, prince? Where, without the shed blood of clan backing that spared you your miserable life? What have I done, but invoke the debt owed, that you refused to honour with decency?'

His sorrow palpable, Arithon regarded her. 'You claim I've abandoned my oath of service.' The lyranthe's voice faltered beneath his stilled hands; diminished, until the closed chamber harboured no sound, and almost no vestige of movement. While Talvish and Mearn caught their breaths, and Sidir braced for explosion, Fionn Areth held poised, as a raven might wait, to crow over the scent of felled carrion.

Arithon laid his irreplaceable instrument down on the divan beside him. Jewels flashed, mute, and fine clothing whispered as he knelt to his youthful plaintiff. 'Before every power, living or dead, I will answer if I am forsworn. But not this way, Jeynsa! You have little idea of the cost you've incurred when you chose to cry me down for sacrifice!'

'I'll see how it ends,' the girl flung back, bitter. 'You will rise to uphold the name of your ancestry. Or else show us false colours, and lay bare your soul as a quitter.'

Through the vibrating air, overburdened with heat, someone's arid snort of contempt: 'Bombast and melodrama! Are we meant to applaud?'

Dame Dawr emerged from the door of her bedchamber, her steel hair swept up in a knot and nailed with an ebony pin. 'I've seen many an embarrassing jape in my time. Never a comic charade to match this!' One frail step, two, she marched into the room, propped on the stout arm of a servant. 'Your Grace! Only babes act out on the floor, before they have mastered the aplomb to stand erect on two feet!'

As Arithon rose, chastened, the raptor's glance fixed next on Jeynsa. 'Young lady, your liege *lord* serves more than crown office. Under his calling as Masterbard, I've asked him to favour my home with his music. You were invited here at his request. But no private quarrel excuses the fact that I am your hostess. I shall overlook your unkempt hair and dress, provided that you mend your execrable manners and display the civility fit for your breeding!'

Tirade finished, she greeted Sidir with respect. Her nippish nod acknowledged Talvish. For Fionn Areth, who reddened and doffed his rough cap, she softened her battle-axe glare. 'A grass-lander, and without pretensions, I see! My salutations, young man. You've upstaged the oldest blood of Rathain, to the mortified shame of great ancestry. Please sit down. If you're chilled as you look, Cresiden here would be pleased to serve you peach brandy.'

Pert head turned, chin lifted, Dame Dawr declared, 'I shall sit, now.'

Her man-servant eased her into a chair, brought a quilt, then wrapped her frail limbs into the semblance of comfort. She subsided, lips clamped, and her breathing too short. No one else, even Arithon, dared to make comment, that in fact, the brief stint of passion had drained her. Tintless skin and bright eyes, the grandame huddled up like a bird. She failed to snap at Mearn's worried survey, or jab with snide wit, when Fionn Areth refused to risk countrified wits to the seduction of her rare liquor.

Lest her stamina fail, there could be no delay. Arithon took up his shining lyranthe. He bowed to Dame Dawr, a rueful arch to his brows that might have been suppressed mirth. 'By all means,' he pronounced, 'let us wreck the last shred of our dignity and slay the dragon of self-importance.' Forthwith, he ignored the footstool set out. To play for the lady in his stature as Masterbard, he embraced the clown, and plonked his richly clothed rump on her carpet.

The lyranthe spoke, instantly. A shouted chord in a major key that raked over fourteen silver-wound strings tuned to superb, ringing pitch. The musician followed his opening with a burst of merriment fit to banish ill humour. Foolery spoke in his phrasing. Once, twice, three times, his deft fingers slipped, a tripping, deliberate change that shocked shifts in key, tone, and timing. The changes tumbled over themselves like epiphanies: in triplets and couplets, drunken slurs and wild dissonance. The bard played the buffoon until his listeners ached, teeth and bones, and the assaulted mind floundered, unable to bear the assault of his catchy invention. Dawr withstood the onslaught, rammed stiff in her shawls like a jangled cat.

Arithon tipped his head to her, then, his strait-laced demeanour beyond all reproach.

Colour bloomed on the old woman's cheeks. Her lips twitched. Then, her wide-opened eyes welled with tears over egg-shell-thin lids. Dame Dawr exploded, not with outrage or scolding, but with unbridled laughter.

The lyranthe captured her mood and responded. The madcap tempo increased. The Masterbard grinned. He took hold, wringing sound through a fiery lift across three major keys. By then, no one could curb the tap of their feet. Had his performance been played for a tavern, he would have had patrons dancing on table-tops, shouting and stamping and free. Here, he played happiness, careless and glad, a soaring cry that evoked a forgotten exultation. Before the composition reached pace, his patroness was weeping. The catharsis burst every dam of held grief and lit Dawr from within like new morning.

No listener could mistake that the tribute was hers. Helplessly swept in, no heart could resist captivation. Sealed separate, they ached: for a celebration of life that recast the hatreds of war as utterly rigid and meaningless.

Unlike the others, Jeynsa s'Valerient had never heard Arithon play. Had never seen art and spirit unleashed with such soul-inspired abandon; nor been touched by a grace that invoked living light, sparked to a transcendent longing. Unprepared, stripped defenceless, she found no retreat, no cranny unscoured inside her. Her torrent of feelings could not be recontained, or stamped out of breathing awareness. The hard knot of mourning she held swelled and burst till she bent in a paroxysm of tears.

Sidir caught her close. He held on through the storm as she drowned, unable to bear the release.

The lyranthe strings spoke, striking air like flung gold, relentless and pure and impassioned. No respite was shown for the Teiren s'Valerient's collapse, or for Dawr's manic flame of delight. Arithon added song to his fabric of harmony, his lyric voice clothed in Paravian.

Translation of the words made no difference. The round vowels and cadenced consonants themselves built the mystical framework. Inspiration fused high art with rhythm, and entrained the bard's purpose, unstoppable.

Arithon played them the rebirth of hope. A vibrant blaze that razed away reason and dissolved earth-bound walls to the expansion of limitless spaces. He gave them a shattering brilliance of joy that devoured the fogs of despair as though pain had *never existed.* Peace such as the forest-born clans had not known, since the departure of the Paravians; and heights that a simple, Araethurian grass-lander had never held enough life to imagine.

Dame Dawr sat transported. Talvish huddled with arms clamped to his breast, sorely tried for the lack that his friend Vhandon could not share the ecstasy of the moment.

Hearing, Mearn s'Brydion saw his vital priorities reordered. Epiphany changed him, nourishing as spring rain, that there were *other things* he would fight to preserve for Fianzia and his unborn child.

Then in trauma and splendour, the peak experience passed. The Masterbard let down his woven thread and drew his creation to closure. Beyond word and string, grace danced in his presence: a tender release of the brilliant focus that supported his consummate artistry. When the last note died, the left quiet cradled an immaculate calm. No one spoke, or applauded. All tears had flowed dry. The reprieve abided, in which Sidir could help Jeynsa back to her feet. With a nod of awed tribute, he acknowledged the bard, then saluted the hostess, who gestured permission to escort the unsteady girl out for privacy.

Fionn Areth sat stunned, until Talvish gripped his shoulder and urged, his whisper not without sympathy, 'If you won't risk Dawr's brandy, we'll seek Dakar. Tonight, he'll damned well share his prize hoard of beer chits and let you get drunk.'

The goatherd arose, flustered. He managed not to trip over his own boots as the field-captain steered him away and propelled him over the threshold.

Mearn remained, and the man-servant, caught at a loss. Neither one dared to disturb the grandame in her regal chair.

A masterbard's empathic awareness alone possessed the unerring instinct. Arithon laid down his instrument. He stood and bowed before the old woman who had asked for his talents as patroness. 'The joy in the song was all yours,' he said softly. 'Mine, the privilege and pleasure to translate.' He raised her withered hand, turned her fingers with their sparkle of fine rings, and kissed her palm with the reverence of family.

Dawr's grasp tightened, strengthless, except for the will that defined her indomitable spirit. 'When you lead them out, those fathers and children and wives who are wise enough to seek refuge, I would beg not to be left behind.'

Although Mearn and the servant could not see Arithon's expression, as a mirror, Dawr's seamed face transformed to a luminous smile.

'You shall be with the first,' the Masterbard promised. Then he straightened, stepped back, recovered his lyranthe, and, on noiseless feet, left the chamber.

The trembling dowager settled back, wrapped in the loving care of her youngest grandson and the kindness of her trusted servant. Because peace in her domicile was always kept sacrosanct, Duke Bransian's authority did not cross her threshold, unasked. That irony twisted the warp thread of fate: for as long as Mearn stayed immured in her presence, he remained oblivious to all else that transpired that night in the citadel.

Cold, whitely shaken, Jeynsa s'Valerient failed in her third attempt to spark the wick of the tallow dip. Her tower chamber was fireless and dark, but not without human comfort. Over her shoulder, Sidir's quiet reach plucked the flint from her trembling fingers.

'Let me.' He drew his knife. A practised rap flaked the stone back to sharpness. Peerless scout, he kept shaved bark in his scrip. The flint was returned, followed by a lit spill that even the most nerve-wracked grasp could not fumble while kindling the pricket.

Wood scraped, from behind. The quiet strength of warm hands guided Jeynsa to sit in the chair just pulled up by the hearth. Sidir did not speak, but crouched by the hob and began to sort the scant logs from kindling within the bronze bin. Soon, he had a clansman's small blaze, which threw off only enough light and heat to take the chill off the bed-clothes he would hang to warm using the towel-rack.

Eased by winter practices known throughout childhood, Jeynsa massaged her shut eyelids, left swollen from weeping. 'I can't stand my ground with him. Not anymore.' For she had seen, finally: in Dame Dawr's exalted abandonment, she confronted the worth of the joy she nearly destroyed out of grief. Her father was dead. To give in to rage was to be consumed by his loss and murder the promise that infused the present. Guilt salvaged nothing. Through the settling pause, while the blaze caught and sang, and a blanket dropped over her shoulders, Jeynsa allowed the grave calm in Sidir's presence to soothe her dashed pride.

He never pressed her, but perched on the settle, hands laced at the patched knees of his leathers. The indoor setting did not nourish his strength. Yet he was himself: his person and habit unchanged from his traditional origins. A stag-horn-handled-dagger with a curved blade for skinning hung at his hip. Not the same steel he had carried from Halwythwood: that heirloom piece had been lost at his branding, lately replaced by an astute gift from Talvish. The raided sword he had never put off, since he came, was cocked back against his tucked ankle. The shorn clan braid, and disfiguring scars he had suffered in her behalf had never been flaunted to diminish her. Until now, that blameless restraint never stung beyond bearing.

Her crushing remorse at last impelled speech. 'How can I serve Rathain as *caithdein*?' she despaired. 'I have not reached the years of my formal majority, and tonight, we both watched the s'Brydion dowager melt like run wax in Prince Arithon's hands.' Jeynsa wiped her stained cheeks. Her tears had spilled over, again. 'Is there any spirit alive who can withstand the masterful force he has learned to wield in compassion?'

Sidir answered, thoughtful. 'Asandir thought you capable, should the sore need arise, and if our liege's willed choice ever threatens the kingdom. He hasn't, tonight. At least, not by my lights, or by the sure instincts passed down through my ancestry.'

Jeynsa sighed. 'I'm glad Mother sent you. Eriegal wouldn't show me your kindness.'

The tall liegeman's glance flicked up. Steady, his blue eyes held burning reproach. 'Eriegal has never found trust in his Grace. That's why he was not sent to Vastmark, by Caolle. No Companion among us has not hated, for loss. But some nurse the wound like a canker.'

'Not you,' Jeynsa challenged.

'Or your mother,' Sidir broached, a tender touch on the flinching pain instilled by her sire's late passing. He added, delicate, 'Did you know Eafinn?'

Jeynsa shivered, raised her knees, and wound her arms tight, with the blanket fringe tickling her moistened cheeks and the soft wool embracing her misery. 'I knew his son better.'

He had been well-loved, that vigorous young man with the flaxen braid and a spirit keen as a raptor. He had gone off to serve with Jieret's doomed war band, and had left no children to further his lineage. The fight to safeguard Prince Arithon's life had claimed too many dead in Daon Ramon Barrens. Sidir had no words, there. Self-honest, he could not absolve his own part: that the same ugly fate would have been his lot had his doomed High Earl not ordered him homeward.

'Father spared you for Feithan,' Jieret's brown-haired daughter declared, as sharp with her own observations. 'That she should not be left alone, after him, as Barach took charge of the lodge tent.'

'Perhaps.' Sidir seldom flinched, no matter how piercing a subject assaulted his dignity. He lived for a mate now, but the path that had saved him had never been his own choice. 'I don't think your mother was all of the reason your father made his decision. Eafinn was dead, and Caolle, gone also, who had served on the horrific campaign waged in Vastmark. That left no one other than me, for your prince. He's not easy to fathom. Everyone fears the potential to overpower that Arithon refuses to wield. Very few know his heart. Fewer still have been offered the gift, or been entrusted to see into his mind, as himself.' A slow breath, then, courageous: 'This is twice, he has shown you.'

Jeynsa swallowed. 'Because of his deep regard for my father, he won't use his initiate defences.'

Sidir smiled. 'You see that much, most clearly. But I suggest you've missed his other intent. The care that he bears you is genuine, and not granted only for Jieret's bequest. His Grace would bring you out, whole, Jeynsa. Will you let go and leave for him?'

'I won't stake him out as hooked bait to get murdered!' she snapped through a ripe flush of shame. 'But must the recovery of my stubborn error come at an untenable cost? Who will cry out for Alestron's free people? Should the lives in the citadel be kept at risk for the sake of Duke Bransian's pride? Who's left to counter the curse that stakes out the s'Brydion as scapegoat to salve the Alliance?'

'I don't have that answer,' Sidir allowed, stern no longer, but only sorrowful. 'You've brought your prince here. That can't be changed. Reaction will happen, now that he's involved. Since the innate compassion you witnessed tonight will never allow him to turn a blind eye, whatever comes, we all reap the price of your bargain.' Before pain could bite deeper, he added, not bitter, 'Arithon's playing touched more than Dame Dawr. I think he unveiled his own boundless hope to remind us we strive in the present. There are no victims, *now*. While we survive, for as long as we love, our future is yet to be written.'

Jeynsa stared at her hands, chapped rough from hard labour. She had no place to turn, except to capitulate, if only to silence her conscience. Sidir held his peace, prepared to make the space to recoup her demolished dignity. While the quiet extended, and the crawling flame-light traced barracks-style wood furnishings, noise intruded. Beyond the shut door, the matched tramp of hobnailed boots ascended the outside stairwell.

Sidir arose. 'That isn't the bearer of friendly news.' His alert, scout's senses picked up the jingle that bespoke heavy weapons and chainmail. Cat fast on his feet, he assumed a guarded stance, just before the latched panel slammed open.

One of the duke's burly sergeants, and more armoured men, packed into the stone-walled landing.

'We've come for Jeynsa,' the officer declared without courtesy.

Sidir weighed the man's presence. Never hurried, his talent for insight digested details: from the fellow's stiff neck, and wind-burned, blunt features shaded beneath his strapped helm, to the bristling hang of his weapons. Last, his glance swept the surly-faced colleagues who crowded the head of the stair. 'Let her change her attire for audience,' he said, reasonable. 'I will stay at hand and accompany her.'

'Duke's orders!' the leading officer snapped. 'She comes now. Alone.'

Deadly calm, Sidir warned Jeynsa to silence. 'Is this an arrest?'

'Move aside, forest man! My lord's will is my duty. Don't try me with insolent arguments!'

Yet Sidir stood his ground. 'You address the one chosen as Teiren s'Valerient,' he reminded. 'A girl not yet in her majority, and subject to her sovereign liege, who is also a guest of s'Brydion. By right, your appeal should be made to Prince Arithon. Since you've spurned my escort, Jeynsa goes nowhere without his Grace's informed consent.'

'Not when she stands on the citadel's turf,' the sergeant insisted, combative. 'Stand down!'

'Sidir!' Jeynsa cried. 'If Bransian's on the muscle, you'll be killed, and for nothing. His soldiers won't gainsay a direct command!'

But the Companion returned a sharp shake of his head. 'I do know where my feal priorities lie.' Cold as spring ice, Sidir challenged the officer, and the nettled men who had cordoned the doorway. 'Now we have a problem,' he declared, no less earnest, and unsheathed his weapons in one fluid movement.

The cramped, street-side tavern where Dakar had been cornered to cash in his hoarded winnings, was packed to bursting. Unemployed citizens hungry for warmth rubbed shoulders with whores and plump, aproned washing-women, and the rust-stained gambesons of off-duty garrison men. Though the evening was young, the crowd already vented rambunctious steam. Raucous noise shook the rafters. Dice games and arm-wrestling had stopped, for the nonce, in favour of running the odds on the contest incited by Talvish.

The fat prophet and the back-country grass-lander faced off to see which one could best hold his drink.

The pair stood, toe to toe inside a ring of cleared space, while Talvish, blond and insolent, used glib talk and the occasional mailed fist to safeguard the packet of ration chits. The task was not tame, since the booty had lightened the pockets of unwary sentries throughout weeks of wrangling card games. Some of the laughter around him was forced; not all of the badgering he fielded was friendly. Shouts belted out between jokes carried menace: the fact the wad was two fingers thick suggested the chance Dakar's partners might have been fleeced.

'He's a slinking Fellowship spellbinder!' a sore loser carped from the side-lines. 'Could have used craft to shuffle the deck! Might've dealt any hand in his favour.'

Talvish quipped back, 'Ever met Asandir? No?' His smile turned evil. 'Then, believe me, you wouldn't care to be in Dakar's boots if he'd maligned his initiate knowledge for cheating.'

'Wouldn't be caught in his boots, standing here,' groused another, a feint jabbed at Talvish.

The shied blow was warded, forcefully brisk. Though playful, the fair swordsman encouraged no nonsense: for the length of the wager he was the available target. No bettor who placed hard-earned coin on the outcome would strike at the pair of contestants. Not while he hoped to collect a lucky sum in recovery. Talvish doled two more chits to the barmaid. His purpose was simple: keep the contentious crowd sweet until Fionn Areth was drunk. Lay him flat long enough to silence his turmoil, while the Masterbard's adept handling of Jeynsa lanced her cankerous grief and let her start healing.

Dakar shouldered the role of buffoon in support. Whatever his reason for amassing beer tabs off half of Duke Bransian's fighting men, he rocked on splayed legs, stripped down to breeches and shirt-sleeves. His portly frame had lost weight, the linen sagged at his waist gathered in by a belt, ineptly punched to tighten the buckle.

'Go on, infant,' he goaded the herder. 'Your turn to down the next tankard. Show us a thirst that can put men to shame! Six piddling rounds are scarcely enough to whet the spit in my whistle!'

'Sheven,' Fionn Areth objected. Black hair in his eyes, he already wobbled like a loose post in a gale. Country-bred obstinacy kept him bolt upright, while the bar-keeper poured the next round and tried not to wince at the tilt in the vessel that captured the beer.

Dakar grinned. 'You won't last eight, milksop.' Blinking, he licked the foam from his moustache and watched his comment strike home.

Fionn Areth flushed purple. 'Go suck on a goat!' Chin out-thrust, his napped stockings bunched at his ankles, he tipped his head back and chugged. Reeled back on his heels, he keeled beyond recovery, then toppled like a felled plank. His own splashed beer caught him full in the face and set him coughing.

The bystanders roared. They banged on the trestles, while the losers screamed, and the elated winners bellowed in triumph. Whichever their lot, the spectacle cut short: Dakar, in midcrow for his easy victory, bent in half, then dropped to his knees.

'Daelion send a confounding wet dream!' yelled an armourer through pealing mayhem. 'Tie score, since the fat lout's gone under!'

In fact, Dakar languished, crouched on his hands, overcome by hammering nausea.

More noise, peppered through by howls of protest over which contestant had succumbed first. Fists swung now, in earnest. Two victims were bloodied as Talvish's oversight became overwhelmed. He threw down the beer chits; leaped over the ravening scramble as opportunistic bystanders cracked heads to snatch. The lightning move hurled him into the circle, as the tap-room seethed into bedlam. No man's intervention could rein in the fight. Too many weeks of stifling pressure frayed tempers to wrathful explosion.

Iron-handed, the field-captain hooked Dakar's arm. His unburdened grip snagged Fionn Areth. Talvish towed away the witlessly fallen, while Dakar, knuckles clenched to his roiling stomach, broke sweat trying to bear his own weight.

'This is an onslaught of prescient vision?' Talvish shouted, hell-bent, as he bashed aside brawlers to reach the rear doorway.

Dakar clipped off a nod. 'The beer's a frank pittance. This is a light drunk. Duck leftwards. That brute's got nail studs in his cudgel.'

'Dharkaron's red glory!' Talvish swore, angry. He kicked down the bull-necked combatant. 'You've done this before?'

A groan answered: not Dakar, but Fionn Areth, objecting. The bumping drag across the brick floor had broken his stupor. Talvish paused, too beset to stand off the rank crowd and still man-handle the grass-lander.

'Pick yourself up!' the field-captain snapped. 'Haul your share and help get us out of here.'

'The yokel's done for,' Dakar gasped between chattering teeth. He lunged, grabbed a trestle, and shoved Talvish off, adding, 'Listen to me! I enspelled the lad's beer. He's not going to rise! Find him a haven and leave him to sleep. He can't cause further trouble, tonight.'

Chilled by *that* note of stark desperation, now suspecting a worse, pending crisis, Talvish assessed the lad's rolled-back eyes, then changed strategy and chose a stout bench. He flopped the near-inert goatherd beneath, then hoped by the Fatemaster's mercy the fool might escape being trampled. Next, he seized Dakar's floundering weight and rammed a ruthless course towards the kitchen.

They burst, stumbling, into the stifling heat of clay ovens, and relative quiet. Cooks and scullions were absent, pans and chopping blocks abandoned to mount a defensive charge on the tap-room. As the smell of stewed onions ripped Dakar to redoubled nausea, Talvish laced forceful fingers in his damp shirt front and hauled him erect. 'Speak! I can't help if I don't know what's happening!'

The Mad Prophet swallowed back swimming sickness. 'Run. Pull your rank.' Clamped teeth and screwed eyes bought no respite from talent. More visions unhinged his senses. 'Commandeer a hitched carriage, and quickly!' The reeling onslaught hit hard and fast, *and showed Sidir,* again, *hard-pressed to the wall by Duke Bransian's guardsmen, and now bleeding from more than one sword-cut.*

Dakar felt a belting slap sting his cheek. The blow scarcely fazed him. Talvish's shout, and the blast of ice-water splashed on his face only left him belaboured and breathless. Dropped by an ache that skewered his chest like the fatal thrust of cold iron, he gasped through roaring darkness, 'Send someone you trust to fetch Arithon, *now*! He'll be with Elaira. If he's laid down wards, break his door and demand his attention! His Grace must bring her and meet us, forthwith.'

'Where, Dakar? *Meet us where?*' The cry seemed to spiral away into nothing.

'Jeynsa's guest-chamber,' groaned Dakar. 'Quickly. Already, we may be too late.' He forced his eyes open, to no avail, as the ceiling fell in and swallowed him.

The bout of oblivion broke, minutes later. Dakar surfaced, flat on his back, on the jouncing seat of an open wagon. Talvish loomed over him, spring-wound to pounce the instant he regained awareness.

Wracked by shuddering horror, Dakar sucked in bracing air. A last image barraged him, ruthlessly sharp. Mercifully, this time, his seared senses stayed clear. 'Sidir's taken a guardsman's sword through the chest.' He pushed off bracing hands and shoved upright, weeping in helpless urgency. 'Just get me there. Fast! He is dying.'

Talvish turned his head, and spoke rapid orders. A driver's whip cracked. In the reeling dark, the galloping cart-horses swerved in their traces. Dakar hung on. Through the rattle of swingle-trees and the jolt of iron wheel rims, the commandeered brewer's wagon veered down a back alley.

'We're almost to the west tower!' the field-captain reported, too much the veteran for hysteria. 'Jeynsa's quarters, you said? Was that instruction accurate?'

The Mad Prophet nodded, dizzied again as his runaway talent spiked lights through his eye-sockets.

'Dharkaron's thrown Spear!' Talvish yanked him straight before he could faint. 'What black-hearted mischief has wrecked tonight's peace?'

Dakar shouldered the misery: no kind words existed for treacherous news. 'The duke's taken the Teiren s'Valerient hostage, with intent to force Arithon's hand.'

Jeopardy

Arithon guarded his privacy through the let-down that followed the performance done for Dame Dawr. Halliron's example had taught him well: the deep
receptivity required to channel his talent needed calm for recovery, and the
fraught tension that gripped the citadel in war-time demanded more strict
shielding, still. Therefore, his wardings enforced a peace he invited none but
Elaira to cross. Since Kyrialt would not be moved from his steadfast watch at
the downstairs portal, the guest tower's ground-floor chamber was refurnished
as quarters appointed for his use and Glendien's.

The snug space above became Elaira's still-room, with pine trestles cluttered
with parchments and ink, mortar and pestle and brazier. The trunks and basketry
hampers that stored her remedies infused the draughts from the stairwell with
the perfume of balsam and herbals. That aromatic astringency sweetened the
air in the bedchamber above, beneath the black beams of the eaves, where the
wind against the latched shutters added traces of sea-salt and frost to the
familiar scents of the healer: a melding of wintergreen, lavender, and chamomile;
of bitter aloe and tannin and willow bark, which persistently clung to Elaira's
clothes.

Her hair harboured the same exotic mélange. Eyes half-lidded, her warm
weight curled with her head rested against his chest, Arithon sifted the rich
locks through his fingers with a touch of matchless tenderness. The long day
begun by his pre-dawn arrival at last drew to a tranquil close.

'There will be a solution,' he murmured, since Elaira would not broach the
subject. 'Your Prime's tyranny over us denies us our right to individual freedom
upheld by the Major Balance.'

Elaira turned her cheek. Green eyes met velvet-grey, and exchanged deep communion, fired through by the flame of frustrated passion. Their discussion had already mapped the fixed obstacles. Had exhausted the obvious avenues, in those shattered, past hours of shared company at Halwythwood: that the Fellowship Sorcerers' power to act in her behalf remained tied by the inexplicable *choice* of her personal quartz. Ath's adepts had been first to unveil the riddle of the crystal's self-made consent. Aligned to her with a persistence that posed an enigma, the stone's willing consciousness, partnered to hers, kept it subservient to the Koriani Order. The stone pendant now rested in Selidie's hands, a powerful game-piece that posed a consummate danger to any outside liaison.

Arithon smiled. The current of joy entrained through his music had not quite tapped out and gone dormant. 'Patience hurts, I agree. But I won't spoil the present.' His thought held cold iron: after his promise to Jeynsa was honoured, the Prime Matriarch had best defend her interests. 'There will be reprieve for us, though at the moment, our limited straits can't imagine it.'

He bent his head then, melted her lips with a kiss that gave physical warmth and the keen signature of his emotion. The caress bestowed comfort, but was not yet matchless: not the grandiloquent melding of spirit *all but* consummated to explosive release three months ago in the night glade at Halwythwood.

Elaira locked her clasp over his loosened silk shirt. At least for tonight, they had each other. All cares could wait. She refused to let the need in her hunger chafe through the vital strength of his hope. His presence alone gifted her beyond words. She nestled close, while in sheer delight, he stroked her dark hair, auburn glints sparkling through his fingers.

In due time, unhurried, they would move on to bed, there to embrace what scant comfort their proscribed straits would allow before the night's fitful sleep claimed them. Or would have, had Kyrialt's step not raced up the outside stair.

The door opened, as quickly, without knock for warning, a departure for the young liegeman. Riled onto his feet, Arithon forgave the intrusion, which had been no thoughtless discourtesy.

Mearn's lady huddled outside in her night-rail. White and shivering, she wore a field officer's cloak draped over her slender shoulders. 'Talvish sent me,' Fianzia announced. 'He said there's been trouble. You're both needed at once. Go directly to Jeynsa's quarters.'

'Where is your husband?' Arithon asked, brisk, as he enfolded her chilled hands in his own and drew her inside his warmed room.

'Mearn's still at Dame Dawr's,' she replied, teeth chattering, while he sat her down in his vacated place at the fireside. There, he peeled off the cloak and made way for Elaira, who wrapped the bearing lady in blankets just stripped off the bed.

'My dear, you shouldn't be out in this state,' the enchantress admonished, as healer. 'Why didn't you dispatch a servant?'

Fianzia shook her head, her blond hair still disarranged from the pillow. 'Talvish said not. For political expediency.' Her enormous, bright eyes tracked Arithon's expression, igniting his feverish concern. 'The captain would not risk having a lackey stopped by the duke's men on the way. You are to know Dakar's suffered an augury that's broached a matter of desperate urgency.'

'Never mind who's in crisis!' Elaira snapped, shocked. 'You aren't going out again in this state, for the health of your unborn child!'

'She'll stay here,' said Arithon, which settled the problem forthwith.

Elaira left the footstool to ease Fianzia's swollen ankles, then snatched her wool over-dress out of the wardrobe. Since she was well-practised to act in emergencies, and more than swift, tying laces, Arithon stamped into his outdoor boots without pause to don leathers or jerkin.

'Be comfortable, lady,' he entreated Fianzia. 'Take whatever you need. Glendien's company will serve you as handmaid until tomorrow, when a closed carriage can come to collect you.' Of the officer's cloak, just tossed aside, he added, 'This belongs to Talvish?' At her nod, he slung on the garment himself. 'If you please? The night's cold enough that the captain won't mind the opportune loan that returns it.'

Last thing, before leaving, he snatched up his Paravian sword and shouldered the strap of his bundled lyranthe. While Elaira raced downstairs to shove some emergency remedies into a satchel, Arithon closed the door firmly behind and gave rapid instruction to Kyrialt. 'Stay here! Stand your guard and let none pass but Mearn! Until I've seen what's pushed Talvish to risk underhand action, the Duke of Alestron himself shall be denied leave to know that the Lady Fianzia bides as our guest.'

The appalling wait ended. At long last, the patter of footsteps broke the quiet of the darkened stairwell. Not soldiers: these arrivals did not pack hobnailed boots or the metallic clangour of weaponry.

'This should be help coming,' Talvish reported, tautly poised at the threshold of Jeynsa's violated guest-chamber. Since the spellbinder remained all too desperately engrossed, the encouragement died without answer. Alone, the field-captain advanced to the stair-head. The night beyond the punched slits of the arrow-loops gave back no cracking echoes of hooves pounding over the cobbles. No grind of iron cart-wheels disrupted the yard. Therefore, the imminent company had engaged no transport, but came at a sprint through the citadel streets. Friend or enemy, at least their approach was discreet.

Talvish gripped his sword, prepared to draw until, emerged out of shadow, below, a slight figure rushed upward, bearing a bundled lyranthe. 'Arithon!'

'Here!' came the instant reply, in a questioning tone that asked volumes. 'Elaira, also. The bearer you trusted to fetch us is safe, under auspice of Rathain's protection.'

Talvish shut his eyes in relief, that the nuances of his jeopardized loyalty had not been overlooked. Then Teir's'Ffalenn and Koriani enchantress reached the landing. Their breathless presence brought a blast of fresh air, whisked in from the cold, starry night. No chase had sent armoured men at their heels, since no signal distress disturbed Arithon's features.

Now the moment had come, even seasoned nerves faltered. Talvish delivered his bad news with gut-sick reluctance. 'Sidir's inside, knocked down with a sword wound.'

'Defending Jeynsa?' Always, in the white pitch of a crisis, Arithon's thought vaulted ahead. 'Why?'

Seen up close, the field-captain's hands were smeared scarlet. More tell-tale stains showed where he had tried to stanch gushing blood with the hem of his surcoat. 'Bransian sent soldiers. They seized her on orders and took her by force.'

Stripped words left no doubt that the battle was lost, with naught left but the wreckage of aftermath: enough to speed Elaira's step over the threshold; and more than Arithon required to guess that his forest liegeman's condition was fatal. Above all, Sidir's oathsworn service was true. Given strength, he still would be upright and fighting.

'Keep our privacy, Talvish,' Arithon appealed. 'I've no words to reward your prompt action, except to lay down Rathain's claim to your service if Bransian's outstepped his titled authority.' A promise, that tonight's abuse would be challenged, and that Talvish's captaincy would have an honourable defence, pending a count of insurgency; the same direct kindness that, heart-felt and fierce, had inspired Sidir's sterling sacrifice.

The accolade maddened, before cruel grief. Talvish snapped. 'Go in and attend to your fallen!'

Crown rank imposed that dire obligation. Arithon visibly steeled harrowed nerves. The calm his spirit would *never* embrace forced a masterbard's empathic discipline. Tears sprang unheeded down Talvish's cheeks, as Rathain's feal prince faced forward and entered the room.

Inside, the burdened air reeked of death. Across trammelled shadows, the flicker of flame-light painted a chamber in shambles: split chairs, a rucked blanket, an upset bench, and a smashed crockery pricket, scattered over the scars gouged by hobnails in the stained floor-boards. Here lay the bunched cloth of a man's tumbled cloak. There, a dropped, clotted blade. Then, sprawled unmoving, the mailed bulk of three strangers' bodies; Arithon stepped over the first, resolute. Savaged senses recorded the detail: the corpse had Jeynsa's poniard struck through one wrist. A gleam of bright silver, clear in the gloom: he identified the hilt of Sidir's hunting dagger sunk into the throat, above a citadel guard sergeant's gorget.

Breath hitched in sharp dread, *that the girl might have suffered an injury during the vehement course of resistance.*

Talvish spoke, from behind, to stem frantic conjecture. 'She's surely alive!

Snatched for leverage. Bransian's men should have kept their strict orders not to retaliate.'

'She's not hurt,' affirmed Arithon. His blood oath, set for her protection in Halwythwood, had not triggered his inner alarms. Sad fact stung afresh: her choice not to grant reciprocity meant he could not reach out, or touch on her mind, or sound with his talent for more direct answers. Clean ethics denied him. Trust in the moment was all he had, that no harm had yet overtaken her.

Sidir's sharp work, meantime, had not left loose ends. No wounded remained to divide concentration, or conflict his affectionate loyalties. Mage-sight affirmed the shocked absence of aura: the duke's henchmen were dead beyond salvage.

Which left the huddled form by the casualty sprawled on the far side of the room. Where a silhouette jammed against the pooled lamplight showed Dakar, brought to his knees, with his hand clasped around the slackened fingers that had reaped the grim price of the sword. The spellbinder choked, unabashedly weeping, as Elaira sank down in support at his side.

Sidir breathed, still. Initiate senses picked up the stammering pulse-beat, which flared static bursts through his faltering presence. From Elaira, as well, Arithon sensed the intensity of focus, as she brought her trained skills as healer to bear.

Eyesight and hearing recorded, unasked: the leap of jerked sinew, as traumatized muscles were thrown into spasm. Skin, wrung too white, and the cut ends of salt-and-black hair, matted with running sweat in extremity.

The body could be made to achieve the unthinkable. Arithon closed the last stride and crouched, met by Dakar, who turned and acknowledged him.

If pain refused speech, the spellbinder's expression transmitted emotion, transparent. Arithon flinched, caught defenceless. All the cankered remorse from a night dell in Vastmark was written over the Mad Prophet's streaked face.

'Just like that shepherd child, taken by wyverns,' he gasped in laid-open distress. 'The beer I swilled in the tavern tonight was to heckle Fionn Areth into a safe stupor. Only now, when it counts? We are losing Sidir! I've pissed away the whole power I had, that could have been used to help ease him!'

Arithon murmured, 'Hush!' At relentless need, his bard's schooling granted at least the appearance of presence. 'You've done enough. We are here, and my liege-sworn's not crossed, yet.'

But already Elaira's taut features showed pity. Her early prognosis was grim.

Sidir lay on his side. Talvish's hand had cut back his clothes when there had been hope of a field-dressing. The blade struck through his bared chest canted right: no heart damage, but a grievous lung wound. His bleeding frothed pink with let fluid.

'I'cuelan am-jiask edael i'tier, Sidir,' the Teir's'Ffalenn said, his Paravian phrased with inconsolable quiet, translated, 'your feal prince attends you.'

The liegeman returned no sign of response. His eyes, squeezed shut, pinched the suffering flesh to his skull, while torn tissue laboured, wrestling against inexorable fate for each separately congested breath. The battle he sustained could not last for long.

Dakar choked off a sob. 'I couldn't hold him! Even to grace him with the last words he might wish to leave his three daughters.'

'He's still fighting!' snapped Elaira.

The adamant, clamped features, that acknowledged no comfort, proved that Sidir hoarded his dwindling strength. His silence supported a frayed concentration, in pursuit of an obstinate, brave will to live.

Arithon swallowed, eyes wet for such courage. The hard task was his, to rise to match the man's blistering resolve, then speak. 'My friend, all you fought for, my hand will put right. Care absolves you of fault. You are free to release your feal burden.'

The next shallow exhale expired, then doggedly, shuddered to inhale. The punishing struggle still would not be relinquished.

'*I'ent cuelan am-jiask edael ameinnt-huell i'tieri*, Sidir!' Arithon repeated, this time phrased in the emphatic form that *claimed* the fullest promise of responsibility. 'What can be done, shall be.' Rathain's prince unsheathed his black sword. Blade laid at his feet, he also unlaced the fleece cover from his lyranthe. 'Elaira?'

Her delicate touch traced across Sidir's breast, completing her rapid assessment. 'The windpipe's deviated too far to the left.' A dire sign, that confirmed chilling failure: Sidir's right lung was already filled, and the pierced chest wall, collapsing. 'We can't pull the sword, either,' Elaira despaired. 'He's bleeding to death. The gush as the steel's drawn will drain him, and flood the drowned airway much faster.'

'Cautery's needed,' Arithon agreed, sorely tried, that Sidir was clanborn, and too natively fluent to mask the grotesque exchange behind ancient language. 'The blade stays in place, then. What do you suggest?'

She hesitated only a moment, tough lady. Then, 'Ath above! We've no time to induce gentle measures. No matter how badly Sidir wants to live, his vigor is ebbing. I'm no adept, with the transcendent power of a sacred grove to tap through! This recall is far outside of my means, except through the invasive use of the knowledge derived from the Koriathain.'

Arithon held her terrified eyes with his own. 'Imposed measures are not in violation if they are used by informed, free consent.' Hammered steady, even under the storm of his human uncertainty, he added, 'You've done this before! Dakar is here also, as a Fellowship initiate, in step with that open practice.'

Elaira spared no sideward glance for the spellbinder's horrified consternation. Tuned into relentless rapport with a suffering that abjured an eased course of release, she curbed doubt. To argue for limits admitted despair, which diminished all effort to nothing.

'A transduction sigil can be made to flash-burn enspelled heat through the metal,' she allowed, though the prospect was frightening. 'But we can't blunt the senses under narcotic herbs. Already, Sidir's too weakened.' The pain would be dreadful, a shock to speed certain death. Elaira shivered. Pinched with distress, she scrubbed fouled hands on her shift and found dauntless courage to finish. 'If we stem the slashed veins, the lung must be drained, and depending on how bad the damage inside, perhaps even forced to regenerate.'

Before she broke under Sidir's demand, Arithon broached the rest for her. 'Then we shall have to halter the living spirit, or he won't survive the harsh course of the surgery.'

Dakar recoiled. 'Ath's own mercy, I can't!' The dread stared him through: a misery ingrained by the hideous failure, as his resource fell short for the mauled girl in Vastmark. Now, sick with drink and undone by the back-lash from a prescient trance, he lacked his basic faculties. 'Don't invite the disaster! I won't watch Sidir's life slip through my inept hands! Not even for you will I try this!'

Arithon bowed his head over his gleaming lyranthe, now unwrapped and braced upright. 'I quite understand.' While Elaira ransacked her satchel for the requisite remedies, he drew up a stool, struck a note, and bent to his tuning.

From flushed rejection, Dakar drained white. 'No. Your Grace, no!' Through the sliding, sweet pitch, ruled fair by the tuning peg, and the ghastly saw of Sidir's ripped chest, the Mad Prophet shouted, 'Past question, Arithon, you *can't* dare to link in consenting rapport with a Koriani enchantress! If Elaira invokes her order's knowledge for you, you'll be bound to Prime Selidie's cause. Dharkaron Avenge and butcher my carcass, before I let you be compromised by a Matriarch's oath of debt!'

'But I'm not doing this for Arithon!' Elaira cracked, cross. 'The healing is Sidir's, underwritten for his sake!'

Dakar's taut face cleared. 'Ah, clever lady!' For the admissible terms of a feal obligation enabled the crown's opening. As Prince of Rathain, under charter law, Arithon was sworn to protect a kingdom subject's born right to freedom; which legality *also* carried the Fellowship's charge, should Selidie outstep her limits.

Stunned cautious, Dakar warned, 'You won't like what befalls if I'm called to defend in the name of the Sorcerer who trained me.' The stakes were unforgiving: for Arithon to rely on a formal intercession, asked under his sanction to rule, the honourable course of reciprocity would be demanded in turn by the Fellowship. His Grace would bend his knee: not to the Prime Matriarch, but to the imposed weight of his ancestral inheritance.

Now, Elaira bristled. 'I will let nobody's talent act through me! Not if Arithon's to be hounded to embrace a coronation by expediency!'

'Peace, beloved!' The appeal broke dissension, cut by the unbearable, pure tone as the treble string sang in trued pitch. 'Sidir's cause won't languish. I have more than one title on which to lay claim to a clear line of authority.'

Dakar glared, slack-jawed. '*You would challenge the Prime Matriarch as Athera's Masterbard?*'

'And on my own resource!' Arithon avowed. 'Sidir is my friend. He is Jieret's appointed replacement for Caolle, to grant Jeynsa the paternal guidance she needs to mature. My debt is personal, and deep enough, that if I must, I'll give all in my power to save him.'

Amid the anguished pause, loud with clinking glass, and the sharp reek of tincture of iodine, Elaira prepared her honed instruments. At relentless speed, she set her boundaries. Yet unlike the past surgery rendered in Merior, she did not proceed in presumption, as she selected the herbals for healing. Her sojourn in Ath's hostel corrected such arrogance. Poised in tender humility, she now sounded out the thread of consciousness underpinning each plant. Then, under intent to mend tissue in partnership with Sidir's desire, *she asked for participation.*

Even Dakar must acknowledge that pause for alignment in accord with the Major Balance. No matter how urgent her need, Elaira suspended opinion. She had to sense whether the channel would open, and grace her willed use with permission. *Only* then could she engage the Koriani sigils of power that heightened remedial efficacy.

Attuned to the peace she required to concentrate, Arithon gentled his stiff ultimatum. 'On all counts, Dakar, you hold my consent. You will use that authority, and without restriction, should my innate talent as musician fail to stay the full course.'

'Impose your acceptance of Rathain's sovereign duty through my ties to the Fellowship?' Dakar crossed his arms, desperate to quell his anguished heart, as in searing language, he qualified, 'Allow this, by force, in a state of extremity? Beware what you say, prince! The blood oath you gave over to Asandir included no term of release! You know I must hold you to your sworn promise, not to permit you to fall into jeopardy!'

'I have no intention of letting things come to that.' Under the sputtering flare of the lamp, as Elaira adjusted the wick, a plucked shower of notes stabbed out in reproof. 'Trust me, I beg you,' Arithon pleaded. 'I protected Feylind. Salvaged the *Evenstar.*'

'And nearly lost all you *were* to the Kralovir cult at Etarra!' Dread and rancour laid bare, Dakar lashed out. 'Without trusting me then, or sharing your strategy beforehand, how dare you rely on me now?'

'I will rise to this!' Arithon stated, determined. 'Stand by me, or leave. I won't shirk the attempt.'

Dakar lost all words. While a dying friend's fingers chilled in his clasp, and the ugly, wet suck of drawn air stretched the seconds, necessity demanded: Sidir's margin for rescue diminished, each moment they wasted in argument.

No more could be done, except to shoulder the adamant watch from the side-lines.

Arithon phrased a final request as Dakar stirred to capitulate. 'Please lace Sidir's hand through Alithiel's grip. If the fight we enact is for a just cause, the sword's enchantment could be moved to speak for him.'

With consummate speed, then, events moved apace. The bard sounded a ringing chord that tested the pitch of his instrument. Elaira knelt, chalk in hand, poised to allow the beguiling draw of his music to amplify her healer's trance. Within the stilled chamber, reeking of death, and still roiled by the discharge of violence, the Prince of Rathain, acting as Masterbard, addressed his prostrate liegeman. 'Can you trust, Sidir?'

Wracked in spasms, near emptied of blood, the Companion opened his tortured eyes.

Arithon's voice all but faltered. 'No! Don't speak! Your right of free choice to survive is acknowledged. If the channel for your consent has been made, let me do the work. I will find it.'

He gripped his fine instrument. Side-tracked the clamour of agonized uncertainty, tipped his dark head, and *listened* with his whole being. Then his hands moved. Touched on metal and wood, that the empathic whisper to forge vital sound might be wedded with fretboard and string. Now, mortal flesh dared not slip from high mastery. Fear and anxiety must have no voice, lest he mar the balance that danced between life and loss.

Arithon opened the phrase for the summoning. Delicate, seeking, he ran the first skein of harmony: sought the bold measures that accessed the keys to the human soul. In rhythm and line, made captive through inspired harmonics, he founded the melody that would play for Sidir his Name.

Partnered with him, entrained to his talent, Elaira inscribed the exacting ciphers for the spelled circle: the matrix, once done for a fisherman in Merior, that would come to shelter the unshielded spirit. Only this time, the consummate weave of meshed talents trod more than the razor's edge of mortality. Initiate skill must *also* thread the unerring path: between Prime Selidie's plot to ensnare Arithon, and the Fellowship Sorcerers' need to preserve Torbrand's irreplaceable crown lineage.

One narrow advantage altered the scales: Arithon's reclaimed mage-sense let him perceive with cleared sight as the ephemeral gold light spun by his notes raised the shimmering construct between them. That delicate framework acknowledged true worth, forming the haven to draw a living awareness clear of its stricken flesh.

Should the bard's gift withstand the arduous course, the enchantress must enact, *without flaw,* the contrary sigils that structured a perilous healing. No longer hampered by Sidir's debilitated pain, with her refigured art uplifted on the wings of the Masterbard's melody, Elaira might stem an ebbing tide long enough to stay the turn of Fate's Wheel.

And if not, if this sinking liegeman reached the end to his striving, the courage must be there, no matter the grief, to play onward and loosen the ties for his passage beyond the veil.

Late Autumn 5671

Reversal

A novice initiate had flirted with one of the Alliance wounded, taken in by Koriathain for healing. Her rash action upset every established activity within the sisterhood's field encampment. Even on distant worlds whose histories predated Athera's compact, the order always had jealously guarded the range of its oathsworn prerogatives. Discipline fell with punitive speed.

The Prime Matriarch called the session of inquiry, despite the late hour's inconvenience. Lirenda's slaved presence was retained for the demeaning service of verifying the actions of the accused, while the formal pavilion was cleared straightaway. By the time the displaced peeresses scuttled out, bearing heaped armloads of books, Prime Selidie sat enthroned in her chair of state, her delicate shoulders regaled in the purple mantle and scarlet-edged robes of high office. No servant came to build up the fire, though lights for reading still burned in the incense-soaked air. The disgraced initiate was kept standing, bolt upright and trembling with fright as she realized her coming interrogation would be impelled through the matrix of a major focus crystal: a gruelling review that entrained thought and mind, and forced past event into present recall. Such intimate analysis was no choice of the subject's, but a forced subjugation of character, made under the absolute terms of the Prime's claim to oath-bound obedience.

The Skyron aquamarine was unveiled for the task, frigidly blue as faceted ice, and as unpleasant to handle; the same jewel, once used to query Elaira, when she had been exposed for her budding attachment to Arithon s'Ffalenn. Then, as now, Lirenda clasped the enabled stone between her bare hands. The waves of dire cold raised by its active field punched her skin into gooseflesh and needled her nerves.

That whip-lash discomfort concerned her far less than her nettled aristocrat's pride: unlike the past trial that harrowed Elaira, this testing was not conducted under the ritual formality reserved for oathbreaking. The Matriarch administered the questions herself. Lirenda was not honoured as the titled Inquisitor. No more the cosseted, superior favourite, groomed to inherit prime power, she was not charged to wield the tuned matrix directly. Instead, her person was fused into the link, made to serve as both reed and sounding-board for the Prime's stripping analysis.

As bearer, not master, Lirenda suffered the probe of each question, inducted through crystal. While the miscreant subject sweated under the throes of involuntary reliving, Lirenda *also* expressed the experience, down to gut-level reaction. Each sordid response became as her own, drawn from the intransigent girl. Tonight's examination carried no heady rush of dominant power, no private thrill of excite- · ment. Instead, the loss of autonomy remade the ordeal into raw degradation.

No escape existed. The teasing, lustful affray in the hospice tent sprang out of concupiscence. Sickened to trembling, Lirenda suffered the wrenching brunt: an exchange nothing like the lyric affair of the heart that had seeded Elaira's rebellious affection. This raging obsession for sex overturned her ordered mind and rampaged through her virgin's senses. She quickened, then quivered, inflamed by desire, until she felt engorged and sullied.

The process bore on, unending, while Selidie conducted her methodical inquiry. 'And how did you touch him?'

A flood of tactile sensation became her heated hands, eagerly fondling forbidden flesh underneath a bed-sheet. The trapped spirit engaged as the proxy witness shivered in mute protest under the relentless onslaught.

'Hold!' The sudden command shattered the entrainment, channelled from the subjugated novice. Hands clenched to the Skyron crystal by reflex, Lirenda reeled, whip-lashed back into the severed awareness of her chill seat in the pavilion, with its scent of stale incense ribboned across the candle-lit dais and cavernous gloom.

Against that stilled back-drop came movement and noise: a senior enchantress had dared to enter and risk interruption. While the released novice swayed upon buckling knees, the cloaked arrival curtseyed in rushed obeisance and delivered her breathless report.

'My Prime, as your will commands. The enchantress posted on lane watch has detected the signature energy evoked by our order's conjury. The signal is the one you predicted, arisen from inside the s'Brydion citadel.'

Unremarked listener, Lirenda was jolted to riveted interest. This reference applied to initiate Elaira, and the glaring urgency of the Prime's machination to entrap the last Prince of Rathain.

'The signature trace has been carefully shielded,' the senior disclosed in crisp recitation. 'We needed meticulous care to be certain. But the resonant ciphers driving the power originate from the sisterhood.'

Selidie's porcelain-doll features seldom showed an expression. The wrapped hands in her lap never moved. But the gleam that sharpened her pellucid eyes shot a flickering charge across the Skyron matrix's active focus. Lirenda sensed *also* the elated thrill that made her Prime pounce on the news.

'The novice set under disciplinary questioning may retire to closed quarters,' Selidie ruled, abrupt beyond etiquette. 'Let the miscreant stay in solitude and consider the gravity of her transgression.' Lest the senior initiate should presume to linger, the next order destroyed the least opening. 'Madam, you will serve as the girl's punitive escort, as well as stay on as her warden. On your way, make sure that the watch is informed. On no account should anyone else broach my privacy until leave is given.'

'Your will, Matriarch.' The elderly peeress bent in compliance, sulky, since the assignment insulted her station and rank. Worse, the shaken novice required support, not yet able to walk unassisted.

Lirenda regarded the pair's weaving departure, perversely glad not to have been dismissed, if her role as Prime Selidie's puppet made her party to Arithon's downfall. More rapid instructions rousted the boy page by the ante-room doorway. He returned, scurrying, with the small coffer stored in the Matriarch's day chest.

The Skyron aquamarine was kept enabled, but relegated to a bronze tripod, while Lirenda's dexterity was pressed to unfasten the chest's warded locks and bronze latches.

'Lay bare the contents,' Selidie demanded. 'But take utmost care! Shield your direct touch as you remove the covering.'

A crystal, then, would be wrapped in the silk. Lirenda peeled the cloth back, unsurprised to encounter the silver chain and quartz pendant that served in rapport with Elaira. The jewel's linked matrix was active, as well. Engaged with the distant enchantress's working, its raised field whispered tingles over Lirenda's sensitized skin. Just how *any* junior initiate could wield power without her attuned focus in hand presented a piquant mystery. The feat should be impossible. Lirenda still sweated the harrowing memory, when one of Arithon's arrogant henchmen had stolen her personal crystal. She had never felt more helpless and humiliated, until her current state of disgrace. Yet no chance was given to study Elaira's singular prowess.

'Our bait draws on her initiate heritage at long last!' The Prime's avid excitement rivalled the cat that measured a mouse-hole for movement. 'Lirenda! You will take up the Skyron focus, again. Search through its kept record and establish rapport through Elaira's vow of obedience. I would tie into her current activity through the matrix of her crystal pendant. Since my subsequent working will be framed through yours, I need a clear line for my purpose. Grant that for me. Absorb the emotional dross through the link we just used to screen the miscreant novice.'

Lirenda could not escape the imperative to take up the Skyron focus. Puppet to the Prime Matriarch's whim, she submerged for the second engagement: found and locked into Elaira's self-signature, indelibly stamped by the order's oath of obedience. That binding permitted the entry for Lirenda to key into the focal point of the personal quartz that the order held hostage. Concentration had to be forced, inflamed as she was by aroused lust from the acts of the flutter-brained novice. Never her own mistress, body or mind, Lirenda did as directed, and enabled the cleared channel for the Prime's will.

The dizzying plunge from the familiar came after, as separate awareness spiralled under and drowned in the well of an altered perception. This time, no feat of endurance prepared her. Even the most rigorous course of experience failed to shield Lirenda's stripped nerves from the glorious havoc . . .

. . . where matched love fabricated a consummate grace, traced to light by a masterbard's music, Dakar stood watch and guard from the side-lines. He had not been idle, since Arithon's word released him from the active circle. His by-standing work had tidied the chamber, then cleared the hazed residue of violent death. The fallen were settled outside the shut door. Talvish would turn the wrapped bodies over for mourning, should relatives come to collect them. No other intrusion could cross the locked threshold. Studded oak had been barred, then warded.

Now, Dakar held his post with an unblinking stare, apprehensive beyond imagining. The moment had long since passed to turn back. Man and Masterbard, Arithon had engaged every faculty to bind the perilous conjury wrought by Elaira.

The constructs that sheltered Sidir's aware essence were in place, and the irrevocable course for his healing, already in motion. Night and darkness outside all but ceased to exist. Under the force of raised power, the enclosing walls seemed to shimmer. Mage-sight could discern the latticed geometry, where the subtle protections caused staid stone to sing in sympathetic vibration. Inside, the shadowy forms of the furnishings loomed dense as ink on the outskirts. Against the cold quiet, the guard rings shone gold, as the difficult working unfolded. The killing sword had been drawn by degrees. An acrid taint of cautery lingered, coiled in the blued smoke that drifted through the configured blaze: which *was* the actualized power, made manifest through the Masterbard's gift, to lift dissonance back into harmony.

Dakar shivered with awe. What he witnessed exhausted all marvels.

Sidir's withdrawn spirit slept, secured in comfort, while the Koriani enchantress laboured to mend his riven body.

Though depleted, the spellbinder was not muddled or drunk. The charged weaving that stitched through the air, and his brief activity had begun to sober his faculties. If he dared not help, his trained awareness could follow the flow of energy, overlaid pattern on pattern. Such dreadfully intricate, dynamic complexity never forgave a mistake. The restoration of organs and internal tissue that Elaira ventured, barehanded, left him dry-mouthed with anxiety.

For the template that nurtured life was left flickering and drained, or else severed outright by damage. Unerring, her touch traced the structural tears, though the track that she followed was thin as a filament, frayed by patches of darkness. Time and again, her skill faltered, lost. The aching pause followed. She listened, poised in seeking silence: holding the ragged gap until the exacting response from the lyranthe could find and key the lost intonation. Where sound answered, revitalized light bloomed again. Slow as agony, each sequence refigured the conduits where nerve and sinew had weakened past holding the imprint that sourced Sidir's Name. One note played false would distort the faint matrix. One mis-stepped rhythm would snarl the harmonic balance off true.

One strand at a time, as the ephemeral web was played back to glittering life, Elaira's precision anchored the restoration, defying entropy through the ciphers taught by Koriathain: force drawn from the collective pool of intent, reined into existence by oath-tied sacrifice, and amplified through a crystal matrix.

Dakar held no illusions. The practice upset his digestion.

'A morbid transmission,' Asandir's patient teaching had explained, long years past on a moonlit hill-side. 'The sisterhood's binding oath forges the transfer of willed choice through constriction. This form of consent always freezes the moment. It anchors, and stops natural expression through movement. Not like a blood-tie, which threads through the essence of Name and draws renewed flow from true being. The promise that affirms the initiate sister stakes life. A fixed structure can never be made to flex. It cannot breathe to admit the spark of unbounded consciousness. Both forms may be reversed, or revoked, if correct steps are observed to unshackle them. But the rigid ones always leave scarring damage, sometimes grave enough to impair survival . . .'

A split hair, Dakar had dismissed at the time, too scattered by his hectic thinking. Now, sweating in the sealed room, he observed the same concept, enacted. As Elaira stapled the rips in shorn tissue, he *saw* the black ribbon of dissonant power, sucked through the placed frame of the cipher: a draining tide, that pulled essence from other life and stamped a hard template for change.

The drawing surge scoured his back-lashed nerves, a *wrongness* that rekindled his nausea. Dakar repressed his instinct to flinch. The risk ran too steep, that a sanctioned crown prince might fall under sway of an oath of debt to the order. Posted as Arithon's trusted defender, the Mad Prophet dared not look away.

And there, his stunned eyes watched the miracle happen, as the bard's line of melody captured the sinister threading. Arithon's counter-measure lilted a phrase, evoking a fair, sweetened resonance. Music lifted into a soaring appeal *that commanded an answering cry of renewal.* Elaira's enchained cipher throbbed, then burned, annealed by white fire into transformation. Dakar watched, spellbound, as the Masterbard's art refigured the oppressive enchantment: captured

the framework, unerring, and rescribed his beloved's intent to serve wholeness. Intrepid, his bright harmony sustained until the stricture blazed clean,
transmuted to joy through free partnership.

Sidir's hurt flesh would heal. Not through the chained power of Koriani
design, but by intimate love, gifted by an inspired spirit, that dared the unknown
to match limitless heart with brave effort.

Time remained the enemy. Shock had to be settled, and blood loss restored,
before the cauterized lung could be reforged in synchronicity with Sidir's being.
The enchantress's delicate concentration must not slip. Nor might the bard's
fingering fail to match the brilliance of her human focus. The blaze of contained
forces swept the shut room, raised sound ringing octave upon octave, until
stone and wood trembled to the waves of unseen harmonics. Exhaustion could
destroy in one moment all of the night's hard-fought progress. Elaira toiled
onward, cranked taut under strain.

She recognized the looming abyss, before Sidir's traumatized flesh could be
stabilized. His vitality ebbed still. The trickling loss might be too great to stem
before the tide turned and the body began to recover. This wounding was
mortal, far more extensive than the mangled forearm, restored for the stricken
young fisherman in Merior.

Dakar found himself weeping. The striving that staved off total failure wrung
him dizzy from holding his breath.

The moment was cruel for the hostile move engendered by Selidie Prime.
Mage-sight detected the taint, a soundless shadow of outside invasion slipped
through the immaculate conjury. Elaira noticed the shift straightaway. A shudder
swept through her. She dared not glance up, or seek the bard's notice, even in
speechless appeal. The disruption inflicted by oath-bound priority could not
be broached: not without risking the grace in the harmony that balanced the
power between them.

But as witness and guardian, Dakar dared not abide. His obligation to
Fellowship interests compelled him, despite risk to Sidir. 'Your Grace, you have
an observer!'

But whether as mage, or master musician, Arithon s'Ffalenn needed no
warning. He chose not to cut off the contact, or abandon the liegeman thrown
deeper in jeopardy. With dreadful delicacy, he rose to the challenge and altered
his playing to compensate. He added another line, at a whisper, to the fine
harmony laid down for healing: a descant theme of close caring, that nipped
and darted in playful counterpoint.

Dakar listened, amazed. The primary composition had not been disturbed.
Still, the progression was wholly Sidir's. Only now, the bard built on a love
for three daughters, brought up to an independent maturity. Extreme sensitivity adjusted a whole chord: captured the rare, open-handed admiration for
the woman who had preferred their raising at Fallowmere, in their father's
absence. Interleaved, as well, was the settled male strength that now cherished

Feithan, and longed for the peace of a traditional marriage. The Masterbard deftly embellished those subtleties above the steadfast foundation.

Only now, the song made as anchor to salvage a friend also plucked at the heartstrings of the furtive listener . . .

. . . the effect on Lirenda was lightning, on thunderbolt. *Everything* her starved spirit had never known – the matchless love of Arithon's partnership, interlaced with Elaira's unbounded regard; the protective tenderness and quiet pride that inflected Sidir's sterling character; the matchless poignancy, sprung from sharp loss, in his constancy through Feithan's mourning – all the human caring and trust that Lirenda had shoved aside in her grasping pursuit of power now flooded her exposed awareness. She plunged headlong: into a range of exalted experience that her proscribed existence could never own.

Already stripped, she had no escape. Lirenda became as the mote seared by fire while the might of the Skyron crystal noosed her subjective awareness.

The dart struck, where no reason might shield the emotional impact. The longing that savaged her broke strength and sanity: sparked the unmerciful heat that remained, unreleased, from her prior linkage with the scapegrace novice.

Lirenda gasped, riven. The iron bond of her Prime Matriarch's subjugation could not stay her response as she shattered . . .

. . . while another, maintaining strict watch at Alestron, observed the dynamic unfoldment: Dakar also witnessed, as Lirenda's reserve exploded beyond containment. For one hanging instant, the shocked pattern blazed as a beacon, torched into wild conflagration. Elaira shuddered, rocked by the wave, while *again*, the bard stretched in improvised fury to compensate. For one, shining moment, the healing was *there*, etched in omnipresent, cold fire: the ciphers to channel Sidir's recovery *also* offered the counterpoint pattern to unleash Lirenda's rebirth from love's starvation.

Yet Prime Selidie lurked, poised as the stilled spider. Her meddling reach was made to extend through the weave wrought for Sidir's recovery. As Lirenda's poise snapped, the Matriarch imposed her overarching directive and engaged the master sigil that commanded all oathsworn initiates, with the power of death over life.

'Avert!' shouted Selidie.

The linked tie to the music's entrainment tore away, leaving Lirenda scorched to a cinder. Her unleashed longing found no safe renewal, but fell back, burned to ashes and withering envy.

Now bare-handed amid the core of the storm, the Prime Matriarch held the emotional leash to Elaira. The move became Selidie's, to break the connection to Arithon's heart. Rip through the seamless current of union, that the ciphers suborned from Koriani influence could no longer regenerate through a masterbard's harmonic infusion. Selidie would snap love's cord. Claim her *due* oath of debt over Rathain's foremost Companion; or else take Sidir's life, and drive his confirmed prince to stand in challenge against her.

Dakar foresaw no victory. 'On your crown oath, Teir's'Ffalenn!' he cried, weeping.

The warning preceded the crude intervention as he braced to invoke the permissions held in his hands. The act ran beyond desecration. The astounding, grand pattern raised up in clear light held too aching a beauty; a brazen feat of sheer innovation that had seemed too magnificent to fail. Yet before the shining coils became poisoned by Selidie's influence, Dakar was obliged to step into the breach. As a Fellowship spellbinder, he must impose Arithon's tie to royal lineage, then back that crown oath and shield Sidir's threatened integrity.

The bard's sensitivity captured the pause before the irrevocable shift. Choice had been forfeit. Law-bound, the crown's watch-dog must serve. The cry that pealed from Arithon's throat held a note of pure despair. Music accompanied. His stark pain, clothed over in melodic sound, wrung protest from the thrumming strings under his hands. The burst shattered air; awoke fire; and bounded through the staid stone of the tower that housed such insufferable dichotomy: *that love for a friend, and a kingdom, and a heart's consort should not be string-tied in duty, but unfettered, and joyful, and free!*

And steel answered. The Paravian sword clasped in Sidir's limp hand blazed incandescent and sang. The wild chord that once Named the winter stars razed into the channel suborned from Elaira's intent. Selidie was forced to match, then counter the risen torrent that refired the contested ciphers.

In her desperation, she reached too far: pulled on the resource lying nearest at hand, that empowered her to drain life from her serving initiates. As her twisting demand gouged through Lirenda and Elaira to fuel her battle for conquest, the sword screamed.

The very air lit, scalded to searing brilliance. The tonal dissonance of beauty and pain, of bright harmony and disruptive violation twined together and hammered vibration through the stone tower. The uncanny shriek ran into the earth. It shuddered the citadel's bed-rock. Far under the threshold of human hearing, it woke the bell-tones of an answering chord, this one shaped by chisel and hammer, through the artistry of centaur masons. Too deep to detect, but apparent to mage-sense, Alithiel's wards summoned a subliminal tremor from Alestron's ancient foundations. Walls raised to protect drummed back their subsonic, bass tone in defence.

Dakar shouted, astonished. All reason had fled. He could not react, could not think, but only rejoice, undone by wonder as the mystical wardings sung into Alithiel's black steel first meshed, then married with the peerless enchantment once wrought to safeguard the life sheltered inside the fortress . . .

. . . Prime Selidie's purchase sheared off at one stroke. While the faceted cut of the Skyron aquamarine failed to chime in concert, its clipped resonance too short to encompass the full range of vibration, her linked senses exploded. Shocked to her core, the Koriani Matriarch was flung backwards, slammed short by the carvings upon her state chair.

Her breathless scream was an animal's.

The icy expanse of the pavilion surrounded her. Not the ringing voice, called from living stone. Never, the shimmering cascade of tone and light that had bespoken the mysteries at the dawn of creation. An old woman, lodged in a young woman's flesh, she was left abandoned in darkness. Inside and out, she felt bereft, desolate as Lirenda's choked sobs, wailing unabated beside her. The moment gave *nothing*. No victory and no triumph. Only the emptiness of disappointment, as the fleeting echo of exaltation faded to deadening blindness.

Recovery

Light died, and sound lapsed to unearthly calm; then, 'You're right, the healing ciphers have shattered. He ought to be dead,' Dakar's shaken voice declared over him; and Sidir stirred awake, eyes opened to lamplight, and a draught that chilled his bloodied skin: of the terrible puncture wound on his chest, no sign remained, and no hitch of agony impaired his breathing . . .

Returned home from Dame Dawr's to hear of his wife's night departure with a desperate message for Arithon s'Ffalenn, Mearn bolts across town in clothing unsuited for riding, and accosts Kyrialt s'Taleyn at the threshold of the state guest-chamber; and news breaks at at first hand, that his duke has defied charter law and snatched a sworn guest as a hostage with intent to suborn a crown prince. . .

In the chill dark, with the Skyron crystal veiled under silk, Selidie Prime broods over her vicious set-back; enraged that the Paravian wards on the citadel could disrupt her planned capture, she stirs, calls the lane watch, and digs for the means to spur Alestron's demise and spring her quarry from his secure love-nest. . .

Late Autumn 5671

IX. Schism

A mid the chill silence of aftermath, the dark and the night seemed oppressive. The frugal fire once made to warm Jeynsa had burned down to smoking ash. Only Elaira's lamp burned within the closed chamber that had narrowly missed becoming the site of a Companion's death-watch. Instead, urgent life now required attendance, with the Teiren s'Valerient's abduction a looming threat wrapped in thorny diplomacy. Dakar filched a cloak from the wardrobe to replace the bloody rags lately cut off Sidir. Upright, left trembling and weak at the knees, the clansman perched on the edge of the bed. The shock of his traumatic healing could not settle without quiet and rest.

His gifted recovery had come at high cost to the pair who had channelled grand conjury. The blanket that, earlier, had eased Jeynsa's distress, now swathed the enchantress, who had crumpled just after the surge of the Paravian wardings. Cradled in Arithon's arms, Elaira languished, unstrung by exhaustion.

Aware that the bard's heightened state also verged on collapse, Dakar faced the necessities. 'We can't stay here. You know this! Duke Bransian won't wait out your weakness, or Sidir's. He'll strike for leverage while we are divided.'

'I realize as much.' Arithon's voice wore the husk of his weariness. After three major workings, without proper sleep, his own demands clamoured for remedy. He was too thinly clad. The shirt and cloth breeches worn throughout the crisis left him cold to the bone as the strain overcame him. The hands that had commanded the lyranthe strings, unfaltering, were no longer faultlessly steady. Since Dakar's scathing regard would miss nothing, Arithon resettled Elaira's slack weight. 'My lady can't argue for bed rest, at any rate.' He sheltered her head against his shoulder, hooked his other arm under her knees, and mustered his compromised strength to arise.

'May Bransian's bones rot in the steaming muck dropped by Dharkaron's Horses!' Dakar railed. He recognized overdrawn faculties, too well: the wheeling faint spells, and patchy vision that whip-lashed through overtaxed senses. 'You shouldn't move, either.' Already ignored, he laced into Sidir, who was doggedly busy with fastening his breeches and no doubt determined to don belt and baldric as if no sapping after-shock troubled him. 'Leave the sword, man! All three of you need a bracing hot tea and unbroken sleep by a fireside!'

The Companion glanced up, his blue eyes still strange with the distance of uncanny experience. 'Kyrialt's unsupported,' he pointed out. 'Lady Glendien's with him. If Alestron's duke has dared to seize Jeynsa, why balk at threatening the wife of a liegeman to hobble our embassy further?' He declared, pale but firm, 'I would fight again before letting that happen.'

'You're not a dumb ox, to keep plodding in harness,' the Mad Prophet fumed, at wit's end. He was wrung out himself. Ready to nap in his boots. 'Nobody else needs a battle tonight. Help me bash the sense of Ath's reason into your crown prince, instead.'

Since his tirade was going to be disregarded, the spellbinder lumbered off his broad backside. He snatched up the wiped sword that had not found a scabbard, then hastened to collect the sheathed steel of Alithiel, and bundle the fleece cover over the lyranthe. His awkward burdens were scarcely secured, when the Prince of Rathain surged erect, bearing Elaira. Dakar freed his right hand. Barely in time, he caught Arithon's collar, and steadied his burdened frame upright. 'Larking goose! The breeze off the wing of a sparrow could fell you. Since you won't let me carry your precious enchantress, stay here. I'll send word on to Kyrialt.'

But a glance had exposed Elaira's waxen pallor. More than weariness sucked her unconscious. One heart-beat more, and the Mad Prophet's shocked, aware touch recorded the flesh, which burned like a furnace beneath Arithon's soaked shirt. The Teir's'Ffalenn was on his feet, though just barely, as the fevers of back-lash raged over him.

'Fiends plague, we're beset!' The spellbinder planted himself to redress slip-shod planning. 'Your enchantress needs a stringent restorative. Much as you hate it, your Grace, you'd be wise to allow me to help.'

Arithon back-stepped. 'Not this time.'

Dakar set his jaw. 'You're played-out!' Rather than suffer the searing explosion, he shouted. 'Do I need a mallet to dunt your thick skulls? *None of you are going anywhere!*'

That moment, someone's mercuric step raced up the outside stairwell. The unknown arrival met Talvish's crisp challenge, followed up by a brisk dialogue.

Then a rap demanded an entry, and Mearn's voice, pitched to spur action, 'I've packed up Fianzia! She's sent to Dame Dawr, whose borrowed carriage is waiting outside. I implore that his Grace should accept my suggestion and take sanctuary with my grandame. Shelter under her roof, until I can deal with my brother concerning this churlish assault.' As always, Mearn dispatched obstacles at dizzying speed. 'Don't fret for your retinue. Kyrialt and Glendien can be fetched from the guest-tower suite on the way.'

'And Daelion Fatemaster sang for the hag!' Dakar breathed, eyes rolled in relief. 'Our stinking luck's changed.' Straps and sword harness a dangling threat to ladder the knit in his stockings, he clomped to the chamber's sealed doorway and released his layers of arcane wardings.

Through the crackle as blue bands of energy unbound, he heard Talvish speaking, emphatic. The phrase, *'fatal wounding,'* pocked a shocking gap; then in rising anguish, *'suffered more than our citadel guard's wasted casualties!'*

Mearn's exclamation pierced through the strapped planking. 'All the more, I insist! The royal party must seek diplomatic asylum within Dawr's household.'

Yet even as Dakar raised the bar and fumbled to unfasten the latch, Arithon gave crisp contradiction.

'My people will not turn tail, or compromise the dowager's standing!' When the panel swung open, Rathain's prince added, with delicacy, 'Talvish?'

'Will accompany me,' Mearn insisted, astute. 'I will have his captain's name cleared! Bransian's actions have been inexcusable.' Surged over the threshold, impatient, he paused.

Opal studs glittered to his breathless haste. He had run himself ragged. Nerves, or frenetic distress wracked his bearing as his glance surveyed the left mess of scarlet-stained cloth and smeared flooring. At tactful speed, he measured Sidir, dazed but upright on the bed. Then past Dakar's bulk, the Prince of Rathain, placed with his shoulder set to the wall, and Elaira's form bundled in his arms. 'Your Grace, there's no argument. You will need my backing.'

Which galvanized Talvish, who had hung behind, still on wary guard by the landing. 'Get the living to move,' he said as he reached the doorway. 'I'll handle the sorrow of bringing the liegeman's body.' Resigned to that misery, he gasped, startled white, as though he beheld a corpse walking. *'Sidir!* Ath, what I saw –'

'Alive!' Arithon snapped across his stark shock. 'We raised conjury in time to heal him. To your credit, my friend. Your prompt action made all the difference.'

To Mearn, his Grace added, 'We're stunned as beached fish in the wake of a miracle. Yes, assistance is welcomed. I agree that Dame Dawr's charitable offer of transport is necessary. For tonight's rank embarrassment, by all means, claim your rightful place to act first. Face your brother before I make charges. If you promise to speak for Talvish's good name, my party will retire. We'll remain in our appointed suite in the guest tower, provided that Jeynsa's not harmed or abused. Within limits, you'll have my free rein to clear matters within your close family.'

'That's fair.' Mearn strode on towards the bed. Without care for the blood that might mar his finery, he extended his arm to Sidir. 'Can you stand and walk? For our dead, s'Brydion won't ask compensation if your injury can be forgiven.'

The wronged clansman stared back, too prideful to lean. While Dakar hefted the lyranthe and sword, and scuttled headlong from the chamber, Sidir mustered his dignity and arose to full height. His grave disposition was flint, delivered from wavering balance. 'Until Jeynsa is freed, by crown obligation, I must let my grievance rest in my liege's hands.'

Mearn nodded, white. 'Of course.' Ball-room silk and mussed velvet made his terrier's stance laughable, except for the fierce courage, which placed no blame, but strove only to master the horrific gaffe his brother's rash deed thrust upon him. Mearn held his hand open, determined enough to spit into the teeth of Dharkaron Avenger.

Sidir unbent then. He accepted support, a statement as much made for friendship and faith as to manage the steep, spiral staircase.

More than the staunch clansman's weight became shouldered by the searing flame of Mearn's outrage: through shaming embarrassment, the younger s'Brydion asked, 'How long can you give me, your Grace?'

Rathain's prince did not answer until Talvish's hale strength had relieved his protective grip on Elaira. Only then, green eyes burning, he relented, and said, 'Noon. Inform your duke to be ready for audience. That's as far as I'm willing to compromise.'

Where the carriages of most well-set ladies were scented with rose leaves, patchouli or lavender, Dame Dawr eschewed flowery perfume. Her conveyance smelled of wax polish and leather, and the cinnamon sticks her manic coachman chewed, since the grandame forbade his pipe while on duty. The skinny man in dapper livery looked harmless. Atop the box, with the lines threaded in gloved fists, he drove like Dharkaron's vengeance.

'He once moved supply for Duke Bransian's army,' Arithon warned at the outset.

His fellow passengers scarcely had time to brace, before the closed vehicle jolted and rolled, with Elaira's slack form once again sheltered in her prince's possessive embrace. The four-in-hand bays surged ahead at a gallop, careening through twisting lanes and steep grades, with Dakar rendered green by the sway.

'Learned his teams as a child, running cargo from the Sea Gate,' Arithon filled in, not quite smiling. 'He knows every inch of the citadel, blindfolded, which is good for us, since he'll probably mow down anything shoved in his path.'

'Carries a mace, I noticed that much,' the forest-bred clansman observed, not so dazed, though the rough ride rattled bones and teeth.

'All of Dawr's servants are hardened war veterans.' Arithon closed his eyes. 'Ease your mind. We're in the best hands.'

Crushed against Sidir's shoulder as the coach thundered over the cobbles and rocked through the next hairpin bend, Dakar continued to glare at the prince, who snatched rest in the opposite seat. Mearn and Talvish had left them, presumably on their promised mission to confront the duke. Removed from outside eyes, and at last granted enough noise to forestall the long ears of Dawr's servants, the fraught spellbinder resumed his remonstrance.

'You're stark mad to believe you'll be upright and fit by tomorrow! Don't fool with me, Arithon! Elaira's in shock. Your state's little better. If you expect to have all of your wits for a brangle with s'Brydion authority, think again.'

'I am not going to delegate you as my emissary,' Arithon said without cracking his eyelids. Propped by the carriage's sumptuous upholstery, with his lyranthe and sheathed sword beside him, he ruthlessly quashed the objection. 'Dakar! You won't minister to Elaira. Or me. The task I am giving you won't permit compromise. Guard our door. Set up ward-watch, once we arrive. I need you for that! Kyrialt's risking his life on my orders with naught to defend but steel weaponry.'

Dakar fumed, stout arms folded. While the carriage barrelled onward, he had to concede that priority. Dawr's concern was self-evident. Her coachman held orders not to spare horses in his break-neck dash to deliver them. A checkpoint flashed past, to a shout from the driver. A snapped whip urged fresh speed from the team. If any sentries came forward to challenge, the dowager's cartouche stood them off. Her frail health might demand a physician. If not that, her keen temper was legend: nothing short of the duke's direct orders would bring any rank-and-file man to risk delaying her vehicle. The break-neck ride at least would be brief. The guest tower lay in the next quarter.

Haste counted, if Bransian's underhand ploy should move on their disarray. The instant the carriage rolled to a stop, Arithon flung open the door. His s'Taleyn liegeman was already briefed: Mearn's foresighted gift, that Kyrialt stood at the bridge-head, primed to receive them. The span over the crevice was kept unlit. From behind, the dark doorway threw no silhouette to expose anyone's form as a target.

'Fionn Areth's already inside,' he reported. 'The guard brought him in, hours past, by routine. They'd found him piss drunk and passed out in a heap, during clean-up after a bar brawl.' As he talked, Kyrialt peered into the coach, measuring with his scout's faculties. 'Your Grace? This is back-lash fever, beginning?' No answer was needed. He read all the grim signs. His touch stayed respectful as he reached in and gathered Elaira's limp weight out of Arithon's arms.

His prince let him take her, a shocking concern.

'Inside with her. Quickly. I'll tell Glendien which simples I need on the way to our chamber.' Now wretchedly shivering, Arithon snatched his Paravian sword and lyranthe from the coach seat as he stepped out. 'Bed down in the still-room, it's warmer,' he told Sidir, who seemed steadier.

The tall Companion unfolded his cloaked frame from the carriage, renewed humour alight in his eyes. 'I expect that you want your privacy, liege?'

'Damn well he won't have it!' the Mad Prophet rebutted, and elbowed his way to the forefront. Like a sack of loose stone lofted out of a catapult, he shot after the crown prince's heels.

So brief a snatched rest should not have permitted the speed which saw Arithon over the plank-bridge, to the tower's entry. As Dakar pounded after, prince and Shandian liegeman ducked inside, rounding the cot where Fionn Areth sprawled, loudly snoring amid crumpled blankets. Now forced to give chase at a lumbering sprint, Dakar puffed on, livid, and wheezed his objections while climbing the stair. 'Your Grace! You ought not . . . to be . . . alone . . . in recovery. What if . . . you fall asleep? Or succumb . . . to the fever . . . you've earned . . . from your state . . . of over-extension?' The first landing flashed past. 'Damn all to Dharkaron! *Arithon!* Will you hear *sense*?'

Dakar caught up by the lit door to the still-room, where Arithon languished, one arm braced to the jamb. Glendien was receiving his rapid instructions, while Kyrialt bore Elaira ahead to the empty bedchamber above.

Dakar mopped his soaked face. Swore through hitched breaths in brothel vernacular, as he moved to block Arithon's path.

'I won't have you as nurse-maid,' Rathain's crown prince attacked. 'In fact, I'll have no one's intrusion at all.'

'Your permissions,' Dakar threatened, pink fingers clutched to the door-frame in hopes of a bulwark.

He was shoved aside.

'Revoked!' Arithon reeled past, dodging through the burdened work trestles with their crocks of salts and herbs, then the looming gleam of the still, the covered baskets, and glass mortar and pestle. He needed both hands to keep his wracked balance.

'Blood oaths are not malleable,' Dakar snarled back. 'The one sworn at Athir still binds you!'

'Then guard the door!' Arithon commanded, regardless. 'We shall do well enough. *You're not my keeper!* And more than one method can heal the surge of overload that afflicts us.'

Dakar flushed beet red. 'You don't *dare*!' Yet stunned eyesight confirmed the outrageous suspicion by noting which remedies Glendien bundled. 'Arithon! You randy fool!'

His shout earned the clanswoman's laughter. 'And you're not the black pot berating the kettle?' she gibed in her warm, southcoast accent.

Dakar ignored her. Lashed white by fresh panic, he launched his stout frame through the clutter of the herbalist's paraphernalia. Jostled Glendien sideways, as his frantic rush broached the darkened spiral of the upper stairwell.

'Did you learn nothing by your past failure in Halwythwood?' he cried in desperate appeal. 'Arithon, please! You have everything to lose, if you pursue this with your faculties compromised!'

Still, nobody listened.

Panting fit to drop, the Mad Prophet reached the threshold above, just as Kyrialt straightened from laying Elaira down on the feather-bed by the casement. The sheets were remade, surely Glendien's work, done with forethought since Fianzia's departure.

One lamp burned low. By that febrile light, Arithon shed his sword, then unwrapped his lyranthe. His chipped-quartz expression left no further doubt: he was set upon claiming his place at his enchantress's side straightaway.

'I can't let you try this.' Dakar bulled forward, only to wince as a crippling grip latched his forearm.

'You will not stay to watch! No matter the cause.' Arithon's clamped fingers steered the spellbinder backwards, then spun him around and thrust his resistant bulk back outside. 'This hour is mine!'

Beyond all persuasion, the Prince of Rathain dismissed Kyrialt. Then he kicked the door shut upon Dakar's appalled protests and sealed the latch with a binding that showered white sparks.

'Don't!' Dakar yelped, as the rebuffed liegeman surged forward. 'You'll just blister your hands, and for nothing. You're not going in, now. And neither am I. Not again. No matter which Fellowship Sorcerer shows up brandishing self-righteous thunderbolts.'

'How else will Glendien deliver the simples?' Kyrialt grumbled with blunt practicality.

'She won't. Not tonight.' Dakar sighed. 'Ath's mercy go with them. They'll bide on their own.' He let his knees give, then. Slumped into a crouch at the stair-head, he jammed his exasperated fingers through his frizzled hair. 'Have your wife leave the kettle and packets outside. His Grace will have to fetch for himself if he's got the wits left to realize he still needs them.'

The wind had dropped to a whisper, then stilled, the brisk scent left by the rain-storm overlaid by a stinging, fresh frost. Talvish huddled into the oiled-wool cloak, returned from his loan to Fianzia. Off duty, but still armed since the side trip to Dame Dawr's that had ended inside a wrecked tavern, he paused on the exposed trail leading upward to the outcrop that crowned the inner citadel. There, Watch Keep's squat crenels cut a stark outline against the starred sky. Shadowed by his helm, his jade eyes surveyed Mearn, who had paused on the grass where the open stair carved into the steep terrain.

'Are you sure, Captain?' the youngest brother s'Brydion asked. 'Be certain, now. Or turn back.' The odd opal stud flared errant fire, as he shivered in his jewelled doublet. The rapier at his waist was no weapon for war-time; he had always hated the blood sport of the hunt. Even so, his taut frame had the set of a man who was pressed beyond desperate, and dangerous.

Nor was his plea spurious.

Talvish's mood also eschewed humour. 'Go up there, you're going to need backing, my friend.'

Mearn's slim shoulders recoiled. The sentries on duty below had not paused to question their passage: none of the watch sergeants realized, yet, that aught was amiss in the citadel. The check-point stayed relaxed, and the routine of the night guard, flat quiet, throughout their wary approach. Yet *nothing* was ordinary.

Somewhere, the man who had skewered Sidir in a fight on Duke Bransian's orders still believed that Jeynsa's abduction could be covered in secret.

'The word of a clan girl, still in her minority, against three dead soldiers, and one of those a respected veteran in the duke's right-hand pocket? The story won't have to stretch much to seem plausible.' Mearn had seen his last illusions stripped off. Shocked reaction now rocked his foundation.

Talvish refused to withdraw his concern. 'Mearn, you need my witness, as well as my sword. I won't risk the chance, that a covert attack for extortion could be white-washed with impunity.'

The indecent plot had been carried too far. Everything pointed towards Bransian's intention to frame Jeynsa's reaction as impolitic youth, then pin a murderous breach of guest relations upon Rathain's crown delegation.

'Discredit Arithon's standing in public, and our law could demand restitution as forfeit!' Mearn anguished, 'We won't have till noon. My brother's planned his strategy to entrap. He'll push through the assize in the morning. We have too much fear and resentment, run rampant. High feelings will raise hysterical sentiment against every shred of hard evidence.' Mearn grimaced in sickened disgust. 'We are better than this. Or we were, once, as a founding family.'

Yet that had been before the unrest of four kingdoms had come to roost on the s'Brydion ancestral seat. The night view from the cornice spread out unremitting: the dense sprawl of the enemy campfires on the mainland a closed ring that relentlessly grew, as inbound ships daily unloaded fresh levies brought in from Shand.

'Like plaguing locusts,' Talvish remarked, bitter with the wound left by Vhandon's absence. 'Such effortful wreckage, and for nothing more than a liar who preaches a threat from diverging ideas.'

'How that poison has twisted our standards, as well.' The unspoken question remained: just how far had Bransian's insanity led them? Who *else* beyond Liesse, and quite likely Sindelle, had spun tonight's threads of deceit? Mearn measured the turn of the stars overhead. 'Let's move, then. My feet are freezing, and my bollock sack's sucked up so tight, I'm likely to squeak in falsetto.'

The visceral hurt festered, that the truth must be walked without quarter. Talvish's tact understood that brute fact, though a brother might agonize over the need to expose the infamy of his family. 'More than my sword at your back,' he said gently. Knowing his act was now informed treason against Alestron's titled duke, the blond captain climbed the stair and overreached his authority. His voice delivered the password to the watch, with intent to suborn the mirror man's relay.

The return challenge came, and found Mearn snapped back into feisty recovery. 'Priority orders!' he rapped, and without saying whose, shoved into the tower the instant the portal was unbolted. 'Upstairs! No delay.' He barged past the sergeant posted inside. 'Send signal in code and recall Sevrand from the harbour mouth garrison. I'll receive him here. If the boatman takes his time with the skiff, or the winch crew's asleep at the cliff-head, I *will* string them up in the galley-men's bar and pink their stripped navels as targets.'

Uneasy quiet reigned over the guest suite that housed the Crown Prince of Rathain. Dakar kept red-eyed watch. Having set the requested stiff ring of wards, he was left to chew over his frothing anxiety. His scrying already ascertained that Jeynsa in fact was detained without bodily harm. Fionn Areth slept off his drunken stupor, oblivious, while Kyrialt gave his weapons a scouring polish and settled to nap beside Glendien. Sidir slept also, his muscled frame sprawled on the carpeted floor of the still-room. He had dressed in fresh leathers. Except for a draught of restorative tea, he rejected the comfort of coddling. Stoic through crises, he snatched a scout's rest, with his cleaned steel laid alongside, and his limbs covered by his weather-stained mantle.

No one dared assay the stairway, above. The shut door yielded none of its secrets.

Which brooding concern, Arithon s'Ffalenn had no intent to dispel. He had been forced on the alert for too long, immersed in strict demand to the volatile currents of wielding high conjury. Rest was now imperative, and more: he needed his faculties, and Elaira's, restored at a speed that left no room for safety.

The duke's berserk temperament was too deadly dangerous. His hackled fury would not brook defeat: the trapped pawn in his hands remained in harm's way, with no sureties placed on the outcome. None of Rathain's feal party were secure until Bransian could be set in his place.

'Bright powers attend us,' Arithon murmured, crying inward for patience and strength. He must snatch this moment of unbroken peace, push what resource he had to renew his frayed focus, and reground the alignment of overstressed senses.

Jeynsa's hot predicament *must* wait for morning. Else the outrage sparked by tonight's wrongful injuries would shatter his grip on constraint. The charge placed before him claimed absolute precedence: Elaira's recovery lay under his care. Arithon steadied his jangled nerves. More than love, more than his next breath, he needed her settled and well. To which end, the direct path was both the most pleasurable, and the most fraught with pitfalls.

The bed and the room were still generously warm, the fire built up for Fianzia reduced to glimmering coals. Rather than pile on a new log, Arithon pinched out the candle-lamp. Soft dark left the ambient glow from the hearth to define the chamber's spare furnishings. He worked, hoarding strength, each calm preparation accomplished in economical stages.

Two decoctions of simples soon steamed in glazed mugs. The unwrapped lyranthe awaited nearby, silver strings shining ruby. Alithiel was unsheathed also. Arithon laid the black blade on the mattress, where he then reclined, tucked into the coverlets beside his beloved. Flesh to stripped flesh, he cradled Elaira, while his trembling fingers smoothed her unbraided hair.

He was foolishly dizzy. Not just from the risen flashes of heat that raked him over in back-lash. The close scent of her turned all his senses: lavender mingled with traces of birch smoke, from the brazier that had heated her reme-dies. He caressed her skin, smooth as moon-rinsed marble. Stroked her neck, where the pulse raced too rapidly.

This time, in truth, the hour was his. As the partnership forged in the cottage at Merior had been foredoomed from the outset, this night was not going to strand them with yet another tormented parting. Sidir's unorthodox healing had opened the way. Grace and caring now must guard this safe passage.

Mage and musician, Arithon began to trace Elaira's inert form with his touch. He did not massage, but admired: a lingering, sweet courtship pitched first to realign her depleted vitality. As he moved, he raised mage-sight, and laced his own rhythm through hers. Linked his own breathing and heart-beat, which already rebounded from the restoratives he had dosed for himself. He soothed, coaxed, and quieted. As time passed, his stroking hands turned to stimulate, then to tease the response of awakened arousal. Her life signs his music, his desire her kindling flame, he opened the flux points and drew on the depths of initiate knowledge to weave. Female to his male, he led her depleted exhaus-tion into a yearning thirst to seek ecstasy.

As he had in the cottage in Merior, his spirit called hers back to blazing awareness, as no other living force could.

When, at due length, her eyes opened to meet him, the need in them burned him, unstoppable.

'You realize what I'm asking,' he opened, contrite. 'A flawed gift, under need to rebuild balance soonest, while pushed in the quicksands of crisis. I could wish –'

Her touch brushed his lips. One finger, caressing, damped his torrent of apology. She gave back the soaring grace of her smile. 'By my choice, as well. No matter whether the stones in the headland should shake down the stars and the moon.'

'This is not Rathain,' he reassured her. 'Nowhere near the volatile interface that quickens the flow within the free wilds.' That truth she would see: no ripple of silver-hazed power aligned with the flux lines, strung active between them. Only the coals in the fire-place burnished the tenderness, mirrored as his own, on her features. 'My crown prince's attunement will not rouse the land in Melhalla, or stun any sleepers from rest.'

'Unless they're unrighteously listening.' Her sly humour up-ended his heart, as she matched joy with visceral bravery. 'Only one of your teas will be necessary.'

The cup with the simple to prevent conception met her parted lips, held in his steadied hand. After she swallowed the bitter-sweet dregs, he kissed her until heightened pleasure destroyed thought, ravished breath, and dazzled the senses.

'I trust you,' she murmured through urgency. 'Completely. Without end, and before the beginning.'

Wordless, he laced her trembling fingers through the black steel of Alithiel's grip. Then, gently relentless, he closed his taut grasp. Caged her hand with his own, as his aching flesh quivered with unbearable suspension against her.

'You are unsurpassed.' Arithon cradled her one instant more. Then he laid his cheek against hers. Drowned in the exotic scent of her hair, he savoured the irrevocable, last moment, then launched them both over the brink. The poised spiral unleashed, while move for move, she cried out with exquisite welcome and matched him.

The fair moment enraptured them with light and song, and was not left unrequited. Starved desire achieved union, as a sword's steel, unsheathed, exploded to shimmering light. Alithiel blazed and belled into bright harmony, with the Paravian wards in the citadel also arisen in resonant defence. The embedded Koriani sigil to enforce fertility was cut off, inert, its insidious spring trap held latent. For this rarefied interval, within secured walls, the dark force of Selidie's power could not strike through or entangle her targeted victims.

More than Dakar sensed the subliminal, marrow-deep tone, as the wardings imbued in Paravian stonework shuddered the rock of the headland. His outburst of swearing sprang in equal measure from horrified fury and shattered relief. Neither sentiment was shared by the Koriani Matriarch.

Prime Selidie recoiled from the venomous sting that curbed the reach of her oath-bonded mastery. She sat awake, still enthroned in her chair, within the night-dark pavilion. As the connection that channelled her live tie to Elaira scattered into burst static, she did not rail against set-back. Her rage stayed cold. Though her direct plot might be temporarily thwarted, her breathless laugh became prelude to a crow of triumph.

None were present to listen. Only the inconsequential boy page had been retained to attend her. Lirenda was packed off to bed with a posset, and the diligent circle of senior scryers dismissed, their task momentarily complete. Wrapped against the cold air, her porcelain face tintless, the Koriani Matriarch murmured over the crystal array left actively poised on her side-table. 'Our too-clever quarry has taken the bait! Arithon has engaged, and accepted my challenge.'

Time and folly would snare him. The insatiable fruit of his consummate love would fan tonight's blaze towards careless addiction.

Selidie avowed to hasten that mis-step. Every power and pawn within her grasp would be pressured to flush her royal prey. To that end, she must break the Paravian wardings that championed Arithon's foothold. The peerless defences in the citadel walls would have to be breached, or abandoned. Alestron's defeat would wrest back her opening to resume pursuit upon open ground.

Prime Selidie freed the stiffened claws that remained of her fire-scarred hands. Her fumbling touch engaged the first of two crystals left tuned for her use by the scryers. Her choice by-passed the one which reflected the anchorage behind Lugger's Islet where the Sunwheel ships waylaid by Vhandon's refugees were being refitted as war prizes by Parrien's sea-wolves. First, her crippled fingers stroked the crystal linked to Lysaer s'Ilessid, lying asleep in the Alliance war camp . . .

Something was wrong. Sulfin Evend awoke to the certainty. If he did not possess an initiate awareness, the grand oath he had sworn at Althain Tower enhanced his innate sensitivity. Whatever had nagged him to gooseflesh would not let him settle or sleep.

His quarters were quiet, as much as could be, in the pavilion that commanded a war camp that sprawled, tens of thousands of men strong. In the dark before dawn, the outside activity sounded nothing more than routine: wagons lumbered in from the fringes bearing supply, and cut fire-wood for the bread ovens. Chattering laundresses lugged their buckets to the river, and horse-boys led their roped strings of destriers from the picket lines to graze and drink. Bits jingled. Men swore. A smith's hammer clanged. Farther afield, the perimeter scouts could be heard, bugling their skirmishers in from a pre-dawn patrol.

Day upon day, fighting ironclad boredom, the fettlesome mass of trained troops trampled over the occupied turf that surrounded Alestron.

Sulfin Evend measured the background tone of complaint, well aware that he needed to shake up morale yet again.

The mud was still heavy from yesterday's storm. Men in miserable, damp clothing and rust-streaked mail poured too much silver into the hands of the trollops. The women sold comfort, till their thin-stretched services soured to carping disputes. Today would demand another harsh drill, with each brutal exercise set to unstring such rank-and-file idleness, mind and sinew. Sulfin Evend tossed off his blankets. Anxiety rode him too hard to wait for his equerry, or kindle the candle-lamp. Unlike the Divine Prince, he kept his partitioned quarters pitch dark. No call to emergency would catch him blundering and dazzled without his night-vision. Sulfin Evend snatched for the breeches hung from the nail on the tent-pole.

His fingers swiped air.

'Damn *all* to Sithaer for meddling nuisances!' he gasped in the pre-dawn chill. Lysaer's prim valet had ignored sense, again. Shouted threats never stopped his twitching fingers from coddling everything within reach.

Bare skin puckered, Sulfin Evend groped onwards by touch and flung open his foot-locker. Two clean shirts flew aside. Then a tied pair of stockings. These had been laundered and folded with a *ridiculous* cachet of mint. Now swearing fit to raise fire and storm, the Lord Commander thrashed deeper and hooked the spare breeches that should, by his lights, have been topmost.

Half-clad, trailing laces, he snagged his belt, retrieved a flung shirt, then clawed on the gambeson left at the foot of his bed. He caught up his byrnie. Prepared to shrug on the bunched mail – and damn all to the hair that pinched out of his tousled head in the process – when the dog-faithful valet barged in from behind.

'Go and scorch the fur off Dharkaron's black bollocks!' snarled Sulfin Evend, annoyed. 'You can hang the idea of a gentleman's shave. My stubble stays put, for the drill field.'

No sound, from the servant, beyond a caught breath.

Which raised the ugly, belated awareness: the man carried no basin and razor. He had not struck a light. Caught by the shine through the crack in the door flap, he was not groomed or composed, but trembling on bare feet in his night-shirt.

Hands clenched in the mail he had yet to put on, Sulfin Evend dropped inquiry and sprinted. The stuffy valet would curl up and die, before showing his naked legs to an officer: which breach of etiquette meant Lysaer s'Ilessid was threatened by trouble too dire to contemplate.

Sulfin Evend burst from his quarters. Beyond, the broad trestles loomed as they should, spread over with markers and tactical maps. The rowed chairs stood empty, beneath the staked hooks with their darkened horn lanterns. Reduced light burned, at night: a paned sconce with a flickering candle stub. The page boys who had neglected the wick snoozed in a sprawl beside the swagged dais. A third, younger child had dozed off while blacking the Divine Prince's boots. The grimed rag he had dropped puddled over his feet, as he stirred in bleary confusion.

'Fetch the Sunwheel guardsmen on watch at the entry!' Sulfin Evend thundered in passing. 'Move! Get them now!' Still packing the mail shirt, he vaulted a stool, kicked a felt hassock tumbling, then charged straight on over a chest and two tables. Counters scattered. A chart of the estuary flapped in his wake, blizzarding white paper galleys. A glass ink-well overset with a tinkle. While the puffing valet dodged his trail of debris, the Lord Commander crashed through the emblazoned curtains into the avatar's suite.

The taint warned him first: not quite a smell, but a lingering suggestion of shadow, half-seen. Always, when steered by his latent clan lineage, Sulfin Evend recognized the presence of Koriani conjury. Now the order's target was Lysaer, already driven awake by the shock of another invasive nightmare.

This one seeded terror. Sulfin Evend met those unseeing, blue eyes, enamel hard, and vicious with the madness of Desh-thiere's curse. All finesse was forfeit. He hurled the mail shirt.

The steel links sailed, ringing, unfurled like a net that scythed a whistling course through the air. The mass struck the avatar full in the face. Lysaer staggered backwards. The edge of his camp mattress tripped him. He crashed, flailing, into the coverlet.

Sulfin Evend's tigerish spring pounced on top. He fisted both hands in the miring steel links. Ruthless under panic, he pressed the weight down, while the fit body he straddled, then pinned, thrashed with manic strength underneath him.

The candle kept blazing nearby had a solid bronze stand, twined with dragons. Bucked off balance, Sulfin Evend snatched for the base. He swung the flanged edge like a bludgeon, hit Lysaer through the mail shirt, and dropped him on the quilts like felled meat. Now two crises faced him: the flung candle that spattered hot wax and fire in a rolling spray on the carpet; and the chance his crazed liege might arouse and fight back with a light strike.

The Lord Commander moved on the exigent threat first. Ripped the belt from his waist and noosed Lysaer's wrists. Then he snatched the filled pitcher from the washstand. Sulfin Evend threw the vessel and its sloshing contents, still athwart the mattress, with one knee gouged into the chest of the Blessed Prince. The burgeoning flames became doused in a splash of smashed porcelain and water.

The valet arrived, panting. 'Merciful Light!' He snapped the flap shut, too late for decorum. The staring page boy outside was already riveted. Sulfin Evend dared not respond, or take time to amend the disastrous appearances. He tugged away the dead weight of the mail and exposed Lysaer's slackened face. Then swore aloud for the blood, vividly welling through the golden hair nested in the rumpled bed-clothes.

'Let me, please, my lord.' The valet clutched a towel, prepared to minister to the fallen. His gaunt form leaned in and fussed with the sheets, while Sulfin Evend dropped the offensive armour and inspected the damage at speed.

Lysaer suffered a split scalp, but no worse. The moment the copious bleeding was stemmed, the wound could be treated by stitching.

'Send for crushed ice and tincture of iodine,' the Lord Commander snapped, gruff. Relief became fury. 'Ath above! Did nobody hear my straight warning? Koriathain will dare to waylay any pawn for use on their infernal chessboard! Your master's nightmares weren't caused by the Spinner of Darkness, but witchcraft, fashioned for suborning influence. Don't be complacent. This fit was provoked. Selidie Prime surely wants to manipulate an attack on the s'Brydion citadel.'

More bodies entered: fighting men, by their heavy-set tramp. Were they not the hoped-for, trustworthy honour guard, the damage spread beyond remedy.

'I want a fresh light!' snapped Sulfin Evend. 'Then dispatch the faster of those two pages to roust out the camp physician.'

No one moved for a lamp. Instead, the crowding footfalls advanced into a cordoning presence behind him. Sulfin Evend hedged a glance at the valet, who looked rabbit scared, but still moved to salvage the upset candle. The fact that the servant left the bedside by one step reassured Sulfin Evend that the men at close quarters were his own, hand-picked to hold true under knowledge of Lysaer's afflicted madness. Ranne and Fennick guarding his back meant that others, who were disastrously ignorant, had crowded into the entry. These posed an outraged knot of obstruction, muttering in surprise, then exchanging veiled accusations regarding their commander's untoward activity.

If the valet's timely foresight had spread the blanket overtop of Lysaer's lashed wrists, Sulfin Evend's abrasive explosion upset any politic story that the avatar might have fallen by accident.

Already, the first incensed outcry arose. 'Have you taken leave of your wits, Lord Commander?'

More zealots joined the declaiming chorus. 'Or are you possessed?'

'What blasphemous folly could make you suggest that our heaven-sent avatar might be vulnerable to Koriathain?'

Sulfin Evend locked his offended teeth. He dared not admit to his outbred clan lineage. The least whiff of suspicion that he owned wild talent, and Lysaer's rabid following would fetch in a priest to put him on trial, if not arraign him for burning.

The valet shuffled back, the lit candle in hand. No help, that the damning tableau now looked worse: Sulfin Evend placed ruthless priorities first and attended the head wound's necessities. At least the towel compress caught most of the blood. Perhaps a mixed blessing: Lysaer s'Ilessid stirred back to consciousness under the fluttering flame. His blue eyes flickered open, confused. Healthy reflex contracted his pupils. He was not concussed, or insane, only hurting, and stung to his aristocrat's bones by the public assault on his dignity.

'Get out!' he demanded, succinct as flung ice. 'If my first commander has lost his aplomb and stooped to a brawling fight, don't expect me to welcome the dumbfounded audience!'

But the bullheaded captain on loan from Kalesh was quite beyond shame. 'Has his Lordship, Sulfin Evend, just dared to suggest that mere witches might set your Divine Grace under a spell of compulsion?'

Lysaer's flattened frame stiffened. Peeled raw himself by that surgical stare, Sulfin Evend stood off, while the valet, inured to all blistering pressure, fluttered in with a robe for his master's bare shoulders.

'I heard what your senior officer claimed!' the Blessed Prince demurred, angry. Assisted to sit upright, but ignoring the garment, Lysaer sat cloaked in blankets and surveyed the gawkers until every man had flushed red. 'In fact, Sulfin Evend lost his temper first. He made his insolent point well enough, as you see by the marks on my person. His gaffe excuses nobody else's bad manners! I serve my own reprimands. This one shall stay private. *Get out!*'

They went. At a stumbling run, clashing armoured elbows and swords in a crowding rush through the tent-flap. Which left the impervious valet, still hopefully clutching the dressing-robe; and Sulfin Evend, shivering unarmed in his halfway-laced gambeson. The blast of divine censure fell with swift fury, since the servant could not regale glittering finery on a man perched upright with his wrists bound.

'I have an errand I need run to the Mayor of Tirans.' Despite snarled hair, Lysaer's royal breeding somehow had regained peerless majesty. 'The instant I have my hands freed for the writ, I charge you to ride post and place the delivery before his closed council.'

Which curt dismissal saddled his foremost commander of armies with a courier's ride to shatter the sternest endurance. Sulfin Evend dropped to his knees, swiped off the crumpled silk coverlet, and loosed the cinched belt that clamped his liege's now-bloodless limbs. 'You were attacked,' he said under his urgent breath. 'Koriathain will strike at you again. My absence does nothing but weaken you.'

'I was assaulted,' Lysaer corrected, imperious. 'A pity.' He rubbed his grooved skin, then unexpectedly smiled. His sunny humour was all too collected and sane, with his gashed scalp streaking ribbons across his fair skin. 'You'll accomplish my bidding at diligent speed, if only to make your hot-foot return to bolster my threadbare precautions.'

'I tell you, the Prime Matriarch weaves a new plot. She will not stay her hand!' Neck muscles bunched, all but choked by fear, Sulfin Evend shuddered under the tug of his instincts. 'Your uneasy dreams are not sown by your nemesis!' Before the insidious threat of the curse, he reasoned his point with more tact. 'You've reviewed my patrols. Crack troops and priest sensitives have done their exemplary work. No skulking sorcerer has slipped past our guard and entered the s'Brydion citadel.'

'You can't swear to that claim,' Lysaer pointed out, serene in his mantle of bed-clothes.

Sulfin Evend stifled his scathing protest. Clammy sweat soaked his shirt. One wrong word might re-spark the volatile tension. He could *never* divulge his convincing rebuttal: the memory, stark as a branding in daylight, of Arithon's promise sworn at Sanpashir. The half-brother cursed as enemy was prodigally gifted, but not murderous by nature, or criminal.

'Lysaer, I beg you! Don't risk this, alone.' Against his stiff grain, Sulfin Evend pleaded to turn the cold wind of disaster. 'Throw me in lock-up. Leave the key in the care of your honourable valet. Dharkaron's fell vengeance, clap me in irons, but don't strip yourself of my watch. Not when arcane means might twist a fell snare to make you a Koriani puppet.'

But the glaring mistake could not be unmade. A subordinate had been caught raising a hand against the divine spirit made flesh. Angry followers would turn on the offending target. Rumour and outcry could raise a deadly recoil, and on that, Lysaer's ruler's perception was matchless. 'You have left me no choice, friend.' He stood with regret, accepted the valet's ministrations, and let the gold-and-white mantle settle over his shoulders. 'I cannot waive the apparent offence. Go, and my bristling dog-pack can be tongue-lashed and leashed, and yanked back to fawning heel. Stay, and you're asking to get a cur's stab in the back, by a rival.'

Late Autumn 5671

Second Audience

Mearn's supposition concerning his brother's intentions proved to be disastrously wrong. No formal assize was called, for the morning. After spending the night in a windowless cell, trussed and shouting herself hoarse, Jeynsa was hauled into Duke Bransian's presence with a sack tied over her head. Even bound wrist and ankle, her struggles tested the strength of two muscular guardsmen. After dragging her out of the dungeon, and into the stuffy clerk's chamber used to take prisoners' statements, both soldiers had bleeding fingers. The larger one limped from a kicked shin.

'She bites!' the burly captain exclaimed. Unscorched by Liesse's horrified censure, he dealt his charge a jarring, hard shake and shoved her before the oak table. 'Clamps her damned jaws till she's scored to the bone, fast as a murdering weasel!'

The girl kept up her crazed scuffling, even then. The men-at-arms had to strap her into a chair before anyone dared to loose the draw-string that fastened the muffling burlap. The cloth was yanked off. Underneath, her flushed face was tear-stained and grazed, and her cropped walnut hair, spiked to cowlicks. The lad's clothing worn to mix yesterday's mortar now had dried blood-stains flecked over the lye. If appearance suggested a hysterical child, rumpled after a tantrum, Jeynsa's opening salvo held withering irony. 'My liege turned his back on this town, once before. Had I the same foresight, I should have trampled your ducal standard into the midden!'

The same brute whose sword thrust had undone Sidir clouted her with his mailed fist. 'Mind your tongue, girl! You think you've seen trouble? Things could get worse.'

The blow left her dizzy. Her lip split and one cheekbone skinned, Jeynsa granted his snarling less regard than a yapping lap-dog.

The room where they held her was still belowground, though the stonewalls were whitewashed. The stout furnishing underneath her had shackle-bolts for felons. Although the claw-footed table confronting her contained a rolled document, quill pen, and ink, no lawful tribunal filled the bench seats. Instead of Alestron's hound-faced justiciar, Duke Bransian stood with crossed arms in his war-time mail and field surcoat. He looked red in the eyes, even hag-ridden, as he rocked on his toes with feral impatience. Shadowed by his taut bulk, Liesse showed calm distance, perched strait-laced atop the state dais. Her lush hair was pinned, brown coils piled above a cinnamon gown and a necklet of rubies. Beyond the ranked guardsmen, stationed behind, the only other official at hand was Alestron's high chancellor, hen-pecked and grey, with his knobby, scrubbed hands folded into the lap of his floor-length black robe.

Jeynsa had only bravado to set against their predacious regard. She protested, though helpless pain and raw grief threatened to drain the heart out of her. 'You claim to live by the old law sanctions. Then where are my rights?'

'This is not about honour,' Liesse declared, across Bransian's bellow for silence. 'Not justice, or fairness to you, on whatever count of mishandling. You are here only for the direct expediency of keeping Alestron's citizens alive and defended.'

Jeynsa raised her bruised chin. Eyes narrowed, she spat. 'The charge I would broach is criminal murder.'

Duke Bransian braced his huge fists on the table, which jostled the clerkly contents. 'You dare say to me that one fallen man is worth all the lives under my seal of office! Wives, craftsfolk, children, and babes? Should your swordsman, who died on his feet in a fight, matter more than a town under threat of invasion?'

'Name Sidir!' Jeynsa challenged. 'He was a free-wilds clansman, and nobody's bondsman assigned for demeaning protection.' Despite fury and effort, the fear in her showed: she could not stop trembling.

Liesse tapped the trestle with a censuring finger, dark eyes also beyond regret. 'Could you hold his life above ten thousand families, doomed to suffer a famine? Does his fate outweigh the rapine and pillage that the heel of a conquering war host will bring us? A sword thrust is quick. Have you ever watched a child die of starvation? A young woman forced till she's haemorrhaged?'

'Yes!' Jeynsa shouted. 'I've seen infants perish of starvation and cold, and all manner of forced brutality, done by head-hunters. You forget. I was never brought up in a palace.' Afraid, not yet panicked, she glowered at the duke, who now paced like an irritable bear. 'I don't see what any of this has to do with a breach of guest welcome, or assault and an unprovoked act of butchery.'

Bransian met her spitting fury with frosty eyes and a curt nod to his chancellor. 'We are hard, but not foolish.'

The fussy official stirred out of furled quiet, slipped the ribbon from the scroll, and twitched a state document across the table.

'Read,' snapped the duke. 'Then sign your name here, before witnesses. Do that, and you walk out of here, safe. Your crown prince won't be forced to defend your hysterical story, or answer a case with no witnesses. You can end this, now, quietly. Or have the same verdict dragged out in sordid detail through the shame of a hearing in public ceremony.'

Jeynsa clamped her jaw. Scanned the offered reprieve, while the last vestige of colour drained out of her freckled face. Before she completed the offensive last lines, she glanced up, breathing quickly. 'Lies!' she gasped. 'Vicious slander on top of vile extortion. Smear Sidir's faultless service by a false claim that he moved out of hand, and *attacked your guardsmen without provocation?*'

'A dead man's good name,' Liesse stated, prim. 'The liegeman's past suffering any dishonour. Give us your word. That's a painless exchange for Prince Arithon's debt, that could spare every innocent life in this citadel.'

Jeynsa shook her head, speechless.

'Is your stiff neck worth so much?' The chancellor leaned forward with overbearing impatience. 'How can you not act for the greater good? Are you spineless? Why not use the power that's yours to save others, hand-picked as you are for an office that can bind the will of a sovereign king? The blood of sacrifice here has already been paid! Don't make Sidir's loss be in vain. Not when your sensibility, and his reputation, might buy many thousands their future survival.'

Which pressure threw too harsh a weight upon Jeynsa's uncertain young shoulders. 'The choice you place on me is not mine to make!'

'Don't be a braying ass!' Bransian hurled his state chair aside. He loomed over the table, the nights of sleepless rage and balked weeks of inaction smoking off his ox frame. 'None of us can afford to choke over principle! Not with Alestron's domain being pillaged by Lysaer's dog-packs of fanatics!' His flicked gesture summoned.

One of the paired guardsmen approached Jeynsa's chair. Steel rasped as he unsheathed his sword and cut the lashed binding, which freed her right hand for the pen.

'Sign, girl!' the duke snapped. 'I'm griped from watching you preach on your backside. No one's got time for your quibbling.'

Her pale green eyes spilled her furious tears. Still, Jeynsa battled her ebbing composure. Left only the grit of her ancestry, she argued: as Asandir's choice for Rathain's *caithdein*, charged to stand at the right hand of princes with no shield but bare flesh and her conscience. 'You won't change his Grace's stance in this way! Or deliver your people from jeopardy. Not by asking me to endorse your misrule through hiding betrayal and murder.'

'Pretty words. Empty threats. You've no leverage to bargain!' Bransian stared her down, beyond quarter. 'Realize how little your breathing life means! You and your crown prince together are not worth the horrific burden of suffering, if the unholy Alliance keeps us besieged through the winter.'

The chancellor regarded his knuckles, distressed, while Liesse pressed her ringed hands to her lips, quick enough to stifle her outcry as the poised guardsman was beckoned to move. Fast as the whirlwind spun out of control, past a line that had long since been crossed, the man-at-arms laid the chill edge of his blade against the tendons of the Teiren s'Valerient's other, strapped wrist.

'Sign your name, Jeynsa!' Overpowering within the stifling, shut room, Bransian bored in, beyond mercy. 'Or find out how dying can be made to hurt. Your corpse can as easily fall with Sidir's, cashiered as evidence to set your prince under mandate. Alive or not, you will serve as my proof that Rathain's delegation spurned guest oath and turned weapons against us.'

'Where are your witnesses?' the chancellor pressed. 'You can't escape harm, except by your signature. After all, Sidir's body will be found in your chamber, with the slaughter of three liveried guardsmen. Your dagger, I'm told, left a crippling stroke. The man with your blood on his blade will be cleared upon grounds that you resisted his lawful arrest.'

'Then be my witness, now!' Jeynsa seized the pen. She hooked the cut-glass well of ink that awaited beside the draughted parchment. Fear spoiled her fierceness. But never her nerve, that had been her sire's and grandsire's before her, as she dipped the quill nib. 'Your methods are dirty,' she pronounced in rife scorn. 'Nastier than anything I've ever seen from the slinking ranks of town head-hunters.'

Quaking and pale, she met the eyes of the duchess, but found Liesse turned beyond sane appeal and hardened to stone by weak character.

'This, for Sidir's memory? I should be ashamed.' Jeynsa snapped the poised quill, then back-handed the uncorked ink-well.

The flung contents flooded the offending document. Spatters sullied Alestron's bull blazon, on the breast of the duke's scarlet surcoat.

Bransian roared. His swordsman lifted his weapon and swung. Jeynsa snatched the split second. As the blade was upraised, she rammed her freed hand to the table edge and shoved with all of her panicked strength. The oak chair overbalanced, and toppled. Her strapped frame was borne over backwards. The heavy, carved finials clouted into the guardsman, who stumbled, his flailing sword stroke gone wild. The blade hissed downwards, sliced through her trousers and hose, and bit into her calf.

Jolted by terror, Jeynsa expected to die. Trussed without recourse, slammed breathless and bleeding, she squeezed her eyes shut on a wheeling view of the ceiling. The trampling thud of rushed boots around her merged with someone's shrill shout. Then the door-panel crashed open. More armoured bodies poured in from the outside corridor. The floor-boards under the upset chair pounded and shook to the melee.

'I've found them!' pealed a male voice in fierce triumph.

Another sword, drawn above her, belled against steel, near enough that Jeynsa cringed from the violent eddy of air. An edged weapon nipped the cuff of her boot, struck off someone's whining parry. Her courage snapped. She sobbed outright, while somebody's fists seized her chair with sharp force, and hurled her helpless frame upright.

'We have you safe!' said Talvish's voice, by her ear. He bundled her face against his rough mantle, drew his knife, and bent to slice through her trouser cuff. 'Mearn and Sevrand are both here,' he explained, as his competent grasp jerked her gashed clothing away, and stanched the red gush of her leg wound. 'They've brought the tower guard, who are lawful. Rest assured. You won't limp once you've healed, and criminal charges are already filed. Though Alestron's justiciar cursed to be served in his bed, you need do no more than hang on long enough to deliver your testimony concerning what happened last night in your chamber.'

Jeynsa found she had no strength to move. Despite Talvish's solid assurance, binding up her fresh injury, she shivered with traumatized terror. 'You risk being discredited!' She had seen the rabid wolf in Duke Bransian's eyes, that abjured every decency.

'Hush!' Talvish urged, still involved with the field dressing.

As he spoke, trying to quiet her, Jeynsa shouted him down. 'The duke wanted my signature to condemn Sidir as a murderer and call in the debt to the Crown of Rathain!' The muffling folds of the officer's cloak obscured her frantic words. She struggled, then hammered at Talvish's shoulder until he straightened to listen.

Still kneeling, his blond head level with hers, he ended her wildcat fit by gripping her forearms. 'Jeynsa!' Her flooded eyes met his steady gaze, until she had to acknowledge: he *had* heard the grim worst. Still, the core of his calm stayed unbroken.

As she subsided, shuddering, Talvish unleashed his sly smile. 'My brave lady, *attend to Mearn*!'

In fact, the shouting across the jostled table raised a noise to roust the lost dead out of Sithaer. While Liesse wept, appalled, and the chancellor hunched his stiff neck in his high, sable collar, Bransian's blustering rage lost wind before stone-walled dismay.

Which left Mearn, spitting mad, and still speaking. Backed by Sevrand, and a mailed wall of men-at-arms taken from watch off the battlements, the youngest s'Brydion sibling hurled down a thrown gauntlet of accusations. 'But we have living testament. Worse, you're outfaced by a clear line of appeal that can be made to extend back to Althain Tower. Dakar's Sighted talent saw all of what happened, when your henchmen took orders for an illegal assault against Jeynsa.'

'Are you serious?' Bransian roared, cornered. 'At the word of a drunk, you'd *lie down* for the wheels of Dharkaron's Black Chariot? Spit your guts on a pike for an egg-sucking dandy! You can't toy with the madness of bringing this matter before the Fellowship Sorcerers!'

Mearn's tirade cut through. 'Don't play the excuse, that Sethvir is preoccupied! Enough power resides *here* to roast your plucked goose, arse down on the fires of calumny! Based on Dakar's vision, Talvish sent summons to Arithon Teir's'Ffalenn, who moved at speed and brought in Elaira.' Mearn's blistering triumph held no joy at all, as he levelled the scathing last line. 'Sidir has survived!'

At Jeynsa's gasp of astonished disbelief, the youngest of Dawr's grandsons threw her a curt nod, then drove on with his nailing account.

'The Companion was recovered through an act of grand conjury, performed by trained witnesses, one of them Athera's Masterbard! Three talents observed the Paravian wards, and the black sword, Alithiel, rise and wake for the wronged liegeman's healing. They bear a just cause. Beyond any poisonous shadow of doubt, you've got no leg left to stand on. I have informed your herald. Call a proper assize, brother! Expose our family's shame to the public's review and risk dividing our ranks in a siege! Or else do what's best for the rule of Alestron. Stand forward to answer Prince Arithon's demand for a closed hearing at noon. Then beg on your knees that your injury to the Teiren s'Valerient doesn't inflame him past hope of granting a settlement in private!'

The duke sat for the royal inquiry, sullen with hobbled rage for the twist that had reined in his scheme by state process. Like the ox stung by the goad in the flank, he bent to Liesse's insistence and changed his ink-splattered surcoat. Clean, but not cowed, he convened the assembly in the small ward-room, used by the elite troop of the citadel guard. The narrow space with its thin lancet windows and thick walls gave excuse to weed down the attendance.

Mearn and Sevrand were present. Armed and in family colours, they flanked the central chair, prepared in the unwanted event they might be called on to adjudicate. Liesse appeared also, too sharp-eyed for humility, her seat at the right hand of the chancellor. That prim stick was tasked with the pen to record, in place of the scribe nobody wished to indoctrinate. The captain of the tower watch held the threshold, with his company arrived in formation outside.

Past question, the mood at the dais was grim, an atmosphere drenched in pent peril and sweat, thick enough to cut with a cleaver.

Against that cranked silence, which abjured all apology, Prince Arithon arrived on the punctual stroke of the hour. He came formally clad in the green, silver, and black of Rathain, the rich doublet from Dame Dawr a sharp contrast with the forest scout's leathers worn for the forced audience, the day prior. A glitter of storm-scud and lightning overtop, the black mantle from Davien the Betrayer draped over his Grace's trim shoulders. He did not bring Dakar. Though he was entitled to a Fellowship presence, none but Sidir attended him. Not Jeynsa, whose complaint had already been made. Nor Elaira, whose split loyalty to the sisterhood might become misconstrued as a threat.

As crown prince to subjects who were the wronged parties, Rathain held the right to bear arms; could have demanded of Alestron's own captains an honour guard to vouchsafe his person.

Arithon brought only the clothes on his body. Alithiel's black hilt did not hang at his side. The clan Companion's blades at his back were his sole, inadequate protection: a fact still the subject of singeing contention, by the measure of Sidir's fixed frown.

Each footfall a shout in the inimical quiet, Arithon approached the dais. He stopped. His right-hand liegeman stayed a half step behind. For an ugly, drawn second, he did nothing at all. Only acknowledged Mearn's impassive quiet, and Sevrand's clamped jaw, and Duke Bransian's vicious, braced carriage, which suggested a mouth clipped shut with a staple *just in case* the shade of a Sorcerer saw fit to attend his ignominy.

Yet Arithon had entrained no higher authority. Instead of a ringing list of accusations, he probed, gently quiet, 'What did you want?'

The question fell with such lack of censure that Liesse masked her face with ringed hands. Before her silenced sobbing, the chancellor shut his eyes and looked sick to his soul. Most stunned of all, Duke Bransian sat tongue-tied. His huge hands clenched, empty, offered no fight against which to rail and bluster.

Arithon sighed. Moved. Drew out a rolled parchment carried tucked underneath his silk sleeve. 'No one needs to make statements. Or review the discomfort of what's already done. Everything that could have been said is in writing, set under a truth seal by Dakar, in standing as Asandir's apprentice.' The document in hand was placed on the table, where it sat untouched as a coiled snake.

'Read it, or burn it,' said the Prince of Rathain. 'Just say what s'Brydion wished to accomplish and let proceedings begin there.'

'You would overlook double-cross?' Mearn ventured, shocked.

Beside him, Sevrand sat quartz-white and poleaxed. Liesse swayed, faint. The chancellor braced her, while Bransian hunched as though forced to chew rocks, without finesse for words past drawn weapons.

'My lord Duke,' the chancellor implored, bent sidewards for an urgent whisper. 'Beware of clever tricks! Take extreme care how you answer!'

The outburst caused Arithon Teir's'Ffalenn to raise his eyebrows with patent impatience. 'By all means, look yourself in the eye!' he rebuked. 'I will not stand here for the counsel of clerks!' Then, to Bransian, with that steely tone refined to silk, 'You can't speak for your motives in straightforward language, or acknowledge the fear in your heart?'

Another step brought Arithon up to the dais. 'Then let me try.' Still, he unleashed no reviling outrage. 'I would understand, of all men living,' he dared to suggest. 'If you thought a few lives could buy the opening to spare many thousands of innocents, that was the same ugly premise I used, when my half-brother's war host invaded, at Vastmark. I was wrong, then. Just how wrong, to my sorrow, I lived to find out. May you never bear that harsh pain of regret. Language fails in the description.'

As Liesse broke down, weeping, Arithon resumed with spare courtesy. 'Three of your most loyal guardsmen lie dead. Two of Rathain's subjects suffered injury for the same cause, which you thought a justifiable price to end Alestron's deadlocked predicament. Five hale defenders struck down, and for naught! I would have no more. Here, before witnesses, I concede once again. I pledge the help *that you already had* to break off this siege and disband the Alliance campaign at your walls.'

Bransian stirred. Alestron's bull blazon glittered to his heaved breath, and his brows bunched into a frown of bafflement. 'Damn your gall, prince! You said you would not fight to kill.'

'I fight to win *lives*,' Arithon corrected. Masterbard, sorcerer, his crisp diction crackled against living bone, and echoed off polished stonewalls. 'Here are my terms! I will brook no appeal, or this sordid case will be made public to revoke your vested authority!'

Before the stunned chancellor could wield his pen, the list emerged like a shot salvo. 'Talvish's service now belongs to Rathain. He may accept your orders. Even fight for your cause. But for all that he does, he will answer to me, and follow my lead when I ask for him. Consider him free of your feal obligation, though the sensible choice should allow him to keep his captaincy while the citadel's besieged. For your guardsman, whose weapon struck my liegeman down, and whose blade was raised to harm Jeynsa, this difference: his oath-bound loyalty stays with Alestron! But his sword-arm and fighting strength are owed to Sidir, until the hour the Teiren s'Valerient is delivered safe and sound to her family in Halwythwood!'

No one moved through the moment, as Rathain's prince turned on his heel and walked out, trailed by his forestborn clansman.

The thunder-clap of relief that surged through the chamber dropped Liesse into Bransian's consuming embrace. The chancellor was reduced to a quivering wreck, with Mearn left too thoughtfully silent.

'That man's beyond dangerous,' Sevrand declared, shaken. Draped limp in his chair, he regarded his slim cousin, who had forced through the honourable settlement just rendered with such frightening lack of hard argument. 'We could live to regret. I hope you know what you're doing, leaving that creature loose in our midst.'

Mearn stood up and stretched. 'Does anyone presume, where that spirit's concerned?' He should have looked kicked to a pulp as the rest, except for the manic, gambler's gleam veiled in his half-lidded eyes. 'I wouldn't care to be standing in Lysaer's gilded boots,' he declared with scorching irony. 'Or be numbered among his Grace of Rathain's declared enemies. We are, one might say, in the fold with the blessed. Though I doubt that Sidir will be lenient with the wretch who ran a sword's length of cold steel through his chest.'

Autumn 5671

Nightmare

The day arrived, foreseen and long dreaded by the coterie of Ath's adepts who attended the Warden at Althain Tower: Sethvir had weakened too far to arise. He lay on his cot like a weather-worn effigy carved out of alabaster. No breathing flesh should lie so still. Shrunken and calm, his form never moved, not a muscle twitch or a tremor. The slack knuckles on the scarlet blanket seemed too brittle to have wielded the pen that recorded five centuries of Athera's history in gracefully miniature script.

He would not waken, now. The vast reach of the Sorcerer's aura had ebbed to a cobweb, too frail for the stabilizing infusions that once were arranged, using crystal. The way of Ath's Brotherhood forbade intervention. Where the world's weave was interconnected, they could not act in direct influence: and Sethvir owned the Paravian's gift of the earth-sense, a power that ranged beyond their learned auspices. While Luhaine prowled in and out, his ghost presence fraught with the Fellowship's lapsed charge of burdens, the adepts kept vigil at the Warden's side.

Day and night, their gentle hands husbanded the waning flicker of life.

Amid tomb-like quiet that was not yet death, one candle was always kept burning. The open casement let in the shine of stars and moon, and today, cold blue sky and a flood of white sunlight. A capricious breeze teased at the wool-blanket, and combed through Sethvir's beard and hair, cascading over the pillow. Five adepts minded his presence that noon: one at right and left side, and another pair at head and feet. The last was seated off to the side, tasked with tracking the subtle, wandering course of the Sorcerer's beleaguered spirit.

For Sethvir's inner mind still rode the flux tides that mapped all event on Athera. Hour upon exhaustive hour, he clung yet to the duty left in his care since the last centaur guardian's departure. Paravian survival could not be relinquished. The Sorcerer fought on without let-up. Dying, he still grappled to stem the leaks in three damaged grimwards. The ending approached. Breathing flesh proved too fallible. Stark will could not counter his dwindling strength, or stem the leaching forces that brought dissolution. While his body became reduced to a husk, the purposeful course of his dreams held the last, fading splendour of his vitality.

Unclothed thought often found the Sorcerer seated in a meadow of young grass, beside a rushing spring stream. While yellow pollen sifted over his frame, his bare feet would be plonked in the swift, running water, and his chin rested on the crossed arms propped upon his tucked knees. Othertimes, he travelled in giant's strides over ice-capped peaks, or wandered as a wisp on the wind's vagrant currents, across skyscapes of towering clouds where sunbeams sliced gold across the cold vault of the atmosphere.

The adept stationed as listener mapped each of Sethvir's restless journeys: over polar ice-cap, and seething volcanic vent, and once, through the indigo deeps where fish with serrated teeth devoured teeming prey in the tropical sea.

Then shrinking attrition claimed its harsh toll. The inner thrust of Sethvir's journeys slowed down and ceased. The meadow became the recurrent meeting-place where outside spirits held visitation. In that shimmering realm, that was nowhere and everywhere, Luhaine often shared information, or exchanged strained conversations that hobbled his argumentative lecturing.

Today, another turn of ill news had brought Kharadmon from his guard on the star wards. At his call, Sethvir's presence was not in the accustomed place, skipping stones for the leaping trout. Instead, an adept of Ath's Brotherhood strode across the seamed scar that once had channelled the freshwater brook. His figure shimmered too brilliantly white in a dreamscape that no longer sang of renewal. Amid grass that had burned to a sun-scorched brown, his arrival was scarcely needed to confirm the desperate turn for the worse.

'How far?' Kharadmon paused, whirling dusty air in sore agitation. He had not been prepared. 'How deeply has the Warden been drawn towards oblivion?' Such a miserable handful of words, to express a grieving rage beyond outlet. Or the galvanic fear: that Asandir might be lost, consumed by the corrosive Scarpdale grimward, and past hope of returning alive.

The whole of *Athera* lay in the balance, if Althain's Warden should fail. And he must: the impossible burden upheld for two years far outmatched any one Fellowship Sorcerer.

The adept answered gently. 'Even you cannot pass, where Sethvir has gone.' His thought-form lamented far more than the state of the creek-bed. 'There is only one being who can safely go to the place where your colleague is dreaming.'

'Damn his name to Sithaer and Dharkaron Avenge, that we should fall so far into jeopardy!' Kharadmon howled in abject despair. 'I should tear up the roots of the Mathorns myself, before asking for help from that quarter!'

The adept bowed his head.

'You already know why I've come.' The discorporate Sorcerer's anguished presence roved to and fro, rattling through the dry grass and seed-stalks. 'Luhaine's whining aside, I've just been dangerously singed. You've noticed the blight that now poisons the flux line that crosses the square at Avenor?'

'Our hostel at Northerly has been adversely affected,' the adept affirmed, but without remonstrance. 'Leaves shrivel and fall in the grove, there. Were you told any sooner, what could you have done?'

'Nothing!' Kharadmon's frustration rang loud, where the breeze had ceased dancing. 'Without Asandir or Ciladis, we're hobbled as babes, fit to piss nowhere else but the cradle.'

For the latent terror Sethvir most feared now brewed a disaster: the skulls of the four dragon hatchlings once enslaved for black augury had been left unwarded too long. Their angry ghosts stirred. Daily becoming more self-aware, they soon would remember their defiled origin.

'The Light's faithful?' Kharadmon ranted on. 'They'll pray! Beseech their false prince for his spouting falsehoods, while the flesh of Tysan's defenceless citizens gets stripped off their standing bones. Today, next week, Ath knows when, those bleating sheep are going to be squatting bang over the birth of a new grimward!' The Sorcerer's tirade reflected his agonized helplessness. 'Did Sethvir believe, in his depleted state, that he also could contain that unravelling chaos?'

'He went,' the adept stated. Such was his sorrow, he might have stopped hearts. 'Could you have kept him from trying?'

'Yes!' Kharadmon's incandescent rage rippled through the etheric landscape. 'I would have looped time! Tied Sethvir's heroic entrails in knots, before watching him leap into self-sacrifice.'

The adept looked up, then, saddened for the pain that served him such savage censure. 'When your Warden chose, he told me this: that he would have the world fair and green, and kept fit for Asandir's home-coming.'

A shade had no tears. Kharadmon left in a shriek of whisked air, lest the parched rocks in the gully should be made to weep in his place.

His wake of whipped dust dimmed the air a long time, before settling. Serene beyond tarnish, Ath's adept shook the film out of his white robe. Alone, he kept the last space for hope, with his beacon light steady and burning.

The peril was not overwhelming, as yet. A pressure that scraped the nerves to unease, or a formless weight, suggestive of threat, that infused the surrounding site where the dungeon tower had collapsed overtop of Avenor's state treasury. The four hatchling skulls buried under the slagged rubble were interred past recovery, with their unquiet ghosts not yet coalesced to a deranging vortex.

Yet Sethvir's dreaming sensed them: as the flare of a burn might inflame tender skin, although here, he retained no real sense of his body's awareness.

His naked being knew only will, focused by the knowledge Athera was threatened. For the consciousness trapped within those slaughtered bones had been freed. Once the enraged spirits recalled their demise, their death-screams would resurge, unleashing explosive destruction.

No warding to limit the damage was possible, given Sethvir's weakened state. Ranged beyond his slack flesh, he had no protection. Only the lulling spells of deep calm: the grip of a polar winter's vast silence; the stillness that threaded the darkest nights, and the inbreath of being that paused living thought at the nadir between the moon's phases. Such a thin tissue, to stay the eruptive storm as the murdered hatchlings awoke. Nigh as insubstantial as the drake shades he fought to suppress, Sethvir knitted the circles of quiet that were all he had left as a shielding defence. He worked, hazed each second by stalking peril. He would perish, and worse, once the drakes' memory roused. His comatose body at Althain Tower lacked the vitality to anchor him.

Sethvir faced that risk, since no other Fellowship Sorcerer at hand might withstand the dire peril. Discorporate, Kharadmon and Luhaine could not survive the proximity to a drake shade. Verrain, as master spellbinder, was not able to weave wardings with sufficient subtlety.

Sunk deep below ground, and beleaguered by weakness, Sethvir proceeded with laborious care. Layer by layer, he sifted through textures of mineral and slagged glass, melted iron and ash. He crept at a snail's pace, touched each particle of smashed brick, char, and soil, sounding for their separate Names. Due permissions were asked and granted. The infusion of peace he presented, each time, was accepted by willing consent. Patient listening taxed his exhaustion: laid him wide open to the conjured serenity shaped by his striving.

How long might he endure without hope of relief? Each moment sapped his dwindling life-stream. Hours or days, no immaculate focus was going to extend his survival.

Sethvir felt cast adrift. Scarpdale's grimward itself was a drain his patched wardings could never stem, with the fate of his overdue colleague already consigned to that bottomless spiral. Lose himself, and Asandir might also fall: how far, no mind knew. A grimward's existence was as bleak a chaos as the sacred groves of Ath's Brotherhood were ruled fair by the fire of creation. The one could not exist without the living possibility of the other: limitless love held all of the dark, and the dark, the potentials of light and shade beyond measure. The beauty and pain, the grotesque and the graceful loomed the thread of a boundless universe. By its vast, inexhaustible nature, greater mystery outmatched every limiting framework.

A being made flesh could not grapple such paradox, or embrace the infinite irony. Sethvir wrestled at the brink. How easily he might be cozened to give in, release the harsh ties to his compromised destiny and soar free. More than the charge of the dragon's trust bound him: he held also for care, strengthened by the redemption once graced by Athera's Paravians.

Despite vigilance, the heart's need wore and tore him, fraying the steadfast loyalty holding live spirit to his inert flesh. One more fleck of Named gravel, and one more bed of powdered ash, and Althain's Warden succumbed. For one faint instant, weakness flawed his braid of spelled calm.

He tumbled, unmoored. His instinctive reach for Asandir's help escaped his prudent restraint. Sethvir plunged down and down. Through layers of deep soil and rock, unable to brake, his awareness carved a meteor's trail into the molten iron that seethed at the planet's core. He did not rest there, but hurled beyond, crashed past remembrance of his solid form. His senses became stripped. Unwilling to release the imperative charge to defend the survival of the old races, his unseated awareness sped relentlessly through the frail barriers he had stitched to stem Scarpdale's breached grimward.

A fleeting impression left the vague sense that *something* crossed his plummeting path.

Then the dead drake's dreaming closed over and drowned him . . .

. . . in chaos that shredded both substance and thought. Sethvir whirled through pinwheels of fire and rain that fouled his mage-sense. Ash clogged his vision. Winds boiled dark clouds like whipped lead and sulphur, laced in lightning, while thunder boomed, fit to shatter his last awareness.

No ground existed to define up or down. Star and sunlight had never shone here, nor had the leafed shoot of any green plant unfurled from a seed, seeking flower. All things ran formless, ungoverned, bled into jangled sensation. A dragon's thoughts were not fashioned for the mind of a man: any more than the rage of its death-scream could be tamed by mortal reason or masterful striving.

Here, tucked into a knot of clenched limbs, Asandir still guarded the spark that once had been a living black horse. At strength's end, he held, beyond reach of rescue, with Isfarenn's spirit tucked safe in his hands . . .

That instant, Sethvir's tumbling awareness snapped short. He cried out, yanked back from the brink. His savaged senses resurged, familiar dimensions restored with a pain that all but flayed spirit from flesh. He awoke: not to his body in Althain Tower, but to the ruined, ephemeral meadow, beside the gulch of a vanished stream.

Davien perched on a boulder beside him, clad in the vivid colours of harvest. Dark brows and black eyes unsmiling, he toyed with a stem of dry grass. Seeds loosened by his teasing fingers blew in the parched wind that also whipped his streaked hair.

'Where is your censure, now?' he inquired, but this time, bitter challenge came tempered.

'I have you to thank that I did not plunge all the way to unending oblivion.' Sethvir's scraped whisper acknowledged the grim certainty: the vision of Asandir's current straits was not drawn from the loom of his earth-sense.

'Which living drake brokered the bargain you've made, to peer inside of a grimward?'

'Should that matter?' The turned-up corner of Davien's mouth always lent his expression a cynical twist. 'We might be dedicated to the same concepts, but never by sharing alliances.'

The words carried glass edges: yet never before had Fellowship desperation walked this narrow a precipice. Althain's Warden resisted the need to cry mercy. He had been rescued, once. Asandir's life was the bargaining chip, tossed like the stripped bone between them.

'Everything matters,' Sethvir declared. 'Are you here to assist? Or will you gloat while a pending disaster obliterates all of Avenor?'

'I am here to tender your choice,' said Davien. 'As I forewarned, the hour has come. Salvage the compact and try for Asandir's rescue, and your hope to achieve a crowned monarchy wanes. Our Teir's'Ffalenn will be left most cruelly unsupported in his moment of greatest need.'

Sethvir captured the delicate change, his tender question above venal spite. '*Our* Teir's'Ffalenn?'

A dream beyond flesh, Davien bent his head. He stared at his restless, artisan's fingers, that wrought wonders from unruly genius. 'The galling truth?' he admitted at last. 'Arithon is more than I realized. A crown prince in heart, if not willing to be caged by the joyless demands of high office.'

Too enervated to smile, even for a startling concession, come too late to be counted a victory, Sethvir watched the wind winnow up ochre dust from the parched stream-bed. 'His Grace was your weapon, you said, fitted best to champion the cause of humanity. You trained him to fashion his own cutting-edge. And he has, far beyond the rare brilliance you once thought to facet from the raw diamond. First at Etarra and also, outside hope, at the King's Grove in Selkwood. Why should you regret?'

Davien laughed and stood up. 'Do I, in fact?'

'Enough that you've asked me to say who should be marked out for sacrifice,' Sethvir observed. 'Though you might prove me wrong, and still do as you please, the same way the cat plays out his pinned mouse for morbid amusement.'

Such a soft ambush, to set a cold sting to the viscera. Davien raised his eyebrows. 'Should you not blame Ciladis, as well? How inconvenient, that his disappearance should force the resumption of dialogue between us.' Beyond merciful quarter, the Betrayer struck twice. 'You dare not try to quell those stirred hatchlings again. Even past counting Asandir's threatened fate, your drained reserves can't be nursed to recovery. The rise of a new vortex will wrack this world. Past ruin, we're doomed. My friend, if you haven't staged your good-byes, someone ought to point out that your life-force has bled ghostly thin.'

'Too thin for a fight.' In the haven far gone from the lush meadow, Althain's

Warden closed tired eyes. 'Why fence with sharp words? You haven't mentioned the dire cost to yourself, should you opt to restore your fractured support. If you think I don't care, you're mistaken, Davien. I have no right to direct any course that would lead you to crippling servitude. Before the peril you *might* shoulder for us, my stake in the matter becomes nothing at all, if not arrogance, pretence and mockery.'

The pause hung, while the wind devils swayed through the rock clefts. Sethvir did not need mage-sight to know that the Sorcerer's spirit had left him. Nothing else broke the dream's desolation. He was alone, perhaps facing the end of all striving. Like Asandir, Sethvir held no more options. He must hunker down. Cling to the receding essence of life and three grimwards, while enduring the agony of fresh suspense.

For if Davien felt moved to commit, and if action led him to shoulder a risk beyond the pale of all human cognizance, which one of his adamant, capricious loyalties would rule the course of the Fellowship's destiny?

Late Autumn 5671

Threads

Far westward, the merchant brig *Evenstar* sets sail from Telmandir, laden down with grain, flour, dry beans, and salt meat; the fine linen, rare herbals, and tinctures for healing; and the barrels of raw spirits granted as relief by the High King of Havish, and bound for Alestron's besieged defenders . . .

Days later, ahead of the next autumn storm building off the Cildein coast, the war fleet under Parrien s'Brydion and Vhandon's armed company leaves the haven behind Lugger's Islet, this time using prize hulls to mask their planned raid on Alestron's entrenched enemies . . .

While Sulfin Evend lathers horseflesh on his errand to Tirans, and Lysaer tosses in the restless dreams influenced by Koriathain, a water-drop falls within a sealed chamber, under the Mathorn Mountains: its downward course is uninterrupted, while the brooding form of an eagle looks on, the splash races ring-ripples across the black well of a virgin spring . . .

X. Hammer and Anvil

T hrough the fortnight that followed Duke Bransian's act of misrule, and redress to the Crown of Rathain, the citizens of Alestron waited, suspended between Lysaer's standing war host and the poised sword of unwritten destiny. Tension sang on the air. Each dawn arrived like an unplucked note that burned the heart with pent silence. The sentries remained vigilant on the walls. Grim officers doled out the dwindling rations, while the hollow-eyed clerks maintained the tallies that marked the slow plunge towards starvation.

The season turned. Relentless, the shortening days brought a winter that held no relief. The citadel's routine ground onwards, unchanged, despite the shame suppressed in the furore that brought them the Master of Shadow.

Man, woman, and child, Alestron's people awaited Prince Arithon's promised response.

He gave them no act of saving conjury. No grand plan to counteract the ongoing siege. No word, no sign, and no encouraging gesture salved their unalloyed worry. The ringing declaration of assistance wore thin, with the first creeping whispers abroad that Rathain's prince had misled with a falsehood.

Beneath day-to-day drills, and through the wailing of displaced families, the frustrated urge to disrupt the cold stalemate built into devouring need. Mage-sense unveiled far more: in the glassine bubble of rage, as the Koriani Prime spun her provocative nightmares to force Lysaer's cursed explosion; in the seething of enemy troops on shorn hills, by manic turns sick and craving for home, then the visceral thrill of a violent engagement.

If Elaira stayed immersed in her calling as healer, and Dakar found numbness through sleep, no such outlet was open to Arithon. The fanatical pitch of deluded belief that shackled his half-brother's following bled into the flux and inflamed his rogue foresight. Let down his barriers, he could see too far: the posited future of each misled spirit could sweep him to abject despair. His words could not sway them, or shift their blinded fate. Understanding could not grant him heart's ease. Branded by doctrine as minion of evil, and maligned for his own warped campaigns from the past, Arithon could do nothing for folk whose fears demanded a simplistic world, punch-cut into darkness or light.

Truth gave him no solace. The short-sighted concept of fair-weather day never *could* rule supreme, without night, and not parch the green earth, or freeze the timeless, dynamic creation that birthed wholeness through the unseen play of the mysteries.

With nowhere to turn, Arithon sought for the deeper balance within Paravian masonry. Hour upon hour, with Sidir at his back, and Kyrialt guarding the guest-quarters, he sat wrapped against the blustering cold, listening in depth to the chiselled blocks first laid to defend against drakefire. On the high battlement, Rathain's prince harkened by starlight. He tuned his ear to frequencies unknown to men, while the quarter moon sailed bright as shaved silver above. In those still moments, carved in light and black shadow, the rainbow colours that lay hidden between seemed to shimmer, scarcely veiled from his questing senses. Sound whispered. The mighty chord that underpinned the great stones' aware fastenings eluded his straining cognizance. Arithon heard with a masterbard's ear what might never be placed into melody.

Immersed as he was, he paid little heed to the tramp of Bransian's sentries. They skirted his position, all noise and bluster, or else mincing with unsettled nerves. The careless who trod inadvertently close were warned off by Sidir, whose stripping glance had grown more formidable since his arcane healing. Even the least sensitive soldier must acknowledge his uncompromised character, which had drawn steel to the death without hesitation for his sworn loyalty.

Arithon mapped the cap-stones of the crenels, then moved on to the massive rock that buttressed the fortress foundations. Nothing disrupted his methodical care: not the blistering prod of Fionn Areth's sharp words, or Sevrand's impatience, which arrived in a huff and demanded action.

More blunt than the grass-lander, or the armed sentries, the testy heir to the ducal seat was not deferred by the forest-bred liegeman. Brash and dangerous, Sevrand bore in, imposing in chainmail and broadsword. 'Ath above, prince! When in Sithaer will you snap out of your mooning and move to uphold our defence?'

Since Arithon chose not to answer, Sidir bristled. 'My liege will respond when he's ready!'

'Hah!' Sevrand snorted. 'More likely he'll continue to squat like a gargoyle till he sprouts lichens on our south wall.' Eyes narrowed, he regarded the prince's tucked form. 'Such lack of courage would rival the blooms on a ditch-growing daisy.'

Unlike Erlien s'Taleyn, this hulking young man had no cause to respect the murderous agility masked behind delicate fingers: which, right now, stayed folded in infuriating calm over the Teir's'Ffalenn's drawn-up knees. No guess might fathom such obtuse behaviour. Strained silence offered no answer. The s'Brydion heir grew bored soon enough, poking at an unspeaking target. To Sidir's cool relief, Sevrand stamped off to vent his hot energy sparring.

Naught else could be done but endure the long days. Under full sunlight, or exposed to the wind that moaned in north gusts through the battlements, Arithon crouched with his ear to chill stone, immersed in the depths of tranced calm. At intervals, cued perhaps by his mage-sense, he spoke: asked delicate questions in the lilted cadence of ancient Paravian. Such moments, his tone held a longing and hope fit to challenge the gates of despair. His stretched pauses extended, as though he expected an answer that came, but never quite reached completion.

Outspoken gossip soon claimed he was mad as a dog's midnight howling, or else foolish as the wool-gathering dreamer. Arithon disregarded such comments. He eschewed the tedium of explaining himself; gave no word in defence, even to the mothers who brought gaunt, tearful children, or the harrowed fathers who begged for encouragement. The gift of s'Ahelas far-sight was his, crossed with the forevision of s'Dieneval: no biddable talent, to stay within bounds, or observe the niceties of convenience. Still raw with that wakening, Arithon traced his way with cold patience. He sought the mystical wardings laced into the stonework, made respectful by the unforgiving aware-ness that what he encountered might not be controlled.

When his faculties tired, he would rise, hollow-eyed, and slip through the back lanes. Often masked under shadow, he might eat in a public tavern, unnoticed while in plain sight. Except that Sidir's tacit presence never left his unarmed shoulder; no matter how polite the approach, or how eloquent the appeal, the clansman backed his liege's odd choice to stay distanced from the distraught populace.

Arithon found his surcease in the guest tower, snugged in the loft chamber, and the scents of the herbals wafted upstairs from the still-room. His enchantress embraced his fraught presence then, and gentled his reserve with humour. Many an evening he played his lyranthe, a furious cascade of wild harmony and fugue, while she mixed her tinctures and remedies. Often as not, his cathartic melody was pitched to increase their efficacy. As though all the agony ignored in the streets could be salved by the balm set into a sick infant's cough syrup.

'Beloved, you have not asked,' he said once, in late evening when the fire burned low, and the quiet wrapped like fine velvet about them.

Elaira raised her eyes to meet his. A smile turned her lips, almost laughter, despite the harsh tide of public opinion caused by his relentless discipline. 'You haven't been badgered to mincemeat by everyone else's impatience? You know that Jeynsa kicked Fionn Areth out on his arse for daring the presumption, that Paravian wardings are biddable?'

Arithon sighed. He laid aside his exquisite instrument, arose, and tucked a strayed wisp back into the ribbon that fastened her braid. 'No one's answered that riddle. If a key exists, I'm determined to find it.'

'Or not.' Elaira returned his needful embrace. While the fragrances of honey and cinnamon met his swift, inhaled breath, she laced her hands at the base of his neck. The muscle was rock-hard with tension. 'You've taken too much weight on your shoulders. You can't spare everyone's threatened life with only your two mortal hands.'

'Could I stop trying?' he asked. 'Who would I be, then?' Green eyes wide open, he savoured her face. Each candle-lit detail became more exquisite with the delight of his familiarity.

'My own love,' she chaffed. 'You are freezing! Didn't you notice?'

'I had.' He gathered her up, herb-stained skirts and mussed braid and soft laughter. She held him close as he bore her to bed, chilled, and half-unspun from the depth of his seeking. Aware that such cherished nights must stay numbered until the Prime's plotting was thwarted, Elaira gave without stint. Morning came, always, too quickly. She let him go, open-handed, and smothered her grief for each moment that his restless quest commanded his absence.

Small things became gifts: given Sidir's bold lead, Kyrialt accepted the enchantress as royal mate under his oath of crown service. That grace lent the strength to match Glendien's saucy flirting with dignified tolerance. If not ties of friendship, Elaira could teach her the principles behind the ways Ath's adepts mixed their simples. The young woman often accompanied her efforts to ease the suffering populace. Willing enough to dirty her hands, Glendien helped treat the chilblains in the garrison, as well as the coughs and the elders' sore joints and complaints. If her wildness sometimes strained Elaira's schooled patience, or her passionate jabs incessantly sought to tease Arithon's masculine instincts, no provocation she could devise shifted anyone's inner composure.

Doggedly set, the Prince of Rathain pursued the old wisdom imbued in the citadel and never once broached the inevitable sacrifice: that Jeynsa's deliverance must come at the cost of the protected love shared with Elaira.

'We will find this, again,' he avowed in the dark, while the black sword murmured star song around them. He cupped her face. Kissed her lips with a tenderness fit to sear spirit and flesh incandescent. 'Whatever comes, know that I live and breathe for the day that no obstacle stands between us.'

Immersed deeply enough to track his intent, etched into the light of his being, Elaira sensed the reach of his focus. His defiant promise was a blind claim, with the future uncertain before them. Torbrand's descendant: *he would brook no half-measures.* Though the twined glory they had nearly experienced in Halwythwood could only be glimpsed, through the citadel's warding, his vow affirmed that commitment. As clear in his heart was the love in the choice that had claimed his blood oath at Athir: the imperative drive to uphold the mysteries sustaining Paravian survival. He had come too far to abandon that charge, which *also* demanded her place at his side, in the ecstasy of freed union.

'For this, we exist,' she agreed, melted into his living embrace. She let the musician's hands, that fore-promised the brightening hope of the world, uplift her, cherished and close. 'I will be there for you, whatever the trial demanded to secure our freedom.'

And the night fled again. Alone in the icy, steel gleam of dawn, Elaira ate her light meal. She loaded her satchel for the day's rounds, while Glendien grumbled at being rousted from bed, despite Kyrialt's warmth being absent.

'Your man's out to fetch water,' Elaira replied, tart, while the stinging epithets continued, muffled under wool-blankets. She added without sympathy, 'If you dally to bathe, I'll be at the barracks, treating yesterday's toll of bashed fingers and aching heads.'

Crisp words reached coherence. 'Are you mad?' Glendien's tangled, bright hair emerged into daylight. 'There's not enough spirits left in this citadel to drive any drunk to a hangover.'

'You'd be surprised.' Elaira flung on her mantle. 'There's still the odd stash that hoarders like Dakar lose, gambling.'

Glendien fixed her with a distempered glance as she swept past the work-table towards the stair. 'You aren't going alone. The mood in the citadel's ugly enough to make Kyrialt spit like a hackled cat.'

'He has that choice,' the enchantress agreed. 'I was not born to soothe his taxed temperament.'

Elaira departed without hearing the retort fired back in forest-bred accents. Given such driving hunger for novelty, Glendien would kiss her man into submission, and probably catch up by sunrise.

Outside, hooded against the chill mist, Elaira stepped onto the narrow foot-bridge over the chasm. At the arch of the span, she encountered Duke Bransian, planted four-square in her path. Relieved his armed pique at least had avoided Kyrialt's hair-trigger instincts, the enchantress seized the initiative. 'Whether or not your complaint can be answered, I will have you step aside.'

'I say your prince means to forswear his promise,' Bransian declared, despite himself rubbing the crick that yesterday's sparring had set in his neck. Hard-bitten and mean as an aging lion, and too proud to ask for restoratives, he snarled, 'What else does his Grace buy, except wasted time? How long should we dangle our hopes on his wool-gathering?'

Before he ran on, lamenting the grain shortage, or the recent movements of enemy troops observed by the men keeping harbour-side watch, Elaira rejected the premise. 'My lord of Alestron, we already know the extent of your citizens' predicament.'

'Aye, well!' groused Bransian. 'You should be aware if your Prime is involved. I've seen her nefarious meddling before! Her stirring fingers might raise Lysaer's curse. This war is nothing straightforward or canny. What sort of stake does your sisterhood hold? Are they angling for our defeat?'

The duke sucked a faxed breath, while Elaira confronted his challenge, unflinching. She would not lie; could not disclaim that Selidie Prime was not playing on Lysaer's warped instincts with ill intent. Yet before allowing the insult, that her beloved's activity was aimless cowardice, she cut the duke's thundering bluster short shrift. 'You won't shift the Teir's'Ffalenn's choices through me! Learn from your mistakes. Save your effort.'

'Well, my people aren't his Grace's bargaining chips!' Bransian rebuked with vexed warning. 'Not like those duped shepherd bowmen at Vastmark, to play at cold-cock war and posture for his tricks of sleight-of-hand conjury.'

'No, not this time!' Elaira snapped, white. 'However you push, his Grace knows your bull-headed methods too well. He's awake to the error that bought his past blood debts and too wise to be goaded through temper. You'll not press him. Or move him to solve this with weapons, however you angle to try.'

Bransian raised his brows in reproof, while the wind tugged at the iron-grey hair that poked from beneath his cap helm. 'Don't claim the bland pacifist he postures in public! Or is it not true, that the Prince of Rathain never sleeps, except by his unsheathed sword?'

'Yes,' Elaira said, steadfast. 'Because the star song the Paravians laid into the steel sings him to safe harbour, and guards his integrity.'

Yet Bransian had a deaf ear for all nuance. He edged aside, finally, allowed her to pass, since no threat of arms could unseat the enchantress's uncompromised honesty.

Another day passed, and another. Then, as the turn of the tide might begin with the whisper sown by an eddy, the deadlocked grip of the siege shifted its precarious balance.

Duke Bransian was back in his element the instant the incoming mirror signal brought the messenger banging on his bed-chamber door. Urgent speech, through the panel, let in breaking news: the deathless stagnation had broken. Enemy forces now crossed their drawn line for a sortie in the dark before dawn.

'The watch turrets have spied furtive movement, ashore!' gasped the breathless young man that Liesse tripped the latch and admitted. 'Seems a sneak effort to launch skiffs carried in over land. They'll shortly be trying to breach our inside harbour from behind the guarded chain.'

'About time we had an opportune target!' The duke thrashed off the bed-clothes, his scowl melted into an effusive mood as he snatched for his clothing and weapons. 'Lysaer's Lord Commander's got ice in his veins. Kept his battle-lines planted so long, it's a wonder his troops haven't sprouted like daisies.' Clad enough for decency, Bransian bowled past his wife. With his boots left abandoned in her outstretched hands, he bolted, still talking apace. 'We'll give the poor bastards a fitting retort, since ours are foamed white at the mouth for the chance to bash heads.'

Minutes later, his familiar hulked form loomed over the sea-side embrasure. With fists braced on the battlement, he heard the details from the captain on duty, whose crisp speech was not Mearn's. The youngest s'Brydion sibling had not stood that post since the forced assize for Rathain's formal settlement.

Bransian grinned. 'If the fools think we're napping, we'll let them come in.'

His lazy stretch unkinked the sleep from his bones. His breech laces half-tied, he stood on bare feet, hauberk and mail tossed on over his night-shirt, and his helm crammed atop his mussed hair. Too rushed to trifle with buck-ling his sword-belt, he had brought his weapon unsheathed. The massive blade lay on the wall at hand's reach, while he strained to peer through the dark-ness. 'Ath! Just look at yon pack of foxes creeping in! They'll have my warm welcome. Get the Sea Gate's heavy mangonels trained. Then I want six of the arbalests that hurl lesser stones, and not shafts. Mount four of those under the wharf-side embrasure. Have the others set on piled rocks, flush with the boards of the docks. We've got calm, and the low tide in our favour. The platforms need do no more than keep the torsion ropes dry, and the men will only get wet as they crank the winch and release.'

'We've had the mangonels swivelled, first thing.' The captain coughed behind his mailed fist. 'But the arbalests? Man! Those cockle-shell boats will explode into slivers, to some Sunwheel officer's shame. He'll be on his knees wailing for Light, once the first boulders plonk into the laps of his oarsmen.'

Bransian rubbed brisk hands in the cold and bellowed for someone to fetch him a cloak. 'We're the life of the party, waging a war. If Lysaer's faithful can't sort that out, they'll take what we sock in their guts till they're mumbling their unhallowed creed to the Fatemaster. Just keep our men quiet! I want these tres-passers in close enough to get stomped like the flies on a dog pile.'

The Light's covert sappers never drifted under the Sea Gate wharf to make landfall as they had planned. Alestron's trained crews placed their harbourfront engines, and on the duke's signal, let fire. The foray was systematically smashed into drift-wood and silenced disaster. Dawn broke, with no more shrilling, agonized screams. A flotsam of corpses and wrecked planks rode the ebb tide, with Bransian spouting his manic ebullience.

'Numbskulls!' he declared, launched off to scrounge a late breakfast. 'Had the arse itch from sitting through sermons, then puckered up their eager, young lips and kissed face-to-face with stupidity. One can hope that lot never lived long enough to plough bastards onto a wench. War could get too easy if the ignorant breed sires up clutches of idiot soldiers.'

If the duke was happy, noon gave rise to elation when the pre-dawn assault proved to be a feint for a subsequent effort, to infiltrate the ruined town and place archers across the tidal chasm. Alestron's drilled crews responded forthwith. Shot slung from the trebuchets brought down the infested walls, with the enemy screams loud on the midday breeze, and their mangled bones and bloody, crushed flesh macerated under the ruin.

'Where's your mincing, wee snip of a masterbard, now?' Bransian crowed in high fettle to Talvish. Since the blond captain's company was vindictively reassigned the drudge labour of scrubbing the privies, the duke liked to snipe with disparaging comments. 'Is his Grace still dithering, one ear clapped to cold rock, insisting our fight can be won without bloodshed?'

When the victim shrugged off that sour baiting, the duke added, loud enough to reach anyone else within earshot. 'Ought to fetch your prince here. Show him how virile men get things done! Or do you really believe you'll live to grow old at the heels of a cringing moppet?'

Talvish grinned. His easy nature did not come unglued, despite the disfavour earned by his changed loyalty. 'If any of us survive to die free, then someone must shift the Alliance war host away from your gates. That can't be accomplished by hurling a few rocks, however much fun you have trying.'

In fact, today's petty attacks only jabbed every veteran instinct. Arithon's presence must wake Desh-thiere's curse: each aggressive move meant that Lysaer slipped closer to the plunge to untenable madness.

As Bransian must realize also, underneath his chaffing slurs. 'I can't trust you, perhaps, now you're Arithon's puppet. Still, I know you well enough to ask why you aren't speaking your mind, when that ornery glint in your eye says Dharkaron's Five Horses are riding you.'

Yet Talvish's fierce worry stayed tucked in reserve: that surely, the Teir's'Ffalenn might be the more vulnerable to his half-brother's assault, now that the yoke of cursed influence had been lifted. Arithon would not lose restraint at this pass. Regrounded in mastery, he *could* reject the use of dire force, even if need demanded a fight to defend himself.

Stonewalled to the last by Talvish's silence, the duke sought the final word. 'Hear fair warning, my friend! If Arithon continues to sit on his arse, waiting for rocks to hatch chicks, one of my sentries is certain to lose his natural temper and knife him.'

'Through Sidir's ready sword,' Talvish said, straight-faced.

To which stark rebuff, Bransian stalked off with a jingle of steel to target his grousing elsewhere.

No mounting pressure of public disgust swerved Arithon from his abstruse cause. By then, he tapped the stonework in the Mathiell Gate's left-side drum-tower. Clad in his worn leathers and Davien's rich cloak, he sat as still as the day, limned in the ice-fall of sunlight, while the wintry air quivered off the warmed rock, scoured a bleached white by the elements. He had not shifted position for hours, while time's stream seemed to part and slip past him. Sidir stood his ground with a hunter's fixed patience, until afternoon waned, and a saffron sunset stained the low-lying cloud banks.

Arithon arose then with an air of finality. Unspeaking, he wended his way towards the guest tower. As he walked through Alestron's darkening thorough-fares, the evening around him stayed cheerless: another severe cut had short-ened the rations. Children wailed in the tent shelters jumbled into the muddied practice grounds. Taut-faced mothers complained. Angry young men met on the street-corners, while the tired town guard hauled water by hand, and shoveled the reeking cart-loads of waste, brusque to the point of explosion. If Sidir met such hardship with forest-bred stoicism, Alestron's folk were never bred to endure such pinching uncertainty.

The Companion noted the changed, glass-stark edge to his liege's habit of silence, yet had the wisdom to withhold his questions. He endured the catcalls dogging their heels, perhaps recalling the past, once, Rathain's prince had carved whistles to distract the toddlers when crisis had shadowed Deshir's threatened clans during childhood. The frivolity had masked an active defence.

Others had no such experience to bolster the onslaught of mounting pres-sure. Though Fionn Areth vented balked steam in the taverns with Dakar, and Kyrialt fretted to redirect Glendien's shameless badgering, Arithon did not unburden. He kept his own counsel until the late night, when he was alone with Elaira. 'I found no good news, beloved.'

They curled together on the wooden bench before the banked fire, while the north gusts whined down the flue and flicked sparks across the slate apron. The chill huddled them beneath a shared blanket, as the sparse fuel burned down. Elaira traced the jet hair at Arithon's nape, raising shivers deep in his viscera. 'I daresay your diligent hours of study cannot have been wasted effort.'

'No.' The lift of his chin denoted the pain sprung from his cutting frustra-tion. 'But my best hope has foundered. All of my gifts, to the limit of talent, have granted no avenue to spare Bransian's domain. The Paravian wardings laid into this citadel are too deep a force. They cannot be moved to man's bidding. However I ask, or assay strains of harmony, I can't find the key to turn such a power to serve in relief.' Anguish broke through as he admitted, 'Though I would spare lives, the greater mysteries are too wild for our mortal reckoning!'

Elaira laid her head on his chest. The same distressed beat raced his pulse. Arithon was a spirit that *always would* argue the sting of a hard-fought defeat.

'I can spare Jeynsa, maybe,' he allowed, for the first time broaching the prospect of failure. Even with his face muffled in her scented hair, his strained doubt could no longer be masked. Or the uncertainty, as he added, 'How much more than that, only Daelion knows! The lyranthe can't speak here. Her sound is too refined. I've no help to call on. Just what inadequate skills I can weave through the purpose the Paravians forged into Alithiel.'

'Those things are not small. And you are no less, Teir's'Ffalenn.'

Yet amid the silence that fell as the coals flickered down into darkness, the enchantress sensed the fibre of the innermost man. Before others, she shared the decision locked in his Masterbard's heart.

'You will act on the morrow,' she stated.

He moved. Tipped up her face, that he could meet her eyes, his own deep as evergreen ravaged by winter. Before she cried out, he savoured a kiss that was poignantly bitter-sweet. 'I must. Though Dharkaron knows, I could wish that every bright star would fall from Ath's heavens, beforehand.'

One last night, they would have, to indulge their rare love, held secure by the stones of the citadel. His arms closed. Linked to his enchantress with all his fierce strength, he swept her up and bore her, cherished as song, to the bed. There she could not do aught but succour his need, and savour the joy only found in his matchless presence.

Attack visited the deserted outer fortress again before dawn. Repeated light strikes unleashed by Lysaer rattled the casements and shuddered the guest keep's foundations. The black sky rinsed red. Fire silhouetted the drum-towers flanking the Mathiell Gate. Across the tide-race, vacant buildings exploded, masonry unravelled to rubble. Tossed wreckage flew air-borne. The crenels that once hung the Wyntok Gate melted to slag and collapsed into the flooding channel. Steam clogged the cold air, while the scent of brimstone wafted across Alestron's secure inner battlements.

Although Lysaer's display claimed no lives, and ruined no more than the blasted ground of the outlying town, the virulent power of his inborn gift sowed fresh fear. However Duke Bransian encouraged his troops, he could not stem shaken morale. The refugee families packed in the baileys turned on a breath from hungry, to desperate.

Seasoned sentries quailed at their posts. Livid, they watched the bulwarks that had sheltered their homes since their birth become cratered to wreckage. Today, from the warded walls of the heights, they were made aware that the Paravian protections safeguarded no more than their breathing flesh.

The purposeful life they had promised their loved ones had lost direction. Day upon day, they could only sustain their meaningless, sorry existence.

Lysaer's cursed might possessed no moral bounds, and no conscience. Man, or woman, or innocent child who set foot outside the citadel would become just as wantonly reduced to ash. The duke's people were helpless as cornered rats. They had risked everything, holding their ground for no more than the gleam on a principle.

Tomorrow changed nothing. They would starve without rescue, their children's well-being at risk for a bankrupted future. Hope died, and laughter, along with every wistful, sweet fancy that offered them warmth and happiness.

Despair struck, of a depth to darken the dawn. If Arithon might have acted before, the staging-point for his effort now suffered a cruel reverse. From difficult, he faced a feat beyond hardship.

His farewell to Elaira had already been said. Arisen by the stripped thread of his courage, and wearing yesterday's garments, he seemed insubstantial in forest leathers, dyed black, and the mantle stitched with silver embroidery, gifted by the whim of a Sorcerer. What lay beyond words had been conveyed by his tenderest care, and the intimate congress exchanged through the night. He bent his head, touched his cheek to Elaira's raised palm. Then he took up the sword, forged at Isaer from star-fallen metal by the artistry of three ancient races.

When Sidir arrived, Rathain's prince knelt, the traditional acknowledgement of crown obligation bonded under sworn service. 'Liegeman,' he stated, formally brief, 'enact my royal charge for the sake of your kingdom. The task I lay on you, before life and death: safeguard Jeynsa. Return home with all speed to your people, and Feithan, and defend the free wilds of Halwythwood.' Arithon straightened. The grave parting that could not find a care-free smile became a firm clasp of wrists. 'Ath's grace, and bright guidance guard all your days.'

Sidir was near weeping, as Rathain's heir stepped out. Last of Torbrand's lineage, he did not go alone: at his back on this critical hour went Shand's honour-gift of Kyrialt, once Teir's'Taleyn. Overmatched by his muscular escort, Arithon did not look back, but crossed the narrow foot-bridge, under the rose light of dawn. Cat-slender, he did not seem any force to stand down the cursed rage that now creased the air with crackling, white bolts.

While stone rumbled and shook, slagged to gouts of red magma, Arithon made his way through the twisting narrows of the citadel's streets. By the stairs laid by centaur masons, his rapid step took him upwards, towards Watch Keep. He did not go unremarked. Some, stiffly solemn, saw him pass with resentment. Where once they had followed, expectant with hope, a fortnight of his isolate silences had poisoned goodwill to rebuff. Some jeered. More, whose craft shops were being razed by the violence of a cursed half-brother, called out insults, blaming their bitter misfortunes on Duke Bransian's ill-starred alliance.

'Why should s'Ilessid attack, but for you, Teir's'Ffalenn?'

And once, with venom, 'Why else, bastard-born!'

A red-faced wife hurled a bucket of slop hard on the heels of the prince. 'Perhaps we suffer for the low fact that your blood-line was saved by a harlot!'

The hatred that burdened the morning was palpable, while the ground shook to Lysaer's assault. The ugly crowd by the wayside kept shouting, their mood *almost* pitched to throw stones. None dared raise a hand. Kyrialt's presence denoted the living witness of Shand, and the crown scion they reviled still remained Fellowship-sanctioned. His person might not be touched, although outraged voices decried that his fickle character shamed his royal station.

If Arithon heard, his indifference appeared unassailable. A wraith in dark clothes, he stepped through the wreathed smoke and mist, that the sun's early rays pierced above the steep eaves of the roof-tops. He made his way beyond the last, guttered drain, where the paving lapsed into mud footpaths. The frost-brown grass of the commons no longer grazed cattle or goats. He walked on, shocked by the recoil that slammed through the headland at each strike from his half-brother's hand.

Here, the glaring charge of shed light made his features seem spun from white glass. Arithon did not look aside. As day brightened, Kyrialt saw what Alestron's goodwives could not: that contact with the earth seemed to flinch through drawn flesh. His Grace would not speak, now. Each breath deliberate, he forged ahead up the steep, switched-back trail.

The tower at the crest of the promontory stayed under vigilant patrol. Two sentries challenged, surprised by the invasion of their staked turf.

'Give way!' stated Arithon, past heed for propriety. 'On peril of your lives, do not stop me.'

'Watchword, first!' came the bristled response. The guards were large men, chapped red from exposure. Entrusted for courage, they were also afraid, with the light raging on in actinic bursts and the rolling thunder of concussive report.

Arithon had no statement to give. His fixated stare never wavered. While he showed no aggression, and his sword remained sheathed, point down in the folds of his mantle, the fact he came armed riled the sentries.

'Hold your weapons!' Kyrialt snapped. 'His Grace is in mage-trance!' Shown dubious scorn, he said with crisp authority, 'Yes! I do know the signs. I watched him raise the centaur wardings on Selkwood, and again, when he faced the mysteries that hallow the King's Grove in Alland.'

While the bearded soldiers glared in suspicion, they still must acknowledge the prince's sworn man.

'Let my liege pass!' Kyrialt appealed. 'By the name of my family, I will swear surety for his harmless intentions.'

Which stark declaration could not be ignored: the s'Taleyn sire's belligerent honesty was held in widespread renown. If Kyrialt stood false on Lord Erlien's reputation, the Kingdom of Shand would owe the s'Brydion no less than a crown reparation.

Prince Arithon pronounced with a quiet but ominous edge, 'I have not come to abet my half-brother's destruction, or to inflame the grip of Desh-thiere's curse.'

Since no man alive might guess his intent, the sentries must strike or stand down. They moved, not for Kyrialt's word in the end, or for royalty's forth-right insistence.

'Our duke's gone up ahead of you,' warned the taller guardsman. 'Try him at your own risk.'

Arithon entered the squat tower that commanded the view surrounding the citadel and the spread of the signal turrets overlooking the harbour. Inside, past the ground-level ward-room, a spiral stair led to a second chamber, where a ladder accessed the wind-swept catwalk above. Through the flurry of men startled up from their posts, Arithon mounted the rungs.

Kyrialt's worried agility followed, while Bransian's truculent bellow filtered down through the open hatch. 'Bedamned if I like this unnerving assault! Surely such force serves some evil design beyond an accursed fit of madness.'

'Lysaer has a purpose.' Black hair wind tousled, green eyes wide in trance, Arithon emerged through the trap. Sword in hand, his mantle on fire with silver embroidery, he stood up on the gust-raked battlement, with its fire-pan and signal mirrors sheltered by a peaked roof, ringed around by a catwalk for archers. The sun's red disk, risen, threw Bransian's shadow, and cast the slighter man into eclipse.

The duke's narrowed eyes showed contempt as he turned. 'Upstart sorcerer. Can you know?'

Wind flapped the mantle, and scattered blood high-lights across the rich threadwork. 'I have seen on the tides of s'Ahelas far-sight.' With an ominous calm, Arithon added, 'Pound enough force through the headland, and even firm bed-rock will shear.'

'Lysaer seeks to tumble the *cliff* into the estuary?' Bransian's scowl darkened. 'That excessive display won't breach our walls!'

'Not at once.' Arithon's manner stayed queerly remote. 'They will send sappers. Mine the scarp under your warded walls, as your crews at the trebuchets falter.'

The duke spat. 'Not while I live to prevent them!'

'You won't,' stated Arithon, and on that shocked note, side-stepped, and moved to the rim of the battlement.

'I could kill, for your insolence!' Duke Bransian howled, while Kyrialt cleared the trap-door at speed and placed his own person between.

The duke goaded, furious, 'What are you worth, prince? A few paltry visions, delivered too late?'

But Arithon seemed beyond provocation. Immersed as a dancer who followed a melody nobody else could perceive, he turned back his mantle and drew Alithiel. He touched the flat of the upright blade against his forehead for a suspended instant. Then, as though reverent, he lifted the sword. Mortal man, and the first of his kind who *ever* attempted to wield the black steel's primal purpose, he apologized first for presumption.

Then, the duke's rage a gathering storm at his back, and Lysaer's cursed fury destroying a hill-side before him, he bowed his head. Softly as a whisper, he started to sing.

The melody emerged with the beat of a dirge, cadenced in measured Paravian. His spare a cappella delivered each note with the ringing purity struck off tempered steel. At the crux, no one present could do aught but listen as Athera's Masterbard engaged his art.

Sorrow spoke through him, the veil of indifference torn away. The fortnight just spent in strict silence had never been what it seemed: every moment Arithon had not deigned to comment, throughout days and nights, as he listened into the secretive quiet of stone, *he had not been oblivious*. Never had he distanced himself from the misery of Alestron's populace. Nothing escaped his exacting attention: not the wails of a single distressed infant; never, the cries of frustrated anger; no word and no sight and no hurt, however inconsequential. Not once had Arithon closed his mind or heart to the pain and privation around him. Masterbard, sorcerer, attention to myriad detail wove his invention. The groans of the deprived, and the strained exhaustion of soldiers, and the lost laughter of children crafted his lines. Like the filled vessel painstakingly emptied, *all* that he held, he poured into song, while the sundering boom of Lysaer's assault framed his ominous refrain.

That raw light flared and cracked incandescent reflections off the Paravian sword he held upright. Spear-shaft straight, Arithon sang of himself. His humility scoured, for a depth of experience that fell too far short of the wisdom that *might* have disarmed a cursed conflict. All the ache of his short-falls, every prior defeat he had suffered and forgiven within Kewar's maze, he restated in sorrowful honesty.

He sang of hope, forgotten, and joy abandoned, and the balm of healing and peace. Then, as the tears streamed down Kyrialt's cheeks, and Duke Bransian covered his face before his stunned officer, Arithon forged his heart-wrenching melody into a blazing appeal. To the magics imbued in the sword, whose latent force held the power of air to inspire the freedom of lifting transcendence, he asked: for grace, and in human admission of fault, a demand that begged footing for change.

The sword shimmered, then lit. Incandescent, the opal runes streamed sound and light. This was not only the chord that had once Named the winter constellations, but something *other*, that upended belief. As though Arithon's song had spun the first overture, the sword's response flowered as no living ear had heard, and no history at Althain Tower had ever recorded: a sound that climbed register and entered fast silence, underscored by a light that waxed blinding as a refined star come to earth.

The shock travelled outward. Its unleashed force ranged through the citadel like bolt lightning that engendered no following thunder-clap. Only pure energy, sweet as a struck chime.

Rathain's prince grasped the sword. Alone, he sustained its vibration, a note beyond hearing that answered the searing appeal in his question by harmony.

The miracle could not be contained within walls: on the mainland, Lysaer s'Ilessid collapsed. His crazed, elemental explosions cut short as he dropped unharmed at the feet of his banner-bearer. Still, the clarion cry of Alithiel ranged outward, unstoppable. More than Alestron's folk were affected. Every spirit enthralled by the Alliance's cause, no matter which side of the conflict, all were compelled to take pause: from camp-followers to grooms at the picket lines, to the servants who polished their dedicate officer's boots.

On a note beyond hearing, those who loved war heard only rage, and these would seek solace in fighting. Others who yearned for creative peace moved to abandon the field and return to their distant homes, or, in the case of Alestron's free citizens, to uproot their families and claim life, resettled amid the free wilds. While the untamed grace forged by Alithiel sustained, hostilities calmed, with the blockade in the estuary paralyzed.

Sidir heard the call, and Elaira, and Jeynsa. Each one felt the tingling touch on the heart; heard the clarion cry to seek liberty. They would leave the citadel by the Sea Gate, packed onto galleys and barges and small craft amid throngs of parents, who sang as they gathered things needful for uncertain journeys. The opening promised was granted, that day, to all who sought a new beginning.

Not least in the upwelling surge of release, Dame Dawr woke, replete in the warmth of her bed. Eyes unsealed, she found the keys to her joy, but not anymore in the flesh: frail age rested at last with the knowledge her heirs had been offered their chance to survive her.

'I am well content,' she told her devoted man-servant, then smiled with the fresh bloom of girlhood. Her last breath blessed the Masterbard's name, as loved beyond pain, her dauntless spirit was lifted to soar on the flame of ecstatic departure.

Mayhem

The note Arithon raised off Alithiel's drawn blade also struck the engaged crystal used by Koriathain to guard their field camp. The ancient quartz shattered, blasted to flying shards and a puff of glassine, white powder. The stone's demise rent the outer wards of protection, which raised a shriek of pure rage from the senior enchantress who minded the watch. Upset roused the camp. A frantic stampede of ranking initiates rushed to restore the smashed defences, and bolster the inside wards, now set under threat.

No sister paused to stand upon dignity, while the deep security of the order's compound was threatened. The Prime herself burst from the curtained enclosure that served as her private quarters. Pale hair in tangles, and her cream flesh clad in naught but her shift, Selidie surveyed the damage with furious eyes.

Chaos tore through the neat rows of her healers' tents. Whatever the plague just unleashed on the sisterhood, the whirlwind unravelled the spells which secured the set stakes against mischance. Guy-ropes cracked to the belly of canvas, flogged in the gusts to thrashed seams.

'Get me the lane watch!' Prime Selidie screamed. She slapped off the hands of the distraught novice, arrived in her wake in the foolish pursuit of regaling her in proper dress. 'Bring the sister on duty here. Now!'

'She knows nothing!' a breathless fourth-rank responded, just come in, and blotting a laid-open cheek. 'Only a clash of arcane frequencies fit to raise fire and storm could seed such an onslaught against us.'

'Bane of my existence!' Prime Selidie snapped at the trembling young initiate, who still cowered, clutching her mantle. 'Find the senior peeress. Send her to me!'

The central wardings were *not* going to hold: as the cresting wave hammered the mastered defences, laced over the inner pavilions, the crystals focused as anchors keened under mounting stress. Selidie faced the horrific disaster: every major focus jewel in her keeping could soon be exposed to this hammering threat. Irreplaceable tools, each one was required to spear-head the Koriani agenda. Wrapped in silk were Elaira's personal quartz, and the most rarefied wands attuned for healing, as well as the ancient set of matched tourmalines that had shielded the Prime's entourage for centuries before the order's Atheran residence. In its box, priceless, the Skyron aquamarine stood second to the disastrously compromised Great Waystone.

'I'll have a living wall raised!' the Prime cried as the gaunt peeress arrived at a breathless run. 'Go! In my name, make this happen!'

'Madam, your will!' The rattled senior bolted to gather the resident inner circle, and create the tranced shield from the breathing flesh of their sister initiates.

Selidie shouted more orders to direct her hysterical servants. While the upset outside ripped her compound to havoc, inside her central pavilion, attendants and boy wards collided in the rush to lock and seal precious items inside wood chests lined in copper. Dust blew in on the knifing, chill air. Banners streamed, unruly, and cracked their pole standards. Upheaved stakes with their over-turned sigils of guard whistled air-borne, and tore the stout canvas that sheltered the Alliance wounded. Screams arose through the hubbub, shrill with panic and pain, as the ridge-pole on one of the healers' tents snapped its mortised sockets and toppled.

A seeress's rallying cry sent more initiates scrambling to stem the disaster, while others, snatched from the throes of activity, became culled to build the tranced circle to buffer the beseiged encampment. Crisis forced novices and seasoned enchantresses to act side by side, in their dash to assist. They linked hands, encircled the main pavilion, and melded their powers, subservient to their Prime's will. Knowledge perfected through millennia of practice steadied their combined effort. Against uncertainty and terror, their ragged chant rose, blended into a gull's cry of female voices, welded into aligned strength.

What a crystal focal point could not sustain, human resource must counter. Each sister recognized her stark peril: in service, her life was expendable. Under oath to her Prime, each one might be used or discarded for the greater need of the order. At any cost, the boundary they secured must not fail. And no guarded line they might raise could outlast the fallible stamina of breathing flesh. Sharp under that pressure, Selidie accepted her overrobe. She sat down, discomposed, while her flinching maidservant combed and dressed her fly-away hair. Throughout, she demanded Lirenda's attendance, speaking through the tug of the brush and the rake of gemmed combs that pinned up her coiffure. 'Find out what's happened! By any means! The order cannot afford the weakness of ignorance.'

No crystal might be risked for a scrying. Whatever beset their luckless encampment, the effects were too volatile for a fixed matrix. More orders summoned three younger novices as vessels to be tapped for straight power. As they knelt, obedient, the prime cipher commanded: their green talents were pooled to spear-head Lirenda's expedient probe. The response the former First Senior unveiled fanned cold fury to redoubled outrage. For the force at large was of *Arithon's* making, a swell of pitched sound that threatened to strip every focus crystal within reach. Worse, the ranging harmonics up-ended resonant spellcraft, unravelling the flux contained by chained sigils into ungoverned mayhem.

'The conjury itself is a Paravian working,' the head peeress determined at length. 'Its vectored intent will not harm life and limb. But all quartz under load will be damaged. Ones not in work are at risk of being energetically stripped of their imprinted records.'

'That's quite enough to destroy our initiative, expunge our kept archives, and rifle our innermost secrets!' Prime Selidie snarled. 'This goes beyond provocation and insolence!'

Actual facts proved demeaningly worse, as the early reports trickled in from outside: the order was not the intentional target, but the by-standing casualty of a disruption aimed at the Alliance's war camp. The first of the distraught afflicted poured in, as the Prime's narrow feet were being laced into her shoes. The sisterhood's healers received hardened camp-followers and drudges with chapped hands, each bearing startling tales: that an enthrallment arranged by the Spinner of Darkness was clearing the Alliance campaign field. A wave of desertion swept Lysaer's encampments. Whole companies disbanded, harnessing the teams that moved supply, or seizing the ox-trains that man-oeuvred the siege engines. The laden wagons were all rolling out. They left in no order, oblivious to the outcries of dedicate officers. Galleys vacated the seaward blockade, then sailed, loaded down with trained troops. Most men had abandoned their armour and tents, and even their surcoats and weaponry. Others marched with the clothes on their backs, their kit knapsacks crammed with provender filched from the cook-shacks.

Prime Selidie listened and took stock. By now, she could hear the spontaneous migration that clogged the trade-road. Snatches of riotous laughter and singing carried in on the morning breeze. 'Where is Lysaer s'Ilessid?'

No one knew. Loose rumour conflicted. Some folk claimed he had ascended to Athlieria, riding the flash of a light-bolt. Others insisted he had jumped, or fallen, from the unstable scarp and drowned in the tide-race by the citadel. The starry-eyed fools who lounged, swilling ale, swore the Blessed Lord had stormed into the citadel and demolished the s'Brydion duke and his brothers. The gamut had just one common thread: the white horse with its gleaming caparisons was found wandering riderless, by one of the grooms.

A chit, big-bellied with a soldier's get, guffawed when she was questioned further. 'What use has an avatar for a mount, when at whim, he might claim heaven's wings?'

By noon, a more credible story came with a foot-page who asked for a tincture. 'A small band of loyal officers with the honour guard brought a draped litter into the command tent. Their burden was delivered into the care of my divine Lordship's valet.' The same servant had sent him, the page added with pride. 'I've been asked to collect a remedy to reduce fever.'

'The wind-bag pretender has knocked himself prostrate!' the Prime's withered attendant declared. An acerbic woman whose decades of service adhered to benign practicality, she banged down a tray piled with tea-cakes, as though nibbling might ease the Prime's furious strain and quiet the bellowing upset. 'Such a profligate waste of elemental force! Ought to clip the s'Ilessid man's arrogance, to be flat on his rear, sweating back-lash.'

Prime Selidie had no opinion to add. Now clothed in state, enthroned in her chair, she seethed in silenced frustration. Her plot to play Lysaer through the curse, and the pressured assault she had hoped to unleash on the citadel, had become summarily thwarted. The malice that narrowed her beautiful eyes fore-promised a vengeful retort. 'We must seize the moment. Find an alternative angle, force a reverse, and recoup our advantage.'

That, or bow to an appalling defeat, with the primary crystals brought in from offworld destroyed beyond hope of replacement. The enchantresses now holding the precarious, last wardings were only human, and fallible. Once their circle collapsed, the blow to the order did not bear imagining.

'Time!' snapped Prime Selidie. 'How long can Arithon stand in the breach, upholding Paravian magecraft?' Could any master initiate endure the wild onslaught this brazen act must have summoned?

No one knew.

While the ranging assault wore on through the day, and the trial of resistance endured without let-up, the stop-gap placement of flesh-and-blood conjury stood off the derangement, just barely. Selidie fumed, a flushed doll mantled in violet. Before exhaustion unstrung her ranked talent, she must shoulder the risk and send out the best of her untried young girls. Knowledge was power: she rejected pity and dispatched the ones who were not yet sworn in, or attuned to bear a quartz crystal. With them went hand-picked, talentless servants trusted for their sharp eyes. Impatient, while her sent agents were abroad, the Prime hounded the crowding petitioners. She sifted through their petty accounts, seeking answers amid the coarse dialect of the washing-women and camp-followers who came asking for talismans. The latest included officers' equerries, whose excited complaints described an outbreak of inexplicable, comatose sleep.

That curiosity seemed worth pursuit. A first-level healer was given the errand. 'Strip your personal crystal,' Prime Selidie commanded. 'Take a copper amulet stamped with sigils for fiend bane, but alter the closing cipher to act for your own protection. If that construct holds off this Paravian crafting, go out on field rounds. Avoid the deserters. Stay unobtrusive. Examine these victims of unnatural sleep and bring back your findings forthwith!'

The young woman returned from the war camp, flushed and gasping with pain. The skin at her hip was blistered raw where the wardings in copper had stressed, and singed through her satchel. 'The defences held, madam, but for only an hour,' she related, trembling before the Prime's chair. 'I bore the discomfort until the hot metal set the cloth wrapping aflame.'

The remains of the stamped strip showed softened edges and fusing. 'Exposed for more time, the inscribed seals would have run molten!' exclaimed the shocked sister called in to consult.

'Sit, child!' Selidie urged her young charge. 'Be at ease. You've done well.' Her peremptory wave dispatched an attendant for burn salve and dressings. 'What did you find out in the officers' tents?'

The shaken girl resumed her report. 'This is no malady. The afflicted appear to be deeply asleep. Their minds are not broken. Their life signs do not labour. Though I could not scan auras without my crystal, I detected no harmful effects on these victims.' A gasped break, as a healer cut the singed shift away from the seared flesh underneath. 'The state seems like a profound suspension of spirit, as though the stricken are dreaming.' The queer correlation took longer to sort, that those who lay prostrate by Arithon's working were men of unshakeable devotion to Lysaer's cause.

The sixth-rank senior ventured her opinion. 'If they waken, they would make a singular weapon to prosecute war with cold fury.'

Which suggested a core following, its dross stripped away, pitched to spearhead a relentless blood-bath. Extreme fanatics would wield the Light's cause ahead of their own survival. The concept gave even Prime Selidie pause. Past question, today's action was shifting the balance by removing the temperate hearts who might have settled for truce.

The Prime's delicate jaw hardened. She withheld her orders to disband the healers' camp or retire the central pavilion. Ruled by fixed purpose and stubborn fury, no Koriani Matriarch would yield to a crown prince's hand. Not before testing all options. Since Lirenda's experience knew the Teir's'Ffalenn best, Prime Selidie ploughed into her captive mind and ransacked for fresh inspiration.

One memory emerged, clear as the noon daylight, drawn from a past encounter. Years before, in a baiting exchange with Lirenda, Arithon had seized control of a Koriani scrying by asserting his bardic talent through air. Today's assault also rode on the winds. Dispersed upon the effortless breeze, such a crafting acknowledged no boundary. Logic suggested that an earth spell might run this bold assault to ground.

A gleam spiking her glance, Selidie discarded her forced rapport with Lirenda and spoke her next string of instructions. 'I want more copper talismans fashioned for baneward! Immerse these in water inside of a clay jug, stamped with seals to dissipate fire. Then find me a girl volunteer, or better, a boy ward who's due for a reprimand. Have him take several such constructs outside. Find out whether their charms can be trusted to frame a stable defence!'

'Earth sigils! How clever!' exclaimed the senior peeress, cut off straightaway for impertinence. 'Your will, of course, Matriarch.' Before the Prime's glowering censure, everyone fled but Lirenda, whose choice stayed proscribed.

The Matriarch paced. Up and down the lush carpet, over copper-thread patterns for ward and guard, the rich train of her robe hissed behind her. Pale, predatory, she trembled with nerves. The chants holding the protective circle outside came and went through the punching gusts that billowed the tent pavilion. While chill draughts leached the meagre heat thrown off by the braziers, Lirenda received no release. Forced to stay crouched upon a low hassock, she remained, disregarded as an idle tool until the Prime's need called for use of her talent.

Time crawled, until midafternoon, when word arrived that the stricken sleeper had reawakened. The frightened man-servant who returned for the order's learned help was dismayed to find his case heard in the presence of Selidie Prime. His master, he said, had stumbled erect, acting like a changed creature.

'He could not stop weeping. Then he ordered his tent and belongings packed straightaway to move out. Plaguing dreams,' the distraught fellow insisted, afraid for his charge's derangement. 'My lord sees nothing else but a horrific future, and claims that he witnessed his beloved family, broken and crying.'

The servant was given a strong sedative to assuage his stressed officer's grieving. Once he was sent off, Selidie called for additional counsel from the encampment's most advanced healer.

'By the servant's account, this bizarre phenomenon would appear to be slanted against Lysaer's favour,' the third-rank grey robe appraised. A raw-boned, kind woman, she flushed with unease before the high chain of command. Her skills revolved around day-to-day troubles, her best work beneath the Prime's notice. But not now, with the hospice reeling from the strange powers wrought in the citadel.

'Elaborate! At once.' Selidie's supremacy brooked no delays: by the sisterhood's oath, she demanded.

The sweating healer unburdened. 'The Light's dedicates might become sapped of conviction while they are deeply asleep. Suppose they arise afterward with their priorities reordered by dreaming? We don't know the range of the tonal harmonic a Paravian influence might engender, far less understand how that arcane force impacts an untrained human consciousness! If time's track is altered, these victims might visit a posited future. Whose morale would not crumple, if a husband was able to sense his abandoned wife's pain, or the bitter despair of his children?'

'We would see Lysaer's laid siege on Alestron torn apart at one stroke.'

Prime Selidie thumped her gloved wrist on the chair arm. She would *not* see her coveted quarry uncaged. Fierce rage broke all bounds, that Arithon s'Ffalenn might slip through her grasp with bloodless impunity.

'I will break this unnatural compulsion that's afflicting the Alliance followers!' the Prime Matriarch vowed. Since her useless hands could not cast the complex chains of sigils to weave the conjury, she fumed for the fact that she must demand help. Then fresh news arrived: that the construct which paired the clay jug with the talismans proved out her hopeful theory: an earth-linked defence could deflect the worst impact of Arithon's unorthodox working.

Deadly, now given the ground for response, Prime Selidie settled back in her chair. She would ply her fulcrum and shift the offensive back in her order's favour.

'Where is Parrien s'Brydion's renegade fleet? Fetch me an able seeress! One with natural talent. I want her to meld with the earth's flux without using a crystal matrix. Then have her link her birth-born gifts through Lirenda's power, directly. Move quickly!' Selidie gestured with incandescent anticipation. 'Find me the position of Alestron's war galleys at once!'

Bold timing must play Parrien's weakness into her order's design. Selidie smiled, inwardly smug. She could fashion a warding, grounded through earth, that would shelter those ship's companies from the effects of Arithon's influence. Then, through more sigils, the men's discontent could be pushed into mounting an assault on the mainland. They would strike while chaos distressed Lysaer's troops. No s'Brydion sea-wolf would question the source of their vicious drive to attack. Steered through hell-bent desire, who among them would not snatch the chance to cut a swath through the ranks of their enemies?

Evening fell, chased in by a searing north wind, and the lowering cloud of a storm front. Snow would fall, blinding, within a few hours, a hardship that posed a back-handed blessing to any who risked crossing the battle-lines. Heavy drifts buried the tracks of all fugitives: both those who fled from the ranks of the war host, and others, braving the white-out blizzard, who chose to abandon the pent misery at Alestron.

Cloaked in unobtrusive, plain clothes, the small party sent under the charge of Sidir rowed across the north bay of the estuary, packed into an open boat. The ebbing tide sped their passage, helped on by the rising wind. Scudded eight leagues past the citadel's watch beacons, they landed far outside of the chain that guarded the inner harbour. There, the huddle of chilled fugitives commandeered a farm-cart and rattled southward over the frozen ruts of the trade-road. Against the fast-falling dark, buffeted by whipping gusts, they unhitched the mule, reloaded the provisions in packs, and prepared to turn off the main thoroughfare.

Safety lay leagues from the site. Well past the Paravian standing stone that demarked the south bounds of Melhalla, the plain of Orvandir's free wilds rolled, wind-raked, a dangerous, exposed passage to reach Lord Erlien's secured encampment inside of Selkwood.

'Your lady?' Sidir inquired of Mearn, whose distracted concern fixed on Fianzia's gravid condition.

'Bearing up.' No complaint, but the bitterly agonized regret: that his wife's near-term pregnancy not only threatened the life of their cherished child but might fatally slow the escape, and hamper safe passage for all of them.

Sidir clapped Mearn's shoulder with brisk encouragement. 'Townsman! Our clans have birthed babes under hostile pursuit for more years than you've been alive. Trust our hardened experience.' His new bow crossed his shoulder, a powerful statement of forest-bred prowess. He would hunt the wary, dun deer at their grazing and trap the swift hare in the hollows. 'We won't starve.'

Mearn protested. 'But Fianzia –'

'Your lady,' snapped Sidir, 'will ride in a litter. Jeynsa knows how to cut the green boughs and weave withies. We won't suffer too much. This storm's nothing worse than we've handled with our women, caught out on Daon Ramon Barrens.'

'Then we rest in your hands,' Mearn gouged back, resentful. The unpleasant odds raised his hackles. Scavenging packs of league trackers were deadly, without adding the unpredictable motivations of Alliance deserters and refugee craftsmen. Though their party had slipped past the Alliance sentries and left behind the drawn lines of the siege, soon enough, the trade-roads and the open country-side would be jammed by today's unplanned exodus. No one might second-guess the result. Too many rough men were left foot-loose. Armed companies who had abandoned a strict discipline soon would encounter the pressures of short supply. Renegade soldiers and homeless civilians might try who knew what lawless acts out of desperation.

A wife so near term could not run, or withstand prolonged chill and privation. The grim husband was not sanguine. Mearn faced his precarious future with only two northern clan allies, Bransian's indebted captain, and four of his most trusted retainers. Family honour protested. Too many of Alestron's free citizens must be left at large to find their own way. That they might be guided by the odd field veteran, or seek protection with other rank-and-file men also leaving defence of the citadel scarcely settled his strident unease. 'I feel remiss. More than my forebears would brand me a coward for leaving blood-bound obligations.'

Turned to help Fianzia down from the tail-gate, Mearn almost rammed into Sidir, who had not moved: tempered lifelong by unjust persecution, the Companion gave the ideal of s'Brydion nobility short shrift. 'You *are* the living name of your family, now, and your wife's unborn heir, the hope of your future lineage!'

Mearn stared, lips pinched shut. The shock stayed too fresh, that Sevrand had chosen to stand beside Bransian inside the beleaguered citadel.

Sidir added, emphatic, 'Don't think for one moment you've chosen wrongly, or that the lives you protect are not paramount! If you try to turn back, Ath forgive, I must stop you! Good man, I would do so, that one day your child survives to applaud my priorities.'

'There is nothing to salvage, if your lineage dies here,' Jeynsa stated, come up beside him. 'You know your lady is too close to birth to endure the slow pace of group travel.'

Fianzia's cold fingers touched Mearn's turned cheek. This once, even her razor tongue did not upbraid his uncertainty. Words and tradition offered no comfort. Nor could the sound backing of old charter law ease the sting of exiled displacement. A clansman's place was to guard his progeny, and a father, to attend his child's birth and ensure a stable succession.

Neither Jeynsa nor Sidir would cave in to argument. Mearn set his teeth. Still bristling, he braced to steady his wife, who would bear the brunt in the trial to come. He *must* abide. Yet nobody living could salve his torn heart, or make him feel other than mortified. The rank fear persisted, that Fianzia might die under hardship in childbed. Winter would wait upon no human mercy. Their precious first-born might freeze, a corpse left to rot in an unmarked cairn.

A fierce slap on his shoulder caused him to spin, enraged for the offensive presumption.

Sidir snapped backwards and missed getting stabbed by the reflexive thrust of Mearn's dagger. Perverse creature, the forest-bred liegeman was smiling. 'Bide easy! We have a hard journey of fifteen leagues to reach the Paravian marker, but there, in a hidden place shored up with boulders, the clans have dug out a snug hideaway. The chamber's kept stocked with food and necessities for scouts pressed by hot-foot pursuit. We'll have secure shelter, I promise. But we've got to move before the deep snow.'

'Southward!' Disgruntled embarrassment stiffened Mearn's back as he resheathed his blade. 'What's on the plain of Orvandir for us?' Durn and Six Towers would not welcome his family name, now. Nor could swift flight reach the safe enclaves in Alland before Fianzia's pending travail.

Sidir shook his head, his weathered features softened to laughter. 'Mearn! You've been mewed up behind walls for too long. We are not going to Alland! Or north, to East Halla, but up-country to the reed-banks of the River Methyl. This cold snap will freeze that placid current to ice. We'll make speed in comfort on a carved sledge. Give me a fortnight, and this mule kept sound, and your lady will lie in under Verrain's protection, inside the fortress at Methisle.'

At which moment, when flagging hope dared to rekindle, the change none had noticed was pointed out by the garrison captain assigned to guard Sidir's return journey to Halwythwood. 'Your liege's Koriani enchantress has left us,' he said, striding in from rear-guard. 'And no, I did not see her leave.' As though any man might have swerved an initiate sister from her chosen course.

'Let her go!' Sidir stated, gruff. 'Elaira has her own business. She knows she could have asked for my help, had she needed the hand of a friend.' In harsh truth, Arithon's woman remained oath-bound to her Prime. Whether she wanted solitude, or if her order's command had remanded her to close service, she could scarcely continue backing clan interests without raising a scalding embarrassment.

'The minion of Selidie Prime can't share our right to claim Fellowship sanctuary at Methisle,' Fianzia reminded.

Resolute, Sidir hurried his small party south, while the risen north gusts nipped hard at their heels and lashed at the mule's heavy coat. They went, touched by grief as the night fell around them, and Elaira failed to return. Sidir could not speak of his desolation, or admit that her courage and indefatigable spirit were going to be sorely missed. Duty commanded Rathain's steadfast liegeman. If his heart cried out, and his worry chafed over Elaira's secretive departure, his feal priorities stayed unremitting. His crown prince had given him only *one* charge, and no margin to risk careless failure.

Elaira hung back, a snatched pause intended to seize the precaution of scrying. Since their landing ashore, an aberrant pulse in the lane tide had flicked at her trained sensitivity. Her foreboding stayed silent: that the earth's natural flux wore the tingling stamp of a sigil-based conjury, sure mark of the Prime Circle's meddling. Too much lay at stake to dismiss the order's on-going agenda. Afraid to stay ignorant, Elaira slipped off. While Sidir's escort saw Jeynsa and Mearn's forlorn household away, she ducked into a thicket and crouched out of sight, where the brush broke the brunt of the wind. A cup of water poured from her hip-flask now lay tucked between her wrapped hands. She closed her eyes, settled into trance, and gently engaged her deep faculties.

A moment passed, two. Already forewarned of the spell's driving imprint, the enchantress eased towards listening focus. Breath caught, and flesh shuddered, as the horror of what she encountered snapped her probe into harrowing clarity. The Prime's bid for ruin ignited the spark on a tinder-box primed for disaster.

While the storm closed, and the song of Alithiel spun the effortful grace for two warfaring forces to suspend their hostilities, Parrien s'Brydion and his ragtag fleet of galleys rampaged into the estuary. Vision unveiled the raw savagery of the crews, galvanized to exact vengeance. Whipped on by Selidie's vile design, their passion had also been warded, denied the unilateral mitigation unleashed by the Paravian sword's active influence.

Like mad wolves, they would venture ashore before dawn. With no alert sentry to cry the alarm, their angry steel would carve a lethal course through the unaware ranks of their enemies.

Revulsion snapped Elaira's tight concentration. Wrenched back to herself, shivering under the frigid gusts that rattled the bare twigs around her, she wept for the brutal assault on Arithon's painstaking integrity.

Past question, if Selidie's conjury held, and this ugly counterstroke happened unchecked, *every* humane effort to spare pointless bloodshed would go up in flames, and for naught.

Worse still, if Mearn discovered the unconscionable spellcraft laid against his older brother, nothing would stop him from turning around in attempt to salvage the threat to his kinsman.

Chilled and alone, Elaira claimed that task. For Arithon, and not least for Fianzia's child, who should not bear the sorrow of growing up fatherless, she measured her dearth of options. Though her reckless choice risked the fate of a Koriani oath breaker, she shoved through the trackless wilds and made her way towards the north road. Buffeted by the hard force of the storm that whirled spindrift off the thrashed harbour, she clutched her billowing mantle about her. The boat on the strand was a useless wish. She lacked the main strength to launch the small craft, or row its deadweight through the whitecaps. She must fare by land, and grasp any means to speed her way back to the citadel.

Elaira paced herself at a determined jog, crashing through the scrub, till she reached the iced ruts of the trade-road. Under snowfall, she avoided the light spilled from the first wayside inn. The gabled structure now served as an outpost for armies. Noise spilled from a tap-room well-stocked with beer. Despite the tempting aromas of fresh bread and stew, leaked from the bustling kitchen, Elaira ignored hunger. The worsening blizzard helped blindside the sentries. A shadow half-glimpsed, she masked her woman's form in a shameless glamour and purloined a mount from the stables. The mare was fresh and willing, with a courier's Sunwheel seal on her saddle-cloth. Urged to reckless speed, parting the marching columns of men who forsook the Light's service to make their way home, the creature bore Elaira unchallenged into the burning, cold dark.

Decision

The water-drop fell through the closed vault of stone, built under the Mathorn Mountains. The splash upon impact exploded through colours: in darkness, light bloomed on black water. The spark birthed a ring-ripple, spreading an image across the spring that welled over the intricate spirals of ciphers carved into the rim.

The poised Sorcerer surveyed the vision displayed in the seclusion of his sealed haven. Davien's chiselled features showed no expression. His dark eyes stayed fixed as stamped rivets. The gleam of the living scene under reflection flickered high lights across his stilled face, as event moved apace at the seat of s'Brydion rule, and across the snowed vales at the verge of the estuary . . .

Breaking dawn wrapped the headland in howling storm. Scudded snow stewed the shallows to a salt rime of slush, where the fleet of lean galleys raked in and dropped anchor off the grey shore-line. Grim men launched tenders. They packed the oar benches, and jammed, crouched in mail, on the bilge-boards, armed and seething for war. Few spoke, as the bows ploughed the spume and bucked over the breaking combers. Unseen and unheard, they leaped the thwarts and rammed through the surf. Snow silenced their landfall; muffled their concerted charge as they fell on the Light's outer lines and attacked all that moved without warning.

The thud of whetted steel and the cries of the slaughtered blended into the scream of the gale. Blood splashed stainless snow, as clotted blades reaped unwary targets one after the next. Berserk with revenge, Parrien drove his ship's companies to attack, unaware of the spell-wrought tangle of sigils that lashed his grief to a spree of blind massacre.

'They're not fighting!' cried Vhandon, shocked by the sight of a Sunwheel sentry cut down, with no move made to unsheathe his weapon. Another man crumpled without a shocked outcry, that might have forewarned his hapless fellows. 'Something's not canny.' Sickened, the steadfast field-captain reached out. His fist locked on Parrien's gore-soaked wrist and checked his swinging blade in midstroke.

'I swear,' Vhandon shouted, 'for decency's sake, we ought to take pause and fall back. Something terrible is amiss, here!'

Parrien spat past his bared teeth and snarled, 'Who grieved for the reaping when Keldmar was burned with the best of our field-troop?' The bereaved brother wrenched his arm free and surged onward, protesting over his shoulder. 'Lysaer razed our folk to dead ash in a moment. We aren't here killing farmers. Or cutting down helpless young girls and small children, tying up straw shocks at harvest!'

That festering outrage remained too raw. Alestron's sea-wolves would brook no restraint, now. After balked months off the blockaded coast, hungry and helplessly hobbled, the ship's crews seized upon Parrien's passion. Amid the blanketing blast of the gale, they chewed their relentless course through the outlying Alliance entrenchments; except for Vhandon, who stopped, shivering.

He stayed, soaked and forlorn, while the tumult swept past. Masked in white-out snowfall, cut by cruel north wind, he listened as the screams of the dying dwindled into the howling elements.

Cold of heart, he longed for release: for the clean ferocity of a winter storm, roaring wild off the deeps of the Cildein. In childhood, he recalled the whiskered patterns of frost, stitched like a crazed seamstress's lacework across the glass of his mother's windows. Without knowing why, Vhandon wept. Something tugged at his core: an unseen note whispered of warm, secure days, and the forgotten sweetness of family happiness; of the languid summers, spent teaching the burly s'Brydion brothers to skip stones in the brook, while the boisterous rule of Bransian's father had guarded the tiered walls of the citadel. Then, no man who honed his war skills had ever imagined a future where Alestron's proud heritage could fall into jeopardy.

Through an uprush of wistful sorrow and tears, Vhandon heard the chord that healed all killing rage, also thrumming through the howling air. Veteran campaigner, he scrubbed his wet cheeks. Lowered his ice-crusted bracer and listened, while ice-crystals pinged off his helm and snagged in his stubble of beard. He strained to discern through the hiss of whipped snow that drifted around his stained boots. The presence of such an uncanny singing had uplifted him once, before this. Recollection stayed vivid, of the moment Alithiel's raised cry had spared the *Evenstar*'s crew from a fiend plague sent by Koriathain.

Vhandon shuddered, afraid. He wondered if today's murderous madness might also dance to an outside influence. Epiphany followed that thought like a thunder-clap, that *Selidie Prime would never give up her effort to bring Arithon down!* Parrien's men could be her ready tools, to offset Alithiel's grace.

A witch's sigil might as readily blind vengeance-bent men, as inflame a wave of wild *iyats.* Vhandon gasped, horrified. The slack troops who guarded the Alliance lines might be bound under Alithiel's peace, while the Prime's twisted plot to smash Arithon's credibility turned them into hapless targets. Parrien's advance would not pause for mercy. Thousands would die without voicing an outcry, or acquitting themselves in a fair fight.

Snow fell, and swirled. The savage wind battered the terrified man who kicked his mired boots free and sprinted. 'Dharkaron's bloody vengeance!' Vhandon despaired.

If Parrien fell afoul of a Koriani plot, he still hacked his way forward, unaware that his grief was the Prime's eager wedge to betray the citadel's chance for salvation . . .

Davien hissed an oath through his teeth, a fist bunched in his flame-coloured mantle. His stance seemed a statement of fury, contained, while the next droplet fell, and shattered the imprinted vista of slaughter that mowed down the dazed ranks of the Alliance's most faithful . . .

An image re-formed, this view showing a weary courier's mount labouring through knee-high drifts. The slight, muffled rider slouched with exhaustion, still on her hell-bent course after a harrowing night in the saddle. She had slipped past the s'Brydion guard at the keeps that defended the harbour chain. Masked by small spellcraft and snowfall, she drew rein at last under the loom of the watch turret across from the quay. Her gloved hands were trembling. Rumpled by storm, she dismounted. The low shore-line here did not cut the wind. Gusts screamed, dimming the high, tower beacon that overlooked Alestron's closed harbour. Across the chopped narrows, the ramparts flanking the wharf at the Sea Gate nestled under the shadow of the upper citadel, had the view not been obscured. The foaming hiss of the breakers flung off rime spray, knife-edged and bitter with salt.

Undaunted, Elaira shoved back her hood. Tangled hair lashed her cheek as she shouted, thin as a bird's call through rampaging weather.

She was initiate Koriathain, also versed in the mysteries of Ath's adepts. Her determined voice reached the alert sentries above. The man they sent down heard her desperate appeal, and agreed urgent word must be sent to the citadel.

The enchantress had risked outright wrath from her order to bear the horrific news: an assault spear-headed by Parrien's men ignited a certain disaster.

The sentry's man urged Elaira to shelter inside, shocked distress threaded through his apology. 'Lady, we cannot take action at once!' The gale raged too fierce to launch an oared boat. Clogging snowfall defeated a mirror signal. 'The outside watch posts are silenced and blinded, until this rough weather abates.' No message in code might cross the harbour to warn Bransian's inside garrison.

'I am sorry, my lady,' the keep's officer confirmed. He dared not waste a valiant man's life, with the channel pitched to white froth. 'No more can be done until the tide's changed, and the worst of the storm has blown past us . . .'

The image pool shivered. As though something massive stirred in the depths, far under the earth where the source lay, a disturbance ruffled the mirror-smooth stillness where Elaira's reflection pressed shaken hands to her face to dam sudden tears of despair.

'No!' Davien protested. 'I would see the enchantress through Alestron's gates! She is the sole anchor to balance the recoil as Prince Arithon faces this set-back! If I'm not free to grant her assistance, leave me the assurance, beyond question, that her Teir's'Ffalenn will not stand alone.'

But the Sorcerer's heart-felt appeal went unheard, an unsettling precedent in this secret place, wrought out of his busy genius for crafting, and another's: a power whose will had slept, acquiescent with calm, until now: for the dreaming partnership had awakened, on terms of a bargain come due.

The next droplet fell. Not of Davien's summoning, its ripple of impact erased the framed scene at Alestron. Now, the fathomless well of the spring gave nothing back but jet darkness. Sourced in the secretive earth, it spilled virgin water, sealed away from air or light and untouched by the quickening stir of the world's wind.

Davien swore aloud. 'Ath above, you are heartless!'

A glimmer arose from the unmarked deeps, flaring yellow-gold as a lamp, or the fire that glanced off the eye of a dragon. The light shimmered, fleeting, then dissolved: into a cruel place of sifted, rained ash, cut through by a jagged canyon.

Stacks of oppressive, striated basalt hemmed in the horizon. Heat and smoke laced with the flat tang of mineral scoured through Davien's flared nostrils.

The warning stopped thought: *almost*, he could sense the spirit and flesh of the colleague entrapped inside Scarpdale's torn grimward. Asandir's will held. His unflagging courage could not last much longer: attrition ground down the resilient strength that a Fellowship Sorcerer could renew, but never from that place.

'Not yet!' Davien flattened his palm in a gesture that was both plea and negation. 'Not yet! Ath's sweet grace, for my wrecked peace of mind, one thing more before I submit.'

Sensation receded. The aurora of rainbow-hued light where the water sluiced over the ciphered inscription seemed a living presence no more. Yet a whisper that was not quite sound, not quite voice, rang through the carved spirals that channelled the play of electromagnetics.

The vibration loosed the next water-drop, falling, a strike that shattered the obsidian polish of the spring's surface. Another scene formed like an eyeblink in time, showing a sun-washed, blue-tiled room, where a family shared an uneasy breakfast around the scrubbed boards of a trestle . . .

The neat kitchen at Innish lay far removed from the blizzard that beset Alestron. Warmed by the light of southlands morning, cosy with the aromas of jam and fresh bread, Jinesse tied back her fly-away hair with a strand of pastel yarn. Seated alongside, her husband Tharrick confronted her adult twins, his weathered face lined with concern.

The impasse that had Fiark discomposed in his chair erupted to his sudden anger. 'Don't try me on that score! Arithon sent a letter three months ago. His terms were straightforward. The Alliance's reach has grown too pervasive. All associates linked to the s'Ffalenn name are endangered. His Grace demanded a suspension of every activity handled in his behalf.'

Blond braid still matted with the off-shore salt left unwashed since her brig had made landfall, Feylind replaced her glower with a wicked smile. 'And did you?'

Fiark flushed. He looked away first. That stark precedent made Jinesse bite her lip and choke back an outcry. Beside her, a staunch bulwark, Tharrick laced his callused hand through her fingers beneath the table.

'No,' Fiark confessed to his twin. 'I didn't. And not only because of that desert-bred steward. His queer, stubborn service makes the *Khetienn*'s crew mind their backs like they're creeping around a poked bee's nest.'

Feylind's triumphant grin brightened with teeth. 'The runt creature's a pest! I'm amazed no one's stranded him. Did he claim he'd skewer you for a roasted goat if you slackened your guard over Mother Dark's Chosen?'

A twisted smile twitched Fiark's lips, prelude to his chagrined laughter. 'Something like that.'

Settled back with crossed arms, Feylind nodded. 'The mad imp threatened me once, a warning never to lapse in my care for Arithon's interests. I've no doubt he'd stick me with his carving knife, too, if he thought that my loyalty faltered.' Warmed up to her pitch, she laced in, again. 'Which is why you will not shift my cargo but sign off on the manifest King Eldir's entrusted to relieve the siege at Alestron.'

'Please,' whispered Jinesse, her throat too tight. 'Daughter, I beg you! Think of your two growing children.'

Feylind swallowed. 'Mother, I have.' Her quiet appeal also included Tharrick, quite stripped of her seafaring bluster. 'The little ones are as much Fiark's and Corra's, as Teive's and mine.'

To which her mate added, 'I have to agree. To our own, we are exotic, strange visitors, while your home has soothed the skinned knees of first steps, and provided the constancy of their raising.'

Fiark said nothing, a declaration that shouted. In fact, the scrappy desertman had told him much more, then made him swear a *frightening* vow to hold that revealed knowledge secret. For the Biedar tribes of the Sanpashir desert, the survival of Arithon Teir's'Ffalenn ran beyond an imperative necessity. Fiark loved his twin sister as life itself. Yet far more than his own family's fate hung in the fragile balance.

To the ship's mate who held Feylind's love, he asked, grim, 'You won't argue our case? When you turn your flag in front of the Alliance armed forces, there'll be no reprieve. If you survive the course, you'll be branded past pardon as renegade shipping.'

'This is my choice, also,' Teive declared, unabashed. 'I saw what Arithon risked when Feylind and *Evenstar* lay under threat by his enemies.' Huge, rope-burned hands toyed with the child's tin spoon, borrowed to drizzle honey over the pan bread that languished, untouched, on the crockery. The metal bent, under his whitened knuckles. 'His Grace would have died rather than forfeit our interests. Could I live with myself as a father if I ignored his need, now?'

'He gave us all that we have here, at Innish,' Tharrick said in startling support. As Jinesse paled, he cut short her aggrieved protest, firmly and straight from the heart. 'Not least, you were there! You saw his hand heal when he spared my wrecked life, after I wronged him in Merior.'

A retired ex-guardsman, once cashiered by Alestron over a miscalled charge of lapsed duty, Tharrick enclosed his trembling wife into his protective embrace. As she sobbed against his broad shoulder, he inclined his grey head in tribute to the stepdaughter who spoke, bold as brass, for her right to take action.

'I can't go with you, Feylind,' Tharrick declared. 'I don't agree with Duke Bransian's policies, or his hard hand with the men who serve under him. Yet the enemies that gnaw at Alestron's sea flank would have long since defeated a lesser man. The aggression which secures his citadel has always provided the linch-pin that defends the clan legacy protecting East Halla's free wilds. The s'Brydion lineage might be faulted for arrogance, yet that short-fall lends no grounds to condemn a whole people. Lysaer's move to create an Alliance rallying cry, and burn them to the ground as a scapegoat cannot be met with a blind eye.'

'You will help! I thought so!' Feylind crowed with fierce pride.

Her gratitude caught the breath of the man who stood for the blood father once lost to the sea. Tharrick sighed. His nod was not grudging. Despite his reservation, that the perilous course Feylind must sail defied every sensible reckoning, he gave what he had to offer. 'For your hare-brained courage, I'll disclose the code signals you'll need to bring you safely into the citadel's harbour.'

Which left Fiark, tight-lipped and silent in the fine broadcloth he wore as shore factor. He might never recover. Beside Feylind's feckless craving for maritime thrills, and her careless penchant for ship's slops, he was ever the settled, meticulous presence. Quite his twin's opposite, for all that they were as two halves of the selfsame spirit.

His blue eyes matched hers, across the plank-table, identically bright with regret. 'If I don't endorse your ship's papers through excise, you'd burn the *Evenstar*'s honest registry forthwith and run this cargo through Kalesh as contraband.'

Like echo, between them, the past spoke in memory, bearing Arithon's cry of stripped anguish. *'Dhirken died!'*

'I know what I'm risking,' Feylind declared.

Fiark raised his fair eyebrows. Troubled beyond any words to express, he pressed anyway. 'Do you? I hope so.' He swallowed, then touched Jinesse in a gentle appeal. 'Mother. My sister is bound to go. I can't withhold my part. The weight of a clerk's stamp on a ship's document won't make any damned difference. Since Dharkaron's Black Spear itself could not stay her, I'm asking you to give over to her Prince Arithon's royal signet. Return the ring. Rescind his Grace's oath, that our lives require his pledge of protection . . .'

The next droplet of water plummeted downwards. Its splash struck the spring, bitter as acid, and unequivocal. The scene within Jinesse's kitchen dissolved as the ring-ripple fled, bringing darkness.

Time could not be stopped. A summons arose on the strength of a promise not to be withheld any longer.

Davien bowed his head. His whisper raised a plaintive echo within the domed walls of the chamber. 'Fly well. Fly alone. Find your strengths, my wild falcon.'

For the Sorcerer saw his worst fear become manifest: he would not be free to stand in support through the harrowing hour of Arithon's need. All of the future hung in fate's balance, while older loyalties, and an ancient binding, lay beyond his might to rescind.

Another drop fell. In the space where the Sorcerer's form stood erect, warm-blooded and breathing, *alive,* now an eagle's winged form shimmered like an explosion amid the stilled air. Wings spread, it soared but a motionless instant. Then its presence melted into the droplet, still falling, lit now by a searing white spark.

The mote struck the spring, dissolved by the splash, while the pin-point of light winnowed separate. At the crux, the pattern of consciousness that comprised a Fellowship Sorcerer did not reclaim human form.

Davien's presence was not borne away as a man, to resolve in another location. Instead, the blazing fleck plunged downward into the deeps that sourced the well's spring. Suspended, it fell like a star *as though through forever*, then vanished.

Frail light became utterly swallowed: into the pupil of a wide, living eye, brilliant as a midsummer sun flared golden at sunrise.

Dragon

The rock-chamber shatters, an explosion that avalanches ice, snow, and ejected boulders down-slope in a remote vale in the Mathorns; where a dumb-struck clan scout on routine patrol beholds what no mortal man on Athera has dreamed: the sight of a great drake as she blares in challenge, launches aloft, and soars westward on outspread, vaned wings . . .

By winter sundown, the dragon's flight rakes over the brick towers surrounding Avenor's Sunwheel Square; while the Light's High Priest whimpers in fear, the creature from eldritch legend dives in, screaming rage, and on a fiery breath, razes every building, every grand hall and mansion, then craters the blasted ground underneath to excise the stolen skulls of four murdered hatchlings . . .

While the pyre of Lysaer's wrecked capital smokes in death and ruin behind, the golden drake wheels with a thunder of wings; linked with the matrix of Davien's spirit, the great wyrm Seshkrozchiel, once the mate of Haspastion, blazes south-east towards Lanshire, and the site of the Scarpdale grimward . . .

XI. Second Turning

At tide's ebb on the southcoast, while the *Evenstar* set full sail for Alestron, far northward, the gale off the Cildein abated to smothering snowfall. In Melhalla, the flakes mounded over the edged drifts, and settled cold swaths in the hollows. All movement along the coast's trade-roads mired down. The post inns, then the haylofts and carriage sheds became jammed with the misery of stranded travellers. Frustrated caravan drovers and stalled couriers clashed in hot argument over space to bed down, the available resources long since overwhelmed: first by an influx of rootless, armed men, then by straggling refugees, overburdened with bundled belongings and wailing children. As the blizzard paralyzed the surrounding countryside, the flood of humanity leaving Alestron sowed clogging emotional snarls into the natural flux currents.

If Alithiel's song had defused killing enmity, nothing might ease the flaring energies sparked by such desperate crowding.

The Koriani seers received the sharp brunt, as the storm static cleared, and the lane flow reopened for scrying. Prime Selidie's galled mood had not settled. Though the wrecked healers' tents had been set right, resecured and defended by earth wards, she had no tolerance left to field set-backs.

'I cannot serve the order's best interests, or make my next choices groping and blind!' The senior who had just complained that her exhausted circle of talent required leave was sent packing. 'Until I decide to retire myself,' said the Prime, 'you will sort any meaningful news from the dross and ascertain that I'm kept informed!'

'Matriarch, by your will.' The rebuffed peeress curtseyed, rushed as she rejoined the sisters just tasked to uphold their assignment.

All fever-pitch purpose remained unassuaged, with the order's threatened future at stake. Selidie dared to allow for no weakness. Dedication moulded her stance: the secret body of knowledge she guarded permitted no flinching weakness. While Sethvir's dire straits kept the Fellowship hobbled, no Sorcerer's resource would quash her. Nothing must challenge her latest bid to wrest back Koriani supremacy.

To that end, Lirenda's slaved talent now augmented another circle of six senior peeresses. Their combined labour powered the sigils that steered Parrien's obsessive revenge. The inflammatory act was almost too easy, the man's heated temperament inviting the spur that fused discontent into discord, while the subordinate sympathy of his ship's companies drew them into the web of entrapment. Though one seasoned captain had not succumbed, he was left alone to approach the nerve-jumpy watch at the Sea Gate. Few campaigners would attempt the volatile charge of informing Alestron's duke.

Vhandon became the stickling exception. The lone seeress appointed to dog his each move affirmed his unflagging persistence. He could not be swerved from the chilling awareness that he must win through before Arithon's mage-taught resources faltered. The moment Alithiel's conjury faded, the dedicate core of the Alliance command would shake off mazed dreams and encounter the swath of Parrien's unbridled butchery. As appalled shock recoiled to fury, Alestron's reivers caught still at large would be cut off and killed out of hand.

'The pressure stays on!' Prime Selidie exhorted. 'Keep those ship's companies wreaking blind havoc up until the last moment.'

The two opposed factions must ignite the explosion. Who lived and who died did not matter. Athera's backwater culture and knowledge could never outweigh the wider legacy of millennia: not with the lore of *thousands* of worlds hanging in the greater balance. All of mankind's prior history lay at stake, proscribed by an archaic compact. The Paravian presence had withdrawn, long since. Alestron's struggle upheld a doomed cause, no more and no less than the opportune sacrifice to leverage humanity's claim to inherit Athera.

To that purpose, the sisterhood's resource must juggle each pawn for the endgame. Prime Selidie beckoned the seeress assigned to keep watch on Elaira. 'I must know. Has the initiate snapped under pressure and tried to forewarn the Prince of Rathain?'

The senior came forward, an upright traditional swathed in rustling silk. Her careful step bespoke the frailty bestowed by longevity bindings, and the austere character that tightened her wrinkled lips. 'Matriarch, by your will, I have seen. Elaira remains in the shoreside watch turret. As you hoped, the rambunctious charge of the storm concealed our cast line of disruption. We've successfully foiled her primary talent. When her working through water failed to flag Dakar's attention within the citadel, she deepened her trance and tried to reach Arithon s'Ffalenn by linked empathy. That channel lies past our means to befoul, however, that barrier posed us no set-back.'

'Elaborate!' interrupted the Koriani Prime, her clawed fingers twitching. 'Was the song of the Paravian sword the factor that bought interference?'

The prim seeress curtseyed. 'Matriarch, yes. Elaira's empathic call was overwhelmed by the cascading flow of harmonics. She can't surmount the obstruction at distance. The male partner's entrained focus must stay immaculate. Through her efforts, we've found that Arithon's being sustains the conduit for the grand conjury. Even a master initiate's sensitivity cannot pierce through the veils of Alithiel's enchantment.'

Prime Selidie tucked her maimed limbs under her purple mantle. Satisfaction warmed her, bone deep. Despite the day's toll of surprise damages, she had recouped the footing to seize the high ground. At long last, the string of reverses unfolded in line with her careful plan: her quarry moved in lock-step towards his doom. Compassion incarnate, Arithon would stay on course with supreme endurance. Since the half-brother's following fed upon fear and the impetus of their fixed hatred, the sword's powers were pitched to dissolve the entanglements driving a curse-driven siege. To ensure Jeynsa's safety, and seed hope for a peace that might spare Alestron's clan sovereignty, Rathain's prince must extend his prodigious reserves until talent and strength were played out.

'How long before the tide changes to flood?' Prime Selidie asked the hovering subordinate.

'Two hours past noon.' The ancient fluttered a dismissive hand. 'The young captain at the harbour-side beacon can't launch a boat to try crossing before then, though he's grasped the stakes that spur Elaira. Once the current's in favour, his men will have orders to row her across to the Sea Gate.'

'Straight into my net!' the Prime whispered, elated. The glittering strand that perfected her snare *required* that Elaira should spurn the sisterhood's interests. Love must keep her bound to Arithon's side. That irresistible, fatal attraction would tie his will at the citadel's fall, and finally close the Koriani fist on the reins of his destiny.

While Selidie excused the older seeress to resume her vigilant post, movement at the pavilion's entry presaged another disturbance. A sister broke protocol and shoved in without leave, barging over two protesting fourth-rank peeresses. Breathless, she argued that her breaking news carried imperative urgency.

'Silence!' snapped Selidie.

The uproar cut off. Both indignant seniors stifled their rebuke. 'Let me weigh the gravity of the offence,' the Prime said. 'If, in fact, this mannerless claim proves to be a spurious impertinence!'

The flushed miscreant curtseyed, knee bent to the floor in relief. 'Matriarch, your will be done, this is no insignificant development.'

'Come here, girl. Speak up!' Selidie measured the petitioner's approach, not forgiving or lenient. 'You're the initiate assigned to review the inbound dispatch from our western lane watch? Then I gather the storm's subsided enough to allow a transmission that's not routine.'

'Yes, Matriarch.' Beneath the high dais, placed under the lofty vantage of the Prime's chair, the second-rank seeress was properly fearful. Her water-stained hem betrayed trembling knees; her clenched fingers, rapt dread and excitement. 'Forgive my presumption! But this news is momentous. The Fellowship Sorcerers have dared to flout history, and wakened the might of a dragon.'

'Ah!' Selidie barely stifled her triumphant shout. 'When have the mighty been so sorely tried?' Her smile showed teeth. 'Get on with your list, girl. Tell me our dragon-skull wards at Avenor have become the first drakish casualty!'

The initiate seeress stared in blank shock. 'Lysaer's royal capital has been razed to the ground. No mercy was shown to the hapless inhabitants! Thousands have died. The injured and burned who survive have no shelter. More wander, lawless, sacking the hamlets, or crowding the byres and trade inns. They will face disease. Folk are desperate and starving, left with too little resource, and no store-sheds for grain, even if ships can bring relief help.'

The bleak picture unfolded, beyond damning words: winter seas slowed the galleys. Supply would be hampered, with Havish's ports closed off to Tysan's chained oarsmen by crown decree. The distressed initiate fought for the composure to finish her daunting report. 'Though the courier's relays are in disarray, some of our sisters already pack for emergency travel from Hanshire. They act to forestall sickness, since Lysaer's examiner has fallen too hard on the local talent.' Few herbalists and trained healers remained to attend such a massive number of casualties.

Before Selidie's calm, which displayed no shock over the horrific damages, the seeress lost courage and faltered.

The moment hung, sharp as etched light through a crystal, until a senior bearing five red bands of rank seized charge and inquired, 'By your leave, Matriarch? Had you foreseen this might happen? Why weren't we warned to prepare?'

For the ugly conjecture held power to terrify: that the disaster caused by the hatchlings' remains had been no misfortunate accident. If Avenor had been purposefully exposed to such peril, then the wholesale destruction of Lysaer's ruling seat had been seeded by a long-range design: a choice that harked back to Morriel Prime, the reigning Matriarch's deceased predecessor.

Selidie surveyed the stunned sisters at hand, from the lowly grey robes who fetched and carried as drudges, to the eldest crones in their graded red bands of seniority. Ironic, that she, as the youngest of them, should be censured by their regard. Selidie's iron nerve never flinched. Her control showed the glacial reserve that upheld her tradition of power. Her mantle was *ancient*. Far older than recent tenure on Athera, her responsibilities sank tap-roots into a past that once had spanned networks of starfaring empires: cultures more vast and varied than today's sheltered underlings had wits to imagine.

'Do you think, after this, that Lysaer s'Ilessid or his Alliance can afford to turn a blind eye? Or that he will keep his insufferable arrogance, or rise up in dispute of our claim that humanity's future's endangered? With Avenor in ruins, the statesman in him must rise to respond. The Fellowship's supreme disregard for mankind's well-being will force a review of alliances.' Unblinking, Selidie unveiled the hideous badge of defeat left by Davien's vicious guile: *stumps of useless fingers, seared livid with scars, could not even lift a cup of hot tea, or arrange a lace skirt, or pull the jewelled shaft of a hairpin.* 'How many cripples shall we lament?' the Prime cried to drive home her venomous conclusion. 'Even the High King of Havish will have a rough time excusing the purpose that's raised a great drake for a flight of rampaging massacre.'

Hush gripped the pavilion again, while the Matriarch's regard raked over her oathsworn. Seated and standing, and linked in avid circles, they were as stopped puppets on a stage of draped canvas, painted in pallid skin and poised jewels under the flickering candles. Each one, a live piece at her Prime's beck and call. This was as it should be: the order had cause. The weapon was forged to strike at need, wielded always without question. Only Lirenda's furious gaze masked the outrage of wider awareness.

Selidie spared that downtrodden tool no glance of acknowledgement. Informed or not, the sisterhood's power stayed under her sovereign charge. Her status in the order's hierarchy would not be threatened today. Her higher purpose must reign, with fate's axis poised to unseat the Fellowship Sorcerers.

'We are at war, ladies!' Selidie declared. 'A battle we must win at all costs or risk losing our dedicate mission to act in mankind's behalf. For far too long, we've been ground down and silenced! I tell you now, as your Prime, that I guard an untold wealth of knowledge, a heritage swept aside and unjustly gagged by the tyranny of the compact. We were forced in duress to accept this world's terms during sanctuary. Since that hour, our ideals have stayed clipped by oppression!'

'Then this news of Avenor's demise is aligned with your will?' the distraught senior peeress ventured outright.

'Not welcome, except that the Fellowship of Seven are trapped in extreme disarray.' Selidie never moved: could not ruffle a statuesque fold of clothing, or risk snagging coiffed hair, that would require a servant's attendance. Only the flash of her amethyst brooch betrayed her excitement. 'I mourn for the deaths of the children and innocents crushed down for Paravian interests! Tysan's sisterhouses will bear the brunt of their suffering. Let our own hands minister to those shattered lives, and lend succour to what can be salvaged. Our order shall act to ease hurt and grief through inexhaustible mercy.'

To that end, the distressed junior seeress on lane watch was granted the Prime's curt dismissal. 'Go out, serve your post. Send my word back to Tysan. Our oathsworn are to render assistance with all speed and resource.'

The initiate curtseyed and rushed her retreat, fast followed by the rest of the white-ranked sisters, remanded to their work in the healers' tents. At the heels of their reordered departure, the Matriarch resumed her address to her chosen. 'We must pursue our cause with dauntless conviction! The terror just visited upon Lysaer's realm proves that Davien and his colleagues are set on the run. They will be too preoccupied to guard their backs, or disrupt the course of our affairs. We are poised,' declared Selidie. 'I insist on your faith as I seize our bold opening to hobble our age-old oppressors.'

Only the crowning cipher remained. 'Take Arithon Teir's'Ffalenn when the citadel falls, and the end game delivers our triumph.'

Sulfin Evend abhorred delays, when fury stuck spurs in his haste. Already well overdue on the road, *still* blistered by the excuses served up by Tirans' mayor, whose vindictive manoeuvring arose out of spite, since Lysaer's cutthroat state-craft stampeded the town's elders, and usurped their pompous authority. While their young men marched in the ranks at Alestron, and their flag snapped underneath the Sunwheel of the Alliance, the baiting chance to discomfit the Light's Lord Commander posed too choice a temptation.

Only the fettle of a Hanshire aristocrat let Sulfin Evend temper his killing rage: an ally run through at sword-point would serve none but his wolf pack of rivals. Since the bloodless alternative meant cooling his heels, Sulfin Evend spurned the next banquet. He pulled rank and bullied the gate sentries. Shouted over their stammered protests, then stymied their captain's adamant plea for a state escort with language fit to shame the whores in the war camp.

Five days on the road, with two more spent crawling against an eastshore blizzard, Sulfin Evend exchewed the temptation of rest in a warm bed at Kalesh. He changed horses, cursed the wet saddle, and turned west till the deepening snow bogged his pace. Wrapped in pearl overcast, he was by now beyond cold and bone-tired, jarred to the teeth from a hack with slab shoulders and jolting gaits.

No discomfort made him shed the rough anonymity of his field-issue over-cloak: the smart trappings beneath would draw too much notice. Better, he felt, to suffer mean treatment before risking the pitfalls of title that might stall his urgent progress. Alone, with only sheathed steel at his side, he pushed on until his spent mount stumbled under him. The next wayside tavern at last loomed ahead, doubtless jammed beyond wretched capacity.

The gabled monstrosity nestled behind a ramshackle paling that also supported an expanded post-station to milk the traffic of war. Too likely the coach yard would be green planks, laid across squelching mud. Sulfin Evend drew rein in the snow-banks outside. Dismounted, limping with aches, and frozen half-stupid, he slogged toward the gate and braced to endure the crush of unwashed bodies and sour ale, and the greasy reek of onions boiled with salt beef. Perhaps a relief, after the wine sauces and snide jabs inflicted by

Tirans' spurned mayor. Lip curled, Sulfin Evend barked out a laugh. No vile indignity would stand in his way as he closed the last leg of his journey.

Or so he thought, as he entered the enclosure and breasted the seething commotion.

'No room, and no beds, here!' snapped the blanket-wrapped man he shouldered aside to make way for his horse. Three more women stood up, shaking snow from their skirts, to clear his path towards the stable. Fist clutched on soaked reins, Sulfin Evend shoved into a space that held standing room only.

Families huddled in every available cranny. More bedded down in the open corrals by the ox barn. Dogs yapped underfoot. The apron by the stable was beyond crammed, yoked teams and steaming draught horses tied shoulder to shoulder in pickets.

Alone, and unrecognized in his mud-stained wool, Sulfin Evend squared his jaw and ploughed forward. Where language failed, he engaged blunt force, elbowing bodies and displacing a fat merchant with a back-handed cuff of his bracer. Folk shuffled aside, ignoring his rank urgency. Most murmured, apologized, even smiled as though they were moonstruck.

Sulfin Evend sucked in a vexed breath, tripped over an upset bucket, then found himself stalled as a screaming toddler crashed headlong into his knee. He righted the mite and almost collided with a Sunwheel soldier, who shed his white cloak, unabashed, and passed over the garment to shelter the shrieking child. The urchin was no paragon. Foul-tongued as the poxed get of a camp-follower, to judge by his soiled motley and cross-gartered rags, with his unlikely benefactor one of Lysaer's elite, unmistakably Etarran. What anomaly *possessed* such a pedigree officer: first to stray from his post, far less to grant charity to riff-raff?

Sulfin Evend checked a field bellow, fit to soil the miscreant gentleman's linen. Instinct gave warning, that more was afoot here than travellers caught out by the storm. Destitute older men; grandmothers; matrons and toothless babes were perched on crates of fluffed chickens. Wet baggage and tied canvas shelters had been jammed helter-skelter between the slats of parked ox drays. Crowded in misery inside farm-carts were pregnant sweethearts and girls, crying children and tousled young boys, tucked in blankets amid oddments of household gear, tatterdemalion sacks, and stacked barrels. Beneath wind-tattered tarps, Sulfin Evend sighted hogsheads branded with Alliance seals, then more bales and crates bearing the tally marks from the pursers who logged in supply for the cook-shacks. The alarming tumult showed every sign of an on-going refugee exodus.

'Dharkaron avenge the Fatemaster's born fool!' The Light's Lord Commander jerked his hood low, as much to muffle his smouldering rage, as to mask his distinctive features. *His untoward absence had lasted too long.* With Lysaer unguarded, the well-ordered siege left behind at Alestron appeared to be coming unravelled. By whose stroke of meddling, he shuddered to guess: the details in front of him failed to add up. Past the oddly delinquent captain at arms, who seemed shorn of his natural arrogance, Sulfin Evend caught the snap of clan accents from a cluster of craftsfolk. An inconceivable shock, that folk from Alestron should dare show their faces outside the duke's citadel. Yet, there they sat, sharing bread with armed troops, who appeared on the lam as deserters. No companies had been slated for legitimate leave; nor were these rank-and-file men billeted under the hare-brained Etarran officer. In shameless display, their field accoutrements and garrison blazons were exposed to haphazard view: astounding behaviour for a pack of slackers, larking off for a binge in Kalesh.

The Light's Lord Commander gripped a circumspect hand over the soaked flap of his over-cloak to keep his gold braid out of sight. He was alone, and outnumbered, upon slippery footing if he was seen and backed into a fight. He brushed cautious shoulders with a whistling sergeant, passed two pikemen hooting at someone's raw joke, before he was able to flag down a groom and surrender his lathered gelding. Beset by alarm, he realized the chills that ruffled his skin had *nothing* to do with wet clothes.

'Find me a fresh mount,' he told the harried boy, then eased his demand with five silvers. 'I see that you're busy. Do what you can. I'll double my gift if the remount's a runner, and rested enough to make speed. I'll be outside, meantime. Tell the inn matron I'll pay if someone can bring a hot meal and packed fare from the kitchen.'

'Sir, at your pleasure,' the boy promised, pleased, his raw fingers stowing the coins as he took the blown horse.

Sulfin Evend moved upslope from the puddled ox urine and tucked up in the lee of the timber wall. From that covert vantage, amid whirling snow, he listened, intent as a predator. Frolicking children raced at his feet. The chatter of women rode the storm-deadened air, through the jingling stamp of the harness teams. The shared mood of the men also seemed knit by an incongruous camaraderie. Whatever event had disrupted the warfront, these folk were not fleeing a debacle.

Prompted, perhaps, by his inborn clan talent, Sulfin Evend recalled the interview forced on him by the wild tribes of Sanpashir: when Arithon Teir's'Ffalenn, cracked to flinching recoil, had voiced his ultimatum concerning the s'Brydion stand at Alestron. '*I will not live their death! Not ever by my willing consent, nor as the Mistwraith's curse-blinded accomplice.*'

Unbidden thought followed, that the bizarre behaviour seen here might be a working by the same sorcerer's hand. Beneath laughter and gossip, through the banter exchanged between travellers, Sulfin Evend *almost* recaptured the grandiloquent depth of experience, when Arithon had torn himself free, as Desh-thiere's influence entangled his aura.

The chill air seemed suddenly too thin to breathe. Sulfin Evend leaned against the rough paling, dizzied by the untoward possibility. Surely as the blood that once welled from his veins, sealing his pledge to a Sorcerer, *the eerie touch he observed was no conjury wrought by Koriathain*!

With Lysaer's plight still his foremost concern, Sulfin Evend flagged down a talkative matron. 'Have you heard aught of the Prince Exalted?'

She smiled. 'Come in from the north, have you?' Her gaiety sparkled, out of place amid the leaden gloom. 'Rumours are flying. Some say the avatar touched off a light-bolt that birthed us a miracle.'

A bystander took issue. 'No, woman! I've heard from a witness. The Blessed Prince has ascended on wings and bestowed the gift of Ath's grace.'

That argument sparked off others, each voice with a different opinion.

'By the Light, no such thing!'

'Truth spoke, and Shadow's corruption was vanquished!'

'We are saved by the dawning of goodness and hope, and the war host is being disbanded.'

Sulfin Evend scraped at his stubbled chin and carefully kept his own counsel. Skin, bone, and viscera, he knew the development was no curse-bound ploy of Lysaer's. The enthusiastic disclaimers around him exposed a ringing, uncanny harmony: a tingling echo that spoke through the heart, to quit senseless striving and conflict. If a masterbard's gift for ethereal music *could* be fashioned to unseat Desh-thiere's hold, the spectre of ruin and war might escape the fraught grief of a blood-bath. The outside possibility awoke admiration. 'By Ath, as an ally, you don't pull your strokes!'

For, yet again, memory cited the evidence: as Lysaer's dark nemesis cried out in appeal, flayed raw by his tormented past: '*Depend on my absence,*' Arithon had promised. '*I will weather the conflict at the fringes of the free wilds, and assist the escape of survivors.*'

The Light's Lord Commander drew in a slow breath. His sudden hope could burn too fiercely bright, that his own insupportable burden of honour might find a painless reprieve. While the press closed around him, and the relentless storm soaked his mantle, Sulfin Evend became aware that somebody shouted. A flustered maid from the kitchen endeavoured to snag his attention.

'My lord?' Cheap crockery chinked as she flounced, peering across her burdened tray with quizzical exasperation. 'You wished supper and a packed meal for the road? The groom says your mount's being saddled directly. Eat now, or not at all.'

The post-horse could not arrive fast enough.

Sulfin Evend pitched her a handful of coin. The hot meal abandoned without second thought, he snapped up the packet of courier's rations and strode straightaway towards the stables. He would girth up the fresh nag's saddle himself, then scorch the track to Alestron and reappraise his neglected command.

Snowfall sifted over the citadel, scrim patterns of white on grey blurring the onset of afternoon. Through the windless, oppressive cold, Alithiel's song slid a knifing cry of pure sound clothed in scintillant light. Up close, the effect undid reason and pain. The yearning heart lifted towards laughter. Watch Keep, where Arithon launched his stand for peace, became the lit flame of a beacon. There, the hot star aligned by the sword struck a chord beyond sense and reason. Sustained harmonics charged the air to find voice, tuned to joy by the dance of grand conjury.

The effect did not ride the free mind past volition, or cancel willed choice and conviction. Those who wished to live free of armed strife departed the citadel's surrounds. The sword's music let the garrison who stayed by their duke help the families who opted to leave. Side by side with their fellows, who chanced a new life, their strength worked the winch at the Sea Gate. Steady assistance directed the evacuation under the cover of storm. Gloved in blanketing murk, and buoyed on the ebb-tide, the packed galleys and boats left the anchorage.

Now, as the flow in the channel reversed, churned by the eddies that presaged the flood, the last huddled children and matrons were gone. Capped in fresh snow-drifts, the wharf-side loomed empty. Reduced in number, the guard manned their posts. Others slept, touched by unearthly dreams, while the sword on the Watch Keep still blazed, its streaming, wild power unfaltering. Arithon sustained the summoning now to stall the renewal of latent hostilities. The travellers in flight from both camps must have time and leeway to secure their escape.

Hush gripped the citadel throughout the weaving. Weapons and runners stood idle. If the sentries on guard lost their focus to day-dreams, neither the duke or his captains at arms made rounds to upbraid slackened vigilance. In the vast quiet, above emptied streets, the war paused, its antipathy shrouded.

Arithon chased his intent without respite. Atop the squat tower that commanded the promontory, the exhaustive hours of prolonged exposure proved bright beyond mortal tolerance. Few could withstand the unshielded force of Alithiel's active proximity. Dakar was the exception. The change instilled by his experience at Rockfell let him manage the overwhelming surge of aligned flux. His measured stints, standing vigil at Arithon's side, left Talvish and Rathain's informal rear-guard to secure the drum-tower's lower ward-room.

There, the thick fieldstone walls damped the ranging, glass edge of the sword's fierce vibration. If no fire burned for the shortage of fuel, the trestles and benches were sheltered from the cruellest bite of the weather. With Glendien gone to assist in the kitchens, the present occupants made two, beside Talvish: Fionn Areth, who clung against sound advice, and the young forest liegeman from Shand. Though cheerful by nature, Kyrialt s'Taleyn stayed loath to grant any town-bred ally his trust.

Without Sidir, whose talent for insight surpassed prejudice, no one could gauge honest mettle with the same infallible accuracy. The lack of that guidance, and the sensible absence of Elaira, left Talvish adrift as the duke's displaced veteran.

'Your toss,' Fionn Areth sniped from the gloom that oppressed the austere stone chamber.

Talvish leaned across the gouged planks and scooped up the dice to defend his staked coppers. But for the fallow gold glint of his hair, he was a lithe shadow, terse and self-contained through inaction. A soldier's fust of damp wool was his element, while the icy draughts wafted snow through the arrow-loops and puddled the hollowed stone floor. 'Will you never lay off cutthroat games before you're landed in debt to your short hairs?'

The Araethurian shrugged. Jeynsa's stabbing wit had hardened his patience. Sometimes, he remembered that silence beat words in the flaying heat of rejoinder.

Talvish rolled, six and five. 'Fleeced!' he crowed, laughing. 'Skinned you stark naked as a spring goat.'

The shied coin of his winning might have bruised flesh. Talvish's reflex fielded the catch, nearly as fast as a clan scout's feral reaction.

Kyrialt marked his speed with a measuring eye. If he refused gambling, he was not inured to the company. 'Don't cry broke to me,' he teased the grass-lander. 'I've no useless freight of coinage at hand for a wastrel like you to borrow.'

Fionn Areth flexed chilled fingers, bored enough to pounce back. 'Straightly said, for a brigand brought up to seize trade goods.'

Talvish's keen observation had watched Sidir react under town-biased insult. *Always* the Companion relied on the cues of his hunter's instinct. The war-captain sensed that same subtlety, now, as Kyrialt tracked the Araethurian's tone of voice and responded to match the intent.

'Disappointed, are you, that I was raised to weaponry rather than stuck wringing cheese out of goat's milk?' Yet where Sidir invariably cut off discussion to guard the deep scars of past history, Kyrialt's buoyant nature preferred kindness. 'Why challenge the man who'd be willing to teach you? If sharper skills are the wish of your heart, you might ask me to spare time for lessons.' While his gad-fly reeled, set at speechless loss, the clan liegeman added, 'Here's Dakar.'

Whatever alerted his forest acuity, a moment elapsed before Talvish detected the stolid tread descending from the topside battlement. Low grumbling followed, past the stairwell portal, while numbed fingers fumbled the door-latch. Then the Mad Prophet shoved his way in, gusting fresh cold through the chamber.

Talvish preferred the crude recourse of language. 'What's changed?'

'Nothing.' Past chattering teeth, Dakar let fly in frustration. 'I can't see with a Fellowship Sorcerer's vision! This use of Alithiel's virtue's a precedent, and I don't have access to Sethvir's library.' Unlike everyone else, Rathain's prince was not freezing. The sword's emanation deflected the wind and melted the snow for a three-yard radius.

Kyrialt tested gently, 'His Grace hasn't moved?'

'Less than a carved statue, for all I've seen.' Dakar kicked out a bench and plonked his ample rump. 'I can't touch him, besides.' He pitched off crusted gloves, beat his bloodless fingers. 'If I venture too close, the same as before, I lose every hold on my faculties.'

To Fionn Areth's fast breath, Dakar snapped, 'I don't know! If Arithon's damaged his mind, he's past helping. I can't reach through the well of Alithiel's influence, even to test his defences. Who knows if he suffers from wasting attrition, or if his auric field's locked into stasis?' Miserable and shivering, Dakar shrugged. 'No more can be done.'

Except wait as they had, and keep anxious vigil, and hope that the sword's wild conjury left its wielder the means to awaken to sanity.

'I'm stripped of loose coin,' Fionn Areth complained. 'Unless you can stake me a purse from thin air?'

'Wine,' Dakar amended with a vicious edge. 'Mulled to steaming, and sweetened with sugar and cinnamon, *if* I possessed such a fanciful talent. Which I don't. You'd have to beg Asandir.'

No answering banter arose from Kyrialt, to ease the Mad Prophet's wrecked peace. Talvish straightened, first warned by that quiet, then clapped a swift fist to his sword-hilt, the same instant the tensed clansman shot to his feet.

'We have inbound company!' Kyrialt snapped in warning. 'Two men. One's the duke's heir, by the swaggering tread.'

Then Talvish picked out the jingle of mail. Also snatched bits of talk, pitched with concern, too muffled as yet to decipher. The over-loud bass was Sevrand's; the other's more measured responses were burred with sapping exhaustion: *but known.*

A prickling chill chased Talvish's spine. *'Vhandon?'* Faster, this time, than forestborn reflex, he crossed the dank chamber. His gauntleted hand flung wide the strapped door. Three running steps more, and he captured his stumbling friend in a bear hug. 'Vhandon! Daelion wept!' Fighting for words through his startled emotion, he gasped, 'I thought you had perished with Keldmar's field-troop!'

Through the swirling snow at the threshold, the bulkier figure side-stepped the reunion: Sevrand entered the Watch Keep amid a kicked scatter of ice clods. Harsh weather never saw him wear a hood. His matted clan braid wore a blood-sparkle of stone: the ruby pendant received from a sweetheart, and his only frivolous sentiment. The cape-shouldered cloak slung over his byrnie clinked to the hang of his weapons: his usual long sword, and an ugly spiked mace, thrust through a studded belt. The steel ring at his hip held a favourite notched boarding axe, which suggested he had come directly from watch at the Sea Gate.

'Trouble?' snapped Talvish, while Vhandon came in and relieved his tired frame on a bench.

Sevrand grunted. 'What's changed?' Then, 'Sithaer's bleak death! The damned fire's put out?' Pitched to grousing before anyone could reply, 'Jackasses locked up the wood bin, *again*? Damn the seneschal's prissy-fist rationing!' The behemoth's stride passed down from his great-grandsire impelled Alestron's titled heir to the hearth, where he unslung the axe and demolished the hasp.

'Does no good, hounding us to hoard logs, while our sentries freeze themselves useless!' Spun on his heel with an armload of kindling, Sevrand jerked his chin towards Fionn Areth. 'Off your lazy arse! A good man's nipped with frost-bite. Clear the grate and help lay a fire.'

But Kyrialt's silent, impeccable handling attended to that chore already. Since his forest practice could not be surpassed, Fionn Areth snatched up the storm-sodden cloak peeled from Vhandon's shuddering shoulders. As he hung the stained cloth to dry, rushed converse delivered the news that had sparked Sevrand's temper: Parrien s'Brydion's war fleet had run the blockade and made landfall, hell-bent on a vengeful assault.

'. . . a hot-headed folly turned wrong from the first,' the veteran captain was explaining, while the spurt of new flame in the hearth lit Dakar's riveted features in profile.

Vhandon pressed on, soaked to the skin, and haggard with sleepless exertion. 'There's an uncanny sigil at play behind this. Koriathain are meddling with Parrien's rage. His men have succumbed, too, driven to berserk slaughter. I think we're seeing a ruinous ploy to twist Arithon's working into an unconscionable massacre. The witches don't care who dies in the breach. We're facing the repeat of the *Evenstar*'s nightmare, but for stakes raised beyond all imagining.'

'How long?' Dakar broke in, distressed. The horrific damage already stopped thought; raised redoubled agony over the prospect of Arithon's future recoil. If Rathain's prince regained full awareness after the sword's song released, he must encounter the shattering brunt of the murders inflicted against him.

Talvish was scarcely a heart-beat behind. 'When did Parrien's crazed foray begin?'

Vhandon glanced up, harrowed. 'Today's dawn.' Against widening shock, as even the goatherd measured the on-going consequence, he qualified, 'Storm's wrecked visibility. Signal couldn't get through to the watch at the Sea Gate. That's why I've brought in the warning myself. Arithon's use of the sword has been turned! Enemies softened under its influence are being hacked down in cold blood!'

'The Alliance will call his Grace to the account,' Talvish summed up in crisp outrage. 'Added against diabolical luck, we're caught at flood-tide, which leaves Parrien exposed without recourse.'

Dakar shoved to his feet, stunned by the crux: stop Arithon's engaged conjury with Alithiel, *as if anyone could*, then Lysaer s'Ilessid would recover his wits. The whip-lash of Desh-thiere's cursed influence would face a butcher's toll of dead allies. Past question, the duke's brother and his suborned compan-ies would die, razed to ash in the virulent counter-strike.

Sevrand slammed his axe-head into a bench. Iced braid dripping, eyes baleful, he accosted the Mad Prophet. 'You'll do something, spellbinder. Handle this *now*! I don't want to see how my cousin will meet the loss of his last, loyal brother!'

'He won't wait,' Vhandon stated. S'Brydion of Alestron did not forsake family. Bransian would attack, and wrest Parrien clear, and try to fight his ensorcelled fleet's crews back to safety. 'This moment, the troops are being hand-picked to storm the Alliance encampment.'

'Fatemaster blindfold the eyes of the fool!' Dakar swore with grim venom.

Sevrand said nothing but bashed past the trestle and snapped the fat spell-binder up by his shirt front. 'Answer me, prophet! What have you seen?'

'Your untimely inheritance!' Dakar retorted. 'War prowess can't save this! You're facing a Koriani circle at work! Fly out in high passion, and your duke's effort must fail. He'll get trapped himself and deliver his rescue party straight into Prime Selidie's conjury!'

Sevrand jammed his quarry against the stonewall, intractable as a gored mastiff. 'Miserable coward!'

'No,' Dakar shrilled. 'A similar horror occurred at Vastmark. Happened the year before you were born.' He gagged, fighting the mailed knuckles gouging his windpipe. 'I swear by the puncture scar left in my back by Bransian's arrow as proof!'

'Truth!' Vhandon shouted, before Sevrand's hazed fury yanked the lodged boarding axe free. 'Morriel Prime once used such a snare in an attempt to assas-sinate Arithon. The Warden of Althain sent Asandir to weigh out the formal account. The charge rested: malign arcane influence, with the culpable opening excused as an action of war. Not cold-blooded murder by ambush, although the unsavoury circumstance certainly called for it.'

The heir to the citadel loosed an inchoate growl. While Talvish's blocking arm quelled Fionn Areth, Sevrand slackened his death grip, but did not let go.

Dangled on his stretched toes, eyes limpid, Dakar continued to reason. 'Even the best of your men will succumb. Their courage will just feed the blaze of Selidie's plot all the hotter!'

'Then back the bitch off!' Sevrand snarled. 'No, I don't care how!' Strained cloth ripped under his twisting grip. 'You are Fellowship-trained to uphold the compact, and this filthy violation against free will amounts to possessive enslave-ment!'

Never more brave, Dakar clung to dignity. 'My stance must guard Arithon.'

While Talvish shoved Fionn Areth away, Vhandon drove his weary frame upright. Both war-captains knew that action was futile. Short of death, they could not salve Sevrand's galled pride or stop the cascade of disaster: much as Dakar appeared the soft fool, he was anything but defenceless.

That moment, the latch clicked. The oak door hissed open, although no gust had hurled its swinging weight.

'What you need is a talisman,' a voice of firm calm interjected across the influx of flurrying snow. Uninvited, the precipitous arrival strode in: a slender form, swathed in a cloak stained with salt from a fast passage across the estuary.

'Elaira?' Kyrialt moved first, braced her shoulder and guided her to the fireside. He sat her down, this time ruffled to more than alarmed concern. 'Ath above, lady! What folly possessed you?'

For the enchantress's wilful return to the citadel posed no gift to her Teir's'Ffalenn's interests. Already he was under siege for his life. With her safety gone forfeit, her presence now served as Arithon's heart-rending hindrance.

'My Prime's matchless cruelty, what else?' Elaira touched the anxious liegeman aside, then flicked a drilling, cold stare towards Sevrand. 'I suggest you let go. We need the Fellowship's spellbinder breathing. Unless you don't want your cousin's doomed march to fetch Parrien curbed?'

The duke's heir turned his head and changed target. 'You have a better strategy in mind?'

Dropped with a jar to his heels that snapped teeth, the Mad Prophet barged his erstwhile tormentor aside and confronted the enchantress headlong. 'No talisman, lady!' he snapped, afraid. 'You can't challenge the force of a crystal-sworn oath! Cross your Prime's will here and now, even as the Fellowship's agent, I can't lift a finger to save you.' His misery palpable, he finished, forlorn, 'I don't own the straight access to power!'

As the plea failed to thaw her fixed stare, Dakar slid to his knees at her feet. 'Elaira! I beg you. Don't challenge your order. The horror will ruin your man's very heart! For Daelion's pity! Get out while you can! Keep faith, and trust Arithon's game plan.'

'I won't forge the talisman,' Elaira said, clipped. 'You will, and you can, once you're given the template. I'll show you the keys to unlock the seals used to fashion Selidie's sigil.' The enchantress bent her head then and stared at the soaked leather that gloved her trembling hands. 'I am not breaking orders. My Prime's directive, which has not changed, is to stand guard for Arithon Teir's'Ffalenn.'

When no one spoke, she swallowed, then added, 'You know, and I, what this atrocity will do to his mind if Parrien's warped revenge is not broken.'

Dakar made a move, strangled short, drained from green to stark bloodless as Elaira looked up.

He matched her regard, unable to spare her. 'You *realize* that your Matriarch desires you here! That she's driven you back to Alestron.'

Elaira shuddered. Past tired, wracked by an incandescence of pain, she admitted, 'If I suspected before, now I'm horridly certain.'

Dakar stood, spun away, ploughed through Sevrand and Talvish, then ducked

Fionn Areth's rapt interest. Not quite fast enough: he collided with Kyrialt, whose forestborn swiftness clamped an iron-clad fist on his arm.

'What did you see!' the young liegeman from Shand hissed into the Mad Prophet's ear.

'Nothing!' Ripped by the sucking faintness that foreran a true augury, Dakar bit his tongue, hard. *He rejected the prophecy! Forced back* the shredding clamour of talent that strained to unstring his composure. If he strangled the vision, he could not stem his dread. He knew, *Ath he knew,* and Kyrialt guessed also: that somehow, an irretrievable nexus had passed, sealing a future that would unleash a fixed consequence, bitterly final.

Of two destinies, posited, one had been lost when Arithon's beloved re-entered the citadel.

Seshkrozchiel

Conversations with dragons were never a linear experience, with concepts as words, laid one after the next into a logical sequence. Although Drakish language formed as other tongues, by varied sounds packaged in syllables, the meaning translated through vibration and symbol became enlivened by moving images charged with emotion. Such bursts evoked energy that branched through dimensions, swirling eddies that gathered to nexus points. The reactive tapestry could explode, across time. As the dreaming of dragons directed the power to weave or alter creation, a human addressed them, alive to that peril.

Davien's flaunting genius attended the prospect with no less than dauntless focus. Excess passion could kill by such an exchange; and decidedly, he was furious.

'Our Fellowship's relentlessly difficult trial has been made immeasurably worse!' His subsequent pause, stark as a walled barrier, marked the deliberate shift: from drakish vowels that scraped like grinding rock, into limpid politeness. He framed the Name of the being he tasked with exacting care: to the least tender nuance of letter and line, his respectful tone matched and then *cancelled* the discord of his accusation. 'Seshkrozchiel.'

The razor's edge trembled upon the stilled air, and unchained no rash probabilities: yet.

The dragon crouched with curled tail at the stony crest of a rise. Behind her, the northern ridge of the Storlains thrust upwards, wisped in smoke from a fumarole. Before her slant snout, the flat wastes of Scarpdale unrolled like straw carpet, the dead grass tufted over the swaths of old lava flows pricked with bare trees and leaden patches of ice. To mage-sight, the creature was blinding-bright – cloaked in living fire, laced layer on layer through an auric field that burned like an aurora, rising eighty-five spans from the needle-points of her dorsal spikes.

Human perception saw only tangible form, and *still* failed to encompass Seshkrozchiel's being. Her sheer size, at close quarters, towered over the landscape, massive enough to break rock with the indolent flick of a tail-tip. The curving arc of a fore-claw, alone, stood the height of the tallest man. Golden scales cast a scintillant, unearthly glimmer, with sovereign disdain for the overcast. She burned in mad glory. Blazing yellow, her slit-pupilled eyes held the terrible glare of the sun.

No need for the scorching, ash-scented breath that steamed on the winter air: where the incendiary puff might blister and kill, her concerted stare could annihilate.

Davien embraced patience. A pin-point fleck of consciousness cupped within the dragon's mailed talons, he need not fret over the mishaps prone to befall hapless flesh. Yet even discorporate, he was cautiously wise. Enough not to press like a fool for the answers today's incumbent peril left dangling. Dragons *never* spoke without forethought. The eldest of their kind, a hand's count in number, expressed themselves scarcely, if ever at all.

Seldom to rarely, when they courted anger, and Seshkrozchiel's rage towered over his own with a might that could shatter planets.

Her scaly eyelids lowered, considering. The gesture slitted the blazing, domed eyes, until thought/voice emerged as a whisper, listing reasons with gossamer delicacy. '*Abuse to kin. These young were stolen, while yet unborn. Murdered! Then left in the horror of death-pain. A malignant threat . . .*' The pause came, for the balancing. If, in chill fact, her willed choice included reconciliation. Seshkrozchiel's lids lowered farther, the hot gleam of her glance all but thrown into eclipse. Melody trilled through her finishing phrases, the harmonics *precisely* intoned to annul the agony fated to the hapless clutch. '*Ath's gift to the world being your charge to safeguard, Sorcerer! The Paravians' survival was threatened!*'

The spark that was Davien did not seethe in response; *dared not*. Bound to the service of dragons for two Ages, he kept his response hammered level. 'It is deemed . . . a wrongness, by humans . . . to slaughter their living.' The last word alone wrought the lifting of resonance: and its tonal meaning declared unequivocal terms: *that which is individual is precious beyond value.* Suggestively gentle, no more than a wisp, the Sorcerer's thought finished. '*The day's two-legged dead were innocent/unaware. Their ten-fingered (individual) hands did not seed this painful dishonour to egg-young.*'

The drake flared her nostrils. Warning only: no breath issued forth. The wait for her reply extended. '*None of ours, these two-legged.*' A lag, into which more pictures streamed, of offences that stemmed from such (individual!) busyness: of Etarra, and Jaelot, and other – hives – that leached refined light from the lane flux. The drake's breath released, uncurling fresh steam. Her aura expanded in majestic display, all fire and wrath! Then shrank back to the chiaroscuro emanation of boredom. The debated issue lay beneath her contempt. Source-of-being for such irritation might as easily *be* deranged on an afterthought, with such upstart two-legged erased from Athera's existence.

A curl of smoke twined, reeking of sulphur. *'Mankind!'* the drake hissed in the sting of subsonics. *That* thought framed a nexus. Near, and present, it stirred probabilities, as though reluctant to dissipate.

Davien withstood the heat, which ached beyond flesh. He absorbed the left ripple, a contest of wills most deadly and real, if not quite permitted to manifest. The Sorcerer outmatched the dragon's displeasure, though at heart, he was a volatile spirit, disenchanted with stasis. Ciladis was the more gifted ambassador; had excelled at soothing down the dicey nuance encountered in conference with drakes. Here, even Luhaine's slavish perfection would have revelled in nitpicking details.

Davien quashed irascibility, that Sethvir, on a *bad* day was better inclined to manage this perilous dialogue.

He faced this pass, alone.

In the calm after impact, he avowed by imperative, 'I am such a man.'

The golden eyes shut. More steam wisps vented: the drakish equivalent of laughter, perhaps, or an affronted rejection, coloured by lofty disdain. *'No such man!'* said Seshkrozchiel in ringing pronouncement, balanced by one word, all harmony. *'Ours!'* As the dead in the blasted ruin of Avenor had not been; Athera's dragons acknowledged no compact.

'Ours!' the drake repeated, a stabbing reminder of a dreaming once spun by an enclave at Corith. Seven spirits had answered: created by dragons, or else summoned into confluency by match, the warp thread of their destiny woven through the weft thread of a fate arisen by their traits of character. The Seven's origin as free-will beings, or not, did not signify, by Seshkrozchiel's reckoning. *'You are ours, made here to defend what is threatened!'* The after-note that described *just what* was protected sustained a cascade of evocative longing: the ineffable essence of the mysteries and the trifold dancing of Athera's Paravians.

Before these, the two-leggeds who despoiled were as nothing, and the workings of them, less than naught.

All music, Davien contradicted, striking the keys that shouted a triumph. 'They matter!'

Golden eyes snapped wide open, ablaze. The dragon regarded the spark of the Sorcerer with blistering query and challenge.

Davien resisted her thundering expectation, that demanded his chastened retraction. Commanded, in fact, though his stance overturned the bent of his former priorities. He did not retort, as he might have done. Did not satisfy pride through the scathing rebuttal that *was* the Teir's'Ffalenn's aura pattern.

Out of vital necessity, he would not draw Seshkrozchiel's attention to that man! Or risk turning her eye anywhere near the bloody affray that contorted Alestron.

The Sorcerer stilled *all* concepts. He gave Seshkrozchiel *silence*. Restraint, quite as terrifying as the coruscating consciousness whose ebon claws and fixed purpose now caged him.

Davien stayed adamant. Born to free choice, and no creation of drakish dreaming, *he knew who he was:* had seen his true Name illumined in grace in the presence of Athera's Paravians. Tenacious, his being reserved that firm boundary, come what may.

The dragon half lidded her eyes once again. This time, the stiff gust of her breath described whimsy. *'The task at hand is not one a string-puppet servant might fashion!'* The music that tendered the balance arrived, searing the statement to irony. *'Daedanthic. Fire Hands! In fullness, your Name is recognized.'*

The discorporate Sorcerer returned no submission, an insouciance to incense Luhaine's tidy nature. Davien waited, viced into a state that froze thought. Time measured the moments, meaningless to dragons. Their being did not acknowledge the values that gave mortal hours their frantic significance. Despite the pause that expected reply, the Sorcerer stayed self-contained, steadfast as a night-blazing star.

Above *everything*, he did not incline towards the east, or ponder the warfront dividing East Halla.

The dragon Seshkrozchiel abided, poised also. Her sun-shifted shadow etched the cold ground. Yet behind golden eyes, she was no longer still: her thread of awareness longed for the mineral pools that steamed and belched, boiled by the suppressed magma underlying the volcanic crater behind her. The itch rode her to wallow, scour her vanes and wing leather clean and burnish away the tarnish of soot that Avenor had left on her belly scales.

For all her want, another dreaming demanded, as lane tide, and star flux, and the errant dance of probability moved into a stately conjunction. Seshkrozchiel stood. She stiffened her dorsal spines to a chime of bright scales, lashed her forked tail, and arched her sinuous neck. Wide yellow, her eyes, as she lifted her fore-claw, that nestled the presence of Davien, also known as Betrayer.

'Our portal draws nigh,' Seshkrozchiel announced. *'My own, is your mind still committed? Has your heart's desire stayed true, that we should venture the opening?'*

The blue-white spark, that had seemed imprisoned by curving black talons was not, any longer, in evidence. Its nexus point burned, still vivid, still bright, but no more in the open.

The Sorcerer's awareness now seated amid the black depths of the dragon's left pupil.

'We go forth,' Davien said, a whisper that scribed a line between warning and caution.

Seshkrozchiel dipped her horned crest. Not acquiescence, as her answer shrilled danger. *'Sorcerer! So mote the way be.'*

The great drake reared rampant. Her kite wings unfurled. The movement raised wind. Fanned boulders shot air-borne. Static jumped from charged dust, became lacework and lightning, which crackled across the whipped air. Then came the shattering thunder of lift, as the dragon's leather-clad down-stroke hammered the elements at full strength. Seshkrozchiel launched upwards, an arrow of gold aimed into the heavens. She slashed an S-curve, roared, and levelled out, spines flat to her back and clawed talons folded, while her whip tail extended, graceful vanes steering. Her course bent over the bared vales of Scarpdale, for the purpose of piercing the moil inside a grimward.

She would dare to disrupt a ghost-kin from his dreaming. *This was no unhatched youngling's unreconciled remnant, but a grown drake slain in battle whose agonized death-scream stayed unquiet, and restlessly bitter.* A living dragon might cross his tempestuous shade and weave new creation to make scatheless passage.

But the Fellowship's field Sorcerer, entrapped within, tied yet to his failing flesh, and another, an unshielded spark stripped discorporate, must establish themselves by their own Voice. Seshkrozchiel could grant the safe escort inside, but not guarantee safe return.

Once any being touched into the fabric spun by a ghost dragon's insanity, contact triggered a chain of live interaction. Quickened awareness would meet the stuff of raw chaos, and engage an explosive response. The corporate mage held the anchor of his breathing flesh, for as long as life might sustain him. But not the one borne inside as pure spirit: Davien lacked substance, at risk of melding into the mad one's inchoate pain. The stakes were not malleable, or tame. The two Sorcerers called into service must secure their own Name against the fury of a drake shade's last reckoning. *If they could.*

War Camp

After two days of brutal riding, and one night's snatched rest, demanded by reeling weariness, Sulfin Evend closed the last stretch of road on approach to Alestron. The snowfall had lifted, replaced by a north wind that scoured the air clean as paned glass. Five hours before dawn, the blanketed landscape gleamed, polished to silver and shadow beneath a moonless sky spattered with starlight. The Light's Lord Commander rode yet without escort, down a swathed thoroughfare bearing no traffic.

The way seemed too eerily empty, in fact: snow masked the road, unmarred by cart ruts. No trampled trails left by couriers' mounts rumpled the pristine drifts. If the pervasive desolation sprang from the arcane flood of melody first noted as he by-passed Kalesh, the working strengthened with each passing league. On approach to the citadel, near to the perimeter of Lysaer's encampment, the surging harmony tugged at the mind with ever-more-insistent urgency.

Sulfin Evend rode as though wrapped in a dream. The music sustained him, moment to moment. The refined strains soared beyond hearing, alive to the seer's talent bred into s'Gannley descent: a true gift, once latent, now called into flower by his oathsworn tie to the Fellowship. If the uncanny resonance did not arouse visions, he stayed in the saddle by rote, his hand on the rein insubstantial.

The reliable gelding ploughed onwards, trail-wise enough to make its own way back to shelter. Quiet reigned over the frozen terrain, except for the crack of burdened snow sliding off smothered branches. The jinking tracks left by the tumbled-off clods seemed all the movement left in the world.

Sulfin Evend had stopped counting the sentries absent from check-points and watch sites. The uncanny allure of the conjury sapped any purposeful drive to make war. The beguiling song was not a compulsion; no man had been lured by main force. The summons cried peace, until longing seeded an ache to pursue a life of deeper meaning, and fear dispelled through the release of laughter. Into the night, the mystical weave raised the beauty of bare trees to a presence that tried mortal senses to witness.

Sulfin Evend heard his true self in that call. He did not serve here as commander at arms, but as a man sworn to the weal of the land, and a friend, devoted to Lysaer's protection. Almost, he felt lifted with joy for a home-coming, but for the wistful pull of regret, that he had no beloved woman awaiting, and no children to grace him with welcome. Desire beckoned, that he might shift his course, and steer his feal obligations to closure. Infused by such hope, he descended a slope and rounded a bend in the trade-road.

Ahead lay the site that the caravans dreaded, and a crossing the more-experienced couriers took pains to avoid, after dark. A thicket of young oaks shadowed the thoroughfare where the winding Paravian track from old Tirans merged with the approach to Alestron's snug harbour. Ghosts from the past often haunted that place, confections of lit floss and moonbeams that might tease the unguarded mind into madness. No such apparitions walked the night, now. Sulfin Evend saw only the vista of snow, painted in mystery and wells of deep shadow beneath the ice glimmer of starlight.

He forged ahead, while the gelding crashed through the drifts, eager to reach oats and stabling.

In the swale, where the grace of Paravians had trodden, ecstatic memory still lingered. Formless, the poignant loss tore the heart, enhanced by the present, belling cascade unleashed by the tones of grand conjury. One step to the next, the effervescent whisper swelled into a deafening cry. Sulfin Evend gasped, reeling, as Sighted vision welled up and crashed over him. He moved, wrapped in light. The singing echo of exalted passage remained: stamped into the ageless recall of stone, laced through the frost-layered black soil, and even stitched like a ribbon of silvery quiet into the blanketing air. The very elements shouted remembrance: a burst of lilting, ecstatic elation, as if sun-children played their crystalline flutes just past the reach of a thought, or the ranging call of a centaur's spine horn still rang bright harmonics through Atwood.

Sulfin Evend clung to the neck of his mount, shameless with need to steady his wheeling senses. As the horse crossed the hollow and topped the next rise, the view opened ahead, the rolling hills of East Halla spread under a sky deep as indigo silk. The guarded shore of Alestron's harbour unfolded, serene, ringed by the ancient signal turrets, with the citadel sited above the dark water, notching the crest of the promontory. No torches burned there. The siege imposed cruel privation. By contrast, the Alliance tents would be lit, with hot food to offset chilled exhaustion. Anxious and tired, Sulfin Evend approached the shack that marked the far boundary of the encampment.

The wooden shelter loomed at the roadside. No posted sentry called challenge. Another deserted check-point among many: yet on instinct, Sulfin Evend reined the horse in. A prickling pause awoke chilly foreboding. Though nothing untoward met his searching glance, an indefinable *something* stitched discord across the night's flawless fabric of harmony. Where the fresh horses for the outriding patrols should be picketed, not a groom was in evidence, nor even one living animal: no change, from dozens of other positions, left understaffed or abandoned. But the gelding beneath him snorted, uneasy. It pawed, reluctant, when Sulfin Evend dug in his heels.

Then his Sighted vision snagged on the subliminal *wrongness*: a faint, clogging haze coiled into the air, streamered like wisps in a current. Sulfin Evend rode into that creeping fog, rocked to a shudder of dread.

Then the gelding broke stride underneath him and stumbled, brought to its knees by a buried obstruction beneath the thick snow. Sulfin Evend pitched from the saddle and sprawled headlong into a corpse.

Stiff hands, hoared with frost and hardened with rigor, and frozen glass eyes stared back from the caved-in drift.

Sulfin Evend shouted in jolted recoil. No scout came running. No enemy archer fired from ambush. The eerie, unnatural quiet persisted, unbroken by bugle or drums. The night was *altogether* too still for a war camp that should have roused to his alarm.

Sulfin Evend shoved upright, his frayed nerves back in hand. He had seen enough battle-field carnage; men torn apart by the uncanny predators in a grimward, and whole companies burned to wracked skeletons by Lysaer's cursed fits of destruction. He had helped dispose of the ghastly, hacked dead, with entrails picked over by vultures. *Why should this sorry casualty prompt such a harrowing rush of revulsion?*

These butchered remains were beyond human suffering. The flesh was frozen to marble, and the blood, congealed from the gaping wounds. This man had been cut down from behind, slashed and stabbed in a frenzy of slaughter.

The Light's Lord Commander was not squeamish. Yet he felt unmoored as he reeled erect. When his spur snagged on another pathetic rag bundle, he realized: the odd humps strewn about in the snow entombed other soldiers: every hapless wretch once assigned to the check-point had fallen here as a casualty.

'Dharkaron's Black Spear!' Rage laced him, charged by the awareness: *that the blued film of haze clinging over this place was the shocked essence of life, released by the untimely slaughter.* As if the sprawled dead continued to bleed, subtle ether protesting the violence of their sundering.

Unmanned by that taint, Sulfin Evend gave way, hands clutched to his belly and retching. While his horse blundered off with its fallen reins trailing, he wept, unable to grapple the dichotomy imposed by his ancestral talent. Not set against the ethereal chord that still embraced his refined senses. Spun gold and crystal, such pure exaltation should *not* coexist alongside this visceral wreckage: men whose vital hopes and camaraderie had been torn to ruin, untimely.

Suspicion struck hard: that the unearthly draw of such beauty *might have been* unleashed for just such a cold turn of treachery.

'Ath above! Teir's'Ffalenn, you will answer for this!' If the Master of Shadow had played him false, and spun fair lies at Sanpashir, the Light's Lord Commander would never rest. Nor would any soldier under his captaincy forsake arms, before just pursuit brought a reckoning.

Whipped on by anguish, Sulfin Evend groped for his sword. He would swear his vengeance upon killing steel. Yet the instant his gloved hand closed on his weapon, the harmonic chord that suffused his awareness lanced his mind and woke dazzling light. He crashed to his knees, overset as a Sighted vision poured through. The unstoppable torrent was impelled by his blood-sworn obligation. The *caithdein's* line bred to serve Tysan's throne was not endowed with prophetic foresight. The seers of s'Gannley unveiled the *past*, illumined by truth fit to partner the s'Ilessid gift of royal justice . . .

. . . *the blizzard had not yet rolled in off the Cildein, and the guard stationed at the Alliance check-point had been diligent when the mystical chord of grand conjury first unfurled across the cold, morning vales of East Halla. The effect did not maze the wits of the sentries, or unstring their mindful initiative. Instead, the note sounded the key to the heart, and refined their innate discernment. Men who longed for their families laid down their weapons. Ones who craved peace left their posts. Others, whose dedicate will embraced warfare, remained dutybound without faltering. Day passed, while the war camp divided itself: some to abandon their commissions and leave, and others, to pursue the validation they sought amid conflict. The exodus was conducted with calm. No officer raised accusations for derelict duty or gave chase to prevent the desertion.*

As night fell, the snowfall closed in like a shroud, blurring the distinction between clan refugee and town-born aggressor whose faces turned homeward. The departing procession of ox drays and wagons ploughed through the rutted drifts. Laden galleys set sail down the estuary, while fishing craft and small tenders slipped from Alestron's closed harbour, towing more burdened, oared boats. The mismatched flotilla rode the ebb tide, unmolested by hostile action.

Dawn brought the marauders. They came with an errant, inbound war fleet, crewed by men rendered deaf to the burgeoning song. They landed like wraiths on the bank of the estuary, masked by the rampaging storm. Parrien s'Brydion would seize his revenge: strike a fierce blow, and tear into the flank of the enemies who had killed his older brother. Sighted vision hid nothing. The scintillant wrongness shrilled through, that the anger driving the foray was warped. Parrien's natural rage had been skewed. The horrific taint also twisted the men he commanded. Each one drew his weapon and slew, befogged by a clouding red haze that whipped their ambush into an aberrant slaughter.

Hanshire born, Sulfin Evend had witnessed Koriani workings enough to recognize his perception: the driving spells of compulsion laid here had been forged by the sister-hood's sigils . . .

The horrific vision became swept aside by the urgency of one thought: that if Arithon had tried a masterbard's intervention to disarm the cursed threat on the warfront, then Selidie Prime had spiked his brave effort with an unconscionable sabotage. After the massacre done in cold blood, outraged troops would leap to retaliate. The next to fall victim was going to be Lysaer, as the cursed pawn of Desh-thiere's design. Sulfin Evend aroused, wrist deep in cold snow, seared back to resharpened focus. He shoved to his feet, ran and caught his loose mount, then vaulted astride, and abandoned the dead to their forlorn unrest. For the sake of the living, he dug in his spurs to reach the Alliance war camp.

The hell-bent course of the Light's Lord Commander was not the only purposeful movement abroad on the dark, snow-bound vales. Wadded up in three cloaks, and puffing through the ice in his beard, the Mad Prophet closed long-suffering eyes and swore like a bull-trampled meat-packer. Frustration found him mired thigh deep in a gulch.

'Bollocks sucked up tight as burrowing rabbits?' The insolent teen in scout's leathers beside him flashed a grin, all bright teeth underneath a draped mantle. 'Get used to the misery. We have company approaching. He's alone on the road. Mounted, and moving west at grim speed on a horse that's already spent under him.'

Which assessment was altogether *too* accurate for a town-raised sprig of a boy: even one sniping sharp, and bred up to serve Alestron's warmongering field-troop.

Dakar abandoned his tirade to stare. And mage-sight delivered the shattering truth: that the *chit* was in fact a clanblood huntress, foisted here without anyone's asking. 'Dharkaron's thundering Chariot! Glendien! Your husband's probably choosing his knives to mince us both into weasel bait.'

'Kyrialt knows better. I look after myself,' the minx declared without conscience. Under the slouched hood, her fox-brush eyebrows shot up. 'You need my specialized talent, besides. Or you'd rather yon rider, whoever he is, climbs up your blind butt with no warning?'

Dakar conceded her pesky point. He had no choice. Sprawled in the surrounding snow with red weapons, the murdering fools from Parrien's war fleet lay felled in the throes of spelled sleep. He had not dared to risk the exposure of asking warped minds for permission. He had just dropped them, hard, and bedamned to the hindmost for the rough salvage of their sorry lives. The penalty stung now, a lashing recoil that would only get worse, the longer he pushed without rest. He could not let up, no matter the peril his endeavour faced by exposure. The culprits of the ill-starred slaughter were stopped, but the Koriani spells of compulsion laid on them had yet to be grappled and broken.

The lead-based talisman fashioned to break the Prime's sigils had been a nasty and difficult labour. The construct still pained him: a vicious headache, pounding the meat of his brain.

Glendien gushed, oblivious to her outraged companions, caught blindsided by the cheeky female insinuated into their midst. 'I like mayhem, forbye.' Her taunts rang too cheerful, since *her* private parts scarcely suffered, groin deep in a snow-drift.

'Not to mention,' she declared, an elbow jabbed into Dakar's plump ribs, 'we get to ding an enemy rider stark senseless. Might argue for reason to lift your dab spellcraft and wake Parrien up to defend himself.'

Dakar wanted to strangle her. 'Try that, and you might fetch his blade through your throat. Parrien loves his fighting too well, and that sigil still warps him for slaughter.' The sleep spell that dropped the brute *still* stung his hands, while his bones wore the bruising reverberation.

Glendien shrugged. 'Takes a rock-splitting maul to turn a s'Brydion head.' A quizzical glance unveiled ginger eyebrows arched with reproof. 'If you aren't planning to take down that horseman, I'm not laughing. Very soon, the fool's going to plough his labouring horse overtop of us.'

'Then lie down for me, wench!' Dakar flexed his fingers, prepared to shape conjury with a mean twist to stifle her gadding impertinence. 'Yon Alliance flunkey will see us as corpses, and may an unpleasant sprawl in the snow chill the sauce off your motherless tongue!'

Glendien snugged into her cloak fast enough to avoid the first cast – for *no movement* – intended to flop her face-down in the drift.

Dakar granted the eight men that Vhandon had sent a more graceful space to prepare. Once they had settled in prostrate comfort, he widened the spell template wrought to hobble Prime Selidie's victims. When his escort rested in oblivious peace, he set about stitching a veil of illusion. Lent the grisly tableau of congealed blood on dropped weapons, his living companions soon were made to appear as cold dead on a field of brute carnage. Revulsion ought to hasten the on-coming rider away without morbid lingering.

The Mad Prophet hunkered down in the gulch. The delay would cost dearly. Ahead lay a brutal course of tight conjury, with no guessing how long the Teir's'Ffalenn could continue to sustain Alithiel's exalted cascade. The mystical power awake in that chord remained all that suppressed Lysaer's curse-riddled instincts. No help could speed tonight's unpleasant work. The Fellowship Sorcerers had not answered the compact's charge to break the Matriarch's snare of delusion.

'May the almighty wheels of Dharkaron's Black Chariot mill the witches to crumbling dust!' Dakar would rather suck mortified flesh as a maggot than befoul himself touching Prime Selidie's treacherous web.

For mage-sight unmasked the vile lines of entrapment spun by her conniving. Parrien's warped passion fed itself off the light cords of affection and loyalty held between him and his fellows. The shared grief for lost comrades had been parasitized like a life-sucking network of fungus: a destructive compulsion that replaced rational thought with an insatiable thirst for ruin. The insidious weave overshadowed the worry posed by one incoming rider. Dakar could support no such minor distraction. While the talisman shielded him from falling prey to Selidie's draining compulsion, he enclosed every man of Parrien's suborned company under a protective boundary, then began the painstaking array of counterwards.

His work was not practised. An apprentice spellbinder lacked the strait strength and experience. Each man victimized through desire for vengeance must be wrested clear, one by one. Every strangling tie isolated, then singly severed, that Dakar might turn their flow counter: run the malign energy to ground under seal, then rebalance the void with the calm intent to hold harmless. Taut focus absorbed him. A careless mistake could lay him wide open to a Koriani attack.

Now critically engaged, he felt someone's insistent tug at his elbow. The rousting shake went on, cringing his nerves until his tranced focus upended.

Then Glendien's whisper drilled into his ear. 'Wake *up*, you incompetent lard sack!'

'Damned fool hussy!' Dakar flung out a tingling hand, snagged her wrist in a grip that hissed her caught breath through her teeth. 'Woman, why aren't you prostrate and dreaming, and what *idiot* mischief keeps shoving you in backside first and well over your carroty head?'

'Look, damn you! The rider!' Desperation broke through Glendien's welling tears for the pinching abuse to her forearm. 'Fault my scout's instinct later, *he's no pesky courier!*'

Fellowship trained, and facile with Sight, Dakar unreeled an outward channel for scrying. He captured the inbound horse, very close! Then the patterned aura of the mounted man burned through complacence and dazzled: the gold that bespoke a gifted talent, laced through by the glittering, indigo strands that denoted a *caithdein*'s oath, sworn to the Sorcerers.

'Blazing Sithaer!' swore Dakar, appalled. His veiling illusion must blindside no less than the Light's Lord Commander himself: a creature imbued by s'Gannley descent, who *would* Sight-read weavings of craft and event, plain as written text on a page. Sulfin Evend could stare straight through all simple work, with the wretched lead talisman an ugly presence nigh impossible to mask from attention.

'We're lost!' Dakar reeled for the crushing defeat that sold out every man who relied on him. His only choice was to give himself up. Negotiate, against hope, that a battle-trained officer would accept Parrien's slaughter with equanimity, and in such an improbable mood of restraint, be convinced to heed a stranger, as Fellowship emissary.

'Craven!' snapped Glendien. 'You will not fail us, now! My lineage carries the hunter's inheritance. But I can't bend the lane flux widely enough. You'll have to extend my short reach.'

The Mad Prophet snatched her offering. 'Take my hands! Quickly! Hide nothing more than our breathing lives and the resonance raised by this talisman.'

Glendien gasped. 'You *want* Selidie's sigil-borne craft left exposed?'

'Let rightful blame come to roost where it's due,' snapped Dakar, centred back into tranced concentration. Ath bless, that Alestron's obligation came under the Crown of Melhalla. To spare clanblood under the precepts of old law, straightforward permission must answer. He gathered the meticulous forms in the blaze of Glendien's initiative, that borrowed the semblance of stone and bare twig, then added the icy profusion of water contained into numberless snowflakes. These framed a pattern, invoked as a binding, to let the hunter blend into the natural landscape. *Here* became a mirror, amplified to reflect the night terrain, strewn over with corpses: the view any predator expected to see, based on the assumptions of fixated senses.

While Glendien melded the ripples of grand conjury against the back-drop of lane flux, the spellbinder entrained his awareness to hers, then engaged his initiate knowledge to expand the mild ring of her influence. His intervention locked down *just in time*! The errant horseman arrived, driving fast round the bend in the road. His mount's brisk canter thudded the ground, *much too close*! Clods of snow churned up by shod hooves pelted over the prone men, vacant stares unresponsive to peril, and slack limbs helplessly vulnerable.

A snarl of rife fury, the rider's gasped curse; then the whipped gelding leaped over the gulch. Dakar trembled under a shower of ice, as its blowing bulk thundered over his head and passed by, hell-bent for the Alliance war camp.

The Sunwheel pavilion that housed the Divine Prince was lit, despite the late hour. More, the enclosure was packed with the noise of an on-going officers' conference. Men from a dozen town companies crowded against the broad trestle, spread over with tactical maps, troop counters, and the scale-model siege engines to demonstrate strategy. No such thoughtful council impelled tonight's gathering. Voices clashed, laced by insurgency. No heads turned to look, as the tent-flap twitched open. No combatant paused to notice the cloaked figure who entered, chilled yet from the saddle.

'. . . a mad and unthinkable proposition!' shouted the westshore's ranked captain, stabbing an adamant finger. 'We must withdraw the troops. Now! Abandon this siege. Make a swift return by sea and relieve Tysan's crown seat at Avenor!'

'Such a journey, in winter? That's fanciful folly!' The advisor assigned from Kalesh slammed the planks with a meaty fist.

While map counters jounced and pinged like flung shot, more objection shrilled from the side-lines. 'You couldn't stage such a move! Or deploy enough men to make a damned difference before the spring.'

That heated point became trampled by the hard-bitten Etarran, left in charge of the field at Alestron. 'Today's crisis would already be settled before our galleys sailed halfway round the continent!'

More contenders clamoured, a deafening chorus demanding instant redress: here, a man urged retaliation for the scores of unburied dead. There, a pack of garrison captains howled for punitive action against an upsurge of desertions.

'We're facing a disastrous outbreak of crumbling morale!'

'Troubles enough, right here where we stand. This campaign's under sore threat of failure!'

'But damage to Tysan's crown regency? Surely disaster on that scale claims precedence!' That yelp, no soldier's, came from the seneschal, who managed the ledgers and finance. His clerkly objections became shouted down.

'We're no pack of nurse-maids employed by the guilds! We took arms to fight Shadow! Not to salve the set-backs to trade, or to guard against the hard-luck losses of merchants.'

Steel flashed, as a hothead waved a drawn blade. 'Should our assured victory here be abandoned, and for naught but crying hysterics?'

Fists shook, to clashing volleys of insults. The smaller disturbance that ruffled the crowd pushed inward, largely unnoticed. Still muffled, the traveller elbowed up to the forefront. As the disarranged officers spun to take umbrage, or snarled to bar his advance, a glance at the face beneath the draped hood forgave the insistent passage. Near enough, now, to gain view of the trestle, the arrival caught a whiff of exotic perfume.

That fair scent as foul warning, he realized what had thrashed the campaign to backbiting discord.

Flooded in candlelight, the majestic, stilled figure in the head chair would *always* command the eye first: Lysaer s'Ilessid, regaled in white and gold, and groomed to the glacial polish that screamed danger to any who knew him. The clasped hands were carved marble, gleaming with rings; the butter-cap hair a combed halo. Before his carved seat, as resplendent in purple velvet banded with red, a slender young woman perched with both hands clasped in a muff of white lynx. The Prime Matriarch of the Koriathain was arrived in state, a striking pale cameo with steel-hard eyes next to her mousy attendant.

That woman, also, did not deign to rise. Her arranged poise displayed icy calm, while the mounting uproar destroyed decorum, despite the distraught herald's appeals.

The pit trap was well baited, with the cream of the war camp's command ripe for shame, just ahead of the rope snubbed to hang them. Had tempers not flared, the veteran officers should have recalled Lysaer's ruthless style, when driving a divisive argument to sharp cohesion.

Sulfin Evend straight-armed his way through the last ranks to the trestle.

Accosted the self-contained creature in her Matriarch's purple as he tossed down wet gloves, with nary a pause to turn back his hood, or declare his titled identity. 'What brings you here, you blood-sucking witch?'

Electrically angry, he bowed with neat grace to acknowledge Lysaer s'Ilessid. Then he resumed his ferocious tirade, as his uncivil entry tore through the surrounding uproar. 'Don't claim you mean well by any man here! Or that you do us less than lethal harm! Not after I've seen the carnage your meddling has left strewn on the roadway inbound from Kalesh!' Bitter and blazing, Sulfin Evend glared down at the Koriani Prime, who never moved. Unruffled, unwavering, her settled regard endorsed none but the Light's Blessed Prince.

'My Lord Commander, just returned to our lines from the north,' Lysaer introduced with suave interest. He inclined his fair head, a lordly gesture that offered no apology for the sting of a favourite's affront. 'Answer my officer, Matriarch. His absence has kept him uninformed. Let him share the bad tidings that brought you.'

Prime Selidie rapped a command to her grey-robed attendant, who lifted a silk-bundled parcel, tenderly guarded between watchful hands.

'If your lordship will deign to see?' Her subservient courtesy suggested rebuke as she unveiled a shimmering quartz sphere. 'Please attend.'

Arms folded, feet braced, and eyes tight with suspicion, Sulfin Evend shoved off his hood. He held his steady gaze on the crystal, although the stone and its entrained spells of scrying set an ache in his teeth. He endured with clamped patience as the Koriani sister unfolded a scene of disastrous impact: *a wakened dragon flew free on Athera*. Sulfin Evend witnessed the horrific rain of death and fire just visited upon Tysan's defenceless citizens. The restored council hall at Avenor was laid waste: smoke and ash, all the buildings in Sunwheel Square, with their towering, golden brick keeps. The distressed murmurs and gasps, from behind, raised no comment from Sulfin Evend. When the grim scene dispersed, the Light's Lord Commander snapped, terse, 'When did this happen?'

'Yesterday's sunset,' the seeress replied, her prim hands busy wrapping the crystal. 'Our sisterhood's healers attend the survivors and shelter the displaced and infirm.'

Sulfin Evend bestowed no praise for such charity. 'Am I to presume that this' – the flick of a dismissive hand encompassed the Prime Matriarch – '*visit*' – the verb cracked in withering irony – 'offers Lysaer s'Ilessid your proposal to seal a Koriani pact of alliance?'

Selidie did not appear pained. But a rising flush spoiled her spring-lily complexion as she engaged his direct confrontation. 'Why object to our heartfelt offer of help? You speak out of rancour. A grudge from your spurned family that's two decades old scarcely serves the well-being of a people in sore need of their regent's defence.'

'A clever claim, truly.' Sulfin Evend's tight smile invited attack. 'Don't play me for a fool. I'm not blind. Or amenable, since both of us know the deadly nature of the little – shall we term them 'artifacts' – that Hanshire's magnanimous sisterhouse saw fit to lend through my father! Whose counsel cajoled him to extend such a peril to serve the cause of the Light? Such an ugly *dangerous* tool, and a potent gift, perhaps sown as a gambit, that one day might risk summoning the wrath of a dragon! Don't claim you're ignorant, or surprised such a monster has aroused to wreak punitive havoc!'

To Lysaer, whose royal bearing never escaped constraint, the Lord Commander pursued with acid delicacy, 'Tell me this, as Tysan's appointed protector: did you misplace the contents of the iron-bound coffer once bestowed by my uncle, Raiett Raven? Were the objects deemed lost when the treasury vault collapsed in the course of your brangle with necromancers?'

A diamond flashed, jerked by Lysaer's caught breath. His eyes, never soft, gleamed bright as chipped sapphire: he had always owned courage. Exposed to the riveted ranks of his faithful, he chose not to lie or evade. 'As you've detailed, this happened. I have to say, yes.'

Sulfin Evend regarded the Prime Matriarch with venom. 'Madam,' he said, low-voiced, 'I rest my rough case.' Then he added, unwilling to risk his turned back, even to grant his liege deference, 'May I suggest that you send this scheming creature back to her lair? Then allow me to dismiss these men, pending my martial orders! We need a close talk in private, my liege. There are certain *particular* facts you should know before you find yourself hobbled in promises that steer us towards certain disaster.'

Silk hissed, as Prime Selidie arose from her chair. Her pale, aqua eyes raked across her accuser, daggered with glittering malice. 'No thanks, and no welcome. I shall not forget.' She inclined her fair head to Prince Lysaer, while the unsettled gathering of officers shifted clear of her startling, swift anger.

'Your offer's been heard, madam.' Lysaer issued no platitudes. The flick of a ringed hand confirmed his magisterial dismissal. 'I remain unconvinced of your order's intentions. At my leave, you will return to your own, by safe-conduct and under armed escort.'

'Captain Ebrar!' Sulfin Evend barked, fast, to dispatch the watch officer. 'See to your sovereign's request. Send the two women packing!'

Token insult, and more than a prideful mistake, to haze with a show of force; steel posed a useless threat to a Koriani Prime Matriarch. Selidie acknowledged defeat without flourish. Incensed that her sisterhood's bargain was forfeit, she swept out, followed in mute obedience by her initiate.

The disgruntled garrison officers found themselves just as summarily excused.

'I have seen our harsh toll of fallen already!' Sulfin Evend cut across their exigent demands. 'I am well aware that we've suffered desertion, and more, that uncanny designs have disrupted our troops, and visited murder upon our watch-posts.' As the loudest contenders shoved forward, unsatisfied, the Lord Commander rapped out brisk orders before the debate could revive.

'You will let our casualties lie as they are! The dead are past suffering. Tomorrow, they can be brought in and tended. I would have their remains respectfully handled! Not trampled over by hot-headed forays, or an ill-starred rush to seize vengeance! Our retort, when it comes, will be savage, *well-planned*, and made worthy of their valiant sacrifice. Leave your prince to my conference. His justice won't fail you. Meantime, I want an accounting of stores. A complete list of every man missing. Those tallies will be in my hands before noon, with docked pay shares attached for inaccuracy!'

Assigned to that course of exhaustive work, the chastened officers cleared the pavilion. The last grumbling cadre had scarcely moved out, when the royal valet shot like a gangling hare from his master's personal quarters. His gratitude met Sulfin Evend's hard stance with a gush of effusive relief.

'You're returned, and none too soon. We're in need your steadying presence more than you may ever know.' A bob of his clipped head, then, 'Allow me the honour?'

Without pause, his fussy, peremptory hands reached to peel off the plain cloak. Belt and baldric came after, and with tsking disapproval, the travel-stained ruin of the dress surcoat trimmed in gold for state banquets. To the surprise of Lysaer s'Ilessid, Sulfin Evend endured the servant's deft touch without a whisper of protest.

Early Winter 5671

Vigils

Under moonless night sky, Dakar dissolves the final tie binding the fleet's crewmen to Koriani compulsion, then clears the last forms and smashes the makeshift lead talisman; and as the freed victims stir, groaning, around him, he strides forward and shakes Parrien s'Brydion by the scruff: 'Up with you, fellow! Move these wretches out! You've still got possession of your sorry lives, but nobody's safe until we have you inside the citadel . . .'

Herded from the Alliance encampment by a suspicious armed escort, Prime Selidie maintains her cankerous silence into the closed sanctuary of her pavilion; and before servants can remove her state clothing, she accosts the senior on watch: 'That Hanshireman is a black bane in the path of humanity's progress! I want him dead, or driven insane, and removed from s'Ilessid influence . . . !'

Atop Watch Keep, Arithon Teir's'Ffalenn stands unbending, the sword Alithiel blazing like a live star in his fixed hands; while Elaira keeps vigil, Kyrialt's concerned question brings anguished tears as she answers, 'How long? By Ath's glory, how can he keep on, sustaining a light that no mortal was fashioned to harness . . . ?'

Early Winter 5671

XII. Third Turning

U sual roles had reversed, with Lysaer fretted and pacing the carpet, while his war commander sprawled in an upholstered chair. Sulfin Evend toyed with a full mug of tea. His horse-stained leathers had been whisked away, along with his soiled shirt and caked boots. Now, his fisted hand propped his scrubbed jaw, still pink from a shave, while sore muscles relaxed in a thick woollen robe, lined inside with cosseting silk. Altogether, he was content not to move. A busy triumph for the opposition: the royal valet had snatched shameless advantage of an active man's sapping exhaustion.

'You're not drinking,' Lysaer observed. Paused between rounds, he leaned on the washstand. Beside him, the bed had not been turned down. Sleepless energy rode him, even in stillness, as he qualified with his back turned, 'The tea brought by my servant is only spiced. Not drugged with valerian, this time. I needed this audience worse than your claim for an overdue rest.'

Sulfin Evend measured the too-rigid set to the shoulders, beneath their flawless gold trim and velvet. The mild tone did not fool him. 'Face me,' he said. 'The wine in your goblet is also untouched. You don't drink, either, when you're nursing distrust.' In private, they might broach the dangerous topics too volatile for the dedicate officers. 'I will speak as you ask for the truth.'

'Very well.' Lysaer straightened and turned around. 'The Koriani Prime Matriarch went without fight. Too easily, in fact.'

'You don't like the sugary after-taste, either.' Sulfin Evend inclined his head. 'Selidie possibly has what she wants. Outraged troops will seethe to attack any target, if she seeks to ignite open warfare. Or she bowed out because my case

387

against her bit too painfully close to the bone. That's more likely. Having lost the initiative, her best option would be to hope the same facts might see us divided.'

Behind regal bearing, Lysaer's blue eyes were troubled. Quite terrifying, in fact, for their stripped vulnerability, as he regarded the war-captain who was ally and friend; and also chancy to cross as errant lightning, when his deep sensibilities conflicted. 'You confided, once, that your uncle Raiett never lied. Yet there has been a falsehood told to me while in your presence. When the dragon-skull wards were brought before Avenor's high council, and the arcane properties first engaged to mask our intent from the Sorcerers, I was assured that the artifacts were mislaid by the Koriathain. That Hanshire's men salvaged them after the rebellion, when one of the order's enclaves burned down.'

The Lord Commander closed his chapped hand on the mug and drank, with his steel gaze dead level. 'Raiett's gift for evasion was without peer. He seldom admitted to all of the facts. Never, if an omission suited his hidden purposes.' A next sip accepted goodwill at a word, that the strong tea was only a restorative. 'My uncle may well have known that the dragonet skulls' recovery wasn't a kept secret from the Koriathain. If he implied tension between contentious parties, the impression misled you, since none existed. The sisterhood always has worked hand in glove with the mayor's council of Hanshire. Raiett pursued power, in all of its forms. He could have held more than your interests at heart, aligned to an ambitious agenda. Quite possibly, up to his end in your service, he was still my father's pawn, after all.'

'And Hanshire hates royalty,' Lysaer stated, crisp. He snapped into movement, all scintillant fire thrown off by candle-lit gems. 'Why didn't you warn me when those hatchling skulls were first unveiled in my presence?' Unspoken, the remorse behind the hot fury driving his frenetic steps: *Avenor had fallen! People were dead for an ignorant error, kept under an unexplained silence.*

Sulfin Evend set his cup down before his tension shattered the crockery. 'Lysaer! Stop blaming yourself. I can't apologize for my callow youth. I was a rebel, cast into disgrace. Not all of my father's unsavoury intrigues were made known to me, then or now!' The rebuttal rang abrasively loud. Too relaxed from the luxuries, and too tired to field thorny inquiry, Sulfin Evend fought to keep his sharp focus: Lysaer was anything but a fool over the betrayals of striving politics.

'Don't ever lean on my family, my liege. Never dare set your trust in them.' Against a calm that was not complacency, alive to the quivering danger, the Light's Lord Commander chose the straight course, which might win salvation, or trigger disaster. Beyond pride, he aired the unsavoury history that had shadowed his paternal name for generations. 'Our mayors have always traded dark secrets. My sire learned the practice at his grandfather's knee, and Raiett was his closest confidant. Remember that Hanshire's provided a roost for

Koriathain all the way back to the uprising! The town's history is ugly, its past record core-rotten with treason. The hotbed of ill craft and entangled jealousy began there, with the dissenting minds that fermented the crown massacre intended to unseat the compact.'

'My regency breeds dens of adders aplenty,' Lysaer declared, but could not hold the mask of regal objectivity over the fresh wound underneath. 'What secretive innuendo moved you to accost the Prime Matriarch with a long-term, hostile conspiracy made hand in glove with your estranged relatives?' Was family blood thicker than any sworn oath? *'How can I be sure I can trust you?'*

The accusation broke across distanced shouts from outside, as a cook's brat chased a dog run amok, and a strumpet shrieked with lewd laughter. By contrast, the diligent rustle of the polishing rag lent no comfort, nearer at hand. The valet would be listening with a keen ear, while he cleaned soiled gear in the servant's closet.

Sulfin Evend ignored his commander's tuned instinct and closed out the distractions at large in the war camp. Survival right now relied on the taut figure, demanding straight answer, before him; whose coiled stillness must be adroitly handled, despite faculties flattened with weariness. Second chances were forfeit. Miscall one response, and curse-bound reaction would spin irretrievably wrong. Subtle changes made the prospect more daunting, as if tonight's altercation somehow carried a different thrust. The soft tread on the carpet had suggested retreat, not the pantherish stalk of aggression. Lysaer assumed no airs behind his state clothing. The pique that rejected the vintage wine was not princely confidence, crying the ruler's self-sacrifice, or the false avatar, mouthing the righteous fire of platitudes that promised triumph and glory. *This yawning break was in fact hesitation.* The ringed fingers that gouged restless prints in stuffed furnishings exposed a mortal man, cut to the soul by desperate entreaty. Sulfin Evend reassessed what he saw with stark care.

This night, netted under the mystical song that spun grace to placate hostilities, the tormented spirit in bright diamonds and gold was not insular, or sealed blind by the Mistwraith's ruthless compulsion.

More, the Light's Lord Commander realized he might speak, and be fully heard. The shattering grief evoked by such a stunned leap of conscience became terrifying for its limitless power to hurt. Sulfin Evend forced patience. While the heart in him tore, the wounded creature before him paced and trembled, ripped naked by the judder of reflections chased across dazzling finery.

'Where did you learn what you told us, tonight?' pressed Lysaer, and this time, as appointed regent of Tysan, he questioned in sovereign demand.

Sulfin Evend chose disclosure, direct as a grace blow. 'I was warned by the Warden of Althain. From my return, until the night that your treasury burned, I was given no opening to act, far less to advise you that we might harbour the lurking seed of a potential catastrophe. You wanted the s'Brydion,' he added.

'However I pleaded against that pursuit, your compromised faculties rendered me powerless.'

Lysaer stopped as though shot. His tortured eyes closed. Apparently the words touched an echo, inside him. Eventually, he said, 'Once, my half-brother told me that my father's hatred lent him no kindly foothold on which to negotiate.' Tears trembled, behind a tight throat, while the diamonds blazed on through an agonized battle to stay at grips with *what might be* natural reason. 'Did Sethvir also tell you that my dead wife, Talith, was not suborned to betray me?'

Sulfin Evend ceased breathing.

'I have had that nightmare,' Prince Lysaer revealed. 'That she was put aside while still innocent.' Though her unfaithful conception was not a staged ploy, one had to admit the lost love of his heart had been raised as a pedigree Etarran: too prideful, when estranged from his regard, and not above wreaking a ruinous price for his bitter abandonment. 'Don't tell me,' said Lysaer. 'I can't bring her back.' Unwilling to rail in effusive distress, he killed the unbearable subject. 'Enough hurt has been done, beyond any of mine.'

The reference extended far past the dearth of affection shown the son, Kevor, and the bloodless political expediency that brought his mother, Ellaine, to ill treatment. Spurred to keep pace, Sulfin Evend confronted his own bitter recall: the appalling cruelty of Earl Jieret's fate, and the honest allies destroyed in the deranged fit of fury that wrecked the campaign in Daon Ramon. He dared not stay silent before those raised ghosts! This pain was sanity, if a harsh trial he would *never* have sought, wracked in the breach as sole witness. 'You know you are cursed.'

'Every hour, since the failed coronation at Etarra,' Lysaer s'Ilessid admitted, distraught. His mouth tightened. 'Every breath, and each moment that rage swallows reason. Did you think I don't thrash in the unending nightmare? Or that this interval, where I can *hope* I'll wake up, is not bought through a constant struggle?' He glanced up, blue eyes limpid. 'I am as the candle, set aflame at the wick, and without the means to stop myself burning.'

'Merciful Ath,' Sulfin Evend whispered, wrung white. 'I did not choose wrong to stand by you, my friend.'

Lysaer moved again, lest the quagmire of his haunted past suck him down to hand-wringing self-pity. From table, to bedstead, to clothes-chest, to chair, revulsion dogged his circuitous flight. 'Three days ago, something terrible shifted aside. As if a ray of light I'd forgotten touched through a black cloud of hate. When I came to myself, I was burning a cliff head to magma! Such arrogance sought to sunder the tidal rip, and bridge the channel surrounding the citadel with fallen buildings and rubble. The Sunwheel officers with me were cheering. How they chafed for the hour of Alestron's defeat! Cried out, in my name, for the walls to be scaled and thrown down for the sake of the Light. I watched them clamour, eager for rapine. They would see clan children put to the sword, no matter if they were not forest-bred raiders, but civilized people, born into families of hardworking craftsmen. I have built and led a *war host* to this!'

'Not your true self,' Sulfin Evend said quickly. As though to soothe down a whipped horse, he insisted, 'We are not our mistakes. You can always change course. Rise above the destruction engendered through you by the Mistwraith's design and seek better choices.'

'Could I?' The anguish blazed. Lysaer snatched up the wine. Liquid slopped as he hurled the goblet into the brazier that heated his quarters. The flames shot up, blue, while the glass fragments scattered, bright as flung tears on the carpet. 'I have enslaved criminals. Broken their spirits in chains on my galleys where once, common decency would have lifted such misery from inhumane bondage. A just prince serves a sentence that preserves a man's dignity. Once, I thought I knew who I was! I believed my own goodness could never have ridden a storm that sought visceral thrill by crazed butchery.' He paused, stared through by a hollow silence that gibbered with *legions* of dead. 'The shadow lurks in my own heart, won't you see? The foothold for obsession has been, all along, the spoiled, overheated, *childish* urge to punish my faithless mother's prized bastard!'

'Yesterday's happened!' Sulfin Evend snapped, blunt. 'You can bleed yourself with recriminations until you crack under self-punishment! Or you can stand firm. Take honest stock of the resource you have, and bear up, keep on striving and heal. My watch officer told me you were brought in by litter, laid out from over-extension.'

Lysaer snorted. 'A convincing act.' Met by disbelief, he folded his arms and leaned on the support for the tapestry that walled the enclosure. When he laughed, his chiding, wry humour was new, and beyond either man's startled experience. 'My fine, strait-laced officer, why should you look poleaxed? If I actually had been prostrate, throughout, you would have returned to the wreck of a dozen sorties! Believe me, I was all too wakefully able! Our warmongering garrisons have none of your sense. My little collapse had to be staged. A puling embarrassment, and the only convincing excuse I could find to absent myself and get my train of fanatics to quit the field.'

'They would turn on you,' Sulfin Evend allowed. He had faced the same fervour, all but died on the knives of the zealots whose weakness demanded the splendour of hailing a saviour. The threat took on a sinister edge, aware as he now was, that a grandiloquent chord of high conjury became all that checked the raw flame of dissent; how much worse, when that steadying influence waned, and the curse-driven conflict resurfaced? 'We are two, and outnumbered,' Sulfin Evend said, thoughtful. 'Like the horse that's been savaged to leap, or fall prey, you've managed to keep things distracted.'

'By hopping through hoops and crab-stepping sideways.' Lysaer shrugged. He might have poured wine, were his fingers not shaking. 'We have weathered, waiting upon your return. Held out, and cajoled Kalesh and Adruin from ravening bloodshed. Ranne and Fennick and your picked cadre of watch-dogs have strong-armed the resistance through extended manoeuvres and drills.'

Until breaking news of the ruin at Avenor upset such unbiased care-taking; Lysaer's darkened eyes and frenetic exhaustion told over the difficult ground. He had been alone, the apex of a fractious host still thousands strong, who viewed him as a punitive avatar. They would force his promise to answer the hatred they pinned on the Spinner of Darkness.

Sulfin Evend rubbed his tight forehead, rushed by the pulse-pounding kick of the tea. The courage stunned *thought*, that the velvet-clad shoulders before him were not yet bowed by defeat.

'They are afraid,' Lysaer admitted with sorrow. 'My own doing. I've abetted Desh-thiere's bleak purpose too well.' He shuddered, wrung by his relentless dread. 'The poison I carry inside will not rest. I don't know how long I may have, before I'm overtaken again.'

How could one man answer this appeal for help, far beyond mortal means to deliver? Desh-thiere's blight was not vanquished. The harmonic working that bought this fragile reprieve was, at best hope, a temporary remedy. Sulfin Evend surveyed the wracked creature before him and saw a frail vessel pushed nigh unto breaking. To broach an appeal to call in the Fellowship *would* provoke a cursed back-lash Lysaer was untrained to survive. Tonight's admissions had skirted the sore: an abiding distrust of arcane wisdom and sorcerers, begun by the Rauven mages' early rejection. Sulfin Evend *dared not* petition Sethvir. Even *if*, one-on-one, Desh-thiere's threat might be handled by strapping Lysaer immobile, the desperate course could not be tried in a war camp with a pack mind-set: men armed and trained, then whipped to blind faith in an invincible, coveted idol.

'How can I go on?' Lysaer said, distraught. 'There are no safe-guards for what I've set loose. Whether I will, or not, death and ruin will happen. I am naked and shieldless to stop such momentum.'

'Then fight against Desh-thiere's incursion with me!' Sulfin Evend implored. 'Make a stand, for your own sake! I won't abandon your side, or revile the effort, no matter how sorry your stumbling failures.'

'I can't retire.' The protest was not arrogance: gadding hatred would raise a new figure-head under which to seek destructive outlet. Lysaer found a chair, let his knees give, and sat, ringed hands shoved through the hair at his temples. 'Nor can you reverse what's become a fixated doctrine.'

'An ambitious rival would just take my place,' Sulfin Evend agreed.

'You could lose your life!' Lysaer straightened and stared. 'The late trip to Tirans was barely enough to divert your upset the last time.'

'All right. That worrisome thorn is well justified. We can't rein back what's already in motion, but only try steering the juggernaut.' Sulfin Evend stood up. He crossed to the side-table, poured a fresh goblet and set the offering beside

Lysaer's damp fingers. 'Drink, man. We're planning. First toss the companies who crave action a sop.'

'Avenor?' Lysaer raised the glass for an unsteady sip.

'This attack by drakefire gives you reason enough to board ship and go back to Tysan. Gather Avenor's tried captains yourself. Sail out of here fast as the weather allows and get clear. I'll serve the most belligerent companies with marching orders, make them pack up and follow your lead. They'll be staged westward, after your advance guard, on the pretext of working salvage after the disaster.'

'You'll stay on here in my name?' The golden liquid shimmered, yet another bell-wether of unrest.

'You must go without me!' Sulfin Evend implored. 'If you stay, we are utterly lost, once you break.' *When,* and not *if*; this was no moment to flinch from that fact. 'Command of the East Halla campaign remains mine. I will set Kalesh and Adruin on their ears, bang recalcitrant heads, and find out if ennui and bad storms can't wear down the resolve upholding the siege.'

Lysaer set down his filled glass with a click. 'My dear friend, your noble course is predestined to fail. Don't you see? A great drake flies free. The only fortress built to withstand attack by a dragon lies under an old blood clan duke who has subverted Tysan's regency. We can't condone spies sent as sanctioned ambassadors! Whatever state information was leaked, Mearn's and Parrien's actions served us with treason. Without the Light's fervour, we might stage a pardon for Bransian, since he was not present to handle his brothers. Given time, we could stall, perhaps even mitigate some of the damaging charges. But not at this pass!' Too much engaged resource rode on an outcome emotionally pitched for collision. 'The Alliance has attached too many factions whose vindication will not brook forgiveness.'

Sulfin Evend leaned across and picked up the abandoned wine goblet. 'Still, that doesn't grant us the licence to throw up our hands and give way.' Against Lysaer's dread, the Light's Lord Commander raised the crystal in toast and saluted doomed valor with humour. 'I'll enjoy giving Selidie Prime a sick headache!'

His grim glance locked to Lysaer's, Sulfin Evend acknowledged the relief: that his utmost effort also must ensure that the innocent were not brutalized, should Alestron fall in defeat.

The small boat, which had crossed Dakar's party of rescuers from the citadel, and Parrien's flotilla of anchored prizes, still rode off the spit across from the harbour mouth. Against breaking dawn, the fugitive fleet was exposed, surrounded by hostile forces and stripped of the covering storm. The free port that might offer Alestron's flag a safe haven lay far beyond these confined waters. Worse, as the tide changed to flood, the fierce rip of the ebb built too swiftly to buck if the ships tried the crossing to Alestron. Even rested, strong oarsmen would be overmatched; and the after-shock from Prime Selidie's compulsion had left Parrien's companies exhausted.

The covert procession stumbling out of the brush scarcely resembled the attackers who had made their rapacious landing the day before. Returned, forlorn, to the wind-raked shingle, the men were beaten and flagging. Short tempers prevailed as the ships' officers took stock and tallied what Parrien's suborned obsession would cost them.

Not all of the s'Brydion galleys might be saved.

'Interfering witches should die for this!' One peppery captain spat in disgust. More grumbled threats couched in gory detail, promising plans for revenge. Deadlocked wills argued the case for retreat, as the bitter wind whined over ice-crusted dune grass, and thrashed the winter-bare heath.

'To Sithaer with Koriathain! We'll fix things, right here!' A weathered first mate with a jut to his jaw pounced first on the saving asset. 'Nab the fat ninny. Somebody ask if he's got the clout to blindside that forsaken blockade.'

Dakar was snagged under the armpits and presented to Parrien's disgruntled senior command.

'Can you?' asked the biggest, stroking his befouled boarding axe. 'Conjure a dab little net of deception to let us raise sail and slip down the channel?'

'Awake, this time, mind you!' another shoved in, pained by frost-bite from last night's forced nap in the open. While the duke's brother watched with unchastened grey eyes, hedged about by Vhandon's picked escort, the loaded inquiry stretched.

'Blundering jackasses!' Feet plugged in the sand like a hefted bull-terrier, Dakar said, 'You'd spit in the teeth of Dame Fortune when she's already smiling full in your face?' The tiresome, on-going need to shape counterwards killed his patience with brangling s'Brydion aggression. 'This far, by my grace, you've got whole skins. Push that luck, keep on the muscle, and you'll find your crews stranded here. I won't look back. Not though you plead like poxed whores, crying for my skilled attention.'

'Peace!' thundered Parrien in his deep voice. 'If you're daring to map out our future yourself, tell us straight up what you're planning.'

Reluctant men turned Dakar loose without pummelling. If he wanted to sulk, he forwent the indulgence. Only tugged his mussed clothing to rights and talked fast, jostled by sea-wolves who pushed in to hear what his trained talent might offer them.

The news was unhappy: only a few of the galleys could risk the fraught passage on the out-bound tide. Those picked to depart must go lightly masked, the sharp look-out at Kalesh and Adruin turned aside by a binding akin to Glendien's knack for concealment. Against the meddling interest of Koriathain, little could be tried, past a talisman keyed with ciphers for misdirection.

'I can't guarantee such defences will work!' Dakar said, buffeted in the gusts that parted his beard and snapped through his ginger-and-salt hair. Chilled by the warnings of a back-lash fever, and alarmed as each minute brightened towards daylight, he snarled down Parrien's objection. 'You have no choice! The best ships leave without you. As the target spear-heading Prime Selidie's trap, I can't send you along. Your active protection requires my presence, and the Fellowship's stake in Prince Arithon's lineage commands my return to the citadel.'

'We don't leave the gift of sound hulls to our enemies,' the most grizzled veteran howled.

'Bravo!' Dakar mimed applause. 'How splendid to see someone thinking with more than the brainless edge on a sword-blade!' For of course, the sensible option stayed pitiless: four of the prize galleys had to be culled, then holed and scuttled in the channel. The rest would sail, which left the last, to be boarded and manned by all of the stranded crews. 'Hand-pick your best oarsmen for the sprint into port.'

No seasoned mariner gainsaid that necessity: with the tide turning counter, the shifts at the bench must serve in short relays, breaking their backs at a double-time stroke lest the rip current should overpower them.

'Ah, we agree!' Parrien grinned. 'There's no safety in stalling!' He shrugged, his massive arms folded across his spattered bracers and surcoat. 'We shove off now. If I don't want a nurse-maid in tow, or a chivvying flight back to the fortress, you can't risk the loss, or break your stricture of free permission by trying to stop me.'

'I won't have to.' Dumpy and tousled, his doughy features nipped pink with cold, the Mad Prophet should have appeared ludicrous, holding his ground. Yet the fierce smile that split his beard was utterly unsubmissive. 'Your duke wants you out of Prime Selidie's reach. That means going home, with eight loyal men under orders to knock you down, if need be.' His gesture deferred to Vhandon's armed guard, ripe for a picked fight, with clean weapons.

'Strike at your own, or back down,' snapped their sergeant, who was well-matched for size and armed prowess. 'You cannot accompany the out-bound fleet, Parrien! Your very presence poses a threat, the ships and men under you a hot liability to your family's welfare and survival.'

'Forewarned is forearmed,' the glib culprit quipped.

Yet Dakar's stiff silence refused stabbing humour. He need not respond, since the changing tide waited for nobody. Already the winkling, first riffles curled into the sucking swirl of deep eddies. The returning vessel must strike out at once, or forfeit her margin of safety.

The determined glint in Parrien's eyes enlivened his shout to set the men under him moving. To hear him, his fleet would part forces, as planned, with four of the prize galleys sacrificed to lend the muscle to breast the rough current.

The loading began, to the scrape of harnessed weapons on chainmail. Amid the scramble to launch the beached tenders, Glendien elbowed her way to the fore and splashed through the shallows. Her gadding positioned her at Dakar's heels, as the surge of the launch plunged the leading craft through the breakers.

'Don't let Parrien fool you,' she gasped, ducking spray as the keel smacked over a tumbling crest. 'That's one stubborn idiot set for a mutiny, if I'm any judge of bad character.'

Dakar blew streaming water from his moustache. 'If you say so, child.'

Glendien hissed an oath, not about to be patronized. 'Watch your back, bucko. The brute will cast back off, once we're set on the dock.'

'He can try.' The Mad Prophet turned a cold shoulder and stowed his bulk on the rocking stern seat. Since sopped cuffs posed a misery, exposed to the wind, he tucked under his cloak like a storm-rumpled owl. 'The night's been hard enough. I'm going to sleep.'

The boat bobbled, as more passengers scrambled aboard. The seamen who steadied the craft waded deeper. Their practised, hard shove, which sloshed up the bilge, caught Glendien by surprise. Forest-bred, and no sailor, she reacted in time. Escaped a raw soaking, but lost her objective: Dakar slouched, already loutishly snoring. No poking jab in the ribs disrupted his complacent nap.

'Pack yer hopes in, lass!' said the grinning, armed bear who threaded his oars amidships. 'Fat lubber won't move. Not for anyone's joy, short of heaving him overboard.'

Glendien scowled. 'Lumpish male follies don't impress me one whit.' But in fact, she found herself stymied as neatly as Parrien. If the spellbinder had a contingency plan, no one would disclose the arrangement.

The white-capped crossing proceeded, unpleasant, with the open boats doused at each stroke. No one was dry when the tenders snubbed under the flagship, tossing at anchor. While the huddled occupants clambered aboard, two hardy men remained at the oars and ran out the line to the pinnace brought across from the citadel. The smaller vessel would be taken in tow, salvaged on hope, since she must be cut loose if the surge in the channel set too much drag on the galley.

While the boatswain cried orders to man the main benches, and the drum-beat called for a backwater stroke to slacken the cable and winch up the anchor, Dakar turned green and sought refuge below to conjure his promised protections. Glendien stayed in the lee of the foredeck. While the reduced fleet prepared to part company, she trained all her forest-bred instincts upon Parrien s'Brydion.

The fellow was nearly as tall as his brother, built to the same bulk and imposing fitness. His square, scarred fists were as well versed at arms. The grey eyes were more restless, opaque as filed iron, and the soft tread, a hungry tiger's. Where Bransian cropped his fair hair for a mail coif, this brother liked to fight helmless. His mink-brown braid was tied in the old style, with blunt chin and squared jaw kept clean-shaven. Against leathery tan, a mariner's squint sharpened his ornery scowl, though the family retainers showed cheerful good grace towards his barbs, reviling their interference. The slight limp, and the stiffening bruises inflicted by Selidie's ill-usage only showed when he believed no one was watching.

Discomfort scarcely hampered his wits, since he caught Glendien staring. 'I'm a married man, minx! Admire the view and get over it while the shrill terror's not here for a scolding.'

Laughter made staying annoyed with him difficult. Glendien bared her splendid white teeth. 'Who says I'm interested, bravo?'

'The tart look in your eyes, wench. More truthful than a woman's tongue, any day. Learned *that* from the wife for survival.' If the quip covered subterfuge, his player's mask held. Parrien's seamanship and his handling of men maintained an exemplary standard. When the strength of the ebb tore the heart from the rowers, he jumped down and claimed a place at the bench, then hauled the oar for two back-cracking shifts, shouting bawdy jokes for encouragement.

The lone galley reeled onward. A snagged bone in the teeth of the vicious current, she cleaved up spray, side-slipped in her clawing effort to thread the tight channel. She battled past the creamed beach of the south point, nearly swept onto the shoaling rocks. There, the reeling pinnace was jettisoned. No one watched, as the current hurled the abandoned vessel aground in an explosion of spars. The rowers had no attention to spare, beyond driving their oars. The hissing, rushed waters wrenched their practised stroke ragged. The galley slewed, an unruly beast wreathed in spume as she breasted the mill-race between the outcrops at the sentinels' towers.

The change happened like the shift into dream, as the prow shot over the lowered chain and entered the anchorage. The beleaguered galley wallowed into flat water, her bilges awash, and her gasping men beaten dizzy.

The last shift at the benches drove her, limping, through the ripple of calm waters, and brought her at last to the Sea Gate. Thrown ropes from ashore were secured to the bitts. Oars run in, the flag galley was warped to the dock.

Her salt-crusted thwart scarcely hove alongside, when a mantled figure detached from the men cleating her fast to the bollards. A leap off the rail saw the arrival aboard, where the wind snatched back the hood of a silk-lined mantle. Streaming a banner of shining, dark hair, the slight person descended the companionway to the oar deck, side-stepped a crewman's lecherous grab, and caught Parrien's neck in an embrace.

'You great oaf! Welcome home,' said the woman, and fastened a lamprey's kiss on his lips.

The man went without air for a very long time. When he did raise his head, Glendien supposed by his curses that the wife's presence posed a hellish nuisance.

'You will disembark, now!' he snapped, both fists working to peel himself from her locked arms. 'Tiassa!'

'Snorting ox! Muscle won't win this. I won't.' Twined to him, the lady laughed in his teeth. To Glendien's admiration, she met his challenge with taunts, as the galley's rough company gathered to stare. 'The harbour chain's raised. Your brother's left orders to keep you penned in. If you try defiance, that's well and good, since I'm present and coming along.'

'Over my carcass!' Parrien roared.

'Assuredly!' Tiassa tossed back her loosened hair and smiled with honeyed indulgence. 'A sensible somebody should ding your dense head with a ballast rock! Or else Prime Selidie nets you again with another pestiferous sigil.'

While Glendien watched, the compromised husband swept his chattering wife into his arms. The deck crewmen cheered. Others slapped their knees, sniggering. Yet before outraged manhood contained her impertinence, or contrived to deposit her back on the wharf, a cold voice cut in from behind.

'She stays with you, Parrien!' The Fellowship spellbinder had come above deck, sick nausea notwithstanding. 'On land or sea, and by her free will, Tiassa remains at your side. And before you ask, yes! I've held her permission to back that decision since yesterday.'

'Ath above, your contingency!' Glendien crowed, then looked on with salacious enjoyment: Dakar, upright and wobbling on rubbery legs, still managed an astonishing note of command before Parrien's blistering fury.

'Do you truly want Tiassa placed at grave risk? Outside of these walls, you cannot protect her! If the Koriani Prime turns on you again, *as she will*, your close ties to your wife will cause her to succumb. Your lady will share the disaster provoked by Selidie's unclean little binding.'

'Don't think I'll forget this!' Parrien threatened.

'Swine! Put me down.' Tiassa punched her mate in the shoulder until he caved in and released her. 'Look at yourself, idiot. You reek like the slaughter-house. Plan your dastard's revenge as you like. But for those of us liking our company civilized, spare us the horror and bathe yourself first!'

Parrien s'Brydion glanced at his hands. Then noted the vile stains on his harness: the blood and spattered brains and dried filth left after his vicious night's action. The unpleasant stench hit him: clothing and mail and crusted weapons, his person was wholly befouled. He could not account for the number of his slaughtered victims: persons he did not recall striking down, not in forthright battle, or anything near his right mind.

'Ath's own mercy!' he gasped, overcome.

Aware that he folded to heave up his guts, Tiassa grabbed hold of his elbow. Her yell summoned Vhandon's by-standing sergeant. 'Help get him away!' To her reeling husband, she said gently, 'Just let's take you home.'

The crisis was broken. Once Parrien s'Brydion was dispatched ashore, the wearied crew secured the war galley. Her hatches were battened and her sea-going gear stowed without further protest. Yet when Glendien turned to congratulate Dakar on his wily strategy, she discovered the spellbinder gone.

Only one clever man who bent, tying fenders, seemed aware of that quiet departure. 'Fellow's gone up to Watch Keep, at speed. Said that Prince Arithon's faltering, and soon to come out of the uncanny trance that sustains the Paravian sword.'

The astonishing word was signalled from the shore beacons: that the duty watch had sighted a gathering panoply surrounding Lysaer's state galley. The glittering vessel had an assembled, armed escort, with every sign the flotilla intended to cast off and sail on the ebb still running apace down the estuary. The avatar's boarding could not be mistaken, acclaimed as he was by a fanfare of drums and the flourish of trumpets that echoed across open water.

For whatever reason, Lysaer s'Ilessid looked to be leaving his rabid campaign. Excitement stormed through the citadel's streets. Set against the triumph of Parrien's secure recovery, high feelings blazed up, incandescent.

As the garrison upholding Alestron's defence gave vent to explosive relief, men on guard at the walls yelled and hurled snowballs, laughing like boys. Women wept over their laundry tubs. A crew digging out drifts to clear the choked thoroughfare danced to the mad scrape of a fiddle played through a tavern window. Speculation chased rumour: without the horrific threat posed by Lysaer's elemental light, Bransian's troops could thrash human numbers. Rampant fears shrank, the burden of dread returned to known ground, and commonplace weapons of steel. Hope resurfaced, unquenchable, that the killing siege might be repulsed, and s'Brydion sovereignty salvaged, unbroken.

Dakar caught wind of the momentous change as he puffed on his way towards the promontory. His effort to flag down a dray, bound uptown, nearly saw him run down by the whooping driver.

'Damn all sour luck for the tits of a hag!' Tripped onto his arse from his narrow escape, the spellbinder slapped ice from his boot cuffs and righted himself. Mage-wise, he found no cause for rambunctious joy: this manic celebration over Lysaer's retreat was desperately premature. Urgency drove him. He *must* reach Watch Keep and raise Arithon's awareness ahead of the Sunwheel flagship's departure.

'Drunk made things easier!' he groused, wheezing onwards over iced cobbles. He hugged the verge, while the duke's feisty officers thundered on by, mounted on horses with steel caulks to manage slick footing. When the next clattered up alongside, Dakar whirled about and accosted him. 'Ravening lunatic! Have you people nothing worthwhile to do beyond trouncing exhausted pedestrians?'

'You don't want a ride up to the heights?' Talvish extended a powerful, gloved hand with a second mount on a lead rein. While the upstaged Mad

Prophet clambered astride, the blond captain added, concerned, 'Can you hurry? Elaira says we've got trouble.'

'She was much too polite!' Dakar jabbed in his heels, clinging through the buck as the goaded horse galloped. Unashamed, that they were the high-handed riders now scattering hapless foot traffic, the spellbinder shouted as Talvish spurred alongside. 'The channelled effect of Alithiel's peace has a limited range of influence! If Lysaer's recovered his natural awareness enough to stand off Desh-thiere's geas, he's not healed. The sword's influence on him will fade, with distance. Brace up for the back-lash! His cleared reason will snap before his ship clears the estuary!'

The breathless warning paused, through the swerve, as the horses plunged abreast through a postern. They broke past and pounded up the switched-back lane fronted with fieldstone houses, as Talvish captured the gist. 'The s'Ilessid will fall prey to the curse off Adruin? He'll have half an armed war fleet under his hand! Then you're fretting over the fate of the escaping refugees fleeing the war front?'

Deserted soldiers and clansfolk still would be bogged down in disordered retreat: easy prey for a battle flotilla manned for aggressive speed and hard action.

Dakar hauled on the reins. While his scrambling mount leaped over a hand-cart, and the elderly man hauling buckets shrilled insults, he gasped, 'Lysaer will turn and slaughter those people outright! A tragic mistake. Better such fury should fall on us here, than destroy every life that Prince Arithon's risked untold peril trying to salvage.'

Atop Watch Keep, the Paravian sword was still blazing. A scintillant halo of rainbows shimmered against the noon brilliance of day. Arithon's erect stance had never changed, a miracle no less than terrifying. The more so, given the naked necessity of disrupting a channelled trance deeper than human knowledge. If the Sorcerers might have tracked his experience, none appeared for a consultation.

Which short-fall Fionn Areth was swift to berate from his perch, obstructing the turnpike stair. 'Well, what use if all that vaunted wisdom leaves us stewed in the heat of the crisis?'

Kyrialt never paused, fingers flying as he stripped off his knives and unbuckled his sword-belt. Intent on the venture to break Arithon's conjury, he minded the skittering edge of tuned instinct that warned him against bearing arms. 'The Fellowship of Seven don't plonk on their arses, doing nothing but spout off blind judgements.'

While the grass-lander flushed, the clansman's keen scrutiny measured the Koriani enchantress. 'You don't like this, lady.'

'Am I transparent?' Elaira tugged the hair she had freshly rebraided clear of her damp mantle and chafed the hands tucked back into cold gloves. Although she had slept since her brutal sea-crossing, clothes had not dried in the droughty keep. 'I don't like meddling outside of my depth. Who has ever experienced a living Paravian?'

'I have.'

Kyrialt whirled towards the entry, blasted by the breeze let in by the Mad Prophet's return.

'I was a child,' Dakar qualified, fumbling to reset the latch. 'Dragging at Asandir's heels, and too young to fathom the commitment required of an apprenticeship. Awe can't begin to describe the experience. I feel that way, now.' Breathless and red from his break-neck ride, he faced the prospect ahead with shuddering trepidation. 'Ready to faint clean away to escape. I was told, afterwards, that I stayed comatose for three days.'

'You don't have that option,' Kyrialt declared. The sheared glance that followed speedily shifted Fionn Areth's recalcitrant presence.

'I don't have sense!' Dakar stated in acid correction. 'Be certain you wish to risk yourself, Kyrialt. We are likely confronting the spun coil of fate, at the risk of ecstatic insanity.'

But the clansman already led off up the stair, accompanied by Elaira. Dakar shuffled after them. Fresh sores on his knees made him wince. Haste in a saddle had never agreed with him. Talvish, outside, tended to the hot horses, while he, still the floundering, unstable seer, was left holding the almighty stick: a Fellowship charge to safeguard an intemperate prince, blood offshoot of three radical lineages endowed with explosive, rogue talent. Beyond dry-mouthed terror, he settled for grumbling. 'If I'd been Sethvir, depend on the certainty! I'd have left young Dari s'Ahelas unfit to breed fettlesome offspring.'

'Won't flourish by stalling,' Kyrialt admonished, lost from sight up the ward-room ladder.

'What can you hope to accomplish?' snapped Dakar, huffing a lapsed distance behind.

'Whatever will serve.' Kyrialt stepped out onto the battlement, his dazzled sight masked behind a raised forearm. 'If nothing else, I can offer my muscle if somebody needs to be carried.' He steadied Elaira on the glaze ice, unruffled by the gust that billowed her mantle.

Dakar emerged also, eyes scalded to tears. The beacon flare of the Paravian sword slapped flesh with near-flaying intensity. Beyond visible light, the fierce emanation knifed through skin and bone, ringing through shivering marrow. The rarefied sound defied hearing and ran tingling through the deep viscera.

Kyrialt's gallant courage lasted one step, before he crashed onto his knees. Elaira stayed upright, unabashedly crying, while Dakar reeled through a dizzy attempt to frame wardings. The shield failed. Alithiel's resonance stripped away reason and muddled the most steadfast purpose. If Fionn Areth had ventured the stairwell, no one kept the resource to notice.

The prince on his feet with the raised sword in hand seemed unreachable. Not poised on a catwalk ten paces away, under sky like an indigo canopy.

Here, the soaring chord of grand conjury seemed to wheel the vaulting of heaven and earth. Breathing caught, whirled to melodic ecstasy, while the spirit exploded, deluged by fiery colour that burned with a hope beyond dreaming. Dakar stumbled, plunged to the wrists in chill snow. The sensation jolted his already shocked nerves. He realized, afraid, that he was played-out, too exhausted from his foray ashore to handle the requisite focus. If Kyrialt might freeze from exposure, or Elaira take harm for his failure, the urgency for saving action drained from him as so much meaningless noise.

'Get up!'

The shout drilled his ear, dissonant through the music's beguiling majesty. Dakar groaned as the busy clasp of chilled fingers tugged at his flaccid hands.

'Get up! Now! I will need your help.'

Elaira's features swam into view, with her determined strength forcing him upright.

'Back me!' she snapped. 'I will forge the focus. Just follow my lead and grant me an anchor.'

Grounding, Dakar realized through fuzzy awareness. She asked for a corded tie to the earth. Any means to resist the ethereal harmony that scattered the senses. The stone tower itself might fulfil that need. He only required the presence to work and establish the link by permission. The staid shadow arrived at his side would be Kyrialt, fighting for the recovery to help brace his reeling balance.

That human support lent the foothold to rally his frayed self-command. Dakar tightened his boundaries. While the sword's song rushed through him, he narrowed his focus upon the blocks of sturdy Elssine granite beneath him. This would not be the interlocked masonry of the citadel walls, crafted by Ilitharis Paravians. The spellbinder prepared himself for the brute difference: a man-made shaping, chiselled by force. Teeth set to endure, he reached for the impacting stress of close contact.

Instead, all his references were swept away by the torrent evoked by Alithiel.

Dakar tumbled into a living framework, *immersed in the structure of mineral itself*: a joyful dance that rang, layer on layer, multi-faceted beyond imagining. A play of consciousness, never dormant or fixed, but aware of itself across the full arc of eternity. The requisite permissions were *given*, a shout of vibration that knew him and acknowledged his kinship, under true Name. Welcomed by the comfort of a seamless partnership, Dakar offered Elaira the haven to launch her vaulting leap to seek Arithon's subsumed awareness.

Where she went, how far or how perilous the mystical course of her journeying, the untrained onlooker lacked the resource to see. Yet none standing witness escaped the moment when Alithiel's unfurled power snuffed out.

Light failed. Exquisite harmonics collapsed, torn to silence. Heart and mind, the uplifted spirit was pitched back into earth-bound existence. The pain of separation wrenched out a scream, as ecstasy dissolved into inconsolable weeping.

Unable to withstand the shock, traumatized by a tumbling fall that slammed like the bars of a cage, Dakar embraced the faint that hurled him into oblivion.

Early Winter 5671

Shock Wave

The scream as the silenced cry of Alithiel stranded Lysaer s'Ilessid at the mercy of Desh-thiere's curse carried far beyond the coast of Melhalla. In distanced Atainia, within the hushed chamber where vigil was kept in the fast quiet of Althain Tower, the adepts attending Sethvir sensed the anguished echo. The forceful surge of event stamped the flux, resounding through the tenuous tie linking the Warden's earth-sense.

The young man posted as listener for the Sorcerer shared the inconsolable impact as the baleful scene blazed into vision . . .

. . . wracked by an onslaught of agonized pain, Lysaer pitched to his knees on the deck of the Sunwheel flagship. The officers at hand for his ceremonious departure stared in shock, unaware as his compromised will battled to resist his doomed plight. Desh-thiere's curse made a mockery of his human effort. Weeping, he scarcely heard the shouts of his trusted honour guard. Before the stunned deck crew, poised to cast off for the run down the estuary, he fought the unnatural urge to wreak violence, to no avail. The blind thrust of aggression inside him broke into ungovernable rage. The rags of held sanity shone through, even then: the light-bolt unleashed as he shattered ripped off his fist and burst harmlessly skywards.

The star-burst explosion raised cheers from his dazzled following, and cast crazy-quilt shadows from the towers of the besieged citadel.

The planned retreat to Avenor could not happen now. Lysaer's cruel defeat, made precipitate by Alithiel's silence, *would* spare the innocent lives, already in flight to escape the blood conflict; but at the cost of a dire set-back for Sulfin

Evend, and the remaining s'Brydion defenders whose choices had committed them to the battle-line . . .

'Merciful grace! Ath grant a redress from the throes of such suffering!' murmured the robed adept.

His colleagues bowed their heads, rendered speechless by the news of Lysaer's relapse. Their pause acknowledged sorrow upon sorrow, while their tireless care served the Sorcerer's dwindled vitality. If hope had diminished, they refused despair. Sethvir was kept guarded. His blankets were constantly warmed by the fireside to drive the creeping chill from his flesh. Day and night, fragrant herbs burned in the grate to freshen the sick-room air.

'Our Fellowship cannot help spare the princes entrapped by the siege at Alestron.' The rust-grained cry emerged from the pallet, where voice had been dormant for weeks. Sethvir of the Fellowship opened blank eyes. Unseeing, his gaze stayed fixed on the ceiling, beyond the least spark of cognition.

The female adept posted by his pillow did not try his taxed spirit with questions. Frightened, she turned in appeal towards the listener, calm as carved onyx beside her. 'Bear only passive witness, I beg you. Althain's Warden must not arouse! In his state of suspension, the transition to wakeful awareness might finish him.'

The gifted young talent raised a hand in acknowledgement, while still immersed in deep trance: and another shimmering shower of vision cascaded from flux current to imprint . . .

. . . washed, but not sanguine, Parrien s'Brydion accosted the duke in black anger over his compulsory home-coming. 'Since when do we crawl belly down like whipped curs before meddling Koriathain? For shame, brother! Our father would weep, or disown us all for a pack of slinking cowards. Here's half the prizes we seized, scuttled outright! Holed and sunk in the channel by our own hands, and all for your cosseting me like a girl who's never been tested by bloodshed!'

Elbows braced on the tactical maps heaped in his private study, Bransian sighed. He looked aged. Full chainmail and surcoat no longer filled out his angular frame, or the unmasked bones pressed against haggard flesh. Despite wasting hardship, with no end in sight, Bransian matched his sibling, stare for accusing stare.

Then he said, against an unnatural quiet that blistered for deathless conviction, 'Ath above, Parrien! I happen to know *just* how foul it feels, to be used as a witch's kicked game piece!' He could never forget: the dismal hour on a Vastmark slope, when his own coerced hatred had launched an arrow to murder the last Teir's'Ffalenn. 'Did you really think I could stand back and permit the same hideous plight for a brother?'

Parrien swiped at the wet snag of hair missed out of his hasty battle braid.

'May Daelion Fatemaster's two-eyed vigilance drop the pox on all Koriathain!' He shrugged. 'If weapons would serve, I'd exterminate the lot.' He caved in with the bad grace of a dog dragged off a bitch in ripe heat. 'I don't like being caged in a broody hen's box, to peck, cackling, over the nest-eggs. If you don't mind, I'll just duck the wife's lashing tongue and join Sevrand to belt down neat whisky.'

Which was a fine intention, to tame disgruntled spirits, if the citadel's stores had not been hoarding the last jug for medicinal emergencies . . .

As the image frayed into the entropy imposed by Sethvir's draining illness, the listener stirred, his dusky skin ruffled up by a chill. He measured the expectant faces around him. As though hope breathed through heart-break, his fellow adepts shared the moment's spontaneous suspension. Gathered to honor the Warden of Althain, they understood without words, the atrophied flesh left so frighteningly uninhabited could no longer be eased by their ministrations. After long months spent enduring the downward spiral, the awareness drew their senses into collective alignment.

Today, the cosy room with its tidied clothes-chests and lit candle seemed touched by more than stilled air, crawling with empty shadows.

'Change,' murmured the elder adept on guard at Sethvir's right side. 'Death or life, the balance stands poised.'

The white brotherhood understood hard-fought passages. Wise to the mysteries, trained healers without parallel, they knew the failing body often gathered its reserves, prior to passing the Wheel. The departing spirit would rally one last time before crossing over. Sethvir's opened eyes showed them no change. His marble pallor as yet displayed no rosy tinge of quickened pulse.

Yet *again* came the sense of a resharpened shift toward purposeful focus. The listener recorded another flare from the frayed web of the Sorcerer's earth-sense, then the upwelling flash of evocative vision . . .

. . . Dakar the Mad Prophet, tucked abed and undone by despair. The loss of Alithiel's music inflicted a lethargy too wide to bridge over. The ache sliced his heart, inconsolable. *He had no wish to live.* The savourless air he drew into his lungs felt darkened to desolate silence.

The song that flooded his being with the wonders that danced past the veil had ceased. Life itself paled before such grand invention. All determined endeavour seemed diminished, as vacant and pointlessly wasteful.

Hands shook his slack shoulders with biting force. 'Dakar! Get a grip, man.' Arithon's badgering urgency stung. 'Rouse yourself, now! You must raise active will. Make the effort, or you won't survive this!'

But the future extended, lightlessly bleak. Dakar shut his eyes in rejection.

'Fetch my lyranthe!' snapped Arithon, angry. 'I am not resigned! If I could withstand a sunchild's presence and return from the King's Grove in Shand, you can pull yourself back from the edge and rejoin the fight to stay with us!'

'For what reason under Ath's sky?' Dakar shivered, weeping. Crushed under by shame, he covered his face before bearing the burden of his inadequacy.

'Your master would tell you.' Arithon answered through slicing harmonics, as his deft hurry tuned silver-wound strings. 'A transcendent encounter's dropped you at the crux where too many aspirants give way. All your hard-won wisdom is needed, my friend. You can never rest, after what you've experienced. Rise to the fresh challenge. Even though you can't see, yet, search for new and deeper meaning! I promise this much: the way cannot open unless you stay present!'

The lyranthe spoke then, as the Masterbard's talent lifted sound and harmonic into evocative fugue. His song blazed a course of unparalleled courage: *that today's wakened pain and solitary separation carried a meaning beyond present knowing. Amid the unassuaged, longing awareness – that now understood an existence surrounded by still wider grandeur – must refound its pioneering delight. Seek, anew, the profound recognition: that each individual was cherished by Name, and supported to further its quest for adventure, fired by limitless welcome . . .*

The tonic surge evoked by the Masterbard's artistry rushed through the listener's poised focus, and sparked joy like the chiming note struck off a tuning fork.

On the pallet, Sethvir caught his breath with a gasp. '*Ath iel i'cuel'an alesstaierient, Teir's'Ffalenn,*' he whispered in awe.

'What's happening?' Cloth rustled, as the female adept by the Sorcerer's feet shot up straight, surprised by the flush of revitalized energy that flicked through his weakened tissues.

The listener shook his head. 'I'm not sure.' Past question, the erratic images framed by Sethvir's earth-sense were *not* due to Arithon's unfolding melody in distant Melhalla. That healing was pitched for Dakar's affliction, with the Warden's spontaneous response no more than a grateful acknowledgement.

Now, against waiting stillness, the north wind hissed over Althain Tower's obdurate stonework, and scoured the glaze ice off the high sills. Inside, nothing stirred but the candle-flame, fluttered by draughts through the case-ment. Sethvir's opened eyes remained vacant. His slow breaths subsided, with his snowy hair and combed beard spilled like floss across the crisp linen. The adepts maintained their tuned attention, beyond the expectation that the Sorcerer's consciousness might ever spiral back into quickened awareness.

He would cross the Wheel. The adepts braced for that grief. Their creed disallowed intervention, even for a parting that would rock the world.

Alone, the listener applied his superb talent. The vast well of the Sorcerer's earth-sense stayed drained, but the silence was no longer empty. *Something* stirred there. An inchoate, foreboding sense of near movement, elusive beyond known experience. Frowning, his folded hands quiet, the adept groped after the source. Echoes scattered before him. His deft probes shot back, rebounding as though, from the source of unformed possibility, a rolling wave sharply crested.

And broke!

The listener shouted, whirled into confusion by a surge of raw power beyond his trained depth. His warning cry left no chance for his fellows to dissolve their rapport. Interlinked, they were also flung into recoil as Sethvir's submerged consciousness snapped free, the live thread of his essence slung out of the fatal entanglement that bridged the gaps in Scarpdale's damaged grimward.

The catalyst driving the frightening change stormed over distance and flooded the scent of ozone into the chamber. Sethvir's flaccid fingers bunched into fists. The adepts stationed next to his pallet cried out, tossed by the shock wave as he arched into convulsion. Smoothed blankets dragged. Arranged pillows tumbled. The paroxysm wrenched tremors through the Sorcerer's frame, while a fiery shimmer wrapped his skeletal form, head to feet. The adepts' refined senses were bedazzled. Their wide-ranging quietude shattered. As the Warden's dimmed auric fields roared up into searing brilliance, the blast all but knocked his wise healers to black-out prostration.

A static play of small lightning laced through Sethvir's presence. Everything touched by the arcane display lost form, solid outlines dissolved into coruscating energy. The dissolute patterning changed just as fast, respun back to firm continuity as though the whole cloth of existence went fluid, or turned itself inside out. The transition crackled like sparks leaping a gap, with familiar experience reshaped afresh by split-second frames of remembrance.

The only spirit not frightened witless was the Sorcerer, wracked in contortion on the mussed bed. Then the fire-storm subsided. The harsh spasm let go. In candleless dark, Sethvir lay quite still, his wide-lashed, turquoise eyes fully awake. 'Seshkrozchiel!' The unaccustomed speech grated. 'Ware dragon!'

While the six adepts strove to rally dazed wits, the ranging link of the Warden's earth-sense resurged. His split-second awareness sorted and mapped the locale of three other Fellowship colleagues: *Traithe, still in Atwood, protected by the raised bounds of Paravian wardings; Luhaine, traversing the sea-bottom to relieve a fault-line that threatened an old Paravian binding; then Kharadmon, rousted at need from the task he assisted at Methisle Fortress . . .*

His summoned arrival raised a shriek of wind through the shutter no one had time to unlatch to admit him. Rushed, even for a discorporate spirit, he cracked, without greeting, 'I've noticed the active vortex in Lanshire. Do I gather the Betrayer's rash bargain came due?'

Sethvir coughed. 'Yes.' As the great drake had served in the caverns at Kewar, respinning lost flesh from the void, now the pacted reckoning reversed, and burdened the renegade Sorcerer. 'Davien owes Seshkrozchiel his promised repayment.'

'A momentous achievement,' Kharadmon declared, tart. 'Don't, please, expect me to feel sorry for him.' A clipped pause acknowledged the assembled adepts, whose healing care should have been supported by that errant spirit's delinquent service. 'I cannot sympathize with Davien at this pass. You were left too far gone!'

Sethvir raised his eyebrows, and husked, 'You won't shed old grudges? We were not abandoned. Our colleague left Kewar and responded in time.'

Kharadmon huffed. *'In time?'* Blankets flapped. A dropped pillow tumbled, and Sethvir's beard became whirled into snags by the breeze of that scathing rebuttal. 'Not by my lights! Never, while you are weakened enough that a shade has to sit on your atrophied chest to keep you pinned flat in a sick-bed.'

Moved at last to steady the ruffled adepts, the discorporate Sorcerer ran on, 'Sethvir's in recovery because the wardings that secure Scarpdale's grimward are down. Yes. Dismantled. The leaks aren't just breached, they're eliminated.'

Against the collective, rapt stares of dismay, Kharadmon completed his heck-ling reassurance. 'My word, you are safe here! Athera won't face destruction by rampant chaos. Not today, anyhow. You have never witnessed a live dragon dreaming the active thread of creation?'

But the listener already beheld the effect. Tuned into rapport with Sethvir's earth-sense, his awed witness shared the vast hole, punched through Lanshire's winter terrain . . .

. . . *a coruscating blackness shimmered and flared, ringed by live fire and ominous lightning that pulsed like a heart-beat.*

The rippling edge altered perception like smoke: as though the framework that underpinned form ran fluid as moving thought. Stones and trees came and went, reft by curtains of light, clothed and reclothed by the warp and weft currents of consciousness.

Beyond that strange boundary, nothing seemed touched. Not an errant breeze stirred the sere grasses. Each rock and scrub tree, cloud and live creature of Scarpdale's landscape unreeled, serene and intact by the cataclysmic might of Seshkrozchiel's will . . .

The listener bowed his head. 'Events move beyond the sage reach of our counsel.' His fellow adepts must acknowledge: such raw power as this eclipsed them. Seshkrozchiel's dreaming outstripped the mystical light, held guarded within the groves of their brotherhood's hostels.

'Our commitment is final,' Kharadmon affirmed as his essence settled to rest. 'Fellowship destiny lies with the dragons. Their dream aligned us for

Paravian survival, and even a strand casting can't show the outcome Davien's unleashed in our midst.'

Now, great drake and Sorcerer broached the unknown. Seshkrozchiel's trespass against a grimwarded ghost would not receive a sane welcome. Her powers now matched an unquiet rage, and locked forces in trumpeting challenge. For the price of the Warden of Althain's life, two other Fellowship Sorcerers braved that merciless maelstrom. Hapless motes in the titanic struggle, Davien and Asandir stood at risk, their joined plight also guarding the stranded shade of the stallion, Isfarenn.

'How shall I serve the moment?' Kharadmon asked of Sethvir. 'Although, like the ant asked to quarry the boulder, brute force with a chisel works better. I have no more hope than a match in a gale-wind to right things should this rescue turn sour.'

The Warden's lips twitched, almost an amused smile. 'Can you manage the patience? I need a courier's support, running messages, until I've regained the strength to stand upright.'

Kharadmon pounced. 'The Koriani Matriarch needs a licking reminder that we're not neglectfully tolerant?'

'Send her packing!' said Sethvir, balefully sharp. 'Far and fast, since her sisterhood's meddling has dared to apply arcane power for bloodshed. No Prime can manipulate Alestron's cursed quarrel as her personal battle-field under the compact! Once her order's been quashed, there's a short, petty list. Warn Verrain at Methisle to expect state visitors. Then we'll need to refigure the wards over Atwood: first to admit refugees into clan shelter, then to dispatch Traithe out to Methisle by way of the focus at old Tirans.'

'Those Paravian defences will tie up my resource,' Kharadmon snapped, impatient, since harrying witches was his style of choice entertainment. 'You'd trust Luhaine to answer your next call for help?'

'He'll have to.' Sethvir closed his eyes. 'For Asandir's sake. Did you think your rank tongue's not a trial for anyone in need of a restful recovery?'

'I don't bury corpses!' Kharadmon warned. For no masking platitude eased their dire straits, or the fate of the Fellowship's field Sorcerer. 'We dance as the handmaidens to calamity, yet.'

Sethvir had no rejoinder. His harrowing task here at Althain Tower had won no space for reprieve: two other slipped grimwards required repair. If the flaws in their shielding were minor, as yet, such latent peril could not be left to wait on the crisis now raging in Scarpdale.

'Your Fellowship will rise to the challenge ahead,' the listener ventured in tacit support. 'Nor should you fear for the worst at Alestron. The transcendent note Arithon called forth from Alithiel woke his cursed half-brother to forgotten vision. Lysaer s'Ilessid found tears for his blindness, if only for a brief interval.'

Sethvir shared that optimism. 'It's the self-blinding belief in the absence of grace that seeds our cold measure of despair.'

Kharadmon snorted, a self-contained tempest that snapped towards the casement. 'I don't care horse apples what *might* go wrong, when we've got a dragon at large, flying down the throat of disaster! I am gone,' he declared, 'to reap the tame whirlwind, flip skirts, and prod insolent Koriathain.'

Evenstar

Wind thrummed through three courses of sails and taut rigging, and salt air wore spray like the dazzle of diamonds. The brig *Evenstar* frisked through the waves of the Cildein. Above, thin clouds streamed like white feathers on a sky of deep blue. For Feylind, no finer pleasure existed than the rushing course carved by a deepwater keel. Her exuberant laughter, then the fond quip from the sailhand who spliced a chafed line by the mizzenmast reached Teive, where he stood taking sights by the stern-rail.

Smiling, he watched the rejoinder: the flippant swish of his woman's yellow braid, as she tossed her head, *so*, then gave the sailor a playful cuff and capped it with a pithy remark. The hoots of the men bending on the repaired mainsail blew aft, with the roll, as the brig knifed over a crest.

Froth flew on the wind. Even the clamp-jawed old quartermaster cracked a grin. Such moments were like perfect jewels, unremarked until they were threatened. Almost, the azure brilliance of day could eclipse anxious thought of the heading just changed at the turn of the watch.

The *Evenstar* breasted the whipped seas of winter, cleaving a churned silver wake for the fortified port of Adruin. The run she attempted had no safe precedent. A Sunwheel flag snapped above the streamed pendant proclaiming her Innish registry, and her manifest listed resupply for the army, encamped on the field at Alestron. Teive sucked in a breath, unwilling to examine what awaited beyond the blockade's outer check-point. His cherished captain would not reconsider her course. Arithon Teir's'Ffalenn had enabled her heart's desire. His friendship acknowledged the bold exuberance that took after her fisherman father, who had died young on the raging sea. For the masterful gift that acknowledged her calling, and placed the keys to navigation in her eager hands, Feylind would not stint the loyalty given since childhood back in Merior.

Neither would Teive relinquish his place as first mate on the deck at her side.

'This brig is Feylind's bulwark,' he told the staid helmsman, whose frown bespoke shared concern for the rumours flying downcoast. The war host besieging Alestron was said to be fifty thousand strong. 'Whatever comes, we stand behind her. Arithon gave all he had to preserve our independence when we were beset by Koriathain. To do less in return is not in Feylind's nature.' Nor could anyone who loved her diminish that genuine quality.

The same pranking gusts that gave her delight also hastened the *Evenstar*'s passage to relieve the beset s'Brydion garrison. Tide and wind were in favour. The brig would breach the mouth of the inlet by midafternoon, where the bristling bother of war-time inspection would stall them in port through the ebb. Teive's pent frustration almost relished the prospect of baiting the officials to enliven the delay.

'Ran over us last time like scrabbling cockroaches, poking in crannies and corners.' Since the *Evenstar* never ran contraband goods, such tireless exploration and knocking taps against bulkheads uncovered no secret hidey-holes. The commerce she carried lay stacked, roped, and netted in plain sight, no boon to the prying of suspicious customs men. 'They'll leave us gnashing their teeth in frustration.'

Teive would give anything to watch their squawking peeve, once the brig unveiled her true colours. Down to the racy, sleek line of her keel, she had never been the douce vessel presented by Fiark's documents, and sea-going trade was not a safe calling for the tame of heart, too stuffy to thrive on the intoxicant fire of freedom.

The mate rubbed his chapped fingers, wicked with anticipation. 'We'll have a night on the town to remember, before we slip our cable and flip off the authorities for gawping post turtles and thieves.'

The brisk wind held fair throughout the day, then backed as a cloud front loomed eastward. When *Evenstar* bowled past the headland for landfall, with sailhands aloft to strike topgallants, the turmoil that choked Adruin's harbour exceeded the mate's scathing prediction.

'Will you look at that mess!' Feylind declared, awed. Come aft from the foredeck, she joined Teive by the helm, a sharp eye on the beacons that range-marked the channel. Since *Evenstar* had sailed these close waters before, the captain disdained to hire a pilot. Her vexed snort deplored the taints of tarred pilings and the slop-bucket reek blown off the slave-bearing galleys. 'It's a gossiping *conclave*, just made to foul tempers and cause constipation.'

No one answered, at once. The quartermaster minded his heading, while the leadsman placed in the martingale stays sounded the mark each half minute. Abreast of the estuary, *Evenstar* tacked. While the sail crew hauled taut, she passed the outer buoy, stripped of her netting and trimmed up for port. The ring shank and stock lashings were cleared, and the anchor off the bow. While the hands at the cat-head bent on the chain-cable, Teive surveyed the harbour-side, hove into view as the brig gybed and rounded the cliff head. Beneath Adruin's blunt battlements, the clutter of masts obscured the roofs of the sea quarter. More crowded at wharf-side: hulls packed and jostled inside of the breakwater close as seined fish. From cod-smacks, to lean war galleys, to merchant vessels built beamy and broad, with chafing gear blackened with mildew, every deck appeared bundled with cargo. Lashed luggage vied with crowding passengers, live-stock, and families tending their squalling young.

'Dharkaron's backside!' groused the brig's quartermaster, his creased fists turning the spokes without gloves, and the set to his mouth a hazed mastiff's. 'You'll feel your way in under topsails through *that*?'

'Surely not.' Feylind flipped back her braid, sign enough that she leaped for the challenge. 'Teive?'

'We're set to let go.' The forward crew at the capstan stayed steady, although the jammed anchorage would have daunted a master galley-man under full banks of oars. A crisp glance at the number and size of the vessels crammed chock-a-block between moorings, with a slacking tide and the wind blowing aft, and the mate gave his considered opinion. 'The chain's sound enough. Love, are you feeling cheeky?'

Feylind whooped. 'Aye! So I am! We'll be coming head-on.' If the brig's copper took damage, they would have ample time, not to mention the use of Cattrick's deft skills, once into safe port at Alestron. 'Just watch that new boy with the check stoppers, and advise the hands. We'll double bitt, and I'll have their bollocks if we're paid cheap!'

'What, smash against our own flukes and rake down wind on some mad-as-hornets war galley?' The mate snorted. 'Ours would die, first.' He left the capstan, still grinning. His captain's aggressive style would grey the hair of the poor salts caught riding alee. Pitched to enjoy their invective, he bounded up the forward companion-way, ready to relay smart orders.

'All hands!' called Feylind. 'Bring ship to anchor! Stand by to shorten sail!'

On deck and aloft, the brig's crew manned braces, hauled taut, and clewed up billowing canvas. *Evenstar* trampled in, wind and tide running aft, towards the last slice of open water.

'Let go!' Feylind shouted. The cock-billed anchor splashed, and the clatter of iron through the hawse hammered over the mate's yell to man the port capstan.

Well-braced as the range on her cable ran out, the *Evenstar* caught. Water snapped from taut rope as she swung beam to, brought up short with a rattle of spars. The anchor bit deep, and held, and she settled, neatly snugged between moorings.

Feylind's glance swept the mismatched flotilla poised to depart on the ebb.

'Want to place bets? Which tubs're most likely to foul their tackle, on tending. We may as well sit on our buttocks and watch.' The curl to her lip promised trouble for the entourage putting out from the customs shack.

The brig's partridge-neat purser appeared, the ship's papers in hand, and his tailored broadcloth like a preened raven among gulls, where the idle hands lined the portside rail to ogle. Their gossips' tongues already chewed over the massive, oared barge that approached, festooned with white bunting. Scrolls of gilt bright-work shone like flash jewellery as her rowers threaded the maze between rocking hulls and striped anchor buoys.

'Look there!' carped the boatswain. 'Carve me for a mark! That's how the racketing dastards are spending the fees they collect for mooring and wharfage?'

'*That's* the excisemen's infernal new toy?' The mate's outrage gained heat. 'Is the harbour-master bonked out of his head? They'll be bleeding us just to meet damages.'

Sure enough, the ungainly vessel caught an eddy and veered. Oars flashed, to a volley of curses. Crews on two Sunwheel galleys scrambled to sheer their vessels to windward in avoidance. In fact, the tub bearing in *was* flying Adruin's colours, above the port-master's fluttering orange ensign.

'Fools,' Teive declared. 'Fur and silk! And those hats! Ath! You'd think all that prinked-out officialdom would tempt the Light's archers to play them for pincushions. Humping mother o'joy!' That, as the craft's starboard oar bank nearly capsized a lighterman. 'Dharkaron's Five Horses and Chariot would be handier in sixteen fathoms than that rig.'

Then, as the barge slewed again, and sideswiped a hapless courier, Teive's lively glance crossed with Feylind's, whose amusement had vanished like scud over sunlight. 'Midships!' she barked. 'Fetch out the dock fenders! Lively! Bedamned if I'll sashay into Alestron and face Cattrick with yon lubber's gold leaf scarring our strakes!'

Since the mate's choice vernacular was fit to scale fish, the customhouse vessel straightened her course and pulled alongside without mishap. Four men in uniformed braid came aboard to assist Adruin's pouch-faced exciseman. That overdressed worthy required a hoist, since his tinselled cloth and ermine were much too fine to risk to salt-water stains. While Teive watched the proceedings with open, round eyes, the ship's bursar presented the Evenstar's lists, and Feylind told over a barrel of lies, her manner as always irascible.

'Resupply for the war host?' The balding exciseman stroked his jowls with a jewelled glove. He yawned. 'Seems routine. Though the limes from Southshire, now, they should warrant a luxury tax.' He winked, and cleared his throat. 'That's if they weren't bound to support the Light's campaign at Alestron.' His nudge appeared affable. Yet the cold, weighing eye behind his spectacles probed for the salacious temptation: the same fruit would command more than premium price, sold into the winter black market.

Feylind gave back her narrow-eyed stare. 'You covet those limes, mister?

Then count them, or confiscate the bothersome lot!' Her shrug implied insult. 'Alliance didn't deal square, understand? Refused to pay near what those beauties are worth! Damned well you know the port towns up and down here are all sweating blood under embargo. Nothing moves, these days. Not unless there's a troop destination and a spotless white bow with a puckering Sunwheel seal on it!'

'Not *like* you have problems with smugglers,' the mate sniped. 'Even if tide-currents in these parts weren't Sithaer's gift to a gouging pilot, damned estuary's clapped up tight in blockade as the slew on a westshore virgin.'

Feylind snapped again, before the official could stiffen his back at Teive's cheek. 'You planning to crawl all over us on forced inspection? Then, fancy man, I suggest you jump to it. I'm wanting my crew out with buckets and holy-stones to scour the decks where you stand!'

Set on notice for their fine furs and swank finery, the officials demanded due oversight nonetheless. Whistling sailhands enacted Teive's order to unbatten the hatches. Since the hold's contents matched the lading list that changed hands, the brig suffered through the invasion and received the requisite port stamps. Mooring fees paid, she was cleared to weigh anchor on the flood-tide.

'Don't let your crew linger town-side past midnight,' the exciseman warned as he filed the discharge documents in his case, then tucked his sweetening pay inside his glittering waistcoat. 'Short-handed galleys are likely to press them. The Light's captains'll snatch anyone hale if they're drunk, or up to no good, hanging idle.'

'No problem.' Teive flashed his most affable smile. 'Any's not rousted from port, then good riddance. Late for the tide, late forever on *Evenstar*. Laggard hands scrounge themselves a new berth without their quit pay and their sea chest.' The smile turned arch. 'Sir! Such expensive furs, I declare. And those boots! You'll want a hoist in the bosun's chair, surely?'

The portly peacock was off-loaded, and the barge shoved off to a warbling fanfare of trumpets. Teive stood, bemused, and even the quartermaster chuckled over the erratic departure that bumped from moored vessel, to anchor buoy, to snagged cable, with the oarsmen straining their brass-buttoned doublets in the roil as the ebb gained force in the channel. 'Enough to give honest rowers the gripes. Didn't the pudding-faced chap with the badges look like a fat whore who'd sat hard aground on her tackle? And wasn't yon warning of press-gangs a shocking kindness, since we last ran a cargo through here?'

'We're feeding the fanatics who're making them rich,' Feylind surmised with dour humour. 'And the bung-hole they're spit-licking for favour'd be Lysaer's. Praise his false Light, such convenience is useful. Before the sun sets, I want a glass in a tavern that hasn't been scoured in brine.'

Night fell, under cloud cold and dense as a blanket. *Evenstar*'s crew set sail under lanterns, pitching before a following wind, with the flood in the estuary pulling five knots, the race under the keel sucking into swift eddies. The gusts breathed of ice, harbinger of a fresh storm inbound off the Cildein.

'We'll have a fast passage,' Teive remarked from the dark. His arm circled Feylind's cloaked shoulder, where she huddled alee of the wheel mount. 'Too fast, maybe. More than a merchant craft warrants.'

The rocky channel became a white froth in the rip, with the war-time patrol in tight force, and the light buoys and torch towers marking the shore-line unlit to discourage smuggling. As the fire-pans at Adruin's harbour fell astern, and the crew aloft unbrailed the topsails to gain headway, the black hills of East Halla scalloped the sky's edge, looming on the port side. Inside the narrows, the hazard of the opposite shore lay scarcely two leagues off the starboard rail. The quartermaster obeyed the command to head off, bearing westward down the tight estuary. *Evenstar* curtseyed, and ran with the elements, laced foam splashed off her bobstays drenching the leadsman who sounded the mark.

'Not fast enough,' Feylind declared, almost reckless. The hand under her mantle stayed clasped to the chain that hung the signet ring of Rathain: Arithon's token to honour an oath made to comfort her grieving mother. Every inch the brash captain, Feylind flinched from the thought of her own children, safe back at Innish. 'I don't like posturing under a Sunwheel banner, even out of necessity.'

The shoreside news had unsettled her nerves: a horrific revenge wrought by Parrien's fleet, and an uncanny event no one's words could describe, but which had incited the refugee waves of desertion from both sides of the entrenched campaign. If no one had witnessed the usage of Shadow, the Spinner of Darkness was said to be active, supporting Alestron in arcane liaison. Past question, starvation threatened the citadel. The defenders remained hemmed in without recourse, drawn critically low on supplies.

Now the hour was ripe to deliver King Eldir's relief. Feylind let go of Prince Arithon's ring and regarded the mate at her side. A solid form, sensibly muffled, his face was obscured by the night. Always, his warmth allowed her to lean on the comfort of his close presence. 'Regrets, Teive?'

'No.' *Evenstar*'s first officer grinned. 'In fact, never.' Head tipped to mark the hands' progress aloft, he called for the crew at the braces to trim the main-yards and haul taut. 'This brig's our home, love. If we're going to pile her onto a shoal, I'd rather be pushing the odds for a friend. Not smashed to ruin by wretched luck, or a random bout of bad weather.' He added, content, 'Everything won't be stage dressing, besides. I'd have the relieving tackles set on the tiller under conditions tonight.'

Weather thrummed through the stays. The fore-sails cracked, shadowed out by the main in the swooping veer of the gusts. Back-up gear would be needed to surmount the strain on the ship's steerage as the bucking tide scoured the channel.

'Speed us on, then.' Feylind laughed. 'Give me the thrill of the careening run before riding a blizzard at anchor inside this bottle-neck. We'd have three cables out, and be tending for tide, chased by plagues of fiends on a storm charge.'

Inside the s'Brydion stronghold, the state of scant supply became critical. The added provender from Parrien's galley could not alleviate the relentless short-fall. Since the stores drawn to support the refugee exodus, the granary echoed, near empty. While the barrels of ship's biscuit, salt meat, and ground barley were raised by hoist from the Sea Gate, and the flag galley was berthed in the caverns, the duke's council-men convened for consultation. Two of them coughed with green colds. The others twiddled with their useless quill pens, or sat idle-handed, their mood grave, as they heard through Alestron's Lord Seneschal.

Standing, his robes belted to his gaunt waist, and his whey-face pushed beyond haggard, that staunch worthy had no hopeful news. 'We already face weakness. Famine will claim the first lives before the turn of the year.'

Outside the closed chamber, with the chilly gloom a pervasive lead overlay, the watch paced the walls above nearly deserted town streets. Gulls soared and called, forlorn flecks of white buffeted by the stiffening breeze. Against the atmosphere of sullen resistance, and a garrison braced to resignation, one restless spirit's pursuit stayed unfazed by desperate hardship.

Fionn Areth was left with loose time on his hands after Jeynsa's departure. Freed also from the cold eye of Sidir, and excused from troop chores since Talvish's change of allegiance, the Araethurian ducked under Vhandon's over-sight in hot pursuit of Parrien's oarsmen. Seafarers talked. Cooped up for months on end with their fellows, they fed like sharks on the blood of past scandal. Given Parrien s'Brydion's outspoken grudge against Rathain's prince, his beached crew might divulge the man's criminal history in full-blown, scurrilous detail.

Persistence unearthed a striking reward: the master shipwright who had betrayed Arithon's piracy at Riverton eighteen years ago had claimed sanctuary from Lysaer s'Ilessid under ducal protection. He was here at Alestron, still. Given the name, Fionn Areth ventured down to the wharf-side to search out a craftsman called Cattrick.

The inquiry landed him at the chandler's, which anywhere else would be a weathered shed, attached to a sail-loft, and a small foundry. At Alestron, the cavernous edifice was built into the buttressed stone of the sea-quarter bastion. Besides sundry ships' fittings, the blacksmith also forged tempered points for the arbalests. If the blockade against maritime trade had crimped commerce, demand had not slackened to idleness. Hemp rope and new chain, tanned ox-hides and tackles, and intricate joinery were also required for war. The fortified warehouse was not empty when Fionn Areth sauntered in from the dock-side.

Cloud-grey light stamped his brief silhouette. Then the plank door swung shut, leaving him in deep gloom, felted with the scents of pine and hot tar, overlaid by the taint of a fish oil lamp. His arrival met the hung silence of more than one paused conversation. Fionn Areth advanced. Hedged by tiered shelving packed with boxes and bales, and baskets glinting with cleats, he found himself pinned by the avid stares of a dozen rough-mannered craftsmen.

'Ath's glory,' declared one unshaven brute. 'Before my two eyes, we're getting a visit from Fellowship-sanctioned blood royalty.'

'Is he now?' That pealing jibe arose from a dimmed corner, underlaid by the scrape of stiff rope. A hunched figure, half-hidden, cackled with glee. 'Then, buckos, sit up and ask why he's here. Won't be for our light entertainment.'

Fionn Areth stifled his grass-lander's drawl and announced to the ham-fisted gathering, 'I'm looking for Cattrick.'

'Ah! So you could be.' Another gruff snigger: the wizened old splicer perched on a stool. His claw fingers busied with lacing an eye-splice, the unkempt creature declared, 'In that case, we're left awesome curious.' While his cronies lounged, grinning, the spokesman licked a spatulate thumb. 'Come here, fellow.'

'Do I know you?' Fionn Areth demanded, his brisk imitation of Arithon's tone used to further his prying inquiry.

'Bad question.' Removed from the dizzying reek of the lamp, the cantankerous inquisitor swung his beaked face towards the approaching tread. His porcelain-white eyes were quite blind. 'You, at least, are not Arithon s'Ffalenn,' he observed with supercilious certainty. 'Your feet are too heavy, your voice is too loud, and stripling? You're poorly informed in the bargain. Yon cocky, wee sorcerer knows me by name, mocked up in an Araethurian twang, or speaking the birth-born lack of it.'

Someone else quipped, 'Who'd forget you, old snake. Mug as ugly as yours could scare bones from the grave on a screaming flight to the devil.'

Another man lounging nearby slapped his knee, to hooting mirth from his comrades. 'Can't hoodwink Ivel, boy. You must be the double. Why's a goatherd come here seeking Cattrick?'

Dice clattered across an up-ended barrel, as three burly longshoremen turned their backs and resumed an on-going game. The fourth and the largest among them ignored the thrown score. Rough-cut and corded with muscle beneath his leather jerkin, he straightened and tipped back a battered felt hat.

Fionn Areth confronted the squint of a measuring eye. The craftsman's bristled jaw jutted as he said in the lazy vowels of the southcoast, 'Better speak, infant. Don't claim you were sent. His Grace won't deliver his words in the mouth of another.'

Snide as a whip-crack, the splicer took issue. 'Are we mean-spirited? Ungrateful?' He freed a callused hand in magnanimous invitation. 'Let the lad speak! What's the harm? We're not bored? Since the dock-side bawds flitted, we should pant for the chance to enjoy his command performance.'

Fionn Areth shrugged his cloak straight, too brazen to shrink before ridicule. 'Cattrick might prefer to receive my inquiry in private.'

'My stars!' Ivel thumped his thin chest. 'It's a closet spat? A tiff between lovers? Or no! Lend us your tender confidence, young sir. You're here to confess that for weeks, from a distance, you've been nursing a moon-calf obsession.'

Laughter from the bystanders cut off to a bang as the huge man at the dice game kicked over his seat and surged upright. He towered. Brown hair tinged with white tumbled to his broad shoulders, while fists like mauls braced with ominous care on the barrel top. 'What makes you *think*, boy? Since we're not delicate, why the implication you might be privy to everyone's secrets?'

Fionn Areth snapped up his chin. 'You're Cattrick? The same master ship-wright who played on both sides, then turned coat until every staked interest at Riverton was betrayed to the opposite party? I want the reason you spurned Lysaer's employ, and why, since the day you took sanctuary with s'Brydion, Arithon s'Ffalenn doesn't speak to you.'

'Or to you, evidently,' the blind splicer attacked. 'Whose side claims *your* loyalty, hinnysop?'

Before Fionn Areth could retort, the snide dicer shoved forward to thrash him. A rabbit-fast nip behind the tiered shelving might buy him the moment to run. Hold his ground, and he would catch a bout of ham-fisted unpleasant-ness.

Except, at that moment, the latched door breezed open and let in one of Bransian's warmongering sentries. 'Cattrick!' The bursting shout rattled the sheaves in the tackles. 'Half of my lot of winnings to you if my latest wager pays off. My coin's laid on, that a merchant brig built to your lines flies a Sunwheel flag in the estuary.'

'What? Is this rape, or extortion?' The huge man bashed over the barrel. Dice flew, and a flittering hail of small coins. Cattrick batted them out of the air, cobra quick, as he roared away in bass umbrage, 'Yon's no ship o' mine, butty! Or be sure I'll throttle the pirate myself, for putting a prize won in battle to a shameful endeavour. Don't claim that brig's running supply for the war camp! Not off a design I've sweated my own blood to keep close to my chest as a baby. Nor would I sell out to s'Ilessid, though his princely blue eyes should leak tears o' gold royals, and beg with a sealed pardon for granting the privilege.'

The shipwright plunged forward. His charge met Fionn Areth, planted four-square in the path to the doorway.

One crashing blow knocked the grass-lander sprawling. The young man struck the shelving, hands pressed to his face, while a tipped box of rivets showered over his head. Cattrick snatched his prey from the spill. Fist snagged in black hair, he said, snarling, 'Insolent whelp! You'll tell me *later* what gives you the right to think I should answer for what occurred in my yard back in Tysan.'

The Southshireman dumped his brute hold straightaway. Fionn Areth dropped to his knees amid the scattered hardware. Stomped rivets clinked across the gouged floor-boards as the cantankerous shipwright followed the betting sentry into the street. The idlers crowding the chandler's surged after, hell-bent on enjoying the outcome.

Which left Fionn Areth to nurse his bruised face in the splicer's obstreperous company.

'You think you hurt now, pup? Then count yourself warned. Cattrick's meaner than a gaffed shark, once he's crossed.' Thoughtful, in darkness, the old craftsman resumed weaving plies with the speed of experience. 'Don't press your luck. The last time a born fool messed with his business, the wretch wore the burn scars the rest of his life. You've got no sick taste for punishment? Then scarper while nobody's looking.'

Fionn Areth said nothing, his bitten tongue busy with counting his battered teeth. Some were knocked loose. Sleeve pressed to his split mouth, he swore at Parrien's seamen, whose malice had neglected to mention the exiled shipwright's vile temper. The grass-lander grappled for balance and stood. Snow scooped from a drift would ease his bruises, since he had every intention of pursuing his grievance onto the Sea Gate battlement.

When Fionn Areth arrived, out of breath, atop the rectangular keep, Cattrick leaned over the bay-side crenel, surrounded by his motley friends from the chandler's. The ship's glass he held was trained on the narrows between the keeps guarding the harbour chain. The tide was poised to turn. Under black cloud, the roiled water heaved pewter, chopped by the rip current's whitecaps. The brig under survey bucked the frothing crests, head to wind and her tan-bark sails slatting.

Fionn Areth had observed enough ships in the channel to recognize one in distress. Whatever the difficulty, her heaving stern swung in danger of ramming against the spiked links.

Even as he jockeyed for vantage, a by-standing expert expounded, 'That ship's not caught aback. She's damaged her rudder.'

Cattrick grunted agreement, the glass glued against his lined squint. 'Tiller rope's snapped. They'll have a relieving tackle taking the strain. See the press by the quarterdeck hatch? Crew's scrambling to rig a replacement.'

Though the sentry still fidgeted over his bet, he knew not to push for his answer. In daylight, the ornery shipwright looked all of his six decades, skin dark as the varnish laid on weathered teak, and his whiskers a silver-tipped wolf pelt.

Out on the vessel, a lantern flashed, twice.

'Signal!' snapped Cattrick. He straightened and shoved the glass at the soldier. 'Read out the code, man.' Still glaring, he spun, his battered felt hat clapped onto his head by a snatching fist. 'Fetch Arithon!' he shouted, straight at Fionn Areth. 'That's Feylind's brig, *Evenstar*, caught by the tide. She's flying the Sunwheel under a ruse, and knowing her mettle, her damaged steering is likely a blindsiding mock-up. We've got only minutes before she strikes the chain. *Someone must open the harbour mouth!'*

Else the ship-killing barrier would chew the brig's planks, beam on in a broaching sea.

Through the scream of the wind, the rapt sentry affirmed the shipwright's early assessment. 'Signal,' he agreed. 'And she's friendly, for sure. The garrison manning the keeps at the headland are being asked to stage a mock fight. At their first flight of arrows, the brig will show a merchant's cowardice, and drop her flags in surrender.'

'Is Feylind aboard?' Fionn Areth asked, urgent. But knowing the captain, he already guessed: only her errant style, and Teive's courage, would dare the challenge of sailing straight under the Alliance blockade.

'Run!' bellowed Cattrick. 'That's my ship, caught aback! If she falls to Lysaer's campaign as a prize, I will pound you senseless, then shred your child's equipment for crab bait!'

Early Winter 5671

Moves

Arrived through the Paravian circle at old Tirans, inside the wards sealing Atwood, Kharadmon updates Traithe concerning the misgivings left by his recent errand: 'I don't *like* surprises! *The Prime Matriarch was too busy!* When I came to demand that her sisterhood's meddlers pack up her camp at Alestron, she was one jump ahead of Sethvir's intent, with tents folded, already leaving . . .'

Fighting to help his stricken liege resist Desh-thiere's curse-bound insanity, Sulfin Evend relies on Prince Arithon's promise *never* to shoulder an active defence at Alestron: 'Hang on, friend,' the Lord Commander implores, 'bear up and withstand this!' which Lysaer does, up until the set-back news breaks, that a brig laden down with supply has lost steering, positioned to fall into enemy hands and prolong the siege into midwinter . . .

Sprinted to the top of a south-facing battlement, Arithon s'Ffalenn bears shocking witness as a light-bolt arcs out, pitched to strike the lone brig pinned against the chain at the harbour mouth; and despite Dakar's shouted dismay, he reacts before thought, his launched Shadow unfolding too late to quite shield the explosive impact . . .

XIII. Stormed Fortress

arrien's war galley was relaunched from her secure berth in the caverns, bearing the armed men and tackle to tow in the charred hulk of the brig. She crossed the closed harbour, cleaving against wind and the slackening tide, and wrapped under cover of Arithon's Shadow. He stood exposed on the open foredeck. Braced on his feet, his wool mantle snapped in the contrary gusts, he had no thought to spare Talvish, on guard at his shoulder in Kyrialt's stead for his practised experience at sea. Mage-trained focus, unwavering, still sought to defend the floundering ship in the estuary. Overhead, the crack of inbound light-bolts exploded to star-bursts one after the next, their slamming reports a continuous thunder. Hot wind and searing steam from the onslaught whipped the rowers, acrid with charred timber and the edged scent of lightning.

Parrien's captaincy drove the warcraft ahead, her men pitched to fight before losing the *Evenstar*'s drifting hull, or risking her cargo. Battle nerves overcame any fear. Where a sailing craft must bow to the elements, tacking for headway in confined waters, an oared ship could cut a straight course. Handily as the galley clove the grey chop, swift progress did little for the shattered survivors clinging on the crippled brig.

An Alliance patrol ship already closed in, her withering assault launched to finish the avatar's pre-emptive strike. Fanatics, her boarders swarmed *Evenstar*'s rail, undaunted by the threat of Darkness. Their heroic foray would capture her load of provisions, or else flood her hold to thwart the citadel's relief.

Sevrand's guard in the watchtowers flanking the narrows responded with arrows and steel. Barbed lances and shot shrieked from their seaward arbalests. While sheets of white light roared in overhead, absorbed by defences of Shadow, the lethal cross-fire whined and thumped into charred wood, or ripped down the zealots who rushed to put *Evenstar*'s stranded sailhands to the sword.

'Arithon, *no*! You cannot help!' Talvish laid urgent hands on the prince to thwart him from displacing a hand at the benches and seizing an oar. 'Steady on, liege! Best to maintain your cover of Darkness. Let the duke's fighting seamen to do as they've been trained since they were beardless lads!'

Yet the wait came too hard. 'That's Feylind's brig, out there!'

'Ath preserve, don't I know!' Talvish ruthlessly strengthened his grip. 'If her captain's alive, trust this galley's endeavour. We'll reach her and strive for a recovery!'

Against the anguished cry of the heart, while the screams of the burned and the wounded shrilled from the brig's exposed deck, the war galley shot through the spray knifed off her plunging bow. Parrien shouted, exhorting more speed. Momentarily, the double-time stroke suspended as the oar banks enacted a shift change. The horn-call sounded. The drum boomed again. Soaked looms lapped the sea and drove the prow into the narrows. The vessel leaped forward, while the struggle to reclaim the *Evenstar*'s hulk raged ahead with undaunted ferocity.

Through the flickering tangle of levin bolts and hurled Shadow, the watch keeps were launching fast lighters crammed with able men. The small craft plunged into the fray, protected by covering volleys from the towers' sharp-shooting bowmen. A swarm of stirred hornets, the boats' crews stormed the brig. Assault parties grappled and boarded. Desperate for food stores, or else driven by the bottled rage nursed over weeks of inaction, they swarmed through the smoke, some falling to hostile arrows. The rest became an unstoppable force. They threshed through the Light's self-righteous invaders and mowed down all standing resistance.

By the moment that Parrien's galley hove in, the disputed deck was retaken. The listing hulk was being shackled by hawsers, and rigged tackles warped the heavy bow. Streaming cinders and smoke, *Evenstar* would be hauled into secure waters behind the raised harbour chain. Men at the windlass inside the west watch keep prepared to toss lines to haul her into the calm shallows.

Seen near at hand, the scope of devastation smashed hope. All three masts were razed stumps. The singed decks were entangled with smouldering tackle, crashed from aloft, still aflame. Across blackened planks, lodged in the splinters and wreckage, lay the sprawled bodies of the brave fallen: the burned and the broken; the moaning wounded, stricken by arrows; and the bleeding, hacked sailors, butchered outright by enemy hatred.

Arithon owned a trained seaman's agility. While the galley manoeuvred at speed alongside, he displaced a deck-hand, unlashed a halyard, then slung himself over the closing span of chopped water. Two steps behind, Talvish was left to snatch the dropped line on the back-swing. He followed, while his liege landed running amid the brig's carnage. As he caught up, Arithon and five citadel men were wrestling aside the charred boom of *Evenstar*'s downed spanker.

Underneath, they exposed several bodies, one unmistakably the quarter-master, crushed against the black stump of the wheel mount and the melted bronze binnacle. Between the glaring flash of each light-bolt, and the flung Shadow that muzzled the back-flash, dead flesh glimmered, reduced to paper-grey ash and seared bone. Two others lay bundled amid the remains of a seafarer's oiled mantle, reduced to singed wool and stinking, scorched meat. Arithon crouched. Barehanded, before stupefied action could stop him, he eased the crisped corpse aside and peeled back the underlying layer of scorched fabric. Found Feylind beneath: spared because her first mate, Teive, had thrown himself over her. His staunch love had sheltered her struggling form against the deck while flaming canvas seared him alive.

Nor was his cherished captain unscathed. Arithon sank to his knees at her side. He restarted his stopped breath. Slapped bloodlessly white by the horrific impact, Talvish knelt also, nearly as fast. He gathered her battered head in his hands. Rested her shuddering weight in his lap, to ease the strained gasps as her blistered lungs laboured for air.

Which left Arithon, stricken, to assess the wracked ruin of her. The limbs flayed by burns; the ripped torso with too many white, splintered bones punched through pulp, where the weight of the gaff rig and spanker boom had smashed her encumbered flesh.

'*Tae'thadra!*' he choked. His eyes were streaming. 'My dear! Most brave, and always a tigress. Of course, you would hoist sail and come. Did you blindside your brother and Tharrick as well? Daunt your mother with your drawn cutlass?'

Talvish eased the wracked braid from Feylind's split lips. Her blue eyes stayed open and urgent. 'No such thing,' she husked, her whisper a thread through the raging howl of the elements. While Arithon's gift quenched his half-brother's cursed fury, she chose her words with spare strength. 'My choice was a gang-up agreement.' A brief struggle ensued. She could not move her arm. Her right shoulder had been stripped to gristle. Her chest heaved. 'The chain. At my neck.'

There, a remnant of tarnished metal remained, stitched through the blood and stuck cinders. Arithon might have balked from sheer grief, had her expectant sight ever left him. For the adamant need in her dying request, he reached out and gently untangled the links from her fouled shirt. His own signet flashed back, green emerald and white gold: unwanted token of an oath renounced, and his pledge of honour to keep her from harm.

'I grew up,' Feylind grated. 'You will make no apologies.'

'You were ever your own mistress,' Arithon allowed. Through tears, he stayed steady. Strict training let him use what voice he had left to ease her closure through comfort. 'Love does not cage freedom. I am nothing if not humbled by the devotion and courage that led you to defy the Alliance.'

'The stores,' Feylind gasped. 'King Eldir's relief?'

Around them, through the efforts of Parrien's men, the initial reports were being relayed to the war galley's watch officer: two crewmen below had died defending the locked hatches that accessed the hold.

'The cargo's secure,' Talvish supplied, 'every cask, net, and barrel of flour untouched. I gather you've brought limes from Southshire as well, to spare us from the scourge of scurvy.'

Feylind coughed. Her distant eyes closed. The fingers too damaged to clasp Arithon's hand quivered, useless, so much capable muscle, shredded to mangled flesh. The harsh whisper resumed, as pain leached her fierce spirit. 'Then, my prince, live well. Accept that I'm satisfied.'

But Arithon was not resigned. The agony of this parting would not rest, for the helplessness that stripped him naked. 'You leave us two children. As my own wards, they shall not want. Never mind that you tried to set my pledge aside, they inherit my claim of protection.'

Feylind's lips turned. The wisp of her most stubborn smile trembled briefly. 'When were they ever not under your charge?'

For one man had filled the empty shoes abandoned by her drowned father. The same generous heart granted Fiark his vocation, and restored Tharrick to the pride of manhood which husbanded Jinesse's healing and peace. For Arithon's caring, a tight family remained, respected and secure at Innish.

'I had my brig,' Feylind whispered. 'A mentor's bright friendship. And Teive.' She shared her last smile: not the imp's grin of the laughing mischievous sprite who ran barefoot on white sands at Merior. This was the fulfilled tribute for her first mate and staunch lover, who had needed no vows to stand firm at her side throughout every madcap endeavour. 'Enough,' Feylind finished. 'I've had every desire held dear for the natural course of a lifetime.'

The struggle reached an end, after that, too swiftly for even Arithon's talent to sing her a masterbard's crossing. Quickly, without dwelling, Feylind passed beyond reach. Arithon shed his cloak. Since he was left too tear-blind to see, Talvish's hands helped to wrap her, along with the bones that remained of her best beloved. The pair of them received her preference for burial, sewn into sailcloth and consigned to the sea. The brief eulogy was spoken, while around Rathain's prince and his silent liegeman, the heaped tackle and decks were cleared of their burden of dead. No wounded from *Evenstar*'s company remained: Lysaer's assault had swept all exposed hands. The blockade patrol's rapacious strike had felled the cook, while the two merchant seamen stationed below finished their doomed stand at the hatches.

The tribute to courage was never more poignant: still blanketed by active wards raised of Shadow, Parrien's war galley was being laden with the stores salvaged from the brig's hold. The men rigged the hoist from the sound vessel's mast, working fast, since the storm wind was rising. They emptied the hull of the last cask, sack, and barrel, and down to the precious nets of ripe limes. Amid such disposition, the pending gale broke, a black anvil squall line that howled down the funnelling throat of the estuary. At the ebb-tide, against the fierce eddies that sucked through the winched links of the harbour chain, and under the flickering reports of spat light-bolts, the blizzard came on like whipped smoke. Snow shrouded the singed timbers and stubbed masts in white; masked over the horror and blood, and the broken, charred wood that one day could see repair under Cattrick's sharp eye; or might not.

The prince who wept with his returned signet in hand was too stricken with grief to make his will known on the matter.

For Sulfin Evend, the storm's savage onslaught became a back-handed gift as he sought to arrest the cascade that hurled the Alliance war host towards certain disaster. A raging mob faced him, massed against the handful of officers called out to stem burgeoning mayhem. Among the green captains and unseasoned men, the sharp, surprise strike of wrought Shadow had seeded ungovernable terror. Few of his ranked veterans had ever known the sorcerous works of Arithon s'Ffalenn, beyond the wild tales bandied about in the taverns. Now, with the estuary gripped under darkness at noon, the orderly encampment seethed with confusion. The shrill garble of horn-calls piercing the snowfall bespoke the on-going struggle to curb spreading panic.

The ground shook. Another shock slammed through the Lord Commander's racing feet as, again, a retort by Shadow deflected. The recoil blasted an untenanted stretch of the far shore-line. Sulfin Evend shouted to direct his gawping officers. He waved the furled flag on the staff clenched in his armoured fist: a peace-keeping forethought, shoved at him by the royal valet in the tumult of Lysaer's first salvo.

'Deploy your lines! Now!' he bellowed, across the heaving press of armed bodies. 'We have to establish a cordon!'

He must not cry vengeance upon the perfidious Prince of Rathain. *Not yet*: caught in the breach by mass fear, he stared down the prospect of death on the swords of Lysaer's fervent followers. *All* remained blind to the danger, instilled by horrific experience. Devout faith placed their lives in deadly jeopardy, the most lethal threat never Shadow at all, but the afflicted insanity of the Mistwraith's design, driving the man they hailed avatar.

Against a repeat of the tragedy that had razed his crack troops once before, Sulfin Evend had naught but bare wits, as events moved too fast to contain. Lysaer s'Ilessid wielded his mighty gift from the top of an unused siege tower, with the clamouring crowd packed beneath. The stair entry was choked. Everyone, down to the grimiest pot-boy, had thronged to observe the sizzling bolts arching outward. Each ground-shaking strike left them trembling as the concussive blasts creased the gusts into shock waves of heat. The mind-numbing, *inconceivable* phenomenon followed, as Shadow erupted, dense as thrown felt, from a placement just inside the harbour mouth. Each bedazzling outlay of Lysaer's gifted power sank into that void and unravelled.

Now, discipline fractured into the fighting frenzy impelled by galvanic fear.

Sulfin Evend faced the onset of riot, his seasoned officers too few. Past campaigns against Arithon s'Ffalenn had destroyed countless thousands of lives. The troops stampeding the siege tower stair demanded their Blessed Prince's due protection. All effort to turn them became battered down, the thin cordon chewed apart under rampaging panic.

'Death to the Spinner of Darkness!'

'Strike the minion of evil to Sithaer!'

Trampling men rocked the wheeled base of the platform, crying the name of their avatar. Rage, frustration, and outright terror seethed into a rallying cry for the grandiose cause.

'Rip down the s'Brydion citadel!'

'Burn the black traitors who shelter the s'Ffalenn bastard!'

'Tear down the defences, stone by set stone! With swords and bare hands if need be!'

Their jostling shoved Sulfin Evend aside. Cut off and deafened by shattering noise, he could never regroup his smashed line. Anxiety spurred him. *Every second that Lysaer succumbed to the curse increased the prospect of a mass immolation.*

Since Sulfin Evend refused to draw steel against his own men, the fool flagstaff must serve. He used the blunt pole as a quarterstave and leveraged his way to the choked stair.

There, braced shoulder to shoulder, two of Lysaer's elite honour guard held off the press, entrenched behind the tow-chains that their harried enterprise had wrapped taut as a barrier between the post stanchions.

'Go up, lord, you'll be trapped,' one screamed over the din.

'I know!' Sulfin Evend reversed the flagstaff. Bronze knurl exchanged for the sharpened finial, he jabbed until the yammering fanatics caved into recoil. While one petrified guard loosed the chain from behind, the other snatched the neck of his surcoat and pulled him inside the planked stairwell.

'Work fast,' his breathless rescuer pleaded. 'We can't last here for long. Ranne and Fennick keep the rearguard, above.'

Sulfin Evend saluted such bravery and ran. The steep ascent snatched the wind from him, weighed down as he was by his chainmail. Stout timbers stung to the vibration of the light-bolts; and rocked as well, as the vicious throng surged to displace the valiant pair down below. Swaying on the first landing, Sulfin Evend cursed outright.

The low vantage was useless. He could not see over the crowd to know if his earlier orders had been followed: whether Avenor's core companies had been deployed to stem the disastrous rush to launch boats. His best captains were tasked to seize priority command and direct the Light's war galleys to pull back the blockade. No more ships must risk a spear-head assault against the s'Brydion keeps at the harbour chain! *Should their Lord Commander fail to recover his upset authority, Lysaer's powerful offensive might set fire to those allied vessels. Their hapless crewmen could be burned alive, entrapped between a curse-driven assault, and the wrought Shadow that sheltered the s'Brydion enemy.*

Sulfin Evend avowed he would see himself dead, first. Before ruin, he would put Lysaer to the sword. Slaughter his liege outright, rather than give free rein to the madness that had ravaged the field at Daon Ramon.

Left naught beyond faith, that his best squad of shock troops in fact handled the precarious line at the beachhead, the Light's Lord Commander rushed into the breach. Whipped by on-coming storm, deafened by the colliding violence of the unnatural elements, he had only bravado to tame the raging pack mind-set, below.

Sulfin Evend unfurled the white banner. Snapped out its glittering, golden device where the streaming crack of the gusts caught gold-tinsel thread in the flash of the levin bolts. He seized on shameless drama: waved the gilt Sunwheel before the whelming spectacle of Lysaer's manic assault.

'There will be an attack!' His cry for retribution *had to* rivet the rampaging mob. As craning heads turned, he spun the flagstaff. Draped the device from the railing, with his form looming over the livid arc of the Sunwheel. There, standing tall, he shouted again. *'There will be an attack!* One that will not trample roughshod over wise deployment and tactical reason!'

'Kill the Spinner of Darkness!'

'Strike now!'

'Let the sorcerer burn!'

Sulfin Evend raised a mailed fist. Regaled in his badges and surcoat, he met the hysterical clamour with the force that had earned supreme rank. 'Are we insane? A pack of rank fools? Did you think I would waste our best lives in this war, only for glory and death? What *cause* sacrifices great men to the enemy? *I will authorize no such irresponsible move!'*

Sulfin Evend unstrapped his spiked helm. Against howling dissent, buffeted by the thunderous crack as each blasting light-bolt ripped skywards, he taunted the teeth of mass discontent; risked the fatal arrow a rival might loose to assassinate. While his better officers flushed with chastened shame, he resumed his peeling tirade. 'A war council will convene in the central pavilion! Stand there! Form up in parade lines and display the loyalty every one of you swore to uphold. Wait for instruction from your liege lord! After Lysaer s'Ilessid has done wielding Light to soften the lines of the enemy, he will honour the men among you with his presence.'

The dissenters nearest the tower's base quieted. None could dispute that their mortal-forged steel was no match for a sorcerer wielding raw Darkness.

Sulfin Evend seized on that slight hesitation. 'See to your gear, soldiers! Sharpen your weapons! Cool your rash tempers, which will only attract infestations of plaguing *iyats*! On my word, under the name of s'Ilessid, I *promise* you'll see action taken. Our drawn weapons will shed enemy blood before midnight! By sure steps, I would have you survive to take victory home to your families!'

The restless crowd milled. The cry for redress against arcane adversity blunted the shrill edge of fear. Sense *had* to prevail, as in the tossed channel, the outrushing tide would hamper the crossing of troops. Better, the winter gale swiftly worsened. Risen gusts streamed the troop banners, and lost them, as swirling snow thickened and pelted. Comfort inside a warmed pavilion must surely outweigh the prospect of battle under such adverse conditions. More officers breasted the bawling press. Their shouts to form ranks by cohort met resistance, but not overt insubordination. Now the men vented steam in euphoric excitement. Rank and file, they would soon pack the cook-shacks to chew over their forthcoming deployment.

Shown the dire hand of the Spinner of Darkness, most accepted the word of their Lord Commander: the siege would shift strategy towards an aggressive attack. The salvage of *Evenstar*'s stores must buy the defenders no more borrowed time; nor would the slaughtering raid done by Parrien's fleet escape a fierce reparation.

From the scaffold platform, Sulfin Evend's black rage could all but be felt, as he shouted to hasten the laggards. 'Alestron will fall! If the stones of the citadel's foundation must be mined and hurled one by one into the race in the chasm, I will leave no toe-hold for the Master of Shadow. The muzzle comes off, as of this hour. Your enemy shall be broken.'

As the loud-mouthed stragglers were dispersed towards camp, the view opened at last, to show the blockade patrol ship limping in under gapped oar strokes. She listed, deck and railings splintered by rock shot. Half her pummelled crewmen were likely dead, with as many maimed from the ferocious defence launched from the keeps at the harbour chain. Shadow aside, the s'Brydion garrison were masters of war beyond parallel.

To breach their fast citadel became no mean feat, even under the skeleton companies manning their walls since the exodus. Sulfin Evend viewed the harsh prospect, unflinching. For all dangers paled before the impossible action lying ahead of him, now. Granted a cleared field as the last gaggle of protesters were bridled by burly sergeants, the Light's Lord Commander left the white banner draped over the rail. He resumed his ascent of the siege-tower with no choice but confront the stark madness unleashed by the curse of Deshthiere.

He could not move quickly. The plank risers were treacherous, shaken by gusts and made slippery by fresh snow.

Worse, Ranne met him on the landing above, the chisel-cut frown above his hawk nose riding him haggard with worry. 'I have to say that black crows will hatch eaglets before you could withstand this onslaught, alive.'

'You say? Then the damnable crows will just have to brood their miraculous eggs and oblige!' Sulfin Evend ducked past.

Morose for that failure, Ranne shouldered grim duty and pursued.

Fennick's Camris-born toughness withstood the cold wind, halfway up to the next tier. 'No sign yet, of slacking,' he greeted, looking fraught. 'Lord? Your only course is to wait out the fit and pray that Lysaer wears himself down to unconsciousness.' His glance clung to hope, though his freckled face had blisters from more than windburn. This near the top scaffold, the back-lashing heat of each light-burst hissed downward in punishing blasts.

'I know.' The bitten resurgence of the Hanshire aristocrat meant the warning would be disregarded. Mean as a ferret, Sulfin Evend refused pity as the guardsman's kind features drained white.

'You're not going up there!' Fennick gasped, shocked.

Ranne kept his silence, beyond distressed. Their past mistake, that once lost them Tysan's young prince, now haunted the tension between them.

'Someone must try!' Sulfin Evend insisted, despite his dread terror. 'Deshthiere's curse has prevailed. Lysaer can't break off! You know this! If he's not shaken free, he won't come down standing upright.' *If he came down at all.* More likely the madness would drive him to death, as the platform ignited beneath him.

'This cannot happen,' Sulfin Evend resolved. 'I have promised the masses an Alliance council of war that he must be left fit to mediate!'

The man styled as avatar dared not collapse while the Master of Shadow threatened the warfront. The least sign of weakness could not be shielded. Anyone who presumed to usurp Lysaer's place would be killed in cold blood for presumption.

'My lord, we won't find your charred carcass to bury!' Fennick despaired, while Ranne more discreetly gathered himself to block the stair's upward access.

'I have to go!' Sulfin Evend ignored the loyal protests, laid open. 'Nobody else is equipped to survive.' The blasting barrage on the s'Brydion harbour mouth *would* be turned upon helping hands in assault. 'I do know the measure of danger I face.'

'But not how to solve the insane confrontation,' Fennick argued.

'Then I will have to trust that somewhere, somehow, I can discover an answer.' Sulfin Evend showed teeth as he drew a firm breath. 'There are no sureties. I will not live in fear! We cannot hang back and still serve our commitment to the troops under us.'

What could be done, but salute such rash courage? Ranne edged aside, face turned in rife misery, while Fennick closed a mailed hand on his Lord Commander's left bracer. 'Go in grace, then, my lord!' He let go with regret. 'Bring yourself down in one piece, if you can.' Though endangered as well, he rejected retreat. 'Count on the fact that this stair stays secure, with both of our swords at your back.'

Far more likely, Sulfin Evend thought wildly, they would all meet flaming oblivion. He adjusted his mail shirt, eased the sword at his hip for quick action, then mounted the plank stair, bent against the onrushing storm that screamed through the gaps in pegged scaffolding. The nailed cover of hides slapped like shot in the gusts, while the pelting snow blanked visibility, and reduced him to a featureless shadow.

The top platform loomed over him, much too soon. Not that planning could help. Above, the sky split to a sizzling light-bolt. The strike briefly lit the white flakes to gold foil, then curdled their shimmer to billowing steam. The melt pattered down, glazing the board stair with treacherous ice. Sulfin Evend edged upward, hammered by the thunder-clap echoes slamming back off the bay. The siege tower shuddered, belted by every recoil of stress-heated air.

Sulfin Evend clawed towards the hatch, forced to grip with both hands, lashed and blinded by the turbulence. He scrubbed tears from blurred vision, and at last glimpsed Lysaer's form beside the rope tackles that lowered the siege tower's drawbridge. Blond hair tangled, his gold trim and fine mantle soot-stained and frayed to singed threads, he howled, fixated on havoc as his next strike hissed aloft.

Dazzled and rocked by the crash of concussion, Sulfin Evend staggered, off-balanced by the whip-crack of his streaming surcoat. He clung, fighting the buck of stressed timbers, and cleared the closed well of the stairway.

Now in the open, his last safety was forfeit. Cruel quandary confronted him: the wracked figure that stood, hurling light-bolts, was no man, but a force single-mindedly pitched to strike down the Spinner of Darkness. *Anything* moving to thwart that directive would be blasted to ash without recourse. The friend poised to coax a cursed mind back to reason could expect to become razed down as an enemy target.

The dichotomy wounded, straight to the heart: that the same bard whose rare talent had called down the shining notes to frame peace should have turned in assault, wielding Shadow. By that one act, Arithon *knew*: reflex must trigger the hideous change and drive his half-brother under the fury of Desh-thiere's murderous insanity.

'Damn your hypocritical promise to Sithaer!' Sulfin Evend snarled in his helpless agony. He possessed no mage training. No exalted grasp of the mysteries. Upbringing at Hanshire had taught him hedge simples, not the disciplined grace for grand conjury. Conviction alone, backed by his mortal care, would not leave his accursed liege abandoned.

Sulfin Evend poised himself. Between the release of white levin bolts, he ignored sapping fear, committed himself, and called out to Lysaer by name.

The avatar spun from the railing and faced him. Flint eyes showed no human awareness. From snarling, bared teeth to flexed hands and torn clothing, this was a possessed creature, become the instrument for an undying revenge. Sized up like meat by that soulless regard, Sulfin Evend choked down his sickened revulsion.

'Lysaer!' he shouted.

'You've come here to meddle!' the mad voice denounced.

'Fight back!' Though the plea felt like grasping for straws in a maelstrom, Sulfin Evend resumed with the scorn of his haughty origins. 'Man and prince, you have birthright! Reclaim your human intelligence!'

Twice before, intervention had snapped through his liege's berserk retaliation. But never before across the antipathy roused by the half-brother's Shadow.

The mistake defied remedy. Lysaer's fury twisted. Feral will revelled, triumph run amok on the intoxicate thrill of destruction. Hands lifted, Desh-thiere's puppet gathered himself. Light blazed for the fire-storm that would torch all insolent interference to ashes.

Never mind the close target would also ignite the siege platform's timbers like kindling.

Unable to run, beyond futile hope, Sulfin Evend flung up a shielding forearm. He cried out, desperate to touch the heart of the man who was lost, imprisoned as the raving antagonist. The grief would not rest, that this animal ferocity would kill: *the most staunch of friends and Tysan's two most reliable liegeman undone without thought, by the Mistwraith's design.*

Sulfin Evend could do naught except crouch on tucked knees, braced to receive a fireball's end without screaming.

That helpless gesture checked fate for a moment. Shocked to be met by unmoving surrender, Lysaer recoiled in hesitation. Light burned in his hands, an arrested force that seared the winter air like unsheathed magma.

Sulfin Evend choked, scarcely able to breathe, as his raced thought lamented the failure: that *once*, a grand harmony channelled through by a Masterbard's talent had broken the Mistwraith's delusion long enough to revive the self-honest yearning for peace. *If only* his cursed liege could be offered the footing to touch that drowned fragment of memory.

Against the dazzling blast of raw light held poised to annihilate, entreaty threw even the need for survival into eclipse. Sulfin Evend cried, shattered, 'Lysaer, you have to believe in yourself!'

The levin bolt crackled, arrested again.

On that livid instant, insight seemed to pierce *through* the shattering blast. *Sulfin Evend felt his perceptions slow down.* On-coming event showed as red-gold flame, laid against finer light, that punched past his galvanic fear. A jolting shock of pure wonder snapped through, that *he did in fact See*! Need forced open the flood-gates: the inherent talent, awake through his oath, raised the heritage of s'Gannley. Gifted by vision, the filigree pattern etched about Lysaer's form *was* no less than the veil of the man's living aura.

Through arrested terror, Sulfin Evend watched the flow surrounding the s'Illessid become muddy again, rifted over by insatiable darkness. He shouted, aghast, using the same phrase. 'You have to believe in yourself!'

Again, came the coiling retreat of the murk. He spoke quickly, before the tide faltered. *'Lysaer! Fight the curse. I know you're not helpless!'*

The pale lightness resurged. At some deep, innate level, Lysaer was responding.

Granted that opening, however slight, Sulfin Evend poured all he had into seeking clear words of encouragement. 'You can listen, Lysaer. Claim your natural self!' Guided onwards by the gilt sheen of the aura, which strengthened upon reinforcement, Sulfin Evend kept faith, adjusting his phrases to bolster the struggle against Desh-thiere's obdurate binding.

'Lysaer! You have to choose! Hold out for the love that knows kindness first!'

Through the crackle of bared light, and the howl of the storm, a pealing scream tore from the throat of a prince, locked into an agonized conflict.

As the curse ripped back, stronger, contending for dominance, the Lord Commander exhorted. 'We have more than this moment! You can hold firm. Think! Lysaer!' While the flickering light flared and battled the dark tendrils wound through his friend's subtle presence, Sulfin Evend dared more. 'True justice suspends judgement! You have been well-taught! I entreat you to weigh every angle and seek, until you achieve balanced insight.'

Against nerve-cracking threat, his Sight *tracked* the trapped will, embattled within Lysaer's being.

'The fair ruler does not bow to rage, or act in summary execution.' Choked by tears, Sulfin Evend bowed his head, his opened hands offered up in appeal. 'Step forward, Lysaer. Come downstairs on your feet!' Tenderly careful to avoid direct threat, or make any reference to Shadow, the Lord Commander fed confidence. 'Together, we can prevail as before. I believe in you, even at risk of my life! Come down! Let us plan by our wits and triumph through the clean use of our human strategy.'

He talked, while the icy wind lashed him numb. 'Help me, liege. We will do this in partnership. For rightness, for peace, and not for the wiles of fell entities sealed under Rockfell Peak!'

Under the wracking, cruel conflict, the poised flare of raised light flickered out. Lysaer had successfully bridled his gift. One reprieve might win others. Sulfin Evend spoke faster. 'We will advance methodically, by well-planned stages. Claim yourself, and strike for a triumph won with forthright honour.'

Eyes shut, now guided purely by love, Sulfin Evend fanned the lit ember of hope. Talking until he was raggedly hoarse, he kept on, until by a miracle, or iron persistence, he felt Lysaer's trembling touch brush against his outstretched palms.

Sulfin Evend closed his hands, firm. The tears welled up, blinding, as he caught his friend close. Through a shattering precedent, the ferocity of Desh-thiere's curse stayed beaten back, and held in abeyance.

The Light's Lord Commander seized his victory and stood. He bundled his shivering charge beneath the shared warmth of his mantle. 'Come down, Lysaer. My liege, we can do this! One step at a time. Be assured, I will not ever leave you.'

Attack came under the white-out blanket of snow, in deepest night with the wind died back to a whisper. Amid fallen quiet, advance teams of sappers and moles crept in over the drifted landscape. They came covered under the squat frames of the sows, which had their wheels replaced by waxed runners. By water, borne on the silent current, oared galleys rode the breast of the tide, gliding up to the harbour-mouth keeps. Their castle-built prows had been fitted out with blunt towers of hide-covered scaffolding and bridges that nuzzled against the high battlements.

The s'Brydion sentries were not caught by surprise. The garrison responded with vicious tenacity. They hurled hails of rocks from the wet ropes of the catapults; shot quarrels from arbalests and rained pots of hot oil down on the enemy crews shielded under soaked hides and stout framing.

Numbers told hardest. For each fallen man, the Alliance fielded ten more, fresh and eager to kill for the Light. Sevrand's companies grappled each oncoming wave. Numbed fingers notched arrows, hurled lances, and spanned cross-bows, with brilliant effect, though the sifting fall of the blizzard blinded the marksmen down to three yards.

From the harbour-side watch turrets, s'Brydion defenders hurled flaming rags and fire-pots in fierce effort to disable the floating siege towers. When the soaked planks on the galleys failed to ignite, they fought hand to hand, against yelling hordes who rushed them from the platforms and swarmed over the glass-studded crenels. With sword and pike, sprayed in blood, they met the on-coming invaders with bitter, then desperate resistance, their drilled skill at arms and inspired heroics sustained without reinforcement. Snow muffled their horn-calls. The reserve force that guarded the citadel slept, uninformed throughout the grim hours of darkness.

With no lull in the storm front, a candle-lamp signal relayed by mirror could not pierce the gloom past twenty paces.

Therefore, the ugly news broke with the dawn: that a third of the shore-side watch turrets were fallen, with the last of them crumbling under punishment by sappers, or battling invasion with crippling losses. The small boat with the messenger pulled in through driving snow at the Sea Gate, his sloshing bilge wracked with dying men, and his slumped oarsmen bristled with arrows. Elaira and Glendien were called to attend them, while the hastily bandaged young officer was rushed away to report to Duke Bransian.

This was not defeat by the overwhelming horror of fire-borne Light, but the relentless ferocity of superior numbers, applied with blunt force.

Alestron's emergency council of war dissolved into a rapid deployment, not for relief, but in counter-attack to hold the battle-line long enough to enact an ordered retreat. The staring fact could not be redressed: that Alithiel's clarion cry to serve peace had stripped the defences under full strength. Where fewer troops could man the great engines, and still mount a barrage of hurled fire-shot, chained balls, and barbed quarrels, the storm robbed that advantage. The smothering snowfall showed no sign of slacking, after the lull. Stiffening gusts snapped the ice off the crenels as the gale-wind reversed, and rose, snarling.

Inevitably, Vhandon became the duke's spokesman to approach the Teir's'Ffalenn.

The chamber equipped as Elaira's still-room was deserted. Since the enchantress was yet engaged in spelled surgery to salvage the traumatically wounded, the first hurdle the veteran captain encountered was the Shandian liegeman, in full arms and clan leathers at Arithon's chamber door. Kyrialt bristled, prepared to deny entrance, though the raised voices within proved Rathain's prince was not sleeping.

'You're not here for condolences,' the young man surmised, through the *bang*! as something solid hammered onto the floor-boards. 'I suggest you come later.'

'Or not at all.' In no mood to prevaricate, Vhandon yanked off his helm. Cramped in the dim stairwell, he clawed clotted ice from his nape and cut to the brutal chase. 'I'm not here for the eulogy, but to appeal on state auspices. Feylind's free-booting venture is costing the citadel a butcher's toll in men's lives.'

'That's Melhalla's affair,' Kyrialt stated, cool. 'Show respect. We are mourning the grace of Shand's fallen.'

'Don't cry histrionics!' snapped Vhandon, through more muffled thumps, and renewed argument in the shut chamber. Eyes like chipped slate yielded no quarter for anyone's believed emotion. 'I knew Feylind well enough! A volatile spirit, and her own mistress, she died of her adult will. No cosseting order of Arithon's could sway her brash mind-set. He sees this, past doubt. Never coddle him!'

Through a locked pause, the fighting heart of each man sized the other one up: the older campaigner with blunt-set jaw prepared to lash callow youth into line, and the younger tempted to use cheek against the bark of a senior captain who relied upon strong-arm authority to cow his subordinate troops.

Then Dakar's hounding anguish pierced the wood door. 'Arithon! No! The concept's unthinkable!'

Vhandon sighed. 'Don't worry. I wish I was anywhere else! But the mission is mine. Since I backed the *Evenstar*'s past affray at sea, I saw his Grace cherish Feylind as he would his own daughter. He'll be gone beyond heart-sore and desolate.'

Naked honesty always won Kyrialt's respect. 'Go gently, then,' he said in grave warning, then stood down and let Vhandon past.

The field-captain rattled the latch to announce company, and swung open the studded door. Under the storm-lit glare from the casements, no head turned to meet him as he stepped through.

Dakar stood by an upset frame chair, railing in petrified conscience. 'No way will I back this! Not even for my Fellowship master's sworn charge.'

Arithon opposed him from the bench seat at the trestle. *Too apparently calm,* he said nothing at all, while the unsettled third party spun at last and faced the breached doorway, his silver-blond hair disarrayed.

'Vhan!' Talvish blurted. 'Thank Ath, someone had the good sense to send you!'

That tone, cranked shrill by relief, impelled Vhandon to tackle the impasse headlong. 'Elaira should be here,' he opened, point-blank. As the prince's angered glance flicked to rake him, Vhandon steadied with uncritical tenderness, 'She could guide us through her understanding.'

'The duke's orders brought you?' Arithon responded. Against the flat glare, detail emerged slowly: despite punishing grief, he had upkept his grooming. His changed clothes were neat, picked for comfort and warmth, of unadorned linen and wool. The scrubbed fingers laid on the trestle did not bear Rathain's ring, a raw enough statement.

'I can't argue that Feylind had the free right to risk death as she pleased,' Arithon added, bald-faced. 'But I was not ready to let her go.' He acknowledged the fact: his impulsive defence had sought to guard his vulnerable love first, before any need to secure threatened stores for the sake of the beleaguered citadel.

'For that one moment, she was larger than all of us,' Vhandon agreed with lancing force. 'And do you sulk now, resenting the fact? Feylind crossed over the Wheel, content, and well satisfied by her accomplishment.'

The sudden breath forced through Dakar's teeth crackled across the pained silence. Talvish winced, also. Which signals foreran the blatant disaster, that Vhandon's astute guess had missed the sore mark.

Arithon's quiet attained the glass edge that defended his most-guarded privacy. While Talvish swore softly, and Dakar cringed, afraid of on-coming explosion, Rathain's prince spoke again, all impervious lightness, 'Duke Bransian wants you to petition for my use of Shadow to repulse the attack on the harbour. I refuse. Go back and report.'

Vhandon tested that walled resistance with the obvious, since he had no better angle. 'Alestron suffers today because of your unveiled presence.'

'Which is precisely why I cannot help!' Such taut stillness hurt, as the snow-filtered daylight intensified the pallor of Arithon's public face. 'This assault is the work of battle-trained troops, using conventional weapons.'

Talvish leaped to illuminate Vhandon's incomprehension. 'For Lysaer's frail hold on sanity, can't you see?'

Which statement slashed through the veil of decorum. Arithon bent his head, fingers shoved through dark hair. 'Dakar,' he pleaded.

Leave permitted the explanation, that cut too close to the visceral bone. The Mad Prophet righted his kicked chair, and sat. Where tact could not serve, the spellbinder tried for gentleness. 'When Arithon loosed his gift of Shadow, the s'Ilessid half-brother fell under the curse of Desh-thiere.'

'We all bore witness.' Vhandon caught Talvish's signalled encouragement, and moved closer. War steel scraped across tension as he dared the bench and assumed the seat opposite. Then he said, but not as the duke's henchman, 'What's changed?'

'Everything,' said Dakar, undone. 'Arithon knows through the strength he required to hold the brig's active defence: *Lysaer did not spend himself to self-immolation.* He did not attack until he collapsed. This time, somehow, he recovered himself. Reason prevailed! Something allowed him to bridle the geas-bent drive to annihilate.'

Talvish picked up, from the leaned stance just taken as rear-guard against the door-jamb. 'Arithon believes that the transcendent chord he channelled by waking Alithiel may have seeded the grace for Lysaer to seek healing. If his kinsman now fights to recover free will, then *anything* that his Grace does in behalf of the citadel might tip that frail effort into deadly jeopardy.'

'Strike now with Shadow to spare the duke's men, and I would destroy the very dawning of hope, as my brother strives to hold his own ground against Desh-thiere's active incursion.' Arithon lifted his face, beyond distressed. 'I can't violate trust, in that fashion.' The Paravian sword's power, just granted for change, demanded his utmost restraint. He must honour each individual's choice, no matter the course of the outcome. 'Every soldier who remains here under arms stayed because he believed in his place.' Through sudden, springing tears of bereavement, Arithon opened his empty palms. 'Just as Feylind placed herself at risk for conviction, I have to keep my heart open and permit the folk on both sides of the siege the same open range of free choice!'

Full meaning hit hard: *that whatever Arithon might personally want, Bransian's men-at-arms must be left to make their own way.* 'That's a damned raw consolation,' Vhandon commented, gruff.

'But the prince is right.' Dakar shouldered the unpractised attempt to ease inconsolable pain. 'Sometimes there are no victims to save, and nothing is broken that should be fixed. What purpose is served? We cannot lose sight of the actual rift. Desh-thiere's malice lies at the root of this conflict.'

'Unless Lysaer grapples the curse on his own terms, the same debacle will happen again, in another arena and on a field as unbearably tragic as this one. I must grant my brother the opening to stop! If he can,' added Arithon, although beyond question he was left aghast, and quite terrified by the necessity.

'Then why were you arguing?' Vhandon bore in, cued by Talvish's tension, that Dakar's upset sensibilities were not yet laid to rest.

'Ath above!' cried Arithon, goaded at last to exasperation. 'Like the man with his fist in the teeth of the tiger, you would taunt my temper and ask! Very well. Since this is not my picked battle to fight, our fraught disagreement arose over how I should take my safe leave of the citadel.'

Vhandon caught himself gripping the trestle until his mailed fingers gouged wood. Dread rode him, roughshod, that Elaira's absence perhaps was a lethal mistake. He forced the issue, since no one else would. 'And the terms in dispute?'

Dakar yanked at his beard with both fists. 'By daring to walk the unknown, past tried limits! Arithon wants to waken Alithiel again, in trust the sword's voice can stabilize his half-brother's compromised gift of royal justice. Which can happen but one way, that I can project!'

Rathain's prince cut in, to side-step histrionics. 'By creating the perceptual appearance I've perished, we can blindside the curse of Desh-thiere.' As Talvish drew breath, he rammed over protestation. 'Jieret and I did this once, with success, to spirit me away from the war host in Daon Ramon!'

Dakar shouted back, quite unmindful of Vhandon, caught in the vicious cross-fire. 'Never this! Not binding your consciousness under, with the sword's note of transcendent change aroused into actualized force! I touched that raised field for only an instant, and almost unravelled my earthly identity! You immersed for *three days*, and –'

'Never for one moment did I stand alone!' Arithon pealed back through the frightened clamour. 'The living grace within that grand chord gave me back, hale and whole!'

'From how near to the edge?' the spellbinder snapped, obstinate, 'You've told us straight out! You don't recall the transitional course that led you into that trance state, far *less* understand any step on the path that restored you to present awareness!' Horrified from his mage-wise perspective, Dakar slammed to his feet, smashing his chair over backwards again. 'This lies past my depth! And yours as well! We need Fellowship counsel for guidance.'

'I am willing to stand on crown auspices and ask,' Prince Arithon agreed. If his hands, on the table, appeared quite relaxed, his lowered gaze refused Dakar's adamance.

Vhandon recognized that evasion too well. Alongside Talvish, he saw the looming crux. The prince who was Masterbard *was going to act*. His risky endeavour would leap forward on courage, without guarantee that a Sorcerer would have the freed resource to back his appeal.

Early Winter 5671

Foil

Midnight passed by before the last broadhead had been removed from the duke's arrow-shot wounded. Elaira roused from the close focus of surgery, blurred under the lassitude caused by extended trance. The shift from altered vision slowed her acuity as she washed her stained hands and fumbled the reach for clean bandaging.

'No matter my dear.' The kindly voice at her elbow belonged to the raw-boned matron who served the garrison as master healer. 'My people can bind up that wound and mix possets. Let them handle those chores. You need sleep.'

Eyes shut as her head swam, Elaira accepted the gift, beyond grateful. The man under her care was now stable. She could pause to ground her awareness. Her form seemed adrift in the cavernous gloom, the swept floor of the sail-loft crammed with makeshift bedding, under demand as a hospice. The lingering tang of tan-bark canvas and hemp rope wrapped the stilled air like a blanket, stitched through by the sweetening fragrance of herbs and the bite of burn salves and iodine. The smells whirled her dizzy, taxed as she was, and verging on feverish back-lash.

'Come away, lady,' the healer urged gently. A tactful, warm hand hooked her elbow, since the earnest staff bearing the remedies could not do their work till she moved.

Elaira bowed to necessity, allowed the woman's spare help to rise onto her feet.

'We'll give you a bed,' the healer suggested in mild remonstrance.

Elaira smiled for her earnest kindness. 'Thank you, but no. I'll rest in my own quarters. I need only pack up my satchel.'

'No cause for that,' the woman assured. 'Your assistant has your things stowed in order already.'

Surprised, Elaira stepped forward too quickly. 'Glendien's still here? But I dismissed her two hours ago!'

The healer's firm grip saved her reeling balance. 'Then the forest woman knew better than to leave you to handle such menial labour!' The chiding acknowledged the rows of stilled men, eased and softly breathing, despite having been on death's door-step. 'I loaned the young woman a blanket. She will have napped as she waited.'

Yet across the dimmed floor-boards, over-sensitized mage-sight captured the flicker of movement. Glendien was urgently coming to meet them, already wrapped for cold weather.

Concern stirred Elaira's lagged wits. She tugged free of the healer's solicitude, and inquired, 'What's amiss?'

For a second figure accompanied the clanswoman, one bearing the grim glint of arms with purposeful readiness. Blunt-cut grey hair and saturnine competence identified Bransian's prized field-captain, Vhandon. The honed faculties of a Koriani enchantress read trouble: that scarred, dead-pan face masked an anxious stride as the soldier flanked Glendien, and shoved the enchantress's outdoor mantle into her nerveless hands.

'What's happened?' Alarmed, Elaira accepted the cloth, while reflex leaped outward, reaching for Arithon by empathic instinct.

She encountered a barrier. A warding, laid down with shocking, stark force, that distanced her as a stranger. *'Beloved! What have you done? Why am I closed out?'* Her inner cry strangled against that razed line, as desperate, she clamoured for access. Recognition slapped back in rebound: the boundary was none of his Grace's own, but a construct of the Mad Prophet's, founded upon the blood oath to survive once granted to Asandir.

'You already know,' Glendien surmised, a wrenching shift that forced displaced awareness back into the echoing sail-loft.

'Know what?' snapped Elaira through shaken distress.

Vhandon explained quickly. 'They mean to waken Alithiel. Then try the same binding that tied Arithon's spirit into the sword, to evade Lysaer's berserk chase in Daon Ramon.'

'How long since the spellbinder crafted the wards?' Elaira pealed in breaking anguish. She pulled on the cloak, fumbling the clasp at her throat. 'Why in the name of Ath didn't you fetch me?' But the reason was obvious: the lives of the stricken men here had required her services, uninterrupted.

Vhandon's smart reaction caught hold of her forearm. He steered for the loft stair, still talking apace. A carriage and pair were in harness to take her. 'Talvish got Dawr's coachman to handle the lines. Nobody matches his skill in a pinch. He'll have you across town in no time.'

Yet that saving forethought could not speed their course until *after* the men at the lift platform brought her aloft from the sea quarter. 'Just pray we're in time.' Elaira managed the stair, shamelessly leaning on Vhandon's strength to steady her vertigo.

Glendien trailed, the slung satchel of remedies chinking complaint at her hip. 'Are you sure that a Fellowship spellbinder's misjudged, and the Masterbard's tactic won't work?'

'Don't be a fool!' Elaira snapped, white. 'Arithon's despondency over Feylind's loss has to colour the handling of his decision. Also, s'Brydion defenders are dying. He would act to disarm conflict soonest!' She finished, distraught, 'I trusted Dakar! Relied on his sense to stay my love's hand, at least long enough to be sure he'd recovered his wise equilibrium.'

'The note in the sword ought to shield him,' Vhandon offered in stout re-assurance.

Elaira shook her head, weak at the knees in stark fear. 'Not today.' The exalted song *was* the unstoppable impetus that impelled transcendent change. She recalled the fierce allure of its promise. *Too well*: even the memory haunted, an echo to last all her days. 'In Arithon's aggrieved state of conflicted interest, the pure stream of that power could lift him too far to hold on to human iden-tity.'

Glendien still clung to impervious optimism. 'His Grace wakened the last time.'

'I know how he came back!' Elaira corrected. Her voice caught, wrung breath-less: she hoped it was just the shock of the icy night air, let in through the ground-level postern. 'My love reached the open gate to his heart. Dakar backed my appeal. He used the oath sworn to the Sorcerer, and on that blood binding, collected him.'

Vhandon's care caught her missed step as she slipped in the alley beyond. Above the loft's buttressed roof, stars burned against a black zenith. The storm had chased off to a spanking north wind, that whipped loosened snow off the cornices. Someone shouted, ahead. More cries arose, past the chandler's ware-house. A company of men jogged past in tight purpose, then more runners, sprinting with flittering torches. The commotion increased, spurred by the moan of a horn-call. A bugle shrilled, nearer: three blasts for alarm, while a drift of oily smoke that reeked of burned hide swirled up from the breastworks, at the quay-side.

'You'll be fielding more wounded,' said Elaira, torn sick.

'The sea-quarter walls are under attack?' Glendien snatched at the satchel to protect the packed glass from the turmoil as they shoved through the tram-pled street.

'Aye, lass! There's fighting.' Vhandon ducked through a side alley, either taking a short cut, or clearing them off the main thoroughfare to avoid a careening sledge, overburdened with barrels and stone-shot.

From the left-side square keep, the jingle and thump of a chain-sling being loaded sounded across hurried footfalls. Then the whistling slam of another's release sliced a sergeant's barked call to span arbalests.

'Inevitable consequence, after the strategic rock that Feylind's taunt pitched through the hornet's nest.' The field-captain urged the two women to run. 'The harbour-side watch turrets have fallen. We'll be facing the same zealot sappers. The great horn's cried warning. Means the enemy's got galley-borne siege platforms also, nosing up for assault on our wharf-side battlements.'

'You'll be needed elsewhere,' Elaira insisted. The frigid air braced her. Exhaustion had become thrown into eclipse as they whisked from the by-way, and threaded the rush of armed men pounding down the next street. 'I can manage from here.'

'No.' Vhandon's spare glance scarcely gave her acknowledgement. 'You'll require my vested authority. The garrison will have cordoned the windlass platform. Under active defence, they'll demand check-point passwords. The lift gear gets fired if Sevrand's guard fails, and the Sea Gate bailey becomes overtaken.' He added, 'Come on! You're nobody's burden! My command post is rightfully topside!'

The dash through the dock quarter ended, replaced by the slow agony of the exposed ride up the cliff-side. There, the wind's whistling thrum through the winch cables lashed every patch of bare flesh. Then the cruel chill was forgotten, as the overhead vista unveiled the Alliance assault on the harbour-front. Oared warships thrashed in, their prow-mounted belfries lurid in the orange light. Ranged against them, fire-shot and smouldering oil arced over black water and broke, streaming cinders down the plank siege towers, swathed in their protective, soaked hide. Screams and cries spiralled upwards, cut by horn-calls and shouts, while the barrage of arrows and crossbolts whined more-ominous notes through the gusts. Under the massive sally, the dark teeth of the battlements seemed outlined in torch-flame, and the seething glints that were men, mere reflections thrown off moving armour.

Vhandon's grim quiet defeated talk, and quenched even Glendien's saucy rejoinders. Elaira endured, tightly wrapped in her cloak. Despair squeezed her hollow, that no healer's skills could accommodate tonight's toll of maimed and war-wounded. Far worse, she might not reach Arithon in time to avert his rash plan. Shivering as the lift platform wrenched to a stop, she stepped off into Talvish's arms.

One glance, and his lean hand cupped her nape, hiding her sudden tears against his mantle. 'You should never have been here,' he said in strait pain. 'Though, Ath's mercy, there's nobody else can touch Arithon's heart and disarm his defences as you can.' A brief word of gratitude acknowledged Vhandon. Then he bundled her past the cordon of sentries and into the waiting carriage. Glendien managed a scrambling entry. Then the door slammed. The skilled coachman grasped the lines and snapped his tasselled whip, driving the snorting team into their collars.

Elaira laid her head back as the vehicle surged forward, eyes shut and shallow breaths steadied. Use of her training reined in jagged fear and sustained her through the jouncing passage. When the carriage arrived, and Talvish jumped down from the groom's perch, she no longer required his ready support.

Across the plank-bridge, with Glendien following, she rushed the staircase towards Arithon's quarters, braced for a fight, and prepared to match adamant force against Dakar's wardings. Instead, she confronted the shocking reverse: the doorway stood open before her. The fear blinded, that she was too late, with the ritual binding of Arithon's spirit already complete. Yet Kyrialt guarded the head of the landing, his unrestrained welcome unstringing her dark net of panic.

'They chose not to go forward!' Elaira exclaimed. 'Has wise council prevailed?' Then, caught by the driving anxiety behind the clan liegeman's relief, *'What happened?'*

'The Paravian sword would not rouse for this hour's cry of appeal,' the young liegeman revealed. 'You are needed, if only to console the raw heart-ache left by that failure.'

Elaira gasped, fuming, 'Consolation is not the course I have in mind.' She brushed past, with Glendien panting at heel to share in the thrill of explosion.

Except Kyrialt's grip closed on his wife's wrist. No regret for brisk handling, he snapped her short. 'You, my most brazen, are not going in there! The Koriani mate's ripped enough to taste blood. While she goes for the throat, her man doesn't need such as you, whetting teeth for a lunge at his bollocks.'

Before Glendien's protesting jerk could break free, Elaira slammed the strapped oak panel with a thud to bang chips from stone masonry.

Inside the shut chamber, the light shone too thin, the flickering fish-oil lamp fiercely trimmed to spare fuel. What the low flame obscured, mage-sight must unveil through taut patience. Poised to one side, Dakar's defenceless misery would have caused his retreat, had Elaira's instinctive gesture not stopped him. Unwilling to apologize for duty-bound trust, he endured, his beard and screwed hair reflecting the strain on plump features.

'Did you think I would shout?' Elaira snapped, saddened. 'Then your past choice in Halwythwood has taught you nothing!'

She moved onwards, searching gaze shifted to the other stilled figure, found seated under the Mad Prophet's shadow. Arithon's wide-opened eyes met her as she reached the trestle where Alithiel rested, unsheathed. The black steel abided, its gateway to mystery opaque. The glassine rune inlay gleamed coldly quiescent, all prismatic rainbows muted. Like the blade's shuttered promise, the beautiful, bard's hands on the boards did not shift as, unflinching, the man accepted her furious scrutiny.

'You saw no other way to spare Fionn Areth,' Elaira apprised at delicate length.

The sigh of relief was Dakar's, released by the startling grace of her empathy.

'No one else realized,' he stated, gruff. 'At the outset, I didn't perceive that wretched angle, either.'

Elaira found the bench, pulled the seat out, and perched. Her chilled fingers were too numbed to grapple the fastenings to shed her mantle. Bone-tired, and edging on sickness herself from the ingrained reek of dried blood and iodine, she swallowed. The straightforward ease of her honesty faltered, as she picked her spare words through like thorns. 'The grass-lander's stubborn. He has not grown enough to concede that forgiveness does not demand punishment. We may have to accept that he can't be extricated. If not, our lapse in protection at this pass may not be accounted a failure.'

'Your own heart would not rest,' Prince Arithon said. Nothing more. Yet the sure, fluid move that broke his stillness arose too fast to assimilate. Poised behind her, he slid his hands under and through her pinned hair and eased the wrapped braid from confinement. Beneath the fall of her crimped auburn locks, his touch mapped the wire-strung ache in her neck, then lightly shifted in a proprietary caress across the mantle that dragged at her collar-bones. The loop catch slid free. The burdensome wool tumbled onto the floor, replaced by his warmth as he straddled the bench and drew her shaking frame into his embrace.

His dangling response stayed unfinished, until her head nestled into his shoulder. 'After all, you once left Fionn's fate in my hands. *The right choice.* I will not abdicate.'

Dakar's leashed calm suggested an argument forced into simmering abeyance. Elaira tried anyway. The issue had to be thrashed over again, if only for form's sake, and despite the cruel culpability that her own oath-tied burden forced her to weather. She steeled for the course. 'What comes of your commitment if the goatherd's free will insists otherwise?'

Arithon's clasped fingers tightened and held. 'Then he chooses. But with the clear road to claim freedom opened and secured before him.'

And *that* sparked explosion, an incensed cry torn from her stung heart. 'Not at the cost of your sacrifice! Arithon! If Feylind were alive, she'd back this fight, tooth and nail by innate woman's wisdom. My hurt is not blameless! *I helped shapechange that child.* You can't lift that pain from me, however you try. Fionn Areth himself never asked for your help. He has not offered a trustworthy friendship. I will not see your life thrown to risk for an undervalued relationship!'

Arithon waited, steady. The torrent that broke loose was too friable, begun in lone anguish on the cold, Araethurian night when the order's might had compelled an untenably harsh set of choices. 'Fionn's character, or lack of it, does not revoke his birthright.' The correction was careful, almost too mild to declare an unbreachable stance. 'Rathain's chartered provenance makes that boy's cause mine for what he has suffered in violation. As a subject under crown auspices, he bears my explicit claim of protection.'

Upwelling tears snapped Elaira's last poise. Dakar seized the moment and arose on quiet feet, assured he could quit the arena. Love's tenacity must now secure the thread of Rathain's threatened legacy. The armed core of Arithon's will was exposed, and the pitfall that terrorized foresight: that if the extreme escape plan went forward, and a repeat attempt could unleash Alithiel's power, with the last Teir's'Ffalenn moved to imbue his stripped spirit into the awakened sword, the ungrateful ally might snatch that opportune opening for his betrayal.

The muted clink of the door-latch signalled the gift of the couple's privacy. No other disturbance would visit tonight, to intrude on that haven of shared solitude. Arithon laid his cheek overtop of Elaira's head. While the lamp-flame fluttered, and silence settled, fragrant with the herbal mélange wafted up from the downstairs still-room, he cradled her searing flood of distress.

Unrushed, at due length, he addressed her in soft quiet, 'This is not about Fionn Areth, entirely.'

A shudder raked through her. 'You know me too well.'

'Ah, beloved!' Tenderness infused Arithon's touch as he mapped the true source of her misery. 'You are regretting your return to the citadel. Don't. Did you fear that my measure to disarm this cursed conflict may also have been tried in your behalf?'

Not waiting for answer, Arithon shifted his grip. He tipped her cupped face to his matchless regard. 'Do you know of your worth to me? Hush! Words can't fathom the substance. Forget the conniving hooks of your Matriarch. Regrets of all kind are not seemly. My joy in your presence remains without fault, no matter what straits lie against us.' As her eyes welled again and spilled over, he smiled. 'Never doubt.' He bent farther and kissed. The salt tears on her lips were absorbed, then melted away by an onslaught of caring too sweet for denial.

Dakar kept his jagged urgency hidden from Kyrialt's sight. He dodged from the stairwell into the still-room, grateful that Glendien's tasked work engrossed her with restocking the remedies. He moved abreast of her, yawning, then flipped off a critical comment that hackled her to a flush.

'Braying jackass!' Glaring daggers, she snapped, 'Where were you? Bent over kissing your bollocks while the brave fallen lay in their blood, dying?'

'Why, bouncing the jennet,' Dakar cracked with a smirk. She flailed at him with a pestle. He ducked, chased safely past striking range. Out of the far door without flagging her inquisitive instincts, he dropped his buffoonery and bolted for the ground floor. Outside the guest keep, his pounding rush collided with Talvish, striding inbound across the foot-bridge, since squaring affairs with the coachman.

Rammed to a grunt on sharp impact, the swordsman's field reflexes saved them both from a tumble into the snowy ravine. 'Fiends plague, Dakar!' Mail-clad fingers relaxed their vexed grasp and shoved the spellbinder back upright.

'If you've unearthed another rough crisis, we've got trouble ganged up on all fronts already.'

Chill slid like a blade through Dakar's layered cloaks. No mistaking *that* tone of urgent concern, though the scud of cloud obscured the expression beneath the guardsman's spiked helm. 'The Alliance's whelming assault has begun?'

'On-going, and laying on pressure like vengeance.' Talvish darted an un-settled glance to his rear, that the action took place without him. 'Sea Gate's holding out. Can't last, up against Lysaer's perishing numbers. The duke's critical short-fall's going to be the hard fact that we're now under strength.'

Which was Arithon's doing; blame would come to roost. Talvish's razor-thin nerves gave that warning.

The Mad Prophet tugged his rumpled cloak back to rights, uneasy for another reason. 'Where is Fionn Areth?'

Talvish frowned. 'Haven't seen him.' He was on fighting edge: *that fast*, he fielded the change in pursuit. 'Not since he delivered the wretched bad news, that *Evenstar*'d snagged in a lash-up.'

'Can I ask your assistance to find him?' Dakar blurted, 'I have a bad feeling.'

Talvish expelled a fretted breath, his poise now charged to leashed light-ning. 'My liege? Was his late feckless enterprise thwarted?'

'Diverted, for now,' Dakar reported. 'He's settled with Elaira. She sees well enough. Expect she will try the time-honoured gift to serve his obdurate grief consolation. Kyrialt's guard will handle the door. We haven't much time. Will you help?'

'Bad feeling, or augury?' Talvish rapped out, then swore over Dakar's clammed-up silence. 'Never mind. His Grace doesn't know?'

'I'm not foolish!' The Mad Prophet clutched two-handed to batten his billowing cloak. 'Though, Ath wept! Stalking a live stream of prescience past the thickets of s'Ahelas far-sight felt like hopping live toads through a fire pit.'

'Let's move on it, then!' Talvish wheeled back across the plank-bridge. 'Damned well I don't like leaving Arithon now. But worse, if we're caught blindsided again by some ugly prophetic vision!'

'Premonition,' Dakar qualified, tart. 'Not quite the same thing.' Short legs pumping to match the tall veteran's fast clip, he puffed too hard to lament the dismissal of the loaned four-in-hand coach.

The citadel streets teemed with frenetic activity. Hand-carts packed rag tinder, and sheaves of arrows and crossbolts. The larger drays bearing stone-shot and oil casks were pulled by sweating men, the oxen long since butchered to feed the populace. Courier's relays sent from the duke's command eyrie threaded through, run on foot or mounted on small, agile horses. The riders passed off their sealed batons with fresh orders at speed, and received in turn the breathless reports dispatched from the fighting at harbour-side.

Through drifting smoke and ragged torch-light, stumbling in the chopped slush, Dakar croaked for a reprieve. A misstep that tore the nails in his boot-heel bounced him off a wagon's pinned tail-gate.

He yelped, hopping lame, as the flapping leather tripped him again. Forced to rip off the hindrance, he sliced his thumb. 'Dharkaron's vengeance! Why bother hauling these forsaken rocks?'

'The trebuchets can't bear on a target, close in.' Talvish shouted above the rumble of wheels and the clatter of messenger ponies. 'Small shot's for the catapults and the large arbalests. They'll heat the rocks red. Then lever them into the sling beds for firing through the hide shielding that covers the galleys landing the siege towers. Or else drop them down upon enemy heads through the murder holes in the barbicans.'

Where Dakar would have lagged, to escape being trampled, Talvish snatched his stout wrist and towed him headlong. The duke's men still honoured their ex-captain's prowess. As his insistent questions crossed their fraught activity, supporting the Sea Gate defences, several brief facts were ascertained: Fionn Areth was not ensconced with Lord Bransian, nor with Parrien's posted lookout at Watch Keep. He had not tagged along with the armed guard attending the s'Brydion wives still in residence.

Moving apace, Talvish snapped in pared summary, 'That leaves Vhandon's command. He's assigned at the winch platform, handling resupply for the battle-front.' To get there, they flagged down a fast-moving wagon and hitched a ride to the cliff-side bastion.

The smoke drift thickened, fouled by the reek of singed hide and the rolling billows thrown off by torched oil. Coughing behind his mailed fist, Talvish croaked to the driver, who answered, yelling through the rag tied across nose and mouth.

'Aye, fires enough. Siege towers, mostly.' The burly man veered for a galloping messenger. While his sweated team skidded, he steadied the lines, coaxing still more reckless speed. His scrambling wheel-horse swung the tight corner, shod hooves nicking up sparks. 'Bad, on the dock quarter,' the man shouted, as the cart rumbled beneath the arched entries of the guild-halls. Above, the three-story facades were faced granite, with flat roofs notched with crenels, as battlements. The unflinching driver whipped his horses on, the hubs of his vehicle clearing the chipped balustrades of the bottom stairs by a cat's whisker.

'Sevrand's got shipwrights to whip-saw through the bollards on the south wharf,' he told Talvish, who clung to the load, alert as a leopard poised in a half crouch. 'Else the enemy might've winched them up with a capstan and seized the tarred logs for a ram.'

'That near, they've tried landing?' Dakar exclaimed.

'It's a gang-up swarm,' said the driver, morose. A clattering slide down the last, icy incline reined the wagon up short at the press by the windlass. His imp's grin flashed sidewards. 'Here you are, then.'

Talvish vaulted down, belting out a shrill whistle.

The signal brought Vhandon, bearing full arms, in a running charge from the lift shack. Where his bark met resistance, he elbowed through the pack-train of burdened stevedores. 'There's trouble, Tal?'

'Aye. Maybe.' Talvish gestured towards Dakar, who was still wedged fast between the stacked casks in the cart. 'Yon prophet's gone lathered. Where's Fionn Areth?'

'Not here.' Vhandon instinctively vaulted ahead. 'You think that boy might try to upstage Feylind's heroics and offer himself in Prince Arithon's stead as a sacrifice?'

'No.' Dakar grunted, straining not to cough as thicker smoke streamed from the harbour-front. 'Much worse, more's the pity.'

Vhandon was less tolerant of gut-shrinking cowardice. 'The grassland rat's hopped off to turn coat? Dharkaron Avenger's Black Spear! I'll wring his slinking, goatherder's neck! Damned fast as that, if he thinks to crack open a postern gate and betray us.'

'He wouldn't.' Dakar redoubled his struggles, red-faced. 'Not consciously. At least, not yet.'

As one partnered move, Vhandon and Talvish grabbed hold of the stout prophet's arms and slung him headlong from the wagon-bed.

'Then say what you've seen!' Vhandon bellowed. 'Talk fast!'

'Prime Selidie's immersed in a fresh round of conjury!' Dakar yelped, stung by the harsh impact to his mangled boot-heel. 'Her activity's too busy for anything innocent. The posited horror's quite real, that Fionn Areth may pack a masked sigil very like the one tagged on Elaira as a specific trap to snare Arithon.'

'What harm could it do?' the two swordsmen asked as one voice.

'Could the working crack through the Paravian wardings?' The new question came from the by-standing watch sergeant, just barged in to query his diverted captain.

'I don't know.' Dakar shut his eyes, abruptly wrung sick as his senses plunged into vision *again*. As before, he captured the flickered impression . . .

. . . *of Prime Selidie, bent above the flame of a black candle, her pale hair twisted and pinned at her crown like a coil of adders. Across from her, serving for her burn-scarred hands, Lirenda sat, dark as twinned night. Neat fingers laced chains of lightning-sharp seals over the cloth of an effigy: a man's crude figure, painted over with runes, and wound in gold wire stamped crosswise with sigils . . .*

Then the gut-wringing wave of raw vision released. The Mad Prophet gasped, propped upright in the grasp of the impatient sergeant.

'Vhandon?' Dakar craned his neck, senses swimming, while the buffeting press jostled past, muscled men rolling barrels, or burdened with sacks of small shot. Someone nearby was swearing mayhem over the nuisance of obstructive idlers.

The sergeant said something.

Dakar understood that he needed to move, or risk getting trampled. The absence of Vhandon's authority gave short shrift to his debilitating fits and histrionics. He yelled anyhow, then spotted Talvish's tall form on the winch platform, lowering from the cliff rim. The watch sergeant in charge refused to flag down the windlass team to let the spellbinder join the descent.

'No civilian goes down! Duke's orders. Now clear yourself out of the warfront before someone spits your fool gut on a pike!'

'Ath's own grace, I've just signed that boy's death warrant!' Dakar shivered and wept, while the duty-bound officer hurled him aside without sympathy.

Left at loose ends, exhausted, Dakar crumpled against a stone buttress, out of harm's way. Woe betide him for his jelly-legged weakness, and Dharkaron's curse on the lapses brought on by his unruly talent. For if the paired veterans caught up with the Araethurian, they would act first for Alestron's security: take down the suborned double by expedient force, then settle their frank questions afterward.

Bid and Opening

A terrier would release a live rat from its teeth, before Fionn Areth gave up a chase driven by an obsession. Never mind that the moment was inopportune, with the Sea Gate's defences at wharf-side being stormed under full-scale assault. The roaring noise all but deafened thought. Unfazed by strayed quarrels that hissed down and cracked, striking sparks off the cobbles and chimneys, the goatherder scuttled through the deserted fish-market, and ducked into the darkened alleys laced through the dock quarter. His footsteps passed the shuttered fronts of the wine-shops, and the galleries of emptied brothels. Scarcely one street removed, the enemy siege platforms rammed in and engaged Alestron's defenders. Steel clashed, and men shouted, where skirmishers raged in close combat. Through the ink palls of smoke, under the notched peaks of the dormers, the Araethurian raced in furtive quiet, while the scream of hot stone-shot creased the night air, and starved rats skittered into the culverts.

No torches burned in these tangled by-ways, the oppressive gloom flitted with shadows cast by the red arcs of fire-arrows. Against the shoreside bedlam, and the officers' trumpet blasts, the Araethurian found what he sought: two men calling comments in broad-vowelled southcoast accents.

Fionn Areth changed course and followed. From doorway to warehouse, past the silled well by the cooper's shack, he tailed his quarry: a pair of muscular sawyers bearing tools on their shoulders, split away from the crew just returned from demolishing the trade wharf. Unaware that two crack field-captains scoured in search of his whereabouts from liftside, the Araethurian chased in single-minded pursuit of the rogue master shipwright, Cattrick.

That errand led down a ramp through an arch, customarily kept locked and guarded. The entry to Alestron's secretive dry dock did not admit prying strangers. Yet tonight, with the walls under dire assault, Fionn Areth crept through, unchallenged. He plunged down a dank stair tunnelled beneath the paved street. Ahead, the sawyers' voices threw muddled echoes off vaulted brick, where the passage intersected the sewer laced under the cliff head. A pine knot blazed in a fixed bracket by a stone landing, jutted into the eddied black current. Several empty pole skiffs were left moored to crusted green rings. Again, the short garrison had upset the roster. The routine sentries were re-assigned elsewhere, with the men he shadowed already afloat and making headway downstream.

Fionn Areth muffled the chink of his sword, untied the next boat, and launched off through the underground drain that unfolded in darkness ahead of him. Swift current nudged his craft down the closed water-way, then into the high, buttressed cavern where Alestron's warmongering dukes berthed their ships for refit and laid the new keels for their rapacious fleet.

There, also, Parrien's seamen had warped the charred hulk that remained of the *Evenstar*. Sorrowfully ravaged, she floated, lit by the gleam of fish-oil lamps that winked into view past the low mouth of the channel. The once-graceful curve of her stern-rail was shattered. Fionn Areth saw that the wheel mount was gone, and the mizzen rat-lines burned wholesale. Beyond her wracked fore-deck, her shorn bowsprit jutted over spangles of yellow reflection. Her jib-boom still trailed tattered rigging. The parted port chain stay dangled, submerged, beneath the singed breasts of her star-crowned figure-head.

Nestled in the wreckage, also, was a man, slung in the gloom of her beak-head. Expert hands were quite busy, threading new blocks to the freshly spliced bobstays. Beside him, the flash of a knife showed another, clearing away the snapped cordage.

If the ghosts of her crew seemed scarcely departed, the wracked main-deck crawled with activity. The lantern hanging above the main pin-rail rimmed the heads of more men, wielding tools at the mainmast.

'Steady on! Lower as she goes!' The booming command, unmistakably Cattrick's, raised the creak of a burdened sheave. Movement stirred overhead, as the shipwork's massive tackle and rope eased a net of casks towards the open hatch.

The sawyers in the pole-boat up ahead skimmed alongside the berthed hull. They hailed their fellows, tied off to the bollards, then collected their saws and debarked. Someone's comment raised rowdy laughter. To more ribald whistles, the pair crossed the plank gangway and boarded the derelict brig.

Brazen as brass, Fionn Areth did likewise. He first presumed the work aimed for a salvage, until he stumbled over a pile of burlap. Experience with Talvish's troops made their musty scent too familiar: the sacks contained lint floss. His blunder fetched him up against a cache of split pine, green and sap-sticky with pitch. The wrecked hull packed torch kindling, taken from weapon stores, and wound over for business with oil-soaked rags.

His racket drew notice. Someone's hard fists seized his collar and wrist from behind. Twisted into an arm-lock, Fionn Areth was hauled up, yelling, and dealt a shove that staggered him onto his knees. More angry craftsmen closed in a circle. Then a capped sea-boot hammered him flat, grinding into his spine and pinning him helpless.

The light shifted sharply. Somebody lifted the hung lantern down and thrust the hot glass towards his face.

'Daelion's black cock and my arm left for shark bait, here's a right fish's tit!' The observer ran on, thick with dock-side vernacular, in answer to Cattrick's piqued question. 'It's the goatherding doggo come snooping back to get himself fleeced for a gelding!'

The master shipwright said, whetted by malice, 'He'd best have a sharp reason. I don't toss the prize to a mudclod who's hell-bent on crossing my bow for a second time.'

Fionn Areth refused to be cowed. As more hecklers clustered, he demanded, 'Does Arithon know you're here scuttling this brig?'

'Scuttle her? Us?' Another jab from his captor, then more grumbles, as rough fingers twisted his sword-belt and seized his prized weapon as forfeit.

'Stripling may know how to butcher a billy,' someone sneered to a companion. 'Can't thole a fished mast from a gate-post!'

'I haven't slaughtered a goat in two years,' Fionn Areth protested. 'Mind that steel carefully. It's made to hack flesh. Should honest ignorance make me an enemy?'

The offensive grind of the boot-heel let up. Disarmed and permitted to scramble erect, the Araethurian dabbed scuffed blood from his chin. He glared, while the bullying shipwrights weighed over his fate.

'Aren't proven our friend,' the most baleful declared. 'Don't say you're not poking your hayseedy snoot into what isn't your business.'

Such guarded industry effected impressive repairs: already, new timber rose from the stump of the mainmast, the splice fastened by a girdling of spars and strapped iron. The supports had been nailed, then woolded in place with over-laid wrappings of hawser. Cattrick's barked order drove three sweating men back to their neglected labour. The boom of their mallets resounded, as wedges were hammered under the rope to tighten the coils.

As others sauntered back to their work, Fionn Areth sighted another party, mounting a replacement rudder under the sterncounter.

'Salvage?' he asked, not wholly convinced. 'Then what's in the casks you just dropped off the lift? Don't mistake my inexperience for stupidity. Nobody loads on dry lint and oil for caulking the seams in sprung planking!'

'What's *your* stake?' challenged Cattrick, shouldered in to take charge. His jutted jaw and frowning squint forgave nothing of the bungled impression begun at the chandler's. Clad in tar-grimed motley, a spliced cluster of dead-eyes clutched in his massive fist, he declared, 'My take's no murky secret. If

Sevrand's watch fails and the Sea Gate goes down, I won't be leaving a seaworthy prize for the enemy. Sweet keel that she is, the *Evenstar*'s going back under sail. One last run to remember her slaughtered crew, my own blood cousin among them.'

The belated truth dawned. 'Dharkaron Avenge!' Fionn Areth grinned. 'You'll launch her off and crash through the Light's water-borne siege towers as a tinder-box fire-ship?'

No one answered. The round of furtive glances instead suggested a vengeful conspiracy: neither Duke Bransian nor Arithon Teir's'Ffalenn had issued these craftsmen with orders. The opportune chance, seized while Sevrand's crack sentries were fighting elsewhere, left Fionn Areth caught in predicament. These shipwrights dared not risk that his loose tongue might foil their free-booting sabotage.

'Why not ask for my help?' the grass-lander suggested with cheerful humour. 'No question, you folk are doing what Teive and Feylind would have wanted.'

The lantern-jawed joiner who had knocked him down turned in appeal towards his master. 'Could use the hand, truly. Don't need our skilled knowledge to run the waxed string we're threading for the slow-match fuses.'

Cattrick's bunched scowl darkened. 'He's your trouble, then, and the nails in your coffin should aught go wrong. Mark me! If the blighted yokel yaps off, I'll club him senseless and drown him.'

Despite the contempt for his back-country origin, a man born and raised on the downs knew how to shoulder hard work. Service with Alestron's veteran troops had thrashed out the habit of petty complaint. Fionn Areth bored holes and fed string with a will through the confines of sail-room and steerage. The craftsmen alongside of him shared his discomforts. They cursed the same banged shins and skinned knees, crawling over the grates in the bilges. Stressed under tight quarters, even their stiff, southcoast attitude must acknowledge his diligence.

'Why did you come sniping after us, anyhow?' asked the bearded fellow who unreeled the waxed string past the stanchions to the starboard chain-locker. With cable removed, the rust-stained compartment reeked of mildew, damp with chill to numb ungloved fingers.

Fionn Areth crawled in and accepted the passed ball of twine. Jammed against the gouged wood, working by glimmered light through the hawse-hole, he said cautiously, 'I wanted to consult with Cattrick.'

'Did you now?' The ruddy caulker beside him squirmed sidewards, busy applying a brush of hot tar to stick the floss batting under the overhead deck-beams. 'Whatever for, butty? He's never passed griff for the asking before.'

'You wanted to try a new trade besides goat sticking?' gibed the little sail-maker, crammed farthest forward.

'No.' Fionn Areth disregarded the next round of laughter. He fed the treated string to the man, who stitched through the affixed tinder with a curved needle, grunting to the odd jab from his neighbour. 'I wanted to ask why you lot chose Alestron above the royal shipworks in Tysan.'

By Parrien's word, Cattrick and his labourers were the only others who had seen paid service under both Lysaer s'Ilessid and Arithon s'Ffalenn. His portion completed, Fionn Areth squeezed out, stretching his kinked back as he finished his contentious point. 'The s'Brydion duke had cause to turn, bound under a title that's tied to clan law.'

The dangling puzzle remained: that Cattrick was a town citizen from Southshire, with family and kin ties in Shand. Since the coastal ports had declared for the Light, his choice to betray the Divine Prince had stranded him as an exile. If the sacrifice was made in Prince Arithon's behalf, there had been no reunion, and no warmth extended in fellowship.

'You don't have to like a man to respect him,' the caulker remarked, head poked out of the chain-locker. Tar-brush clamped in his teeth, he emerged before granting his dour admission. 'Master o' Shadow worked the crews plenty hard. But his silver was timely. No one could say that his terms weren't fair.'

'You sweated under his Grace, also?' Fionn Areth inquired, then caught the bundle of batt sacks he was thrown. Choked by puffed dust, he heard his answer through a paroxysm of sneezes.

'Most of us did, son. Though make no mistake, we don't bow and scrape over titles. Mostly our loyalty's given to Cattrick, and Ath bear witness, the affray back in Tysan left him and us on raw terms with the Koriathain.'

Since the reference applied to a past oath of debt, discharged against Arithon's interests, Fionn Areth wisely withheld from untoward comment. As the work progressed down the starboard decks, the laid fuses and oiled kindling made ready for reiving, the story was left to surface in unforced conversation: of the underhand plot that had placed the shipyard labourers under arraignment at Riverton, then the brutal ordeal that put them to the question by the order's coercive spellcraft.

'Sisterhood used their trained seers with spelled crystals to break a man's mind!' the sail-maker said in cold anger.

The caulker shuddered, and brandished his brush. 'Shrinks my gut to remember. No breathing human should suffer such horror, nor any creature born living in Ath's creation.'

'Damned witches want the Teir's'Ffalenn taken down as their captive trophy,' the stout sail-maker ran on with fresh venom. 'For spite's sake, I'd thwart them. All here who survived their cruel handling would deny the Prime Matriarch's satisfaction.'

'Nothing to what the bitches did to your face!' Unbent enough to show brutish sympathy, the caulker clapped Fionn Areth on the shoulder. 'Can't have liked being rigged out as their decoy.'

'Less than you know,' Fionn Areth allowed, beyond words for the depth of his rancour.

The labour crept forward in the cold dark, by the trembling flame of the lantern. The very fact the activity passed unquestioned bespoke a garrison pressed hard by short numbers. No one mentioned the fear that the cavern might be cut off if the battle outside changed to rout. Now and again the force of the assault rumbled echoes beneath the stone vaulting. The massive, grilled gates of the tidal lock shuddered on their tracks, jostled by disturbed eddies of current as siege rams shocked the harbour-side wall. Othertimes, muffled shouts filtered in, or the distanced clangour of weapons, as the enemy galleys thrashed in at full stroke, and ploughed into bitter resistance.

Fionn Areth blinked sweat from his eyes, galled to have been disbarred from the fight with the veterans in Vhandon's company. Ever and always, his spell-turned appearance placed his character under question. Few trusted his loyalties. No one he befriended asked for his thoughts. However he strove for a life of his own, wherever he wished to grant loyalty, his place was presumed, either hobbled or cast into bitter eclipse by the dictates of the Teir's'Ffalenn.

Now masked in the shadow of the brig's lower hold, the young grass-lander served unstinting amid the rough company of the shipyard labourers: men well-respected for their independence, who argued with forthright opinions. Already, his stubborn grit earned their praise. His quaint quips prompted chaffing and laughter. When the fire-ship sailed, and he volunteered, he avowed that *this time* he might win an acceptance on the unbiased strength of his merits.

His bold moment approached. The topside repairs now finished apace, the pounding of mallets replaced by loose talk. The splashing thump of oar strokes from outside the hull signalled the launch of the long-boats. At Cattrick's brusque order, the unreeled warp lines hissed down. Spliced ends slapped the water, to bumping scrapes as the men in the tenders made fast the tow cables to warp the brig into the lock.

'Best wrap up here,' urged the sail-maker, while the last batt and wick string was tarred into place, and the joiner collected his tools.

Fionn Areth followed the crowd at the hatch, using touch where the lantern's gleam faltered. Emerged on the main-deck, he brushed off his grimed clothes. Shoulders squared and chin raised, he lit off to appease Cattrick.

The irascible master shipwright stood braced at the portside railing, the frizzled hair in a sailhand's queue set apart from the caps of his fellows. The Araethurian's confiscated sword had been shoved through a loop in his apron. His back stayed turned as he shouted praise over the dusty sacks bearing mill stamps, tossed up to the deck by his ankles.

'Flour?' Fionn Areth said in puzzled inquiry.

'Aye, lad.' The sail-maker flashed a blood-letting grin. 'Loft that stuff into the air down below, you'll witness one baleful explosion.'

'Not our hold, peggy,' a bystander decried. 'We're sending the long-boats with picked crews, ahead. They'll scull in and grapple those Sunwheel galleys, then waft flour in pokes through the oar-ports. While everyone's folded double and coughing, our *Evenstar* slips in behind. She'll serve up our prearranged packet o' hell, and torch off Dharkaron's own vengeance.'

'I want to go with them,' Fionn Areth announced, unable to check-rein his eagerness. 'Let me pull an oar. Or at the least, bide on *Evenstar*'s hulk with a slow match.'

Talk froze. Through the choked silence, Cattrick spun from the rail to dress down the impertinence. 'Why?' A step forward brought his narrowed stare closer. '*Why?*' The stripped demand blistered. 'You've shared our company for less than one hour! What did you think? That the counterfeit mug of a prince gives you the born right to collaborate?'

Fionn Areth burned scarlet. 'No! Like you and yours, I'm not sworn to Rathain, or reduced to a Koriani pawn dropped into the Teir's'Ffalenn's pocket!'

Cattrick gave back his least civil smile. 'I'd say not,' he agreed.

No warning was given, nor any kindly support from the craftsmen clustered behind. Fionn Areth never saw whose hand turned against him. He felt only the blow that hammered his nape, and dropped him straight down into darkness.

Awareness returned to a shattering headache and the misery of numbed extremities. Fionn Areth groaned. His shuddering breath brought the smell of damp wood, and his hearing, the slosh of salt water. Queasy with dizziness, and hounded by pain, he found that Cattrick's wrangling scoundrels had dumped him in the bilge of a long-boat. Spinning vision showed him that the craft was moored to a piling by the dry dock. His wrists were bound, hands in front of him. Another rope lashed his ankles. The deserted quiet meant the *Evenstar* had already embarked.

'Motherless sons of a goat-humping dog!' Fionn Areth shivered, furious. If he laid eyes on the shipwrights again, he would carve that vile ancestry into their livers. But before retribution, he had to win free. His untoward bout of unconsciousness left him half-stunned by the cold.

Most of the lamps he remembered were gone. By the fluttering light that remained, he discovered his long sword, jutted over the stern seat. The hilt was placed within easy reach, a reprieve that earned no forgiveness. Fionn Areth muttered another ripe curse, and awkwardly manoeuvred himself upright. As he suspected, the brig's berth was empty, the weir gates cranked shut and locked since the vessel's stealthy departure.

Outraged as he wrestled to unsheathe his steel, Fionn Areth made out smatterings of muffled talk beyond the strapped grille and planking. His savage ignominy galled all the worse for the fact that some loudmouth still cracked jokes at his absent expense. 'Dharkaron spear those two-faced rats for the maggots!'

Cattrick's covert foray had scarcely been launched: the primed hull was settled inside of the closed lock, forced to wait while the sluices let down the water. The sea-level egress, which accessed the harbour, had yet to draw clear of immersion.

The Araethurian braced his blade and hacked rope with fever-pitched fury. Head down and back turned, he encountered changed fortune: the sturdy curve of the long-boat's thwart shielded him. He was not battered flat as a *boom* like trapped thunder blasted a breach through the weir gates behind him.

Breach

Entrained on the warfront from her distanced vantage, Prime Selidie ends her incantation, then bids Lirenda to cut the tie of compulsion forced onto a dying shipwright; while before her, a ship's ceremonial effigy burns, incited to premature explosion, she praises her Senior Circle: 'Out of set-back, we triumph! Alestron's sea-side defences are weakened for the Alliance attackers to seize fatal access . . .'

Still thwarted by the ornery watch at the lift, the Mad Prophet cries warning, overcome as Seer's vision shows the lower lock gateway torched into ruinous flame; *the disaster he fears does not stem from Fionn Areth,* but springs instead from a latent imprint in crystal, held over a shipwright since Riverton: a discarded pawn and an innocent man, until passage outside the Paravian defences left him prey to the wiles of Koriathain . . .

Shocked by the unforeseen blast that demolishes the shipwork's lower weir gate, Vhandon and Talvish take pause on the wharf-side battlement, their search for Fionn Areth lapsed in the face of staring disaster: below their snatched vantage, white water thrashes out through the breached cut, while enemy war galleys equipped with siege platforms ram upstream for aggressive assault . . .

XIV. Sortie

T he concussive force of the blast lurched the long-boat, and tossed Fionn Areth onto his side. Half-trussed and still helpless, he cringed under the pelt of exploded debris. Burst iron and flaming splinters raked overhead and splashed, hissing, extinguished to steam. Strong current spun the craft's keel as the gaping hole in the lock's upper gate flooded water in a violent gush from the cavern. His danger turned urgent. The boat where he languished had ferried the flour: for ease of unloading, her painter had been snubbed tight to the dockside. As the reservoir dropped, the shortened line would upend the bow and dangle the boat from the mooring cleat. Fionn Areth would be spilled from the stern. Unable to swim, or cut his bonds loose, he would drown in the fierce eddy sucked out through the weir.

Frantic fear clutched him, that he would die here, victim of the master shipwright's betrayal.

The canting floor-boards gave him no purchase. Toppled over again, he sprawled, face-down on bruised wrists. Worse, the sword that might free his tied limbs had tumbled under the stern seat.

'Damn your name, Cattrick!' he gasped through his teeth.

'Aren't you short-sightedly quick to lay blame?' an irascible voice remarked from the catwalk above. The long-boat rocked sharply. The treacherous craftsman himself leaped aboard, returned like the fiend to bedevil him. Cattrick paused to wedge an oil cask in the prow, then drew his rigger's knife and cut the painter away from the bollard.

Fionn Areth recoiled as the same blade licked towards him. Convinced a rife traitor had returned to finish him, he shouted. But the sharp steel that flashed down only nipped the frayed cords at his ankles and wrists.

'Move!' Cattrick snapped. 'Shift your useless arse off those oars!' Hurled onto the bench seat as the drifting craft slewed, snatched by the rough ebb, he unshipped the looms. Shot the shafts through the rowlocks and dug a hard stroke against the roiling water.

The jerk overset the goatherd again. Cracked into the thwart, he was reviled by the southcoaster's curses, then blistered for clumsiness.

'Right yourself, ninny, and unsnag that sword!' Cattrick snarled, beset. The vicious current slapped waves at the bow, for each battled surge of seized headway. 'By Dharkaron's Black Spear, you'd best know your business at arms! I've no stomach for hauling deadweight.'

Already pummelled to bleeding indignity, Fionn Areth snatched for his fallen weapon. Hilt clenched in hand, he whipped the blade free and turned on the rogue who tormented him. 'Give me one reason to keep you alive! That was a cowardly underhand blow you have dealt the s'Brydion garrison!'

'Put up that steel, you blow-hard ram! I have not left the duke's service.' Gashed on his brow where a billet had grazed him, Cattrick showed teeth as he wrestled the oars by main strength. 'Rave on as you like! Just forget about killing. If my stroke lags for an instant, we're dead, threshed to rags in the weir gate.'

The sword stayed, a line scribed against fire where the wrack of breached timbers crackled, ablaze. 'Then talk!' snapped Fionn Areth. 'Convince me! You have until we reach the stone pier. That's more time then you've ever listened to me, and twice over your brute fists have trampled civility.'

'You're a cheeky wee rat!' Cattrick grinned, eyebrows raised despite his dire straits, until the quick blade darted in and snicked through the points on his jerkin. Since his blood would spill next, he added, quite cool, 'The only reason I stayed on that dock was to secure the winch on the weir gate. We keep Sevrand's trust! With his sentries called off to bolster the battle-front, we shouldered the watch, here. Now the cussed lock shaft's blown open, the upper conduit has to be closed against the invasion!'

'Your claim holds no proof,' said the goatherd, unmoved.

Cattrick heaved on the oars. 'I don't know what went wrong!' Strained to the limit of muscular prowess, his anguish might still mask deceit. 'Our effort was genuine. Alestron's our home. The shipworks are my livelihood. I held the rear-guard to cover my crew. *The fire-ship was meant to be launched in the open!*'

Fionn Areth's disparaging glare made the shipwright unburden. 'Only the men who volunteered to lob flour through the galleys were to be at risk of deadly exposure. The hulk's other hands had my orders to disembark! Let the brig go on under sail with her tiller lashed for self-steering as the slow fuses ignited. They were meant to come in! Shut the lower lock, and stay safe as the sortie began. My timing should have seen them inside the defences *far* ahead of the final explosion. *Are you listening?* I am not spouting nonsense! The sluices that flood the main shaft only operate from inside the dry dock's cavern.'

'How convenient.' Fionn Areth refused to withdraw. 'Nobody's left to gainsay your story. You could be spoon-feeding me a sweet pack of lies.'

'No knife in your ribs!' Cattrick snapped, vicious. 'Thrash out the self-evident truth, you blind fool! You've been holding that sword all along by *my* grace! Because between us, however that foray turned bad, the break in the lock's wrecked the Sea Gate's integrity. Before giving the accursed Alliance free passage, I need your help! There's no one but us to secure the postern from the sewer until Sevrand's company sends in armed relief.'

'How do I know you'll fight and not run?' Fionn Areth hurled back. 'Or was there another reason why you sold Arithon off to Koriathain, then turned again on Tysan's crown interests and scarpered from Riverton on charges of felony?'

The shipwright glared daggers. Sweat slicked his craggy temples. Speech would not come freely past his seething rancour, or the breathless exertion that bucked the long-boat against the rushing current. Inch by hard-won inch, his strokes managed headway, the splash of lapped oars gouging bubbles of foam through the sucking black eddies.

'Speak fast!' cracked the goatherd, the replicate image of Arithon's features a more searing advocate than he imagined.

Cattrick admitted in stiff discomfort, 'I had a demonstrative point to be made. Koriathain used their oath of debt on my name in dishonour, and made me their unscrupulous tool to cause harm.' His next enraged oar-stroke plunged the long-boat through the arch to the underground water-way. 'Nobody *ever* has owned me, that way. I wanted my stand on that matter made clear.'

'That's cold.' Yet even as he let fly with denouncement, Fionn Areth was raked by a chill.

'You say, bantling!' The master shipwright barked a sour laugh. 'We're far more alike than indifferent over our desire for fierce independence. Whose side will you take? Don't claim you can't choose. I won't cut you slack if you're dithering.'

Yet this pass, the grass-lander could not be provoked. 'If you worked for yourself, or decried the shame on your character, that doesn't forgive your smeared record, today. How do I know you weren't out for sabotage?'

'Gut-ripping shark!' Cattrick's face twisted. 'My dead aren't enough? *You think I set the spark off that slaughtered them?*'

Silence answered. The targeting sword never wavered, despite the hard thrust of the oars that slapped wavelets against the slimed passage-way. Now the plunge of each stroke stirred up plumes of muck. The water was dropping. Once, then again, the long-boat's keel scraped over the sediment shoaling the channel.

'All right!' snarled Cattrick. 'I'll give. But first, I'll have your promise you'll stand at the pier in defence of the citadel.'

'For my part, that issue was never in question.' Fionn Areth need not wait to prove his resolve. The boat grounded out. Their forward progress must continue afoot, breasting the flood in the shallows. Prepared as the shipwright abandoned his seat, the Araethurian leaped overboard.

His feet sank into mud. The icy water swirled knee deep, and wrung the very breath out of him. Rocked by the swift current, he snatched left-handed and braced, as the boat slewed and threatened to sweep him off balance. His sword-arm stayed trained: the disingenuous craftsman had not plunged in after him.

In trust, or necessity, Cattrick had turned his broad back to salvage the cask from the bow. 'Loose the boat, goat-boy. She's no use to us, now. For sweet luck, she might hammer a few foes downstream. Best if she dives off the edge of the weir and knocks some armoured grapplers off their boarding ramps.'

Past question, the margin for bickering philosophies had to be running thin. The echoing clash of a ram boomed behind: one of the galley-borne siege towers closed in. Assault would tear through the remains of the weir gate. With the ferocious ebb drawing down the high water, the conduit where craftsman and grass-lander waded would fast be spilled dry, wide open to hostile invasion.

Yet even the closing promise of ruin did not move Fionn Areth. Bone stubborn, or else suicidally brave, he continued his interrogation. 'If your good intentions oppose the Alliance and Lysaer's declared cause, I'd know why!'

Cattrick swore murder and shouldered the keg. The steel at his back was no bristling feint, but aimed by rampaging emotion that might strike to kill in a heart-beat. Slogging ahead, each fled second precious, he spoke fast. 'I was just a paid craftsman who carried a grudge, until the day of the official inspection that followed Lysaer's misplayed foray at Corith. The Blessed Prince sat in my chart loft and examined the ships' plans I'd sketched in false lines. Lysaer had scant knowledge of deepwater craft. He lacked the expertise to recognize the subtlety of my sabotage. I thought him self-blinded enough to be gulled, until Mearn s'Brydion made his entry and forced the conversation into exposure.'

Cattrick snatched a deep breath. The rough features shadowed by the hefted cask *perhaps* matched his ringing bitterness. 'I was shown the creature behind the state mask. The manipulative brain clothed in flawless charisma. *Lysaer knows men!* Reads us with the ease of a mariner's chart. Past all question, he sensed that I would play him false. My calm reserve was all poisoned duplicity, yet he did nothing. Said nothing! Never once guarded the lives of his own jeopardized sail crews. He let them walk into my trap just to leverage a plot for his own strategic benefit. Lysaer s'Ilessid has mind, but no heart! Whether such nerveless conviction is caused by Desh-thiere's curse, or if the flaw springs from calculated ambition, I committed my course, then and there. I could serve with a pirate who valued his people. But not bow down, knowing, for no more than coin, and watch my life's work become used in live chess for a righteous quest without mercy.'

They had reached the stone pier. Cattrick stopped, braced for the sword's finishing thrust. He chose not to plead. 'If you won't defend to buy time for the citadel, you will have to strike. I won't change coat now for coercion.'

The moment paused, hanging, fraught with the echoing, triumphant shouts of armed enemies, burst through to the unmanned dry dock. Against the on-coming noise of invasion, a thin ring of steel sheared the gloom.

'I saw Arithon's face, after bearing your word that Feylind's brig was pinned down with all hands aboard.' The truth written there had surpassed all deceit: that Rathain's prince had no shield against honest tears for the unalloyed sorrow of casualties. Fionn Areth stepped forward, sword sheathed at his side, and offered his steadfast apology. 'I've got tinder, if you need my help with the oil. Then count on my stand in the passage.'

Paired as they had been through much of their professional lives, Vhandon and Talvish matched desperate strides through the tangled streets of the dock quarter. They had outdistanced the cohort of garrison men, stripped by neces-sity from the melee on the walls: a fighting force that could ill be spared, called away to thwart the imminent threat to the shipworks' broken rear postern. Pounding at a sprint, strained lungs burning in the frigid air and feet skidding on icy cobbles, the two captains shared the grim certainty that the Koriathain's made decoy of Arithon would be found embroiled at the site of disaster.

'I'll kill him,' gasped Vhandon, ripped raw with remorse.

Talvish just ran, having nothing to say. Both men had given their friendship to the surly Araethurian. They had done their utmost to mentor his conflicted character, beyond any other green recruit because, like Arithon, they had believed in his salvage. The trauma that had mauled his innate identity and twisted his idealism into contentiousness had been a flaw born from cruel exploitation.

To the end, all had striven to keep an unbroken integrity with the victim, that he might build his own footing for trust.

Now that kind-hearted mistake came to roost. The reckoning impelled the most harsh acknowledgement: that, all along, the grass-lander was the made instrument of the Prime Matriarch's fashioning. In life, his sole purpose had been viciously crafted to snare the Prince of Rathain. Excuses were forfeit, before the staring fact: danger stalked Arithon without remission in the long shadow cast by his enemies. The anguished captains spurred their brutal pace. However the weir at the cut had been breached, that event posed the crippling blow to drive Alestron to final defeat.

Once invaded, the cavern defences could not be recouped. The dry dock gave the enemy a defensible access, with the warren of sewers too extensive to flush without crippling losses. A mass influx of sappers would mine under the cliffs. Before the walls crumpled, no more could be done but hamper the final incursion. Allow Sevrand's forces enough borrowed time to stage a doomed retreat to the upper citadel. The crushing impact of impending conquest could scarcely be mourned, far less measured.

The heroic effort of two driven men could not cross the sea quarter any faster. Past the wharf-side's dark shop-fronts, through the cramped gutters between masonry warehouses, and under the railed balconies of the back-alley brothels that no longer roared with the lusty abandon of deck-hands on leave, Vhandon and Talvish rushed ahead with a will fit to burst mind and sinew. The awareness, that all they had done was for naught, added torment to searing exhaustion.

'Think of your brave daughter!' gasped Talvish, not able to bear the mute agony on Vhandon's face. 'She is far from this place, and quite free. She chose life! Arithon's summoning granted that grace. Remember her, above failure!'

Alestron might fall. But the Light's hollow cause could never obliterate the record of Bransian's unbroken defiance. Because Arithon had come, Vhandon had a legacy: grandchildren who would grow up in peace, informed of the citadel's resistance. Unlike his lost eldest, a son who had farmed and been killed by the blast of Lysaer's suborned power; or his tempestuous youngest, who served yet under arms with the duke's elite guard.

'For Fionn Areth?' snapped Vhandon, not one whit consoled. 'The Teir's'Ffalenn shall not be told! Let his Grace never know whose black-handed ingratitude caused our undoing.'

Around the next corner, both veterans coughed, eyes streaming under the roil of smoke choking an avenue well-known since their boyhood. Guided by instinct, lashed by cruel grief, they pressed forward on guts and necessity.

Their fight must deny the Prime Matriarch's prize. Accord between them required no words: Desh-thiere's curse, and the meddling of Koriani politics drove Alestron towards hostile conquest. Citizens would be on fire to lay blame. As their anguish turned in reproach on the Masterbard, they would accuse Arithon for the suffering heaped on the undermanned garrison.

'Can't spare his Grace from public censure unless we take the grass-lander first,' Talvish said in grim assessment.

'Too much has gone wrong,' Vhandon agreed.

Brothers in arms, they raced past the shut doors of the guild-hall, where excise stamps with the s'Brydion blazon had endorsed fair commerce throughout an unbroken succession. Beyond lay the arched postern that guarded the maze of the underground sewer.

The night street between as yet remained empty. No hordes of armed enemies charged from the gap, yet.

'Ath bless!' gasped Vhandon.

He and Talvish drew their swords as one movement. Shoulder to shoulder, they rushed down the ramped passage. The steel gate within was not locked or guarded. But an on-coming clangour of weapons scattered echoes off the vaulted conduit. Somewhere ahead, a living defender sweated in hard-fought retreat.

Talvish forced his reserves and quickened pace. 'If that's the sentry, he's sorely beset.'

'Tiring, also,' Vhandon observed, his trained ear attuned to the sword-play. 'Else wounded.' Through the stressed ring of steel, hazed to frenzied crescendo, he added, 'Won't leave him to enemies, whoever he is. Hold at the grille!' Without further word, he shoved onwards into the gloom.

'Damn your fool heroics!' Talvish followed, fraught to match Vhandon's gruelling lead. 'You're not going alone!' As fragmented swearing sliced back up the corridor, he flashed his most insolent grin. 'No, friend! I don't take your ranked orders, since I'm no longer Duke Bransian's officer.'

'Alestron might suffer for that change in loyalty!' Yet Vhandon's barked protest failed to shake off the blond swordsman's insistent protection.

At the bend, where a pine-knot torch should have burned, they encountered an empty bracket. The mooring rings wore severed knots: someone's ingenuity had taken the pole-boats and rigged them for incendiary tinder. A cloud of black smoke billowed up the drained passageway, rank with burned oil and noisome, singed meat. The screams were not pretty as men burned alive, ambushed by the conflagration.

Talvish coughed. 'You hear? They're cursing the Spinner of Darkness for sabotage.'

'Here's hope!' Vhandon snarled. 'Perhaps they've mistaken the rat-handed goatherd for somebody else! Confusion to the enemy.' He ploughed into the murk and bellowed ahead. 'Friends of the citadel!'

The feat with the oil was not going to last. Fouled air and dizzying exertion sapped stamina. Ragged footsteps approached, in flight where the glow of set flame stained the fumes lurid orange. Backlit by the pall, two blurred figures rushed upward, both of them doubled and choking. As the fire subsided, more stymied enemies pursued, crowding in numbers behind them.

The man in rear-guard whirled at bay. Sword steel spoke again: alone, without armour, that berserk defender challenged the on-coming fray. 'Go on! You can't help!' he screamed after his running companion.

The other, still wielding an oar as a bludgeon, dropped the shaft and clenched a ripped forearm. His clothes were a craftsman's, sodden and rent. He belted onwards up the drained sewer, determined and rasping for breath.

'Run! *Shut the grille!*' The yell was Fionn Areth's. Unable to glance backwards, engaged beyond fear, he reeled through lightning parries, forced into back-stepping retreat. He fought beyond hope. No swordsman's prowess could surmount such pressure. Only slow the inevitable, a harried bone in the teeth of the crushing onslaught about to roll over him.

'Cattrick?' snapped Talvish, wrenched out of stride as the wounded fugitive slammed headlong into him.

'We're undone.' Through blood and soot, carved bone deep and in agony, the burly southcoaster sagged to his knees. 'Koriathain kept a secretive hold on my shipwrights. Must have done, since the affray at Riverton! They were suborned. Forced to suicide and made to turn our own fire-ship against us. I'm sorry. The dry dock's overrun by the enemy! We were two, up against a pitched company.'

The whine of a quarrel creased through the clogged air. Unarmoured flesh caught the marksman's cruel accuracy. Cattrick jerked and crashed over like a kicked post, wracked to spasms in Talvish's arms.

Ahead, Fionn Areth still laboured, engaged on all fronts by Alliance shock troops. Brute men in full arms, outfitted for hacking assault on the walls, with straight blade and spiked axe. However brave, no single hand with a sword could hold the tight corridor against them. Somewhere down the passage, the enemy bowman would be furiously cranking to span his discharged weapon. That one would, at cool leisure, pick off the nuisance that snarled the Alliance advance.

'My fight!' Vhandon shouted over his shoulder. 'Tal, I'm equipped for this fracas. You're not.'

Painful truth: still on posted duty, the older captain wore his breast-plate and mail; his blond partner, reassigned as crown liegeman, had no more than strapped bracers and studded brigandine.

'Talvish, no nonsense!' Vhandon cried in the breach. 'Save your prince. Take the rear-guard. For all of our sakes! You must go back and secure the postern!'

Before Talvish could shed the killed weight of the shipwright, Vhandon's forward charge clashed with the brute swing of the axe-man. His solid parry came in saving time. Fionn Areth recouped his slipped footing, rallied, and resteadied his stroke in the grace of relief.

'Go back, Tal!' Vhandon pealed, now committed past argument. 'Man the gate!' Matched shoulder to shoulder in practised defence, the grey-haired captain sensed the grass-lander's rhythm. He compensated by professional instinct. Allied with his protégé, strength and untried weaknesses, he matched stroke for stroke in the gruelling press. Trusted fate, as if his left side relied on the skill of a veteran comrade.

One instant, for sight to record the bright moment, as the Araethurian reached for his latent potential, quickened by confidence to skilled refinement. Given his place, he rose to match the dauntless experience of the man beside him.

'I'll hold your retreat!' Talvish cried in ripped anguish, while the clash of stressed metal commingled with blood scent, and the reek of the dying befouled the corridor.

Vhandon objected. 'You have one task left!' To the other grown man he had taught, who dauntlessly matched his prowess in battle, and who claimed the respect of a lifelong friendship, he pleaded, 'Talvish! Get topside! Aid Sevrand's relief. Then go on and serve where you're oathsworn! If you can, if the garrison holds, tell my son that I pass with no thought but a father's love for him.'

'I'll do better than that,' Talvish snapped, streaming tears. 'I will take the same word to your daughter and grandchildren, after my liege is delivered alive and seen safe past the citadel walls!'

Nothing remained but to turn, after that, and race hell-bent back up the conduit. Talvish slammed shut the massive, grilled gate. He shot the bar with numbed fingers, then rammed closed the iron-strapped siege doors beyond. He sealed off the breached corridor, scant seconds ahead of the battering storm that assailed the locked barrier with screaming ferocity.

Duty accomplished, cheek laid against the cold, studded oak, Talvish grieved in anguished salute: to a comrade more treasured than kin, and also for Fionn Areth, who would never receive his apology, or know a peer's due respect for a man's place, served on the battle-line. As Sevrand's reserves arrived in re-inforcement, Talvish wept still. *Naught more could be done.* Tears were too small a thing, and too bitter, to honour his fallen. The unflinching courage of Vhandon, and Arithon's brash double, Fionn Areth Caid' An, who wrote his last act in crossed steel and smoke, without ever disclosing his purpose in life or discover-ing his innate identity. As Sidir once foretold, the untried bow had been strung. The arrow, now launched, had flown true.

Accosted by women on both exposed flanks, while squared off with the duke front and centre, Parrien s'Brydion looked up from the noisome task of cleaning his befouled field gear. All eyes watched him, expectant. Poleaxed with surprise, he stared at his brother, brows raised and blunt jaw dropped open.

Bransian simply glared, forearms folded and his back jammed against the shut door. Whether the lordly request just delivered singed his brother to outrage, the crisis at hand forced the risk.

'You're loonie, man!' Parrien groused at due length. 'Daft as a dog yipping under the moon.' Even stripped down to his breeches and boots, he posed a menacing adversary. Early sun streaming in through the casement exposed his chafed skin and patched blisters. Over these, blotched in plum, the bruises from his berserk foray mottled his strapping torso. His scarred shoulders crowded the pastel chamber, knavish against the fussy rosettes a past carver had gilded to adorn a lady's tea room.

This morning, the pretty nook served as an armoury, claimed for its east-facing windows. A cast-plaster ceiling conserved the sun's heat without fuel, for which Parrien endured the squawks of his wife to dry the soaked fleece of his gambeson. The cosy scents of patchouli and rose were lost under the reek of wet sheepskin, and the rancourous bristle of argument.

Anger building in volcanic waves, Parrien rammed his stained rag in the sand bucket and stabbed a grimed finger at his elder brother. 'You'll be kissing up to a dumb sack of rocks before I'll behave like a whining ambassador. Not again! I will *not* lick the carpet for Arithon's favour, or plead your case for his cantankerous pardon. Not while we've got sappers and rams crawling over us like teeming lice on a trollop! I'd lay down my arms, first. Wave my bare arse at the forsaken *enemy* before mincing talk like a slithering lawyer.'

'You're afraid of him,' Liesse accused: a mistake. Parrien's wife clamped her lip in pearl teeth, her hissed inbreath a stifled explosion.

Parrien slammed down his clogged byrnie. 'Easier to suffer a mule with a cow kick than listen to your claptrap dithering.' Furious to be kept from the fighting, he locked horns. 'Does *nobody* recall the wrecked state of our flagship the last time I tried reasoning with Arithon? Send Vhandon! By now, he ought to know how to cosset the pesky runt. And, forbye, he won't drag our family name to disgrace.'

Silence answered. Even Liesse's raw-boned features whitened.

Parrien narrowed unforgiving, grey eyes. 'Spit me on a pike for telling the truth. We could yet find ourselves raked over live coals, under censure by Fellowship Sorcerers.'

The duke's calm smashed precident. 'Vhandon's dead.'

Against reeling shock, the Lady Tiassa regretted her neglect for civility, despite today's barging intrusion. A servant should have had mulled wine at hand to ease breaking word of fresh tragedy.

As if any token refreshment could soften a loss such as this: raw pain now exposed, unbearably sober, the Lord of Alestron rubbed his temples. 'We lost Vhan to heroics down in the conduit. He was holding the postern gate from the shipworks. That's why I'm tasking you, Parrien. The sea quarter's falling. Our straits turn from worse to desperate.'

Parrien recoiled in stunned disbelief. 'Ath! I never imagined we'd come to this.' For Vhandon, an inconceivable rat's end in a culvert, with no friend at hand, and no veteran's honours to brighten the torch at the pyre side. Savaged by heart-break, Parrien's voice burred for the stalwart captain who had finished the edge on his sword-play. 'If we've jettisoned pride, and we're going to go down, I might as well be the first on my knees. Though Daelion wept! It's a miserable case we've got left, and cold grounds to try bargaining with Rathain's crown prince.'

Reclad in full arms, now respectably polished, Parrien s'Brydion emerged at midmorning to handle his brother's request. His frame of mind stayed unpleasantly volatile, result of the fur-ripping row with Tiassa that still nipped his heels on departure. Beyond his hazed nerves, he itched in fine wool, tongue-lashed into his parade surcoat.

'She won't be appeased. I should gag her tart's mouth,' fumed Parrien under his breath.

The wife's sniping rang on, *despite* the oak door he slammed shut behind him.

'You barbaric lummox!' she bawled through the planks. 'Who should listen to you? Whirling your sword like a windmill in a squall, and breathing fire to lambast the tapestries! Mule-brained ox! You'll need every trapping of decency just to be let into the prince's apartments. That's if Arithon's disposed to receive you at all, misused as he's been on the excuse of diplomacy.'

From eight strides along, the offended husband bellowed over his shoulder. 'I'll be nobody's fawning lap spaniel, woman! You might have gotten me tricked up in bows, but don't expect I'll nose up to yon royal bastard, ears perked and curly tail wagging.' Still bristling, Parrien tramped under the carriage arch. 'The gold thread just makes the bull on my chest a prime target for cross-fire, besides!'

Outside, the crammed street held convulsed pandemonium. Noise and misery rode with the crawling progress of supply from the lift: stock from the warehouses needed for war, cleared away from the encroaching enemy. What could not be salvaged, the men-at-arms burned. The acrid fumes of torched oil and searing hides dimmed the sun, and deadened the notes of the horn-calls. The bass roar from the battle-front pounded on, unrelenting since the breach at the cut was disastrously widening. The boom of the rams now beat deep refrain to the quick-time drums on the galleys.

Parrien ached as never before. Always, Alestron's brutal campaigns had been fought in the field, the wrack of fresh losses at remove from the ancestral seat. At every familiar street-corner and shop-front, Sevrand's begrimed officers pushed their mauled companies through the throes of a routing retreat. Hand-carts bore the wounded, if only those hale enough to survive the extraction. Parrien beheld the ghastly pallor of the smoke-poisoned. He heard the moans of the unconscious burned, swathed amid the seeping stains fouling their blankets. Not all were fighting men. Some were street beggars and matrons; worse than these, the scorched team of boys, who had been hauling water to replenish the fire buckets. Non-combatants fell as readily to the withering crossfire launched where the siege platforms landed.

The procession stitched horror the length of the thoroughfare, until Parrien wished he could stifle the groans of the dazed. Many sprawled, stricken with arrows or crossbolts the overtaxed healers could not snatch time to draw. Delayed treatment of any war wound brought on poisoning that demanded intervention by trained knowledge or birth-gifted talent. This was not open ground, where the rear-guard reserves could maintain a safe camp for convalescent recovery. Truth pursued, unremitting: Vhandon's death had been the first of too many. On the harbour-side battlements, and in the breached weir, Alestron's best would be dying. More would be sacrificed for every agonized minute the lift winch stayed operative. Each countryman spared, and each casualty withdrawn, exacted a cost in let blood.

Parrien elbowed through the grim press, buffeted by the mauled and the battered. The charnel reek made his errand seem a futile appeal against ruin that loomed beyond salvage. Beneath the bronze lamp where he had kissed his first sweetheart, a child with a singed arm and a bucket of crossbolts wept tears on a stalled wagon's buckboard. A grimy bread-baker stooped on the cobbles nearby, wrapping clay pots for the catapults. His bony frame seemed unfamiliar and sad: once the fellow had been merry and fat, dicing in comfort with Mearn.

Parrien sidled past, overwhelmed. He could not shake the upset of Vhandon's passing, or watch as the misery of slaughter overran the inner walls of the citadel: revetments and gates he had never imagined could yield by force to hostility. More wounded limped by. Then two women in tears, bearing a brother laid out on a litter. Their fate would be sealed, as the defences crumbled: to die fighting or to suffer alive, forced as spoils amid brawling conquest. Both seemed tenderly young. *Under age to be married,* Parrien agonized. *Why should they have stayed? With sweet life before them, why had they not seized the freedom once granted by Arithon's mercy?*

'Bless your caring, we couldn't.' A fearful glance in a soot-streaked face met his unwitting question, just spoken aloud.

'Our father was ailing. Too weakened to travel. We had no one else to take care of him.'

'I'm sorry,' snapped Parrien. His gruff pity did nothing to ease their plight. Unwanted, the blazing reflection resurged, of the Masterbard's exhortation: *'Your defence at Alestron will be written in blood. I foresee this!'*

Pride stung. Iron nerve faltered. Parrien plunged into the by-way. Head down, mailed grip locked on the hilt of his sword, he gave way to retching distress. *All of these faces were known to him.* Even here, he could feel the pounding of enemy sappers assaulting the cliff-head. Sows with steel-tipped rams chewed into the stone that supported the oldest bastions. Inexorably, *now*, the Sea Gate was crumbling. Beneath full sun, in the sparkling north wind that *should have* gouged diamonds out of fresh snowfall, the heart of the town he had known all his days wore the harrowing cloth of a nightmare.

Never more clearly, and desperately late, he encountered the pain in the Masterbard's cry of forewarning. To face the same man in today's flooding shame required unparalleled courage. Parrien stumbled. Reeling on towards the keep that housed Rathain's delegation, he shook off the hand that grappled his arm; ignored the brusque shout that waylaid him.

Whoever accosted him, he turned his back.

Until a mailed fist clamped his shoulder and spun him about: *that* wrenched a berserker's roar from his throat. He failed to draw steel, because Talvish's blow chopped his wrist with disabling ferocity.

'His Grace is not here!' cracked the duke's former captain. 'If you seek my liege, I'll take you myself. Though with fairness, be warned, you may risk being cut off from your family.'

Parrien blinked. 'Arithon's running amok in the sea quarter? Ath wept! Whatever for?'

But Talvish's urgency brooked no delay. Parrien pushed to match the harsh pace, hampered by his state trappings.

One stride back, and still shouting, he chased Talvish's lead up the revetment ladder that short-cut the packed streets. 'Sevrand's post is withdrawn. The rear-guard's coming in. War-horn's sounded the signal already, and depend on my word, the winch lift will be ashes by noon! What feat can yon shifty rat's cunning achieve when the harbour keep's swarming with enemies?'

Talvish vanished into the coiling smoke billowed up from the wrack at the water-front. 'You'll ask that in Arithon's presence! If you dare.' Through hacked coughing, he added, 'Trust my guess? His Grace doesn't plan to come back. The guest suite's stripped bare. The enchantress and Rathain's feal following have gone downside, every parcel of remedies packed along with them.'

They found Arithon s'Ffalenn in the sail-loft at the chandler's, made over as hospice to succour the injured too stricken to move. There, where the crash of the enemy's incursion shocked vibrations through walls and floor-boards, Parrien first heard the notes that a masterbard's skill wrought to fuse shattered bone and torn ligaments. The sweet clarity pierced the dust-sifted air like the chime of steel rings, dropped onto sheet glass. The harmonics sheared the dross from the mind, and lifted the spirit into ineffable joy.

Caught within the dimmed stairway, Parrien s'Brydion lost a gasping breath and crumpled onto his knees. Mailed fingers pressed into his face to stop tears, he tried and failed to recover. One gasping shudder followed the next, until he was helplessly weeping. If he thought he had ever known beauty before, the musician's winged mastery reformed him.

Talvish, beside him, was better prepared. Aboard the *Khetienn*, seventeen years before, he had witnessed the first, explorative measures an exacting practice had shaped to enact today's healing. In matchless splendour, the bard's talent redressed suffering, bleak disharmony knitted to wholeness. Now, far-sight and initiate mastery evoked a fresh edge of refinement: the cascading melody brought to full flower might have balanced a stone on the wisp of a moonbeam.

'You won't die, though your heart's fit to burst,' Talvish managed. His fraught grip braced the larger man's weight, while the seconds flowed past, gilded in exquisite sound. Thoughts wrung still, the chance-met observer could only endure, while the dynamic framework of life was made whole, and the revivified spirit unfolded and ached for a balance precocious and glorious.

Scarcely bearable, the onslaught found closure at last. Spent strings dwindled into taut silence. Roughshod against calm, the clamour of war continued its harsh storm outside. Within, the stark cry for retreat reached crescendo: felled on the stair, Parrien shuddered, unable to rise.

Talvish hauled him erect. 'Your doing taught my liege that entrained sequence. He wasn't born knowing the key to access those rarefied octaves.'

'I once broke his leg?' cracked Parrien, bitter. 'Ath's own mercy!' The depth of such fierce sensitivity daunted. 'What brought your crown prince to return here?'

'His friends, and a life debt.' Talvish climbed onwards, beyond resolute. 'You couldn't have realized. But Arithon renounced your family's alliance for reasons of love. The Seer in him would not be reconciled.'

Which truth fitted too well: laid open by his receptive talents, a masterbard of such stature could never endorse the destruction that ravaged the citadel now. The failing sea-walls were soaked in let blood. That held line could not last. Before sunset, the harbour-side keep would be shattered by the invasion. The brother charged as the ducal ambassador struggled to rally his bludgeoned wits. If he would appeal for the grace of an interview, his plea must be made before the musician engaged the next healing.

Kyrialt kept steadfast guard at the threshold. In forest leathers and clan braid, his formal stance stayed immaculate, until sight of the scarlet s'Brydion colours jabbed him to wary antagonism. State manners could not curb the frowning glare he shot Talvish.

'Let his Grace determine!' the blond liegeman murmured. 'Allow us to pass.' Wan light at the threshold illumined his face, unveiling the fact he was haggard.

Kyrialt's umbrage dissolved into shock. 'Tell me! What's happened? Where's Fionn Areth?'

This time, as grief locked Talvish's speech, Parrien tendered gruff answer. 'I've not seen the goatherd. Vhandon fell holding the breach in the shipworks, and I am not sent with the message for consolation.'

But the High Lord of Alland's past heir proved too seasoned to bait. 'Where his Grace of Rathain is concerned, your family's entangling history predates me. Never show me fresh cause!'

Parrien acknowledged the challenge, teeth bared. Pleased not to be misjudged for his court-dress, he bulled ahead, knowing Talvish would hound every by-play stirred up in the sail-loft.

Two steps stopped him cold. No rife bluster could ease the sight of the torment laid on the rows of stained pallets.

There, shorn of arms, and outside secured walls, the man reviled as the Spinner of Darkness chose to spend the matchless gift of his resource. With Elaira beside him, and Glendien's assistance, he bent his royal knee to administer to the abandoned, the wrecked, and the hopeless. Groaning men lying gutted by pole arms and steel; bundled forms butchered senseless, that laboured to breathe; others scorched beyond recognition by fire. Children bled limp by the loss of a limb, or afflicted with crushed ribs and the cyanotic pallor of flail chest. These lay side by side with brawny smiths and prime craftsmen, once gainfully busy supporting their kinsfolk, and now at death's door from the mangling accidents that struck when the torsion ropes strained and snapped under load on the arbalests and catapults.

The ugliest face of the war sheltered here, where expedient logic begged for the clean end of a mercy stroke.

'Why?' Parrien pealed, riven numb. 'Heal them or not, you can't possibly save them!'

'I would be here, anyway, given what's passed.' The slight figure bearing the lyranthe overheard, aroused from the languor of after-shock. Arithon stood. The state cloth that met his turned glance shouted warning. He touched Elaira's lips in swift reassurance, then handed his heirloom instrument off into Glendien's keeping. Alone by discreet choice, he approached the intrusive s'Brydion petitioner.

Close up, beyond artifice, his severe features were stripped: wide open still to the insight that tapped the well-spring of deep mystery. In unguarded green eyes, Parrien saw his own sorrow, unbearably mirrored. More, the tuned range of subtle awareness mourned every tear yet to be written, the more vividly seen by rogue-talented s'Ahelas vision.

The s'Brydion spokesman reeled before a compassion he felt flawed and unfit to withstand. As the forms of diplomacy failed, the lean hand of the prince steered him wide of the horror sprawled on the cots.

'You have my attention,' said Arithon s'Ffalenn.

Sweating before that initiate awareness, Parrien needled, 'Why not just flay my thick skin with an axe?'

Arithon fielded the jab with neutrality. 'I'd save the discomfort. Masks drop without bleeding.'

'Not on this turf,' Parrien countered. 'We grew up stretching Kalesh's spies on the rack, and our mother died screaming, poisoned by Adruin's assassins.' Stripped of pride, his appeal emerged without effort, unleashed by his torrent of longing. 'For my brother, and the sake of this law-bound clan holding, your Grace can do nothing more than attend to the hopelessly wounded?'

'The born right to live that's given each person was never assigned to my keeping. Nor could I force sense against the grain of your duke's short-sighted decisions.' Arithon inclined his head to acknowledge Elaira, who had dragged up two sail-maker's stools to smooth the thorny audience.

After Parrien, the crown prince seated himself. Now the extent of his weariness showed. In tight lines at his eyes, and in the searing constraint imposed by the *Evenstar*'s defeat. Yet Arithon would not bow to grief. A spirit forged by the trials of Kewar's maze, his reserves could match lacerating distress with frank tenderness. 'The present moment holds all our strengths. I have not given over my hope! Of those futures left that my choice can still influence, I act for the one that unfolds with least death. Many of your citadel's folk may go free.' As Parrien's composure threatened to break, he assured, 'Even yet!' Careful to salve wounded dignity, Arithon waited a moment, then qualified. 'If the Mistwraith's influence can be disarmed, then my half-brother's insane enmity will become temporarily suspended.'

Long enough, maybe, to blunt the brutality driving the inevitable conquest. Respect, before reticence, allowed Parrien to grasp that unpleasant gist.

'I cannot salvage your stake in the citadel,' Arithon said finally. 'Yet if the s'Ilessid royal gift can be freed from the curse, we can steward the chance of just treatment for your civilian survivors.'

No fool, Parrien sprang to the crux. 'I should retire without fuss? Accept Lysaer's criminal charges? Daelion's fate, prince! You will just stand aside, while your s'Brydion *spies* get arraigned by s'Ilessid for treason?' Now shadowed by Talvish's defensive presence, closed in behind his right shoulder, Parrien blazed with honest agony, 'We as good as married our honour to yours, Teir's'Ffalenn! I see we were only a sop, all along, to be thrown to the jaws of your enemies.'

'Your own enemies, since Riverton!' snapped Arithon. Annoyed, but not vicious, his crisp outrage answered. 'Before that hour, the s'Brydion name was untainted. Mearn's post as ambassador stayed above all suspicion! Dare you recall, Parrien? I once fought your bullheaded choice to a standstill! You broke my right leg. Overrode my appeal, that Lysaer's royal shipworks should be left to bide without your killing spree of reprisal!'

'We made that mistake, and on our own merits,' Parrien was swift to admit. 'We have lived by the sword for too long. Our friendships are forthright, and founded on passion. We also decided to help Princess Ellaine. She was not abandoned to wrestle a plight that trapped her as a helpless game-piece.'

When Arithon said nothing, Parrien bore in, probing hard to smoke out flinching weakness. 'In fact, are you Torbrand's most pithless descendant, to shelter the peace at all costs? If you do hold the power to sway Lysaer's hatred, then our blood-line sees an ignominious end because you gagged on a principle! Can you sit back on your string plucker's arse and, like the rank coward, do nothing?'

'But I have not done nothing,' Arithon corrected. He stood up and bowed. 'Alone of your kindred, Mearn saved his family when I invoked the Paravian sword to enact intervention. Fianzia's first-born will arrive in two weeks, under the protection of Verrain at Methisle. By the gift of forevision bred into my ancestry, I have Seen that child's Naming! On grounds of succession, your brother's appeal is already met.' Unfazed as the larger man shoved to his feet, Arithon dismissed, 'I have no more patience! Go and tell Bransian on my royal oath: your ancestral lineage survives beyond question.'

Parrien's electrified surge to draw steel was arrested on Talvish's sword-point. 'No, brother! Not here. Not now, against this man. Indulge your blind rage, and you will murder hope. Trust me, I beg you! If you press this fight, you will have abandoned your own wife and children. On my word, by my years of true service, my liege has not told you everything!'

'Then explain!' snarled Parrien to Arithon's turned back. 'Straightaway and in unvarnished language, say why I shouldn't drop you both to rot alongside your doomed lot of carrion.'

'In fact he must die, at least by appearance,' a breathless voice interjected. The intrusion was Dakar's, barged through without leave as he made his rushed entry. In the teeth of Parrien's suspicion, he added, 'Sparing the sentiment, these wounded also offer the key to salvage the threat being taken with Rathain's crown heritage.'

'Where's Fionn Areth?' asked Arithon, spun volte-face in a sharp change of subject. 'Dakar! Why isn't the grass-lander with you?'

The Mad Prophet ran over that question, roughshod. 'Shall I remind you as Fellowship spokesman? I answer a higher authority than yours! Your Grace, clear this room. We have run out of time! Only *one* life inside this doomed rock pile is not considered replaceable!'

As Parrien purpled, and Talvish changed stance in vain hope to forestall a royal explosion, the Mad Prophet shed his cloak and slumped on a stool, unstrung by puffing exertion.

'You risk moving too late!' he accosted the prince, beyond caring whose temper might savage him. 'The mule-headed sentries permitted my passage because at this moment, enemy sappers are working the rock to crack the underground cisterns. The sea quarter's condemned, and Parrien's stranded. The duke's guard are torching the lift.'

Early Winter 5671

First Betrayal

In forest-bred stillness overlooked since the latest intrusive arrival, Kyrialt observed Parrien's disrupted audience from his posted watch at the threshold. He kept his ear tuned through Dakar's bitter news, and the brutal shock, that the duke's expedient sacrifice of the sea quarter had left a brother cut off from his kinsfolk. Amid the raised voices, Arithon's cracking-fast question repeated.

Again, Rathain's prince demanded the reason for Fionn Areth's unexplained absence.

The forced pause hung, electrified.

Kyrialt tensed, no longer on guard for a posited threat from the stairwell. From *inside* the door, the sharp rise in tension bristled his nape in dire warning. Hunter's instinct reacted. He moved on the turmoil that converged at the front of the sail-loft.

Talvish's pallor snagged his eye first. Kyrialt mapped that bleak reticence and knew: *the grass-lander's fate had gone badly, somehow tied to Vhandon's demise.* Talvish's lapsed attention, as he scrambled for words to break tragedy, opened the gates to disaster.

Kyrialt charged, silent, knife and sword drawn in stride. Alerted to violence with preternatural clarity, he locked on to Parrien's overdrawn tension. *Saw,* as the moment's insupportable pressure drove the man's shattered fibre past breaking.

Parrien raised a lightning, mailed fist. He slapped Talvish's ready sword-point aside, drew cold steel, and lunged to strike Arithon: *who was unarmed, and caught unaware, entrained as he was on the nascent distress behind the spellbinder's evasions.*

Kyrialt extended muscle and sinew, past time to voice any outcry. A fraught fraction too late, he pushed his athletic faculties beyond thought of self-preservation. The blade he thrust between Parrien's stroke hit and slid with a clashed scream of metal.

The assault that *should have* stabbed home was turned. But the driving momentum, unstoppably launched, deflected its razor cut downward. The slashing impetus carved Arithon from midriff to hip. There, the murdering weapon snagged bone, and wrenched a deep gash through the viscera.

Kyrialt vented his distraught anguish, above Glendien's harrowing shout. 'Alestron's reprieve will never be bought by selling my liege to your enemies!'

Yet all recourse was spent. Talvish, caught flat-footed, *was moving*. But Kyrialt's intervention blocked his direct response.

As Arithon folded, the befouled long sword jerked clear.

Parrien snarled, 'His Grace meant to play dead! By Ath, should I wait and abandon the lives of my own threatened family?' His riposte launched to finish his foiled assassination.

Kyrialt let his hurled bulk drive in between. Unbalanced already, his sacrificed footing committed beyond all recovery, he caught the force of the strike in his back. Then slammed into the floor-boards, aware he was dying. Beside him, crumpled and bleeding, Rathain's prince lay curled in fraught agony.

Still living: what distressed voice his bard's talent could raise was pitched across belling steel, a gasped plea that begged restraint for the life of Parrien s'Brydion. 'Tiassa's children should not grow up fatherless! Talvish! Honour my royal word as promised for Dame Dawr's legacy!'

Then Elaira arrived. Her whipped skirts brushed the grazed skin of Kyrialt's cheek. Masked his view of his liege as she dropped on her knees to attend what should not be salvaged.

Kyrialt raised his chin. Shuddered. 'No lady! On my oath.' Which freed her to turn and look after her stricken beloved.

Son born to the flower of a *caithdein*'s lineage, Kyrialt s'Taleyn had no more strength nor acuity left for his scout's faculties to track the fight left abandoned. He could not see whether the spellbinder's art might curb treachery under the law of the compact. The rank jet of blood soaked through shirt and leathers. His veins emptied with the pumped gush of a severed artery. The end would be quick. Unlike the lingering pain of the wounding that he had tried, and failed, to spare Arithon. Kyrialt shut his eyes in despair. Already, vitality faded. Dizziness up-ended his senses, air-starved despite his raced breathing.

'Kyrialt! Husband!' The grip that supported him through the ebb matched his last wish, being Glendien's. He barely felt the spellbinder's furious hands, wadding cloth to stem his rushed bleeding.

'Davien's cloak,' Kyrialt entreated, thread thin. The limp fingers clutched in his wife's frantic clasp were unable to close as he faltered.

'Rest easy,' said Dakar. Speech came from far off. 'Crown honour attends you. Trust my word, we'll secure the life of your prince in your absence.'

Kyrialt smiled. His awareness recorded Glendien's tears, then her hair, fallen warm on his face as she kissed his lips and eased his heart through the wracking, last spasms.

The serenity to set warding circles was lost, the chance ruined, to engage the intricate preparations for securing the live spirit outside its dormant casing of flesh. Now, the throes of a dire wounding smashed the hope of controlled intervention to slip Arithon past the Alliance war host and disarm Lysaer's cursed affliction. Dakar wiped bloodied hands, paralyzed by anxiety. *He dared make no other grievous mistakes.* If this bitter crisis careened beyond salvage, by his own wretched prophecy, the Teir's'Ffalenn's death would smash the course of the Fellowship Sorcerers' future reunity.

For Kyrialt, nothing more could be done. Most brave, his swift passage was over. While Glendien shrouded her husband's stilled form, Talvish restrained Parrien's sprawled frame with the strap leather of belt and baldric. Both men bled from fresh sword-cuts, though the disabling blow had been Dakar's, an oak stool snatched at need and shied into the s'Brydion nape from behind. Whether or not the felon was damaged, the Mad Prophet faced the more urgent priority. He sank to his knees on the spattered floor, laced his hands in black hair, and cradled Arithon's head.

Rathain's prince was still conscious. The wracking shock of the wound that had felled him rocked through him in waves of agony. Elaira had cut his stained clothing away, laying bare the horrendous damage.

One glance left Dakar wheeling and faint. He said fiercely, 'Don't you dare leave us, your Grace!'

Pooled in running blood, the gash that crossed Arithon's stomach was not threatening. Severed muscles could mend. The diaphragm was not pierced. Unlike the tender flesh of the groin, where the terrible sword stroke had ended. Dakar's belly heaved into revolt. Twice, he mangled the cantrips attempted to ease back afflicted suffering.

'Give over!' Elaira cut in, stark as steel. 'Trust my recent training with Ath's adepts, and my natural skill as a healer.'

Wrists rinsed scarlet, she worked. A crystal poised in a delicate hand was invoked for a probing assessment. Dakar's gorge rose again. The nerve in him quailed, that a quartz matrix bound to the Matriarch's service should be invoked for Rathain's royal legacy. Then Arithon raised a dreadful, rasping croak. 'She guards my integrity. Always. Dakar, look again.'

'Beloved!' chided Elaira, most gently. Her eyes streamed with tears. However she trembled with terrified pain, her expedient touch stayed viced steady. 'Don't speak!'

In fact, Dakar saw his concern laid to rest: her lit shaft of quartz was Atheran in origin. Scried insight disclosed the honest acquisition, gifted from a wise woman who sold simples in Highscarp. Rapt with the crystal's tuned focus,

Elaira stitched subtle light in accord with the Major Balance. Through each check for surety the spellbinder made, the meticulous permissions *had* correctly served balance. Though a Koriani sigil would have worked faster, for Arithon's safety, the enchantress used gentler means to stanch the cut veins in his savaged flesh.

The horrific rip through the viscera must wait. Bleeding and shock would kill before sepsis. Dakar swallowed back resurgent nausea, *knowing*: the prognosis of gut wounds was never assured, or easy to minister against the onset of insurmountable anguish. No surcease might relieve Arithon's effort to muffle his harrowing screams.

Dakar measured bad odds. Though the binding of Davien's Five Centuries Fountain held the potential to stay the fatal course of the sword-thrust, the oncoming Alliance invasion left no safety to nurse a prolonged convalescence. Arithon could not command his talent. Pain unstrung the immaculate focus required to spiritwalk under his own resource, and all of their planning was ashes. The transmigration of spirit accomplished before in Daon Ramon could not be attempted to disarm Desh-thiere's curse, or smuggle his vacated body across enemy lines.

If, in icy truth, the same arcane ruse could blind-side Lysaer's talent-sensitive priests. The doubt on that score had already been thrashed under jangling argument.

'Whatever you do, decide your course quickly!' Talvish snapped in bald warning. Despite injuries, he had recovered his sword to assume the lapsed guard at the threshold. 'Sevrand's force has withdrawn! Can you not hear the noise?' Already, the Light's zealots mowed through the last resistance defending the harbourfront. 'We're going to have looters inside a few minutes! I can't hold the influx off very long, if I'm forced to a stand in the stairwell.'

'Don't try!' cried Elaira. 'Your liege needs you alive!' Unswerving, attentive, she cupped Arithon's cheek. 'Hush. I'll speak for you. I can track every thought in your mind. We'll accomplish what's needed.' While her touch with the crystal continued to weave an unerring course of swift cautery, she relayed instructions.

'Dakar! You're to strip off Parrien's state surcoat. Burn the cloth in the grate and untie his clan braid. Then bundle the man naked into a cot. Poultice his head and start binding his wounds as though you're a healer in training. Talvish! Dig through that pile of used clothing and pick out a Sunwheel surcoat. No argument! Just do as I say. Several men who once wore them lie here with the fallen, brought in from the battlement. You're now asked to languish as one of my wounded. Slump on that empty stool as if faint, awaiting your due turn for treatment. Glendien! Lock Arithon's lyranthe in my larger remedy trunk. Move anything out to make room. Then I'm going to need that Sorcerer's cloak! Look inside the brass-handled hamper.'

Glendien left the side of her dead without ceremony. Born to forest customs, that placed exigent survival before mourning, she took action and shortly arrived with Davien's mantle clutched in her arms. The bordered edge of the night-black wool glittered, laced with patterns of silver embroidery.

The thread *would* contain spellcraft.

Before Dakar's hot protest, that the Betrayer's work could not fail to invoke unknown consequences, Elaira cut in, 'Would you rather fall back on the arts of my order? Arithon's free choice must run contrary!'

'You have trusted too much!' the spellbinder reproached the prince with shut eyes, who gasped bleeding.

'Then set faith in Kyrialt, who didn't!' Ravaged and pale, the young widow hung on by her obdurate spirit. 'You will honour my husband's last word in this life and wrap his feal prince in the Sorcerer's garment!'

'Hurry.' Elaira laid her dimmed crystal aside. She caught Davien's mantle in frantic, wet hands. Heart laid bare, yet without hesitation, she spread the cloth over Arithon's wracked form, head to feet. Dark wool settled, for one hanging instant turned as deep as the primordial void. The brilliant embroidery *sieved down through the weave*, dissolved to ephemeral light that sank into the prostrate body beneath.

Black fabric remained, an unmarked, plain cloak. But the shrouded man *did not wear the familiar semblance of Arithon*. Again, Dakar viewed the guise of the blind elder, last assumed when Rathain's prince stalked the Kralovir cult at Etarra. Just as before, Davien's craft appeared seamless. Even as mage-gifted Sight read the aura, the Sorcerer's finesse masked the etheric stamp left by Fellowship sanction and royal identity.

The feat occurred with such speed that Dakar shivered with gooseflesh. 'Merciful Ath! Would that I *knew* how that working was done!'

If Elaira was shaken, her healer's attention already rallied to measure the changeling spell's impact.

'Arithon's unconscious,' she announced, undone by relief. 'Davien's enchantment has stabilized his erratic pulse and lifted him quite beyond pain.' Which was well, for the moment. Her beloved would not feel the brute course of the treatment their effort demanded to save him. 'Glendien! I'll need that plank trestle cleared. Let's bear his Grace up with the utmost of care, since I can't accomplish refined surgery crouched on the floor.'

Talvish's prior projection proved wrong. The sail-loft over the chandler's was not barraged by pillagers fired with the passion of conquest. What thundered up the stair in hobnailed boots was a Sunwheel officer, in crisp command of a task squad. His duty, to mop up an ordered assault, encountered no futile last stand; no suicidal charge by panicked citizens trapped by the harbour keep's downfall. The door he kicked in broke a stifling quiet, cut across by the piteous moans of the prostrate. His raking glance scarcely absorbed the rowed cots, before Glendien scalded him scarlet.

'Idiot man! Take your warmongering elsewhere! No one lies here but the sick and the maimed.'

'You say, forest bitch!' yelled a soldier from the landing behind. 'My sword says your accent makes you the Light's enemy!'

Before his startled sergeant-at-arms could agree, or snap a reprimand for impertinence, Elaira arose from the trestle, both hands stained with gore to the elbow. 'Sir! You've dared to break into a Koriani hospice. If your man speaks ill of our novice again, I will silence his rank tongue.' As the lead officer straightened, *fast*, to apologize, she cut him short. 'Leave this place! Here, where we undertake a charitable service, your steel and your blundering pose an offence.'

Shamed stiff, the sergeant refused to be cowed. 'I go nowhere, enchantress. With all due respect, you are harbouring Alliance traitors, if not outright minions of Shadow.'

'Glendien,' said Elaira, her voice dripping ice. 'Deal with this. Now!' Back turned, she resumed her grisly work, where nobody's eyes wished to linger. Her blanketed charge displayed a hideous sword wound, a gashed length of pink gut laid out on the plank for cleaning. The stink lingered, beyond ripe. What the woman's fingers were stitching with spells would wring a staid veteran to heave up his breakfast.

The barbaric redhead laced in straightaway, a scathing reminder that Koriathain did not take sides. 'By all means,' she challenged with venomous sweetness, 'march in like butchers and clobber your own. Your dumb interference comes at your own peril!'

The officer took pause. His survey by then had swept past the cots, and covered the farthest, dimmed alcove. There was a blond casualty who reeled on a stool. He did have an ugly slash on the wrist, stanched with the wadded hem of a Sunwheel surcoat. Not yet convinced – the chap might be an imposter – the sergeant regrouped and tried reason. 'If you truly have any Alliance men sheltered here, then you'll have to show me firm proof.'

'Koriathain don't lie!' cracked Elaira. 'Inspect and be quick! You'll see faces you recognize. But I warn! Show all due respect for the ones not your own. If anyone under the sisterhood's care takes harm by your prodding, if I'm forced to stir to mix a fresh posset, or if Glendien must reset a bandage, be sure I will visit my undying curse on the manhood of every last wretch in your company.'

Before the hazed officer could protest, Glendien lit in ahead of him. 'Can you be so arrogant?'

'Have you no need at all for our skilled help to attend to your mortally wounded?' Elaira pealed, pushed beyond tolerance.

The sergeant blanched. 'Sisters, forgive. My duty commands me.' He waved a subordinate forward with the curt imprecation to review the bedridden casualties. 'And touch nothing!'

'Aye, sir!' Horror met the man's flinching glance. Pity tore, for the mangled children and unconscious boys, who languished past hope of a hale recovery.

The crippling wounds, the ghastly, weeping burns, and the blistering reek of strong unguents wore down brash nerve and sapped the will to continue.

'These two are ours,' the man-at-arms verified. He glanced up in sweating appeal, that his senior officer would choose to be satisfied.

Again, Elaira seized the initiative. 'Have your bearers bring the worst cases here. You'll find litters, there. Yes! Propped in the corner. I'm sorry one's burdened with the sheeted dead. The corpse goes wherever you're planning to burn the citadel's fallen. If you'll hear my suggestion, take the fat servant with you. He knows enough to set the bleeders in field dressings, and bind splints so the broken bones and the paralyzed can be moved without further trauma.'

Dusk fell, palled in smoke, which fore-promised a night limned in the flitter of torches as the assault companies came in, worn, off the siege front. Shouts criss-crossed the Alliance camp, as replacement companies from Etarra marched aboard waiting galleys to shoulder the relief watch inside the broached harbour. The troop change proceeded with seamless discipline, as Sulfin Evend returned to the calm surrounds of the Light's high command tent. Fast strides and a nod from the guard at the threshold admitted him. He plunged past the rich hangings of the ante-room, the ruddy crackle of pitch pine outside replaced by the polished glimmer of candle-lamps.

Ranne's sombre report met his rushed arrival at the tapestry that partitioned the trestle and tactical maps. 'No change,' he assured, in reference to Lysaer.

'I came as fast as I could.' Sulfin Evend slowed down. Shut his eyes, and swore out of simmering distaste. The row between officers, just broken up, already clamoured towards riot concerning the upcoming seizure of spoils.

'Bulls in the porcelain shop?' Ranne murmured in sympathy.

'I told the grasping fools I'd wring their necks if they unleashed their troops like raiders on a stricken caravan!' The discomfited twitch of broad shoulders resettled the Lord Commander's mussed surcoat, but not the burdensome weight of his mail. 'Except, to be fair, the damned clansmen don't rape.' Remiss for his bad temper, Sulfin Evend concluded, 'It's the head-hunters' lewd vicious-ness that incites our fresh troops to rude expectations and swaggering.'

Past the flap, the large trestle and siege models remained in place for debates over strategy. The rowed chairs stood empty, the last stage of the battle already closed. If the velvet-and-wood furnishings escaped the grime of war, the taint of char and oiled steel rode the air, oppressive as everywhere else.

Sulfin Evend encountered Lysaer, standing, back turned to the entrance. Ranne's reliable eye had not sweetened the truth. Under stainless white cloth and gold trim, the crown regent's carriage reflected the strain of a sleepless night. Inexperience might not see beyond his innate majesty. But the more intimate survey sensed a pressured stillness that trembled like an indrawn breath, denied from explosive release.

The fight to resist Desh-thiere's geas never ceased. Hard against flinching nerves and hazed will, the hateful drive flamed on consuming course to shatter the veneer of sanity.

'The body's not his,' announced Lysaer s'Ilessid, quite aware of whose presence invaded his fraught need for solitude.

If his opening seemed casual as a tea-room discussion, Sulfin Evend dared not rely on appearances. Straightaway, he approached the draped plank by the lamp. Flipped back the stained sheet, and exposed the muddy, mauled corpse retrieved after the melee that swept the sea quarter caverns, and now delivered here by his diligent second officer. The light unveiled a young man with black hair. The green eyes were dulled glass, and the angled cheek-bones, crusted over with blood. Feature for feature, the face was the same, recalled from the past encounter at Sanpashir.

Memory resurged, fit to raise the gorge for the ring of forthright conviction: *'Nothing I know could force me to this!'* Arithon Teir's'Ffalenn had insisted. *'No concept of honour will be made the cause to destroy another clan enclave of women and children.'* That ringing, clear voice, gifted to render a masterbard's music, also had carved a living miracle. Sulfin Evend bristled to primal rage. He could not reconcile the unearthly, grand chord, which had founded the bid for Lysaer's redemption, evoked as well through callous duplicity to gull his effortless trust. The murderous liar had moved with such grace! Even laughed with engaged abandon.

And there, reason snagged on the glaring discrepancy. In death, one detail mismatched the impression left by the bastard's live presence. These awkward hands, nicked with wounds, were all wrong: the wrist-bones too coarse, that suggested the stocky frame of a labourer. In fact, no old scar seared by a past light-bolt marred the stiffened right forearm.

Sulfin Evend reined in his unruly emotions. 'I agree,' he told Lysaer. 'This would seem an imposter. Though the likeness is quite astonishing. Your priests did not sense any residue laid by a worked enchantment?'

'None.' Not moving, which was no good sign, Lysaer added, 'I still feel the gnaw of the curse in my vitals. Which would not be so, if the Master of Shadow had crossed Fate's Wheel.'

Sulfin Evend lowered the shroud and stepped back. *Every instinct he had shouted wrongness.* 'If we are supposed to be duped, this faked carcass lacks the murderous artifice we've always met on the field.'

No one had died, beyond mundane casualties. No spectacular provocation had been staged to upset the campaign's ordered progress. The broadscale chaos unleashed on the troops who had marched upon Vastmark and Daon Ramon gave the lie to a ruse of such obvious transparency.

Frowning, Sulfin Evend hooked a chair, spun the seat to face Lysaer, and perched. His uneasy senses shrilled with the need to stay vigilant. Lysaer's volatile state remained driven past surcease by Arithon's close proximity. Each passing hour, that peril increased as the pressure leached his reserves.

While the siege approached closure, Sulfin Evend had no choice but to keep watch at his liege's shoulder. No one else had the talented Sight to prevail, if crisis broke in his absence. He could not stand down, though the arduous demands of the upstepped campaign wrung him to blinding exhaustion. The befogging ache pierced his bones, to sleep like a rock where he rested.

'What is your intent?' he probed at quiet length. 'It might suit our purpose, and perhaps blunt the rabid aggression of conquest, if we let the ceremonial burning to rest the shade of a sorcerer go forward.'

'You want that diversion to lend the free rein to investigate on your own,' Lysaer surmised. 'For what gain?' He turned around, his cranked tension unveiled by the bruised rings that shadowed his eye-sockets. His state collar glittered under the force required to steady his breathing. 'Who handles the parade of appeals to the Light, if you are not here, and I have to answer directly? My Sunwheel priests already realize the Spinner of Darkness still lives. You wanted the guiding presence of talent. I haven't the means to blindside that array of trained sensitivity! Gag them outright, and I cannot mislead the dedicate fervour of the rank and file with lies. Not without sending them to self-destruction, since the criminal sorcerer is surely at large, and quite busy supporting the s'Brydion resistance. As well as I, you must realize our victory progresses too easily to be trusted.'

'The risk mounts, the tighter we corner our prey,' Sulfin Evend agreed. 'The object is not to fall for his wiles but to take him down clean, before spending the lives of the war host positioned to flush him. That calls for swift stalking ahead of the lines. You can't act there with covert anonymity, my friend.' In unvarnished honesty, the fear could not rest, that a direct encounter must trigger the insane ferocity of Desh-thiere's curse.

Worse, the sensitive discussion could not stay private. Warned first by Ranne's challenge, then the sound of an approaching tread from without, Sulfin Evend shifted his form of address on delivery of his ultimatum. 'If you try, Blessed Lord, we have thrown away sense! Might just as well pin your bleeding heart on the gauntlet we throw to the enemy!'

Lysaer inclined his fair head to the senior officer who entered, the dangerous, deep glitter roused in his blue eyes a threat that seized on distraction. 'You have a recent development to report?'

'I bring triumph, Divine Prince!' The man bowed in worship, his soiled surcoat and gear arrived straight from the battle-front. 'Alestron's sea quarter bailey is ours. All resistance is routed, though our push for complete occupation is hampered. The s'Brydion defenders launch cross-fire from the upper citadel. They have set the harbourfront burning.'

'Rise and sit.' Lysaer flicked imperious, ringed fingers to summon his valet. 'My servant will bring wine. Once you are comfortable, your Lord Commander will share your account.'

The report that followed was mostly routine. While Lysaer paced to bridle frayed nerves, a list of casualties changed hands, followed by a detailed assessment of the numbers who could fight again after rest and refreshment. Sulfin Evend heard out the names. He asked after the performance of his squad sergeants, then pounced on the lapse, that one company was late in at the watch change.

'That would be Gevard's division, from Telzen,' the staff captain disclosed, flushed. 'Those squads stayed on to oversee transfer of the wounded, and help the Koriani enchantress whose hospice required moving to secure turf on the mainland.'

'*What?*' Sulfin Evend's barked incredulity shocked Lysaer from midstride to standstill. With a gesture to forestall undue divine interest, the Lord Commander demanded, 'What Koriathain? Why was I not informed? Since when have we had more witches sticking their noses into Alliance affairs?'

'One sister, my lord, and her novice assistant.' The staff captain cleared his throat, set aback. 'She is most diligently tending our casualties. Unlike the ones with the gaudy pavilions, this healer does not put on airs. She flaunts no silk mantle and attaches no retinue beyond a male servant who runs menial errands. If you would judge her harshly, she's saving our men. Her conjury has spared many injured we would have lost without her learned practice.'

'Where is she now?' snapped Sulfin Evend, shoved to his feet.

'Adruin's galley, my lord. The ship's master agreed to bring her convalescent charges across. He had little choice, after the hospice she kept in the sail-loft was set ablaze. Since the rest of the harbourfront's burning past salvage, she was offered safe passage and a tent shelter next to the war camp.'

On one knee before thought, Sulfin Evend presented his rapid appeal to the white-and-gold majesty of the Blessed Prince. His request for leave was placed without pride, under the name of true service. 'My Lord Regent of Tysan, let me intercept that galley before she makes landing among us.'

For the thornier handling of Arithon's demise had to wait. At least until he thwarted this bald-faced attempt to insinuate another Koriani presence in the teeth of the Alliance campaign.

Dark Hour

By sundown, a biting east wind razed the estuary, whipping gusts that hampered the loading of Adruin's out-bound galley. With the sabotaged wharf left a mangle of sunk timber, and the upper-tier catapults busy hammering ruin on any ship caught within range, the craft lay tied in close to the battered stonewalls. A rough gangway lashed from loose planks and moored tenders boarded the assault troops due for leave from the harbourfront. Elaira attended her wounded, beleaguered, on the vessel's exposed upper deck. If the freezing weather endangered her critical cases, the blaze in the sail-loft forestalled better handling. The Alliance captain's offer of transport defrayed the certain destruction that swept through the sea-quarter streets.

'That's setting your crown prince, stunned helpless, within the cursed reach of his half-brother's fury,' Dakar accosted Talvish in a searing whisper. 'Not to mention, we'll be under the itching noses of the Light's watch-dog priests!' Dockside, the pair of them grunted to heft the locked chest that hid the Paravian sword and the heirloom lyranthe. While the enemy assisted the on-going task of hauling their litter-bound casualties across the heaving span from the ruined landing, any snatched conversation was risky.

Yet the blond liegeman, who gimped with his sword-arm strapped up, only backed Elaira's decision. 'How else to challenge the Alliance's cordon?' He tipped his chin towards the lights of the patrol galleys raking to and fro across the closed harbour mouth. 'We're bang in the midst of those blood-feeding sharks! Bravado alone cannot jack a small boat, or slip past that accursed blockade! We will cross alive if we go under sanction by Lysaer's officers.'

But the persistent hunch to the Mad Prophet's shoulders decried the logical option.

'Trust Davien's working!' Talvish urged in clipped haste. 'Our chances are sure to be better ashore, where our leaving won't be as nakedly obvious.'

Against Dakar's steamed silence, and all better sense, Arithon's wrapped form was bundled aboard by two Sunwheel soldiers, under Glendien's rapacious oversight. Talvish perched atop the stowed trunk, strategically placed in close reach, as the galley's crew raced the changed tide to cast off.

The vessel embarked under cover of darkness. She surged into the icy race of black water to a blare of horns, and the crackling flutter of her Adruin registry and Sunwheel pennant. Errant danger increased as the oarsmen dug in, driven at double-stroke pace. As they pulled the ship clear of the looming cliff, only nightfall and speed could foil the defenders' hurled shot. Under hot fire from the upper citadel, the galley ran, lanterns shuttered. Her zigzagged course dodging the whistle and splash of lofted boulders unleashed by the trebuchets.

A glancing hit splintered the yardarm and topmast. Deck-hands sprang to jettison the entangled wreckage, while a luckless by-stander writhed underneath, screaming with a compound fracture. The bone-setting left Elaira too engrossed for worry, or Glendien's shattering grief. The clanswoman mixed remedies without anyone's prompting, while Dakar, reluctant, wound cantrips to ease the seaman's piteous suffering. Throughout, Arithon lay senseless. Kept under Talvish's tacit watch, his condition stayed changeless, while the galley bore off, and the tumult of battle fell away astern.

Parrien also remained blessed by unconsciousness, while beyond the wake thrashed up by the oars, the stamped silhouette of the citadel brooded over a necklet of flame. The conflagration streamed from roof to roof, roaring throughout the tight streets of the sea-quarter bailey. The galley made steady headway through the fouled air, until the rolling billows of smoke chased away on the wind off the Cildein.

Beyond range of the trebuchets, the deck-officer ordered the lamps kindled. Sailhands at work on the mangled rigging began whistling as the oar-stroke was relaxed, then suspended for the blockade challenge. Throughout the parade review for security, Rathain's delegation stayed beneath notice, too obviously busy soothing the wretch with the fracture, and ministering to the line-up of others who sustained gashes and splinters. In deference to the critically wounded, Adruin's galley was passed in brisk order. She rowed past the gutted keeps at the harbour mouth, and changed course for a shore-line entrenched with the Alliance war camp.

'More lives stand in jeopardy than you can possibly imagine,' Dakar snapped to Elaira, still flushed to sweat from restraint of the seaman just strapped into splints.

The enchantress returned a nettled glance. 'I prefer freezing chill and overzealous protection to the certainty of a roasting. You aren't busy enough? We've run short of blankets. Glendien needs you to borrow spare cloaks from the rank-and-file men who are sheltered belowdecks.'

She turned her back, forced the semblance of calm as she addressed the badgering pressure of too many helpers. Since her talent tended Alliance men, now, every movement she made tripped over the hindrance, as soldiers with wounded comrades aboard crowded in to assist. She put them to work. Some fetched and carried, while others rigged makeshift sailcloth or strung hammocks to shelter the injured against the rough crossing. If Glendien was just as raggedly hand-tied attending the stricken, Talvish had contrived to position his body to shield his unconscious liege from the spray off the foredeck. The covert restraint galled him, that his masquerade in a Sunwheel surcoat permitted no more without risk of undue attention.

That misery lasted, until Elaira made rounds to ascertain the prince's stitched loin had withstood the trauma of loading. 'You! Blond chap with the sword wounds! I don't care blazes where you've placed your loyalty. Your sound arm is needed. Steady that grandfather's hammock, forthwith. The gut wound he's suffered fares ill, set to swinging. I won't lose a life to your lazy comfort. Keep him under your charge till he's brought to safe landfall, or believe this, you'll answer to me!'

Arithon's exposure was not the sole pitfall to strain her inadequate resource: Parrien s'Brydion also languished among her prostrate wounded. The trump blow dealt by Dakar would not leave him harmless. Already his groggy awareness resurged in the sting of the freshening air. Elaira sensed his prideful rage at her back, as, stripped naked in blankets, he found himself hog-tied and bandaged on a galley flying the hated flag of Adruin. His curdling howl did little good. The poultice that packed his bludgeoned nape also bound his thick jawbone and gagged him.

'You are hurting, dear man?' Elaira knelt at his shoulder, called for a candlelamp, and flared the light in his face. His murderous glower left her unfazed through a pitiless examination. 'Awake, and past fortunate to be so,' she murmured. 'Head trauma is unpredictably dangerous!'

The affront she tossed back into Parrien's teeth stayed whetted beneath smiling honey. 'Your life is thus far preserved, an *astounding* grace brought by unbiased compassion. You are nicely concussed, which makes it unsafe to dose you on soporifics. Therefore, your sad suffering must be endured. Do I have to warn? The unwise move on your part could prove fatal, with my sympathy stretched beyond snapping. Act the fool, and your get will be raised by your widow, for I will not stir to save you.'

Since his clenched fists were chilled, she called for a hammock and a dry cloak. Then she took further pains to steer Glendien clear, and set Dakar to post sharp watch over him.

In due time, the galley approached the far shore. The slap of the waves slackened as she neared the cove landing, and the glimmer of torch-light unveiled the teeming sprawl of the war camp. Raucous noise as the off-watch companies let off steam rebounded across the black water, wind-snatched talk cut by jubilant shouts, celebrating the day's massive victory. Beyond the relief ranks, packed in wait on the strand for their turn to press the engagement, the cookfires warmed rowdy singers. Their infectious high spirits spurred shipboard morale. Sternwards, a sergeant was cracking a joke, while the deck-hands itched to lay hands on their beer, and romp with nubile harlots.

'Beggin' yer pardon, sweet,' one ventured to Glendien with a lusty grin. 'There's whores like their play hot and rough, and some strumpets too bawdy to settle for a dullard husband.'

'Has your itching male pucker *replaced* your runt brain?' the clanswoman retorted, en route to empty a slop bucket. 'Yap such to your mother, she'd flay your rank tongue. That's if you're not a pimp's rut yourself, bred for naught but a swaggering jackal.'

To whoops from his fellows, the seaman laughed back. 'Virgin witch!' he sniped, flagrantly ripe for a dousing. 'What would you know of the wicked delights found in an evening's dalliance?'

'Enough to hobble your play in the sheets,' Elaira cut in from the sidelines. Arrived from the shadows, *just in time,* she forestalled her posed novice's folly.

The men scattered to their posts, while Glendien paused at the leeward rail: not to break, despite her pale face, and the grief that fought welling tears. 'I can handle them.'

'You can't,' contradicted Elaira. 'But where there's no choice, we'll bear up. Take a minute. We shall need iron nerves for the hazards on landing.'

The weariness also sucked through her in waves, anxiety chafed by the effusive crew, and the relapses caused by the open-air passage. She also snatched refuge, aching and cold; beyond drained from the wearing hours of subterfuge, and sharp-focused use of strong magecraft. No sigils had buttressed her healing, throughout. Only the free use of crystal, as taught by Ath's adepts.

'You're unwell,' remarked Glendien. 'Worn thin and pressed near to overextension.'

'I will manage,' Elaira insisted, a ruefully honest glance darted sidewards.

'You couldn't.' The clanswoman flashed a bitter-sweet grin. 'But since when does helplessness stop any woman whose beloved requires protection?'

The moment was shattered by a brisk hail from the sloop, scudding in under sail from the shore-line. Shouted orders disrupted the inbound routine for a conference with the galley's captain. While the drum changed beat to backwater the oars, the ship's mate sprang to brighten the forward candle-lamp. His poised light unveiled the streaming pennant that declared the approach of a Light-sanctioned courier.

'Dharkaron Avenger show mercy to idiots,' the Mad Prophet huffed, arrived at Elaira's right side. 'Here's the prickling gamut, no question.'

For the array of the banners shouted ill luck, if not an outright disaster. The top-ranking officer of the Alliance had requisitioned this craft from her out-bound run down the strait. Commandeered *here* by that supreme authority, the impasse would place their tissue-thin ploy under gruelling examination.

'Rinse that bucket clean,' Elaira barked to move Glendien. 'Stow it in my locked remedy trunk, now, though you'll have to displace the fellow with the strapped forearm who's parked on top!'

Dakar spoke, near as swiftly. 'You'll be challenged by the Lord Commander at Arms, Sulfin Evend –'

But Elaira cut off the untoward speech as she glanced in affront towards the on-coming vessel. 'Only a heartless brute and a fool would obstruct my order's mission to succour the wounded.'

'No doubt you'll endure nothing worse than formalities,' declared the breathless fore-deck officer from Adruin. He had come up behind to oversee crew, sent pounding to run out the anchor. Dakar was forced silent. While the captain's bawled orders had the oar banks run in, and the middle deck men deployed fenders, the sloop luffed her sails. Agleam with lamps, she grappled for boarding.

'The man will be civil, whoever he is,' Elaira cracked, annoyed, then shoved off with straight back to tackle the unnerving interview.

Dakar pursued. Staggered over the wallowing deck, he let his inept footing fetch him into the enchantress's elbow. Entangled in skirts, through effusive apologies, he demolished her resolute platitudes. 'The creature's outbred clan, of s'Gannley descent, a *caithdein's* direct line that sees everything!'

'Your flapped nerves are a bother!' Elaira lashed back. In feigned fury to distance the curious, she added, 'By all means, make yourself scarce if you're cowed. Gold badges, or not, the man shouldn't be hard to intimidate.'

Yet the frantic, raced pulse in her wrist told the truth, as Dakar's crushing grasp let her go. She did know, altogether too well, whom they faced in their effort to spirit off Arithon: *the errant son of Hanshire's conniving mayor was most expertly versed, and unafraid of the Koriathain.*

Amid shaken confidence, the stopped galley was seized by two dozen Sunwheel guardsmen. They were of first-rate caliber. Deployed on the main-deck, they *already* suspected her presence: the ordered detainment of the hospice wounded occurred with alarming speed. The uninvolved soldiers and onlooking deck crew were crowded well back from that firmly drawn line. More, the indignant complaint of Adruin's sea-captain met drawn steel, a warning to cede his ship's rights and stand down before Sunwheel priority.

'We're here on account of your unsanctioned passengers, brought under the auspices of the Koriathain,' the invading sergeant at arms told the disgruntled galley-men. 'Hold your tongues and stay quiet! The sooner our Lord Commander is satisfied, the earlier your scheduled course resumes without fuss and delay.'

While the overshadowing presence of Lysaer's first war officer mounted the side battens behind, Elaira seized her last moment to take stock of the fugitives inside her quarantined company. Glendien, ensconced with the hurt children in plausibly protective dismay; she had dispatched the bucket, since Talvish was also safely displaced from his post at Prince Arithon's side. His blond head just showed, where he crouched tucked in blankets, in shadow behind the remedy chest. Dakar also bowed to the sensible course, his technique used before to deflect Lysaer's arcane examiners. His seer's aura drawn down to an unremarkable muddle, he hunched at the side-lines, holding the hand of a delirious matron who suffered disfiguring burns.

The hammock that held Arithon swayed unattended. *Surely* beneath notice: Davien's disguise rendered him as a feeble old man, unobtrusive amid the savagely mauled and the fevered who languished, unconscious. Yet the desperate wild card lurked alongside, still triced up in wound linen and rage: Parrien s'Brydion watched with scorching grey eyes, when the Light's Lord Commander strode under the candle-lamp on the deck.

Apparently warned that no purple robe awaited his scouring survey, Sulfin Evend demanded, 'Let the Koriani sister among you stand forward!'

His predatory distrust strangled thought. Elaira knew not to try bluster as she rallied her poise and stepped towards him. The instant impression screamed self-assured power: from compact strength in full arms, which wore trappings of rank as inconsequential, to the unrelaxed hands, no stranger to steel, and campaign scars, unabashed in plain sight. Then surface appearances were swept aside by the glittering *hatred* that lurked in his tiercel's eyes, raking her.

'What do you fear?' she asked, soft as moonlight, and backed by a healer's conviction.

His weathered skin drained, a shock that did nothing to blunt his ferocity. 'You were not invited!' Dark hair and hard stance, he still carried the stamp of his privileged origins. 'Everywhere your accursed order appears, they bring the scourge of their hidden purposes.'

'I have known that unpleasantness,' Elaira agreed. Work-worn, *too tired*, she sensed his sharp talent beating at her innate balance. 'I am not in regalia, or wearing white ribbons of rank. As you seem familiar with some of our ways, the lack of attire should tell you my practice is not attached to a sisterhouse.'

He was not without courtesy. A stiff word to his sergeant fetched a chair from the stern cabin, placed underneath the hung lamp. She accepted the grace. Chapped hands folded, she observed, while Sulfin Evend contained his sultry impatience before her. Such unease, wrapped in stillness, was too well controlled. The night breeze and the riffling flame rebounded off his spotless accoutrements. Confrontational, silent, he allowed her to read him, the cynical slant to his glance quite aware that her talent would plumb his aura. The exposure amused him. While this ceded the truth, that he did in fact carry an oath-bound tie to the Fellowship, the gift was not free. His rapacious alertness did not miss, in turn, that the groans of her wounded spurred her own vulnerability.

Nonetheless, she had enough brazen nerve not to volunteer information.

The order's wandering independents were a tough breed. They did not visit Hanshire. If he asked, she would cite him the reason.

But instead, Sulfin Evend waved his men back. His inquiry claimed the semblance of privacy, as much to limit the risk she posed him, through blood-letting exposure. At close quarters, Elaira grasped that, like her, he was unmanageable: the same dogged perception guided his honesty.

When he took up her thrown gauntlet at last, the sting was not pulled from his challenge. 'I have just rid myself of three pavilions' worth of your viciously meddling sisters.'

'They are not my concern,' Elaira said carefully. 'You see here the extent of my charitable service. If meddling saves lives, then that has been my calling. The wounded and sick suffer for your delay. Some might die of neglect, while you hamper me.'

'Charitable service? Your protestations ache my back teeth!' Sulfin Evend bore in, 'Don't offend me, with caring. You've insinuated yourself a free passage to bring *who knows what* within reach of my war camp.'

Which woke rage, that his hazing implied a Prime Matriarch's hand, plying intrigues. 'You are here to serve Lysaer with steadfast defence, defined by a love that won't waver?' Shown his angry surprise, Elaira attacked. 'Then take off the blindfold of your past resentment. Look again! My purpose and yours are not set at odds. Your distrust here harms only the innocent.'

'But *are* they innocent?' Sulfin Evend glared back, uncowed. 'Some will be, I warrant. But all of them?'

'The distrustful commander must see for himself?' Elaira denounced, peeled to acid. 'Then why not be less thorough? You could choose to get us all out of the cold. Send me packing straight off with an escort. I won't need more than a cart for the stricken. Just leave me those few the camp's healers don't have the trained skill to keep on the mend.'

'Sly vixen!' exclaimed Sulfin Evend, amazed, while the cold-blooded strategist that never slept sized up her bold offer for tactics. 'Maybe you're telling me half of the truth. Shall we test your sincerity first? Since I'm versed with war injuries, your offer's accepted if I'm left to choose. Who goes and who stays damned well ought to pose us a shockingly riveting chess match!'

Elaira measured his adamant will. Met those focused, hawk's eyes, and gauged his amusement: he *dared* lure her on. Against the unknown stake she withheld, he would match ploy for ploy until he uncovered her secret.

'Soonest started,' she snapped, and stood for the contest, cornered at last by his stature.

The commitment he kept was too ruthlessly sure, the past grievance he held against the order's seniors, quite likely a just call of honour. Yet that history lay above her rank to question. She would risk her oath if she tried. Therefore, she must rise to call this man's bluff. Ride the chance, that event would not force her hand. Rather than seal her Prime's clever entrapment, with sigils invoked to shield Arithon, Elaira played the least damaging card and bid for disarming subterfuge.

'I would have you stay clear,' Sulfin Evend declared, disallowing the arcane distraction that might tip the scales in her favour. He unhooked the glass lamp. Beckoned two men to cover his back, then commenced with the harrowing tour of her wounded.

Elaira held firm, torn ragged by fear. Sulfin Evend analyzed all his details with adversarial intensity. *Everything* now relied on the others to withstand his ruthless inspection. She was Koriathain, disciplined to school the least nuance of expression and bearing. Dakar could rely on initiate practice to stay ignored as a servant. Yet the trained eye could scarcely miss Talvish's tension, crouched beyond the remedy trunk. Or the sullen, trapped blaze of Parrien's resentment, although he had the sense to lie back with shut eyes, feigning unconsciousness.

Sulfin Evend peeled back blankets, unreservedly thorough. He searched faces, and with unsurprising, skilled knowledge, probed the wounds beneath neatly strapped bandages. His explorative touch caused no harm. He was polite towards the hurt women, and unthreatening to the tearful child. Yet his fixated search was not going to be satisfied. Never, before he ascertained the afflicted did not harbour fugitives in prime health.

Elaira endured, despite screaming nerves. Forthright evidence must exonerate her character. As Sulfin Evend made rounds, she had to admire: his choices were just as he winnowed the superficially hurt from the dangerously infirm. For the wagon, he singled out two women with burns. Then a child with a crippling fracture. Next, a soldier whose leg threatened sepsis, and another whose chest cut progressed to filled lungs. Arithon ought to be passed as he seemed: an old man with a near-fatal gut wound. If Parrien was recognized, the dilated eye of a genuine head injury should remand him to non-partisan Koriani protection. Glendien's talent was real enough. The claim of a sisterhood novitiate ought to shield her forest-bred origins from the persecution; and Talvish wore a Sunwheel surcoat, over gashes won fair, by the sword.

All would be well, if no one cracked under pressure, or gave way to needless stupidity.

Nonetheless, Elaira closed a damp hand on her crystal. She aligned her inner awareness, *prepared*, as Sulfin Evend dismissed a young girl with a crossbolt puncture. Neat on his feet, despite the heaving deck, his progress reached Arithon's hammock. There, he took pause, his rapt focus resharpened. *Something* snagged his rapacious attention. The icy chill followed, as Elaira recalled Arithon mentioning that this man's uncle, Raiett, had detected Davien's wrought disguise during an interrogation by Kralovir necromancers. Disastrously late, she grasped Dakar's frantic warning: a *caithdein*'s direct line would see everything!

Sulfin Evend possessed the gifted heritage of a teir's'Gannley, awakened through Fellowship auspices. Intuition arisen from hand-picked descent *surely might recognize the attuned binding borne by a sanctioned crown prince.* Even if only subliminal awareness picked up the unconscious connection.

While Elaira looked on with stifled anxiety, Sulfin Evend peeled back the blankets. He lifted the cloth of the unmarked black cloak and perused the stained evidence of a wounding, quite real, and invasive enough to inflict the fresh onset of fever.

'You earned someone's vicious enmity, old man,' he murmured, nettled by the hunch this was not just any civilian casualty. Frowning, Sulfin Evend extended his survey over the invalid's body. Those exquisite, fine hands; the lithe bones and cat's build; surely they woke recognition?

'You!' he gasped, his bitterness plain as a shout to the ear of the mage-trained.

And Elaira's breath froze: for her shared empathy stirred to the shattering sense that the disturbance roused Arithon back towards cognizance.

Talvish would not see, his vantage obscured by the blanket.

But the fogged eyes within Arithon's falsely aged visage were open and searching for light. No doubt blind except for initiate mage-sight, he groaned and started to stir. Agony caught him short; a hissed gasp, as every razor-cut nerve exploded to ruthless sensation. Rathain's prince languished, laid out in the hammock, and quite unable to move. Confused, convalescent, he came fully awake: alert to the furious oppressor poised over him, stunned yet by the shock of encounter.

Endangered, possibly fighting delirium, he mustered the rags of his resource. Elaira could follow by heart-tied rapport, as auric imprint let him identify his antagonist.

'Full circle,' Arithon managed at a frayed whisper. 'The eldest of the Biedar foresaw this. How will you deal? I still am not your enemy, for all that I had to break my past promise to stand clear of the fight at Alestron.'

His shadow had answered to spare Feylind's life. For that, he would ask no man's pardon. As Talvish well knew, by the wary movement that stirred in the gloom past the remedy trunk. The wounded liegeman gathered himself to enact a foredoomed intervention. Dakar might act also, protection being forfeit, and Sulfin Evend lashed into impenetrable rage by Arithon's presumed betrayal.

The paired guardsmen stationed on duty behind failed to notice the building danger: they had no cause to fear a wounded old man, not inside a bristling cordon at battle-strength in full arms.

'I will not act,' said Prince Arithon in stark calm. 'If I'd wanted you dead, you would have gone down, blindfolded and bound in the caverns.'

If the statement pleaded a line of appeal, Sulfin Evend stayed torn. His watch-dog guardsmen sensed no alarm yet. But Koriani-trained instincts were screaming.

Elaira firmed her heated grip on the crystal tucked beneath her draped cuff. Eyes open, thought stilled, she divided awareness to access the stone's focal matrix. The sigils required for ascendant domination were ugly, when framed for compulsion. Elaira gathered the resource, regardless. She would not watch Arithon killed out of hand, although nausea raked her in warning: the advanced awareness schooled by Ath's adepts ran utterly counter to all imposed spells of forced mastery.

Through dizzying strain, her beloved's wracked speech laboured on to reach Sulfin Evend. 'You are not at risk, here! Rely on my word, if you won't hear a friend. The enchantress will not entrain any craft to serve my self-preservation!'

Ath above! He asked her straight out to stand off. His compassion yet held out for reason. Or maybe he thought to fall back upon Dakar, *whose auric fields were shut down to muddy the etheric blaze of his talent.* No saving angle existed for back-up, with Sulfin Evend near losing his grip, whip-sawed by conflicted emotion.

Through frantic dread, Elaira sensed Arithon's touch in her mind, gentle as rain in the desert. *'Listen. Beloved, we are not alone.'*

Listen to *what*? The pound of her heart was as thunder. Even as her wracked balance floundered, the aligned crystal held at the ready flared in the palm of her hand. Its matrix opened. A sudden surge of unleashed reassurance flooded her being and steadied her.

'Listen,' sent Arithon, and urgency gave her the access to knowledge she needed: *that the crystal she held had been mined on Athera, its innate consciousness encompassed by Sethvir's earth-linked awareness. The Sorcerer was entrained, back at Althain Tower. As Warden, he had sounded the crown prince's wound through the meticulous care in her healing. Now, Sethvir's tuned sight tracked the peril that threatened aboard Adruin's detained galley.* As Elaira's overset faculties quieted, the Sorcerer's sending touched through to her: *'If there may come a time to rely on your order, this is not the moment. Hold fast.'*

Elaira glanced sidewards: saw the Mad Prophet's fist locked on Glendien's arm to curb her rash interference. The restraint eased the shrill edge of her panic. *What nuance did Fellowship prescience see?* Her frantic reassessment showed nothing else. Only the certain plunge towards disaster, juggernaut swift, still unfolding.

Across the deck, Sulfin Evend's two guards had drawn swords, now distressed as their commander pressed his savage inquiry. 'Lysaer lies in jeopardy as long as you live! The mere fact you breathe is a threat to him.'

'Truth,' allowed Arithon, drained ghostly pale. 'Though I very much doubt my death at your hand will do anything to help save him.'

Which feverish utterance, born of despair, a Biedar forecast had vigorously denied. Sulfin Evend still bore the searing remembrance. The clear force of its imprint also reached Elaira, a Sighted transference likely steered by Sethvir, as the tribal elder's past warning bridged time like a struck flare of lightning: *'Alone on Athera, he is the key to secure your liege's deliverance from jeopardy.'*

'Koriathain have plotted to undermine Lysaer!' Sulfin Evend responded in smoking rebuttal. In the cold dark, under the wind-tossed lantern, his justified fears gained dimension. 'Here and now, I have caught their sneak hands in, again! While I saw a corpse, the stark semblance of yours, delivered to my command tent, the true sorcerer languishes here in disguise. The deadliest foe, masquerading as wounded, being ushered under the false cover of charity into the heart of my war camp!'

'You saw –!' gasped Arithon, while distanced, his friends watched his breath stop. Then restart, on forced need to confirm the unbearable: *that Fionn Areth was dead*. The sorrow, just breaking, a devastating blow his nerves could never assimilate. Not in such harsh pain, pounded to stranded wits, amidst a charged confrontation.

One critical instant, Elaira saw Arithon lose hold on the fact that he faced Lysaer's liegeman, whose loyalty posed lethal peril. While for Sulfin Evend, the split-second silence extended too long for tenuous doubt to stay credible.

'*For there will come the dark hour. His life thread crosses the palm of your hand. The choice is yours,* Seithur, *whether or not to stay blinded,*' the desert elder had forewarned of this fateful meeting.

'How long, before you planned to drive your nemesis over the edge?' pealed the Light's supreme officer.

'My kin and my brother! I have raised no attack on him.' Arithon closed the clouded eyes that veiled any humane expression of grief. He had small breath left. Only the presence to rephrase the gentle closure once used before, at Sanpashir. 'You fight as my nightmare, Lysaer's true *caithdein*. But never in life as my enemy.'

Sulfin Evend's controlled temper broke. He had no thought for the onlooking ship's crew; none for the by-standing wounded. No vision to spare for another wrapped form, slung in the adjacent hammock: a fighting man with his head swathed in poultices, who had listened apace with burning hatred dammed behind his shut eyes. Nary a glance acknowledged the blond soldier with the strapped right arm, crouched by the remedy trunk.

Poised over the s'Ffalenn bastard who was Spinner of Darkness, the Light's Lord Commander unsheathed his sword, perhaps to strike, perhaps only to threaten. Perhaps, as a spirit bound under a *caithdein*'s oath to a Sorcerer, to test the given word of a crown prince, and ascertain whether arcane means or shadow might be turned in foul play against him. No one ever knew: for Parrien s'Brydion rolled out of his hammock, reclaimed by the berserker's geas wrought by the Koriani Prime Matriarch.

Elaira detected the hard glimmer of spells spindled about his strapped form. She had no second to react, and no breath to cry warning, before Parrien's hurled bulk crashed full length, and took Sulfin Evend behind the knees. While the war-captain toppled, and the two Sunwheel guardsmen lunged with bare steel to retaliate, Talvish uncoiled, threw back masking blankets, and drew the black blade of Alithiel left-handed.

Defence of the helpless unbridled the star spells.

Bright sound and dazzling light blazed aloft, dissolving the Matriarch's ties of dark practice. The winter night rang to a chord of pure harmony that shattered the fabric of reason. Ecstatic reaction undid the armed men. Every standing guard in the cordon was hurled off his feet. The vibration coursed through weapons and mail, stinging held steel from their grasping hands. As the Sunwheel ranks crumpled, Talvish stood tall, wrung to tears of relief, while the sword's released power ranged outward. Soldiers and seamen and officers alike were wracked helpless, first crying, then laughing, rocked speechless by waves of wild harmony. The onslaught built, scaling octaves, until solid bone felt recast to struck glass, and flesh shuddered, lifted beyond strife by ineffable tingles of rapture.

If Alithiel's song had been potent before, this explosive release surpassed bearing.

Already flattened, the witnesses overtaken on board the Light's galley became whirled dizzy, then scattered witless. Prone on the deck, or dropped limp in the hold, they succumbed to euphoric unconsciousness. All, beyond the sword's bearer, and two more: the Koriani enchantress, whose hand clasped a quartz still encompassed by Sethvir's sent warding; and the clownish, fat prophet, whose auric fields were shut down far enough to slow the barrage.

Elaira had scarcely a moment to notice the shielding that spared her from the sword's tonal confluence. Her hope, taking flight, became pressing necessity, sped on by word from Althain's Warden.

'Act now, my dear!' Sethvir sent through the crystal. 'Though I realize you'll be concerned for your wounded, the tide in your favour won't wait. Your prince and his retinue must be sailed out of harm's way on the sloop. As a courier, the vessel's officially scheduled. She'll win you free course past Kalesh, where you'll make clean escape through blue water. When Dakar gets seasick, remind him that Parrien s'Brydion knows how to navigate.'

Early Winter 5671

Star Song

While the sloop scuds in brisk winds towards the safety of open waters, Arithon lies senseless in the black weave of Davien's cloak; and although the peal of Alithiel's chord has restored his natural appearance and eased the healing of his dire wound, his shocked spirit has yet to recover awareness since the cry of sheathed steel, fallen silent . . .

Southward, under stars upon the jet sands of Sanpashir where the eldest in service to Mother Dark's Chosen tips her seamed face to the sky, her tears hang the balance between sorrow and hope as she measures the living course of the prophecy: 'Behold the dark hour of the second death! Now Arithon Teir's'Ffalenn rides the song of the sword, with only one way to survive. His fate, and ours, lies with Elaira *anient*! Grant strength for her coming decision . . .'

Hours later, when the Light's stricken men recover awareness aboard Adruin's anchored galley, the count turns up several missing wounded, with the crew off the courier penned in the stern cabin, and their swift sloop, secured under Sunwheel pennons, long gone with the out-bound tide; in their midst, Sulfin Evend swears with savage refrain, that in life, he might *never* cross paths with the Spinner of Darkness again . . .

XV. Athir

A cold, off-shore passage through stormy waters left a man in acute discomfort too much time for reflective thought. When Parrien s'Brydion awakened, mewed up in a berth aboard the jacked messenger sloop, the small vessel rolled hell-bent for the chartless deeps of the Cildein. Creaking timbers and the moan of taut gear told a seaman's emerging senses the craft bearing Arithon's delegation slogged, ill-set, against a cruel headwind. The risen gusts that screamed through the stays presaged worse weather to come. Parrien gritted his teeth. His mad-dog pain found no voice, that all he loved was endangered. He could not guard his doomed family, or spare them from the horrors that followed defeat. Alestron's sad fate lay beyond his reach, while the siege broke the ramparts, behind him.

Worse than the throb of a headache at sea, and the sting of his tender contusions, Parrien faced the distrust of his shipboard captors. The moment the enchantress pronounced his health stable, Talvish arrived, armed, and rousted him.

Chivvied past Glendien's skewering glare, then prodded above deck in a stranger's ill-fitting oilskins, Parrien cursed Dakar's lubberly seamanship as he assessed the sloop's course and condition. Rolling whitecaps thrashed a molten lead sea, sheeting spray off the plunge of the bowsprit. The keel wallowed, awash. Both main and jib-sheet were pinched, and thrumming in waspish protest. Each crest slammed the careening hull, as the north-eastward tack ploughed towards the frayed scud that foreran a trampling storm front.

Whipped by the hanks of his unbraided hair, still clogged with mud from the poultice, Parrien blustered, 'Why hasn't your piratical prince stirred his arse to attend the ham-fisted trim of these sails?'

'Mind your vile tongue!' the spellbinder snarled. Forced in soaked misery to man the rank helm, he ran on, 'His royal appeal in behalf of your life is all that's stayed Glendien's hand. I'd rather have left your fate to the thugs grunting oars aboard Adruin's galley.' Between imprecations, Dakar belaboured his s'Brydion prisoner with understanding that, Arithon being infirm, somebody else was required to navigate.

Parrien licked his teeth. More likely, that inconvenient necessity had been what kept the clan widow's dirk from his ribs. Braced as the salt chased the fur from his mouth, he said carefully, 'Where under sky am I taking us?'

Dakar's staggered gesture encompassed the darkened horizon. 'Anywhere out-bound.' Under contrary wind, despite heaving sickness, he had won as much distance from Alliance pursuit as the courier craft could withstand. 'What course we set later depends upon Arithon, who hasn't returned to aware-ness.'

Which upset was certain to make shipboard life beyond difficult: Parrien understood he was roped by the heels. The Fellowship flunky would scarcely forgive his blood-letting assault on a crown prince. 'A stupid mistake doesn't make me suicidal,' he declared in cornered forbearance. 'If you turn your back now, I won't swap the heading. My death, or your prince's, would just salve the tears of the jackals besetting my family.'

Dakar's hackles outmatched the queasy reflex to render his gorge. 'I should credit the fact that we're in this together? That didn't restrain your killing rage last time.'

Parrien shrugged. He need not apologize when pressed at bay, that s'Brydion reacted for kinsfolk. Since survival demanded, he bent his rapacious attention towards easing the sheets. A cross-staff rummaged out of the stern-locker let him sight the sun's angle at noon. He reset the glass to log elapsed time and determine the moment of sundown. Since plotting required map and dividers, he asked for Talvish to relieve the helm. The belaboured keel settled immedi-ately under the man's more-experienced hand. Wet, but less battered, Parrien left Dakar folded against the lee-rail, then braved the on-going hostilities below to establish a running fix.

With his two wardens topside, the empty stern cabin allowed him free use of the chart nook. His snatched refuge extended, since he could not scribe figures until his numbed fingers got warm.

Fragmented talk filtered through the companion-way, where the Prince of Rathain still languished in febrile unconsciousness. Glendien remained by his midships berth, where the roll of the sloop stayed the mildest. Elaira mean-time braved the noisome task of changing his crusted bandages. 'No sepsis,' she commented, thankful, as the lifted dressing exposed the tender pink of a closing wound. 'The drainage has slackened. I won't need the iodine. Alithiel's chord seems to have healed the grim worst. The fever's less, and his body is mending without any sign of impairment.'

Yet for the spirit strayed too far afield, swept in thrall by the winter stars' singing, no remedy Dakar or Elaira had tried could effect a waking recovery. The Masterbard's gifted awareness stayed lost, strung warp through weft with a harmony past human cognizance. Every effort to summon him through rapport ended in reeling faintness. Against precedent, the enchantress could not touch Arithon's being. Always, the splendour of the grand chord surged through and unravelled her contact.

'He's drifted too far,' she murmured, forsaken and raggedly desolate. While the lantern swung to the sloop's heeling pitch, she masked tears against her clenched fists. Her wisped chestnut braid draped the curve of her neck, and stress bowed her brave shoulders. Through the keen blast of spray through the hatch, as Dakar clumped below on a staggering weave that fetched him up, green, in the galley, Parrien caught snatches of her untenable anguish.

'Three days . . . drive him beyond safe limits . . . can't measure the scope of his danger! Mercy on us . . . try some other more-desperate avenue . . . don't find some way to recall him!'

Dakar left off brewing his peppermint-leaf tisane to kneel at her side. 'Elaira.' Drawn as he was himself, and as sorrowful, he gathered up her distraught hands. 'Stand down. Stay strong. Your beloved is spirit wandering. If he rides the winds, that does not mean he's in fatal danger just yet. The effect of the Five Centuries Fountain should balance his health and grant time to seek wiser means than your order's forced mastery to waken him.'

'You've communed with Sethvir?' Against Elaira's nature, bitterness showed as she pushed off the spellbinder's comfort. 'I've sent to the Warden myself. Called out in appeal through my crystal, repeatedly. Yet I've gotten nothing but silence from Althain Tower!'

Dakar stood with a reluctant sigh, braced his awkward weight, and filled the pot on the gimballed stove. 'Sethvir is still fielding the leaks on two grimwards. Even on good days, nobody fathoms the ways of a Fellowship Sorcerer.'

Anxiety blunted her Koriani perception; else Elaira would have noted the Mad Prophet's veiled lids and suppressed calculation. A nuance apparent to Parrien, caught sidelong from inside the stern cabin; s'Brydion cunning deduced the gist: before losing Rathain's precious blood-line, the Sorcerers would have a salvage plan. If they dissembled now, their abstruse machinations were surely already in motion.

Yet hours passed. Night fell to no change, beyond the climbing shrill of the wind, and squalling flurries that led in the storm front. The little sloop reeled, with Talvish strapped to a jack-line on deck, wrestling to tie reefs into the thrashing sails. One man could not control the rank helm. Parrien kicked Dakar from moaning prostration and forced his jelly-legged weight to assist. Tireless strategist, the s'Brydion also cornered the Mad Prophet's reticence.

'You know our next course change,' he accused straightaway. 'Don't prattle to me that you haven't had your marching orders from Althain's Warden!'

'We'll be making for Athir,' the spellbinder allowed, his discomfort plain through the shared effort to muscle the wheel-spokes. In the roaring dark, his sickly features showed steel: the mulish point past which nobody's mauling might move him. 'Once we've made our safe distance offshore, we'll steer north. No tricks, for my confidence. If you hope for a lawful reprieve from your felony, Parrien, you will chart the journey in safety. Best for all concerned if your crime is reduced from a life-threat down to a wounding. Pray that Arithon s'Ffalenn regains waking awareness before we reach our destined landfall.'

So began the difficult passage upcoast towards the desolate spit on Rathain's eastern shore. Amid testy hostility, and the murk of kept secrets, Arithon lay stilled in his berth. The unearthly peace that settled his features wrenched the heart for its changeless serenity. Opposite Dakar's uneasy reserve, Elaira's fraught worry pervaded the sloop's crowded cabin. Her harrowed focus ascertained that his early assessment had not hedged the truth: the nebulous limbo that gripped her beloved did not *yet* threaten survival. Arithon breathed easily. As long as his muscle tone resisted atrophy, she withheld from trying the arcane means that could entangle his fate with the Koriani Order.

Glendien's grief, also, found no release. In cruel separation from kinsfolk and clan, her mourning for Kyrialt had no outlet, except to assume her husband's abandoned post and guard the stricken crown prince. While Elaira slept, and Dakar groaned under flattening nausea, the clanswoman glared daggers at the duke's brother from her crouch beside Arithon's berth.

Yet the ice in Talvish's silence wore the hardest on Parrien's trapped state of penury. Watch after watch, through black storm and under the glittering, blue mornings feathered with cirrus, the blond swordsman shouldered each stint at the helm with his light humour cast into eclipse.

S'Brydion tenacity broke only once, the hag-ridden temptation too strong to resist when a fisherman hailed off the coast from Perdith rafted up for the purpose of barter. Dakar's odd insistence, that their sloop's onboard stores must be bolstered with long-term provisioning, stayed their passage an hour to onload sealed casks of salt meat and biscuit. With Talvish's muscle immersed with the lading, and the women belowdecks hiding Arithon, Parrien's sneak attempt to stow away on the lugger was thwarted by the spellbinder's detainment for cause, on the outstanding charge of crown justice.

'Only Arithon's word holds your fate in abeyance! As Rathain's prince, he alone can appeal for the grievance of Kyrialt's death, or call a reprieve for your mad act of slaughter against him.' While the cheerful fishermen cast off their lines, the sloop fell away, turned offshore again to duck hostile patrols, and

Eltair Bay's flow of Alliance-flagged commerce through Vaststrait. Dakar planted his obstinate bulk at the helm and shouted down his prisoner's seething rebellion.

'You will make no dire threats!' Knuckles clenched, brown eyes narrowed, he bristled like an unkempt spaniel flaunting a wolf's teeth. 'What had you planned? To browbeat that crew for their fishing craft?'

The pinned fugitive glared back. Arms crossed, he said nothing. Sore desperation did not reason, or answer to brangling morality.

'Forget your suicidal attempt to rejoin the warfront!' snapped Dakar. 'Run like a rogue, Parrien s'Brydion, and you'll face arcane force under rightful reprisal. By my charge to safeguard the royal lineage, you could lawfully be noosed as a murdering criminal.'

Even scalded to shame, Parrien's shrewd instincts gave warning: something *else* lurked beneath Dakar's outburst. Hidden pain, stuck like a thorn in the flesh, hazed his nerves beyond volatile. Set on wary guard, Parrien retired, and left Talvish to steer the next leg of their thrashed, winter passage to Athir.

As night fell again, the next clobbering storm whipped up the Cildein. The sloop reeled and tossed in the shrieking wind, with spars stripped and her helm lashed alee. The savage weather became everyone's gaoler, as hours of frigid, damp misery kept them huddled belowdecks with the galley stove doused to avert wild fire.

Parrien endured in hostile retreat, protectively curled in the forward cabin. Nobody else would dispute that rough berth, banged and corkscrewed by each hissing wave-crest. The wet salt on his cheeks was not due to the deck leak, when someone's invasive touch clasped his shoulder, softly arrived as a moth's wing.

His flinching spin and snarled oath met Elaira.

She held a lit lamp. Her severely neat hair was braided, and her eyes pale as smoke in the dimness. 'Glendien's with Arithon, for the nonce,' she explained, 'and we are not alone, having someone we love in grave jeopardy.' Her voice was unsteady, despite her held calm; a ghost's imprint against the pounding rush of frothed water, and scarcely a plank's width between the storm's fury, and drowning.

'Damn you!' snarled Parrien, before his throat closed with anguish for Tiassa and his four children. 'Why not hold the hand of your hobbled prince? Or do you seek revenge by jabbing my flanks with censure parading as kindness?'

Elaira hung the lamp from the ring in the deck-beam. Unhurried, against the sloop's gyrating roll, she pulled shut the louvred door. Even in anger, one must pity her hands. She had worked herself raw, poulticing wounds and grinding the herbals for astringent remedies. Now, the same dauntless mercy withstood the inimical stare fixed upon her.

She said gently, 'Please understand that your effort has not gone for naught, by steering this craft towards safety.'

His recoil came on a sharply checked breath.

She cut him off. 'Your wife is well, Parrien! Alestron's upper fortress has not yet fallen. I'd show you in full measure, that accepts no one's word, offered as a lame consolation.'

Surely, *past question* the harsh cold made him shudder. Parrien pulled the dank blanket around his bull frame, tucked up his chapped knees, and demanded, 'Why?' He could not remove her. Not if he manhandled her for rank insolence and bashed her backwards through the latched companion-way. Deeper than Tiassa's nerve-stripping rages, this woman: her provocation was *more than* witch-trained. Over and over, she displayed the fibre to match and ameliorate Torbrand's fettlesome lineage.

Parrien fought his tight chest. 'Should my desperate straits matter?'

Elaira attacked through his blistering spite. 'Not for your pride, foolish man, that snarls to hide your heart's weeping. I have come for your wife, who surely would settle the anguish of mind that torments you from sleep.'

Massive and war-scarred before her elfin frame, Parrien propped his jaw on his fists and glowered like a denned animal. 'You don't have that high-handed hold over me!'

The enchantress reached under her mantle and presented a clear crystal sphere. 'Try me?'

Her invitation awaited no answer. Already, her flicked rune cast the scrying his unbearable need in fact could not resist . . .

Night view opened up, of a scene boldly snatched from the midst of the Alliance war camp. There, under lamps in the Sunwheel pavilion, Lord Commander Sulfin Evend stood with Lysaer s'Ilessid, both men clad in the glittering regalia to commemorate the ritual burning and scattered ash of a convicted sorcerer. Which furore now set them in ranked opposition to the officers, who clamoured to close the campaign by unbridled aggression.

'We can take the filthy rat's warren down!'

'Bury the s'Brydion name and lineage in the rubble of their own battlements!'

'End the scourge that has strangled the trade in East Halla, protecting Atwood's barbarians!'

'Flush the lair that's harboured the Spinner of Darkness and furthered the hindrance of Fellowship sorcery!'

Above the howl to drive home a swift conquest, then savage the wreckage for spoils, Sulfin Evend slammed down his fist and gave the riot his icy refusal. 'Alestron's sea quarter is already ours! And you've witnessed the corpse of the Master of Shadow blasted to smoke by invoked Light and the hands of your priests! Impatience at this stage will only waste lives. Our galleys risk sinking each time we stage a new company onto the harbour-side landing. Alestron's last bastions won't need to be cracked, since our sappers have broken the cisterns. More than ever before, we sit tight and wait. Hold the defenders hostage atop their own walls, and let thirst and hunger deliver their surrender into our hands.'

When more outraged yelling disparaged restraint, Lysaer rebuked folly in scalding terms and fierce majesty. 'Are we hungry for death? Addicted to ruin? Has the horror of war and a sorcerer's wiles turned us into despoilers of women and children? Or are we the champions of hardworking craftsfolk, rightfully born to pursue decent lives and build honest security? I say now, under peril of my retribution, we stand proud and hold out for an honourable victory. My leave is not given to tear down a fortress like starving wolves set on a carcass!'

'The s'Ilessid pretender has changed,' murmured Parrien. 'How? Not through Fionn Areth's sorry demise! Don't tell me the burning of a false corpse has blindsided Desh-thiere's curse.'

'The Mistwraith's grip has not lifted,' Elaira affirmed, her grief for the hapless grass-lander's fate limned by the scene in the crystal. 'The staged ritual was a sop done to placate the troops. Endorsed by Lysaer, since Sulfin Evend's sworn witness correlated his curse-driven awareness that his half-brother had quit the arena. Now, Lysaer wrestles the warped urge to pursue on the strength first inspired by Alithiel's harmony. You have bought the distance to make reprieve possible. The farther away we move Arithon's influence, the more the geas wanes, and the more freely Lysaer's innate character can fight to reclaim his abused self-command.'

Unlike the false avatar last seen in Tysan, who inflamed men to wreak righteous slaughter, this sane appeal curbed fanatical zeal and promised mercy through civilian justice. 'Your Lord Commander serves my word of law!' the Blessed Prince appealed in dismissal. 'Arcane workings no longer threaten our conquest! Our lines shall stand firm for an ordered surrender. Every one of you! Carry on by my charge to spare Alestron's survivors from untoward cruelty . . . !'

'Pretty statesmanship won't let my brother back down,' Parrien said in flat irony. 'A cold day in Sithaer, before he bows his neck and flings open our gates to an enemy.'

'I know.' The admission was sorrowful. A pass of the enchantress's hand masked the crystal, then unveiled a flickering change. 'But hope always kindles through striving.'

A fresh view unfolded within the quartz sphere, drawn from another council of war, convened inside the besieged citadel. There, Bransian paced like a shambling lion before the trestle that seated Sevrand, and the dauntless, hard-bitten captains still holding Alestron's defence: heroes, who yet manned the cliff-top embrasures after the fall of the Sea Gate. All were besmirched by cinders and soot. Most gimped in blood-stained bandages. Bransian squinted through smoke-reddened eyes, against all the odds fired by grim purpose. 'I don't care blazes if the cistern's run dry! We are holding the walls! There's drifted ice mounding the inside baileys. More snow-melt running off the slate

roofs that our women are saving in catch barrels. We still have split rock to launch
from the trebuchets, and dulled swords aplenty that can be resharpened. By Ath, we
have the tools left to strike back! I will hear no more grumbling cant over losses! Tiassa
and Sindelle are not whining, as widows, and no s'Brydion babe gives me bawling
complaint that they're cutting their teeth on jerked horse-meat. My own do not falter!
We continue on! Until we are sucking the bones of boiled rats, this fortress will be
protected!'

Under the duke's irascible glare, belief never flagged, that the effort withstanding
the Light's siege might yet win the hour, or find unforeseen intervention . . .

Parrien scrubbed at damp eyes. Through the tacit pause, the enchantress cleared
the spent charge of her scrying and veiled the dimmed crystal back under silk.
Because she did not press, or try him with platitudes, he found civil speech.
'Thank you. I never properly acknowledged the fact that your action spared
me from falling to enemy hands as a hostage.'

'You would have been butchered outright when the sea quarter fell,' Elaira
gave acid correction. 'I shared Arithon's awareness, as he went down.' Agonized
by that memory, but sure of her ground, she finished as she intended. 'His
Grace's plea to stay Talvish's hand was not bleeding-heart mercy, but a surety,
delivered by the rogue far-sight of his s'Ahelas ancestry.'

'You say?' Parrien looked away. Scratched his beard, then heaved a sigh
like a staghound chastised for gutting a warren of rabbits. 'If I owe the runt
sorcerer a life debt, may the rainy day come that he has to collect. Needing
my help just might peel the man down to the lump in the clay that is
human.'

'The lump in the clay has been there all along,' Elaira declaimed, now amused.
'You both don your breeches one leg at a time. Though I swear, the Fatemaster's
list will be written and burned before either of you will admit it.'

Humour lifted the shadow of shame. Parrien could weather the passage to
Athir with at least the semblance of grace. If the Sorcerers made an appearance to try him, he would seize opportunity, rally his courage, and place an
appeal in behalf of his brother.

As if his stubborn resolve was transparent, Elaira laughed with kindly understanding. 'Sometimes such adamant, rock-headed strength opens the path to
create a changed outcome.' Her smile blurred by the swing of the lamp, she
added, 'We are both snagged by fate. But I will not give way to the pointless
belief that I am unworthy, or helpless. That was the one lesson I learned on
the streets, and a stance I chose not to abandon.'

Parrien looked at her. He realized she was not blind, but tenacious, altogether
too well aware her beloved's recovery swung over the abyss. 'Beware of your
Fellowship prophet,' he told her, forthright. 'At Athir, he may turn on your
interests.'

Her poignant smile resurged, rendered brilliant. 'My gratitude, Parrien. But

I need no one's warning. Dakar's intentions and mine lie at odds, beyond question, on the subject of Arithon's future.'

The harsh passage lasted for one fortnight more. Alestron's defences still had not fallen on the wind-swept, fair morning the courier sloop wore into the barren headland, where green ocean rollers smashed to lace spray, at Athir. Lest the exposed anchorage should draw undue notice, the stripped hull was scuttled the moment her supplies and passengers had been ferried ashore. Beyond the heaped dunes, atop a windy hillock, the roofless towers of a Second Age ruin stitched a crazy-quilt maze of stonewalls. An old right of way, winding westward towards Minderl, filled the nights with Paravian haunts. The wan silver gleam of ethereal presence made town-born mariners shy away. No one landed to fill casks at the wells, whose water still ran sweetly clear. Few could endure the cry of the breeze, singing over lost beauty in poignant lament.

Yet clanblood respected the voice of the free wilds, and initiate talent knew how to propitiate ghosts. Dakar invoked need under charter law auspices, for the sake of Rathain's threatened crown prince. Respite was granted, which let Talvish and Parrien's field-guided experience fashion a shelter of sailcloth and spars inside an abandoned courtyard. There, for three days, the small party laired up in wait for assistance from Althain Tower.

Yet the Paravian circle sited at the old ruin did not deliver a Fellowship Sorcerer. No attempt at scried contact raised answer. Sethvir maintained his obdurate silence, while uncertainty shortened balked tempers. Parrien's endless attempts to pick fights moved Talvish to drag him off hunting to fill the stewpot. Arithon regained no sign of awareness, though Elaira fatigued herself, trying. She weathered the cold, lonely nights set apart, with his limp frame clasped in her arms. The rhythm of his breath and heart-beat never once quickened to her murmured speech. His angled features stayed utterly lost, clothed in unearthly serenity. Though she listened, and threw herself into rapport, nothing answered her unpartnered cry but empty distance and vaster quiet. Far beyond the veil, Arithon danced at one with the star song, above the reach of her talent. Each morning, she rose and attended his clothes. Combed his black hair, and changed his linen. With Glendien gone to fetch water and wash, Elaira bared his marble skin and rubbed his raw scar with sweet oil. Until the dread hour that she paused with hitched breath, run chill by the stark recognition: her healer's touch sensed the insipid loss of resiliency in vital tissue.

'We are losing him!' she snapped in despair to Dakar, who sat cracking the marrow from the stewed bones left over from last night's supper. 'If your Sorcerers care for him, why aren't they here? Ath's blinding glory! I cannot bear to watch while his spirit abandons his flesh to slow atrophy!'

'You need not, for much longer,' Dakar said, abstruse. He stopped chewing cartilage, swallowed, and caved. After all, he could not brave Elaira's direct stare. 'I know of a way, only one, to recall him. But the chance taken must come at the cost of your guarding hold on his integrity.'

Elaira shuddered. Desperately tender, she covered the matchless, neat symmetry of Arithon's body: the exquisite hands that had bestowed pleasure on her; that always grasped life with such vivid intensity, now lying bitterly still. Gone was his laughter, along with the passion that sourced the well-spring of his musical talent. Silenced, the rages, so swift to defend his most vulnerable caring.

'Say on,' she demanded, pressed by reckless fear. 'I will not believe that Arithon chose to abandon his fate without fighting.'

'You will not like the method.' Dakar shivered, fussed by his glaring reluctance as he skirted the explosive disclosure. 'Winter solstice, at Athir, can be made to invoke Rathain's sanctioned tie through the land.'

Her recoiling cry, as she grasped the cruel gist, slipped her whitened lips before thought. 'No! That would conceive his child! Under Selidie's binding, I can't ever –'

But the spellbinder whose loyalty upheld the succession met her cringing nerve with no mercy. 'Then Glendien must assay the rite in your place. I have asked her, yes! She's already told me she's willing to try!' Against that horrified jolt of deception; into the teeth of an undying love's speechless fury, he bore in. 'Arithon swore an oath to survive in let blood to the Fellowship Sorcerers! Here, where his Grace knelt before Asandir to receive the seal over the knife-cut, the ocean sand keeps the imprinted charge of that promise. Koriathain! I tell you, on no terms do you realize the cause that marries the realm to an Atheran crown prince.'

Elaira stayed obdurate. 'You will not proceed with this!' Wild-cat angry, poised over her prostrate beloved, she lashed out. 'What friend would dare even *think* to betray him with another woman as surrogate! I'll not grant you the keys to Arithon's heart! Never for your unscrupulous usage to salvage the throne of Rathain.'

Dakar shrugged, already braced for that blast of indelicate argument. 'But I know the keys, lady.' Past grace, he insisted, 'They've been shared already, given into my keeping since the moment Kharadmon disrupted your misspent union in Halwythwood.'

'Dharkaron Avenge me for that violation!' swore Elaira, drained beyond pale. 'You wouldn't!'

Footsteps pelted, outside. Her distress had drawn notice. Glendien burst in, panting and flushed, her red hair soaked, and her clothing half-laced in a sprint from the well that expected to thwart bloody mayhem.

She stepped into a tempest; with her husband's drawn knife at guard point, and measured the furious combatants. Then saw Elaira's fingers, protectively clasped over Arithon's pillowed head. 'You've told her!' she snapped. Her vitriolic glance flicked back to Dakar, who was harrowed enough to cringe outright.

Elaira said, stony, oblivious to the tears that silvered her eyes. 'Glendien? How can you become a consenting party to *this*? You once tested Arithon's inner fibre! Could you sell out his helpless integrity while he's unconscious?'

Yet on that point, clan custom was adamant. 'I cannot let Kyrialt's death go for naught! My own gave himself to save Rathain's blood-line! How could I cavil, when what's asked of me is far less?' Since the naked blade in her hand was now trembling, Glendien rammed the steel into the scabbard. 'Once, Arithon said the life of my husband outweighed his personal dignity. For his honour's sake, should that choice be reversed?' Against Elaira's horrified pain, she defended, 'Would you let his Grace die? That's unnatural jealousy! I've agreed with Dakar. The attempt must go forward. Forget personal sacrifice! This may be the last chance we have to save the descent of Rathain's crown lineage.'

Elaira looked, one to the other, and measured the tenor of raised opposition: Dakar, with his mussed clothing and smudged, moon-calf face far removed from the scapegrace buffoon. Then Glendien's ripe and sensual allure, once defeated in a blazing assault against Arithon's private will, and now reclothed in the razor-sharp mourning of a widow's determination.

'By Ath, you're both serious.' Suspicion pricked through, that the adamant silence imposed by Sethvir *in cold fact may have been deliberate.* 'Tell me, Dakar! Has Althain's Warden withdrawn his counsel on purpose?'

Would the Sorcerers gamble with her wounded pride, that a royal birth might be snatched from the cross-roads of choice set before her?

Yet the spellbinder lacked a Prime Matriarch's connivance, to pour salt on the sting of her misery. 'No. Elaira, I can't lie. Not for this. The Warden bade me to bring us to Athir. Though I must speak for the weal of the land, whose power shall bid for Prince Arithon's life will be left in your hands to decide.'

'My voice casts his lot? Between Fellowship directives and the machinations of Koriathain?' Elaira withstood the urge to shut her streaming eyes; crushed the howling need to go deaf before forcing her harrowed wits to probe further. 'Then Sethvir steered you to this ugly course to restore my love's scattered awareness?'

'No.' Dakar found his courage and matched her regard. 'The inspiration was mine. Once, at Rockfell Peak, I linked awareness with Kharadmon. Rathain was imperilled. Lent the Sorcerer's insight, I observed as Arithon achieved a mastery that harnessed the lane tides. The imprint left me with the access to knowledge. In depth, I saw how the attuned tie at sanctioning binds a crown heir to the realm.'

Beside him, Glendien listened, endurance pitched to withstand grieving loss in support of a need that held meaning.

'That this accursed day had never arrived, or I had not been born to shoulder this sorrow, laid on me.' Elaira sat, shattered beneath the hurtful crux placed before her. 'Leave us! I can't bear your presence, or think!'

The choice became hers. If Arithon was not to be abandoned to death, she must decree which way the brand of lasting betrayal fell on him: to serve love's integrity, she must fulfil the vicious triumph of Selidie's high-stakes conspiracy. The Prime's implanted sigil would run its dire course, and a talented girl-child of her and Arithon's private begetting would be bequeathed to a lifelong enslavement by Koriathain. Or she must forsake the priceless gift of his heart: let Glendien's rape saddle him, or his offspring, with the burden of Rathain's royal heritage, constrained under the law by the Fellowship.

When Talvish returned, by Elaira's request, his sword stood guard for Prince Arithon. His oathsworn hand became her trusted bastion, as she walked the swept shingle to weigh her fate's path, under the cold stars of Athir. Love's grace lent her no surcease from her inner turmoil. She had no guidance, beyond her own heart; no word of reassurance to uplift or buoy her. Only the distanced memory of another night, lit by a fire the Sorcerer Traithe had laid on another desolate shore-line. His word to her then, imparted in kindness, had been of an augury shown to the Warden of Althain. For good or ill, she was the one spirit alive who would come to know Arithon best. *'Should your Master of Shadows fail you, or you fail him, the outcome will call down disaster.'*

A stumbling step, as a coarse stand of dune grass entangled her ankle. Winter wind and sea-spray were not cruel enough to strip her savaged nerves numb. The silvery sheen of the Paravian haunts showed her naught but their silence. Elaira pulled her damp mantle close. She swore herself breathless with rage, then, emptied, scoured her being for the wisdom gained from her study among Ath's adepts. *'How do you feel? What do you believe? Where does your heart's whisper lead you?'*

But the life she was asked to speak for *was not hers.* How did she dare to summon such courage, or fathom a judgement that set her responsible word over Arithon's survival? Give him to death, uncontested, or bid for his life through a binding compromise? Where did love cede her the right?

How would he feel? What did he believe? Where might his heart's whisper lead him?

Above her bowed head, through her agonized turmoil, the winter stars whose clear singing had drawn him past hearing shone down on her tormented grief. She cried to their implacable majesty, broken, 'How would my beloved choose for himself, if he stood here beside me?'

'Listen,' Arithon had said. Once, on the ship's deck, when Sulfin Evend's bared sword gleamed above him, thirsty to kill over principle, his thought had reached her like struck crystal. *'Listen!'*

But here lay only the voice of the land, bare of his human warmth and encouragement. The thrash of the ocean breakers rolled in, their tumbling rush hurling laceworks of foam that erased the print of her footsteps. Elaira sat on the chill crest of a dune. Sensed the place, there on the lonely strand, where a crown prince had sworn on his let blood to live, come whatever cost and against every concept of sacrifice. Knowing that Dakar must honour that oath, she sorted her disparate memories. One by cherished one, she reviewed her encounters with the mated spirit become an inseparable part of her. And there, she found Arithon's unalloyed words, framed by the trust of unbounded rapport, while she had been made one with his innermost being during his passage through Kewar.

'. . . *take my permission here and now,*' he had stated, with regard to the peril of entrapment posed through her by the Matriarch's meddling. '*Should my life become threatened, don't lie, beloved. Even had I not sworn my oath to the Fellowship, I could no more watch you die than cease breathing. My love for you will not suffer false promises. Honour my preference, but only if you are able. For myself, in plain truth, I lack the fibre to hold firm and see you take harm.*'

She *had seen* his depths laid bare to her then: before letting her perish, Arithon would have indebted himself to the Koriani Prime Council a hundred times over.

Could she do any less for his sake and not risk destroying the selfsame integrity by which he held his life sacrosanct?

While, in far-off Sanpashir a Biedar Eldest also shared waking vigil, Elaira addressed the black vault of the sky, mystery written across by the glory of Athera's constellations. These, the same stars whose Paravian Name wove the chord that endowed Alithiel's transcendent harmony, and now held her beloved spirit-bound. 'If I err acting in your behalf,' she addressed his cold absence, 'then I must lean on my faith in our love. Surely, between us, we can find the strength for an unbounded forgiveness.'

Against the raw wind, she arose, the race of her heart at last quieted. She left the shore and re-entered the ruin to shoulder the unthinkable course.

Inside the tent shelter within tumbled walls, a single rushlight stayed burning. A neat, clansman's fire boiled a stew that no one found stomach to sample. Talvish maintained steadfast watch by the pallet, guarding Arithon's inviolate privacy. Parrien looked on, alert as a weasel, as Elaira shoved through the canvas flap.

She faced Dakar and Glendien, then spoke her mind. 'This night, no one sleeps. I will not suffer longer, or stand aside while this limbo of dreaming robs Arithon's health and vitality.'

The spellbinder said nothing. If the clanswoman coveted a personal stake, she laid down the skinning knife used to clean pelts with the grace not to show untoward eagerness. As the tireless pound of the sea through the quiet stripped every vibrating nerve, Talvish made the soft inquiry. 'You'll not wait for the safer timing at solstice, or evoke the crown oath to the kingdom?'

Elaira lost voice. Withstood the awful, terrified moment she needed to bridle her terror. When she answered, she had steadied again, strengthened by icy conviction. 'The realm's throne has no claim, here. Arithon's adamant preference swore the blood oath to preserve his life. He did not bend his will for the weight of a crown when he granted commitment at Athir. I would rather remand him to a fight against enemies than consign him to the stagnation of traps spun by those who call themselves friends.'

Her passion broke through to fresh tears, as, *even now,* the fat spellbinder dared the breath to belabour her with reasoned protest.

'You wish your prince living?' she pealed, past restraint. 'Or dead of the trust that you *will* murder outright if you attempt the false road by manipulative betrayal. We will act now, or not at all, if my hand must direct the proceedings.'

Dakar shoved erect in the tumble of blankets that had not brought the comfort of sleep. 'You're insane!' he lashed out, appalled. 'You will use your love under vow and sell his Grace over to your Prime Matriarch?'

'No,' said Elaira, razed to dread for necessity. 'But I will take the lead in this dangerous dance. I need Glendien's help. And yours also, backed by the authority of the Fellowship Sorcerers. If you'll give clean consent to what has to be tried, here is how we're going to proceed.'

For what she proposed, there were no guarantees. Only bare hope, that Arithon's strayed spirit could respond to her love, impelled by no more than her bonded rapport, kept inviolate and untarnished. Parrien carried the unconscious prince to the site of the Paravian focus. There, Arithon was laid down, wrapped in Davien's black mantle, atop a rough bed of dune grass. If the lane force purling through the patterned stone inlay touched through to his distanced awareness, no colour quickened his flesh. The bitter wind flicked his hair, unregarded, while the darkness attendant upon his slack form remained fathomless as loomed velvet. Dawn seemed far off. The angled features lit by the torch Dakar held seemed no more alive than carved ivory.

Undaunted, Elaira asked Talvish to kneel. As trusted crown liegeman, his solemn oath to stand watch for Prince Arithon must be witnessed and sealed first of all. Elaira embarked upon every small safeguard. No part of the poisonous bargain she struck would be left to lapse, or fall forfeit.

The swordsman bared his blond head and crossed his hands on the hilt of Alithiel. Quiet voice clear through the thrash of the sea, beating the headland at Athir, he declared the terms of life service under which he extended protection. 'As I am appointed my prince's right arm, be assured of my word, sworn in my Name under grace of Ath's light, and upheld by Dharkaron's Black Spear should I falter.'

Elaira raised him with her own hands. Her swift embrace shored up his lanky height, as he lost words for her unbounded courage. 'No friend has done better,' she told him. 'Whatever comes, you hold as worthy a place as any of Jieret's Companions.'

Beneath the unshielded blaze of the stars crowning the sky overhead, she let Talvish go to assume his post on the line that demarked the south quadrant.

Of the barriers woven by Selidie's malice, and the entanglements blood-sworn to a Sorcerer, Elaira did as she must, and called Dakar forward to make disposition. She could not thwart fate without drawing, in part, on the knowledge derived from her order. Therefore, she asked the spellbinder to swear oath of debt, that no blank line should be left for Koriani interests to interpret. 'You will not bind over the Name of Arithon s'Ffalenn,' she decreed with explicit directness. 'The bond will be assumed against the Crown of Rathain, which must answer to Fellowship precepts.'

'Ah, clever!' crowed Parrien, against Dakar's stiff misery. 'Leave it to women, for stickling bargains to strangle posterity!' For the fine point she accomplished by invoking crown law would involve the Sorcerers, should the Prime Matriarch move to collect.

'I am not Sethvir, to read all angles of nuance,' Dakar warned, chilled beyond what the winter air warranted.

Elaira bowed her head. 'I don't claim that vision. My faith rests with your masters, who will keep their covenant. More powerful wisdom than yours, or mine, must determine how tonight's knot unwinds in the future.' *She would not risk their child; never chance the unconscionable betrayal, that the prodigious gifts of the Teir's'Ffalenn's lineage could become the vessel to shape the Prime Matriarch's ambition to groom a successor.*

Dakar ceded his case. To hold Elaira's love clear of the mire, and secure her help to spare Arithon, all else must tread the razor's edge: such brazen effrontery must serve to thwart the enslavement of an unborn child. Rife uncertainty triggered no errant augury, either to warn or to guide him; no contact from Althain Tower forbade, as he handed his torch off to Parrien. Committed, Dakar entered the circle at Athir. He embraced the midnight crest of the lane tide and assumed the binding that crossed the sedition of the Koriathain with Fellowship stakes in Rathain's undetermined accession.

The last, and most critical part became Glendien's, to assume by free choice. Clad in a loose robe that belonged to Elaira, her loose hair scented with herbals, she came forward with her impertinent wit as armour to shield the raw wound of Kyrialt's absence. 'Why sulk?' she accosted Dakar. The provocative pout to her lips was bravado, a poor effort to salvage torn pride. 'Don't we all get what we want in the end?'

'Don't cheapen your sacrifice.' With a depth of awareness untapped through five centuries of whoring debauchery, Dakar plumbed the fierce light in her tawny eyes and tested her feckless dismissal. 'Are you not offering up your own destiny in belated repayment for Arithon's selfless past gesture in Shand?'

'No.' Glendien ran her hands down her supple body, that beyond any question did not bear the quickened seed of her deceased mate. 'I give myself for the land's sake, and Kyrialt. This is not about my past blunders, or any flirtatious temptation to try the mettle of Rathain's prince. Keep your long nose in your own business, spellbinder! Enchantress or not, Elaira is woman enough to honour her private conscience.'

Already, the steps had been clearly laid out, with consent on acceptance made unconditional. The deep binding the enchantress proposed to entrain had been practised since time beyond memory by the order's advanced healers. 'You'll be enveloped by what feels like a normal sleep,' Elaira reassured the clanswoman as she made preparations. 'Throughout the duration, you cannot change course. Although your awareness will not leave your flesh, you will stay gently held under the threshold of waking.'

The Atheran crystal unwrapped in her hand as she scribed the first circle for arcane containment *also* would grant oversight to Althain's Warden. Sethvir could intervene, should objection arise, if his earth-sourced attention was not deferred elsewhere. Elaira evoked no darkening veil of concealment. The boundary laid down by her order's skilled surgeons *only* ensured that no sensation would cross the spelled barrier; they sought by their working to mask fear and pain. Yet since nothing planned here would mar the flesh, Elaira left the last loop in the intricate cipher unclosed.

She told Glendien, 'If you allow Dakar's trust to stand guard for your spirit's integrity, I promise to leave you with the record of what your body has known, to ascertain your dignity stays intact, afterward.'

But never the memory of Arithon's shared heart! That distinction was not left in question.

'My dignity's scarcely at issue,' declared Glendien. 'Ath above, don't I know? Your finicky prince is the one we're wringing ourselves dizzy, protecting.' The spelled circle was joined. She assumed the role given her; permitted Elaira to braid up her hair in the pattern familiar to Arithon's fingers. Provocative lest she should break in retreat, the clanswoman flipped Dakar a sensuous grin and crossed the grand arc of the focus.

Elaira raised the black cloak over Arithon. Endured the moment, unflinching, while the widow stretched out in cat comfort against his limp frame.

As unsettled to uphold the part that was asked of her, Glendien kept her insouciant courage. 'Do your utmost, enchantress. If his Grace will answer the cry of your need, just bring him back to us, singing!'

Elaira masked her face in cold hands. A deep breath lent no steel to fraught nerves. Tears at this pass would not lift the uncertainty: that if Dakar's hand failed her, or if the forces unleashed by the high flux at Athir burned through every herbal decoction, an unspeakable prize might be conceived of tonight's posited union. The most dire precautions might not be enough to wrest the chance-born possibility of a child away from the Koriani Matriarch. But earnest search had uncovered no better option: for Arithon's life's sake, Elaira must finish the frightening course she had charted.

'Parrien?' she summoned, too exposed for false calm. 'Put out the torch, if you please, and come forward.'

For the reckoning demanded that she lie down in trance, then gather the resource to spiritwalk. The surgeon's link, framed by the order's seniors to map internal damage for healing, would then be engaged to fuse her awareness into tuned rapport with Glendien's body. Hours might pass, in that altered state. *No one could map the fraught danger she trod.* If survival relied on her partnered effort to recall Arithon's strayed spirit, someone must keep her vacant flesh warm throughout the arcane transference.

Parrien s'Brydion arrived before her, embarrassed, but prepared to return the kindness he owed her. 'Although merciful grace! I am risking my married skin. Promise! Again! That you'll gag Glendien's tongue and keep this night's work from the twitching ears of my wife.'

Elaira found laughter to lighten his scowl as she allowed her shivering form to be wrapped in his mantle and cradled in his brawny arms. 'Should I have asked Dakar to watch your fresh hands?'

Last sight, against stars, before closing her eyes, the brief flash of teeth through wire beard: Parrien grinned, his bass rejoinder rumbling the chest pillowed under her ear. 'That's the fox set to guarding the hen-house, forbye. Like the mythical silkie, just be back in your own skin before dawn. No pretty woman stays in my lap when the need calls me to stand up and piss!'

Concatenation

The world turned, between breaths. The moonless spin of the stars seemed to hang suspended, momentarily sliced out of time. Farthest south, in Sanpashir, the same hush that gripped the headland at Athir also suffused the darkened desert. There, the revered who was Eldest sat amid the men of her council. Her listening patience sensed the closing cipher Elaira entrained: the glyph that permitted the spirit of one to enter into another, done as an act of shared harmony. The working was recognized from a rite her tribal people had known for uncounted millennia; and a secret that had been stolen away, from an origin that long preceded the diminished enclave now resident on Athera.

Yet the woman that an Araethurian seeress had once called *Fferedon-li* – the same also spoken to become the *affi'enia* forecast by Ath's adepts – as Koriani enchantress, she who was also named *anient* by Fire Hands did not impose the rogue sigil of forced mastery, as taught by her thieving order.

The freely made gift of compliant consent raised the ancient cipher to its original template. The same peaceful melding, formed in sacred ritual by the Biedar initiates to commune with the wise of their departed ancestry, now became repeated upon the Paravian grand focus at Athir.

The elder in service to Mother Dark's Chosen cried out and clapped wrinkled hands. 'Attend on this hour of the new moon! Our part draws nigh as hope for the wandering spirit becomes reborn. She who speaks for his heart must not fail! Or the gifted talent her beloved bears will not waken again in this world.'

Elaira reopened her eyes to cold darkness, clothed in warm flesh that *was not her own*. She steadied herself. Strove not to recoil from the unfamiliar comparison, or reject the vivid awareness of transfer. Discipline let her sink into accepting immersion. Glendien's presence was *there*, but cocooned in serene unconscious-ness. The opened channels for senses and touch recorded her earth-bound surroundings. The beat of the surf on the headland and the whisper of winter wind were the same as ever they had been. Yet the trained reach of initiate talent that extended beyond breathing form was Elaira's, the nuance of her spirit brought across intact for the vital purpose of healing. There, she was not disoriented. Her innate sensitivity thrummed to the pulse of raw lane force, coursing across the inlaid agate pattern that charged the focus circle beneath her. Beyond eyesight, she *knew* the man wrapped in the cloak at her side was the bone-and-blood form of her own best beloved.

Arithon. Urgency for him eclipsed other thought, made exigent as no move-ment met her. His fractious embrace did not welcome her in. Instead, torpid flesh absorbed her living heat, slack limbs and stilled face unresponsive. Elaira endured that grief, as she must. Forlorn, not disheartened, she rejected fear, that their paired strength could be rendered powerless!

The unearthly rapture that drew Arithon away left him deafened to tactile caresses. Mere animate reflex could not bridge that gap or reach his unbounded experience. To recall his consciousness, the ephemeral matrix must be redrawn, then sparked to rekindle his self-awareness. Glendien's form did not matter: the drift in his subtle interface was etheric. Elaira assayed the challenge, shed the herb-scented robe and tucked naked under the silk-lining of Davien's mantle.

Come what may, she steadied to sound the attenuated layers of Arithon's aura. Where Dakar would have gathered the lane flux from the land, then commanded in summons to refire his lapsed will through blood oath and crown obligation, Elaira eschewed overriding demands. Heart and mind, she began with the whispered intimacy born of her consummate love. That terrain, Glendien's fair charms and stern heritage did not own the power to replicate. Where a stranger must wake sensuality by rote, Elaira stitched a treasured and beautiful tapestry, gilded by partnered experience.

The hand laced through Arithon's wind-tumbled hair also knew the charge of his tempestuous passion. The features she cradled with poignant care carried the more vivid recall: of his opened eyes, trained in adoration upon her. If she ran her finger-tips *so*, down cheek and neck, then over his chest and across his vulnerable flank, with precision she *knew* how he preferred her touch. Where he responded to firmness and warmth, and how he shivered, when tendered in lightness. How, engaged in resonant harmony, his initiate focus released, undone in abandon until he became dazed by raptured delirium. She recalled the sweet moment of his hitched breath, as he gathered himself for shared pleasure. *Ached for* the delicious, unbearable pressure, while he shuddered and laughed, raised to match what was freely given.

Always, he reclothed that stunned flood of sensation into a masterful poise: let the fiercely held flame of his ardour fly majestically wild to captivate her surrender in turn.

She had all *his murmured words of endearment; had joined into seamless rapport with the thundering force of his presence, whirled at one with the lane flux in Halwythwood.*

Memories the spellbinder could never recast, except at second hand, pallid reflection. If that searing, grandiloquent spiral had been smashed short of explosive requital, the languid nights Elaira spent in Arithon's embrace at Alestron had rewoven their explicit love into a matchless intimacy. Each moment, and each remembered caress kept, as jewel-bright, in a setting of untarnished tenderness.

Tonight's rite would not breach that trust. If Arithon woke, he would feel, first of all, the inviolate symmetry of union unbroken between them.

Now, the drastic absence of his awareness became her most daunting obstacle. The template Elaira asked his flesh to rebuild denied her the gift of his reassurance. This hour of congress could not cherish, as honey, the tactile joy of senses tuned into concert. Her welling tears must not pain him! Though she felt no trembling, exquisite tension answer the sounding board of his skin, her intent dared not waver. She stroked him over, each fingertip certain in familiar sequence. No matter how one-sided the touch, she persisted, listening with fervent intensity. Seeking, she invited. Provocative, she extended her healer's awareness and *reached,* striking always to raise his reactions, but in the higher octaves of spirit light. To succeed, she had to arouse what extended beyond nerve and flesh.

'Dearest, my own,' she whispered.

Words evoked vibration, even though Arithon's displaced attention ranged beyond human hearing. The reverent appreciation described by her hands enacted a dance that also – *she knew him*! – spoke past his reflexive defences. His living memory, she wove as a net, until her remembrance stretched the cry of true partnership into the realm of exalted creation. The suspenseful caresses were hers, plied with a love that made her regard as the mirror to reflect his very self.

Immaculate concentration steered her, until no exquisite part of him was left cold. Hands laced through his, pressed against his warmed flank, she reached farther, to gather the Name of him. Her own faculties raised to preternatural clarity, she let her pitched adoration lace over and through him. Humility mapped his being in *all* his splendour: embraced, but did not try to bridle the essence of what could never be tamed. She kissed him, a kindling call beyond words, forged out of her matchless devotion. As the flesh she wore for him blazed for his presence, entrained with the light that was spirit, the flux current honed through the focus at Athir infallibly imprinted her fused emotion. As mate to crown prince, the lane force flared up, called to answer the flame of its rightly tuned match. . . .

The dazzling shift in the flux streamered outward. Like the opening note struck from a taut string, raised power laced like ephemeral lightning the length of the seventh lane. Dakar saw the heightened coruscation through mage-sight; felt the prickling surge lift the hair at his nape. His awed gasp breathed hope. 'Ath above! She's called the land's current into response. Do you sense the thrill? The very ground underneath us is quickening!'

Parrien s'Brydion dared not reply. Amid winter dark, a cut shadow defined by the gleam of the stars, he cradled the enchantress's vulnerable flesh in his sheltering arms. Her courageous endeavour *had* to succeed. Else he would forfeit his chance for reprieve from the charge of a crown prince's murder. On Arithon's life hung his family's survival, a grace he had not held the fore-thought to grasp in the furious moment his sword had struck home.

Nothing must upset the spiralling song, or alter the delicate balance. The first coil of the mystery had been unleashed. Latent charge flooded the focus. The agate inlay flickered, then brightened, unveiling to sight the living pulse within the Paravian pattern. Elaira's challenge was fully joined, no avenue left for retreat.

Chilled by his knowledge as Fellowship spellbinder, Dakar trembled before growing fear. Failure now would not forgive a mistake. The grand union Elaira strove to recall must retrace *without error* the experience broken off in the oak glade at Halwythwood. One slip would bring chaos to burn human flesh. Nor could any protection he offered deflect the impact in consequence. The building stream of the flux woke his seer's gift, as the forces entrained by crown heritage raised the pulse of Athera's electromagnetics. The Mad Prophet felt the warning sting through his feet: sensed the hook snag the weave, as the clean emanation from Athir flagged the distant notice of unfriendly interests.

Prime Selidie had scryers busy at Telzen. *Their circle was tracking the lane tide, aware, and poised for a hostile counter-thrust.* Should the raised chord of grand confluence command the conception of a royal heir, the Matriarch lurked to seize full advantage, and snatch her prized stake on the outcome.

Against such betrayal, Talvish's shining loyalty guarded Elaira's south quadrant. There, Dakar acknowledged a choice that outstripped ceremonial precaution. If the Warden at Althain was also entrained, the spellbinder made to stand as the Fellowship's formal witness pleaded by every power of grace! Let him not become the available instrument, hurled into the onrushing breach . . .

Far southward on the black sands of Sanpashir, the circle of tribesmen led by the crone who defended Mother Dark's Chosen *also* noted the sparkling leap as the flux line at Athir blazed active. The shaping event matched the weave of a prophecy, guarded in hope for millennia.

As Eldest, she gave her signal command, whisper soft as the breeze. 'We stand at the crossing. Begin.'

The men in her service accepted the charge, handed down from a history beyond living memory. Into the silence of pending event, poised on the stretched wings of destiny, they blended their gifted voices in song. The power they wound into patterned tonality braided a knowledge that predated language. With gentle reverence, the Biedar elders framed their appeal to summon the wise of their ancestry from beyond the veil. The delicate notes they sustained woke a resonance vivid as unearthly fire. At Athir, their uncanny working caused the inlaid agate focus to echo in subtle refrain.

Sound melded with light, brought to bear through the cipher Elaira had used, unwitting, that harked back to the Biedar tribe's origins . . .

The crux rested on her. She held the focal point for *all* moving forces, immersed, single-minded, in shaping her love as the beacon for Arithon's recovery. No other thought touched her. Her will shone, as crystal. Rapt attention guided her forward. Her regard never left Arithon's features, or she would have seen other powers evoked by her outreach: would have shared the breathtaking cry of the miracle, as the Second Age wisps of Paravian ghosts flocked towards the blaze of the circle.

There, the shades of the past gathered, shining. Limned on the night air like pearlescent floss, came the horned majesty of past centaur guardians, feathered hooves, and tall torsos muscled. They carried the massive, dragon-spine horns slung upon stitched leather cross-belts. Silenced, arms folded, they towered above the diminutive grace of the sunchildren, who whirled, care-free, underfoot. Lost in time, left as a dazzling imprint, the merry dancers spun and leaped to the measures unreeled by the surf. Their joy raised emotion that could *almost* be sensed, though the ethereal peal of their crystalline flutes lay centuries removed from the present. Their wisped movement still held the echo of magic. The stone focus rang to an age-old renewal, from a time that could be yet again: when, as a burning, gold river of flame, the Riathan – the unicorns – might gallop in thundering herds to the summoning, manes tossing and polished horns gleaming.

Living bridge, they had been, to the cry of Ath's glory, free as wind to embody the wildest heart of the mystery.

While Dakar wept, and Parrien sat dumb-struck, and Talvish gripped Alithiel's sheathed hilt, Elaira, rushed dizzy, knew only Arithon. For her, the man sharing Davien's mantle seemed all that existed in the wide world.

She played the dark silk of his hair through her fingers. Kissed his lips with her own, lit to burning. 'Only you. Always. Beloved.'

She rewove the essence of him, strand by sure strand, each line of his body revisited under her hands. The surge of her arousal laid him under bold claim, until singing rapture *must* answer. She savoured by the ineffable music of touch, until his remembrance flooded the core of her: the spare fitness that shaped profound grace when he moved, as treasured as her own heart-beat. Breathed into the reverence of undefiled memory, Elaira poured herself through the high octaves as light. Warp through weft, she gathered him into a fabric of consummate caring. While the focus beneath magnified her emotion, then burgeoned from violet to gold, she wrapped Arithon in love, until the trembling cry of her unpartnered spirit reforged the lost flame of desire.

Beneath her, through reflex, his flesh hardened and rose. She answered him, delicate. Easy and slow, her tenderness whispered, skin on heated skin, fused into surrender past bearing. She eased herself deeper, then deeper, guided by spirit into the tranced clarity that tuned her awareness to the upper registers. The act of the body now a distant echo, she lifted the song to take flight in ecstatic melding. The path was well cherished. Her hands knew the way. He had given the keys: shown her how to access his vulnerable core, there to unwind the spiralling shield of his innermost defences. One by one, Elaira accessed the wide-opened flux points; let her own lowered barriers spark through the breach. Drowned under the blaze of exalted embrace, she laid her cheek on his. Kissed his face with her tears and allowed her twined energies, *ever so gently,* to enter his unguarded heart.

Around her, beneath her, in fixed star above, the lane forces at Athir ignited to actinic fire. At one with her beloved, Elaira was sheeted in fountains of light.

There, at the crux that promised hope and joy, she stilled and *asked* for his inner permissions – and almost lost her grip. The insistent drive towards reflexive completion *nearly* whirled her over the edge. Somewhere, Elaira found purposeful strength. She resisted. Cried out, then held back the consuming plunge, *his and hers,* that must not achieve climax unpartnered.

'Beloved. Arithon!' She gasped the fraught plea to reclaim his awareness. Past the bittermost drive of her need, through the crucible burn that onrushed towards confluence, she must endure, yet. Gentle the savage, animal onslaught, until she poised at the hanging point of trued balance. As the lane forces fired, then towered, then blazed, *she had to sustain the drawn crest by herself.* Withstand the tension, *wait,* and hold on. She must! Shuddering, wrung heart-stopped and breathless with splendour, she fought to stay entrained without snapping until the shattering shout of raised earthforce could ground the uncanny allure of the star song.

Arithon!

She sensed him, *there,* alive and still enraptured. Her yearning spirit reached out to him. First touch, and the tearing sweetness of the chord he experienced ripped down her nerves like white fire. The danger, once started, could not be reversed: that she might not withstand the unbearable edge. Surrender to ecstatic union too far, and she might slip the casing of her borrowed flesh. Lose her tenuous grip in the lane tides at Athir, and she would be swept away, swirled into immersion along with him, there to die entranced to forgetfulness . . .

Dakar's pealed outburst passed unheard in the torrent. 'Don't try!' he warned Talvish. No hand could reach the twined couple, now. The blast of the flux current would hurl even the strongest man off his feet. Every mind in proximity was reeling, all but stunned into black-out unconsciousness as harmonic forces shimmered towards peak.

Sethvir, at Althain, *must be aware.* If the Sorcerer heard, the torrent that razed through his earth-sense did not prompt any saving assistance.

Were the Koriani scryers still entrained, they would be deafened and blinded. No Matriarch's reach could command the unleashing power that fired the flux. Her most potent sigils would become ripped asunder, undone by torrential harmony.

At the centre-pin of the gyre, the choice was unmalleable. Break the cascade, and flesh would burn, wracked skin from bone by chaotic disruption. Or allow the event its unbridled, full course, and let the two spirits entwined at the focus become swept beyond reach past the veil.

'We are losing them both!' Dakar cried in despair.

He could do nothing, *nothing at all*! Only watch, aggrieved, while white light and sound rocked into keening crescendo. Joined at the crux, Elaira and Arithon now led the storm that must release a shower of bright exaltation. Unstoppable force, as the star song entangled with the exploding flare that annealed the land circle at Athir. Joined under such influence, a crown prince and mate *would enact a royal conception*. Rathain's need would bear fruit as due consequence. But at such a cost, the brave heart could not contemplate; nor could thought lament, or seer's talent shift the course of that frightening flash-point . . .

The crone at Sanpashir alone did not falter. The time and the hour had been her kept charge, since her affirmation as keeper of Mother Dark's Chosen. Her word aimed the might fashioned by her male singers for release at the tingling crest. Into the burn of wild forces at Athir, while the lane tide scorched towards peak, the tribe's revered eldest unleashed the full-throated cry that called down the wisdom of Biedar tribe's hallowed ancients. Into the listening pause that ensued, across a gap, torn through time, she also hurled her bold appeal to the Warden at Althain Tower.

'I choose to call in *Anshlien'ya*'s debt!'

Hope's promise, now reclaimed, from another, prior conception enacted five hundred years in the past. When, as an act done in free consent, spun under the influence of the tribes' singing, a young maid who had been the last-born of s'Dieneval's prophets had crossed her blood-line with Shand's royal heritage.

Dari s'Ahelas had sprung from that night's union, and young love, in the heat of Sanpashir's black sands.

Let Sethvir dare to deny the Biedar their right to influence tonight's culmination! The Fellowship Sorcerers *would* yield their fierce claim. *Due answer was owed, for what the desert tribe had granted at the behest of the Ilitharis Guardians*: a bright light for the future, and continuance for a kingdom, when Shand's crown succession had been the inheritance facing sure threat of extinction.

Where Sethvir gave naught but cold silence at Athir, the Biedar crone received the sweet gratitude of his release. *'Madam, I daresay I have little choice but to bow to your foresight on all counts.'*

The crone chuckled, amused. Her grasp stayed firm on the matrix of power that arrested the trembling moment. 'You have seen where this leads as Athera's caretaker?'

Sethvir sighed. *'Not all. But enough. I will have to accept the bitter-sweet sorrow for what your kind must ask of me.'*

The crone narrowed her eyes. Experienced beyond knowing, she never left the least thread of doubt under question. 'Swear your bond now on behalf of your Fellowship.'

'My oath rests, that the father must never hear of the birth, or acknowledge the daughter delivered from this night's mating.' Sethvir's courage was adamant. *'You would not intervene, but through dire necessity.'*

The Biedar eldest inclined her white head. While the winds sang over the trackless dunes, and her singers wove skeins of ephemeral light through the gleam of night's constellations, she whispered the one truth she had to balance the Sorcerer's harrowed decision. 'This child shall come to spare her father, one day, dispossessed of his knowledge of her paternity.'

In his fast eyrie at Althain Tower, Sethvir's distanced eyes welled over. Tears streaked his worn face. He answered aloud to the same winter stars that shone through his eastern casement. 'Then, madam, I beg that you ask for such grace. In free will, by her royal gift of compassion, let Arithon's daughter choose for herself when the time comes to shoulder her fate.'

The crone's wrinkled smile was gentle. 'Caretaker! We are the sworn enemy of the Koriathain, and never the same, to wield arcane power as unscrupulous tyrants! This child, conceived under the old Biedar cipher, will bear the endowment of our tribal ancestry. She will not arrive breathing, *except* by consent! Witness my given word! The path walked by the daughter of Mother Dark's Chosen will stay impeccably true, and quite fearless. Let her raising begin as Dari's, under your own peerless guardianship.'

'For her father's life's sake, then, her life path is yours,' Sethvir whispered, saddened. 'Kept under the Balance, our ends are the same. Proceed with my blessing.'

The crone opened her hands. The forces held captive rushed into release. As an arrow shot flaming through the crested surge unleashed by the confluence at Athir, the convergent array of multiple futures resolved into *one*, with the legacy claimed by the Biedar ancients threading the consummate breach.

A net of gold light unfurled through the cipher Elaira had enacted to share Glendien's flesh.

The binding held true to the cloth of its origin. The enchantress whose intent had reforged the old template stayed entrained by that untarnished thread. Lost to herself, she was not beyond reach of the wisdom that guarded the annals of a mighty tradition. Enraptured by the strains of the star song, entwined with the essence of Arithon, Elaira knew *only* the strength of her love, while the wrought design of Biedar tribe's making unfurled, then surrounded, and granted the grace of benevolent shielding.

Black-out followed the deluging blast, an unconsciousness deep beyond knowing to shelter the fragile flame of mortality. Elaira's exhausted awareness stayed veiled while the blaze of ancestral protection enfolded her being. She was spiralled down, gently. In silence tenacious as her fierce passion, the consciousness of her beloved was also swept out of entrancement. Realigned under the bliss of grand confluence, anchored into the land by his crown tie of attunement, Arithon's strayed spirit became annealed back into his forgotten flesh.

Where he could not have stayed, too long sundered from reason, the wise of the Biedar sang of an ineffable wholeness. Their healing secured the shocked fields of his aura as the surging crest waned, then coiled back towards quiescence. Since hours would pass before he recovered the stream of resurgent sensation, the desert tribe's elders spun him the solace of sleep. Cradled as though Named by a summoning, Arithon rested under the stars, and no longer enthralled in distanced splendour, scattered among them.

Stymie

The exalted release just completed at Athir found Selidie Prime balked outright from her prized objective: Arithon Teir's'Ffalenn was not captive or dead. His talented child, of Elaira's conception, would not be born, or sealed under Koriani auspices. 'We've been thwarted! The babe whose future I engineered to acquire will be carried instead by an ignorant, free-wilds clanswoman!'

The Matriarch's astounded fury smashed through her coquette's poise. She erupted from her seat by the fireside. Her tigerish step and shrill curses disrupted her circle of tranced seniors. A kick of her slippered foot sent two of them scrambling, out of her path.

The dim, curtained chamber, with its wealthy trappings and costly carpet, only heightened her caged agitation. Eyes snapping, Selidie quartered the space commandeered for her use, where the seventh lane's flow crossed through a mansion in the port town of Telzen. The merchant's wife whose claimed debt lent the room had an obsessive penchant for fripperies. A back-handed swipe of the Matriarch's crippled fist sent a glassware vase flying. The trinket smashed against the brick hearth.

Across the tinkling tumble of shards, the Prime muttered, 'Save us all!' This bitter defeat ran beyond inexcusable. *One rebellious initiate's deviation from the steps of established practice had wrought a disastrous break!* Principles influenced by Ath's adepts had opened the gateway to hamper the order's internal affairs. 'Elaira has aroused the sleeping might of our ancient enemy in Sanpashir!'

Dharkaron's hand on her! No miserable, cross-grained third-rank healer should have *mattered* enough to raise the attention of old Biedar power! Who could have foreseen such determined invention might thwart a reigning Prime Matriarch?

Selidie hammered a tapestry in frustration, the gemstones on her embroidered mitts glittering like lightning unleashed. 'Bedamned to the defection of Enithen Tuer!' And worse ill, to plague the lost Sorcerer Ciladis, whose prior meddling in the distant past had denied Koriathain their earlier bid to claim the issue of Meiglin s'Dieneval in the first place!

While Selidie fumed, raging over old scores, Lirenda sat silenced in passive constraint. She received no order to release her entrained state of tranced subservience. The elderly scryer bidden to serve as her Prime's eyes was compelled to maintain her rapt focus as well, her quartz sphere attuned to recapture the event on-going upon the sand point at Athir. Patient, she waited, plying her skills, while the Matriarch raved, and the white-out blaze of confluent energies subsided over the Paravian circle. Minutes passed by, before the flux stream calmed enough for trained talent to garner a stabilized image.

'Your will, Matriarch?' the seeress probed gently. 'I have regained sighted access to the seventh lane focus.'

Selidie paused, pale eyes darting with hope. 'Have we a single point of leverage left?'

The ranked senior sighed. 'Matriarch, none.' Her crisp recap confirmed the rife disappointment: 'The feal liegeman still blocks the south quadrant.'

Selidie hissed through locked teeth. No use, to test that stubborn avenue further. All of Lirenda's usurped power, and every sigil to command binding influence had failed to move Talvish's character. Unassailable loyalty could not be suborned, or pushed by imbalance to sow errant havoc. Whatever coercion the Prime's seniors applied, the true liegeman's aura rejected the conjury slipped through the flux to entrap him.

'Our downfall, that the fellow has no insincere aspect for us to exploit.'

'Then use Parrien again!' Prime Selidie snapped. 'That ready pawn should succumb through his livid resentment towards Rathain's prince.'

'Your pardon, Matriarch.' The seeress sighed again in pressured distress. 'The s'Brydion brother has embraced a truthful regret. The latent channel once forged for our purpose has been closed by a healer's influence.'

'Elaira's doing,' Selidie snarled. Where had the chit found such strength, to release the hurt of a man whose crazed passion had nearly accomplished Arithon's murder? Fuming rage only mounted, as the dismal report kept unfolding. Elaira's adventurous spiritwalk had ended. She now rested, securely resettled within her own flesh.

'Asleep, even if you elect to recall her, or revise her orders through oathsworn obedience.' A slight pause, as the seeress hesitated.

'There's *more*?' Selidie kicked a carved footstool tumbling out of her path. 'Tell me!'

Head ducked, hands laced to still her scared trembling, the seeress delivered the last snagging detail. 'The Biedar weaving has unravelled your inset sigil of conception. We cannot shift the course of our current reversal. The protective veil raised by the desert tribe's ancients will not release Athir's focus until after Prince Arithon's waking. If you wish to command Elaira's return, you must dispatch a galley across Vaststrait to collect her.'

Pushed to the end of resourceful machination, Selidie lashed out again. An enamel bowl sailed, clanging into the wall, to a chipped scatter of plaster. 'And Glendien? What about the clan tart borrowed through consent as surrogate?'

But the scryer's list remained unremitting. 'Awake as well. Taken into Dakar's direct custody.' No need to belabour the unpleasant fact, that a Fellowship spellbinder of Asandir's making would grasp the scope of her rights as a mother with child by royal descent.

Selidie wheeled in livid explosion. 'To our ruin!' How much had Davien the Betrayer foreseen, when he had insisted the fire-brand snip of a wife should accompany Kyrialt's liege-bound course to Alestron? Worse, the feckless young widow could never be touched! *The Sorcerers would shelter both mother and babe: a daughter bred for a peerless rogue talent, made and meant to be claimed under oath of debt and subject to Koriathain!* 'Show me something to mitigate this accursed day!'

But the seeress had no further angle to pursue. Worse, the gloating triumph behind Lirenda's eyes all but mocked the Prime's sore ignominy. Of all initiate witnesses, the fallen favourite alone dared to smirk as the grandiose plan spun through years of conspiracy collapsed into savourless dust. Only Lirenda knew of the ruinous augury Morriel once had garnered through the Great Waystone: the latent danger – not yet defused! – that named Arithon s'Ffalenn as the living cipher who could sunder the Koriani Prime's hope of succession.

Unaware such a massive threat darkened the future, or that Lirenda burned yet for the chance to wrest back her forfeited access to rank, the dutiful seeress gestured over the image captured in her attuned quartz. 'My Prime, if you would engage the Great Waystone –'

'Silence!' Selidie smothered the raced seethe of her blood. She was utterly hobbled, as Lirenda knew also, with fullest demeaning embarrassment! The amethyst focus, which *could have enabled* a stand against Biedar power, was still wretchedly infested by an errant *iyat*. No one else was aware of that plaguing mess, inflicted by Arithon after the misplayed attempt to use Feylind against him. Until means could be found to excise the fiend, the order's supreme tool of mastery remained compromised.

Selidie whirled and stalked back to her chair, molten magma quenched to white ice. Today's board had been swept! Naught else could be done but keep cold watch and wait: poise like the spider, and spin a new web, seeking for means to try fresh intervention.

'This round might be finished,' the Prime Matriarch declared, her barbed malice aimed towards the stilled well of cold *no one* other than she could discern: the rankling affront, lurking in the room's corner through brazen, *unbearable* nerve! That Luhaine's invasive presence should come prying drove the day's toll of insult and injury beyond pardon.

Selidie spat venom between her spare lines. 'But at what cost; the Sorcerer's victory?' Ruined hands tucked in her violet skirts, she glared at the Fellowship shade with fierce hatred. 'As I live and breathe, mark my warning! After Arithon's daughter is born, the Seven had best watch her back night and day, and defend her with unbroken vigilance!'

Luhaine's sole response to the poisonous threat was departure, at thought's speed, for Athir. The next instant, the seeress's quartz sphere went dark, its scried image doused blank by his warding influence.

Dawn-light

While daybreak infuses the focus at Athir, Luhaine engages the tide of the lane force and transports Glendien to safe refuge at Althain Tower; and while Dakar remains to keep guard at the ruin, he knows his part in the past night's events have severed a trust, and that his service to Rathain's crown prince has ended in favour of resuming his former apprenticeship . . .

At Alestron, the drums boom as the war host turns out in resplendent panoply to send off the state galley bearing the Divine Prince; and as the flagship's flotilla embarks, unimpeded, for a return to Tysan to succour Avenor, Sulfin Evend retains full command of the siege as the avatar's voice for the Light . . .

Restored to shelter inside the Second Age ruin, now flushed with resurgent life, Arithon s'Ffalenn wakes under Talvish's guard, wrapped in blankets alongside Elaira; unaware of the crisis that passed in the night, content in the grace of her presence, he winds her sleeping form in his arms and pillows his face in her perfumed hair . . .

XVI. Scarpdale

When Seshkrozchiel took flight to challenge the spectre ensconced in the barrens of Scarpdale, her course did not traverse time and distance. Such bounds did not limit the remnant dreams, when a great drake died unrequited. Neither did a living dragon's perception own any concept for warding or barriers. Form could be made and unmade on a whim. The perception of the world's eldest beings acknowledged no linear beginning and knew no idea for a finite ending.

Seshkrozchiel engaged will to encompass the ranging echoes raised by the haunt's vivid yearnings. The vortex spun by its seething restlessness drove her wing-beats across a shifting montage of dreamscape. She accepted the raging discharge at first as whole cloth: whether stilled, moonlit forest, or hail-pelting storm front, or unfolded valley of volcanic cinder, steaming with the mineral geysers that drake kind preferred to polish their scales. Seshkrozchiel gathered in the streaming emanation that loomed ephemeral thought to full-bodied creation, then altered and remapped the framework to restore Scarpdale's disrupted symmetry.

For Davien, whose presence lodged in her left pupil, the effect was to watch the ground under her wing strokes pale like dye rinsed by flood from a tapestry. Scarpdale had been laid waste since Athera's antiquity, an upland plateau scarred into a barrens when two rival drakes had done furious battle. The vales that summer would mantle in wildflowers now wore wind-swept brown grass and scrub thorn. Chill streamlets meandered, scabbed by winter ice, their stony banks clumped with skeletal trees.

Now, the haunt's warring rage laced the terrain like shed lightning. Set into flux by the tidal bore of its fury, the solid earth would shimmer, then vanish into chaotic patchwork. Sometimes, such vistas framed fragments of memory, tinted by wistful nostalgia: places where dragons had sailed the world's winds, or danced in exuberant, winged aerobatics. Then, Seshkrozchiel's outstretched pinions would glide above forests of towering, summer-crowned oaks. The breeze of her passage rustled green leaves, or else sliced against the screaming gales that combed clouds over serried peaks. Her shadow might ripple across slopes chiselled under groaning, white glaciers. Othertimes, the haunt's recollection shaped an expanse of violet ocean, hurled into spume by a squall, or spread as a dimpled mirror of calm, under streamers of gold sunset cirrus. Flight scribed through the vault of limitless blue skies, noisy with flocking birds, or twisted through updraughts and thunder-head ramparts. At times, tail sculling in serpentine loops, Seshkrozchiel drifted, serene, above deserts clustered with delicate thorn plants. The hillocks lay paint-box purple and mauve, with dry river-beds that stabbed sudden, sun-caught reflections off mica and glittering mineral.

Always, her might flowed across the haunt's errant current of thought. Where she passed, its unquiet creation would fade into shimmering rainbows, then resurge, knitted back into the wintry wilds of Scarpdale.

The shift occurred without visible seam. So precise was the living dragon's restraint on encounter with outside awareness, she dropped nothing: no fragment of chert, no bounding hare, and no flying hawk over frost-dormant tussocks. Not even the sleeping mouse in its den became lost from the face of existence. Seshkrozchiel sensed the template for their return: every frail leaf on its unbudded twig, and each rustling stalk of dead grass. Such presence emerged, individually intact. The passage of wind, cloud, and puddle, and the angle of sun's moving shadow resolved, past reproach for the haunt's renegade interruption.

Yet the dragon knew naught of the creatures she shaped, though her eye imprinted detail with rhythms of memorized poetry: she could number the rings on the carapaces of the tortoises, buried in hibernation, and puzzle together the fragments of egg-shells that had hatched nestling birds the past spring. Despite that vast repertoire, she could not recognize the current of spirit made voice, that underpinned a live being. Her ear could not fathom the tuned identity in the vibration struck off a crystal. Seshkrozchiel enacted these things in command of a masterful majesty, but as a mirror would copy reflections. The unfoldment of Scarpdale occurred by rote, a glorious discipline of assembled nuance, unbiased by cognizant empathy.

Her emotions detected no harmonious communion. Such was the nature given to dragons since the embodiment of Ath's creation.

Today marked the advent of perilous change. As Seshkrozchiel raked through the spiralling vortex sown by the haunt's enraged spirit, she carried the bargain struck with a Fellowship Sorcerer.

Once she had loaned her vast power to Davien, enabling his translation from spirit back into flesh. Now, as her price, called in to curb the desecration arisen from Mankind's mishandling of four dragonets, the Sorcerer's fused being embellished the moving enactment of her awareness. All that Seshkrozchiel perceived shared the dynamic of Davien's experience.

She had always recognized the functionality, *busyness*, and streams of synergistic purpose, where life flourished in crowding abundance. She understood complex efficiency. But this upsurge of surprised pleasure was novel: Davien's joyful delight in the juxtaposed tumble of landscapes shocked the accustomed range of her senses.

'*Beauty,*' Davien supplied, as she queried what was inexplicable.

His human appreciation was utterly new. The artistic leap, found in colour and form, and the esoteric thrill that sparked in response to resplendent invention was *not dragon*. Which bursting discovery wrought wonder and change: Seshkrozchiel grappled a concept that altered her innate perception. Another aspect of *symmetry* bloomed, heretofore unknown to her kind.

'*Attend Scarpdale's wholeness!*' Davien sent in reminder. The intent they pursued must not lapse into bemusement. Else the naked influence of the dead dragon would seize ascendancy and destroy Athera's myriad continuity. Already, the fabric of Lanshire's dales failed to resurge into flawless stability. Seshkrozchiel soared ahead, tail flukes lashing. Her intense cogitation generated energies that fuelled the coruscating flame of her aura: *and something stayed wrong.* Flux emanation streamed from her dorsal spines, as she skimmed the breeze above a verdant prairie. Elk bounded beneath, scattering song-birds. The thickened air languished with late-summer heat, and a clicking chorus of insects.

Davien damped his alarm. Added emotion could only inflame the drake's divergent attention.

'*Hunting a thing,*' Seshkrozchiel responded. Then, with a snarl that snapped off static charge, '*Here! Drakespawn. Their presence has acquired an unnatural life by – ? – not dragon. This anomaly snarls my weaving – ? – ? – is a discord past my understanding. Human perhaps, and not beauty.*'

The grasses rippled beneath her stretched wing leather, stirred by no errant gust. The predators that had chased the elk herd to flight pursued at a bounding sprint. Their bodies were sinuous black. Manes like lions' spilled over slab shoulders that were larger, and more dreadfully lethal. If the Seardluin that gorged on the thrill of blood slaughter were now expunged from Athera, the creatures still prowled in the timeless memory of dragons. Seshkrozchiel was too wise to reshape their forms to run rampant. She unmade the scene where the predators stalked. Yet despite her care, a faint texture remained. The hazy patch lingered, spreading a stain upon Scarpdale's restored continuity. The oddity confounded her effort.

Whatever had mixed with the haunt's remnant fury eluded her peerless experience. She could not *restructure* the imprint found here, which persisted on flowering havoc.

Yet the Sorcerer's sensibilities recognized the copper-sharp reek of pure fear. This thread was human, and most hideously lost in a sharp-focused morass of terror. Before Davien could recoil, the dragon's empathic dreaming captured his distress and loomed the reaction. *Creation ensued.* The dun landscape of Scarpdale unravelled, stone and tree and frost-hardened earth replaced: *by five horsemen outfitted in Hanshire guard's colours pounding at a breakneck gallop over the copper crest of a dune. Their mounts rolled wild eyes. Soaked coats spattered white strings of lather. Hard after the horses' streaming tails streaked the pack of Seardluin, slit eyes fixed in chase as they closed in for slavering massacre.*

Davien knew, cause to consequence, that the graphic impression stamped by their kill could reverberate to infinity. Too late: faster than warning logic, the electrified fright of the victims wracked him into hapless concert. Without flesh to slow his sympathetic response, the mortal reflex to survive joined the naked thrust of the trauma. Agile emotion leaped into sympathy, *and drowned,* identity thrown into blinding eclipse.

The leading Seardluin bunched its hindquarters and sprang.

'Sorcerer! Beware! I cannot hold your essence against such an onslaught!' This vivid encounter with human despair far outstripped Seshkrozchiel's experience.

Davien heard her distress. His stunned wits strove and failed to wrest clear. Where a being enfleshed used stark panic to focus, the displaced spirit convulsed in response with no footing to react. Swept into the intensity of forming event, the discorporate Sorcerer had no shield to deflect the impact of riveted terror.

No choice remained except to reach through. Ride the tide's crest, while grasping for the fragmented template of the riders' personalities. Before death on the claws of a predator's blood-lust, these men had memories. They once knew family; had been someone cherished, with the hopes and workaday disappointments that made up a human experience. Somewhere, forgotten, they owned a true Name in the fullness of Ath's creation. The horses, as well, had been foals by their dams, frisking amid emerald pastures.

Davien thrashed, consumed by terror as the dream's volatile interface exploded around him. Struggle fed the tumultuous torrent as the first lancer fell, and *pain* joined into the clout of reactive sensation.

No haven existed. Only death and shocked fright, endlessly swirled into an ever-more-magnified echo. All but unravelled, Davien sought the referent matrix of stone. The artistry that had built the haven at Kewar snatched for that protective retreat: *a time when his own cry of intolerable anguish sought solace within the Mathorn Mountains.* Mineral moved to an altered interface: slower, more staid, intricate in attentiveness, its nature could absorb the back-lashing storm without losing stability. Snugged into the frame of a pebble, frozen into a winter stream-bed, the Sorcerer coiled back into himself. There, he found, watching, the burning gold eye of Seshkrozchiel, laced through his being.

The dragon had traced his meteoric mis-step. A wing-beat, two, and her meticulous awareness restored Scarpdale's familiar serenity. Trees and dales resurged without any harm done in consequence. Yet the stain, now identified as a human remain, stayed sealed in the weave, congealed into latent potential.

'Haunts left by your kind,' came Seshkrozchiel's thought. 'The dropped thread of their being cannot be spun free of the angry one's dreaming without the grace of Paravian presence.'

A circle of Athlien dancers could untangle these mortally shocked spirits, but no such benefit lay at hand, now. As a spark lodged in stone, surrounded by the snap-frozen patterns of five dying horsemen's rank horror, Davien surveyed the predicament. 'These lancers were lost in the Korias grimward. Not here!'

Seshkrozchiel snorted a tendril of flame, impatience, perhaps, or else drakish amusement. 'And have your colleagues not used the skulls of our dead for convenience, as portals of crossing?'

'That's Asandir's purview!' Davien snapped, tart. 'He's our preferred expert on working through the unpleasant quirks found in grimwards.' Knowledge did nothing to ease present quandary, that the chaos traversed through Seshkrozchiel's partnership was infinitely permeable, as well as reactively telepathic.

Neither was Davien an accomplished masterbard, with the talent to sound the harmonic balance that soothed fright and traumatized pain. Where such gifted empathy might strike the individualized notes to recapture a mazed spirit's identity, a discorporate Sorcerer possessed no earthly form to wrest a salvage from drake-spun insanity.

'My sight holds these beings,' Seshkrozchiel offered.

No progress without risk: 'Show me,' Davien responded.

A hillside dissolved into a snap-frozen tableau, as her precision remembrance mapped horses, marked so, each one differentiated beyond their white stockings and head blazes. Seshkrozchiel respun them in exhaustive detail: from each blacksmith's nail that crimped on steel shoes, to the odd whorls in each sweated coat. The riders likewise bore distinctions: here, a ring with a topaz setting adorned a grimed finger, and there, a man's corded neck was strung with a luck charm. One veteran's nicked gauntlets had fiend banes stamped in tin, and another carried a wash-leather bag containing a worn set of dice. The fellow who turned his fraught glance behind had a scar, remnant of a tumble in childhood. Each blazoned surcoat and horse-troop's accoutrement was worn with unique flair: the gallant demarked from the dour field sergeant, and the insouciant braggart announced by the cocky hang of his weaponry.

Davien weighed the information, as stone: Kharadmon would have split himself, laughing, and worse, Luhaine's lugubrious nature would have revelled in such tedious *nuance.* Patient through desperation, Davien surveyed each being, stilled at the cusp before the agony of violent dismemberment.

The man's ring seemed the opportune place to begin. Metal imprinted emotion most easily, and gemstone would speak to pebble in congruent resonance. The genius that crafted the maze under Kewar well knew how to bare the most hidden facets of character. Davien tapped the ornament's setting and let topaz speak of the wearer, days before this seized fist lashed to drive a frenzied mount for more speed . . .

. . . and like a whisper embedded in calm, the jewel disclosed *a gift received from a sweetheart, as a summer-time pledge for an autumn marriage.* The trace imprint of the woman embodied contentment, while her intimate smile fore-promised delight . . .

Where Davien would have reached for the woman as mirror to seek out the name of the man, Seshkrozchiel's fascination swerved sidewards and plumbed the female yearning displayed by the mate. *Dragon* embraced those human particulars. Entranced into focus, her power of active creation unfurled.

The remembrance of the rider's beloved appeared as though enfleshed within the dream's setting. Wistful, she stood, her hand outstretched, and her blue eyes filled with the unassuaged sorrow caused by her soldier's parting. She cried out for her husband, torn by her heart's longing. That charge of pure *need* resounded across the trapped rider's inchoate terror: *and the lost heard her voice.* Love's potent desire unfurled through the morass, and cascaded change through the polarized flux.

Now, the beleaguered man stood on foot, hard-breathing, bewildered, but cleared in deliverance as the arms of his wife closed around him.

Davien snatched the moment, spoke a swift warding to shield the man's presence, as the essence of self came untangled. Cut free of over-reactive emotion, the dead man's stripped spirit recouped his forgotten autonomy, even as his wife's memory vanished.

'Why am I here?' he asked in distress. *'What fell nightmare entrapped me? I left Valdie at home and rode out on patrol. We were hunting the Master of Shadow.'*

'You entered a grimward,' Davien responded. *'There can be no earthly return from this place. To escape, you must claim the grace of your Name and cross over by way of Fate's Wheel.'*

'Death?' said the man. Displaced in the dream, he regarded his welted hand, still wearing the token bestowed by his heart's beloved. *'My Valdie will be left to mourn as a widow?'*

Davien bolstered his warding with all the tenderness left in the gifted ring. *'Pass on. You will encounter your sweetheart again. The gateway at death is only another form of beginning. Turn around. Step back through, into the hills of Athera. You will find a light there, and a guardian waiting to ease trauma and show the way.'*

The guardsman fingered his mauled surcoat, uncertain. The oathsworn duty he owed to Hanshire ought not to stay unfulfilled. *'We never took down the Spinner of Darkness, or captured the minstrel whose seditious ballads encouraged corruption.'*

Davien chose not to argue philosophy, or denounce the cause against Arithon's life as unjust. *'There's no punishment waiting, no failure,'* he encouraged instead. *'The seat of your being arises from a source that embraces all lives without bias.'*

'You know this?' The man looked up, torn.

'Don't rest on my promise,' Davien replied. *'Step through and find out for yourself.'*

While the yellow eye of Seshkrozchiel looked on, the battered rider turned on his heel. With Scarpdale's winter vista a short pace away, he took his reprieve from the harrows of nightmare, moved on by choice, and the dreaming released him. Whatever awaited, his spirit form faded, recouped through a natural crossing.

'Four more haunts that were human remain, and five beasts.' The dragon's admonishment shimmered with urgency. Scarpdale's threatened stability could not be redressed before each shade's sundered course was resolved. More, the worst yet lay ahead: a fury that raged beyond reach of the hope spoken by the flutes of the Athlien dancers. Grimwarded haunts were recalcitrant beings, stubbornly wedded to vengeance: an impasse Seshkrozchiel's might must contest in irreversible challenge.

For Asandir, the maelstrom whipped against his set will without let-up. Now hunched in the lee of a volcanic rock, he tugged free of the drifted sand miring his feet. He had lost sense of time. Nothing resembling diurnal rhythms existed to measure existence. Darkness and daylight occurred without pattern, and the weather changed at the caprice of the haunt's maddened dreaming. One moment, his skin would be needled with sleet, lashed by a punishing gale. The next breath might bake him beneath glaring sun, or choke him with fouled air poisoned with ash.

Blisters and injuries were sluggish to heal, with his resources taxed to depletion.

Right-handed, he held the fleck of starred light that remained of his cherished black stallion. 'I will see you clear,' he reaffirmed, coughing through the rasp of volcanic cinders.

He had to move. Rising gusts made his shelter untenable. The face of the boulder that once gave him refuge now caught pelting sand as a death-trap.

How many times had Isfarenn nudged him ahead, as his weary steps stumbled or faltered? For how many leagues had the horse borne his tired weight, thrashed by the ugly, unbiddable spite that blasted the elements to primeval havoc? Loyal of heart, more than generous of spirit, the stallion had served until muscle and bravery gave out, for a companion too spent to heal him.

Tears of regret could not ease that sorrow. Some short-falls could never be rectified.

Asandir would not relinquish his protective hold on the horse's spirit, though such loyalty drove him to ruin. Beyond the rock, the gale shrilled, unrelenting. The Sorcerer wrapped his frayed mantle over his face. Punched and buffeted, he pressed into the tumbling gyre, groping forward as a man blinded. To think at all was to embrace despair, outfaced as the shifting grim landscape transformed into ever more vicious hazards at whim. Always, the rugged conditions got worse near the centre-pin of the spiral. Asandir clutched the spark that remained of the stallion one dogged stride after the next.

No telling how far he had yet to go, and no use to dwell on the failure, that his raw toil here must be repeated. At cost of his care for Isfarenn, he could not divide his resources, even to seal the breached grimward behind him.

Sethvir's wasting attrition would suffer the brunt.

This time, the blast that threw Asandir to his knees did not fetch him up under a convenient boulder. Not sand, but a jagged scarp tore his palm, while the flaying wind tattered his clothing. Curled against the wrath of the storm, clinging over an abyss that loomed, fathoms deep, Asandir set his teeth. He must rally his resources. Climb the cliff-face, and walk, before the gale ripped away his frail hold, or scourged his exposed flesh to the bone. The Name of Isfarenn still clutched to his breast, and his left palm extended, Asandir clawed the brutal volcanic stone for a finger's hold to gain purchase. A wind devil tumbled him. Knocked into a slide, coughing out grit, he gouged in his toes and repeated the effort.

Perception up-ended.

The slope flattened under him, and his bloodied hand plunged wrist deep into icy water.

The sting ripped a startled shout from his throat. This was no streamlet wrought from a grimwarded drake, dream-sprung from a single consciousness. The tumbling winter brook carved its course through Athera. Water element splashed across his torn skin, full-bodied and *alive* with the ecstatic synergy of a myriad creation.

'How?' Asandir flung back the rags of his hood. He stared upwards, shocked dumb as he met the massive gold eye of a dragon. She crouched with her foretalons cupped alongside him, her rampant wings stretched above like curved sails, deflecting the wind.

The pocket of Scarpdale restored by her dreaming had granted his ninth-hour respite.

First things first: the Fellowship's field Sorcerer scraped crusted dirt from his streaming eyes. Propped on skinned elbows, he croaked a courteous phrase, stunned to gratitude for the deliverance. Then, shaken down to his final, stripped nerve, he opened his fingers. Too beaten to weep, he whispered his grief-stricken tribute to speed his dead stallion's safe passage.

Throughout, the dragon's fixated gaze burned with impatient inquiry. *'Sorcerer! Wisest if you also accept my secured return to Athera's free wilds.'*

'Sooner would I have abandoned Isfarenn!' Asandir snapped, unequivocal. His steely glance had not missed the presence lodged in the dragon's left pupil. 'Sethvir holds his post at Althain Tower? Then my place is here, without question.'

Asandir gathered his abraded limbs. He arose, braced against an ebon claw to steady his wheeling balance. Already, the ominous change in the breeze revolted his natural instincts. The haunt's vicious dreaming resurged like flood-tide, a boiling swell to unstring the solid footing beneath him. 'I don't need a reason,' he addressed Davien. 'No more than you did, when you left Kewar and sealed your unorthodox bargain.'

Asandir bowed to acknowledge Seshkrozchiel. Grave dignity intact, he asked whether she would mind bearing him. 'I might walk, except my benighted boots are in tatters.'

The dragon regarded his dwarfed presence, unspeaking. Then her over-powering fore-talons moved. Asandir found himself caged in a grip that could have cupped a butterfly's wings without damage. Yet Seshkrozchiel did not spring aloft. Her snout turned, steaming smoke. She presented the huge, yellow disk of her right eye, the slit pupil tall as the Sorcerer. Reflected within that black well of intelligence, Asandir sensed the thundering pulse of her thought. Her awareness stung through him, skin, bone, and viscera, as she contemplated a pattern, *not dragon*.

'Loyalty,' he stated, ineffably gentle. 'A quality honoured by sages and fools, by which humankind finds the courage to trample the reflex for self-preservation.'

Seshkrozchiel snorted a riffle of flame. *'Has the sage or the fool spoken for your decision?'*

Asandir loosed a gasp of hoarse laughter. 'That will depend on the outcome, my friend. Shall we brave the endeavour and see?'

Seshkrozchiel gathered the Sorcerer up. Immaculate in finesse, she unfurled the double-layered vanes of her wings and took flight, with Asandir clasped inside of jet claws. Tail lashing, she steered for the turbulent heart of the gyre, while Scarpdale's sere ground fell away and dissolved. That stabilized presence could not be maintained through the winding last turn of the spiral.

Now, once again, rock-cliffs reared up like ramparts, pocked with fumaroles that belched gritty cinders. The sulphurous air reeked, searing with acid. Asandir tore a rag from his threadbare mantle and muffled his nose and mouth. Spare of word, always, he addressed his discorporate colleague. 'Your action has salvaged Sethvir, beyond question.'

'I should feel honoured?' Davien bit back. *'Your thanks was more eloquent in behalf of the shade of your stallion.'*

'Isfarenn was steadfast,' Asandir agreed.

Provocation met back-lash. *'Surely you long to ask after the fate of your precious crown prince?'*

'Torbrand's get dislikes officious spokesmen,' Asandir declared. 'In the case of Athera's titled Masterbard, should either one of us dare to presume?'

'The rogue gift of prophetic far-sight imposed by s'Dieneval sharpens that talent somewhat,' Davien denounced with sly irony. *'The headache makes Luhaine chase his own tail like a terrier baited with rat scent. Kharadmon rails with epithets, and Sethvir is certain to try himself, scrying, until he's short-tempered and cross-eyed. You're not worried?'*

Asandir's mouth twitched. Stifled amusement made him look raffish, with his silver hair tangled and singed. While the dragon swooped through the noxious clouds, cut by jagged stacks of cooled lava, he said carefully, 'If we survive, I won't need the debate. Arithon's doings have always entangled the hot list of snagging developments.'

Awarded Davien's nettled silence, Asandir's threatened smile broke free, brilliant as sudden lightning. 'Ath's glory! You're vexed? Does that mean his Grace has outmatched every test you've laid on him?'

'You couldn't handle him before Kewar's maze,' Davien attacked without flinching.

Necessity cut off the nipping exchange, as the weather-stripped bones of the haunt loomed ahead, tumbled in unquiet death. Athera's affairs paled as Seshkrozchiel's flight broached the tumult that seeded the gyre. Gusts snapped at her wings. Membranes strained to withstand their mangling force, while her sleek armour of scales shed the blast. Storm charge struck sparks off the spines of her neck where her being contested the corrosive flux. She looped and twisted the dream to force access, then shot, needle straight, through a vast granite arch. Her wings carved upwards, braking her rush. Neat as a cat, she set down on her haunches amid the remains of Scarpdale's grimwarded drake.

Eerie quiet descended. No winds rampaged here. A low hillock arose, bleached to powdery chalk by the flare of the drake's final breaths.

The creature had not perished quietly. Pearlescent shards remained of the rib-cage, tumbled like scythes amid the ridges ploughed up by the thrash of maimed limbs. The tail flukes were a smashed scatter of spines. Even the whorled skull wore the furrows left by gouging talons.

'No skeleton I've seen ever showed such a harsh mauling,' Asandir ventured in shock.

'This combatant failed to secure a life mate.' Here, where the latent charge in the air seemed to strain towards volatile release, Seshkrozchiel constrained her mighty presence to a whisper. *'Three times the young male fought, and thrice lost the contest to a rival. He died of the wounding, in brooding despair. His agony still howls defiance.'* She balanced the sorrowful note with reproof, since most vanquished/unmated who suffered fatality plunged into the sea, their lives quenched without pain in salt water.

Asandir dared an impertinent question. 'Do you also carry the Name for the lost?'

'You presume to know what possesses no substance?' Seshkrozchiel raised the talon-wrapped Sorcerer, her burning gold eye half-lidded in scorching disdain. *'Names for our kind are declared, always forged in the act of a triumphant mating.'*

'So we are told by Athera's historical record,' Asandir allowed with strained dignity. 'Yet wise experience takes no fact for granted, even though scribed in the lore books at Althain Tower. Methurien also claim no innate identity. But by my understanding of Paravian law, as derived from Ciladis's study, that condition is a misperception.'

Steam puffed to the dragon's incensed reproof. *'The Athlien singers failed in sounding the requiem here!'*

Asandir bowed. Unshaken despite his shattered appearance, he stated, 'Today, we do not have that option.'

Empowered yet by his quickened flesh, the Sorcerer could have entered the skull's chamber and effected a transfer back to Athera; yet for Seshkrozchiel to bring Davien through without harm, the discorporate must maintain his subtle awareness amid the dire blast of the haunt's resistence. Davien would be dependent, until the last, that her living strength could master the challenge, victorious.

Since no outside place in the world remained safe with Scarpdale's grimward unbounded, Asandir added, 'We stand or fall here. Our kind do not quench our defeats in the sea! Or forsake a sworn trust by abandonment.'

'Davien's bargain with me was none of your making,' Seshkrozchiel hissed. The provocative thrust of her phrase was kept open, a deliberate danger left dangling.

Asandir raised his eyebrows. His eyes dauntless grey, every whiplashed nerve steady, he sealed her reactive statement. 'Differences don't grant me the arrogance of dismissal. I will honour my colleague's endeavour without prejudice. Let him argue my born right to choose! Free will says I stand at his back.'

Davien kept his own counsel. Even Sethvir never gainsaid the gift of Asandir's forthright commitment.

'Such force could shape diamond.' Seshkrozchiel dipped her massive, horned head. After *beauty* and *loyalty,* she acknowledged *adamance.* Things *not dragon,* but concepts that fitted together in patterns whose nuance was pleasing. She opened her clutched talons and invited the Sorcerer to stand at liberty, nested inside the spiralling curve of the dorsal spine at her brow. Once his perch was secure, she settled from rampant crouch onto her fore-limbs. Her back arched. Snake quick in movement, she darted into engagement: to shatter the derelict skull if she could, and dream the haunt's bones out of Athera's existence.

Where live dragons closing for battle would lunge with a roar that shook sky and earth, this strike was eerily soundless. One moment the emanation off Seshkrozchiel's spines was restrained to luminous quiescence. The next, as though torched to an indigo bonfire, her auric field flared and unfurled.

Everything shattered, swept into pulsating rainbows. Through the deluge of energies, the bones of the drake lit and gleamed golden red as forge-heated metal.

Force met bared force! with a clap like explosion. Although no thunder marked the event, Asandir felt the recoil sleeting chill through his viscera. As Seshkrozchiel's dreaming sought to unmake the wracked skeleton, its wraith arose in pealing wrath to contest her. From *nothing*, a spirit form burst from the ethers. Neat as a bared sword-blade, vicious in splendour, the haunt appeared as a lambent form, wrought out of crystal and gossamer. Its whipping plunge for Seshkrozchiel's throat was ravening fury, distilled. A bolt to serve ruin from bared fangs to lashing tail-tip met indigo fire with a grappling shock. Seshkrozchiel's ebon spines crackled with lightning. Fast as she absorbed the attack, deftly as the electrified blaze of her aura knitted chaos back into stability, the strike sowed rippling back-lash. Asandir and the dragon were buffered by flesh. But Davien's lodged spirit was a naked mote, hurled through the moiling flux. His reactive sensitivity possessed no anchor.

So had Isfarenn's spirit been left vulnerable to the erosion of bounded identity. Alone until rescue, Asandir had staved off the stallion's attrition. Yet no brutal trial by experience prepared for the task of safeguarding his threatened colleague. Failure awaited if he did not try. Sethvir's survival must not come at the cost of Davien's reckless sacrifice. Disruptive, creative, unbridled in passion, his rogue genius had always been the breath and light that impelled fresh angles and change.

Asandir shouted, but words did not carry.

Seshkrozchiel already mounted the hillock, unravelling the bones of fore-claws and rib-cage, and blasting comet-tail bursts towards the skull. She could not disengage without risk to herself, while her dream and the haunt's focused fury collided. Bones re-formed and melted. Shattered glass rainbows warred with lancing dazzles of light, scattershot as hurled mercury. As the haunt raged in spiteful counterpoint, human senses found no familiar expression. Sound could not hold the texture of language. Davien rode without shield at the forefront, embedded within the rampaging thought-stream of the live dragon's visioning.

He could not withstand the naked interface.

Hesitation would kill just as fast as wrong action. Wrapped in the crackling coil of Seshkrozchiel's leading dorsal spine, surrounded by bursts of indigo flame and violet lightning, Asandir shoved his hand into the streaming flux of her aura. He closed his seared fingers. Shut his scalded eyes, gathered his will, and *imagined* the most vivid encounter snatched from the shared annals of Fellowship experience . . .

The year was Third Age 5129, when the inquiry that had turned so terribly wrong convened at Althain Tower. That solstice summons came wrapped in dank chill. Despite the fragrant heat of the birch fire ablaze in the King's

Chamber's hearth, Desh-thiere's leaden mist leached the warmth from the inside air. Outside, its blight dimmed the waning moon, arisen past midnight. Yet the flames in the candle stands were torn by more immediate draughts, as Davien paced in caged fury before the high table, which seated Sethvir, Ciladis, and Asandir. The discorporate witness of Luhaine and Kharadmon breathed a disapproving cold through the gathering.

Only Traithe had been absent. His delay leaving Morvain looked to become chronic, since few deepwater captains dared the risk of lee shoals, left only fog-bells by which to navigate. A century, since the fall of crown law, and a year shy of three troubled decades since the departure of the last Ilitharis guardian: how blindsided their beleaguered Fellowship had been, to presume that their straits could not turn for the worse.

'You might sit,' Asandir snapped, 'since we're asking an honest effort from you, and a fresh avenue for resolution.'

'Hold your council without me.' Davien turned his sharp profile, haggard despite the livid cast lent by the fluttering candles. 'Your hope of a compromise courts disaster.' Hands clenched, black eyes harrowed, he defied with a cornered wolf's wariness. 'I will not be a consenting party to ruin. Or watch as the town populace slides deeper in jeopardy.'

'Then the door must stay barred, until we have your word,' Sethvir declared, pushed at last to consider a drawn line. 'No one but you spurns our Fellowship's covenant. None, since the dream of the dragons laid claim on us! You are the first who has acted outside of our informed backing.'

'I will not cede my liberty,' Davien bristled. The lynx gold of his jerkin no less than immaculate, and his footfall warningly firm, he spun away from his fellows. 'Bedamned to your pussyfoot need to mince through a formal emascu-lation with manners! I'll leave you the choice. Since I won't serve your course to reinstate the crown heirs, you'll just have to step aside gracefully.'

'Not after the bloodshed unleashed by your hand!' Kharadmon hurled into the breach. 'How many infants and children were murdered because the cabal at Hanshire was allowed the free rein to disseminate havoc? Luhaine's left discorporate. Our *pussyfoot mincing* where you are concerned has been altogether too forbearing! No thwarted ideal can excuse your decision to harbour that nest of bigotry and provocation!'

'I'm not laughing,' cracked Davien, 'but surely you jest! Has five thousand years, bearing the trials of high kingship, not killed our precocious crown talent off any faster?'

'Kharadmon speaks out of turn.' Who had the heart left to defend but Ciladis? The most gentle, and the quietest, whose laced brown fingers were trembling still from the intricate spells that fired the sunloop. 'In fact, Davien, you have not been accused. We are hoping you'll explain what went wrong. To weep is not weakness. What price, for our patience, that this cankerous grievance can heal and reach wiser consensus?'

'What's left for me that's not already been said?' Davien stalked to the ebon stone mantel and poised there, whipped to scalding bitterness. He could scarcely speak: the sorrow that shadowed Ciladis's joy posed a misery beyond endurance. Overcome, he buried his face in long fingers, while his shoulder-length tumble of hair caught fire in the uncertain light. 'Shall we perish of tedium?' he asked, hammered flat. His nerve-wracked hands moved. 'Sit and grow moss, while I yap myself silly? Well, I am not yet the lap-dog, too inbred to have any teeth!'

Again, Ciladis addressed the sore point, disarming the cynic with gentleness. 'You insist we were wrong to demand the service of mankind's birthgifted talent.'

Davien exploded back into his tigerish stalk. 'The split that's evolved between town-born and clan is a widening schism that begs our destruction. I will not stand down. If respect for the free wilds' existence cannot be learned, we are lost!'

Luhaine's effort at censure was trampled over by Davien's blazing frustration. 'Have you bothered to think beyond rhetoric? Won't you realize we've sent the wrong blood-lines to exile on Dascen Elur? Let the townsfolk who've grown blinded to Athera's mysteries be dispatched through the West Gate, instead. They will learn the faster to manage themselves on a world of more limited resources.'

Before Luhaine could defend with a lecture, or protest that harsh trial by privation, Davien razed through. 'We have lost our living contact with the Paravians! What's next? How long will you nurture the bones of past policy? Because the more dire disaster will strike! How far should we drift, till we're driven to forsake a bad call and change course to salvage the future? Our burdens here have grown far too weighty to keep the lame pretence of vigilant oversight.'

'Law cannot replace the responsible choice, willingly made out of freedom,' Sethvir agreed with wide-open, mist eyes. He paused through a taut interval, groping to bridge thorny impasse. 'If more problems arise for every solution, we must become more creative. Your wild-card methods have always inspired. If Hanshire's conspirators were left unbridled, you will have had profound reason.'

Davien arched his eyebrows.

Whether or not he meant to provoke, Luhaine pounced to attack. 'Did you hope to incite the towns until we were obliged to revoke their claim under the compact? If so, Paravian presence is gone! We're left to strike balance across the raw ground that hatred has soaked in fresh bloodshed! Does that condemnation suffice, by your lights? You've unleashed enough impetus to force our hand, and not left any avenue open for guidance.'

'How your words in my mouth raise my hackles!' Davien threw up his hands. 'Say again that this is not a staged trial, tailored to fit the renegade criminal roped in for summary judgement! I find the role that you've scripted too pat.

Your string-puppet accused will not dance for the question!' Quick as the turn of a leaf in a storm, the Sorcerer spun on his heel. He strode towards the doorway with a fierce glance back, talking fast to jam Luhaine silent. 'You don't need my presence to bandy conjecture. Carry on, by all means. Enjoy your salacious dissection of character without the bother of my protestations.'

Sethvir's fraught cry for restraint went unheard. His tenure as Warden was too recent, yet, for his colleagues to grasp full significance. Or perhaps Davien sensed the overshadowing gravity. In his wild rage, he might have left the warning suicidally disregarded. The heated moment had fanned Fellowship tempers too high for clear sight: that Althain Tower's Paravian defences had stirred active by their raw dissension.

The warding seal at the doorway had never been meant for restraint. Sethvir's token binding was symbolic, a sincere gesture to confront wounded trust and reforge a confidence torn by the pressures of Desh-thiere's invasion.

Davien broached the drawn line and stepped out. Brilliant as autumn, he vanished into the stairwell, without second thought crossing the focused will of the appointed Warden of Althain Tower.

Asandir was alone, as he leaped in response to the unforeseen crisis. Chair slammed over backwards, the field Sorcerer vaulted the ebony table and launched off in desperate pursuit.

He might have overtaken Davien in time. Intervention, at speed, perhaps could have checked wounded pride and stopped his colleague's incensed departure.

But Kharadmon slammed the door in Asandir's path. 'Let the betrayer go his own way!'

Luhaine's victimized feelings agreed. 'Davien's incessant meddling brings naught but dissent! He'll break our hearts, arguing, while new packs of head-hunters are reiving through the free wilds slaughtering clansfolk –'

'Shehane Althain's aroused!' Sethvir's shout at last broke the clamour.

But the fortunate moment was already lost. Davien encountered the raised might of the tower's guardian centaur, and the vigorous reflex for self-preservation entrapped him, past any recourse save one: the ceremonial dissolution his colleagues enacted to spare him, that stripped the spirit out of living flesh . . .

Convulsed by the acuity of remembered agony, Asandir kept his hand immersed in the violet flux streaming off Seshkrozchiel's dorsal spine. He sustained the recoil. Endured, braced, as the scream of the colleague he would have spared, whole, reechoed across his stretched nerves. If Asandir wept, if he also recalled Ciladis's tears for a judgement forced into premature closure, the hour for grieving was over. The field Sorcerer embraced the experience without falling to the harrowing onslaught of guilt. He had wrestled such emotional echoes before, immersed in the coils of grimwarded haunts. While the imprint razed into the unfolding flux, he knew the live dragon's engagement would capture the shattering resonance.

No barrier deferred the tangling impact. *Creation must follow,* as the tumultuous, past trauma fed the storm of reactive event.

Davien's conscious memory was swept along. His threatened cognizance became riveted as the horrific shock of his error resurged, nightmarishly vivid as direct experience.

Asandir held the line. Fist still clenched in the crackling forces thrown off Seshkrozchiel's dorsal spine, he added his heart-felt appeal to her dream-weave: *that explosive recall of Davien's fatal severance would seed enough charge to bind a discorporate spirit to self-awareness amid lawless upheaval.* And that if his drastic tactic sufficed, such searing coherency might last *long enough* for Seshkrozchiel to unspin the vengeful haunt's fit of battle-fury.

No thought and no time could be spared to examine for wide-ranging consequences. The Fellowship's past action to appease Shehane Althain's defences had been the same: a heart-rending choice of expediency seized in a split second's opening. Crisis had not let them salvage the mis-step that threatened Davien's destruction. Nothing else, now, might shield him from ruin through the bid for Scarpdale's restoration.

Asandir stretched his practised faculties, counterworking the whip-lash effects of grimwarded dissonance. He recognized peril: at no time had the shade of his stallion been cross-linked with a living dragon's awareness. No Fellowship Sorcerer might foresee the outcome sown by Seshkrozchiel's perception. Nor had Asandir witnessed the prior banishment of Hanshire's strayed lancers, or tracked the speed at which her avid attention could freeze the progression of breaking event. Her close survey, by which she mapped the essence of all things *not dragon* would have left even Sethvir's resources reeling.

Asandir received Davien's conflicted torment, rocked by a fear that fused thought and will into ruthless concern for the future; while Davien saw beyond his branding need for redress with a merciless, refigured clarity.

If Kharadmon had been incensed from pain, and Luhaine, still mad with grief for the rebellion's harsh losses, the luminous care behind disparate viewpoints now eclipsed every meaningful truth. Beyond the cruelty of Davien's wracked horror, sparked to salvage abraded identity, Asandir brought the quickened, yearning frustration that once dead-locked the Fellowship's impasse: Ciladis's joy, never robbed by disdain, but overspent by driven exhaustion; the suffering born of Traithe's crippled perception; and not least, the most disastrously misappraised stress of them all: Sethvir's harrowing struggle to master the augmented stream bestowed by the earth link.

Davien's stunned recoil, and Asandir's shock, had no chance to recover. Seshkrozchiel did not perceive as Mankind. Her intent acknowledged no course beyond *victory.* Thus, the entangled energies that were *not dragon* became seized and recast, made her own. A recombinant pattern, snatched from the throes of the Fellowship's failure, would resharpen the cascading thrust of her assault.

'Yours to choose, ancient!' Asandir whispered, undone if his stop-gap strategy should overturn to the detriment of all he held dear.

Seshkrozchiel dreamed.

The resonant print of the warding raised by Shehane Althain struck *skull!* and bone shattered; while the matchless depth of Ciladis's patience overwrote the sting of an unmated defeat into a poignant longing that eased bitter rage into loneliness. The crazed haunt had no footing to stand before *love*: a concept, *not dragon,* strung through Asandir's *adamance,* and Sethvir's *loyalty.* The onslaught awoke flooding sorrow, *for beauty lost:* and the inspiration of new understanding broke the grip of riled insanity. Refigured by change, the intractable drake-spirit knew the unfolding grace of release. It embraced death such as no dragon had known in the course of evolving creation.

While Davien, whose hot-blooded urgency had once impelled a tragic disaster, met the shearing crux of his past ruin again in the flux of a live dragon's dreaming.

Watching, the golden eye of Seshkrozchiel encountered his human *regret.*

The flame of lost desire stood stark as cut diamond. Force kindled reaction, unstoppable. Davien's present, discorporate consciousness launched across a threshold of shifted event. Devoured by a coruscation of rainbows, *he passed through the King's Chamber at Althain Tower.* Then the fleeting impression plunged into oblivion dense as the dark of the womb.

Redemption

Tradition held that change always followed the footsteps of Fellowship Sorcerers. If Glendien had never troubled before with the gravity of ancestral warnings, that reckless attitude had withered amid the blustering days of midwinter. Her capricious exchange with Davien the Betrayer had led to the siege of Alestron and loss of her husband in Rathain's crown service.

Now her womb harboured the next s'Ffalenn heir. Such ties to crown lineage evoked privilege: Glendien accepted the offered grant of a protected residency. The explicit need for her informed consent might have caused her to weigh that decision more carefully; or not. Scoured by grief, she would have seized upon any distraction to numb her fresh heart-ache.

History declared without exception: to cross over the threshold of Althain Tower was to be tested and tried, either to break, or to reforge shrinking weakness into the strengths of true character. Yet Luhaine's expedient transfer had not delivered her to Sethvir. Her needs were met instead by a White Brotherhood adept, who had smiled but answered no questions. The second-floor guest suite was austerely furnished, the swept stone floor warmed with a bright rug, and a south-facing window with diamond panes that let in flooding sunlight. Except for the silence, her room seemed quite ordinary.

Glendien detected no dread currents of power. Even the burn of the flux lines seemed stilled, which warned her the chamber was shielded. Althain Tower lay on the primary lane that flowed through Atainia, where the Great Circle at Isaer's old ruin once hosted the council of the centaur guardians. Transverse lines crossed here, which powered the Sorcerer's Preserve and the axis under the Mathorn Mountains; also the shining track that surged through the old way from Narms, past the marker stone in Daon Ramon Barrens, and the Second Age nexus sited at Ithamon.

Yet no turbulence blazed through Glendien's dreams. She sensed no other voice but the wind, whisking across ancient stonework. Restless despite a night's peaceful sleep, she brushed her red hair for the third time and fretted under the irritation of leaving the tresses unbraided. Never having borne Kyrialt's child, she had no more right to the clan pattern of s'Taleyn; if the s'Ffalenn name had been gifted a traditional weaving, she had no elder of Arithon's lineage to guide her.

'Ath above,' she burst out, as she ripped up a lashing of static. 'I'd rather a bow to go hunting!'

Uncertainty coloured her isolation. She noted no outside bustle of comings and goings; nothing important arose to explain why she should be abandoned to her own devices. Sethvir's hospitality seemed vexingly dull. Her forestborn talent strove, and quite failed, to pierce through the blanketing quiet.

By contrast, every slight comfort was met before asking, until Glendien felt like a cosseted jewel tucked into a velvet-lined box.

That impression broke the next morning when a robed adept arrived at her door. He had bright, dark eyes, the brown skin of a tribesman, and a spry stride that outpaced her ascent of the stairs as he escorted her two floors higher up. There, she was admitted to the King's Chamber and asked to wait on the attendance of a Fellowship Sorcerer. No assurance of welcome soothed her jangled nerves. Instead, her anxiety gave rise to more doubts at the sight of the banners denoting Athera's five kingdoms. The hearth fire did not ease her mounting dread, in this place. Which of the empty, carved chairs at the ebony table had once seated Torbrand s'Ffalenn? Here also, Rathain's first *caithdein* had stood with drawn sword, on the hour the lineage's founder had knelt to seal his crown oath over his blood descendants.

Glendien shivered. One day her child might be called to serve in the grandiloquent weight of such footsteps.

The dyed carpet felt much too rich underneath her irreverent tread. Thick silence itself seemed reproachful. Glendien ran her fingers over the panelling that softened the tower's stonewall. The curly maple all but sang to her touch, fitted with the uncanny rapport that bespoke Paravian joinery. She could not deny the sharp misery that broke her bravado to tears. In dread fact, she felt unfit. Arithon Teir's'Ffalenn had not chosen her as the mother to bear his first child.

'You still can turn back,' a mild voice declared from the doorway.

Breath caught, her pulse pounding, Glendien whirled face about.

The promised Sorcerer stood at the threshold, watching with steely grey eyes. How long had such powerful stillness been present, unnoticed until he had spoken?

Keeping her pinned in his earnest regard, the arrival finished his statement.

'The hour is not yet too late to change your mind and step back. You need not bear the full consequence that will result from your choices at Athir.'

Glendien swallowed. Temper sparked off the raw flint of her fear as she trembled beneath his close survey. 'Do I seem that untrustworthy?'

'No.' Asandir strode fully into the room. Soundless of step, he left the door open, perhaps aware that her forest-bred nerves felt entrapped by closed quarters. His imposing height was clothed in formality: a deep indigo robe bordered with silver that shimmered like summer lightning. He had labourer's hands, close-trimmed nails, and large knuckles, the impression of capable strength unnervingly calloused and ordinary. The Sorcerer accepted her stare. Without comment, he turned one of the ivory-trimmed chairs and sat down. Now settled beneath her regard, he seemed care-worn, even shadowed by signs of a taxing recovery.

Which insight lent nothing, by way of advantage. His conclusion stayed dauntlessly level. 'You keep what is promised, and without complaint. I would have said, Glendien, that you are impetuous.'

She raised her chin. 'No quality fit to endow a crown heir. My pride can withstand your rejection.'

One corner of Asandir's mouth pulled awry. He folded his hands and leaned forward. Lit head to foot by rapt expectation, he urged in silk quiet, 'Continue. What other faults should you list for my censure?' As she flushed scarlet, he added, quite mild, 'Or else say what you actually want. Short and plainly is best, from the heart.'

The cry of her grief for her dead beloved emerged as fresh tears that welled over. She turned her back. Hoped the crude need for retreat came in time, as the silver and black on emerald green of Rathain's royal leopard dissolved from her sight in the flood. Worse, her shaking knees threatened to buckle. The courage that should have raised her fighting spirit ebbed under her crushing anguish.

Perhaps she gasped Kyrialt's name, after all.

For suddenly the Sorcerer's presence was *there*, looming over her wretched misery. A ghost's touch clasped her elbow. She was steadied, then upheld without words through the torrent, regardless of acute embarrassment.

Then Asandir said, 'You've seen everything that was needful, in here. Let's move our discussion outside. Doubtless both of us would prefer the open air.'

Despite brimming eyes, Glendien stared upwards in shocked surprise.

Asandir's quick smile eased his severe face. 'Why else do you think I stay out in the field? Sethvir's the one who likes sitting, mewed up with his piles of books. He's always preferred his fur buskins and comfort, though if you stay, you'll have to excuse his loose habit of letting the blizzards dump snow through the casements.'

Glendien permitted such disarming patter to steer her through the door, and on down the draughty stone stairwell. The Sorcerer allowed her to lean, without comment, as she wavered in threading between the commemorative statues of the Paravians, housed in Althain's ground-floor chamber. Then the awe raised by yester-year's majesty fell behind, closed off by the chased panels at the sallyport threshold. The icy shrill of the draughts through the murder holes under the gate arch restored her. Glendien gulped desperate breaths in the cold, while Asandir manned the winch and unbarred the tower's triple array of defences.

Then the north wind off the Bittern Desert slapped into her aching lungs. Speech was not expected, through the bracing shock, as Sorcerer and clanswoman stepped out. Together they traversed the heath that surrounded Althain Tower. The sere toss of the grass wore rime-frost, but no snow. The blue sky was combed lace, with cirrus. Early sun shot flickers of brittle gold light on the tossing canes of last season's briar. Even at midwinter, the air was alive with the rustle of small animals and bird-song. Nesting wrens liked the ivy on Althain's south wall. Their fluttering, as they gleaned for small insects, seemed to scatter ahead at each footstep. Elsewhere, a jay's squalled retort gave warning of a soaring hawk.

Glendien felt her heart lift. Wind flagged her red hair to fresh tangles. The gusts rippled the indigo velvet of Asandir's mantle, across silence that begged her to talk.

'You'll snag such fine cloth on the thorns,' she ventured at testing length.

'Not the first time, for that.' The Sorcerer's comment seemed wryly amused, though a note like iron struck through his calm as he finished, 'We've both survived amid turbulent times. My last set of leathers came back unfit to wear. Sethvir's sewing replacements. He says any chore that keeps his hands busy helps him sort through his brooding thoughts. You don't enjoy needlework, do you? Our Warden's always been secretly crushed when a guest won't leave him with the mending.'

Glendien shivered, not from the cold. Arms wrapped at her breast, she had not marked the moment when the Sorcerer's touch had abandoned her. 'Should I bear Arithon's child and stay?'

'I can't answer that for you.' Asandir's ranging stride led to the crest of a hillock. The vales rolled away in serried ranks, wind-swept and mottled with violet haze until the edges blurred into distance. Lancing sunlight kissed the mica-flecked rock, sparkling like stars dropped to earth. The Sorcerer's voice seemed woven into the enduring grace of the wilderness. 'You are entitled to ask questions. If I can, I will lend your choice guidance.'

His piercing whistle slashed the clear air; woke the blast of an answering whinny. Amid the high brush, a black colt raised his head, nostrils blowing and ears pricked in his burr-tangled mane. Young, not yet yearling, he flagged his high tail, then stretched his long legs and galloped. He veered, playing tag with the gusts, and joyously kicked up his heels.

'Show-off,' Asandir murmured with fondness.

The animal ploughed to a snorting halt. Eye rolling, he reared. The swift, punching strike of a stockinged foot asserted his bold independence. Then he pranced up to nuzzle the Sorcerer's fingers and try a swift nip if he could. High crest to flat back, the magnificent creature knew his own worth; was proud to own the place he inhabited. He had a narrow, white snip on his nose; one blue, ghost eye, and one brown, that shone deep and bright with intelligence. 'You take after your sire,' Asandir declared. 'A rare gift, born out of a blood-line even a sorcerer can't hold for granted.' Asandir's attention remained on the horse, where his keen insight might not intimidate. 'You might start with the child,' he invited gently.

'My own expectations there scarcely signify.' Glendien let the young stallion snuffle her hair. 'She will be herself, if she's born to this world. You'd know better than I, if she's fated.'

The black colt dipped his head. Asandir's fingers were surprisingly deft, as he feathered through the matted snarls and unstuck the burrs. 'There were portents enough surrounding her conception,' he admitted, sparing words that suggested he might hold reservations. 'This child's heritage will not be straightforward. Elaira's presence is well-marked in the weave. If the bloodstock springs from your lineage, and Arithon's, there was a love summoned that spoke for this spirit. She will bear the mark of that all her days, if you elect to grant birthright. We will raise no child apart from the mother. On that matter, our Fellowship commands no precedent.'

Glendien watched, while fine velvet picked up a careless cargo of burdock; then flecks of chewed grass, as the horse snorted foam and rubbed his head on the Sorcerer's sleeve. 'You don't stand much on ceremony,' she dared to observe.

Asandir grinned. 'Not since I wash my own clothes in the field.' He shoved off the horse. Chided, before his braid trim became torn in the playful grip of bared teeth. 'You! Show some manners. The mares would bite back, for presumption.'

The colt frisked away, neck high and tail streaming. The Sorcerer's gaze at last turned and surveyed her. 'You need to consider what your life would be, without any child born to a marked destiny.'

Glendien bent her thoughts back to Selkwood. Everywhere, there, she found Kyrialt's shadow, dogging her unpartnered footsteps. If she returned, barren, she would be expected to meet clan obligation and further her blood-line. Where, after the flower of s'Taleyn, could she find her match in vivacious audacity? Who, after Arithon, had ever stood forward to lock piquant wit with spiced challenge?

'What's left but sorrow, awaiting in Alland?' Again Glendien's eyes welled up and spilled over. 'Though surely I owe Lord Erlien s'Taleyn the duty of bearing the news of a valiant son's death.'

Heedless of tear stains, Asandir closed her into the warmth of his mantle.

'My dear, you need not concern yourself. The difficult errand's accomplished. Luhaine's been our voice for such consolation, though truly, the High Earl was advised of the loss well beforetime. The gift of his son was Prince Arithon's survival, as Shand's seeress foretold from the outset.'

'Then I cannot go back.' Glendien chose her path, not to become the sorry reminder of a young man's life, cut short for crown duty. 'Kyrialt's sacrifice would have this child secure from the reach of Prince Arithon's enemies.'

'Then stay as you wish.' Asandir smiled. 'Be welcome without any strings. Sethvir's lackadaisical, stocking his larder. You won't pine for excuse to go hunting.'

Only one question remained left to ask. 'Will Prince Arithon ever –'

'No, Glendien. Never.' Asandir's interruption stayed firm. 'Your daughter will shoulder her fate in due time. She must find her way without the concern of her father's aware interference.'

Whether the child might become Rathain's next heir, the Sorcerer also called Kingmaker refused to say. Though the gleam in his far-sighted eyes well suggested his vision might measure the probability, he turned the resolute clanswoman back towards Althain Tower. 'Come in from the cold, Glendien. Sethvir has tea waiting, and I've got another visit to pay before I take leave in departure.'

Davien had not strayed far, since the hour he wakened, restored to flesh and returned to Athera. North of Althain Tower, the incessant winds raked the Bittern Waste into ridges of swept, knife-edged dunes. There, Seshkrozchiel dug herself a deep wallow to scour off soot and polish her dazzling scales. Once clean, she rested, snout laid on her tail fluke, with her wings spread to bask in the sun. The dreaming fire that shimmered off her erect dorsal spines lazed in coils, reduced to a glimmer.

The Sorcerer her bargain still collared was found, seated, back leaned against her left fore-claw. He wore the same summer dress, each button and tie re-created from the hour of the misfortunate gathering: a lynx-gold jerkin and chocolate-brown hose, tucked into neat, calf-skin boots. If his silk shirt was too thin, the rippling warmth thrown off by the dragon drove back winter's chill when Asandir made his appearance. He called, sliding down the slope into the hollow as the day advanced towards midafternoon.

Davien's sardonic, dark eyes regarded the indigo robe, now greyed with grit at the hem-line. 'You shredded your last set of leathers, again,' he declared by way of tart greeting.

'I do have crown business still left at Athir,' Asandir said with mild reproof. He folded his lean length of leg and sat down, unconcerned for his court-styled velvet: his upcoming bout of lane travel would shake out the residual dust. Less sanguine over his horse-slobbered cuffs, he admitted, 'Though a rinse in a stream would not be amiss, in the meantime.' A glance sidewards encompassed a fine, lynx-gold garment, also now a bit less than immaculate. 'You'd forgotten the bother?'

Davien laughed. 'Never.' He rubbed his solid hands against drawn-up shins, pleased, and treasuring the sensation. Before his colleague could ask, he tossed back tousled hair, and said outright, 'I am not going back to announce my prodigal return in Althain Tower's library just yet.'

Asandir waited. If he looked to have the stilled patience of stone, his appearances could be deceptive.

'You aren't breathing,' Davien trounced with shrewd joy. 'Don't say I've dashed your bright hope for a clinging reunion with Sethvir?'

Asandir raised an eyebrow. Behind him, the orb of the dragon was open, as scalding through cloth as noon sunlight. 'I was waiting, hands folded, with meek expectation,' he amended without ruffled nerves. His polite nod acknowledged Seshkrozchiel. Then he added, 'Sethvir chose not to come. He's too busy sewing. When you're done paying court to hackling sensation, you've ever been quick to declare yourself.'

'Luhaine always snaps the hooked bait like a trout.' Davien showed his teeth, very nearly a grin. 'Shall we by-pass the stickling history and cut to the chase? When the dragon has rested, she's agreed we shall mend the two grimwards that still need attention without your assistance. I'll retire to Kewar to repair my own leathers. Though in passing, you may tell Luhaine this: he can ask for my help anytime he wants Prime Selidie and her sisterhood roped back to heel.'

Asandir laughed. 'Let her try meddling with Arithon again, don't rest on your luck. I'll be there before you.' If no mention was made to approach Kharadmon, the field Sorcerer was wise enough to let the unhealed past bide without pressure. 'If you won't take my thanks, then find me content. Isfarenn's colt needs his care-free years to mature, and grimwards afoot are no party.'

Both Sorcerers stood. Further words were not needed. But for the first time since the bloody rebellion that brought massacre to the high kings, a wrist clasp of amity sealed their brisk parting.

Dawn at Athir arrived with spectacular beauty, a blaze to set the very world afire above the Cildein's sparkling surf. Over the fathomless dance of the ocean, the lucent sky brightened, a golden horizon blended in light to a zenith of cloudless indigo. Two figures awaited on the grass knoll beside the Paravian focus, when the Fellowship Sorcerer stepped through the crackling burst of the flux tide at daybreak. Four transfers across latitude from Atainia left his indigo mantle spotlessly neat. Except for a few ragged ends of singed hair, his presence seemed steadfast as ever.

'Asandir! You're a sight for sore eyes.' Dakar strode forward, altogether relieved that his difficult watch should be ending. If his squared shoulders reflected a deepened sense of purpose, he still itched to spill the fresh gossip.

'His Grace recalls nothing beyond the awareness that Elaira's love was the power that recalled him.'

Asandir's gaunt profile turned. He regarded the other, who waited some distance off, and made certain she planned to stay out of earshot. 'The Biedar elders can be an irresistible force, when they choose to take action.' Whether or not the tribe stood as his ally, the Sorcerer held his opinion. 'You're that eager to be away in my company?'

For in fact, the root of the spellbinder's urgency was not his former recalcitrance. The Mad Prophet tucked his round chin in his beard. He tightened his grip on his shapeless brown cloak, tugged in billows by the strafing wind. 'When you've seen the look in Prince Arithon's eyes, you'll know why,' he evaded. 'He's awaiting you inside the ruin. We don't speak, by my preference. I've sworn instead to guard Glendien's trust. But there's not a night that goes by where I don't lie awake, questioning whether the turn of events I helped shape could have been any different.'

'Our prince is still alive,' Asandir said without flinching. 'His blood oath on the matter is not in debate. Though, naturally, I cannot hold you to blame if you can't bear his intimate company.' Tactful before Dakar's naked relief, the Sorcerer's glance surveyed the figure still standing, forlorn, on the rise. 'And Elaira? Does she share your wounding remorse?'

Dakar stared into distance. 'She holds Arithon's true heart. That simplifies conscience. On the subject of Glendien's abrupt departure, the enchantress said what she hadn't been told would not trouble her honest rapport.'

'She's unlikely to breeze in for tea with Sethvir, or chase after Lorn's midwives, digging for scandal.' Asandir's stifled smile suggested sympathy. 'Though if she did, I'd back Althain's Warden. He's always had a touch for bare-faced diversions.'

Dakar shivered. 'All the same, I don't care to watch the exchange you intend for Prince Arithon.'

'I'd prefer that you didn't,' Asandir agreed. 'What business I have to attend should be brief. You have things left to gather? A fishing lugger bound across Vaststrait is scheduled to meet us within the hour.'

Dakar cast a wall-eyed glance at the surf, steep crests curling over in explosive froth from the swells of an outlying tempest. His complexion turned green. 'I'll forgo my breakfast,' he managed, resigned. Then, 'Why under Ath's sky should I choose this?' Rough passages and lane transfers wrung out his gut. Hard riding chafed him to blisters. Travel with Sorcerers was no kind of life to exchange for warm doxies and drunken oblivion.

Yet if he expected a master's sage answer, Asandir had already moved on to address the Koriani enchantress.

The freshening breeze pried at her coiled bronze hair, and the knuckles clenched on the satchel that bundled her healer's remedies. Asandir surveyed the dawn tint of her eyes and the lips that still wore the turbulent flush of Prince Arithon's parting kiss. 'My brave lady,' he opened. 'Do I have to say that our Fellowship owes you a debt beyond any repayment? You chose for a life, come whatever the cost. I salute the sweet gift of that bravery.'

Elaira regarded the Sorcerer whose grave counsel years ago in a seeress's cottage had steered her life's course from the proscribed path set by her order. From silver-grey hair to reactive, poised quiet, he was the same spirit, now. Still, he waited for her to direct the bent of today's conversation.

She shut her eyes. Throat closed, language failed her. Arithon's words, whispered into her ear, still entangled her beyond reason: *'Until forever, beloved,'* he had said. *'Our home together is where your life takes you.'*

The Sorcerer's reserve was unerring: her fight to recover her threatened poise needed none of his help. 'What little thing can our Fellowship give, that's racing your heart-beat to ask of us?' As she seized a deep breath, he added, acerbic, 'Speak in forthright confidence! Rest assured, if you fear an untoward listener, your request has my sealed ward of privacy.'

Elaira gasped with surprised laughter. 'You'd have Prime Selidie smoking with rage if she knew that her will could be thwarted so easily.'

'Then she'd best look out where she sparks off her fires,' Asandir declared with stripped warning.

Speech broke then, an unstoppable torrent. 'I have to return,' Elaira burst out. 'I don't relish the prospect. But one matter of driving importance remains. My personal crystal is still in the Matriarch's keeping. The question persists, why the quartz chose to bind its right to freedom under my vow to the Koriani Order. The riddle posed by the stone must be answered. Nobody else can pursue that course for me, or honour the peculiarity in my stead.'

Asandir sighed. 'Sethvir's earth-sense cannot unravel that quirk, since your quartz was not formed on Athera. Though you're right. The mineral's preference will carry a reason, strange though it seems to our human-based sensibilities. Neither are you one to forsake a friendship that has not turned and betrayed you.'

She had started to shiver. The Fellowship Sorcerer did touch her then, a warm, callused palm laid against her turned cheek as a shield from the bitter wind. 'What do you ask of us? Beyond what our Fellowship already has: Luhaine's surveillance will be ever-present, and Davien has a living dragon at hand, primed to answer your need, should you call him.'

'Save us all!' Elaira recovered her humour. 'What's become of your Fellowship's vaunted restraint?'

'No more damaged grimwards,' Asandir allowed. The steel flash in his eyes bespoke no mirth at all, as he added, 'The gang-up move to protect your good name could get thick, lest Arithon's fury should jump in first and spark the errant explosion.'

'He's pacified,' said Elaira, turned pale at the thought. 'I've promised my hand. He'll have to abide my Prime's interests until the time's fully ripe. Which brings me to ask for your favour. I'd like transport, south.' The long way by the land road was too heavy with memories to endure the cold journey alone.

The Sorcerer in his regaled formality regarded her. 'Brave lady! That's all? For his Grace's life's sake, my Fellowship can do you much better than that.'

When, again, she said nothing, Asandir's amusement resurged. He laced his large fingers through hers and drew her away from the leave she had asked, by way of the Paravian circle. 'Listen well. Sethvir's augury claims that the *Khetienn* will make landfall here, shortly before winter solstice. Prince Arithon will rejoin his ship's company, aboard. He'll have only Talvish, since he's bound on to Selkwood with a Masterbard's condolence for Lord Erlien and Kyrialt's grieving mother. His Grace also owes the same due respects to Fiark and the other family in mourning at Innish. Why not share his journey? A leisurely deepwater passage could set you ashore in the free wilds of Alland. The smugglers' coves there are a short hop to Telzen. Unless, of course, you're delayed by strong weather. Be assured, if that happens, your Prime Matriarch means to retire and sulk in seclusion at Forthmark. That route is best managed by ship, don't you think? You wouldn't be wise, yet, to venture a crossing on foot by way of Sanpashir.'

Elaira grinned. 'I'd report back to my order all in due time?'

'Well yes. Handfast to Rathain, why not please your betrothed a bit longer?' Asandir stared out to sea, a fierce light in his glance, that perhaps matched Sethvir's for dodging connivance. 'What else could your hobbled Prime Matriarch do, except gnaw on the nubs of her bandages till you arrive?'

Entailment

If Asandir's promised conference with Rathain's crown prince was pointed for brevity, the opening moment came as piquantly charged as Dakar's most cringing prediction. Yet where the Mad Prophet presumed that the Sorcerer's entry would meet with a stinging riposte, instead, the staging was set by the lyranthe the bard had just finished restringing. A plangent cascade of melody poured through the spill of new sunlight. The echoes reverberated from old stonewalls, already alive with the whispers of vanished Paravians. Beauty reigned, spun from a minor key that evoked the anguish of parting.

Talvish crouched in the shaded archway just outside of Arithon's presence. His pale head was masked in the crook of an elbow, braced by his upright, sheathed sword. His loyal guard was not dismissed, a relief the man stood up to acknowledge. The Fellowship were sticklers on matters of integrity; and among Seven, Asandir was the most straightforward taskmaster of all. The fact a sworn liegeman was kept on as witness meant this interview would stay restricted to formal crown business.

Yet even a Sorcerer on short timing would not impinge on the art of Athera's Masterbard. The outcry wrung from the raw pain of leave-taking was allowed the matchless, sweet effort to seek a release. When the musician's hand faltered, at last overcome, Asandir let his arrival be known.

He stepped through the arch, heralded by his long shadow.

Inside the tight stonework of Athir's foundation, the sea-wind was reduced to a salt-scented whisper. Arithon perched with his hair tumbled loose, his back braced to a roofless wall. The posture that still nursed a tender scar was wrapped in an oiled cloak, purloined from the sunk courier's crew locker. His borrowed shirt was also too large, and his jerkin, cut down from an outworn cast-off.

Yet nondescript clothing could never hide the stamp of encounter left by Athera's deep mysteries. The eyes that Dakar had been loath to meet snapped upward and challenged intrusion. An unworldly vision lurked in their green depths, a captured echo of glory past reach of the heart's ease to tame.

Swift fingers damped off the strings, faintly thrumming with the last strains of nakedly scalded emotion. To the Sorcerer's silence, Arithon said, 'You've come for Parrien? If so, you don't need formal dress to intimidate. He's been sweating in dread behind snappish pride, until Talvish threatened to grant him relief by clubbing him into unconsciousness.'

Yet the Fellowship emissary refused to be hazed. 'The issue of criminal justice can wait.' His pause left the sunlight vibrating on the stilled air. Where Talvish, behind, sucked his breath in abeyance, Asandir just managed to curb his impulse to chuckle out loud. 'You can unbend and smile, your Grace. I'm not here to berate you for hair-raising risks. The debt, in lives spared, is quite beyond price. I'm sorry you were abandoned to your own devices, and more. Your grief is acknowledged. The cost paid by some of your own came too dear.'

Arithon supported that stripping care, moment upon moment, not breaking. 'I have had Elaira beside me,' he said. 'Sidir will wed Feithan. Mearn's with his wife and new-born, secure under protection at Methisle Fortress, and for my misspent sacrifice in let blood, my writ commands pardon for Parrien.' He stretched out his arm, and retrieved a tied scroll from within the cover for his lyranthe. 'I trust you'll know when to apply this.'

Asandir accepted the offering. Though his glance never flickered, he noted the wax seal, impressed with Rathain's royal leopard. 'You've softened,' he tested. 'Enough to set your signature under the blazon of your crown birthright.'

'Have I?' Arithon's smile unveiled his edged challenge. 'Try this, instead. Shand's *caithdein*, the High Earl of Alland, will place his grievance for Kyrialt's death with the Crown Steward of Melhalla. I suffered a duke's brother's assault subject to her kingdom, also. Kindly as the Teiren's'Callient is, tendering soup to rude strangers, would she brook any less than my sanctioned signature at trial, for a murderer's binding reprieve?'

Asandir's frown remained purposefully grave, although Talvish, behind, caught the impression such bristled composure was kept for appearances. 'Melhalla's charter would not accept less. Never, under my Fellowship's oversight! Not for a wounding stroke meant to be fatal, against the unarmed talent, entitled as Masterbard.'

'Then I rest my case.' His lyranthe protectively tucked in his arms, Arithon did his utmost not to show that the stinging correction struck home. 'My name under seal set against a man's life? Thrown the miring weight of your crown, I will use its power at my convenience.'

'What of the folk still at risk in Alestron?' Asandir inquired point-blank.

While Talvish, behind, recoiled in dread, the Sorcerer bore in, unblinking.

His eyes mirror brilliant, he held out until, beyond mercy, Arithon Teir's'Ffalenn lost the poise for his jabbing defence.

'I thought so.' Asandir's murmur held more than mere gentleness. 'Where you've tried and failed, perhaps I might succeed. Your writ can be honoured where Parrien's concerned, though I will take your liberty to choose the timing to repeal the crown's pending charges. Meantime, let's see what else might be done for the people still trapped under Bransian's protection.'

As Arithon stared, fighting tears, the Sorcerer eased his promise for Alestron's reprieve with even more nerve-stripping tolerance. 'Your *convenience* has done a fine job for three realms. The rude stranger won't find us ungrateful. My earnest gesture awaits you, outside, one that I trust will delight you. If you're done belabouring Talvish's patience? Torbrand also masked over his frightful heroics with no end of testy disclaimers.'

Arithon laughed. 'Who's to blame, there?' Disarmed at last, he set down his lyranthe and stood, now willing to give the grace of a free singer's courtesy. 'I don't guess that my forebear volunteered for your throne. What blandishment did you offer him?'

'Complete your accession,' Asandir said, straight-faced. His height a forcefully shameless advantage, he peered down at the miscreant. 'I promise, your Grace, on that day, you'll find out.'

Gangling as he was, and as marked by hard service, the field Sorcerer owned blinding speed when he chose to move. The roofless courtyard was vacated before Arithon managed his scathing rejoinder: that Jeynsa s'Valerient had certainly proven her mettle to steward the throneless plight of Rathain.

Talvish side-stepped the Sorcerer's precipitate departure, then dodged again, to escape being flattened by a second rushed figure, incoming.

'Just hobble the insolent yap on his Grace!' he groused, pleased, as Elaira flew across the cleared threshold into Arithon's startled embrace.

The battered fishing lugger engaged by the Sorcerer plied a lumbering passage southbound from Athir across the narrows of Vaststrait. Tossing, she rounded the headland at Northstor. Cantankerous as a balked cow, worked to windward, she seeped at the seams, with rust streaked down the strakes at her chain-plates. The ripe stink of mackerel fouling her bilges earned jeering contempt from the galleys passing down wind.

Parrien s'Brydion suffered the ignominious crossing under Fellowship custody, and was not requested to navigate. While the grizzled captain and his hard-bitten hands plied their nets, Dakar underwent a rigorous study of weather wards and elementals. Asandir pushed those new skills to the limit, until the spell-binder grumped that his eyesight sparkled with distortion, and his aching head pounded, near back-lash. The decrepit vessel made port only once: an afternoon's dockage at Perdith to replace a patched sail and reprovision. The harbour officials pinched their disdainful, pink noses, and declined a thorough inspection.

While the fishermen gutted and sold their ripe catch, and Parrien stewed, constrained aboard, the Sorcerer visited a chandler's shop that sewed pennons. He returned, brightly whistling, a streamer of deep, midnight blue rolled up under his arm.

His word set the lugger's crew back ashore, smug and smiling with callused hands stuffed in their smock pockets.

'Save that Sorcerer from all mothering storms!' crowed the craft's relieved captain. What was left, but carousing to celebrate his astounding turn of good fortune? The round sum paid off by Asandir's charter would commission a handier vessel. 'For such brash generosity, we'll have us a tight, snappy lady that'll breast the cold easterlies without straining her caulking.'

'Won't miss the leaks that drizzled the berths.' The fishing crew exchanged a jubilant toast, as their tired old darling cast off. Their derelict, meant for the wreckers come spring, instead ploughed away on her wallowing route south.

Dakar's tasked lessons with wind and water resumed, while Parrien chewed over curses and languished. His slit-eyed ill humour lifted just once, when the lugger wore ship rounding Kalesh, and Asandir unfurled his new pennant to run up the peeling mast. The triangular cloth was slashed, contrary, by a diagonal white bar, with the upper quadrant marked by a six-pointed star: a device not observed by a town on the continent for more than five hundred years.

'Ath!' declared Parrien s'Brydion, awed, his piratical beard allowed to run wild. 'What I'd not give to sit above deck! Lounge at this tub's rail and laugh when the port blockade's excisemen try their damnable sanctions, enforced in the breach by archers with lints tipped in fire!'

'If they don't know the banner,' Asandir agreed, 'the lapse in town history just might go down a bit hard on them.'

Which double-edged warning hushed Parrien, fast, and left Dakar advised to tread softly. The lugger plunged onwards, groaning under loose stays. With the odd flag streaming like night under sunlight, she tacked again, side-slipping in churned foam to leeward. Then change occurred, seamless: wind and tide bowed before her worn tackle. More than the ancient banner declared presence, as her blunt prow came about, and suddenly cut an unerring, straight wake against the roiling ebb.

Fiasco ensued as she sliced the blockade, in flagrant disregard of extortionate fees and war edicts. On both sides of the strait, customs men from Kalesh and Adruin scrambled onto their barges to give chase. Harbour officials in overdone finery yammered threats through their bull-horns.

Commands to heave to and declare for the Light were ignored. The lugger showed them the gouged paint of her stern, as hot pursuit trailed her course through the estuary.

The fire archers, perforce, were commanded to shoot, whereupon the natural bent of wave and weather went crazy. No one agreed, afterward, about squalls in clear air. Yet the evidence stayed incontrovertible. The volleys of arrows bent awry in the gusts and kindled embarrassing wild fires. Errant shafts torched off the customs shacks, first; then the spired roofs of the towns' guild-halls. Both of the mayors' mansions went up, ignited by wind-borne sparks. The blazes blackened the view of the narrows, while the final round the bowmen unleashed quenched harmlessly into the sea.

Strayed in the clogged air, the customs fleet's barges fetched up in a snarl of oars on the shoals. There, the hysterical occupants howled, clinging in soaked misery upon canted decks, until the slack tide permitted a rescue.

The rogue lugger, meantime, thrashed away down the narrows, ramming up spume like a juggernaut. Kalesh dispatched fast couriers at a lathered gallop. By dint of post-horses changed every league, the riders smoked blisters on leather to outstrip the moth-eaten fishing craft's run towards Alestron.

Breaking news of the inbound blockade-runner reached Sulfin Evend at his morning conference in the command tent. He was standing, irritable, sparkling in state regalia, dark hair tied back beneath his shining helm. His mailed fists stayed planted on the table-top where his war council sat dead-locked in another snapping dispute. Day upon day, he was forced to crush the next clamour to waste troops in a frontal assault through the breach at the Sea Gate.

'Damn you all for a flock of rockhead spring rams!' he snapped in his withering accent. 'The citadel's garrison's starving and cold! By now weakened enough to succumb to disease, if not dropping within the next fortnight. Bedamned if you think your bickering can wear down my sensible patience. I'll have no more widows! The victory is ours. Naught's left to be done, beyond wait for it!'

Sudden, rushed footsteps from outside turned heads. The heated talk stalled as a courier burst in through the tent-flap. 'Bad news, your lordships, brought at speed from Kalesh!'

Breathless, the fellow unburdened. 'Sorcery!' he gasped. 'Light save us from evil, with our Blessed Prince gone to Avenor!' Into an atmosphere whiplashed from fractious anger to disbelief, he announced, 'Raise arms! We're set under assault by the powers of Darkness!'

Mayhem erupted. Alarmed officers shoved to their feet. Against their hoarse outcry, Sulfin Evend banged the trestle and raised a field officer's shout. 'Silence! Sit down!'

No one subsided. Blocking the rampage to roust idle troops out for battle, the Light's first commander snatched the hysterical courier by the collar. A shove backed his whining against the oak table, where harder questioning plumbed his message for clarity. 'You mentioned a strange banner flown by a lugger that sails contrary to natural forces?'

'Yes, my Lord!' The pinned courier swallowed. 'The craft bears a flag the port look-outs cannot identify.' Hedged by glittering steel, surrounded by volatile tempers, the stammering description emerged: of a deep blue, triangular streamer, marked with specific white symbols.

'Ath, I know that device.' Sulfin Evend's sharp features turned pale. 'No attack!' He released his grip, a lone voice in the crush, as the Light's fractious officers surged to seize charge.

He flung his state chair against the stampede. Hurled himself bodily into the breach, clubbing back the armed bodies that shoved to displace him. 'Hold your lines, on my order!'

Under dire threat, as the jostling unsheathed killing steel, Sulfin Evend pealed warning. 'Fools! That lugger's defended by powers your Blessed Prince could not thwart. Interfere by assault, and you'll seed wrack and ruin. Stay your swords! Though your faith in the Light might insist that aggression can triumph, weapons cannot prevail! I forbid an attack. At your peril, defy me.'

'Wise choice,' declared a disembodied voice, arrived to a snap of stark cold. The uncanny draught billowed a shrieking rip in the canvas roof overhead. Its tight blast also checked the murdering rush against the staunch ultimatum declared by Lysaer s'Ilessid's foremost captain.

'Oathsworn to the land, Sulfin Evend, you are called to serve!' cracked Kharadmon.

The next instant, the Sorcerer's image unfurled standing four-square before the Alliance's Lord Commander at Arms. 'Under the auspices of the Fellowship of Seven, the assault on Alestron is ended. Your troops make war upon ground ruled under old law, and threaten a citadel defended within charter grant under the Crown of Melhalla. King's justice, as served by the Teiren's'Callient, shall administer the terms by which the combatants will lay down their arms under truce.'

A smile curled the Sorcerer's lips, wickedly framed by his coal-black moustache and spade-point beard. 'At your peril,' Kharadmon repeated with a joy that simmered toward impatience. 'Upset your ranking officer's order and leave me the pleasure of shredding your war camp!'

The hour of summons found Lord Bransian in a temper, haranguing his mutinous cooks. 'I don't care blazes if you pucker up at the taste! You will butcher those rats! Every squeaking wee carcass! Stew their plucked flesh to a mush even your shrinking gut will take kindly. My fighting men can't hold the walls without rations. Serve up what you're given! Or by the unvanquished name of my fathers, you'll be set in chains and left to gnaw your own turds in my rodent-free dungeon!'

The boy runner sent by Sevrand plucked up his courage again. This time, he tugged at the duke's pumping arm. Through stammering fright, his message was finally heard. 'A patched lugger flying the standard of the Fellowship of Seven has tied up to the ruined landing.'

'Dharkaron's black bollocks!' Duke Bransian scowled. 'If this is my cousin's idea of a joke, I'll chop off his right arm to thicken the gruel in that pot.'

Yet the startling truth already wrought change: the hollow-eyed duty watch had pulled a dispirited team off the trebuchets. While the men rigged a new cable to replace the torched lift, the duke pelted to convene his blood family for a Fellowship reception.

'Confound the Sorcerers,' he gasped, hooking clasps, while his wife thrust his scarlet surcoat and state collar past the equerry, just suborned to clean his scuffed boots. 'Why couldn't they have made their timely appearance six months ago, when we weren't reduced to pulling brass tacks and boiling the leather off the good furniture?'

'You gave Kharadmon's diplomacy a blithe lick and a shrug,' Liesse pointed out with acerbity. She added, before fielding obscene imprecations, 'Sindelle and Tiassa are already dressed. And no! There's not a single wax candle left in the citadel, unless you've got a stash tucked away in the armoury.'

'None, you bloodsucking shrew! I have not stooped to lies among family.' Bransian bent his bare head, morose, as the ruby seal on its chain settled around his hunched neck. 'What about lamp oil?'

'Gone up with the Sea Gate.' Liesse sighed. 'Trust me, a spouse with no spine would have poisoned you on your wedding night.' She tied her laced bodice, too bitter and gaunt, and more drawn than the short rations warranted. 'I've taken the liberty of opening Dame Dawr's apartments. The south case-ments there at least will provide light for this cheerless arrival.' But no warmth, the last fuel being reserved for the kitchen's vile stew, by the duke's enforced orders, that morning.

Bransian's chapped lips cracked to show teeth. 'Let the Sorcerer freeze his rump in a cold seat. He can chew on rat's arse, if he's hungry.' But the bite to his bluster was sheer bravado, as his trembling wife surely knew.

'Which of the Seven, do you think?' she whispered in dread, gripping her husband's stout arm in descent through the frigid staircase. 'Sethvir won't have dispatched a shade on this errand.' For no boat and no lift tackle would be needful for a visitation, breezed into their midst.

'It would be Asandir,' Duke Bransian snarled, 'since Traithe would scarcely announce himself flying that brazen pendant! Never bang in the eyes of the blood-sucking towns that host the Alliance's war host.'

Hard on the heels of the scrambling servants who snatched off the sitting-room's dust-sheets, Asandir assumed the winged chair that had once belonged to Dame Dawr. The seat still commanded the space before the stone pilasters of the darkened fire-place . To his left, the latched casements spilled in streaming sun, brilliant day to storm-lit, azure night, where his velvet mantle draped upright shoulders.

Since Bransian s'Brydion was too massive to slink, he stalled until the last moment. Sevrand and both bereaved wives sat in silence, as his bold-as-brass tread crossed the threshold and hammered the carpet. He settled his duchess with immaculate deference. She was forced to fold her hands in her lap, or else risk her lace cuffs to destruction: the scarred trestle pulled in haste from the armoury had stayed bare in the rush to accommodate. Yet the juxtaposed setting of rich comfort and rude function was thrown into eclipse by stilled power, leashed in waiting to address Alestron's duke.

Bransian chose to remain on his feet, his last refuge his heavy-weight muscle.

'Old law still reigns here,' Asandir opened in declarative quiet. 'When did you think you became the exception, wielding the privilege of title above the terms of sworn service accorded to this ancestral seat?'

Though the steel in that gaze raised a glaze of flushed sweat, Bransian answered directly. 'My banner still flies above walls not yet overtaken in conquest. I may not be applauded for every mistake. Fact remains, my defence has not faltered.'

Asandir laced his large fingers; leaned forward, his face chiselled bare of expression. 'Defence by extortion, manipulation, and conspiracy?'

Cloth rustled, down the table. 'Prince Arithon spoke for his liegeman, and Jeynsa, who has been released without harm,' Sevrand dared. A brief pause ensued. 'Lawful terms put the grievance to rest,' he went on in his kinsman's defence.

A mistake: the Sorcerer's drilling attentiveness only resharpened upon the duke's steaming discomfort. 'My selection for the late high earl's post in Daon Ramon, as Arithon's intended *caithdein*, but a girl not yet sworn, in her teens. She was not sent home in corrected disgrace! Intrigue and collusion saw her brave folly reduced to bloodshed and bullying abuse. Rathain may have accepted compensation for damaging injury,' the Sorcerer amended in blistering censure. 'But no foreign prince on Melhalla's ground can usurp the right to declare for the crown's arbitration.'

'We are at war!' Duke Bransian pealed, laid raw as Liesse masked her face to stifle her ashamed tears. 'What of the enemies hounding our walls, laying siege while my people are starving? What of the holocaust that razed our farmsteads, and slaughtered our innocent villagers?'

'The Alliance will disband.' Asandir inclined his silver head in respect to the destitute wives, as he added, 'Each troop returns home to its town of origin, under a Fellowship fiat. Sulfin Evend's commanded to retire to Tysan. He will turn his crack troops to relocate the squatters encamped at the Second Age site at Avenor. That nest of iniquity will be swept clean! No more threats will be issued by a false court against the Kingdom of Havish! Lysaer s'Ilessid shall no longer house his pretensions at the crown seat of Avenor.'

A scraping disturbance arose at the door. Bransian turned his head, met by the mailed tread of his acting captain. The man's hands were the same, in their battered gauntlets, that had wielded steel through a lifetime of loyal campaigns. Only now, he carried the scarlet standard bearing the s'Brydion bull, just run down from the Watch Keep's flagstaff. The folded cloth was remanded to Sevrand, which at last ruffled Bransian's crowing defiance.

'Ath above!' he cried, shocked. 'You can't strike our colours in front of that mincing faker's religion!' Spurred yet by the courage of his stubborn heart, his anguished bellow gained force. 'That abrogates every term of the compact. Rams hard against every principle my ancestors died to preserve.'

'On no terms will I declare a surrender!' Asandir snapped in rebuke. 'The Fellowship's pendant takes sovereignty, here. This citadel holds too much strategic importance to stand at strength under any armed faction's self-serving brutality! Neither will an heir of s'Brydion reign, unless a Paravian presence returns to the continent. I have come to enact Alestron's entailment! This fortress will lie under Fellowship seal, until such time as a centaur guardian may declare in your favour for a reinstatement!'

'Then where will we go?' the deposed duke gasped, pale. The sun through the casements blazed down, too bright. He could not bear the sight of Liesse's bowed shoulders, or face his displaced cousin, or answer for the gaunt desperation endured by his lost brothers' widows. 'There would be no mercy shown by town mayors for the least of my children and kinsfolk. No secure place for any fighting man in my company who's resisted invasion.'

'Your place,' declared Asandir unequivocal, 'will be to serve Atwood's defences henceforward, with your war band kept under arms at your Teiren's'Callient's right hand. Your head of household shall fall to Mearn. He will hold the chieftain's seat on her council, until time determines what honest mettle your lineage matures for review.' The silence was stark as the Sorcerer finished, 'No one else dies for your family pride. The craftsfolk who have held out within the walls will be asked to resettle themselves in the trade towns. Since those who possessed a tuned ear for the mysteries have departed, called out by the song of Alithiel, they remain free to set roots where they please.'

The Sorcerer's unabashed sorrow emerged, then, as his mild closure scored the air like a line of engraving. 'By these terms, your people are granted their right to continued survival.'

Bransian shoved forward and banged on the trestle. Debased by shame, he shook off the imploring hands of his wife and glared down at his Fellowship arbiter. 'Let me die here. Strike me down, before I slink off to the forest, tuck tailed and grovelling.'

Asandir sighed. 'Just once, I might have seen you show the natural grace to apologize.' He stood to full height. Not a silver hair turned as he inclined his head towards the side doorway that led from the bedchamber. 'Dakar? Bring the prisoner, please.'

The spellbinder entered, to the rasp of Tiassa's shocked breath. Short-strided and fat, still fumbling with the role of authority, he ushered in Parrien's aggressive step. But this hour, the larger man's prowess wore the ridicule, tied in restraint as a felon.

'I will read you a choice,' said the Sorcerer softly. 'Parrien's sentence for the murder of Kyrialt s'Taleyn, struck dead while defending a fatal assault on

Athera's titled Masterbard. Or, you accept a quiet exile in Atwood, with your brother exonerated by Arithon Teir's'Ffalenn's sealed reprieve. Cross me again, Bransian, and I burn the royal writ that grants Tiassa's children their blood heritage, and her husband the privilege of retaining an ancestral name.'

Bransian raised his bearded chin. Shut his harrowed eyes, before weeping. Defeat branded him there, a huge, wounded lion torn by too many battles, waged through generations of vicious adversity. 'Tiassa,' he grated, 'set free your bound man.'

Clear sun shone, still, through the casements. Glints sparkled, blood deep, through the rubies in the state collar just unclasped and laid down on the trestle. Then a shadow eclipsed them, not Asandir's: the shaft of winter light illumined the reunion, as Bransian s'Brydion embraced the lost brother that fate had restored at the price of humility. Before Tiassa's joy, and Sindelle's faded mourning, he had nothing to do, and nowhere to turn, except to brace Liesse's tearful distress and step from the chamber in silenced ignominy.

Days later, the Second Age citadel of Alestron stood emptied of people and parading sentries. Dakar stood at the side of the Fellowship Sorcerer on the stilled, midnight eve, when Asandir spoke in actualized Paravian to rock, and mended the cracks in the underground cisterns.

At sunrise on winter solstice, the spellbinder also was granted the gift to bear living witness: as the Sorcerer mounted the height at Watch Keep and declared his address to the wind. Through an appeal to air element's grace, Asandir summoned the power of the wardings the centaurs of old had laced into the citadel's stonework. A heart-beat in time brought his answer. The solid ground sang underfoot, as the light and sound force of the defences blazed active, and ran gilded ribbons of ecstatic joy through flesh and bone, and ephemeral spirit.

How long the Sorcerer and his apprentice endured the struck note that streamed through the eye of eternity, no human senses might measure.

Yet when Asandir shouted the Named rune for ending, the fortress of Alestron lay under seal. No step would trespass here. Man, woman, or child, none might enter unless Mankind's presence was granted leave by Athera's Paravians. The high walls were left silent. Vacant crenels lay washed in a faint, silvered nimbus, until the summoning force of grand mystery dwindled to moonbeams in daylight, then faded quiescent. Nothing spoke then but the cry of a hawk, and the salt-laden gusts off the estuary.

The Sorcerer faced north-westward, and offered his opened hand, palm upwards. His silver-grey eyes appeared fixed into distance, as he touched the listening presence of Sethvir, who awaited, poised at the focus laid into the vault beneath Althain Tower.

'Are you coming?' Asandir admonished the spellbinder, still gawping over the memory of marvels.

Dakar started and yelped, seized by Asandir's fist. Ever and always, the fat seer was granted no warning to brace for the gut-wrenching upset that followed.

'*Reach!*' sent the Warden.

The clasp of Asandir's raised wrist was received, bridged across yawning oblivion.

The next instant, the crag of the citadel stood empty, the only trace of a Fellowship presence the midnight blue and white pennant, streaming above the fast quiet of Watch Keep's squat spire. For passing years that extended to centuries, the men in the crab skiffs that trapped in the estuary, and the caravans bound down the trade-road attested the fact that the cloth never frayed in the grip of the elements. Unlike the worn lugger, that stove in forlorn planks in the next winter storm, and sank under the waves at the landing.

Weavings

Last to board the state galley moored at the quay beside the slagged ruin of Avenor, Lysaer s'Ilessid muses to his Lord Commander at Arms, while the lines are cast off to make sail in the wake of the last flotilla of refugees: 'Regrets? I have many. But none to outmatch my honest need for your strength, as I grope for the foothold to safeguard the future . . .

The tall oaks of Halwythwood bud with new leaves on the day that two trail-weary travellers return to Earl Barach's lodge tent; beside a grown daughter clad in *caithdein's* black, invested by Fellowship presence at Methisle, Feithan weeps for joy in the arms of Sidir, restored to her side on command of a crown prince whose talents would bless her life best through benevolent absence . . .

Far south, amid the black sands of Sanpashir, on the dark moon fallen nearest the spring equinox, the eldest of the Biedar unsheathes an ancient flint knife to cut the birth-cord of an infant successor; and her words, in thick dialect, charge the child to watch over the one named as Mother Dark's Chosen through the trials of the next generation . . .

GLOSSARY

A'LIESSIAD—a wholeness of balance between all beings.

   pronounced: ah-less-ee-ahd

   root meaning: *a'liessiad* – balance, with the prefix for the feminine aspect.

ADRUIN—fortified coastal town located in East Halla, Midhalla. Bitter enemies of the s'Brydion of Alestron, with a running blood feud since the uprising in Third Age 5018.

   pronounced: like 'add ruin'

   root meaning: *adruinne* – to block, or obstruct; or alternatively *al* – over; *duinn* – hand

AFFI'ENIA—name given to Elaira by an adept, meaning dancer in the ancient dialect of the Biedar tribe, but carrying the mystical connotation of 'water dancer', the wise woman who presided over the ritual of rebirth, celebrated on the spring equinox.

   pronounced: affee-yen-yah

   root meaning: *affi'enia* – dancer

AIYENNE—river located in Daon Ramon, Rathain, rising from an underground spring in the Mathorn Mountains, and coming above ground south of the Mathorn Road. Site of the ruinous battle between Earl Jieret's war band, and the Alliance war host under Sulfin Evend, which enabled Arithon's escape to the north in Third Age 5670.

   pronounced: eye-an

   root meaning: *ai'an* – hidden one

ALESTRON—city located in Midhalla, Melhalla. Ruled by Duke Bransian, Teir's'Brydion, and his three brothers. This city did not fall to merchant townsmen in the Third Age uprising that threw down the high kings, but is still ruled by its clanblood heirs.

   pronounced: ah-less-tron

   root meaning: *alesstair* – stubborn; *an* – one

ALITHIEL—one of twelve Blades of Isaer, forged by centaur Ffereton s'Darian from metal taken from a meteorite, and sung by the Athlien with the arcane endowment for transcendent change. Passed through Paravian possession, acquired the secondary name Dael-Farenn, or Kingmaker, since its owners tended to succeed the end of a royal line. Eventually was awarded to Kamridian s'Ffalenn for his valor in defence of the princess Taliennse, early Third Age. Currently in the possession of Arithon.

   pronounced: ah-lith-ee-el

   root meaning: *alith* – star; *iel* – light/ray

ALLAND—principality located in south-eastern Shand. Ruled by the Lord Erlien s'Taleyn, High Earl, and appointed *caithdein* of Shand.

   pronounced: all-and

   root meaning: *a'lind* – pine glen

ALTHAIN TOWER—spire built at the edge of the Bittern Desert, beginning of the Second Age, to house records of Paravian histories. Third Age, became repository for the archives of all five royal houses of men after rebellion, overseen by the Fellowship Sorcerer, Sethvir, named Warden of Althain since Third Age Year 5100.

  pronounced: all-thay-in

  root meaning: *alt* – last; *thein* – tower, sanctuary

  original Paravian pronunciation: alt-thein

ANIENT—Paravian invocation for unity.

  pronounced: an-ee-ent

  root meaning: *an* – one; *ient* – suffix for 'most'

ANSHLIEN'YA—name given to Meiglin s'Dieneval by the desert tribes of Sanpashir, prior to her conception of Dari's'Ahelas, crown heir of Shand, who would bear the rogue talent for far-sighted vision.

  pronounced: ahn-shlee-yen-yah

  root meaning: *anshlien'ya* – Biedar dialect, ancient word for 'dawn;' idiom for 'hope'

ANYN'E AIN S'TEIRDAEL—handfast to my prince.

  pronounced: an-een-ay ay-in s'tay-er-daa-el

  root meaning: *anyn'e* – one with suffix for in potentia; *ain* – my; *s'teirdael* – possessive prefix, 'belonging to' one who holds rulership

ARAETHURA—grass plains in south-west Rathain; principality of the same name in that location. Largely inhabited by Riathan Paravians in the Second Age. Third Age, used as pasture land by widely scattered nomadic shepherds. Fionn Areth's birthplace.

  pronounced: ar-eye-thoo-rah

  root meaning: *araeth* – grass; *era* – place, land

ARITHON—son of Avar, Prince of Rathain, 1,504th Teir's'Ffalenn after founder of the line, Torbrand in Third Age Year One. Also Master of Shadow, the Bane of Desh-thiere, and Halliron Masterbard's successor. First among Mankind to tap the transcendent powers of the sword, Alithiel, and also responsible for the final defeat of the Grey Kralovir necromancers.

  pronounced: ar-i-thon

  root meaning: *arithon* – fate-forger; one who is visionary

ARWENT—river in Araethura, Rathain, that flows from Daenfal Lake through Halwythwood to empty in Instrell Bay.

  pronounced: are-went

  root meaning: *arwient* – swiftest

ASANDIR—Fellowship Sorcerer. Secondary name, Kingmaker, since his hand crowned every High King of Men to rule in the Age of Men (Third Age). After the Mistwraith's conquest, he acted as field agent for the Fellowship's doings across the continent. Also called Fiend-quencher, for his reputation for quelling *iyats*; Storm-breaker and Change-bringer for his past actions when Men first arrived upon Athera.

  pronounced: ah-san-deer

  root meaning: *asan* – heart; *dir* – stone 'heartrock'

ATAINIA—north-eastern principality of Tysan.

pronounced: ah-tay-nee-ah

root meaning: *itain* – the third; *ia* – suffix for 'third domain' original Paravian, *itainia*

ATCHAZ—town located in Alland, Shand. Famed for its silk.

pronounced: at-chaz

root meaning: *atchias* – silk

ATH CREATOR—prime vibration, force behind all life.

pronounced: ath

root meaning: *ath* – prime, first (as opposed to an, one)

ATH'IEL I'CUEL'AN ALESSTAIRIENT—Creator light your extreme persistence/dedication.

pronounced: ahth-ee-el ih-cue-el-ahn ah-less-tay-ree-ent

root meaning: *ath* – prime force of creation; *iel* – light; *i'cuel'an* – you/one or 'your' with prefix meaning shaded towards light intent; *alesstairient* – emphatic form, extreme dedication

ATHERA—name for the world which holds the Five High Kingdoms; four Worldsend Gates; formerly inhabited by dragons, and current home of the Paravian races.

pronounced: ath-air-ah

root meaning: *ath* – prime force; *era* – place 'Ath's world'

ATHIR—Second Age ruin of a Paravian stronghold, located in Ithilt, Rathain. Site of a seventh lane power focus; also where Arithon Teir's'Ffalenn swore his blood oath to survive to the Fellowship Sorcerer, Asandir.

pronounced: ath-ear

root meaning: *ath* – prime; *i'er* – the line/edge

ATHLIEN PARAVIANS—sunchildren, dancers of the crystal flutes. Small race of semimortals, pixie-like, but possessed of great wisdom/keepers of the grand mystery.

pronounced: ath-lee-en

root meaning: *ath* – prime force; *lien* – to love 'Ath-beloved'

ATHLIERIA—a dimension removed from physical time/space, or the exalted that lies past the veil.

pronounced: ath-lee-air-ee-ah

root meaning: *ath* – prime force; *li'eria* – exalted place, with suffix for 'beyond the veil.'

AVENOR—Second Age ruin of a Paravian stronghold. Traditional seat of the s'Ilessid High Kings. Restored to habitation in Third Age 5644. Became the ruling seat of the Alliance of Light in Third Age 5648. Located in Korias, Tysan.

pronounced: ah-ven-or

root meaning: *avie* – stag; *norh* – grove

BARACH—second son of Jieret s'Valerient, and older brother of Jeynsa. Successor to the title, Earl of the North.

    pronounced: bar-ack

    root meaning: *baraich* – linchpin

    root meaning: *bar* – half; *ris* – way

BIEDAR—desert tribe living in Sanpashir, Shand. Also known as the Keepers of the Prophecy. Their sacred weaving at the well produced the conception of Dari s'Ahelas, which crossed the old *caithdein*'s lineage of s'Dieneval with the royal line of s'Ahelas, combining the gifts of prophetic clairvoyance with the Fellowship-endowed penchant for far-sight.

    pronounced: bee-dar

    root meaning: *biehdahrr* – ancient desert dialect for 'lore keepers'

BITTERN DESERT—waste located in Atainia, Tysan, north of Althain Tower. Site of a First Age battle between the great drakes and the Seardluin, permanently destroyed by dragonfire.

    pronounced: bittern

    root meaning: *bityern* – to sear or char

BRANSIAN s'BRYDION—Teir's'Brydion, ruling Duke of Alestron. Husband of Liesse.

    pronounced: bran-see-an

    root meaning: *brand* – temper; *s'i'an* – suffix denoting 'of the one'/the one with temper

CAITHDEIN—(alternate spelling *caith'd'ein*, plural form *caithdeinen*) Paravian name for a high king's first counsellor; also, the one who would stand as regent, or steward, in the absence of the crowned ruler. By heritage, the office also carries responsibility for oversight of crown royalty's fitness to rule.

    pronounced: kay-ith-day-in

    root meaning: *caith* – shadow; *d'ein* – behind the chair 'shadow behind the throne'

CAMRIS—north-central principality of Tysan. Original ruling seat was the city of Erdane.

    pronounced: cam-ris

    root meaning: *caim* – cross; *ris* – way 'cross-road'

CAOLLE—past war-captain of the clans of Deshir, Rathain. First raised, and then served under, Lord Steiven, Earl of the North and *caithdein* of Rathain. Planned the campaign at Vastmark and Dier Kenton Vale for the Master of Shadow. Served Jieret Red-beard, and was feal liegeman of Arithon of Rathain; died of complications from a wound received from his prince while breaking a Koriani attempt to trap his liege in Third Age Year 5653.

    pronounced: kay-all-eh, with the 'e' nearly subliminal

    root meaning: *caille* – stubborn

CARITHWYR—principality in Havish, once a grass-lands breeding ground for the Riathan Paravians. Now produces grain, cattle, fine hides, and also wine.

   pronounced: car-ith-ear

   root meaning: *ci'arithiren* – forgers of the ultimate link with prime power. An old colloquialism for unicorn.

CATTRICK—master shipwright hired to run the royal shipyard at Riverton; once in Arithon's employ at Merior by the Sea, now in charge of the shipworks for Duke Bransian s'Brydion at Alestron.

   pronounced: cat-rick

   root meaning: *ciattiaric* – a knot tied of withies that has the magical property of confusing enemies

CILADIS THE LOST—Fellowship Sorcerer who left the continent in Third Age 5462 in search of the Paravian races after their disappearance following the rebellion.

   pronounced: kill-ah-dis

   root meaning: *cael* – leaf; *adeis* – whisper, compound; *cael'adeis* colloquialism for 'gentleness that abides'

CILDEIN OCEAN—body of water lying off Athera's east coast.

   pronounced: kill-dine

   root meaning: *cailde* – salty; *an* – one

CORITH—island west of Havish in the Westland Sea. Site of an old drake lair, and a ruined First Age foundation. Here the council of Paravians convened during siege, and their appeal brought the Second Dreaming by dragons, which enacted the summoning of the seven who became the Fellowship Sorcerers.

   pronounced: core-ith

   root meaning: *cori* – ships, vessels; *itha* – five

CORRA—wife of Fiark, and mother of his children.

   pronounced: cor-ah

   root meaning: *cor* – ship; *ar'ia* – little etheric being/a benevolent sprite that brings good fortune to shipping endeavours.

CORTEND—company sergeant, under Talvish's command.

   pronounced: core-tend

   root meaning: *koria'tiend* – one who keeps order; orderly spirit

CRESIDEN—Dame Dawr's most trusted man-servant.

   pronounced: cress-i-den

   root meaning: *criess* – honest; *i'den* – light of manner, courteous

D'AEDANTHIC—desert dialect, the name by which the Biedar tribe of Sanpashir refer to Davien.

   pronounced: die-dan-thick

   root meaning: *d'ae* – fire; *danthic* – hands

DAELION FATEMASTER—'entity' formed by set of mortal beliefs, which determine the fate of the spirit after death. If Ath is the prime vibration, or life-force, Daelion is what governs the manifestation of free will.

pronounced: day-el-ee-on

root meaning: *dael* – king, or lord; *i'on* – of fate

DAELION'S WHEEL—cycle of life and the crossing point that is the transition into death.

pronounced: day-el-ee-on

root meaning: *dael* – king or lord; *i'on* – of fate

DAENFAL—town located on the northern shore of Daenfal Lake, which bounds the southern edge of Daon Ramon Barrens in Rathain.

pronounced: dye-en-fall

root meaning: *daen* – clay; *fal* – red

DAKAR THE MAD PROPHET—apprentice to Fellowship Sorcerer, Asandir, during the Third Age following the Conquest of the Mistwraith. Given to spurious prophecies, it was Dakar who forecast the fall of the Kings of Havish in time for the Fellowship to save the heir. He made the Prophecy of West Gate, which forecast the Mistwraith's bane, and also, the Black Rose Prophecy, which called for reunification of the Fellowship. At this time, in the service of Arithon, Prince of Rathain.

pronounced: dah-kar

root meaning: *dakiar* – clumsy

DAON RAMON BARRENS—central principality of Rathain. Site where Riathan Paravians (unicorns) bred and raised their young. Barrens was not appended to the name until the years following the Mistwraith's conquest, when the River Severnir was diverted at the source by a task force under Etarran jurisdiction.

pronounced: day-on-rah-mon

root meaning: *daon* – gold; *ramon* – hills/downs

DARI s'AHELAS—crown heir of Shand who was sent to safety through West Gate to preserve the royal lineage. Born following the death of the last Crown Prince of Shand, subsequently raised and taught by Sethvir to manage the rogue talent of a dual inheritance. Her mother was Meiglin s'Dieneval, last survivor of the old *caithdein*'s lineage of Melhalla, which was widely believed to have perished during the massacre at Tirans. However the pregnant widow of Egan s'Dieneval had escaped the uprising and survived under a false name in a Durn brothel.

pronounced: dar-ee

root meaning: *daer* – to cut

DARKLING—city located on the western side of the Skyshiel Mountains in the Kingdom of Rathain.

pronounced: dark-ling

root meaning: *dierk-linng* – drake eyrie

DASCEN ELUR—splinter world off West Gate, where the heirs of three crown lineages lived in exile, with intent to spare the royal blood-lines from the upheaval that followed the Mistwraith's invasion.

pronounced: das-en el-ur

root meaning: *dascen* – ocean; *e'lier* – small land

DAVIEN THE BETRAYER—Fellowship Sorcerer responsible for provoking the great uprising in Third Age Year 5018, that resulted in the fall of the high kings after Desh-thiere's conquest. Rendered discorporate by the Fellowship's judgement in Third Age 5129. Exiled since, by personal choice. Davien's works included the Five Centuries Fountain near Mearth on the splinter world of the Red Desert through West Gate; the shaft at Rockfell Peak, used by the Sorcerers to imprison harmful entities; the Stair on Rockfell Peak; and also, Kewar Tunnel in the Mathorn Mountains.

    pronounced: dah-vee-en

    root meaning: *dahvi* – fool; *an* – one 'mistaken one'

DAWR s'BRYDION—grandmother of Duke Bransian of Alestron, and his brothers Keldmar, Parrien, and Mearn.

    pronounced: dour

    root meaning: *dwyiar* – vinegar wine

DESHIR—north-western principality of Rathain.

    pronounced: desh-eer

    root meaning: *deshir* – misty

DESH-THIERE—Mistwraith that invaded Athera from the splinter worlds through South Gate in Third Age 4993. Access cut off by Fellowship Sorcerer, Traithe. Battled and contained in West Shand for twenty-five years, until the rebellion splintered the peace, and the high kings were forced to withdraw from the defence lines to attend their disrupted kingdoms. Confined through the combined powers of Lysaer s'Ilessid's gift of Light and Arithon s'Ffalenn's gift of Shadow. Currently imprisoned in a warded flask in Rockfell Pit.

    pronounced: desh-thee-air-e (last 'e' mostly subliminal)

    root meaning: *desh* – mist; *thiere* – ghost or wraith

DHARKARON AVENGER—called Ath's Avenging Angel in legend. Drives a chariot drawn by five horses to convey the guilty to Sithaer. Dharkaron as defined by the adepts of Ath's Brotherhood is that dark thread mortal men weave with Ath, the prime vibration, that creates self-punishment, or the root of guilt.

    pronounced dark-air-on

    root meaning: *dhar* – evil; *khiaron* – one who stands in judgement

DHIRKEN—lady captain of the contraband runner, *Black Drake*. Reputed to have taken over the brig's command by right of arms following her father's death at sea. Died at the hands of Lysaer's allies on the charge of liaison with Arithon s'Ffalenn, Third Age Year 5647.

    pronounced: dur-kin

    root meaning: *dierk* – tough; *an* – one

DIER KENTON VALE—a valley located in the principality of Vastmark, Shand, where Lysaer's war host, thirty-five thousand strong, fought and lost to the Master of Shadow in Third Age 5647, largely decimated in one day by a shale slide. The remainder were harried by a small force of Vastmark shepherds and clan scouts from Shand, under Caolle, who served as Arithon's war-captain, until supplies and loss of morale broke the Alliance campaign.

pronounced: deer ken-ton

root meaning: *dier'kendion* – a jewel with a severe flaw that may result in shearing or cracking.

DURN—town located in Orvandir, Shand. Birthplace of Meiglin s'Dieneval.

pronounced: dern

root meaning: *diern* – a flat plain

EAST HALLA—principality in Melhalla.

pronounced: east hall-ah

root meaning: *hal'lia* – white light

EASTWALL—city located in the Skyshiel Mountains, Rathain.

EAST WARD—fishing and trade town located on the eastern coast of Fallowmere, in Rathain.

EASTTAIR—fortified town located on the East Halla peninsula, in Melhalla.

pronounced: ee-ass-tay-er

root meaning: *e'ast* – small cove; *taer* – calm

EBRAR—an elite captain, dedicate to the Light, serving under Sulfin Evend.

pronounced: ee-brar

root meaning: *ebair* – reliant, steady; *i'er* – the line

ELAIRA—initiate enchantress of the Koriathain, currently serving the order as a wandering independent. Originally a street child, taken on in Morvain for Koriani rearing. Arithon's beloved.

pronounced: ee-layer-ah

root meaning: *e* – prefix, diminutive for small; *laere* – grace

ELDIR s'LORNMEIN—King of Havish and once the last surviving scion of s'Lornmein royal line. Raised as a wool-dyer until the Fellowship Sorcerers crowned him at Ostermere in Third Age 5643 following the defeat of the Mistwraith. Now father of four children.

pronounced: el-deer

root meaning: *elder* – to ponder, to consider, to weigh

ELLAINE—daughter of the Lord Mayor of Erdane, once Princess of Avenor by marriage to Lysaer s'Ilessid, and mother of Kevor s'Ilessid, who became an adept of Ath's Brotherhood.

pronounced: el-lane

not from the Paravian

ELSSINE—town on the coast of Alland, Shand. Best known for its granite quarries and tempered steel.

pronounced: el-seen

root meaning: *elssien* – small pit

ELTAIR BAY—large bay off Cildein Ocean and east coast of Rathain; where the River Severnir was diverted following the Mistwraith's conquest.

pronounced: el-tay-er

root meaning: *al'tieri* – of steel/a shortening of original Paravian name; *dascen al'tieri* – which meant 'ocean of steel,' which referred to the colour of the waves

ENITHEN TUER—seeress living in the town of Erdane. Originally a Koriani sister who encountered the Biedar tribes in Sanpashir, and on the basis of their influence, was freed from her initiate's vow of service by Fellowship Sorcerer Asandir's intervention.

pronounced: en-ith-en too-er

root meaning: *en'wethen* – far-sighted; *tuer* – crone

ERIEGAL—second youngest of the fourteen child survivors of the Tal Quorin massacre known as Jieret's Companions. Renowned as a shrewd tactician, he was ordered to serve Jieret's son Barach as war-captain in the Halwythwood camp rather than fight Lysaer's war host in Daon Ramon Barrens in Third Age Year 5670.

pronounced: air-ee-gall

root meaning: *eriegal* – snake

ERLIEN s'TALEYN—High Earl of Alland; *caithdein* of Shand, chieftain of the forest clansmen of Selkwood. Once fought Arithon s'Ffalenn at sword-point over an issue of law bound over by Melhalla's *caithdein* and also as a trial of a sanctioned crown prince's honest character. Father of Kyrialt s'Taleyn.

pronounced: er-lee-an

root meaning: *aierlyan* – bear; *tal* – branch; *an* – one/first 'of first branch'

ETARRA—trade city built across the Mathorn Pass by townsfolk after the revolt that cast down Ithamon and the High Kings of Rathain. Nest of corruption and intrigue, and policy-maker for the North. Lysaer s'Ilessid was ratified as mayor upon Morfett's death in Third Age Year 5667. Site where Arithon defeated the Kralovir necromancers in Third Age Year 5671. Also the seat of the Alliance armed forces.

pronounced: ee-tar-ah

root meaning: *e* – prefix for small; *taria* – knots

EVENSTAR—first brig stolen from Riverton's royal shipyard by Cattrick's conspiracy with Prince Arithon. Currently of Innish registry, running merchant cargoes under joint ownership of Fiark and his sister Feylind, who is master.

FALLOWMERE—north-eastern principality of Rathain.

pronounced: fal-oh-meer

root meaning: *fal'ei'miere* – literally, tree self-reflection, colloquialism for 'place of perfect trees'

FARSEE—coastal harbour on the Bay of Eltair, located in East Halla, Melhalla.

pronounced: far-see

root meaning: *faersi* – sheltered/muffled

FATE'S WHEEL—see Daelion's Wheel.

FELLOWSHIP OF SEVEN—sorcerers bound to Athera by the summoning dream of the dragons and charged to secure the mysteries that enable Paravian survival. Achieved their redemption from Cianor Sunlord, under the Law of the Major Balance in Second Age Year One. Originators and keepers of the covenant of the compact, made with the Paravian races, to allow Mankind's settlement on Athera in Third Age Year One. Their authority backs charter law, upheld by crown justice and clan oversight of the free wilds.

FEITHAN—widow of Jieret s'Valerient, Earl of the North, and *caithdein* of Rathain, handfast to the Companion, Sidir.

    pronounced: faith-an

    root meaning: *feiathen* – ivy

FEIYD ETH SA—Biedar dialect, from Sanpashir, meaning 'look at this!'

    pronounced: fay-eed-eth-saa

    root meaning: *feiyd* – look; *eth* – at; *sa* – this

FENNICK—man-at-arms from the royal guard at Avenor, once honour guard to Prince Kevor, now reprieved and reassigned as one of Lysaer s'Ilessid's personal guard by Sulfin Evend.

    pronounced: fen-nick

    not from Paravian

FEYLIND—daughter of a Scimlade fisherman and Jinesse, twin sister of Fiark, currently master of *Evenstar*, a merchant brig of Innish registry.

    pronounced: fay-lind

    root meaning: *faelind'an* – outspoken or noisy one

FFEREDON-LI—ancient Paravian word for a healer, literally translated 'bringer of grace' and the name given to Elaira by an Araethurian seeress on the hour of Fionn Areth's birth.

    pronounced: fair-eh-dun-lee

    root meaning: *ffaraton* – maker; *li* – exalted grace

FIANZIA—(ANZIA, diminutive form) wife of Mearn s'Brydion.

    pronounced: fie-an-zee-ah

    root meaning: *ffianzia* – jade

FIARK—son of a Scimlade fisherman and Jinesse, twin brother of Feylind, currently a merchant factor at Innish, also handles all of Arithon's covert shore-side affairs. Husband of Corra.

    pronounced: fee-ark

    root meaning: *fyerk* – to throw or toss

FIONN ARETH CAID'AN—goatherd's child born in Third Age 5647; fated by prophecy to leave home and play a role in the Wars of Light and Shadow. Laid under Koriani spellcraft to mature as Arithon's double, then used as the bait in the order's conspiracy to trap the s'Ffalenn prince. Rescued from execution in Jaelot in 5669-70. Currently in the protective custody of the Prince of Rathain, in company with Vhandon and Talvish at Alestron.

pronounced: fee-on-are-eth cayed-ahn

root meaning: *fionne arith caid an* – one who brings choice

FIRSTMARK—port town located on the shore of Rockbay Harbor, in Radmoore, Melhalla. Known for its wine and hides.

FORTHMARK—city in Vastmark, Shand. Once the site of a hostel of Ath's Brotherhood. By Third Age 5320, the site was abandoned and taken over by the Koriani Order as a healer's hospice.

not from the Paravian

GANISH—trade city located south of Methlas Lake in Orvandir, Shand.

pronounced: gan-eesh

root meaning: *gianish* – a halfway point, a stopping place

GEVARD—officer from the Telzen garrison, allied with the Blessed Prince.

pronounced: gev-ard

not from the Paravian

GLENDIEN—a Shandian clanswoman, wife to Kyrialt s'Taleyn, formerly the heir designate of the High Earl of Alland.

pronounced: glen-dee-en

root meaning: *glyen* – sultry; *dien* – object of beauty

GREAT WAYSTONE—see entry for Waystone.

GRIMWARD—a circle of spells of Paravian making that seal and isolate the dire dreams of dragon haunts, a force with the potential for mass destruction. With the disappearance of the old races, the defences are maintained by embodied Sorcerers of the Fellowship of Seven. There are seventeen separate sites listed at Althain Tower.

HALLIRON SEN ALDUIN—native of Innish who became Masterbard of Athera in Third Age year 5597, after Murchiel. Son of Al'duin, husband of Deartha, and teacher of Arithon s'Ffalenn. Died of an injury dealt by the Mayor of Jaelot in year 5644.

pronounced: hal-eer-on sen al-doo-win

root meaning: *hal* – white; *lyron* – singer; *sen* – denotes paternal descent; *alduin* – scribe

HALWYTHWOOD—forest located in Araethura, Rathain. Current main camp-site of High Earl Barach's band, predominantly survivors of the Battle of Strakewood and Daon Ramon's late war.

pronounced: hall-with-wood

root meaning: *hal* – white; *wythe* – vista

HANHAFFIN—river running through Selkwood in Alland and emptying into the Cildein Ocean.

pronounced: han-haf-fin

root meaning: *hanha* – evergreen; *affein* – a dance step

HANSHIRE—port city on the Westland Sea, coast of Korias, Tysan; reigning official Lord Mayor Garde, father of Sulfin Evend; opposed to royal rule at the time of Avenor's restoration. Haven for Koriathain at the time of the uprising, with strong ties to the Senior Circle.

    pronounced: han-sheer

    root meaning: *hansh* – sand; *era* – place

HASPASTION—ghost of the dragon contained in the grimward located in Radmoore.

    pronounced: has-past-ee-on

    root meaning: *hashpashdion* – Drakish for black thunder

HAVENS—an inlet on the north-eastern shore of Vastmark, Shand, now known as the site of the massacre enacted by the Spinner of Darkness, preceding the Battle of Dier Kenton Vale, Third Age Year 5647.

HAVISH—one of the Five High Kingdoms of Athera as defined by the charters of the Fellowship of Seven. Ruled by Eldir s'Lornmein. Crown heritage: temperance. Device: gold hawk on red field.

    pronounced: hav-ish

    root meaning: *havieshe* – hawk

HIGHSCARP—city sited near the stone quarries on the coast of the Bay of Eltair, located in Daon Ramon, Rathain. Also contains a sisterhouse of the Koriani Order.

HILGRETH—war-captain in Selkwood, under Lord Erlien, High Earl of Alland.

    pronounced: hill-greth

    root meaning: *huell* – one who protects; *gireth* – gauntlet, war glove

I'CUELAN AM-JIASK EDAEL I'ITIER—your feal prince attends you.

    pronounced: ee-kway-lan am-jee-ask ee-dah-el it-ee-er

    root meaning: *i'cuelan* – your, with prefix for 'light' or focused intent; *am-jiask* – state of being bound by faith/feal; *edael* – prince; *i'itier* – one who holds with light/attends

I'ENT CUELAN AM-JIASK EDAEL AMEINNT-HUELL I'TIERI—your feal prince attends, with protective intent—raised to the emphatic state, of personally claiming fullest responsibility, as the oath-bound prince who protects.

    pronounced: ee-ent kway-lan am-jee-ask ee-dah-el am-ee-int hoo-well ee-tee-er-ee

    root meaning: *i'ient* – to hold by light, promise by willing intent; *cuelan* – your; *am-jiask edael* – feal prince; *am* – state of being; *iennt* – by light intent, extreme emphatic form; *huell* – one who protects; *i'tieri* – one who attends

ILITHARIS PARAVIANS—centaurs, one of three semimortal old races; disappeared after the Mistwraith's conquest, the last guardian's departure by Third Age Year 5100. They were the conservators of the earth's mysteries.

    pronounced: i-li-thar-is

    root meaning: *i'lith'earis* – the keeper/preserver of mystery

INNISH—city located on the southcoast of Shand at the delta of the River Ippash. Birthplace of Halliron Masterbard. Formerly known as 'the Jewel of Shand,' this was the site of the high king's winter court, prior to the time of the uprising. Home port of *Evenstar*, and Fiark's business as trade factor.

pronounced: in-ish

root meaning: *inniesh* – a jewel with a pastel tint

ISAER—power focus, built in the First Age in Atainia, Tysan, by the Ilitharis Paravians, to source the defence works of the Paravian keep of the same name.

pronounced: i-say-er

root meaning: *i'saer* – the circle

ISFARENN—etheric Name for the black stallion ridden by Asandir.

pronounced: ees-far-en

root meaning: *is'feron* – speed maker

ISHLIR—town on the eastshore of Orvandir, Shand.

pronounced: ish-leer

root meaning: *ieshlier* – sheltered place

ITHAMON—Historically significant in the First Age, site of a Paravian focus, a Second Age Paravian stronghold, and a Third Age ruin; built on a fifth lane power-node in Daon Ramon Barrens, Rathain, and inhabited until the year of the uprising. Site of the Compass Point Towers, or Sun Towers. Became the seat of the High Kings of Rathain during the Third Age and in Third Age Year 5638 was the site where Princes Lysaer s'Ilessid and Arithon s'Ffalenn battled the Mistwraith to confinement.

pronounced: ith-a-mon

root meaning: *itha* – five; *mon* – needle, spire

ITHILT—peninsula bordering Minderl Bay, in eastern Rathain.

pronounced: ith-ilt

root meaning: *ith* – five; *ealt* – a narrows

ITHISH—city located at the edge of the principality of Vastmark, on the south-coast of Shand. Where the Vastmark wool factors once shipped fleeces.

pronounced: ith-ish

root meaning: *ithish* – fleece or fluffy

I'TISHEALDIANT—to wish, or to bring lightness to a disrupted state/a splash, or shattering ripple raised to the emphatic – idiomatic for the energetic impact of a disruptive event.

pronounced: ih-tee-shee-al-dee-ahnt

root meaning: *i* – prefix to specify by light; *tishealdeant* – splash, emphatic form

IVEL—blind splicer from southcoastal Shand, once hired by Arithon at Merior.

pronounced: ee-vel

root meaning: *iavel* – scathing

IYAT—energy sprite, and minor drake spawn inhabiting Athera, not visible to the eye, manifests in a poltergeist fashion by taking temporary possession of objects. Feeds upon natural energy sources: fire, breaking waves, lightning, and excess emotion where humans gather.

> pronounced: ee-at
>
> root meaning: *iyat* – to break

JAELOT—city located on the coast of Eltair Bay at the southern border of the Kingdom of Rathain. Once a Second Age power site, with a focus circle. Now a merchant city with a reputation for extreme snobbery and bad taste. Also the site where Arithon s'Ffalenn played his eulogy for Halliron Masterbard, which raised the powers of the Paravian focus circle beneath the mayor's palace. The forces of the mysteries and resonant harmonics caused damage to city buildings, watch keeps, and walls, which has since been repaired. Site where Fionn Areth was arraigned for execution, as bait in a Koriani conspiracy that failed to trap Arithon s'Ffalenn.

> pronounced: jay-lot
>
> root meaning: *jielot* – affectation

JERVALD—watch captain of the lower wall garrison at Alestron, under Mearn's command.

> pronounced: jeer-vald
>
> root meaning: *jier* – pointed; *vald* – wit

JEYNSA—daughter of Jieret s'Valerient and Feithan, born Third Age 5653; appointed successor for her father's title, *caithdein* of Rathain.

> pronounced: jay-in-sa
>
> root meaning: *jieyensa* – garnet

JIERET s'VALERIENT—former Earl of the North, clan chief of Deshir; *caithdein* of Rathain, sworn liegeman of Prince Arithon s'Ffalenn. Also son and heir of Lord Steiven. Blood pacted to Arithon by sorcerer's oath prior to the battle of Strakewood Forest. Came to be known by head-hunters as Jieret Red-beard. Father of Jeynsa and Barach. Husband to Feithan. Died by Lysaer s'Ilessid's hand in Daon Ramon Barrens, Third Age Year 5670.

> pronounced: jeer-et
>
> root meaning: *jieret* – thorn

JINESSE—mother of Fiark and Feylind, wife of Tharrick, resident of Innish.

> pronounced: jin-ess-e
>
> root meaning: *jienesse* – to be washed or pale; a wisp

KALESH—town at the mouth of the harbour inlet from the Cildein Ocean, enemy of Alestron.

> pronounced: cal-esh
>
> root meaning: *caille'iesh* – stubborn hold

KEIR'VE ARISH—an insulting embarrassment, idiom for a fool in Biedar tribal dialect.

> pronounced: kee-aar vay aah-ree-ch

root meaning: *keir've arish* – translated as 'one caught with wet feet'

KELDMAR s'BRYDION—younger brother of Duke Bransian of Alestron, older brother of Parrien and Mearn.

pronounced: keld-mar

root meaning: *kiel'd'maeran* – one without pity

KEVOR—son and heir of Lysaer s'Ilessid and Princess Ellaine; born at Avenor in Third Age 5655. At age fourteen, in his father's absence, he exercised royal authority and averted a riot by the panicked citizenry of Avenor. Thought dead by Khadrim fire in Westwood, but survived via an interaction with Ath's Brotherhood. Became an adept in Third Year 5670, at the hostel in Northerly, Tysan.

pronounced: kev-or

root meaning: *kiavor* – high virtue

KEWAR TUNNEL—cavern built beneath the Mathorn Mountains by Davien the Betrayer; contains the maze of conscience, which caused High King Kamridian s'Ffalenn's death. Arithon Teir's'Ffalenn successfully completed the challenge in Third Age Year 5670.

pronounced: key-wahr

root meaning: *kewiar* – a weighing of conscience

KHADRIM—drake-spawned creatures, flying, fire-breathing reptiles that were the scourge of the Second Age. By the Third Age, they had been driven back and confined in the Sorcerers' Preserve in the volcanic peaks in north Tysan.

pronounced: kaa-drim

root meaning: *khadrim* – dragon

KHARADMON—Sorcerer of the Fellowship of Seven; discorporate since rise of Khadrim and Seardluin levelled Paravian stronghold at Ithamon in Second Age 3651. It was by Kharadmon's intervention that the survivors of the attack were sent to safety by means of transfer from the fifth lane power focus. Currently working the wardings to defer a minor invasion of wraiths from Marak.

pronounced: kah-rad-mun

root meaning: *kar'riad en mon* – phrase translates to mean 'twisted thread on the needle' or colloquialism for 'a knot in the works'

KHETIENN—name for a brigantine built at Merior and owned by Arithon; also a small spotted wildcat native to Daon Ramon Barrens that became the s'Ffalenn royal device.

pronounced: key-et-ee-en

root meaning: *kietienn* – small leopard

KORIANI—possessive and singular form of the word 'Koriathain'; see entry.

pronounced: kor-ee-ah-nee

KORIAS—south-western principality of Tysan.

pronounced: kor-ee-as

root meaning: *cor* – ship, vessel; *i'esh* – nest, haven

KORIATHAIN—order of enchantresses ruled by a circle of Seniors, under the power of one Prime Enchantress. They draw their talent from the orphaned children they raise, or from daughters dedicated to service by their parents. Initiation rite involves a vow of consent that ties the spirit to a power crystal keyed to the Prime's control.

> pronounced: kor-ee-ah-thain – to rhyme with 'main'
>
> root meaning: *koriath* – order; *ain* – belonging to

KRALOVIR—term for a sect of necromancers, also called the grey cult, destroyed by Arithon s'Ffalenn in Third Age Year 5671.

> pronounced: kray-low-veer
>
> root meaning: *krial* – name for the rune of crossing; *oveir* – abomination

KYRIALT s'TALEYN—once heir designate and youngest son of the High Earl of Alland, Lord Erlien s'Taleyn, *Caithdein* of Shand, now bestowed as liegeman to Arithon of Rathain as a debt of honour.

> pronounced: key-ree-alt
>
> root meaning: *kyrialt* – word for the rune of crossing with the suffix for 'last,' which is the name for the rune of ending.

LANSHIRE—northernmost principality in the Kingdom of Havish. Name taken from the wastes at Scarpdale, site of First Age battles with Seardluin that blasted the soil to slag.

> pronounced: lahn-sheer-e
>
> root meaning: *lan'hansh'era* – place of hot sands

LAW OF THE MAJOR BALANCE—founding order of the powers of the Fellowship of Seven, as taught by the Paravians. The primary tenet is that no force of nature should be used without consent, or against the will of another consciousness.

LIENRIEL RIVER—crosses the free wilds of Alland, and joins the Hanhaffin inside of Selkwood, in the Kingdom of Shand.

> pronounced: lee-en-ree-ell
>
> root meaning: *lien* – to love; *riel* – silver

LIESSE s'BRYDION—Duchess of Alestron and wife of Duke Bransian.

> pronounced: lee-ess
>
> root meaning: *liesse* – state of accord, based from the word 'a note in harmony'

LIRENDA—former First Senior Enchantress to the Prime, Koriani Order; failed in her assignment to capture Arithon s'Ffalenn for Koriani purposes. Currently under the Prime Matriarch's sentence of punishment.

> pronounced: leer-end-ah
>
> root meaning: *lyron* – singer; *di-ia* – a dissonance – the hyphen denotes a glottal stop

LORN—town on the northcoast of Atainia, Tysan.

> pronounced: lorn
>
> root meaning: *loern* – an Atheran fish.

LUGGER'S ISLET—a barrier island located off the shore of East Halla, popular as a haven for galleys during winter storms.

LUHAINE—Sorcerer of the Fellowship of Seven – discorporate since the fall of Telmandir in Third Age Year 5018. Luhaine's body was pulled down by the mob while he was in ward trance, covering the escape of the royal heir to Havish.

    pronounced: loo-hay-ne

    root meaning: *luirhainon* – defender

LYRANTHE—instrument played by the bards of Athera. Strung with fourteen strings, tuned to seven tones (doubled). Two courses are 'drone strings' set to octaves. Five are melody strings, the lower three courses being octaves, the upper two, in unison.

    pronounced: leer-anth-e (last 'e' being nearly subliminal)

    root meaning: *lyr* – song, *anthe* – box

LYSAER s'ILLESSID—prince of Tysan, 1497th in succession after Halduin, founder of the line in Third Age Year One. Gifted at birth with control of Light, and Bane of Desh-thiere. Also known as Blessed Prince since he declared himself avatar for the following known as the Alliance of Light.

    pronounced: lie-say-er

    root meaning: *lia* – blond, yellow or light, *saer* – circle

MARAK—splinter world, cut off beyond South Gate, left lifeless after creation of the Mistwraith. The original inhabitants were men exiled by the Fellowship from Athera for beliefs or practices that were incompatible with the compact sworn between the Sorcerers and the Paravian races, which permitted human settlement on Athera. Source of the Mistwraith, Desh-thiere, and the free wraiths that threaten Athera.

    pronounced: maer-ak

    root meaning: *m'era'ki* – place held separate

MATHIELL GATE—last gate to the inner citadel in Alestron, Paravian built to withstand the fires of dragons. It was the Mathiell garrison who secured the span guarding incursion from the Wyntok Gate during the uprising that threatened clan rule in Third Age Year 5018.

    pronounced: math-ee-ell

    root meaning: *mon'thiellen* – sky spires

MATHORN MOUNTAINS—range that bisects the Kingdom of Rathain east to west.

    pronounced: math-orn

    root meaning: *mathien* – massive

MEARN s'BRYDION—youngest brother of Duke Bransian of Alestron. Former ducal emissary to Lysaer s'Ilessid's Alliance of Light. Husband of Fianzia.

    pronounced: may-arn

    root meaning: *mierne* – to flit

MEDLIR—name used by Arithon when he travelled incognito with Halliron Masterbard as apprentice in Third Age Years 5638 to 5647.

    pronounced: med-leer

    root meaning: *midlyr* – phrase of melody

MELHALLA—High Kingdom of Athera once ruled by the line of s'Ellestrion. The last prince died in the crossing of the Red Desert. Currently stewarded by the Teiren's'Callient.

    pronounced: mel-hall-ah

    root meaning: *maelhallia* – grand meadows/plain – also word for an open space of any sort.

MEIGLIN s'DIENEVAL—the legitimate daughter born to the widow of Egan s'Dieneval in Third Age 5019, just after his death in the slaughter of the rebellion. Heart's love of the last High King of Shand for one night, just prior to his death while fighting the Mistwraith. A weaving by the Biedar of Sanpashir, done at the behest of the last Centaur Guardian, ensured the union would bring conception, and the birth of Dari's'Ahelas. Also named Anshlien'ya in desert dialect, as the dawn of hope.

    pronounced: mee-glin s-dee-in-ee-vahl

    root meaning: *meiglin* – passion; *dien* – large; *eval* – endowment, gifted talent

MERIOR BY THE SEA—small seaside fishing village on the Scimlade peninsula in Alland, Shand. Once the temporary site of Arithon's shipyard. Birth place of Fiark and Feylind.

    pronounced: mare-ee-or

    root meaning: *merioren* – cottages

METHISLE FORTRESS—a Paravian keep on an islet in Methlas Lake in Orvandir, currently overseen by the Guardian of Methisle, the Master Spellbinder, Verrain.

    pronounced: meth

    root meaning: *meth* – hate

METHURI—METHURIEN (plural form) an *iyat*-related parasite that infested live hosts and altered them for the purpose of creating new hosts. Extinct by the Third Age.

    pronounced: meth-you-ree

    root meaning: *meth'thieri* – hate wraith

MI A'DAELIENT—address given by a liegeman or woman to acknowledge the realm's queen.

    pronounced: mee ah-day-ell-ee-ent

    root meaning: *mi* – my; *a'* – feminine prefix; *daelient* – ruler bearing crown rank.

MINDERL BAY—body of water inside of Crescent Isle, off the eastshore of Rathain.

    pronounced: mind earl

    root meaning: *minderl* – anvil

MISTWRAITH—see Desh-thiere.

MORRIEL—Prime Enchantress of the Koriathain since the Third Age 4212. Instigated the plot to upset the Fellowship's compact, which upset seven of the magnetic lanes on the continent. Her death on winter solstice 5670 left an irregular succession, resolved by the elevation of an incompetent initiate, Selidie, who had been chosen to facilitate an unprincipled act of possession by Morriel, which usurped the young woman's body.

> pronounced: more-real
>
> root meaning: *moar* – greed; *riel* – silver

MORVAIN—city located in the principality of Araethura, Rathain, on the west coast of Instrell Bay. Elaira's birthplace.

> pronounced: mor-vain
>
> root meaning: *morvain* – swindler's market

MYRKAVIA—island located in Rock Bay Harbor, off the coast of Havistock, in Havish.

> pronounced: meer-kay-vee-ah
>
> root meaning: *miere* – reflection; *kavia* – spruce tree

NAI FFIOSH E'ELEN SLIET-TH'I—no false tiny steps.

> pronounced: naye fee-owsh e'el-en slee-et-thee
>
> root meaning: *nai* – no; *ffiosh* – false; *e'elen* – diminutive for short, small, tiny; *sliet-thi* – step with suffix for plural

NARMS—city on the coast of Instrell Bay, built as a craft centre by Men in the early Third Age. Best known for dyeworks.

> pronounced: narms
>
> root meaning: *narms* – colour

NORTHSTOR—trade port at the northern tip of the East Halla peninsula, and Vaststrait.

> pronounced: north stor
>
> root meaning: *stor* – summit or apex of a triangle

ORVANDIR—principality located in north-eastern Shand.

> pronounced: or-van-deer
>
> root meaning: *orvein* – crumbled; *dir* – stone

PARAVIA—name for the continent inhabited by the Paravians, and locale of the Five Kingdoms.

> pronounced: par-ay-vee-ah
>
> root meaning: *para* – great; *i'a* – suffix denoting entityship, and raised to the feminine aspect, which translates as ' inclusive of, or holding the aspect for greatness'

PARAVIAN—name for the three old races that inhabited Athera before Mankind.

Including the centaurs, the sunchildren, and the unicorns, these races never die unless mishap befalls them; they are the world's channel, or direct connection, to Ath Creator.

    pronounced: par-ai-vee-ans

    root meaning: *para* – great; *i'on* – fate or great mystery

PARRIEN s'BRYDION—younger brother of Duke Bransian s'Brydion of Alestron, Keldmar, and older brother of Mearn. Husband of Tiassa. Broke Arithon's leg in Third Age Year 5654, and in restitution awarded Rathain's prince the service of two s'Brydion retainers, Talvish and Vhandon.

    pronounced: par-ee-on

    root meaning: *para ient* – great dart

PELLAIN—trade town located on the inland bounds of East Halla, Melhalla.

    pronounced: pell-ayn

    root meaning: *peil* – odd; *ai'an* – hidden one

PERDITH—trade town located on the east shore in East Halla, Melhalla, known for its armourers.

    pronounced: per-dith

    root meaning: *pirdith* – anvil

QUAID—trade town in Carithwyr, Havish, lying inland along the road from Los Mar to Redburn. Famous for fired clay and brick.

    pronounced: qu-wade

    root meaning: *cruaid* – a clay used for brickmaking.

RAIETT RAVEN—brother of the Mayor of Hanshire; uncle of Sulfin Evend. Considered a master statesman and a bringer of wars. Served as High Chancellor of Etarra, ruling in the absence of the ratified mayor. Died in Arithon's purge of the Grey Kralovir necromancers from Etarra, Third Age 5671.

    pronounced: rayett

    root meaning: *raiett* – carrion bird

RANNE—royal guardsman of Avenor, once honour guard of Prince Kevor, reprieved and reassigned to Lysaer's personal guard by Sulfin Evend.

    pronounced: ran

    root meaning: *ruann* – a fledgling hawk

RATHAIN—High Kingdom of Athera ruled by descendants of Torbrand s'Ffalenn since Third Age Year One. Device: black-and-silver leopard on green field. Arithon Teir's'Ffalenn is sanctioned crown prince, by the hand of Asandir of the Fellowship, in Third Age Year 5638 at Etarra.

    pronounced: rath-ayn

    root meaning: *roth* – brother; *thein* – tower, sanctuary

RAUVEN TOWER—home of the s'Ahelas mages who brought up Arithon s'Ffalenn and trained him to the ways of power. Located on the splinter world, Dascen Elur, through West Gate.

pronounced: raw-ven

root meaning: *rauven* – invocation

REDBURN—town located in a deep inlet in the northern shore of Rockbay Harbor in Havistock, Havish.

pronounced: red-burn

not from the Paravian

RIATHAN PARAVIANS—unicorns, the purest, most direct connection to Ath Creator; the prime vibration channels directly through the horn.

pronounced: ree-ah-than

root meaning: *ria* – to touch; *ath* – prime life-force; *an* – one; *ri'athon* – one who touches divinity

RIVERTON—trade town at the mouth of the Ilswater River, in Korias, Tysan; once the site of Lysaer's royal shipyard, before the site burned by Cattrick's sabotage in Third Age Year 5654.

ROCKBAY HARBOR—body of water located on the southcoast, between Shand and West Shand.

ROCKFELL PEAK—mountain containing Rockfell Pit, used to imprison harmful entities throughout all three Ages. Located in West Halla, Melhalla; became the warded prison for Desh-thiere.

pronounced: rock-fell

not from the Paravian

s'AHELAS—family name for the royal line appointed by the Fellowship Sorcerers in Third Age Year One to rule the High Kingdom of Shand. Gifted geas: far-sight. Also the lineage that carries the latent potential for the rogue talent for far-sight and prophecy, introduced when the *caithdein*'s lineage of s'Dieneval became crossed with the royal line in Third Age 5036, resulting in Dari's birth in winter, 5037.

pronounced: s'ah-hell-as

root meaning: *ahelas* – mage-gifted

SAMAURA—a third-rank Koriani healer.

pronounced: sam-your-ah

root meaning: *s'a'moara* – a woman who holds close, or is tenaciously possessive

SANPASHIR—desert waste on the southcoast of Shand. Home to the desert tribes called Biedar.

pronounced: sahn-pash-eer

root meaning: *san* – black or dark; *pash'era* – place of grit or gravel

SANSHEVAS—town on the south shore in Alland, Shand, known for citrus, sugar, and rum.

pronounced: san-shee-vas

root meaning: *san* – black; *shievas* – flint

SAYSHA—a Koriani Senior with an enhanced talent for telepathy.

pronounced: say-shaa

root meaning: *saisha* – to listen

s'BRYDION—ruling line of the Dukes of Alestron. The only old blood clansmen to maintain rule of a fortified city through the uprising that defeated the rule of the high kings.

pronounced: s-bry-dee-on

root meaning: *baridien* – tenacity

s'CALLIENT—lineage of the *Caithdeinen* of Melhalla, Fellowship chosen to succeed s'Dieneval after the fall of Tirans.

pronounced: scal-lee-ent

root meaning: *caillient* – most extreme form of 'fixed' or stubborn – 'immovable'

SCARPDALE—waste in Lanshire, Havish. Created by a First Age war with Seardluin. Site of the Scarpdale grimward.

pronounced: scarp-dale

not from the Paravian

SCIMLADE TIP—peninsula at the south-east corner of Alland, Shand.

pronounced: skim-laid

root meaning: *scimlait* – curved knife or scythe

SECOND AGE—Marked by the arrival of the Fellowship of Seven at Crater Lake, their called purpose to fight the drake spawn.

s'DIENEVAL—lost lineage of the *Caithdeinen* of Melhalla, the last to carry the title being Egan, who died at the side of his high king in the battle to subdue the Mistwraith. The blood-line carried strong talent for prophecy, and was decimated during the sack of Tirans in the uprising in Third Age Year 5018, with Egan's pregnant wife the sole survivor. Her daughter, Meiglin, was mother of Dari s'Ahelas, crown heir of Shand.

pronounced: s-dee-in-ee-vahl

root meaning: *dien* – large; *eval* – endowment, gifted talent

SEARDLUIN—drake-spawned, vicious, intelligent cat-like predators that roved in packs that sought ruthless slaughter of other living things. Battled to extinction by the middle of the Second Age for the sake of Paravian survival. Remnant recall of them can arise in the dreams of grimwarded drake haunts.

pronounced: seerd-loo-win

root meaning: *seard* – bearded; *luin* – feline

SEITHUR—Biedar tribal dialect, meaning one whose choice will determine the future.

pronounced: see-thur

root meaning: *seithur* – one whose choice affects all generations to come

SELIDIE—young woman initiate appointed by Morriel Prime as a candidate in training for succession. Assumed the office of Prime Matriarch after Morriel's death on winter solstice in Third Age Year 5670, at which time an unprincipled act of possession by Morriel usurped the young woman's body.

pronounced: sell-ih-dee

root meaning: *selyadi* – air sprite

SELKWOOD—forest located in Alland, Shand.

pronounced: selk-wood

root meaning: *selk* – pattern

SESHKROZCHIEL—name for the female dragon who was mated to Haspastion.

pronounced: sesh-crows-chee-ell

root meaning: *seshkrozchiel* – Drakish for blue lightning

SETHVIR—Sorcerer of the Fellowship of Seven, also trained to serve as Warden of Althain since Third Age 5100, when the last centaur guardian departed after the Mistwraith's conquest.

pronounced: seth-veer

root meaning: *seth* – fact; *vaer* – keep

SEVRAND s'BRYDION—heir designate of Duke Bransian of Alestron.

pronounced: sev-rand

root meaning: *sevaer'an'd* – one who travels behind, a follower

s'FFALENN—family name for the royal line appointed by the Fellowship Sorcerers in Third Age Year One to rule the High Kingdom of Rathain. Gifted geas: compassion/empathy.

pronounced: s-fal-en

root meaning: *ffael* – dark, *an* – one

s'GANNLEY—lineage of the Earls of the West, once the Camris princes, now bearing the heritage of *Caithdein* of Tysan. Iamine s'Gannley was the woman founder.

pronounced: sgan-lee

root meaning: *gaen* – guide; *li* – exalted or in harmony

SHADDORN—town located on the Scimlade Tip in Alland, Shand.

pronounced: shad-dorn

root meaning: *shaddiern* – sea turtle

SHAND—High Kingdom on the south-east corner of the Paravian continent, originally ruled by the line of s'Ahelas. Current device, purple-and-gold chevrons, since the adjunct kingdom of West Shand came under high crown rule. The old device was a falcon on a crescent moon, sometimes still showed, backed by the more recent purple-and-gold chevrons.

pronounced: shand – as in 'hand'

root meaning: *shayn* or *shiand* – two/pair

SHANDOR—trade port located on the westshore of Rockbay Harbor, in West Shand.

pronounced: shan-door

root meaning: *cianor* – to shine

SHEHANE ALTHAIN—Ilitharis Paravian who dedicated his spirit as defender and guardian of Althain Tower.

pronounced: shee-hay-na all-thayn

root meaning: *shiehai'en* –to give for the greater good; *alt* – last; *thain* – tower

SHIPSPORT—city located on the Bay of Eltair in the principality of West Halla, Melhalla.

SIDIR—one of the Companions, who were the fourteen boys to survive the Battle of Strakewood. Served Arithon at the Battle of Dier Kenton Vale, and the Havens. Second-in-command of Earl Jieret's war band. Handfast to Feithan, widow of the former Earl of the North.

 pronounced: see-deer

 root meaning: *i'sid'i'er* – one who has stood at the verge of being lost.

s'ILESSID—family name for the royal line appointed by the Fellowship Sorcerers in Third Age Year One to rule the High Kingdom of Tysan. Gifted geas: justice.

 pronounced: s-ill-ess-id

 root meaning: *liessiad* – balance

SILVERMARSH—large bog located south of Daenfal Lake, in West Halla, Melhalla.

SINDELLE—wife of Keldmar s'Brydion of Alestron.

 pronounced: sin-dell-e

 root meaning: *san* – black, dark; *ael* – destiny; *'e* – suffix for future in potentia

SITHAER—mythological equivalent of hell, halls of Dharkaron Avenger's judgement; according to Ath's adepts, that state of being where the prime vibration is not recognized.

 pronounced: sith-air

 root meaning: *sid* – lost; *thiere* – wraith/spirit

SIX TOWERS—trade town located in Orvandir, Shand.

SKYRON FOCUS—large aquamarine focus stone, used by the Koriani Senior Circle for their major magic after the loss of the Great Waystone during the rebellion.

 pronounced: sky-run

 root meaning: *skyron* – colloquialism for shackle; *s'kyr'i'on* – literally 'sorrowful fate'

SKYSHIELS—mountain range that runs north and south along the eastern coast of Rathain.

 pronounced: sky-shee-ells

 root meaning: *skyshia* – to pierce through; *iel* – ray

SLIESHENG DHAVI! AYKRAUK I'IEN KIEL'D'MAER TIEND! – Slinking fool! Scorch your pitiless spirit!

 pronounced: slee-shing dah-vee! aye-croak eh-een kee-eld-may-er tee-end

 root meaning: *sliesheng* – slinking; *dhavi* – fool; *aykrauk* – to scorch; *i'ien* – an ill wish sent upon you, by intent; *kiel'd'maer* – pitiless; *tiend* – spirit

SOUTHSHIRE—town on the southcoast of Alland, Shand, known for shipbuilding.

 pronounced: south-shire

 not from the Paravian

s'TALEYN—lineage of the *Caithdeinen* of Shand.
   pronounced: stall-ay-en
   root meaning: *tal* – branch; *an* – one/first 'of the first branch'
STARBORN—name for the Fellowship Sorcerers used by the Biedar tribe of Sanpashir.
STORLAINS—mountains dividing the Kingdom of Havish.
   pronounced: store-lanes
   root meaning: *storlient* – largest summit, highest divide
STRAKEWOOD—forest in the principality of Deshir, Rathain; site of the battle of Strakewood Forest, where the garrison from Etarra marched against the clans under Steiven s'Valerient and Prince Arithon, in Third Age Year 5638.
   pronounced: strayk-wood similar to 'stray wood'
   root meaning: *streik* – to quicken, to seed
SULFIN EVEND—son of the Mayor of Hanshire who holds the post of Alliance Lord Commander under Lysaer s'Ilessid. Spared Lysaer from his dark binding to the Kralovir Necromancers, and in the course of that awakened the talent of his outbred clan lineage: of s'Gannley descent, through Diarin s'Gannley, who was abducted and forced to marry his great grandsire. Bound to the land in Third Age 5670 when he swore a *caithdein*'s oath at Althain Tower as part of his bargain with Enithen Tuer, who in turn imparted the ceremonial knowledge and the Biedar knife used to sever the etheric cords the cult used to enslave victims.
   pronounced: sool-finn ev-end
   root meaning: *suilfinn eiavend* – colloquialism, diamond mind 'one who is persistent'
SUNCHILDREN—common name for Athlien Paravians, see entry.
SUNLOOP—a device for augury, wrought by the Fellowship Sorcerer Ciladis, and completed in Third Age 5129, which was designed to reflect the first return of sunlight to Paravia, following the Mistwraith's invasion.
s'VALERIENT—family name for the Earls of the North, regents and *caithdein* for the High Kings of Rathain.
   pronounced: val-er-ee-ent
   root meaning: *val* – straight; *erient* – spear

TAL QUORIN—river formed by the confluence of watershed on the southern side of Strakewood, principality of Deshir, Rathain, where traps were laid for Etarra's army in the battle of Strakewood Forest, and where the rape and massacre of Deshir's clan women and children occurred under Lysaer and head-hunters under Pesquil's command in Third Age Year 5638.
   pronounced: tal quar-in
   root meaning: *tal* – branch; *quorin* – canyons
TALITH—Etarran princess; former wife of Lysaer s'Ilessid, estranged from him and incarcerated on charges of consorting with the Master of Shadow. Eventually

murdered by a conspiracy of Avenor's crown council, when an arranged accident caused her fall from Avenor's tower of state in Third Age 5653.

    pronounced: tal-ith – to rhyme with 'gal with'

    root meaning: *tal* – branch; *lith* – to keep/nurture

TALVISH—a clanborn retainer in armed service to s'Brydion at Alestron who was sworn as liegeman to the Prince Arithon as a point of honour.

    pronounced: tall-vish

    root meaning: *talvesh* – reed

TEIDWAR—Biedar dialect for outland strange person who fares through another's place, kinless.

    pronounced: tide-war

    root meaning: *tiedwar* – a traveller who does not belong to the tribe

TEIR—masculine form of a title fixed to a name denoting heirship.

    pronounced: tayer

    root meaning: *teir's* – successor to power

TEIREN—feminine form of Teir.

TEIVE—first mate of the merchant brig *Evenstar* and father of Feylind's two children.

    pronounced: tee-ev

    root meaning: *tierve* – reliable

TELMANDIR—seat of the High Kings of Havish in Lithmere, Havish. Ruined during the uprising in Third Age Year 5018, rebuilt by High King Eldir s'Lornmein after his coronation in Third Age Year 5643.

    pronounced: tel-man-deer

    root meaning: *telman'en* – leaning; *dir* – rock

TELZEN—town on the eastshore of Alland, Shand.

    pronounced: tell-zen

    root meaning: *tielsen* – to saw wood

THARIDOR—trade city on the shores of the Bay of Eltair in Melhalla.

    pronounced: thar-i-door

    root meaning: *tier'i'dur* – keep of stone

THARRICK—former captain of the guard in the city of Alestron assigned charge of the duke's secret armoury; now married to Jinesse and working as a gentleman mercenary guard at Innish.

    pronounced: thar-rick

    root meaning: *thierik* – unkind twist of fate

THIRDMARK—port town located on the eastshore of Rockbay Harbor, Shand.

TIASSA—wife of Parrien s'Brydion of Alestron.

    pronounced: tee-ass-ah

    root meaning: *tias's'a* – a woman of wealth or means

TIENELLE—high-altitude herb valued by mages for its mind-expanding properties. Highly toxic. No antidote. The leaves, dried and smoked, are most potent.

To weaken its powerful side effects and allow safer access to its vision, Koriani enchantresses boil the flowers, then soak tobacco leaves with the brew.

pronounced: tee-an-ell-e ('e' mostly subliminal)

root meaning: *tien* – dream; *iel* – light/ray

TIRANS—trade town located on the East Halla peninsula in Melhalla, also a Second Age ruin, seat of the High Kings of Melhalla, sacked during the uprising in Third Age Year 5018. Site of a Paravian focus circle.

pronounced: tee-rans

root meaning: *tier* – to hold fast, to keep, or to covet

TIRIACS—mountain range to the north of Mirthlvain Swamp, in Midhalla, Melhalla.

pronounced: tie-ree-axe

root meaning: *tieriach* – alloy of metals

TORBRAND s'FFALENN—founder of the s'Ffalenn line appointed by the Fellowship of Seven to rule the High Kingdom of Rathain in Third Age Year One.

pronounced: tor-brand

root meaning: *tor* – sharp, keen; *brand* – temper

TORNIR PEAKS—mountain range on western border in Camris, Tysan. Northern half is actively volcanic, and there the last surviving packs of Khadrim are kept under ward.

pronounced: tor-neer

root meaning: *tor* – sharp, keen; *nier* – tooth

TRAITHE—Sorcerer of the Fellowship of Seven. Solely responsible for the closing of South Gate to deny further entry to the Mistwraith. Traithe lost most of his faculties in the process and was left with a limp. Since it is not known whether he can make the transfer into discorporate existence with his powers impaired, he has retained his physical body.

pronounced: tray-the

root meaning: *traithe* – gentleness

TYSAN—one of the Five High Kingdoms of Athera as defined by the charters of the Fellowship of Seven. Ruled by the s'Ilessid royal line. Device: gold star on blue field.

pronounced: tie-san

root meaning: *tiasen* – rich

VALDIE—widow of a Hanshire lancer who was lost in the Korias grimward in Third Age 5653.

pronounced: val-dee

root meaning: *val* – straight; *die* – pretty object – colloquial for faithfully fair

VARENS—trade town on the shore of Eltair Bay in East Halla, Melhalla.

pronounced: var-ens

root meaning: *var'uens* – keep safe, or lock

VASTMARK—principality located in south-western Shand. Highly mountainous and not served by trade-roads. Its coasts are renowned for shipwrecks. Inhabited by nomadic shepherds and wyverns, non-fire-breathing, smaller relatives of Khadrim. Site of the grand massacre of Lysaer's war host in Third Age 5647.

    pronounced: vast-mark

    root meaning: *vhast* – bare; *mheark* – valley

VASTSTRAIT—narrows linking the Cildein Ocean with the Bay of Eltair on the eastshore-line.

    pronounced: vast-straight

    root meaning: *vhast* – bare

VERRAIN—master spellbinder, trained by Luhaine; stood as Guardian of Mirthlvain when the Fellowship of Seven was left short-handed after the conquest of the Mistwraith.

    pronounced: ver-rain

    root meaning: *ver* – keep; *ria* – touch; *an* – one original Paravian: *verria'an*

VHALZEIN—city located in West Shand, shore of Rockbay Harbor on the border by Havish. Famed for shell-inlaid lacquer furnishings.

    pronounced: val-zeen

    root meaning: from Drakish, *vhchalsckeen* – white sands

VHANDON—a renowned clanborn war-captain of Duke Bransian s'Brydion of Alestron, assigned to Prince Arithon's service as a point of honour in Third Age Year 5654.

    pronounced: van-done

    root meaning: *vhandon* – steadfast

WARDEN OF ALTHAIN—alternative title for the Fellowship Sorcerer, Sethvir, who received custody of Althain Tower and the powers of the earth link from the last centaur guardian to leave the continent of Paravia in Third Age Year 5100.

WAYSTONE—spherical-cut amethyst used by the Koriathain to channel the full power of all enchantresses in their order, lost during the great rebellion that threw down the rule of the high kings, and recovered from Fellowship custody by Lirenda in Third Age Year 5647. Currently useless to the order, due to Arithon's arranged sabotage, which has infiltrated a stray *iyat* into the stone's matrix.

WESTWOOD—forest located north of the Great West Road in Camris, Tysan.

WERPOINT—fishing town and outpost on the north-east coast of Fallowmere, Rathain.

    pronounced: were-point

    root meaning: *wyr* – all, sum as in numerical total.

WEST HALLA—principality located in Kingdom of Melhalla.

pronounced: west hall-ah

root meaning: *hal'lia* – white light

WHITEHOLD—city located on the shore of Eltair Bay, Kingdom of Melhalla.

WILLOWBROOK—stream feeding into the River Lienriel in Selkwood, located in Alland in Shand.

WYNTOK GATE—upper gate in the citadel of Alestron, opening onto the suspended wooden bridge that crosses the tidal moat to the Mathiell Gate.

pronounced: win-tock

root meaning: *wuinn* – vulture; *tiok* – roost

Appendix

Blood Heritage of the Royal Families

The five royal lines of Athera were originally selected by the Paravians, with each of the original founders chosen for a dominant gift of character.

> Torbrand s'Ffalenn, High King of Rathain – Compassion
> Halduin s'Ilessid, High King of Tysan – Justice
> Cindra s'Ahelas, High Queen of Shand – Farsight
> Bwin Evoc s'Lornmein, High King of Havish – Temperance
> Rondeil s'Ellestrion, High King of Melhalla – Wisdom

Each of these individuals gave their willing consent to accept the directive to rule, both for themselves, and for all of their future offspring, for as long as their lineage should survive in participation with Athera's destiny. No distinction was made between matrilineal or patrilineal lines of descent; both were equally favoured. The Fellowship Sorcerers used the initiate magic acquired from the dragons to fix these traits of character as an imperative geas, transferable through all subsequent issue. The prominence of this endowment was not passed on in a linear fashion. The gifts manifest in a 'spread' that seeks outlet through all available blood descendents of the original forebear. Heritability does not pass in equal measure, but flows forward like water, seeking the easiest channel for expression. Descendents who display a natural leaning in character will 'inherit' – or more correctly enact – the gift more intensely than others whose personalities bend in opposing directions. The wider the pool of descendents, the more 'choice' of channel the royal gift will have to seek outlet. For this reason, direct blood descent is never the determinant factor, but rather, which descendant portrays the most emphatic stamp of the progenitor's qualities.

The more descendents there are, the less predetermined the course of the inheritance. Some individuals may show predominance. Others might show little trace, or even none, although all living offspring within the lineage will carry the latent range of the geas' fullest potential.

Where a lineage is sparse, or only one descendent remains, the full force of the royal gift will flow through that individual, and be expressed with indelible emphasis.

This is why the line of descent varies, and may move freely between cousins, or skip generations, and why, without exception, the Fellowship Sorcerers are charged to Name and sanction each crown successor.

To conclude, the degree to which a royal gift expresses is twofold: inherited potency (how many descendents are living to 'carry' the trait) combined with the factor of personal choice that arises as personal character: how each individual is inclined toward their particular forebear's gift in the first place.

In the case of a lone descendent born with a personality not favourably inclined, the gift must still express. That individual would struggle, at odds with the inborn drive, and threshed by internal conflict. For this reason, many offspring and a wide extended family became an imperative preference for royal lines.

The High Kings who ruled during Paravian times had shorter reigns, provided there were sufficient progeny to support an early retirement. Crown office was extremely rigorous – many died young. Some reigned only a month or a year or two – others for a matter of days. A few hardy individuals held the throne for several decades, all dependent on how well, or how many times, they sustained the call to enact a direct liaison with the Paravians. Their perceptions were often dramatically altered after such encounter(s). The strength by which each individual king could surmount the changes varied widely.

Succession of Crown Candidates and *Caithdeinen*

By terms of the compact, the Fellowship of Seven must Name a crown candidate. Any one Sorcerer's innate perception is deep enough, and wide enough, to make such an assessment based upon probability. The task is most often handled by Asandir, as his natural aptitude for executive action makes him the preeminent Sorcerer to serve in the field.

The Crown Prince's appointment is never automatic, and does not pass by direct descent. Nor do kings or any other office decreed by crown charter hold their seats until death – (Unlike town mayors, who are elected or selected by town council, but then rule for life term.) Royal lineages are not replaceable.

They cannot be transplanted from another kingdom's bound line of descent, as the Paravians matched each forebear in resonant accord with the needs of the specific crown territories.

Provided that there are multiple blood relations, including cousins, to select from, the choice follows two factors: first, individual strength of character; and second, the quality of 'natural calling' — this being any candidate (without bias toward male or female) – who displays the best aptitude for the post. Thus, if Arithon s'Ffalenn had possessed more than one relative, he may have passed the character requirement, but his natural calling as musician and initiate master may not have been deemed harmonious to the post. A cousin or relation of strong character, but who displayed more aptitude for the throne (by personal preference finding fulfilment and contentment in the position of arbitration) may have been chosen instead.

The heritable traits of Athera's crown lineages do not *ever* transfer to *caithdeinen* if a last royal line-bearer should die without issue. *Caithdeinen* do administer crown justice in the absence of the king, and this may be an ongoing responsibility if crown rule has passed into a permanent state of stewardship. In this novel's historical setting, this only occurred in Melhalla since the last s'Ellestrion heir died childless. In such a case, succession of that realm's *caithdeinen* will now become Fellowship chosen.

Caithdeinen, or crown stewards, who stand behind a living royal heir, are selected for character and for the ability to think independently. In times of peace, under a crowned High King, they would have been selected from a picked lineage, which could change with times and circumstance. The candidate would be suited to know their crown ruler well, and have the courage to draw clear and honest conclusions. This post would not suit a sycophantic personality, for example.

Proposed successors for *caithdeinen* and other charter seats are usually 'designate.' This term denotes a conditional appointment, bestowed by a council of elders. (Kyrialt s'Taleyn was designate for Shand, as Ianfar s'Gannley now is to Tysan.) An heir designate will inherit *unless* the choice is overruled upon proven grounds of incapacity. The appointment also can be upset by either a crowned High King (who would possess the requisite power of insight acquired through four attuned initiations) or a Fellowship Sorcerer's direct word. Such a ruling would occur prior to or during the ceremony of investiture, where such an authority would be present. An heir chosen by Fellowship auspice automatically becomes invested without question. The investment ceremony then becomes a formality, wherein oath is sworn to uphold the post. Jeynsa s'Valerient, therefore, owns the power of her office by default – she has but to claim the responsibility.

A Fellowship Sorcerer only executes the selection of a *caithdein* if the existing royal lineage should be actively threatened. In this manner, if the crown succession fails, that *caithdein* would stand steward for the throne in fact.

Particulars of Clan Heritage

All old blood lineages were determined by the Paravians at the time Mankind accepted the terms of the compact, yet the 'system' was not closed, and not every family assumed the same function. Some lineages stood for land rule – these guarded the interface between humanity and the Paravians. These individuals possessed Sighted vision or natural talent enough to be charged with protection and preservation of the boundaries of the free wilds.

Other family lines were selected for adamant traits of character. These generally governed a town-based seat, and administered directly to human affairs in those areas where Mankind was free to live with least oversight. Sometimes land rule and town governance were held as dual functions. Checks and balances within the charter system were designed to thwart private concerns and blind ambition from degrading the compact's intent: to hold Athera's great mysteries, which are essential to Paravian survival, in balance with human activity.

Clan seats held solely for governance would rule from a keep town without a focus circle – these were not located within the designate bounds of the free wilds, and were the backbone of charter law before the uprising incited by Davien. They administered the king's justice in accord with those lineages holding the land rule.

The crown was the voice of land rule, and governance, under the charter written by the Fellowship Sorcerers. The sanctioned High Kings enacted the first-hand liaison with the Paravians, and were the protectorate for the free wilds. They presented the petitions to the Centaur guardians, then executed the final arbitration, as the agents of the Fellowship's compact. They appealed, and enacted, Paravian decree, concerning what could and could not be altered to preserve the overall harmony of the land's mysteries.

Each child born into clan lineage was subject to testing at each generation through the trial of Paravian presence. This testing could be refused, in which case, the candidate would revoke his charge to interact with the free wilds. A town-born individual could undergo the same test by free will choice. In rare cases this would occur, and a new lineage might arise from one candidate – just as an older, established lineage might become degraded, weaken and fail. Lacking Paravian presence, in recent generations the determinant factor has blurred. By the time of this novel's setting, the range of human talent cannot be identified with such definitive accuracy. Those individuals with latent or weakened talent are no longer able to prove out the direct function of heritable lineage. Thus, a 'talent deaf' town born will see no apparent reason why the free wilds should not be considered another ripe acre of earth, ready for exploitation. Nor would such a person recognize why the old blood traits were not arbitrary politics.

The prolonged absence of the Paravians now has created a schism that is growing increasingly difficult for each side to reconcile. The non-talented individuals do not discern the wider perceptions of their clan-born fellows. They see no convincing case left for the restraints imposed by the lapsed system of charter law. There is no such division of interests between the old blood lines and those who still follow charter law, since the underlying reason for the Fellowship's restrictions is still actively recognized.

The Designate Free Wilds, and Execution of the Compact

At the forming of the compact, which defined the terms for Mankind's permission to take sanctuary on Athera, the Fellowship Sorcerers had dispatched or contained the worst of the drake spawn. Paravians were in fact leaving their Second Age fortifications, which were tied to the web of Athera's mysteries by means of the focus circles. These structures are intersect points – connections that link the resonant flow between sites that comprise Athera's most exquisitely sensitive ground. The human families required immediate shelter. Those arrivals who already possessed the requisite awareness to inhabit a fortified circle, or who had talent that could be heightened to flower in proximity to such places were appointed charge of them.

The initial grants named in Third Age Year One went to individuals with the strongest heritable family traits – those born talents already able to perceive within the necessary range to handle the guiding purpose of their guardianship. These rulers also were charged to hold sacrosanct the high resonance land that could not be disturbed by any human activity. These areas were designated as sacrosanct areas deep inside the free wilds. Markers were set forth by the Centaur guardians delineating sectors where Mankind was not entitled to trespass.

Other acreage was not so critically reactive. There, new towns were built for those who had less natural 'tolerance' for the higher resonance state of the original Second Age sites. Such land was given over to agriculture and roads in allotments generous enough to allow Mankind to raise children and survive. The governing seats for these settlements had an elected council, presided over by a family lineage chosen for tenacity of character more than aware talent. These seats were appended following Third Age Year One. Here, humanity had license to keep their affairs as they wished, based upon certain precepts laid down by charter right to inhabit that territory. Alestron fell into this category. So did Hanshire. A mixed population lived in these subsidiary towns. The least sensitive people found most comfort in the smaller villages and tended to choose areas furthest from the free wilds.

Therefore, to a certain degree, acclimation to the higher resonance sites determined who came to live where, and who was comfortable setting down roots in each particular locale. This tended to isolate the older lineages to a degree – with marriages evolving with the need to raise a next generation of children able to manage the duties defined by the compact. Mixed bloodlines tended to fail more often, and parents were understandably protective of their offspring's chances of a successful 'testing' against the Paravian presence. Records were kept to track the tried lineages, and note the most favourable crosses.

While the general population in the towns were not inclined toward the traits of expanded awareness, it must be noted: the intuitive propensity to perceive is inherent in all of Mankind. Whether the quality remains latent depends upon how each individual aligns their focus and lifestyle.

Latent gifts of any kind can be awakened. Dormant awareness can be raised through training and initiation. Few town born voluntarily choose such a course, unless pushed by circumstance to change. Most might view the arduous study, and the disorientation of learning to adjust to such an expansion an uncomfortable process. Encounter with a living Paravian was powerful enough to incite an accelerated shift by resonance. Yet the change could shove human perception too far, too fast, and leave what appeared to be a husk with a broken mind. Living amid the free wilds also enhances perception – as would time spent in close proximity to a focus circle, provided that buildings and the life patterns of the surrounding inhabitants did not interfere too much with the delicate frequency of the lane flow.

Throughout the course of the early Third Age, mankind tended to clump into enclaves of greater or lesser sensitivity. Over time, this caused the old lines to strengthen their innate talent, while the less gifted ones devolved to a lower threshold of sensitivity. As centuries passed, half the population came to view the precepts defined by the Fellowship's compact as rote rules without meaning. The factual foundation was forgotten, then lost, lying outside the range of sensory awareness the town-born population understood.

For this reason, most Second Age sites fell to ruin after the uprising. (Jaelot being a rare exception). Town born alive now avoid such places, since crossing the free wilds, or travelling the forbidden ways, or spending time within old ruins, will alter human perception by resonance.

Throughout Third Age history, there were no social strata, or concept of 'nobility' attached to any old lineage gift. Nor was there any stigma attached to the town born without access to active talent. The cultural boundaries were not fixed, but fluid, defined case by case through choice and perceptual awareness. Blood inheritance is not a predetermined prerequisite. Yet without risking comparative insanity, a town born who set out to develop such enhanced sensitivity would require a gradual initiation to assimilate the shift.